Kathleen Winsor is the celebrated author of *Forever Amber*
She has also written four other novels – *Star Money*, *The
Lovers*, *America with Love* and *Wanderers Eastward,
Wanderers West*. Miss Winsor lives in New York City.

D0465889

Kathleen Winsor

Calais

Futura

A *Futura* Book

First published in paperback by
Futura Publications 1980

This edition published by
Futura Publications 1994

To T.M.P.

ISBN 0 7088 1775 0

Printed in England by Clays Ltd, St Ives plc

Futura Publications
A Division of
Macdonald & Co (Publishers)
Brettenham House
Lancaster Place
London WC2E 7EN

'Take all my loves . . .'
WILLIAM SHAKESPEARE

PROLOGUE

1966

Not quite awake, she watched as if a motion picture had appeared behind her lids.

First, the figurine. She had seen it somewhere, recently. A miniature statue carved in ivory, a man and woman naked, the woman lying beneath, legs spread wide, her arms embracing him forcefully. An enameled morning-glory vine bound them together, its flowers tinted purple, the colors bright and vibrant against the ivory figures which, as she watched, slowly increased in size; then began to move.

The man's buttocks rose and pressed forward; the woman's head was flung backward; her body rose and fell in a rhythm to match his.

As they grew larger, the ivory changed to the color of her flesh; her hair turned blonde, his black. The vines writhed and twined about them, following a perfect rhythm of coordination until, as she watched in wonder this reverie which was not quite a dream, there was a burst of activity – bodies, vines, moving, clasping, twining. All at once the vines drew away, releasing the man and woman; a shudder shook their bodies. The vines slowly enclosed them. The figures returned to their original minute size, their ivory and enamel composition – their brief fling at humanity over and done with in moments.

She was wide awake.

She had seen those figures a few days before, a bibelot Granville had shown her, in London, after they had finished the film. He had opened the upper half of a walnut shell which contained them. 'Beautiful workmanship, isn't it? Japanese—'

She had admired the workmanship; he had covered them with the shell, replaced it in the cabinet, yet it seemed she had brought it with her, after all.

She opened her eyes slowly, cautiously, wondering who had sat down beside her as the plane was about to take off, just as she was falling asleep, a man who had immediately opened an attaché case, removed some papers, and begun to read.

With no idea whether an hour had passed, or three or four, she found he was still reading papers, covered with angular hand-writing and curious hieroglyphics which looked like nothing she had seen before.

She glanced at her watch. Three-thirty, and the sun was bright, the ocean scarcely visible through the shield of clouds.

Airplanes served a useful purpose in her life – and that was to provide space in time, the only time free from work.

Perhaps that was because she usually got on a plane after some sequence of events which had left her sleepless for too many hours.

There he was, a warm glowing presence next to her, whose face she had not seen, reading. Reading. When he might be using these few unreal hours to empty his mind, banish the incessant stream of thoughts which collided morning, noon, and night; atoms run amok.

No.

Here was a man who had caught the tiger by the tail and could not let go even at thirty thousand feet, crossing the Atlantic.

Eyes half closed, she looked sideways at him.

His hands were long and narrow-fingered, seemingly fitted for the practice of surgery or music. There was patience, and stillness.

She turned her head quickly and, yes, he was looking at her, a look of concern, as of a man looking at a troubled child. She had frowned at the copulating couple, perhaps? Impossible. She had not frowned for as long as she could remember. Frowning was forbidden.

He was a magician, a mind reader?

'You're all right?' he asked, so that evidently the

lovemakers had reflected some disturbance. But she was struck by the voice: low, professionally trained.

She looked at him directly, her flecked hazel eyes with their black-rimmed irises asking what she had to do with him; she looked out the window.

Faces seen on airplanes were not real faces. They had never been seen before and would never be seen again.

This man, who returned to his reading after the rebuff of the brief direct glance, had come from nowhere and would return there. He was not part of her life. So much the better: *Where there's been no real beginning there can never be any real ending, either.* A bargain, of sorts.

After a time, however, she looked with some curiosity at those symbols.

Whose were they? Not a surgeon's; not a musician's. These were the symbols of an unknown tongue, perhaps an unknown world. Symbols of magic? Symbols without meaning? He was entertaining himself, after all?

The stewardess fixed two trays side by side, and so it seemed they were to be companions in taking airborne communion. She began to eat, slowly, and he took a forkful of steak, still pondering those symbols.

Symbols of a lost civilization? He was an archaeologist. Symbols of the chemical laboratories? He was trying to determine why life had appeared on earth at all? But Michael used no such symbols. Symbols of a sorcerer?

She looked at him again, but only his profile could be seen, and she glanced quickly away, as if she had no right to intrude on his privacy.

But she had seen that the face was elegant, the cheekbones prominent, the nose high-bridged, the black hair covered a beautifully formed head. She could not see his eyes, and so the most important clue to character for her was invisible. He was ignoring her, and she must show him the same courtesy.

Even so, she continued to wonder about him.

Unless it was possible to imagine another person in different ages and circumstances they were not valid people to her. They had one dimension only, the present.

Now – was this his one incarnation?

What other age and station in life might have become him?

He might have been an Egyptian pharaoh, with that look of aloof pride. Or a seventeenth-century Spanish grandee, black cloak flung across the lower part of his face, ready for duels of honor, duels of the flesh – disdainful, intimidating. Or a medieval monk, cowled and robed, poring over illuminated manuscripts as the years went by, unnoticed; quite as he was now ignoring the hours.

He looked slightly familiar, as if she had seen someone who looked like him once – but who, after all, looked like this man?

He turned, saw her watching him, and smiled. This time the smile was quite a different one and, yes, his eyes were gray. An unremarkable although brightly glistening gray.

The smile showed that slightly anguished look of a man watching a woman whose beauty disturbs him. That was a smile she read easily. It appeared on a man's face without his awareness, and it lasted only until there came some warning signal.

She decided to warn him.

'Strangers,' she said, 'may be the only people worth knowing.'

It was certainly not what she believed or ever had believed. Quite the opposite. It was a signal that he was not to have anything to say to her; study his hieroglyphics, and she would study hers. The copulating figures entwined with morning glories were, at least, symbols of life. His were symbols of what – Symbols?

Now, he was looking at the small green jade statue of the goddess Kuan-Yin, lying between her breasts, attached to the center strand of a string of pearls which wound three times around her neck. He looked quickly away, and Arlette smiled, amused by his embarrassment.

He turned back again. 'I'm sorry – I didn't hear what you said.'

Something in his intensity and sober manner was reassuring. He might admire Kuan-Yin, or her breasts, or her face, but he would not try to find out who she was. He would let her be anyone she chose to be.

She began to enjoy herself.

'I said strangers may be the only people worth knowing.'

This time the smile was calculated to alarm him, quick, dazzling, practiced to a perfect reliability for effect. He did not seem alarmed, but the color of his eyes changed slightly, from gray to green, then changed so quickly back again that the colors might have been only a reflection from the late sunlight.

All these appurtenances of an old, old spirit, of one who knew – perhaps – more than she did?

Although that seemed unlikely, since she was convinced that by now, she knew it all. All there was. Or even more than there was – for there might in fact be nothing to know:

When will we know what we know?

Could he tell her that?

' "Strangers may be the only people worth knowing," ' he repeated thoughtfully, and once again she was taken by surprise at the sound of his voice. Voices remained in her memory, even, it seemed, in her blood and the tangle of her veins, in the unknown territory of her body, longer than any other memory, any other impression or experience, but for the sexual encounter.

And this voice – yes, it was extraordinary, like his hands. Like those changing eyes. Like the quiet, the silence, the sense of a warm glow. The voice was a kind of power.

'Strangers offer no threats?' he asked.

'Strangers are the products of our imagination.' She was silent, watching the clouds, while he, she knew, was watching her. 'We can turn them into anything – Egyptian pharaohs, Spanish grandees. Just so they don't tell us who they are in real life. Then it's all over.'

13

She glanced at him quickly, before he had looked up from his study of Kuan-Yin, or her breasts.

'It is an unusually beautiful Kuan-Yin.'

'You recognize her?'

'My favorite deity, ever since my first visit to China.'

'Yes, she's mine too.' She recited, softly, the prayer to the Goddess of Mercy: *'Great mercy, great pity. Save from sorrow. Save from suffering.'* She smiled slightly, but no longer with challenge. Now there was a slight brooding tenderness, also perfected. 'She hasn't always been successful in my case. You've had better luck?'

He smiled; almost, she thought, a smile which reflected what he had seen in her face. 'No one does.'

'Even so, I'm never without her. Ever since I lived in China.'

This did surprise him. 'You lived in China? China's been closed to the outside world for more than twenty-five years. With few exceptions. You've been there – recently?'

'About twelve hundred years ago.'

'I see,' he said soberly, evidently prepared to play the game.

'I was the Supreme One – Empress of China, for all practical purposes.' She smiled confidingly. 'It was an interesting experience.'

'I would think so.' He did not smile.

'I've been wondering what language you're reading. Akkadian? Oh, please don't tell me. That would spoil everything.'

The plane had been slowly descending, and now, as she glanced at him, the full sunlight struck across the upper part of his face and she drew a quick breath, surprised again at the changed color of his eyes, from the glistening gray, impenetrable, to a green, brilliant as emeralds, shining gems:

I will never forget this miracle – or whatever it is.

All at once, Arlette picked up her glass: *'Ten thousand years!'* The toast to the Chinese emperors of twelve

14

hundred years ago. She drank the champagne quickly, tribute to the emerald miracle.

His black eyebrows lifted slightly, in amused appreci-ation. 'L'chaim.' He raised his glass and drained it.

'Is it ancient – that language you're reading?'

He was willing to continue the game. 'It's not an ancient language. It's quite a modern one.' His smile showed the kind of humor exchanged only between friends of long acquaintance.

From the first glance from the corners of her eyes, there had seemed something familiar about him, and yet she knew she had never seen him. That was no face to forget. Certainly not for her, a lifelong student of faces.

It was a face even a casual observer was not likely to forget, for its elegance of bone structure, the brilliance of concentration showing through the gray eyes, the stillness, the sense of glowing warmth.

'And you've learned it. That's remarkable, in its own way. To have found the time – in however many years you've had – to have learned a new language which perhaps no one else can understand. Did you invent it?' She spoke seriously, but there was still the curving smile at the edges of her lips, to let him know they might be serious about all this, but likely were not.

'It's a rather common language. And I suppose you can either learn it quite easily or not at all.'

'Of course.'

'Of course?'

'Like everything else.'

She moved slightly away. Something was happening; the simple male capacity for taking possession of a woman, if his imagination and will were strong enough, before he had touched her.

She looked at him, convinced that only by remaining motionless, looking back at him with the same attention he was giving her, would she be able to dominate this encounter.

But why should either of them care to dominate this

brief period of time, spliced somewhere in the midst of their lives, with no history, no future, no real significance?

She was amused and a little surprised.

Each man can turn you into a virgin all over again.

Wanting and fearing the knowledge, not so much of the man himself but of the world of men; the only world which existed in its pure reality, then vanished, to be forgotten, finally, as if it had never happened. Only some treachery of the imagination: the ivory figures, intertwined, lifeless, beautifully carved; gaining their humanity through their lovemaking, then losing it again when the excitement had run its course.

Quickly, to change the balance between them, she asked: 'You've been to China, you say?'

'I'm returning.'

'Now?' That was news.

'Now.' He smiled, still watching her with that careful intensity.

The plane had been slowly descending for some time, and as she glanced out the window, she found those last rays of sun had become a hazy twilight. The lights of the city rose toward them, and the speaker system advised them that this journey, too, was about to end.

She returned the smile, tipped her head a little, as if to tell him she understood the joke, whatever it might be. 'No one goes to China nowadays.'

'A few.'

'Oh, well. I deserved it, with that fable of having been the Supreme One, twelve hundred years ago. You remember her: Yang Kuei-fei – Jade Ring. She was famous. And yet, I may have been. In another life, on another star. In a way, it's truer than you might be willing to believe.'

The plane settled on the runway, shot forward, and slowed abruptly, then continued toward its port.

'You do believe in stars?' She looked at him seriously. 'Other worlds? Other times we don't know how to imagine?'

'I believe in little else.'

He closed the attaché case, and the stewardess was

giving him a black trench coat, but had nothing to offer her. She had made the trip as she got aboard, wearing only the dark red velvet suit, pale pink chiffon blouse, Kuan-Yin on the strand of pearls.

'May I help you?'

The game is over. This was the Spanish grandee, prepared to offer assistance to any damsel in distress at a great airport.

'Thank you. I am being met.'

She stood up and passed him. It was an old habit with her to make a quick escape from almost any situation, or place. The door opened. Time to go.

Moving rapidly toward the customs office, she realized she had forgotten him, and glanced around.

He was beside her, somewhat taller than she had expected, lean and straight, as a proper Egyptian pharaoh should be. She smiled again, that smile which had left its impression on thousands, millions of men and women by now.

'Good-bye,' she told him gaily, as if she were parting from an old friend.

'Good-bye, Mrs De Forest. And thank you. I enjoyed your performance – as always.'

She continued on her way quickly, and when she glanced around again he was nowhere in sight; possibly he was even more adept at getting through airport crowds than she: *Mrs De Forest*. He had known her all along. She laughed softly, and walked on.

I enjoyed your performance – as always . . .

Edna Frazier was waiting as Arlette came walking at that swift gliding pace which took her through airport crowds as easily as along a beach, a path across the moors, streets of the busiest cities.

She smiled from a distance, and Edna smiled in reply, for they liked each other in spite of being employer and employee, although there remained after seven years the formality which prevented Edna from calling her anything but Miss Morgan; not Mrs De Forest, but Miss Morgan.

They shook hands affectionately, for Edna had left London some months before, and as they walked to where Conrad waited with the car, Arlette questioned her:

Yes, Irma and Conrad had enjoyed their annual vacation in Norway.

Yes, Mr De Forest and Mr Brown had gone to Arizona and California several days ago and were expected back in time for dinner.

Yes, the house was cleaned, polished, painted – there was new upholstery, and new draperies and curtains, identical with the old ones.

'Oh, I'm so glad to be back! There's Conrad!' Another old friend.

They shook hands. 'A pleasant flight, Mrs De Forest?'

Just as Edna had never called her anything but Miss Morgan, so Conrad – chauffeur and butler for as long as Edna had been her secretary – had never called her anything but Mrs De Forest. He worked not for the professional woman, but for the wife, as did his wife, Irma.

Arlette smiled at him, not quite the brilliant smile she had given the stranger just returned from China, but the smile she kept for people like Conrad and Irma, Edna and the Webbs; the stage-doorkeeper and electricians and stagehands; the people who liked to say that Miss Morgan was human even if she was famous. And they knew it, for did she not—

And of course, she did. She had to. She did now. She always would. It was so automatic that however she felt, whatever she was thinking about, there it was: the reliable brilliant smile; the gaiety and warm consideration. The people she depended upon could depend upon her.

'Very pleasant, Conrad. And Miss Frazier tells me your—'

'Very much so, Mrs De Forest. It's always good to be back.'

The big black car drew slowly away from the curb and entered the stream of traffic leaving the airport for the city, and once again she remembered the man she had sat next to from London to New York.

She looked out the car window, hoping to catch another glimpse of him, for he had disappeared through the crowds before she could reply, gone on about his next business as quickly as she had gone to meet Edna and Conrad.

There, she thought. *There he is.*

She leaned forward: *No. Someone else.*

Well, what difference did it make?

Only that it was so unusual nowadays for her to talk to strangers – or even to meet them – civilians, outsiders. And the toast they had exchanged, Arlette lifting her champagne glass, when he had turned toward her as the plane banked and the late afternoon sun struck across the upper part of his face, changing his eyes from the glistening impenetrable gray to a green bright as emeralds:

I will never forget this miracle – or whatever it is.

To commemorate the event, she had lifted her champagne glass: '*Ten thousand years!*'

And with a slight grave smile, he had replied, in the professionally trained voice: 'L'chaim.'

She could hear his voice clearly, for even spoken quietly there was a resonance, yet it was not an actor's voice. Whatever he was, he was not an actor, for she could recognize an actor at sight. Actors were marked by their profession.

Whoever he was, and whether he was teasing her about having just returned from China, as she had teased him about having been the Supreme One, twelve hundred years ago, he was an authority of some kind. That quality conveyed itself from one to another of those who possessed it. It was the indescribable yet unmistakable signal of the world's most secret society, whose initiates recognized one another at a glance.

Medieval monk? Ancient Egyptian pharaoh? Spanish grandee?

Edna had opened her attaché case, set it across her lap, and put on her horn-rimmed glasses as she began to read. She read to Arlette from a carefully edited file. By now she knew what Miss Morgan wanted to hear as well as Miss Morgan knew.

She knew whom Miss Morgan would talk to on the telephone and whom she would not talk to. She knew when Miss Morgan would go to a party and when she would not. She knew when Miss Morgan should be reminded to give a dinner party, and what the guest list was likely to be, as well as the menu and the wines. For while Anthony had collected a connoisseur's cellar, he drank no more than Arlette did – one of the risks of the profession they had decided not to take.

Edna Frazier was blessed not only with competence, but better still, with a lack of envy.

She did not envy Miss Morgan her fame, her success, her adulation; or her beautiful face or her beautiful figure; or her soft blonde hair, which looked as if it had been lightly gilded, which it had. She did not envy her her expensive clothes, her jewelry, or her house. She did not envy Miss Morgan her money, even though she knew how much she had and where it was invested. She did not envy her her friends and admirers, or even her enemies. She did not envy Miss Morgan her handsome husband, or their highly publicized ideal relationship, a significant professional asset, for its rarity.

The car stopped, and Arlette leaned forward, looking up at the four-story brick house, painted a soft buff color, with a scrolled black iron balcony across the second floor, long narrow windows with their shutters painted a smoky black, and a great wisteria vine, its stems the size of her wrist, which once a year festooned the house with purple blossoms.

Arlette got out quickly and met Irma midway up the front steps.

There was none of the formal reserve which was in her greeting to Edna Frazier and Conrad. Irma, whether she had been away for a few days, several weeks or, as this time, for eight months, greeted her as if a favorite child had returned. Irma was not many years older than Arlette, but she had the manner of a woman with her daughter.

'Oh, Mrs De Forest – how long you've been away! Mr De Forest was lonely – even his work did not make him happy. He called from the airport less than half an hour ago. He'll be in time for dinner. Was England good to you this time, Mrs De Forest?'

Edna had slipped by them, no doubt having urgent errands, telephone calls to make in her office on the third floor, before she left for the day, and Arlette and Irma walked into the house.

'England,' said Arlette, 'was – England.'

'Oh, I know, Mrs De Forest.'

She stopped in the foyer, looking into the small drawing room, which, with the dining room and kitchen, occupied the first floor above the street level. 'How beautiful it is. I've missed you, Irma – I've missed everything. I'll never go there again.' So she had said before.

Irma was her benevolent household spirit, and her presence was a charm, a benediction. Nothing could go wrong in Mrs De Forest's life while Irma was there to keep the house as Mrs De Forest liked it, and to cook the meals Mrs and Mr De Forest liked.

The interior was cool, and as Arlette moved into the drawing room, Irma left her, gently as she had arrived.

The room was decorated in soft shades of mauve. The furniture, but for two overstuffed sofas, was Louis XV, upholstered in mauve, deep purple, ash rose, with two or three small chairs covered with crimson velvet.

There were several Impressionist paintings – most of them gifts from Anthony's family – and the collection was rather famous; one or two pictures were usually on loan, and Arlette now walked around to examine each carefully, to discover what had come back, what had gone away, these old friends of the nineteenth century: Renoir and Pisarro, Sisley and Degas:

Hello. Glad to see you've come back to us.

Having greeted the furniture, the flowers, the paintings, she went on to examine the jade collection: bowls of white nephrite, almost transparent; spinach-jade buddhas; and, last of all, a small pale statue of the Goddess of Mercy, Kuan-Yin, to whom Arlette now made obeisance, palms together, head lowered.

'My favorite deity,' he had said, that man beside her on the plane, with his elegant face, the prominent cheekbones and high-bridged nose, which she had studied as attentively as if she had been commanded to remember him always. 'My favorite deity, ever since my first visit to China.'

What must he have thought of her tale of having been Empress of China, twelve hundred years ago? And yet it was true. At least as true as that she was Arlette Morgan today. Mrs Anthony De Forest.

Over the fireplace hung the portrait, done a year ago, of Arlette Morgan as Lady Macbeth: *That most terrible test of any genius*, a nineteenth-century critic had described the part. And so it was.

The portrait was nearly life-size and showed a blonde Lady Macbeth, in a long gray-green dress which looked as if it had collected the Scottish mists through which she seemed to move slowly out of the canvas. Her head was slightly lowered and she gazed straight at Arlette Morgan, studying her with an inquisitive, critical intensity. Her stare was fixed, a little wild, with some unholy rapture, as if the Three Witches had touched her too. Her arms were held high, fingers spread wide with the effort to support the heavy gold crown.

Slowly as from a great distance in time, a time longer than the centuries which separated Arlette Morgan from the Scottish queen, she began to remember who Lady Macbeth had been one year ago.

All at once Arlette shuddered, shaking away the curious fascination of the queen who had bedeviled her life for years before she had dared play her:

Could I play that woman again?

No. She's gone. I have no idea how I did it.

She turned to go upstairs, bathe, dress for dinner. Anthony would be here, perhaps in a few minutes, and they had not seen each other for nearly eight and one half months.

Partway across the room she turned swiftly, as if to catch Lady Macbeth trying to follow her, perhaps to ask that she give her life back to her. Lady Macbeth remained where she had been, and Arlette smiled at her slightly, nodding in brief recognition of what they had been to each other:

Fame is the only treasure that endures.

The pearls she wore, with the goddess Kuan-Yin attached, had been Anthony's gift to her on the opening night of *Macbeth*, and a more surprising gift than any of the others.

It had told her that so far as Anthony was concerned, nothing had changed. She loved him as much as he loved her.

In some sense, she did. But not so very long ago she had loved him without sense. She had loved him without sense, without reason, without self-protection; and, she thought, unluckily, there was no other way to love. The compulsion to protect the self destroyed love before it came to life, and if it came to life and self-protectiveness then asserted itself, the love was killed on the moment.

Her unquestioning vulnerable love for him had lasted

23

for almost all of the eighteen years they had known each other. Or perhaps it had.

.For when she realized she had begun to love him, nothing could have surprised her more. But that seemed to be love's way – it came by surprise, unannounced, unexpected, unwelcome.

And when it went, that was the farewell it made, too. A surprise, unannounced, unexpected, even more unwelcome in its departure than in its arrival.

Now—

. He would appear at any moment – after the longest absence since they had been married – and here she dawdled about the drawing room, examining this picture and that piece of jade, and felt she had not recovered her equilibrium after the plane trip, but was still dazed, part of her in England, part of her here, and part of her still seated beside the man on the plane.

Surely, she had more reason to be returning from China than he could have. Her life, after all, had begun in China.

She had refused his formally courteous offer of help as they got off the plane, then found him beside her as they entered the customs area, quite a tall man, who spoke to her gravely, with only the trace of a smile: 'Good-bye, Mrs De Forest. And thank you. I enjoyed your performance – as always.'

That was the last she had seen of him. When she looked again, he was nowhere in sight.

But, at least, they had been playing the same game, and that pleased her. Even strangers might understand each other, although they almost never did. No better than they were likely to understand each other when the strangeness was gone. But this stranger had passed through her life; he would not reappear: they came from different worlds, read different languages, knew different kinds of people.

She had crossed the landing on her way upstairs when she heard the front door open. There was a silence, and then: 'Arlette?' in Anthony's voice.

PART I
1945

CHAPTER 1

Nothing could be worse than being fifteen years old.

Fifteen was no longer young. Fifteen was not yet old. Fifteen was not old enough for independence, even though she had as much independence as she had time for. Time was a precious commodity, and had been for the past ten years, which were all the years she could remember, day by day, if she should choose to try.

Fifteen was too young to know who you were going to be. Fifteen was too old to be satisfied with who you were so far. Fifteen was the age which knew everything, only to realize by the time the year had gone that everything was yet to be learned. Fifteen was the year when she stood upon the shallow edges of unexperienced time:

When will my life begin?

Lily Malone. Lily Malone. Lily Malone.

She wrote the name a dozen different ways, a hundred different ways. Still, she could not decide if she would continue to be Lily Malone or if she would decide to be someone else someday, once she could think of who she would rather be.

Lily Malone, luckily for her, as she had begun to realize two or three years ago, was destined to be more than a pretty blonde child with hazel eyes, her hair turning less blonde as the years went by, until by the time she had arrived at the age of fifteen, that blonde hair, which had once been the color of her mother's, had become a light brown, streaked blonde by the California sun. This pretty child, who had come to live with Frederick and Valerie Morgan when she was five – their niece and ward – was a beautiful young woman by the age of fifteen.

Her beauty, even so, did not entirely satisfy her. She looked at her mother's picture, the gay smiling young blonde woman, twenty-seven years old, the picture taken shortly before she had been killed, and she yearned to look like her. Blonde hair might produce the miracle.

That photograph stood on Lily's dressing table, the same dressing table which had been in the guest room of her aunt and uncle's house when she had arrived from Chicago.

Like the rest of the large two-story house, it was furnished in light wood furniture, glass-topped desks and tables, yellow and orange flowered upholstery. The house had the joyousness which Valerie had had herself, a Valerie less serious than she had since become, although Lily realized now that even in those days, Valerie Moore Morgan, twenty-five years old and married for one year to Professor Frederick Morgan, who was not quite thirty, must have been a serious young woman to have accepted as her responsibility this child of her husband's sister.

She had installed Lily in the guest room on the second floor, with a bathroom adjoining, at the opposite end of the hall from the bedroom Valerie and Frederick shared. Then she had begun to plan Lily's life, and soon the program was well under way.

A rescue program, Lily thought later, it must have seemed.

For the five-year-old girl who returned with them from Evanston, after the funeral services, was still expecting her mother and father to appear one day and take her back home.

It had been some time, two years, as she now supposed, before she had understood she would never see her parents again. They were dead, not merely absent.

And the fact, once she absorbed it, became all the more incomprehensible, the more bitter, because they had died senselessly, in the midst of a brilliant sunny day driving back from a weekend trip. They had met, coming upon them at the crest of a hill, another car, driven by a man alone, drunk or blinded by the sunlight, who had crossed the white line and driven into them at a speed which wrecked both cars and killed the three occupants.

She put that history together, bit by bit, as if she were

trying to reconstruct the shattered fragments of the windshield, the demolished car, by questioning Valerie and Frederick.

She had questioned them carefully, slowly, asking at first only when her parents would return from their vacation.

She refused to accept a loss which could never be repaired, which would never be transposed into the eagerly anticipated moment of magic surprise, when they would run in to sweep her into their arms, kissing her and laughing. The journey, they would explain, had been so pleasant they had decided to stay a little longer, knowing she and her brother would understand, glad they had seen unknown places, had great adventures they would describe.

It had been their way to tell them stories of their trips, most of them business trips around the nearby states, visiting one or another of the sites where Morgan-Malone Construction Engineers and their affiliated companies were building a bridge, an apartment house, a hotel – these trips had a way of sounding as if they had visited Byzantium and ancient China, distant stars and magical caves of crystals and diamonds.

But as Lily grew older, asking her aunt and uncle one question and another, growing bolder as she began to approach the comprehension of what had happened, those crystal and diamond caves became an image of the shattered windshield: a mirror, reflecting those two handsome young people, both of them laughing – for that was the way she remembered them, and that was what their photographs showed – until the windshield was shattered into a million diamonds, sharp and thin as razor-edged knives, millions of diamonds in the splintering glass, millions of miniature knives, glittering, flying like rain in a high wind. Then they were dead.

It was not, as she had begun to fear, that they had lost interest in her and Michael, sent her away to live with Valerie and Frederick, while Michael stayed in Chicago with their father's brother and his wife and family.

By the time Lily was ten years old, she no longer knew what stories her mother and father, that now legendary couple, Lily and Phillip Malone, had told her and what she had imagined. Essentially, it made no difference. For as long as she believed the conversations had taken place, with all the glory and excitement in their shining eyes and faces, the stories. real or imaginary, remained an abiding link.

Whenever it was, two years or three after they had died, she had come to the realization all at once, as if some clear white light had momentarily blinded her, some unexpected, terrible, yet immediately accepted vision of eternity:

They are dead.

The word, even though she had heard it from time to time, as Valerie and Frederick had tried slowly to accustom her to its meaning, had remained a word in a foreign language.

Then, whenever it had been – perhaps one morning when she awakened early; perhaps in the midst of a game with her school friends; racing over the hillsides covered with purple lupin and yellow spring buttercups – at some moment of activity or serene detachment, the foreign word revealed itself clearly, and she realized she had known its meaning for a very long time.

At fifteen, she had become a confirmed fatalist, convinced that the only way to endure life was to be happy, at whatever cost, and whether the happiness was true or false.

'While you're alive,' she told her uncle Frederick during one of their discussions in his library, where he corrected his students' papers, wrote his lectures, worked on his book about the life of the ordinary people of the Middle Ages in the British Isles – kings and queens and their like having had quite enough said for them. 'While you're alive, you manage to get along some way, don't you? And when you're dead, you don't have to worry about it.'

She was kneeling beside his chair, hands spread flat

across her knees, the signal that she had something serious to discuss.

Frederick knew when she was talking about her mother and father. After a moment he spoke quietly: 'A wise man once said: "*The dead are not absent, but only invisible*." '

Lily thought about this, and all at once she stood up. 'No. They are dead.' She left the room.

No more pretending for her. No more hopes. No more false consolations. They were dead. She had nothing of them but the photographs, some in her room, some in an album in Frederick's study, and on his desk. And the conviction that she would not live to be twenty-eight. After all, her mother had not.

That being so, she was aware of time as a force, rushing her ahead. Every moment must count for something. Whatever she wanted to do, whatever she wanted to have, she must do it immediately, have it immediately.

Other girls had abundant leisure. They expected to live forever. They had not even the sense to realize that today they were ten and tomorrow they would, if they were lucky or unlucky, be eighty, their lives lived out, spent.

And so far as Lily could determine, most of them would have little enough living to show for the years. These girls, for all that she walked to school with them, played with them during recesses, ate lunch with them, went to their parties and invited them to hers, did not and never had seemed quite real to her.

The boys seemed more real or, at least, more interesting: ten years old; eleven years old; twelve years old. At twelve, the current favorite gave her a dramatic demonstration of his passion.

'See that,' Dave Bartlet said to her one night, just as it was getting dark, when he had come to ask her to walk around the block. He raised his fist and punched the glass on the fire-alarm box, and neither flinched nor made a sound when the shattered glass left his hand dripping blood. 'That's to prove I love you.'

But the proof failed of its purpose, for Lily, horror-struck by the splintering glass, ran home and refused to speak to him again.

His successor, Al Hughes, another professor's son, was wiser in the ways of young women, for he bought her candy bars and ten-cent store jewels and invited her to the movies on a Saturday afternoon, an invitation she declined, having no time free for such wasting.

Valerie kept her occupied, when she was not in school, with a variety of private lessons. And Lily was not sorry to miss the movie, for although she was willing to kiss him in broad daylight on the front porch, a theater was dark, and a twelve-year-old boy had begun to seem a type of centaur, astride a dangerous beast.

A part of Lily's education had early begun to include the freedom to range through her uncle's library, as well as Valerie's recommended reading list for growing girls. By the time Lily was fifteen, the list included medical texts on male and female anatomy; two volumes by Freud; two by Havelock Ellis; Kraft-Ebbing, a somewhat more difficult undertaking, since she knew no German and a dictionary made the footnotes laborious, if instructive. She was, by then, the oracle, and her friends came to her when their parents refused to answer their questions, or the girls suspected their parents of essential ignorance anyway.

One of her friends, the daughter of a professor of Greek drama, was a married woman at eighteen, a premature matron, with a baby and a nineteen-year-old husband.

'It's wonderful, Lily,' she assured her when Lily appeared at the hospital. 'The only way to know what it's like is to try it.'

'But what will you do with – it—' Lily gestured toward the baby.

The girl laughed, and seemed to think she had the most amusing toy imaginable.

Lily found the world full of such warnings: freedom was easy to lose. And once lost, freedom was difficult if not impossible to regain. Something in the nature of the loss created walls too high for most girls to scale; and something in that first loss of freedom seemed to cut the will out of them, as if by surgical maneuver.

Anyway, just as she had no time for Saturday afternoon movies, neither had she time for illegitimate babies, made legitimate only by parental stubbornness.

While her twelve-year-old friends talked of how many babies they would have, when they would get married – even before the first fourteen-year-old centaur had invited them to a Saturday matinee – Lily was occupied with other things.

'How many babies are you going to have, Lily?'

'None.'

'How old do you want to be when you get married, Lily?'

'I'm not going to get married. I like freedom too well.'

She did not intend to lose it, ever. She was free now, because she was free to speculate, to imagine the future. Nothing had been set into cement. She intended to keep it that way, and sometimes sang a folk song she had heard at a friend's house:

> *'I never will marry,*
> *Nor be no man's wife.*
> *I mean to live single*
> *All the days of my life.*
> *The shells in the ocean*
> *Shall be my death-bed,*
> *And fish in deep water*
> *Swim over my head . . .'*

Usually she sang the song in a voice too low to be understood, but occasionally she sang it aloud, and once she came upon Frederick, waiting on the landing for her to pass him going downstairs, and saw the troubled expression in his eyes.

But he said nothing, and no doubt supposed the song was a part of the grief she would not surrender, even though she seemed, most of the time, gay and casually happy, occupied with one or another of the projects

Valerie had been inventing for her from the first week she was with them.

Valerie had a degree in anthropology, but although she had done some field work during her post-graduate studies, she had turned her interest to the study of behaviorist psychology. Then Lily Malone entered her house and became the perfect subject for Valerie's Ph.D. thesis: the possibility that childhood need not be a wasteland.

Undoubtedly, their meeting at that moment was a lucky one. Valerie's high good humor, despite her seriousness, her absolute conviction about her convictions, coupled with her willingness to change the direction of an experiment if it did not prove promising, was the one possibility of deflecting her niece's brooding attention from her parents.

'Childhood,' Valerie explained when Lily was eight or nine, 'is usually a fallow period of life, without real stimulus or challenge. And if they're lost, those years between five and twenty, there's no hope of ever becoming what one might otherwise have been.'

Lily did not think of herself as a child, either then or later, but only as Lily Malone — a mysterious personage who dwelt either somewhere inside her or on some distant star in some other century.

But she enjoyed the solutions Valerie provided for repairing the void of childhood, and while her friends were counting their babies in advance, playing hopscotch and jacks, or baseball and basketball, Lily was taking lessons in ballet, although she did not dance on her toes, for the risk of spoiling her feet and legs; swimming; studying French and Spanish under private tutors. Some of the lessons lasted a year. Some of them two years. But they were carefully chosen, as was her reading schedule, for what would fill her world, internal and external.

'Unless you're a professional, no serious event in life ever requires a game of tennis, golf, or bridge,' Valerie told her when she was fifteen and her friends began to learn these accomplishments. 'But to swim and ride superbly – *that* can be your salvation.'

CHAPTER 2

Every year there was a Christmas reunion.

One year Frederick and Valerie and Lily went to Chicago. The next year the Malones brought Michael and their own three children to California, and for ten days the house was noisy, filled with laughter and running up and down stairs, games and presents and Christmas-tree trimmings.

Lily's private studies came to a halt. It was the time the two families had provided for Michael and his sister to remember that they were a part of a larger unit, that once they had had parents, and that now, at least, they had each other.

By the time Lily was twelve and Michael nine, the Christmas reunion – that year at Valerie and Frederick's – brought them together with the customary surprise at the change of the past year; at least Lily was surprised:

We don't look exactly alike any more. I look more like she did, and he looks more like our father did.

Lily's picture of her parents, by that time, was a complete one, composed of conversations with Valerie and Frederick, and of the photographs she had studied, the album of snapshots. Now she thought she knew them, exactly as they must have been: young, ardent, beautiful; both of them strong and vivacious. They seemed to her rare and wonderful beings, those two, with their babies, Lily and Michael, and the fabric she wove was a comfort, and a source of endless despair and bitterness.

Her brother remembered them not at all.

'How could I, Lily?' he had asked reasonably when she had questioned him three years before. 'I was two years old.' Now he was nine.

'Even so,' she had replied. 'Even so.'

Now that three years had elapsed, she intended to put him through another catechism. There was no reason why she must bear this burden of memory and sorrow without his help.

She began to watch him suspiciously during those first few days, as they played with the cousins, ate at the round dining table, the children first, the adults later – although when they were alone Lily ate with Valerie and Frederick, and was encouraged to ask them every question she could imagine.

The game was an old one:

Ask us everything you can think of. Try to find something we can't answer.

But the game was not easy to win. They knew, it seemed, all the answers – and they were learning new ones every day.

'What is it you do, exactly, Uncle Frederick?' she had asked him, entering his study at that hour, about six o'clock in the afternoon, when the last student had gone.

Frederick laid aside his pen and smiled, a reflective, not entirely happy smile. 'What is it I do, Lily?' He gestured at the books which covered every wall and stood piled on the floor. 'I am, I suppose, a student of the *splendid and the bitter past.*'

Lily thought that over carefully. 'So am I.' She gazed at him with the occasional somberness which gave her face a look as of one born with an ancient wisdom.

'I know.' They looked at each other carefully. She reached out her hand as she knelt beside him, and he took it gently. 'She was beautiful. You see that.' There was a photograph on his desk, the four of them taken the day Valerie and Frederick had been married, and now it seemed to Lily to belong to some remote unimaginable past, another century, another era of the world's or their own history.

Neither Valerie nor Frederick was what adults called old, even now, but from her viewpoint at twelve, the Valerie Moore Morgan and Frederick Morgan of the photograph looked unbelievably youthful, untouched.

The four of them, in this informal picture, stood with their arms about one another's waists, smiling directly at the camera with those gay confident smiles of which Lily saw nowadays only an occasional reflection on the faces of her increasingly serious aunt and uncle.

While Lily and Phillip Malone, dead less than a year later, would smile as they had that day, for as long as the picture existed – longer, Lily thought.

There they were, and there they would always be, happy, in love with each other and with the future, with the past, no doubt, since it had been favorably disposed toward them – given them health and good looks and, so far, time to enjoy them.

She was beautiful, that Lily Morgan Malone, blonde-haired, hazel-eyed, with a rapturous smile Lily remembered, with or without photographs to remind her. The smile of greeting; the smile of a temporary parting.

There were other pictures, snapshots taken at picnics, on beaches, with Lily Morgan Malone's blonde hair blowing about her face, and laughter on her mouth. She had gone through her short life, Frederick said, with gaiety and confidence, and laughter had been her most natural expression, even though there was, as Lily saw in some few of the photographs, moments of a solemn, tender, thoughtful, and almost remorseful sadness.

What had caused that? Why should she have been remorseful, even for a moment, when it was to end so quickly? There had not been time for the usual tears and fancies of young and ardent women.

'I suppose, like all of us – she suffered from the unknown grief.'

Lily looked from the photograph to Frederick's serious face: *The unknown grief?*

Was there such a thing? She knew what her grief was. It was as clear and simple and profound as grief could be· the only hope for which all hope was hopeless.

'The unknown grief?'

'Yes, Lily. You feel it, too. Even though you think you

37

know what it is, there's the other part — the part that's missing for all of us.'

'What part is missing — for all of us?'

He touched her face, in that familiar gesture of reassurance, as if he yearned to promise her that, even so, life was not all unbearable loss, irrevocable abandonment, though he had suggested it might be. This student of *the splendid and the bitter past* had also discovered some bitterness in the present?

'Maybe it's only the missing part between the experience of living and the experience of dying. Something which should be there, or so it seems to us, but which we can never be sure of having found.' He looked at the photograph again. 'Some people believe the missing part is love — and there is no other solution for any of us.'

'That's just the way to lose whatever you have found. If you love someone — of course you will lose them.'

'Not always. You must not let yourself believe this loss is the world's pattern for you.' Of all their conversations, upon every subject she could think to bring him, this one had taken the turn most disquieting for her and, it seemed, for Frederick. 'Someday, you may love someone who becomes part of you.'

'And then,' she demanded, 'you are no longer suffering the unknown grief?'

'Perhaps. Perhaps, darling. If I could tell you, I would.' He stood up. 'Come — let's go see what your brother is up to.'

'I know what he's up to. That chemistry set you gave him. He's in the dining room, mixing up all kinds of terrible-smelling things. I think he's going to turn into Mr Hyde before this Christmas vacation is over.'

What, exactly, was Michael doing with a chemistry set — when it was intended he should become an engineer, like his grandfather, his father, his uncle Kenneth?

One of his presents had been given with that destiny in view, an elaborate game for creating bridges, castles, modern apartment buildings. Several had been put up and dismantled, then abandoned in favor of the chemistry set;

Valerie's idea, as Lily knew. For the children had run through their annual psychology tests the year before and Valerie had detected Michael's interest in other things than engineering.

When Lily had asked to be shown exactly where, on the test papers, she had detected it, Valerie could not be explicit. It was there, that was all.

'We'll see,' she had promised Lily. 'Next Christmas.'

Perhaps there was something in those tests Valerie gave them, pretending it was the great game of the year. And so they proved to be, for the children clamored after them and spent two days gathered about the dining table, wherever they were, working at the puzzles with a kind of desperate joy, even though results were never listed, grades never passed out.

The tests, Valerie explained, were an end in themselves. This was not school. But by the time she was ten, Lily had begun to suspect otherwise, for her aunt Valerie was not inclined to waste time, and Valerie was classifying and codifying and indexing them as part of her great experiment, of which Lily Malone was the centerpiece.

Now Michael had taken over the dining room between meals, spreading out his books, his retorts, his multi-colored liquids, and there he was to be found at almost every hour of the day and as late as he was permitted to stay up at night, mixing and swirling, measuring and pouring, too absorbed to hear when they approached him.

Michael was almost Lily's height now, and promised to be, like his father and uncles, rather tall and thin. His hair was brown, like his father's; his eyes were light brown.

How all this could be true, and the matching photographs to prove it, and Michael still not remember anything at all, was a mystery Lily thought must be cracked open, revealed for him to see.

Michael smiled at them swiftly and confidingly, but immediately returned to his measuring. He promptly answered the questions Frederick put to him, without looking up. But when Frederick disappeared, Lily remained at her brother's side, watching him, now and then holding her nose as a puff of smoke went up and an unusually noxious odor filled the room. The windows were wide open, the other doors closed. Dr Caligari had his cabinet to himself, or so he seemed to think – for though Lily had remained after Frederick's departure, Michael did not seem to know she was there.

At last she addressed him in a clear imperative tone: 'Michael.'

He had evidently reached a situation which promised major crisis, for he had moved to another chair and was studying one of the books, underlining as he went.

'Michael,' said Lily, determined to catch his interest even if she had to sweep the chemistry set onto the floor. However, she had a better way. 'Do you know what I'm going to be?'

'Aunt Valerie,' said Michael, still reading, 'says you would make an excellent anthropologist. Or maybe a sociologist. You study people – that's why.'

'Sociologist,' repeated Lily in a soft scornful tone. She stood very straight, lifting her head, as she did when she practiced before her mirror, with the dolls she never played with but set in a row along the wall – witnesses to the high drama of her life, acted before them in brief scenes. 'I am going to be a great actress. Not in the movies. That's not acting. On the stage, where it counts.'

Michael had always been tolerant of the notions and plans of others, and he accepted this announcement calmly. 'They won't like it. The world needs sociologists and anthropologists and worthwhile citizens.'

'What's come over you, Michael? I think you're losing your mind over that chemistry set. I am going to be a great actress. I've played one starring part, and I was a tremendous success.'

'So was I,' said Michael, and seemed eager to please her. 'I played the Spirit of Arithmetic.'

Lily burst into laughter, the laughter which – when she could remember only the present – was natural to her, a gay laugh, joyous, a fountain of laughter, which enchanted her admirers. 'But I,' she assured him, 'played the part of

Antoinette in a play I wrote myself. Guess what it was called.' No use waiting for an answer. '*Adventure*. I wrote it, I directed it, I designed the costumes and stage settings, I organized the ticket sales, and I played the part of a girl who is beautiful and reckless and has one adventure after another. It was produced in the garden.'

She glanced through the window, seeing it all, as if it were taking place at that moment – even though the glorious day had come and gone four years ago and she had been afraid to tell Michael about it until now, when he was too preoccupied to pay strict attention to what she was saying.

She could still see the rows of chairs, with the mothers and fathers of the cast seated in them. There was Lily Malone, wearing Spanish shawls, gypsy skirts, and hoop earrings, pursuing her headlong career while the rest of the cast tried to keep up with her improvisations. She had bowed at the end, as if none of the other players were present.

It had been the most glorious moment of her life, so far.

Yet it had never been repeated.

For the next time she tried to recruit her performers, they wanted to do something else: perhaps they had not enjoyed being the furniture by means of which Lily Malone had demonstrated her charms to all in the neighborhood. And Valerie had remarked that it had been an interesting experiment, but it had taken too much time.

'Play is all very well,' Valerie told her, paraphrasing one of her favorite philosophers, 'provided it detracts from nothing better.'

And that had been the end of Lily's privately produced presentations, nor did she take much interest in the school pageants, with their white cotton wigs and minuets; their crepe-paper roses and crepe-paper butterflies. She participated resentfully, refusing to contribute her sparkle, her vitality, her smile – her best smile, at least – to any such foolish undertakings.

'And you, Michael – what are you going to be?'

'I haven't decided.'

'You're nine years old. Valerie says childhood is usually a wasteland.'

CHAPTER 3

Lily looked at herself in the dressing-table mirror:

I am a haunted house.

Her hair was blonde again, a process which had taken place slowly during the past two years, about which she had consulted the pharmacist with all the secrecy and ardor of Juliet consulting the old friar about the sleep potion, and the final effect had become evident today. She had applied the lotion, washed her hair and wound it on large rollers, and wearing her white robe with a yellow towel around her head, waved good-bye to Valerie and Frederick, setting out to visit friends at the Davis College campus.

To Valerie and Frederick, there was no demarcation between professional friends and personal friends. To Lily, friends who were only friends – like Marjorie Wells – were less interesting than friends who participated crucially in her life, as Barbara Sloan had since Lily had shifted best friends in the eleventh grade. For Barbara was better-looking than Marjorie, and attracted boys from other colleges to her parties and dances, and that in itself made her more a colleague than a friend.

When Frederick and Valerie had gone, Lily went through her routine of ballet exercises, then one half hour of calisthenics and, while she waited for her hair to dry, to see the grand final effect of her subtle experiments (which Valerie and Frederick had been too preoccupied or too tactful to mention), applied a new makeup, just different enough to match the new hair color: a little more mascara, a touch of mauve eye shadow, a lipstick of a deeper pink than the nearly invisible one she had been using.

The makeup had been carefully planned for the effect she wanted to produce. Lily was convinced that only Lily knew what was best for her.

She made no such drastic changes as some of her friends made. She had simply grown up, so it appeared, easily and naturally as a plant, blossoming and ripening with what anyone but Lily would have sworn was the inevitability of natural process.

Not only had Lily known what she wanted and how to go about getting it – more surprising, she seemed to know how to achieve her goals without attracting undue attention to her progress.

'People don't like people who know what they want,' she had confided to Frederick.

He had looked at her, as he sometimes did, as if he were seeing his sister's reincarnation, or some other manifestation of wonder. 'No. But how did you find that out – at your age?' Lily had shrugged, then all at once given that surprising free and open laugh, the one into which she was training an effect of rippling water.

The new makeup, which took half an hour to apply, pleased her. But she avoided looking at the photograph of her mother on the dressing table, to see if the mimicry was accurate.

She ran through the house on her way to the attic, stopping in Frederick's study to look at the picture of the four young people, Valerie in her white silk gown, holding a bouquet dripping long white knotted ribbons, the men in morning clothes, Lily Morgan Malone, as matron of honor, in something which appeared to be chiffon, with a pointed hem, as if giant handkerchiefs had been sewn into the skirt. About her neck was a strand of pearls – the pearls Valerie had placed in Lily's hand the day of her high school graduation.

Lily had accepted them, closed them in her hand, but refused to wear them. They had remained in her dressing-table drawer on graduation night, and had not yet been clasped about her throat. Now and then she looked at them, but could not bring herself to touch them:

Someday, someday, I'll be able to do it . . . when the time comes.

The time had not come.

Not today, either. Even though she had made the great decision to remove some of her mother's dresses from the trunk in the attic. Valerie had told her they were there, that she might examine them if she wished to. But she had not wished to.

Today, for reasons unknown, she raced up the stairs, approached the trunk slowly and cautiously, and all at once flung it open. Before her courage could fail, she began to remove the dresses, carefully, laying them over chairs, until she had strewn eight of them about the dimly lighted room.

The dresses, wrinkled, though they had been carefully packed in tissue paper, looked like a collection of flowers, a scattered bouquet of yellow and mauve blossoms, a bright red one of chiffon, an ivory evening gown of panne velvet. They were cut in the styles of the eight years or so before her mother's death, and so they were now almost twenty years old.

They seemed wonderfully exotic, and all at once she took one, made of something not as sheer as chiffon, a mauve and lavender and purple evening dress, with white water lilies floating across it, and ran downstairs, her heart beating as if she were about to steal something of great value.

She unrolled the curlers, brushed her hair quickly, then bent close to the mirror.

She was blonde, no question as to whether her hair was light brown with blonde streaks; and the color seemed to deepen the hazel of her eyes. Her hair was parted on the right side, and a curve touched the edge of her left eyebrow. But the hair, only slightly waved and reaching her shoulders, did not obscure her face – that face which now surprised her. The slight difference in the color of the hair, in her makeup, and there was a new Lily Malone.

She threw off the robe, slipped the dress over her naked body, and stepped into the high-heeled mauve satin pumps she had worn to the high school graduation dance. She fastened it at the neck in back, and a stranger faced her. She stood straight and surveyed that other woman, her unknown self. The dress fell over her body as if it had been intended for her:

She was the same height I am.

Yet she had known for years how tall her mother had been.

She was the same weight.

She had also known for years how much she had weighed, and that she had been slender yet rounded; that was evident in the photographs. She had been pliant, graceful, perhaps because she loved dancing, and Lily had convinced herself that the woman who had lived as Lily Morgan Malone for twenty-seven years was as familiar to her as she was to herself.

She smiled at the mirror:

Why, of course – that's what she looked like.

She removed the dress, repacked the garments, trying to pretend they had never been worn by anyone, impersonal dresses with no history. But she did not repeat the experiment. It had been too profoundly troubling.

A few weeks later she was in the attic with Valerie, helping to file some of the papers which were fed at a continuous rate into the filing cabinets, and Valerie asked if she would like to see the dresses her mother had worn. Lily shook her head decisively.

'I've seen them.'

Valerie glanced at her, surprised. But Lily was busy putting the files in proper chronology, and clearly intended to say no more about the dresses, no more about the subject of her uncanny resemblance to Lily Morgan Malone.

She thought she had no right to the name, either:

Lily Malone. How can I be Lily Malone?

Michael had not been able – not the first Christmas she had discussed it, nor the next, nor the last one – to give her any satisfaction, although she challenged him upon it each time.

By the last visit, he was done playing with Christmas chemistry sets. He was studying chemistry in school, had abandoned entirely the earlier expectation of being an engineer, and he was not easy to catch in the house, for he was riding his bicycle in fiercely competitive races with his cousins and the boys in the neighborhood. By then, of course, Lily was too grown-up for such childishness, if she had ever been young enough.

Now she was busy dressing up and going to holiday parties and the dances given at Barbara Sloan's house, and seventeen- and eighteen-year-old boys were rapping at the door to carry her away in borrowed family cars.

The boys bored her, most of them, but they were boys, and so they had some interest for that reason if no other.

She had played Circe with one; Cleopatra with another; Helen of Troy with another.

But they got less from her than perhaps they were hoping. She kissed them if she liked them, and would not kiss them if she did not, for there were too many boys eager to escort Lily Malone to a party. Most of her friends had less luck, in these matters as in others, and could not afford Lily's high-handed ruthlessness if they were to enjoy any popularity at all.

'The beauty of a young girl,' remarked Frederick as she entered the living room one night, wearing the mauve silk graduation dress which was her favorite costume – all she would need for the rest of her life, she thought – smiling questioningly at the aunts and uncles, the younger cousins, to ask their approval. 'The beauty of a young girl is indeed an awesome thing to contemplate.'

He spoke in a low tone, overheard only by Lily, who gave him a secretive smile of thanks. For she was realizing the truth of this statement, day by day.

Even the disaster of her appearance in the senior-class production of *Bitter Sweet*, starring Barbara Sloan, while Lily had sung a part as unsuited to her as a part could be, had shaken her confidence only for a day or two. And she had forgiven Barbara, because of the ballroom on the third floor of the big Victorian house, where Barbara and her divorced mother lived – even if she had not forgotten it:

One day, Barbara – one day . . .

Bitter Sweet, after all, had been no test of anything. She was prepared to wait until a worthy one came along.

She was convinced that there were certain *Days of Destiny*, and that the art of living was to recognize them when they came, not to let them pass unattended, as most of her friends seemed to do. And her performance of Manon in *Bitter Sweet* had not been one of those days. It had been a mistake that she had agreed to play the part, but Valerie had argued reasonably that it was the duty of each member of society to cooperate in the common adventures, the rites of passage.

Cooperation. Unselfishness. Duty. Responsibility. Devotion. Those were Valerie's code words. Along with: Atheism. Socialism. Behaviorism. Philosophical anarchy.

Somehow Valerie was able to piece this seemingly disparate patchwork into a unified philosophy, and Valerie was, so far as anyone knew, probably including Valerie, a happy, purposeful woman.

'Your name,' she said to Michael when she found him alone one afternoon, reading in Frederick's study. This was a precious moment, for it had not been easy to come by in the rush and confusion of the holidays.

'My name?'

'Malone. Don't you ever think about it?'

'Should I?'

Lily thought about her name very often, and very often it seemed she had stolen the name, and perhaps in stealing the name had stolen her mother's life:

Lily did not belong to her. Neither did *Malone*.

'Of course, you're not named Phillip.' It was their oldest cousin who had been named Phillip, and he was proud of being named for his handsome dead uncle. 'It's not really our name. It was their name.'

Michael was older than when she had first tried to force

47

him to remember them – anything, something to indicate that they inhabited Michael as they inhabited her.

'I don't understand you, Lily.' He was honestly bewildered. 'They gave us the name, just as they gave us our lives. It's something we have.'

He looked at her seriously, for there were tears in her eyes, and she could do nothing but ignore them and hope they would not become a fountain. She waited, and the danger passed. The tears were brushed away.

'It's all we have,' he said gently.

Lily swore to herself she would never speak of them to him again. He was not evading. He could not remember. Nothing was left from those first two years of his life which he could force into awareness:

Very well, then. I'll remember for both of us.

The memory was always there. It never left her, even when she was most completely concentrated upon something very different: dancing at one of Barbara Sloan's parties: studying for finals; practicing ballet.

Perhaps only Frederick knew that she could be thinking about them when she seemed to be thinking of nothing but how wonderful the world was, with all its secrets, more secrets than she had herself:

And the one great secret, yet to be discovered.

When? She had no idea.

Lily's beauty made her snobbish, unwilling to let the boys who admired her, obeyed her, hoping that one day she would forget what was happening, so causing it to happen. She never did.

The hand slipping too far upward on the inside of her thigh was stopped. The hand caressing her breasts, unfastening her dress or sweater to admire her, for Lily wore nothing but a slip under her clothes, and sometimes not that – the hand, if it belonged to the boy she was going with at that time, was permitted to stroke her breasts; the mouth might move downward over her throat, to her breasts – although the first time that happened she had been so astonished at the pleasure of the sensation she had let it go on too long, and the trousers were unzipped,

48

the hard penis she had never seen, never touched naked, pressed against her closed legs, but she pushed him away.

The temptations had begun and, so she had heard from Marjorie, once begun, there was no stopping them. Marjorie had had an abortion the year before and was embarrassed to admit she did not know who the boy had been. Marjorie was popular and became popular soon again.

Marjorie, thought Lily, was a damned fool. But, nevertheless, there it was; the secret some of her friends had discovered before they were twelve remained a mystery to Lily.

She was not waiting, consciously at least, for the irresistible moment. She was protecting Lily Malone from an experience she might later wish she had not had so soon. Therefore, when they became too insistent, they were banished. She went to Barbara's dances with some-one else.

That was where she met Jack Davidson, the summer after her first freshman semester. Jack was new to these dances, an older man, nineteen, and a junior. Barbara had admitted that she liked him.

'Tell me if you think he's right for me, Lily. You're a good judge of men.'

Lily gave her a slight smile, nodding: *Poor Barbara*.

CHAPTER 4

This was the queenly period of her life.

Circe and Cleopatra and Helen of Troy having had their day, not yet quite recognized for what they had meant to her, she had supposed those incarnations being over and done, no new ones would appear.

She was Lily Malone, no one else.

It had always been easy for Lily to suppose that the experiences of other people were of no great consequence, while her own experiences and responses produced a glow she sometimes thought must be visible as the aurora borealis, turning whatever it enhanced into magical beauty and purpose.

She expected nothing less from life. She demanded nothing less from herself.

The exact nature of this achievement had yet to be determined – despite her proud announcement to Michael, who had never mentioned it again and had probably forgotten it, that one day she would be a great actress.

Valerie and Frederick would be disappointed, and she was less prepared to disappoint them now than when she had been twelve. The devotion they had expended, never with any hint that it was expended for reasons other than love, freely given, had increased her wish to please them.

And so she had enrolled in the two anthropology courses open to freshmen students, and one in sociology.

'This is your choice, Lily?' Frederick had asked.

'It's my choice.'

He smiled slightly, not skeptical, not ironic, since he had never shown her such qualities, although Lily had heard that her uncle's senior and graduate students admired and feared his ironic way of dealing with that splendid and bitter past to which he introduced them.

'It's sometimes better, Lily,' Frederick had said, plainly doubting the urgency of her interest in anthropology and sociology, 'to act as if you know you're right than to wait until you are sure. That day never comes, except for the psychopaths. The rest of us live by guesswork. Some of us guess better than others, but we must learn to trust our guesses.' He had looked at her with shrewd concentration. 'You understand what I'm telling you?'

'I understand.' She did.

She was not to choose their path. She was to choose her own life.

That, she thought, was easier said by him than done by her. Her future, she thought, was fixed – out there somewhere among the aborigines with mud in their hair, as Jack Davidson had remarked the night before, as they danced together and he politely inquired what she was studying.

Not five minutes after he entered the room with Johnny Parker, he had danced with his hostess and then gone directly to Lily – as if Johnny had brought him there for no other purpose than to gaze upon this inaccessible blonde beauty. For that was the reputation she had, and she liked it.

When he had cut in, Lily was dancing with Dave Bartlet, to 'People Will Say We're in Love,' one of Lily's favorites – for she liked songs about love, even though she did not believe in it.

He had laughed aloud when she had replied that she was going to be an anthropologist. Lily looked up quickly. He was some inches taller than she, this young man with curly blond hair and narrow blue eyes, a broad grin, showing fine square white teeth, to match his fine square jaw and shoulders. Lily had thought as he approached that he was unquestionably the most attractive man she had met.

'What's funny about that?' she had demanded. It was such a noble ambition, and so far from her real one, she expected to be taken seriously.

'A girl who looks like you – out in the boondocks with those naked savages in their jockstraps and mud in their hair.'

He held her closer, spun her around, and she forgot her anger in a delicious pleasure and excitement. He knew how to dance, and since she was expert, that made him superior to most of these young men, who shuffled from one foot to the other, scarcely moving from the square yard they had staked out as their territory, or tossed their partners about when a jitterbug record split the air.

Even so, although he had driven her home, asked if he might call her tomorrow, asked if he might see her tomorrow, he had not tried to kiss her. He was, she decided, sophisticated, and that was the greatest compliment she or Barbara would have paid a man – they knew few who might be called, even in their private jokes, sophisticated.

She had thought him more or less sophisticated not to offer to kiss her, and had thought about that puzzle more than if he had behaved as the other young men did, lunging toward her the moment the car stopped, as if she might escape, as quite often she did. That it was sophistication and not indifference was clear from the fact that he had called while she was riding horseback with Valerie. He had called again when she came back, to ask if he could see her tonight, then tomorrow night, or the night after.

Scarcely three weeks after she had met Jack Davidson, her reign over him had been so completely established he would have thrown his cloak in the mud, set out on a crusade among the infidel, gone north to defeat the Irish once and for all, had any such whim occurred to her. And a willing subject, she discovered, was a luxury for a young woman, something quite superior to any of the earlier luxuries of devotion provided by boys like Dave Bartlet and Al Hughes.

There was some slight commotion with Barbara.

The morning after Barbara's dance, Lily was called to the telephone in the midst of having breakfast with Valerie and Frederick, telling them who had been there last night, but saying nothing about the person who had driven her home and talked in the parked car until nearly two o'clock.

Barbara's voice sounded unnatural, and Lily knew she was angry for the first time during their long friendship. Lily had been angry when Barbara had stolen *Bitter Sweet*, but Barbara had not known that.

'When can I see you? I can be there in ten minutes.'

'My horseback riding lesson is at ten. Remember, this is Sunday.'

Remember, this is Sunday, translated to mean: *Remember, this is the day I take all the lessons I don't have time for during the week.*

Horseback riding was at ten, and she was dressed for it,

as Valerie was; this was one of the things they did together. A French teacher came at twelve. If Lily did become an anthropologist, Valerie reasoned, many primitive tribes were in what had once been French colonies. If the reason was a practical one, Lily had private lessons. Otherwise, Valerie preferred Lily to learn among her peers and future competitors. That Lily learned to compete in many things the curriculum did not include was possibly something Valerie guessed, but did not discuss.

'After the French lesson, it's the piano lesson. At five it's—'

'Jack Davidson?'

'At five I'm going to study.'

'I'll be there at five. It will only take a few minutes.'

Lily hung up and studied the carpet:

Is she having an affair with him?

The housekeeper sent Barbara to Lily's room at five o'clock. She rapped peremptorily. 'It's me – Barbara!'

Lily opened the door, wearing her white robe, her hair wrapped in the yellow towel, for Sunday was still the day for experimenting with the blonde hair: gold was the color she was after.

Lily smiled at her friend, as if this were the ordinary Sunday afternoon call. Barbara entered swiftly, glancing about as if she thought Jack Davidson might be hidden there.

Barbara was two years older than Lily, although Lily considered herself wiser than Barbara. She had studied Barbara more carefully than the boys did, and knew that Barbara was a pretty girl, but not beautiful, and so she did not worry about her.

Barbara was a little taller than Lily, and her body was more slender, but for her breasts, unusually ripe for a girl her age. Her buttocks were flat, a negative correlation in Lily's mathematical assessments, and her hands were not long, nor could she use them to the effect Lily achieved with her modern and ballet dancing classes. Her chief claim to notice was her long black hair, which had grown to below her waist, and which she wound into a high chignon, and her large eyes, almost as black as her hair, upon which she relied for her greatest effects, rolling them as if everything in the world interested her. No, Barbara was not subtle, but she had, at least with boys, a soft demure manner which made them imagine her a different girl from the determined willful one Lily knew.

Lily lounged in the overstuffed armchair, her bare feet on a hassock, while Barbara lay on the bed, watching Lily suspiciously. Yet she did not want to end her friendship with Lily. She only wanted Lily to renounce Jack David-son.

Lily now began her so far unrecognized tactic of exaggerated politeness, which she had used for several years as a form of ironic sarcasm. Yet no one had ever recognized it for what it was. They mistook it for modesty, friendliness – even generosity. They began to discuss Jack.

'Oh, he's a little more grown-up than Dave Bartlet or Al Hughes or any of the rest of them. He's going to be an engineer,' Lily added, as if Barbara might find that interesting. It had interested Lily, since her father had been an engineer, and she had tried to imagine, without great success, what his work had been like.

'He came there to meet me, after all,' Barbara said. 'Johnny Parker brought him because he'd seen me on the campus and wanted to meet me. And then you took up all his time.'

'I took up all – his – time?' She gazed thoughtfully at Barbara.

'He spent most of the night dancing with you. And he took you home.' Barbara sat up suddenly and her black eyes flashed. 'Did you ask him to?'

Lily was silent, looking at her friend with thoughtful concern, as if she might be troubled that perhaps Barbara was not feeling well.

'Did he ask to meet you, Barbara, or did you ask Johnny Parker to bring him?'

'I met him once. On the campus. He was with Johnny, and we stopped to talk and—'

'And he asked if he might meet you,' Lily concluded sympathetically. 'Has he ever asked you out?'

'No. But he was going to.'

Lily got up, slipped her hands into the pockets of the floor-length robe, and strolled slowly about the room. All at once she stopped and looked at Barbara.

'Barbara, do you want him?' she inquired gently.

Barbara's face turned pink. 'Do I—'

'Then take him!'

Lily gave a swift outward gesture of both hands, as if not only to give her this precious gift, but to annihilate Jack Davidson in the act. One more inconsequential subject – how little for a queen to bestow?

CHAPTER 5

Jack Davidson was not so easy to give away. He was stubborn and intractable, as the line of his jaw indicated.

He was not amenable to being used as common currency among girls, passed around as escort, bartered for invitations to parties. By the time three weeks had gone by, he had called Lily every day, taken her to lunch twice, been permitted to come to dinner one night to meet Frederick and Valerie, neither of whom seemed enthusiastic – perhaps because they also detected that stubborn persistence.

Barbara never mentioned the Sunday afternoon when she had volunteered to be the source of her own embarrassment, and neither did Lily, and when the next dance was organized, Barbara told her to come with Jack, quite as if that was now taken for granted by all their friends. Certainly it was taken for granted by Jack.

'I love you,' he had told her when Valerie and Frederick had left them alone in the living room.

Lily looked at him in astonishment. He had not yet tried to kiss her, and she had begun to think he was afraid of her. He was sitting at one end of the sofa and Lily at the other, wearing a sweater and skirt, legs curled under her.

He smiled at her expression of surprise, as if he had made some bizarre announcement, and in fact, since Dave Bartlet had first smashed his fist into the fire-alarm box to prove his love, the boys she knew had been as wary of the word as she was.

'I don't know what love is. There isn't any such thing. It's an idea, that's all. I'm never going to fall in love – with you, or anyone else. You may as well forget it.'

But, just as he was not an object for bartering, neither did he forget it.

She went to Barbara's dances with him, and soon found that for all her defensiveness, she had begun to let him kiss her, and within two months had been drawn into a bond of mutual yearning. The dances became of little interest, only the opportunity to have his arms around her, and they left noticeably early, to drive somewhere and park.

Lily had suspected for some time that her sensuality was going to prove a problem, and that it had not only because the boys she knew were not very appealing to her. But Jack was slow in what he did, subtle; he continued to tell her he loved her, he needed her.

'I can't,' she told him one night as they were parked above the city and he had pulled her dress over her head, leaving her naked. 'If you made me pregnant, I'd hate you. And Frederick would kill you. I have things to do.'

He was kneeling before her, and he spread her legs. His hands caressed her breasts, drawing tendrils of exquisite sensation, passing over her body until she felt a warm glow between her legs, a wonderfully pleasurable excitement as his fingers explored her more deeply. But as he was ready to enter her, she pushed angrily against him and he stopped, bowed his head, and she felt his shoulders shake, a shudder passing over them that turned her weak with a longing to share it, feel it inside her.

He left the car for a moment. She pulled the dress on, and combed her hair. Returning to the car, he put his arm about her shoulders, his hand closing over her breast. 'I'm sorry, Lily. You must trust me to be careful – I don't want anything to happen, either. It would be a hell of a thing for both of us.'

'Careful with what?' she demanded. 'One of those damn things that always break?' She had heard horror stories enough on that subject, and continued to hear them from some confiding friend who was waiting out the month in terror. 'I've got to work. I've got to finish school. And I'll be god damned if I'll have an abortion.'

'It doesn't happen as easily as you think. Not if the guy knows what he's doing. Believe me. Don't talk about it now. It's made you angry, and I don't want you to be angry. I want you to—'

'Let you screw me.'

That silenced him, since Lily did not use the word and was somewhat ashamed of having said it now, only to humiliate him.

'To love me,' he said with such honest humility that she might have taken him, after all, but for the determination not to follow the pattern of so many of her friends, not to find her life had been sealed before she had begun to live it.

The desire grew steadily more painful. She wondered if she might go to their doctor for some reliable contraceptive but was afraid of what Valerie and Frederick would think – even if they said nothing – should he tell them.

'Do it to someone else,' she told him cruelly. 'You have, after all.'

'Oh, Lily. What of it?'

She had teased him, pretending to think he was a Don Juan, and so had obliged him to swear that all his experiences had been with one girl. And where was she now? Her parents had found out about it, and they had moved to another town. That was the extent of his sophistication.

But the physical need was not the only threat to the future.

Jack Davidson not only knew how to kiss her and had many ways of doing it; he knew how to stir her longing with his mouth and fingers; how to give her pleasure of such keen intensity she longed for the final pleasure given by that stalk she sometimes held in her hand, caressing its dark red bud. She was ashamed of frustrating him, and ashamed of her fears.

Worse yet, he wanted to marry her. Not now; when they were out of school. And that had begun the first serious quarrel between them.

For not only had Jack given Lily an outline of the map of his future life, but he was insisting that was to be her future life as well.

It had happened one Sunday afternoon, when he had come to take her for a drive, the day after her birthday party, given by Frederick and Valerie the night before. The great day at last: sixteen years. Except, of course, they were still imagining that sixteen was young, while she knew it was quite an advanced age.

She had told Jack remarkably little of what was important to Lily Malone, and nothing whatever of the thought she harbored, a seed, long in germinating, that early boast to Michael:

One day I will be a great actress.

Once a secret was told, its magic was gone.

She had told Jack why she lived with her aunt and uncle, but not about those two handsome young people, Lily Morgan Malone and Philip Malone, who haunted her still.

Is that all? she had asked herself again and again? *Only those few years?*

Given the choice, perhaps they would have chosen not to have lived at all, not to have loved each other, not to have produced Lily and Michael Malone.

Most of her friends never thought of owing their lives to their parents, or to any force of nature. They took it for granted the world had been destined to produce them, never suspecting that here they were, accidental as a leaf, a flower, a dragonfly, a cat.

Life seemed to have no great value for most of them, so she judged by the casual way they approached it. And this, she thought, was because they had never confronted the knowledge that life could be lost as easily as it had been given: a cousin of Barbara's had died years ago. A young sister of Marjorie Wells' had died – some of them had such experiences.

But only Lily, it seemed, carried the forbidden knowledge of what it was to have lost, even before she was in full realization of their existence, the man and woman who had fallen in love, had imagined a world and a future between them – and had not lived to know what it might have been.

These dark dreads, never far from awareness, both increased the urgency of her longing for Jack and filled her with horror as she heard him outlining his plan – as if it were fixed long before the oceans rolled.

Jack evidently thought that nature was wise, nature had foreseen the human species when the first amoeba divided. Nature had foreseen Jack Davidson, separated out from the herd. This life was no phantasmagoria which greeted him. It had been planned only that their generation might arrive in time so they would sit here beside the lake, late one June afternoon, while all around were picnickers on the lawns, strolling about, playing with babies, little children running and screaming.

He would finish college. He would take a master's degree in engineering. He would join a large, or perhaps medium-sized firm, and would build bridges, highways, whatever the firm was assigned to build. They would be married. She might become an anthropologist, at least until the children were born. Three seemed the right number, but if she preferred two, he was agreeable to that.

Lily listened in dismay and increasing revulsion as she sat gazing at the people in the park, while he put the finishing touches to his grand design.

Everything about it seemed ridiculous, and worst of all, stifling. As she listened it began to seem that some internal pressure forced itself against her lungs, threatening the air and life out of her.

For although she had her private view of a family, a handsome dark-haired young man, a beautiful blonde young woman – other families, living out their lives in cumbersome day-by-day encounters, seemed to her a disaster to be avoided at any cost. Marriage, she had long ago concluded, was a vast blotting paper.

'Don't count on me,' she said when he turned to look at her just after he had said she might choose between two children and three.

She laughed bitterly. Here they were, unable even to solve the problem of how they might make love without the risk of any children at all, and he had leaped far ahead to provide them with three children, running and scream-ing and laughing, exactly like those outside the car, carrying balloons, eating ice-cream cones, some of them still too young to do more than wobble a few steps and fall down.

'Lily?'

Lily's eyes narrowed slightly, and she found herself hating him. 'I said,' she replied slowly, 'don't – count – on – me.'

'For what?'

'For anything. For the future. Not even for much of the present.'

He looked mildly surprised, but not alarmed.

'Don't count on me to fall in love with you, Jack. Because I won't.'

He looked somewhat bewildered, and no doubt sup-posed that a girl who responded as she did, who came sensually alive at a touch, who offered him her body for any experiment of pleasure he chose to make, who begged him to find some way they could make love – such a girl must be in love, whether she knew it or not.

But Lily had early developed an aristocratic aversion to lying. Lying, she thought, was for cowards. The truth was her private property, and she gave it or withheld it, as she chose.

She knew what he wanted, and what he wanted was Lily. She did not intimidate him; he was not distressed by her changes from warm to cool and hot to cold; from charming and vivacious to forbidding and silent. Things that might have discouraged another young man did not discourage Jack. Just so, she guessed, would it prove with every man she might ever admire; Jack was a premonition, a prophecy, and she studied him as such. But his ambitions outran her.

'There's no hurry,' he assured her. 'I just wanted you to know how it is.'

All at once her skin burned as if a flamethrower had passed over it, and a brilliant red seemed to fill the inside of her skull. She had a terrifying fear that rage might destroy her unless she escaped him.

She got out of the car, slammed the door, hoping to break the window, and began to run, darting among the picnicking families, running across this green park. She ran without glancing back, as if her life depended upon escaping from this dragon who had looked at her with adoration: *I want to take care of you, Lily,* he had said, with that stubborn tenderness for which she thought she could kill him. *And I'm going to – all your life:*

The hell you are!

She shouted it to herself and ran on, dodging among the children, the couples, who seemed surprised by the sight of her desperate face, her mad flight through this peaceful Sunday afternoon, running across the grass, thick with wild daisies and yellow dandelions, a girl so eager to get somewhere, or get away from somewhere, she had forgotten her shoes.

She did not look around to see if he was following her, that satyr with his plans for houses and babies and a life as calculated as a grid, as fixed, as static, until at last she could run no more, and so she stopped, panting, feeling her heart pounding, not with fear or rage, but with the exertion of running so far and so fast.

She pressed her hand against her ribs, and as her heart slowly went back to its even beat, her breath came more steadily, she fell into a reverie of contemplation of the sunset; it was her responsibility to enjoy the days they had missed, the sunsets which blazed on the evening sky. It was for her, whether the desire be for small things or great ones, to seize all of life she could lay hands upon, grasp it, hold it fast, let it engulf her. That, too, Jack offered her.

She turned slowly when the sun was gone and saw him approaching through the dense late daylight, and all at once she smiled, a wide brilliant forgiving smile, for with that smile, recently learned by her studies at the dressing table, she had in effect seized upon the most formidable weapon of her lifetime. An achievement Valerie would have been astonished to know she valued more than she valued all the lessons Valerie had provided for her.

She stood motionless, watching him, and realized that Jack did not believe even now that she had rejected his plans for the future. Jack, she sometimes thought, had the stupidity which went with knowing too clearly what you wanted, too young. He never suspected that to live a life at all, one must be prepared to change as the day changed, the weeks changed; a year was eternity itself.

But to Jack, at the age of nineteen, all was fixed, all was final.

She could foresee, very clearly, that one day, sooner perhaps than even she expected, they would be apart, and she would forget him as if they had never spent every free moment together.

They stood looking at each other, Lily's smile fading.

He held out his hand, and she put hers into it, confidingly, as if there had been no run for her life. They walked back to the car, and all about them the families were beginning to gather baskets, blankets, wandering children. Lily noticed that these men and women looked at them with some envy in their faces. No doubt their situation, still so early in life, produced in these people a little farther along the road a benevolent envy, which caused Lily to feel a wondering amazement.

For what, after all, had they to envy but the fact that their years upon earth had so far been few and uneventful?

CHAPTER 6

To his surprise, on that heavily rainy January afternoon, the car parked on a hillside, she had offered no last-moment fears, no misgivings, and after a brief pressure and slight momentary pain, she drew a deep sigh, opening herself wider, and held him with all her strength.

There was a rush of pleasure as he moved, slowly, almost cautiously, as if to test her readiness for him, make certain he was welcome there, and soon he moved more swiftly, the pressure inside her grew stronger, more intense, and after some indeterminable period of time, she heard a sound, lost in the cry of her own voice, which sounded strangely in her ears, a distant wail of gratitude, and at last that interior cornucopia, seen by her as filled with red flowers, quite contrary to what the anatomy books showed her, burst apart, fell into collapse, and she lay still, eyes closed, while her legs throbbed and all her body had begun a quivering of nervous relief and release:

Now I know what the world is about. The other secrets I can learn one day. This is the only one that means everything. All the rest are hidden somewhere inside it . . .

He had completed the world and, in a sense, set her free of him; the secret he had carried in his body was his secret no longer. She had it now, a world discovered in this ferment of pleasure, far more terrifying, more violent, this world of sensuality she would only now begin to investigate, that invisible power which had, as she had foreseen, the annihilating force of the ocean itself.

Lily said good-bye to Jack Davidson without ever having told him she loved him. She did not thank him, either, for his tenderness, honesty, devotion; not even for the great discovery he had helped her to make during the two years they spent together.

63

'I believe,' she told him, 'that we each have several incarnations.'

She and Jack were sitting on a blanket beside the car, on a hillside above the city. It was the end of July. Jack was to begin graduate work in August, and Lily would enroll for her senior year, in which her major was now established in anthropology, her minor in sociology.

'I believe we each have several incarnations,' was not the idle comment Jack pretended to take it for. It was the result of a long period of reflection upon time and Jack Davidson, her future, and her feeling about the woman who had lost her life too young.

Jack seemed mildly surprised, and had evidently decided the best defense against Lily's surprises was to deal with them tolerantly, and count for his own salvation on her sensuality.

'One life in one century – and then another—' he suggested, gently ironic.

Lily leaned both arms on her drawn-up knees and gazed across the hills, beyond the stands of pine. 'No.' She spoke softly, and might have been talking to herself. She had, however, something definite to tell him. For his own incarnation had only a week or so until he must become a new Jack Davidson, one who was not Lily Malone's lover. 'Several lives – in the same life.'

She did not glance at Jack, but she could hear the smile in his voice, that brave and stubborn smile of resistance against everything she had tried to tell him about the real nature of their relationship in the present and the future.

'No,' she said, still gazing away into those other lives. This one with Jack was almost over. She had lost interest in it, even though half an hour before, while he made love to her, she had been as pliant, as demanding and responsive as ever. Possibly more than ever, since she was keenly aware that she had no future prospect who would supply her with a similar excitement. 'Two years, Jack, is a long time.'

'Don't think ahead, Lily. We're still young.'

Lily ignored that. She was eighteen, Jack was twenty-one. If he thought that was young, then it was young to him; not to her.

'Life isn't made up of very many two years.'

He drew a deep breath, and that meant that for all his stubborn imperturbability, she had made him apprehensive. 'How can you put a time limit on your feelings? Two years – ten years. I'll love you as long as I live.'

Lily shook her head, dismayed by this young man who could not listen. Perhaps if she were to scream at him. But Lily had no wish to leave ugly memories – not with Jack Davidson, not with anyone. Lily Malone was too valuable to her. Lily Malone was Lily Morgan Malone, one generation removed.

She pulled up a tuft of grass and let it fall. 'Four days left, Jack.' She got up quickly. 'It's time for my ballet lesson.'

Winter, summer, spring, fall, the lessons continued. Nor did she take them as a chore, one more way of expressing her gratitude. They had become necessary as breathing, eating, sleeping.

For all her secretiveness, she had only two important secrets she had never discussed with Valerie and Frederick, with anyone. One was her relationship with Jack Davidson. The other was her first great ambition, hidden since her defeat in the high school production of *Bitter Sweet*.

She would one day become a great actress – an idea of gross incompatibility with her apparent intention of becoming an anthropologist.

Yet, the deeper the idea of acting went, the closer it became to instinct rather than concept, the less inclined she was to talk about it.

She had decided to make one more casting of her fortune.

The fall semester was to provide the University with a new class in drama, and a new professor, Gordon Donahue, who, according to campus and city newspapers, came to them trailing clouds of glory.

He was not just one more boring professor, acquired to impress them with his age, his honors, his unreadable publications, to add luster to the University, if not enthusiasm to the student body. This Gordon Donahue, so the accounts read, had been born in Boston, taken his doctorate of philosophy at Harvard, had spent nearly two years in the Navy during the Second World War, and returned home with a shoulder wound a few months before the war ended. He had spent two years as theater critic, writing for a Boston newspaper and small magazines, had published one book: *Shakespeare's Tragic Men*, and had spent a year teaching the history of drama in the English department at Harvard.

He was thirty, an interesting age to Lily, since despite the sexual sophistication she supposed she had acquired with Jack, she was aware that she still knew nothing about the difference between a boy and a man. She knew only as much about men as she knew from her uncles, from their friends. Now, she could study this man, and study with him.

He would teach a three-credit course: the History of Drama, designed to give a résumé in lectures this fall, and to present an ambitious play of ancient China for a run of one week in the University auditorium next semester.

'It would be fun,' she said, showing Frederick her program. 'Or do you think it's a waste of time?'

He read her list of subjects for her senior year and returned the list to her, smiling, shaking his head a little. There she stood, in her pleated yellow skirt and yellow cashmere sweater, her narrow perfect feet in the sandals she preferred for everything but hiking, looking at him as if she expected some denunciation of her frivolity.

'Of course it's not a waste of time. If we thought the theater was a waste of time we wouldn't have taken you to see everything that comes here.'

'They're going to produce a play.'

'And you want a part in it.'

'Well—' Discovered secrets were embarrassing.

However, once that was settled, she went to the library, got Professor Donahue's book, and read it.

Two hundred students, more or less, would comprise

the class, and she hoped to discover among them no one she knew.

Why she did not want to find a friend, or even an acquaintance there, was a mystery, and yet she felt so keenly that it would be a disaster that she was shocked when Barbara said, 'Are you going to take Donahue's course? I am.'

'Why?' Spots danced before her eyes. She drew in a long, deep breath and looked steadily at Barbara across the lunch table.

Barbara, with her long black hair and black eyes, could far more easily pass herself off as a Chinese concubine of the eighth century than Lily Malone could hope to do. Was Barbara to play Jade Ring in Donahue's fantasy of Chinese history and legend, woven with quotations from the poets and his own imaginary ending for China's most famous tragic love affair?

'I thought it would be amusing. I've heard the play is great fun – love and lust, killings of all kinds, kingdoms destroyed, emperors banished. I can't wait.'

Lily continued to look at her friend, and smiled slightly: *Another Bitter Sweet, is that what you're thinking? No, Barbara. You don't get away with that twice.*

The script of the play would not be available until the beginning of the second semester, but there were numerous histories which contained the story of the Shining Emperor and his beloved Jade Ring, the Supreme One.

'Have you read anything about it?' Lily asked.

'I want to be surprised.'

You will be.

They walked out, Lily on her way to a swimming class; Barbara on her way to meet Dave Bartlet, who remained so constant that Lily supposed Barbara was no more a virgin than she was.

They did not talk about that, and neither had she told Barbara of her intention to say good-bye to Jack Davidson on August fourth, a date she had selected for no exact reason, only that it was as good a date as any other and close enough to her arbitrary period of two years. One month's grace she had allowed him, at that.

Jack would not believe it. Not even when she remarked, as they were driving home from a movie, 'This is the last time I'll see you.'

He looked so astonished that she understood he thought she might say good-bye — but, one day, she would say hello, again.

That was not the way it worked out.

It worked out as Lily had told him it would, and the mystery, which would perhaps remain with him the rest of his life, was how she had known so well, and so early, what their common destiny was to be.

He walked with her to the steps of the low porch. She turned, holding out her hand, as if to a stranger. 'Good night, Jack.' She spoke kindly, a doctor encouraging a sick patient.

They looked at each other seriously, as if each were trying to guess what this moment meant to the other. He took her hand, as on any ordinary night. They did not kiss outside Frederick's house, for the traffic was likely to be heavy at this hour; students, other professors and their wives, dinner guests leaving, after-dinner guests stopping for coffee and brandy.

'Good night, Lily.'

She took the initiative of shaking his hand, a brief cordial hand-shake, which made them effectively strangers again, more strange to each other at that moment than they had been the night he had come to Barbara's, entered the room, and presently approached her as if to claim his rightful property.

'Don't call me tomorrow.'

She turned away, glanced briefly at him as she mounted the steps, and went into the house; within a few seconds the motor started, the car picked up speed rapidly, and there went Jack Davidson, out of her life.

She avoided the gathering in Frederick's library and went directly to her bedroom, where she closed the door and locked it, signal that she was through with the day and ready for sleep, and sat down before the mirror, that most reliable confidante; that same treacherous glass which lied to so many girls, but did not lie to her.

She was, she saw, not at all guilty or ashamed. In fact, she prided herself, more or less, on her cruelty. It was not her fault if she knew, and he did not, that people did not change one another only by believing the change would come about.

By the time for registration, she had put Jack Davidson on her *Ledger of People Who No Longer Count*, and had said nothing to Barbara until Barbara asked her about it, while they were waiting in line.

'Is it true that you and Jack are separated?'

'It's true.'

'But – why? He loved you so much. I've heard he's absolutely broken up.'

'I doubt it.'

'But he was in love with you, Lily. Really and seriously in love.'

'I know.'

Barbara looked troubled. Why? Pity for Jack – or fear for herself, now that Lily was again free to negotiate? 'Sometimes,' said Barbara doubtfully, 'sometimes I don't understand you.'

Lily did not try to answer that, and a few days later heard herself as she lay in a tub of hot water, singing her song:

> '*I never will marry,*
> *Nor be no man's wife.*
> *I mean to live single*
> *All the days of my life . . .*'

Love was not what made the world go round. Love was what stopped you in your tracks. Love made you forget your own best interest. Love, usurper of the spirit, destroyer of the personality, was the force which obliterated the individual.

Who ever heard of anyone in love who could think for himself – or even think of himself?

Where is our life before we have lived it?

CHAPTER 7

A new professor did not ordinarily attract much attention, but even before Gordon Donahue's first class in the History of Drama had opened, Barbara and Lily had seen him walking with another professor or a student.

The first time they saw him in the campus bookstore, they observed him carefully. Barbara concluded: 'He's attractive, isn't he?'

He was leaning one elbow on the counter, his hand on a stack of books, and was turned partly away from them. As if becoming aware that someone was looking at him intently, he glanced around, gave them a courtly nod, and a quick charming smile.

'Do you know him?' Barbara's voice was challenging.

'He's just being polite. My aunt and uncle have met him – one of those welcoming parties. His wife, too.'

'I've seen his wife.'

'Really?' It was never necessary for Lily to elicit information from Barbara by close questioning.

'Little, rather pretty. She could be prettier if she wanted to bother. Brown eyes. Brown hair, pulled back like this—' Barbara drew her palms flat over her ears and arranged a small imaginary chignon low on the nape of her neck. 'She's twenty-six. He's thirty. They have a six-year-old son.'

Lily laughed aloud. 'You've done quite a bit of research.'

'He stoops a little—' They looked at him as he paid his bill; and it was true. Although he was tall, his shoulders had a slight roundness, which made his tweed jacket hang unevenly and gave him a scholarly look. 'That's from a war wound. Hit in the shoulder by a Japanese bullet off Okinawa. He was in the Navy two and a half years.'

'Barbara – what industry.'

He passed them, and there was a smell of honey and

apples from his pipe tobacco. He glanced at them as he went by, a quick, friendly glance.

He's alive, Lily decided, and was surprised, as she always was, to discover someone who seemed fully alive.

Lily sat beside Barbara in the classroom, with two hundred other students, and took notes all that first semester. She was waiting, as she guessed Barbara was waiting, for the spring semester, when the class would present the play he had written; the legend and history of Ming Huang and Jade Ring, the Imperial Concubine.

Historically, the Shining Emperor had surrendered his beloved Jade Ring to his mutinous soldiers to be killed. The country was overrun by an invading army led by his adopted son, the Tartar general An Lu-shan, and Jade Ring and her family were blamed for all troubles.

That is, she had been until Donahue decided to give history an unexpected turn in the interest of ironic fantasy. Now, she did not die until she had seen her lover dead of grief, an exile from his Flowery Middle Kingdom.

'*A subverter of empires*,' Ming Huang had ordered his Chief Eunuch to search out. '*One glance from whom would overthrow a city – two glances an empire!*'

The Eunuch found her nearby, a young woman of eighteen, married to the eighteenth son of the Shining Emperor: '*hair like a cloud – a face of snow and flowers.*'

Reading the play, which was distributed in January, Lily had run to her dressing table and surveyed herself intently:

Of course. Who else – in that class. . . ?

Barbara Sloan, it seemed, had the same notion.

Now, here it was. And none too soon. The time had been ripening without her awareness. The need had been growing stronger. The craving to test herself had become irresistible.

If she did not play Jade Ring, what would become of her grand design for acting? She had told it all once to Michael, and never to anyone again. Not often even to herself. For her two destinies, her own, and Valerie and Frederick's for her, were of a remorseless incompatibility.

71

She read the books Donahue suggested – which most of the class ignored – because these books assuaged her conscience that she was learning, adding to her store of the *Five Cartloads of Books*, which Jade Ring's uncle had assigned, so that when she went to the Palace of the Golden Bells she would not bore the well-read monarch as other favorites had.

One day Lily found what she had been looking for, without having been aware a search was under way: '*The dead have great power over the living*—'

She paused as if she had been struck a blow to the heart.

She took out the strand of pearls given her by Valerie and never once clasped, held them around her neck, looked at herself with long careful intensity, and returned them to the drawer:

The first night I play Jade Ring I will wear them.

The problem, perhaps, was not so simple.

Ming Huang, the Shining Emperor, was a man of formidable assets.

Such-a-One, for they dared not use his name, lest the demons destroy not only the offender but the Flowery Middle Kingdom with him, walked into his throne room each morning to find his loyal subjects prostrate, foreheads to the floor. Slowly he seated himself upon his Dragon Throne while the eunuchs shouted: '*Knock three times!*' Thereupon the loyal subjects knocked their heads upon the floor; then three times more, while at intervals the subjects urged him: '*Live ten thousand years!*'

He had in the minds of his people a dragon's own power. His harem had assembled three thousand of the kingdom's most beautiful women – used and unused. Armies swept across the land or rested peacefully at his command. He played the flute like a nightingale, composed poems to equal those of his court poets. He was a man well worth losing a friend like Barbara Sloan for.

Barbara could play Mei Fei, Jade Ring's predecessor, who had bored the Shining Emperor with her shy and modest demeanor – *even in bed*, the Emperor had complained to his Chief Eunuch. Barbara, after all, had chosen to cultivate that same demure manner.

Even so, it was Barbara who seemed about to capture this Chinese paragon of monarchs.

For she read – according to Donahue's system of rotation – two pages of the part of Jade Ring, and she read with spirit and authority, seeming to have a good enough comprehension that a concubine who was to remain in historical memory for more than a thousand years might have charm, but that had no more to do with the woman than did the kingfisher feathers in her hair.

Lily listened in despair, for Lily had just completed a spiritless reading of Mei Fei, intended to convince Donahue that she was not suited to the part of a banished favorite.

Mei Fei was a worse part than Manon, while Jade Ring was capable of throwing a kingdom into confusion, and her lust for revenge upon the Emperor for his one-night defection to Mei Fei had at last destroyed the Shining Emperor, in Donahue's rewriting of history and legend.

Historically, Jade Ring's affair with An Lu-shan had destroyed monarch, empire, her own family, and she had been hanged by a white silk scarf from a pear tree.

Not so in Donahue's version of their story.

His Jade Ring survived the soldiers' mutiny by sending Mei Fei, disguised as Jade Ring, to be killed – and the real Jade Ring followed the Emperor into exile, to wait for his death.

Listening to Barbara reading this part with such confidence, Lily was enraged.

The scene was Jade Ring's discovery of the Emperor getting out of bed the morning after he had spent the night with Mei Fei, and before he had contrived to return her to the Pepper Chamber, with his three thousand concubines.

'*Long live your Majesty!*' Barbara's voice was heavily sarcastic as she entered the royal bedchamber, where Mei Fei, hidden behind the draperies, was preparing to leave.

'*Your Majesty is late today in giving audience to waiting ministers!*'

The scene proceeded until Jade Ring set about tearing off her jewels and flinging them at the Shining Emperor, screaming: '*Maybe she'd like to have these, too!*'

The screech of rage of a jealous woman was so convincing that the class burst into applause and Barbara glanced sideways at Lily, smiling. The part was hers. Evidently it had not occurred to her there was more to being the Supreme One than a convincing talent for bitchery.

The class, Lily knew, had decided that she was tepid enough for Mei Fei, Barbara turbulent enough for Jade Ring.

When the hour ended, Lily left her seat quickly, ran down the crowded hall to the Women's Room, and made her way to the mirror above the row of washbasins, oblivious of other girls, laughing, talking, making up their faces, touching perfume here and there; no way to use perfume, she knew.

Lily had found her perfume by then, a fragrance of roses, jasmine, and honey, and had decided that so far as the way she smelled, that would do very well for the rest of her life. By now, her clothing, even after being cleaned, was permeated with roses, jasmine, and honey.

She combed her hair and studied her face. *Skin like jade.*

She became aware of Barbara beside her, smiling at her in the mirror.

Lily glanced at her, and would have left without a word, for she was intent upon the next several minutes, which might prove the crucially decisive minutes of Lily Malone's future life, but Barbara spoke to her.

'You will be a wonderful Mei Fei, Lily.'

Lily looked at Barbara in the mirror – Barbara, her best friend.

Even Lily's theft of Jack Davidson had made little difference. Perhaps, Lily thought, because Barbara had not been quite ready for the kind of experience Jack would provide, and she had been more ready for it than she had realized. She had not yet replaced him, or the experience, and had become more inaccessible than ever; while Jack, always in the company of the same girl, now passed her without a nod.

Lily looked at Barbara, who was smiling what she probably considered Jade Ring's bewitching smile. Lily knew better.

Lily had practiced that smile before her dressing-table mirror, at night and in the morning. Whenever she was in her room, she tried on Jade Ring's smile.

For Jade Ring's smile and Jade Ring's breasts – even though they would not appear in this senior-class production without a silk robe over them – were Jade Ring's greatest charms for the Shining Emperor.

Jade Ring smiled when she was gay, but more important she smiled, according to the advice of her uncle, when she was angry:

'*That smile – that bewitching smile!*' he cried at first sight of it. '*Never lose it! Never forget it! When your temper is at its nastiest – when the world collapses – that smile will be your salvation!*'

'Do you think so?' Lily now politely asked Barbara.

'You'll be a charming Mei Fei.'

Lily's face disappeared from the mirror beside Barbara, and she was through the Women's Room and on her way down the hall, leaving Barbara standing there, smiling a secretive rather sly smile, quite wrong for Jade Ring.

She ran up two flights of stairs to Donahue's office.

If she could not convince him that she, not Barbara Sloan, was Jade Ring, then her life was over, then and there. Fate would have decided against her, and for Valerie. This was the day for throwing the sticks.

The door to his office was open. He sat with his feet on the desk, talking to two men students, laughing, which seemed almost as characteristic as his intense seriousness, and he was combing his thick black hair with his fingers.

Lily stopped in the doorway. He saw her and promptly got to his feet. 'Come in, Miss Malone. Please sit down.'

Then, as if his eager display of courtesy had embarrassed

75

him, he frowned, sat down, and continued talking to the two young men with an air of great earnestness. Lily sat in a chair a few feet away, but did not listen to the conversation or even notice who the two young men were. She was watching Gordon Donahue and trying to read his mind:

Why, I'm the one he wants to play Jade Ring.

It's only that damned silly system of reading in rotation.

I'll read what I want him to hear – as soon as these two idiots leave.

She turned her attention upon them, studying first one and then the other. They began to fidget; and after three or four minutes got up to leave. Three men alone – whatever they had been talking about – were easy to disconcert. She moved to another chair opposite him.

Lily wanted no favors from Gordon Donahue. She wanted to play Jade Ring because she was convinced that here, in concrete form, was the great revelation. The ancient Chinese had considered themselves to be surrounded by the spirit world – invisible, but nonetheless influential. They had understood what it was for an individual to be a haunted house.

He looked at her with the intent pleasure of a man looking at a beautiful woman, but a beautiful woman who did not threaten him, since he was not in love with her.

'Well, Miss Malone – what can I do for you?'

'That's what I've come to talk to you about.'

They looked at each other several moments, Donahue waiting for her to tell him whatever she had to say. All at once she smiled at him, Jade Ring's bewitching smile. After a moment, the smile vanished slowly, leaving only a slight upward curve of her lips as she inquired: 'Can Barbara Sloan smile like that?'

CHAPTER 8

The word went around that Lily Malone had gone late Wednesday afternoon to Donahue's office.

Whatever she might have said or done, when the class met on Friday, he announced that today Miss Sloan would read Mei Fei's dialogue and Miss Malone would read Jade Ring's.

The secret balloting for the final parts were counted by the election committee on Monday, and one of its members read the cast aloud, while Donahue sat to one side, gazing at the floor.

Barbara gave a gasp, and a sharp sideways glance at Lily, who looked straight ahead. The casting was complete. The first reading would begin the following Monday; the other volunteers would begin to design costumes and sets; and presently the auditorium would become the Palace of the Golden Bells, where the Shining Emperor took Mei Fei and, fatally, Jade Ring into his curtained Golden Dragon bed. The strange sorrowful passion between China's most respected Emperor and his *subverter of empires* would presently engulf them.

The trouble began before rehearsals got under way.

After the reading of the cast, Gordon Donahue gave the class one last quick smile, combed his hair with his fingers, and left. It might have been any usual ending to the lectures of the semester before, so far as his manner conveyed any political forecasts overthrown, any ambitions gratified or denied, friendships enhanced or destroyed.

Barbara sat staring after him somberly. Lily left Barbara to her private grievance and went out, but paused at the sound of Barbara's voice in the crowded hallway.

'Lily!'

'Yes?'

They faced each other, while passing students glanced

at them curiously. Here were the two campus beauties, best friends since high school, perhaps because they liked each other, perhaps because each had decided the easiest way to keep watch over her chief rival was to make a friend of her.

Even so, Lily had slipped through the network and made her way to Gordon Donahue's office, and there had evidently contrived to work some illicit magic upon him. For it was Lily Malone who had been voted Imperial Concubine, Barbara Sloan the part of the inadequate concubine.

'How did you do it?' Barbara asked in a fierce whisper.

That, Lily reflected, is exactly the tone Mei Fei would use when she realizes that Jade Ring has rescued her from the besieged city for the purpose of saving her own life. That was how Mei Fei should sound when she says: '*And I trusted you — to bring me here.*'

But Lily did not think Barbara was of her own frame of mind — saving, noticing, observing, remembering, all manner of odd scraps of feeling and experience, should they prove useful one day in the fabrication of some character quite different from her own.

'How did I do what?' asked Lily.

'What can I do for you, Miss Malone?' he had asked.

'That's what I've come to talk to you about. What I want, Professor Donahue, if you have ten minutes, is to convince you that I should play Jade Ring.'

Donahue had laughed gently. 'What splendid self-confidence, Miss Malone. I've always admired that in you.'

'This system you have of letting the students read the parts in rotation — that's why Barbara Sloan seems right. Barbara has enough natural bitchery to read Jade Ring just well enough. And I have enough natural vulnerability to read Mei Fei more or less well. But that doesn't mean either of us could play those parts without changing the play's meaning.'

Donahue looked at her thoughtfully. 'You're a very serious young woman, Miss Malone.'

She leaned slightly forward. 'I can play Jade Ring because I understand jealousy – and I understand revenge.'

This surprised him more than Jade Ring's smile.

It occurred to Lily that he was the most charming man she had met, outside her family. The charm was a compound of simplicity, a seemingly uncomplicated wish to please his class, his companions, an intense conviction about himself and about living, as if he found each moment going by him on its way to eternity of high value.

'I know why Jade Ring wanted revenge on the Emperor for taking Mei Fei to bed. Her affair with An Lu-shan only partly satisfied her vengefulness. What she really wanted was to see Ming Huang die. She waited.' Lily paused, then quoted from the play: '*Heaven is vast, the earth is old, time will pass away – but this great wrong shall last forever and ever.*' This Jade Ring said to Ming Huang when the exiled Emperor begged his Taoist priest to summon Jade Ring's reincarnation to him, so that he might see her one last time before he died.

Donahue had the extraordinary listening capacity she believed was possessed only by extraordinary men like her uncle, the only other man she had known to have it. And recently, Michael, young as he was.

It was a gift, and no doubt like any gift which endured, had been carefully cultivated. He listened as a lover might listen, as a concerned devoted relative might listen – as almost no one did listen. Life was so interesting to him that he was willing to pay attention.

'What can you know of jealousy? A girl your age – with your looks—' He gestured slightly, indicating all of her.

'Nothing. And everything.' They looked at each other. '*I know that love is strong as death, and jealousy cruel as the grave.*' She was quiet, wondering how it happened that had come into her mind, a sentence she did not remember having remembered. 'Do I need to know more than that?'

He looked at her with a slight wistfulness, and replied, with an adult's tenderness for youth: 'I hope you never do.'

*

79

Now here stood Barbara, almost nose to nose with her, although Lily tried to back away. 'How did you do it?'

'You heard me read Jade Ring last Friday. Or were you thinking of something else?'

'You went to his office.'

'What of it?'

'Bill Parkman and Bob Murphy saw you there.' Bob Murphy was playing An Lu-shan.

'I didn't say I didn't go. I said – what of it?'

'You were so determined to take that part away from me—'

'Oh, Barbara!' Lily laughed. 'What an idea! I think I can play it better. It's a school play – like *Bitter Sweet*. How important was that? This is one more three-unit course. A little campus notoriety. A chance to fail. Whether you play Jade Ring or Mei Fei won't make any difference in your grade.'

'If you get the part – and it seems you have – everyone will say you're sleeping with him.'

Lily laughed, softly, the conspiratorial laugh which had been cultivated to sound like a distant chime echoing from somewhere in the house, a light and lyrical, curiously provocative sound. 'Are you jealous, Barbara?'

'Of course not. You've been unfair – you've been a bad friend, Lily. And all along I trusted you—' Barbara paused, perhaps aware that even now she was beginning to sound as if she had absorbed the part of Mei Fei. Then she smiled, a small malicious smile, Mei Fei's defeated, vindictive smile. 'I'll be interested to see if you can make the same kind of idiot of Pat Runkle you made of Jack Davidson.'

'I've never met Pat Runkle.'

It was true she had been somewhat taken aback when Patrick Runkle had been assigned the part of Ming Huang. For Pat Runkle had an air of conquest, a reputation of conquest, an accredited history of conquest. Nor did she like anything she had heard about him, which was too much.

During the past two years when he had come to finish

80

his junior and senior years on the campus of this big university, Pat Runkle had become president of the senior class, captain of the football and basketball teams; he had usurped columns of publicity, and behaved as if he had come here for the purpose of general self-aggrandizement before he disappeared back to his native part of the state, or returned to the east, to study at Harvard Business School, his rumored destination.

It was supposed he had come here not because he lacked the grades to finish the last two years at Harvard, but because he, or someone in his family, had decided it would be a good thing if this future leader of industry should know something about the kind of people who lived in a world he had never inhabited – outside the walled gardens of the Imperial Palace of his ancestors.

'I,' Lily assured Barbara, 'will play Jade Ring. He will play Ming Huang. We will cooperate. There will be nothing personal about it.'

'You think.'

'I know.'

Barbara left her with a lingering smile. 'Good luck, Lily . . .'

Barbara was angry. Barbara was jealous. Barbara was envious. None of these were good emanations, and Lily was superstitious about being their recipient.

But as for Patrick Francis Runkle – ridiculous name, which was some comfort, even if it was a famous one – Pat Runkle might have rattled all the other women on the campus, but not Lily Malone.

Not only had she never spoken to him, she did not glance at him when they passed on the campus streets, or sat near each other in the auditorium during Donahue's drama class.

What was a man with Patrick Francis Runkle's future, and past, doing in a drama class? Amusing himself, at their expense. Yet, he had read Ming Huang as if the idea of being China's Shining Emperor came quite naturally to him.

He did have some kind of acting ability, but why he

should have it, where he might have picked it up from his family background and the experiences which had formed him, Lily could not imagine. He was, so far as she was concerned, an exotic creature in the big university, and she was sorry he had chosen to stray in that direction, whatever might be the nature of his search.

Lily decided that if she kept her mind on Jade Ring, she would be safe from Patrick Runkle.

The play quickly began to form in the imaginations of all in the drama class.

The stage was filled with courtiers, and maids-in-waiting, soldiers and Siberian tribesmen, Greeks and Persians, Japanese and Syrians and Turks. To costume this motley group was a major undertaking.

Some students, including Lily, volunteered to supply their own costumes and jewelry. From the small treasury accumulated by last year's production, wigs were bought and hundreds of pieces of ten-cent store jewelry were strung by the wardrobe department into pendants and looped from pronged pins to fasten into shining black wigs. The stock wardrobe was raided; old costumes pulled apart and put together. The scenery was being constructed, and it seemed that if any talent for the theater lay hidden anywhere about the campus, Donahue would discover it.

The excitement became contagious, for until a woman had addled his pate, Ming Huang had presided over the highest culture in Chinese history.

Even in translation the poetry proved intoxicating, and the class developed a secret language of lines from the I Ching, from Taoist and Confucian literature, from Lao-shi and Ti-Po.

Some of the professors had begun to speak of this Gordon Donahue who had appeared stealthily among them, looking a proper professor, with his black hair, his pipe, his not very well-fitted tweed suits, and had proved himself a modern Pied Piper. He made his class forget their responsibilities to French verbs, the study of aboriginal tribes, the ailments of the daily world, which they were expected to learn to cure.

If there was a flaw in this charmed environment Lily had entered, an environment more real than the reality of all her other classes, it was none other than Ming Huang himself.

He was too handsome, with his slightly waved black hair and black eyes, his athlete's body, tall, slender, and muscular, the quick smile which could turn to a surprising look of brooding sullenness, his Scotch-Irish intensity, his rich family. He was too much of everything, and he had too much of everything. Worst of all, he was unscrupulous about taking every advantage of his advantages.

Whether he took the girl to a fraternity dance, a movie, or a supper room for dinner and dancing, he took her later to a motel. And even the motel he patronized was well known, having a reputation as a Bluebeard's Castle, since no girl went there twice.

Once, and they mysteriously disappeared. They were still visible to their friends, but they had become invisible to Pat Runkle. Either he had found a way to protect himself from the disadvantages of being too desirable, not only for his own qualities, perhaps even more for those of his family, or he was as ruthless as Lily thought him to be.

And then one day, when they stood at the side of the stage, watching the other actors, he asked Lily if she would go to the Deke Barn Dance that Saturday night. Lily concentrated her attention on the actors, and did not look at him.

'No, thanks, Pat.'

It was some time before he spoke to her again, except in his persona of Ming Huang addressing Jade Ring.

Presently he began to find ways to tease her. He began to turn their love scenes into real love scenes whenever Donahue's attention was distracted. He passed in back of her, and his hand brushed her buttocks.

She refused to acknowledge that she was aware of him.

83

Yet wherever he had touched her, however his body had pressed briefly against hers, she could feel it, days later. Whatever happened to her, pleasurable or not, seemed to leave its tracks, a permanent marking of her body and memory. It was there forever. She might forget it, or think she had, but it was not so: someone had done something to her. She remembered it always.

Still, she would not, and Pat Runkle knew it, ask Donahue for protection from the Shining Emperor.

A few rehearsals of the most violent activity, Donahue had told them, during the last week, would be enough. Anything more, and each rehearsal would become a struggle for dominance among these inexperienced young actors.

Even so, one day while they rehearsed the scene where the Emperor was to tell Jade Ring that their love was eternal, Lily became aware that Donahue, talking to two professors, had left the auditorium.

'Let's wait until he comes back.'

Pat was smiling at her. 'You're afraid of me, aren't you?'

'That's absurd.'

She looked at him with a face as sullen as his own sometimes was. All at once, this young man, whose allure seemed to her a calculated affront, causing pain which was almost physical, some unlocalized but real condition of protest against his looks, became Ming Huang, serious, speaking of his love, and as Lily listened a dizziness made her long to close her eyes, blot out the face too near, evade his breath, fragrant as incense.

Obviously there were men not as eager as Jack Davidson to settle down with one woman, nor so optimistic that one woman was enough women to settle down with. But, Lily was thinking as he moved nearer, at least he might have the decency to be less desirable, even to women who disliked him. Lily Malone was evidently his one failed conquest, and he was unhappy about it.

There they sat, Ming Huang and Jade Ring, on a hot summer night – while the Tartar General swept over the

Flowery Middle Kingdom. The gardens of the Golden Palace were alight with candles fixed to cassia trees; fountains splashed fragrant water; the Supreme One wore a loose white silk gown.

All of this was more real to Lily than her mauve skirt and cashmere sweater, the auditorium stage with its unshaded lights, its straight-backed chairs and low desks.

'*I am at peace.*' Ming Huang broke in half a box made of a shell and laid one half upon her palm. His face was serious, intent, and Lily gazed at him in dismay, wondering what would become of her ambition to steal every scene when once they appeared before an audience. '*You are one half of this shell, I am the other. Keep it. Place it in my hand when you have closed my eyes for the last time.*'

Lily held the imaginary shell, aware that these were the first words of love she had heard spoken by a man which sounded like love, even though they were the fragments of poetry and fantasy pieced together by Gordon Donahue.

Ming Huang's arms went about her, too slowly and gently for her to protest that this was above and beyond the call of rehearsal duty.

She cast a quick glance in the direction where Gordon Donahue had last been seen, but he had not returned.

The Emperor was smiling at her, that confiding flattering smile which he flashed here and there, using it, she thought, like a yinyang mirror, to confuse and immobilize all rivals, all prey. He went on speaking to her in that voice which was one of his greater attractions, for it contained an almost imperceptible laughter. '*The music of silence*—'

Jade Ring closed her eyes, waiting, vaguely aware that he had bent across her in such a position that neither the students standing around nor Donahue, should he return, could see Lily Malone, only Pat Runkle's broad shoulders and back, concealing her from the waist up.

'*Heaven and earth may pass away, but our love – will last forever*—'

She felt his mouth touch hers, softly, and then his hand

85

was beneath her sweater, moving slowly over her breasts. Before she had recovered enough to move away, he left her. 'That's what I thought.' He was standing, looking down at her and smiling. 'Smooth as jade.' He walked away, while Lily felt a rising rage, as if he had made love to her and left without a word.

CHAPTER 9

Gordon Donahue was walking slowly down the aisle. Pat stood to one side of the stage, his back to her.

Donahue was looking at her questioningly, and all at once Lily stood up, remembering Jade Ring's uncle's advice: '*That bewitching smile! When the world collapses—*'

And so she smiled at Donahue, and he smiled in reply. The class was dismissed. 'Tomorrow we'll do a run-through, without scripts.' Lily descended the stairs at one side of the auditorium, quite as Jade Ring descended from Heaven to appear one last time to the aged Emperor, that he might die in peace.

'Will you look at my makeup? I've been working on it—'

The makeup was a success, he assured her; and by then the concentration upon Jade Ring's face had restored her, although she was still vaguely, pleasurably aware of Pat Runkle's warm practiced hand on her breasts: she had found out something most girls had to go to Bluebeard's Castle to discover: he knew how to touch a woman to get the most response from the slightest pressure.

Lily began to remove Jade Ring's makeup, while Donahue went to advise An Lu-shan, who had got himself up to resemble Dr Fu Manchu. When he came back, she was Lily Malone again, and he sat beside her, as if to tell her something of importance.

'The love scenes are the chief lure of a drama class, for at least half the students.'

'They're not very serious about acting.'

86

What did he see?

'Did you think they were?'

'Why do they take the class?' That was not the question. The question was: *Why did Pat Runkle take the class?*

'How many people do you know who have any real interest in their classes?'

'None.'

He was smiling, watching her more carefully than ever before. 'You do.' He was about to tell her something she must learn and remember. She listened, not immediately aware that he was quoting to her lines which Jade Ring and her uncle spoke. '*You are not like other women. You can only live on life.*'

He means it — and it's true.

She began to feel stronger, more confident. '*I was born with a strange vision.*' She smiled, a little apologetic for the hubris, even if it was Jade Ring's. 'I've always thought so. Perhaps I thought I had to—'

She had told him once why she lived with her aunt and uncle, and he had never mentioned it again.

'There's one other in the class,' he said. 'One person who takes this as seriously as you do. That play. The need to be good at it.'

'Barbara.' She knew better.

'No. Barbara Sloan is serious about Mei Fei — but she is not serious about her own life. She will let it go by, however it goes. She will not try to guide or control her destiny. And, after all, without guidance, there is no destiny. Is there?'

'At least some *fate comes by chance*.'

'*But fate can always be altered by the will of heaven.*'

'And the other one — who is serious?'

'Pat Runkle.'

'But he's a businessman! He's not an actor — except as an excuse to show off.'

'He has a real talent, you know.'

'I know. And he knows.'

'Talent is never a surprise to anyone who has it. Pat Runkle has talent. Whether he will also develop the ability to use that talent—' He shrugged and stood up. It was nearly six o'clock, and they started up the aisle. 'Of course, if he should ever decide to become a professional actor, he'll have to change his name.'

Lily laughed, grateful for something to make fun of Pat Runkle about, even if it was only his name.

Quite unexpectedly, the opening night was one week away.

She had so far refused to contemplate the possibility of a fatal stage fright – whether she would have it, whether it might paralyze her. Even so, she could not forget that when the time came it would come in a rush. Like final examinations.

'Nothing,' Lily said wistfully one afternoon, at the end of rehearsal, 'nothing will ever be as much fun again.'

To her surprise, for she had spoken impulsively, disturbed to realize how much she had come to depend upon the play, there was a brief burst of applause from the others onstage.

'Nothing will,' An Lu-shan agreed. 'It'll be real life from here on out.' He, like most of the cast, would graduate in June. 'And real life, from what I've seen, is no god damn fun at all.'

It seemed, in some curious way they all appeared to feel increasingly as they became better acquainted, not only with one another but even more with the characters, that this was an end of something which would prove to have been vital to all of them.

In this effort to accustom themselves to another time and place, other attitudes toward love and living, in this love story, curiously inverted, they had come to think that for the last time they were experiencing a simple pleasure, unmixed with the pain of real life. The story of Ming Huang and Jade Ring, the destruction of the Flowery Middle Kingdom, had been grand tragedy, once upon a time – and now it was not only a play of dramatic fantasy, it was a form of play.

Even this pleasure had developed its own pain. Rivalries

arose among them, real and intense, however Donahue tried to keep them aware that this was twentieth-century America, not eighth-century China.

No one would have his head chopped off. Jade Ring's uncle's head, kicked about the stage by the soldiers, was a papier-mâché head, not the head of the young man who played him. No one would be put to the Lingering Death, flesh cut off strip by strip. No one would be strangled by a white silk scarf in the powerful hands of the Chief Eunuch – not Mei Fei, not Jade Ring.

No one would be banished to live out her life in the Pepper Chamber, suffering the interminable boredom of the company of three thousand idle women. No one would have his belly hewn open, his guts spilled out upon the bed. The town would not be evacuated, set afire, destroyed by Tartar invaders.

Or would it?

What was, after all, so different about the play and their own lives? These metaphors described their feelings; perhaps, in some sense, their future lives.

Love affairs had begun and ended. No such involvements on such an intense level had occurred in earlier plays presented by the drama class.

Donahue disapproved of the incapacity of some of the actors to distinguish the play and the parts they performed from their true emotions.

'I've never been able to prevent it,' he told Lily. 'They fall in love. They fall out of love. They hate each other. They forgive each other. Even some professionals do it. But it's troublesome, and sometimes, it destroys the play. Inexperienced actors have enough difficulty telling real life from the parts they're playing.'

They paused, in the late bright sunshine, and turned toward each other, Lily listening even to his silence. She listened to him more intently than she had listened to anyone but Frederick, and was vaguely aware of expecting that now he would tell her the final secret.

There was one, somewhere; although what might be its

nature, she could not guess. Perhaps some reason for being alive which she had not yet been able to discover.

The words of the play, spoken by her aloud at rehearsal, the words of the other actors heard again and again, those words ran through her mind like an old song. They seemed to have some eerie connection with the deaths of her young parents: Ming Huang and Jade Ring had taken their lives over where they had left them unfinished, and were to live them out in that other incarnation. She had the conviction that it was a way of giving them a life they had not had the chance to live – an illusion of restitution.

At times the illusion seemed no illusion, but reality itself – and that, perhaps, was when her feelings about Jade Ring and Ming Huang, An Lu-shan, Mei Fei, grew so overpowering there seemed a threat that when the time came she would not be able to keep separate the difference between Lily Malone and Jade Ring, Ming Huang and Pat Runkle, Barbara Sloan and Mei Fei.

As a precaution against Barbara's stealing the play, she had written on a sheet of paper: BARBARA SLOAN, slipped it into an unmarked envelope, sealed it, then put it at the bottom of her sweater drawer.

The next night, as she sat in her room practicing playing the table lute which had been manufactured by a music major, it occurred to her it was even more essential that Ming Huang did not defeat her.

She quickly wrote: PATRICK FRANCIS RUNKLE, and slipped that envelope into the sweater drawer.

Reflecting that the study of anthropology and psychology did have its uses, she took up the lute again.

The capacity to concentrate when and upon what she chose had been as reliable as the beat of her heart.

Not now. Not since Jade Ring had got hold of her. Not since she had gone to live in the Palace of the Golden Bells. Now, whatever else she tried to think about, there arose those other men and women, who moved and talked and took over her feelings:

Whatever happens to me – wherever I go, whoever I know,

wherever I live, I will never lose them. They will be with me always – they will never desert me.

My real home will be the Palace of the Golden Bells.

I, after all, was once Empress of China, the Supreme One.

Suddenly she put the lute aside.

She had no idea why she was crying. But tears came to Lily by surprise – at least when they were not part of the play.

For some minutes she cried silently, and then she began to sob. All at once she realized she was crying not for Lily Malone, but for the young man and woman she had never known, for her memories of them were few, and unreliable.

She looked at the photograph on the desk. There they were: two strangers, for all that she was their incarnation, that she was custodian of their unexperienced joys, their unlived happiness and sorrow. And yet she had lost them, as she could never now lose Ming Huang, or Mei Fei, Kao Li-shi, or An Lu-shan.

The telephone rang, and she started as if at a summons to her beheading. Eight-thirty. No one called at eight-thirty. They knew the rules: No telephoning after seven o'clock Monday through Friday.

Lily picked up the telephone. 'Hello?' Her voice surprised her by its lightness. There was not even the sound of tears.

'Lily?' It was Pat Runkle, and he had never called before. 'Can I see you?'

'Can *you* see *me*?'

With that curious suspiciousness which had come over her ever since she had turned into Jade Ring, she knew he wanted to ask her to give up the part of Jade Ring to Barbara Sloan.

After all, he was taking Barbara to the formal dance concluding the spring semester for his fraternity.

That was the latest news, although Lily had not mentioned it to Barbara and Barbara kept her distance from Lily, apparently hoping she would not be asked if she had lost her mind, going out with Pat Runkle when everyone would know she was an abandoned woman – one more girl who had supposed she could keep out of the Pepper Chamber after her night of glorious notoriety and whatever might go with it.

Pat's voice replied reasonably: 'We have only three more days—'

'What of it! We've rehearsed the damned play too often. We've done all of it too many times to each other!' She paused, not liking the way that sounded, and heard him laugh softly. He was so polite, so humble, that it was clear he would, one way or another, contrive to see her.

'All right, Lily,' he said in that same even voice, which would serve him well when he became a businessman. While all about were losing their heads, Patrick Runkle would make allowance. 'I thought we might talk – maybe find a way to agree about some things we seem to be having trouble with. Half an hour, Lily. May I come?'

'Tonight? No, no. I'm studying—'

'I'll be there in ten minutes.'

Lily ran into the bathroom to repair the damage tears had done, comb her hair, add perfume.

CHAPTER 10

She had not heard Valerie and Frederick return, and hoped they would not before Pat Runkle arrived, for then he would be obliged to discuss social utopias and the need for putting into public ownership everything his family now owned privately. And neither Jade Ring nor Ming Huang would find out what was disturbing each rehearsal.

Gordon Donahue had asked her to wait that afternoon when the class left, and had driven her home. The rehearsal had been the first with the thin rubber masks, made by a professional makeup man, in which Jade Ring must transfer her own face to Mei Fei's and take Mei Fei's unadorned Serving Girl's face for her own.

Bending over Barbara, Lily's hands had begun to

tremble, and something cold and murderous threatened to overpower her.

At last, she had changed the faces of the disguised Serving Girl and the Imperial Concubine, and stepped back, wondering if she would faint. Why this experience had proved so unnerving, she could explain only on the basis that they were amateurs.

'I hope to God, Lily,' Gordon said, 'that you won't let your dislike of either Barbara or Pat affect your playing. You can't control your feelings, but you must, while you're on the stage, obliterate them. Don't forget that Jade Ring *must* smile at Mei Fei when she tells her she is going to have her strangled. If her hatred is obvious – there goes the irony. There goes her revenge.'

'I know, I know.' Lily felt she would rather be strangled herself than play that scene. Obviously, she understood jealousy and revenge better than she had guessed when she had supposed she was bragging. 'I'll try.'

Now, here was Pat Runkle, throwing her a lifeline, and little as she liked to take such emergency measures from his hands, there seemed no alternative.

She opened the door and surprised both of them by giving him Jade Ring's bewitching smile. 'Come in?'

'Let's drive around a little – look—'

He gestured to indicate the soft night, filled with stars and a rising white half-moon. Bad omens, all of them, thought Lily as she went to get her keys and, as an afterthought, a notebook, as if this were to be a seminar.

He drove at a leisurely rate, and was presently winding about the roads in back of the campus, up toward the hilltops. Lily sat silent while Patrick Runkle pointed out the various landmarks below, as if conducting a tour for a visitor just arrived. All at once Lily laughed.

'What's funny?' He was silent. 'You don't like me, Lily.'

'You're Ming Huang to me. No one else.'

'I know.'

She was surprised to find that there was this reasonable, even considerate man, who was also Pat Runkle. He was not only, or not always, the football star, the senior class president, heir to banks, lumber companies, newspapers, orange groves. 'That's why I thought it might be a good idea to get better acquainted.'

He swung the car off the road, switched out the lights, and although it was now so dark she could not see him, she felt his body turn toward her. A moment later, growing more accustomed to the dark, she could see his arm resting across the steering wheel.

'Lily—' Still that same warm, soothing, reassuring voice. 'I may not be the nicest guy you've known or will know. I'm not asking you to like me. I don't think it makes any difference.'

Lily sat confounded. Whatever else, she had not been expecting apologies – if this was an apology. They sat silent, motionless, and he made no move to touch her. Presently, he began to talk again.

'When Jade Ring first comes to the palace, she not only falls in love with Ming Huang – she adores him. It's important that the audience understand this is not a cynical woman, but a young girl – a year younger than you are, Lily.'

'I know that.' She was looking at the lights which shone in houses spread below them. She reminded herself that Lily Malone did not get involved in feuds with anyone, and how it happened that she was at war with her best friend, and with Patrick Runkle, she could only blame on the play itself. The Orient had disoriented her reason; that was it.

Deciding to be cooperative, she offered: 'She has never expected that anything so extraordinary would happen to her. She loves him because he is the Shining Emperor.'

'And because he gives her pleasure, of a kind she has not imagined.'

'I suppose.'

With a surprising sense of defeat and discouragement, Lily rested her elbow against the lowered window and leaned against the door, eyes closed, while she wondered what she could say or do next.

He bent across her, his mouth touched hers, lightly at first, and she found that she had been longing for him as she had never longed for Jack Davidson, or supposed she might long for any man.

The kiss continued for what seemed some interminable time, and she became aware of an invasion of new sensations, from within her body, upon her skin, trailing across her breasts, passing between her thighs.

All at once she pushed against him.

He let her go, and she heard a low laugh, which made her so angry she got out of the car and ran several steps, then turned, and saw him walking toward her slowly. 'Lily?' He was beside her again. 'Lily – I won't do anything you don't want. You know that.'

'It's late. I've got to study. Let's go.'

He followed her back to the car, then all at once caught hold of her, holding her firmly, pulled off the sweater and skirt, and with a quick movement pushed her backward upon the seat, unprotesting and by now helplessly eager, as he bent over, both of them seemingly unaware of what they did, what sounds they made, for some unknown time.

However long it lasted, not very long the first time, a seeming eternity the second, he had still said nothing when they put on their clothes. Lily curled up on the car seat like an abandoned child, and he started down the hillside.

At last she remembered that she had to enter the house, that Valerie and Frederick might not have gone to bed, and took out a comb and lipstick, glancing sideways at Pat Runkle, his face clearly visible in the light from the dashboard.

He was concentrating as carefully upon the road as if they were descending an ice-covered mountain path. His eyes were narrowed, his mouth grim. He looked fiercely angry – and that infuriated her:

I'll always hate him. Why didn't he leave me alone?

Nothing, she was convinced, even while she felt the blood throbbing in her legs, the warmth in her belly, as

95

if he might not have left even now, nothing could have made her so submissive, eager, greedy, but the same deceptive charms with which Ming Huang had appealed to Jade Ring: power, popularity; celebrity. His family cast its shadow before him.

Pat Runkle had been born to luck. And luck was a powerful aphrodisiac. The fragrance of it enveloped its possessor, and drew outsiders nearer, to breathe the air — even if they might not catch the good fortune itself.

He stopped the car, and before the motor was turned off she had opened the door and was out, whirling around with a wild accusatory expression she hoped he could not see.

'We do know more about Ming Huang and Jade Ring now, don't we?'

There was a soft mocking laugh, her own, and she ran up the steps, leaving the car door open.

She heard him slam it as she unlocked the front door. He drove off, picking up speed so swiftly that by the time she entered the living room, to find the lights turned down, the engine was roaring like a police car. When she closed the door, the sound had disappeared, and she walked slowly to her bedroom. At last she went to bed, stupefied by the realization that everything she had thought she knew so well had no truth in it after all. Jack Davidson seemed someone she had only imagined.

They played the next two rehearsals and the first part of the rehearsal on the day of the opening without any acknowledgment that the drive had ended in quite a different way from what they had expected. Or, possibly, it had ended exactly as they had expected, although not at the Golden Dragon Motel.

Lily stood at one side of the stage, in complete costume and makeup, watching Mei Fei pleading with the Chief Eunuch to persuade the Emperor to let her meet the Supreme One. After the weeks of Donahue's guidance, Barbara had turned her Mei Fei from a tedious young girl to a woman of tender charm.

Mei Fei's voice grew more plaintive, and Donahue had taught her to speak with sweetness, the mythical nightingale who had died in trying to outsing a lyre – heartbreaking tones. Yes, Lily told herself, Barbara was learning to act. Or was she only learning to act this one part, as some people could learn to play one piece of music?

She was watching the scene so intently that when a hand touched her shoulder she started.

It was Pat Runkle, beside her, his face troubled. 'Lily—'

It was the first time he had spoken to her – not Jade Ring – since she had jumped out of the car. Now, here he stood, speaking in a voice of tenderness and beguilement, setting her teeth on edge, as if she heard a fingernail scraping a blackboard.

She moved to one side, but did not look at him, only continued to watch Mei Fei. He spoke in a voice so low no one nearby could understand.

'I swear I had nothing like that in mind when I called.'

She glanced at him, and there was Jade Ring's bewitching smile, fresh and magical, practiced so often she was sure it was stamped permanently upon her face:

No doubt, when I die – I will be smiling, just like this.

'What are you talking about, Pat?' Her voice was loud enough to carry to interested neighbors.

Pat moved away, his eyes darkening with a warming flash, and he strode onto the stage, Ming Huang about to encounter Mei Fei in the garden.

'Your eyes are sad, Mei Fei—' He touched her face gently.

And so they were, thought Lily. Sad and, as he said, her mouth was uncertain. Was it Ming Huang Barbara was worrying about, or Pat Runkle?

Once this is over, it'll be a bloody miracle if any of us ever knows for sure who we are again.

For something whimsical or savage or despairing in Gordon Donahue had taken the ancient legend and caused it to be turned inside out and upside down, just as Jade

Ring had substituted her rival for herself when the soldiers demanded her life.

The auditorium was filled with twelve hundred friends and relatives.

Lily's first appearance came early in the play: while Ming Huang was describing to his Chief Eunuch that *subverter of empires*, Jade Ring appeared at the other side of the stage, with her three sisters, her uncle and cousin, and softly played the table lute while her uncle lectured her on the arts of getting and keeping a man.

Lily waited in the wings, breathing deeply, those Yoga breathing exercises she had begun to learn as soon as she had decided to become Jade Ring, and stepped forth on cue, suddenly calm, in a fury of pride and determination to carry everything before her, Pat and Barbara, her own reluctant self.

The play proceeded swiftly, until all at once, as if a loud voice had called out a warning, she became aware of the approaching moment when she must exchange Mei Fei's Serving Girl's face for Jade Ring's ornately painted one.

She stood facing the Emperor, who had given her to his soldiers, and she gazed at him forgivingly. '*I go to die.*'

The Chief Eunuch had ushered Mei Fei, in her Serving Girl's disguise, into the Post House. Jade Ring knelt before a statue of the goddess Kuan-Yin. She bowed her head.

'*Great mercy, great pity,*
Save from sorrow, save from suffering.'
She rose slowly. '*Amidha Buddha!*'

She entered the Post House, and all at once was alert, murderously intent, smiling at Mei Fei, who looked as terrified as Mei Fei must have been, had this moment ever taken place outside Gordon Donahue's imagination.

Lily approached that scene with an uncanny dread, convinced that some grotesque unholy change was being made in her life – that once she had played that scene before an audience she would never again be the person she had been.

A decision would have been made. All her future life would have been committed – to what?

She had no idea.

'*Predestined enemies will always meet in some narrow alleyway.*' Jade Ring's smile was beguiling, and when Mei Fei cried out, Jade Ring asked tenderly: '*Did you suppose that you and I would have nothing more to say to each other?*'

Mei Fei stared at her with hard bitterness. Outside the soldiers had begun to beat the war drums. '*Why must I die – for you? I, who hate you.*'

'*Two women who have loved the same man are seldom good friends, Mei Fei.*'

Jade Ring's smile was serene, and Jade Ring described the tortures Mei Fei would endure if she were turned over to the soldiers, describing the Lingering Death with the delicacy of a connoisseur recalling a favorite relish. '*I offer you – mercy. A quick and painless death, which will not disfigure you.*'

She indicated the Eunuch approaching with the silk sash from Jade Ring's gown held in his hands. The war drums beat louder, then fell ominously silent.

'*Kill me then. What difference does it make? I died long ago.*'

Jade Ring leaned toward Mei Fei, slowly extending one hand to exchange the masks.

Lily's heart stopped beating, then gave a burst. She stood motionless, overcome with horror, unable to send another woman to death in her place.

Mei Fei looked at her steadily as the mask was peeled away, and Jade Ring soothingly passed her hands over Mei Fei's face, fixing her own mask there, transforming Jade Ring into the Serving Girl.

Lily took a step backward. A blackness surrounded her and her ears were ringing, her skin wet with cold sweat, and she felt the stage moving beneath her feet.

She closed her eyes, the darkness faded, and when she opened them after some indeterminate time, Mei Fei had been strangled and the Eunuch was carrying her to the litter. He gave Lily a swift fierce glare of summons, and all at once she was Jade Ring again, disguised now as the Serving Girl.

When at last, still the Serving Girl, she bent over the dead Emperor to close his eyes, the Curtain of Enchantment slowly descended, the transparent curtain upon which was painted the smiling face of Jade Ring. Behind that curtain she submitted to the ritualistic strangling by the Chief Eunuch, was picked up by him, and placed on the bed beside the Emperor.

The lights went out briefly, and as the Eunuch backed off from the two dead lovers, giving a fearful cry of terror and pity: '*Ai ya!*' the Curtain of Enchantment rose slowly and the audience confronted an empty stage: the performance had perhaps been their delusion.

The actors filed across the stage with solemn faces. Lily bowed deeply, until her forehead touched her knees; after a moment she stood upright, giving a movement of her head which flung the long black hair backward with a dramatic flourish.

No such concessions from Pat Runkle. His face was expressionless as he gazed out at them as if he were, indeed, Emperor of China, dead twelve hundred years, with no more interest in them than a dead emperor might be expected to have.

The room where Lily dressed with Barbara and four other girls was so crowded she could scarcely enter, and she found herself being kissed and congratulated, although she did not clearly see who kissed her, nor hear the congratulations, but felt as if she stood in the midst of a windstorm, trying to get her bearings.

'Oh, Lily, Lily, it's finally over! You were wonderful! I was petrified!' Barbara threw her arms about her.

'You were marvelous, Barbara!'

Lily drew in a deep breath and felt her muscles at ease, as if resting after some extraordinarily difficult achievement:

I have a choice. I do have a choice.

She was aware of a vast magnanimity toward all the

world. There was no one to resent, nothing to fear, nothing to dread, no one to hate, no future contests. It seemed the magical moment would last forever.

It lasted, at least, for several seconds, and then she floated easily toward earth, slowly descending into more familiar atmosphere, where she landed gently. There was no sudden disastrous encounter, and she recognized it as the same earth she had known all along; magic, however seemingly real, was vagrant.

The haunted house had a tenant at last: the Jade Ring of history and legend, and Gordon Donahue's fancy.

She unclasped the string of Lily Morgan Malone's pearls and dropped them into her handbag, and went to join her aunt and uncle.

CHAPTER 11

It was clear to Lily as they approached Gordon Donahue's large brown shingled house, where lights burned in every window, that in Valerie and Frederick's opinion, their niece was lost to anthropology.

But it was not so clear to Lily. She remembered too vividly the sickening moment when her heart had stopped beating and the stage shifted treacherously beneath her feet.

They went up the steps, but at the opened doorway Lily let Valerie and Frederick go on while she hesitated, accustoming herself to the idea that this was no longer the T'ang Dynasty, and she was free of Jade Ring – until tomorrow night.

She entered not at all like the star of the show, but so quietly, moving through the room without looking directly at any of them, that they let her go by as if it were Jade Ring's ghost passing.

The members of the class looked strange, with their Caucasian faces, their blonde and brown hair, dressed in dinner jackets and low-cut evening dresses, displaying the bare arms and backs and shoulders not revealed by the costumes of Ming Huang's court, holding cocktail glasses and cigarettes, the young men standing about with their hands in their pockets, sitting with their legs crossed, casual, negligent, with none of the alert dignity Donahue had imposed on them:

Who are they? Do I know them?

She decided she would leave, go home, forget that the ambition to play Jade Ring had ever entered her mind.

She felt Gordon Donahue's hand take firm hold of her wrist, and knew who it was before she looked at him. Then she was outside, going down the stairs, oblivious to the young men and women on their way in, passing her with gay greetings and compliments. Gordon Donahue put his hands on her shoulders as they reached the bottom step and turned her about.

'Don't be foolish.' When she looked at him, it was to find his eyes serious. Why at this particular moment should she decide she was free to come and go as she liked, after her history of fanatic cooperation?

'Why, hello,' she said, as if they had met one afternoon on a campus street. 'How are you?'

'It's over. You did wonderfully well. I'm proud of you.' He sounded like the doctor who had taken out her tonsils.

'Oh, no! There were so many things—'

'Come in – you've met my wife.'

There she was, Marian Donahue, smiling and congratulating her, shaking her hand. She looked to Lily a plain, undecorated, unpretentious, well-meaning, anxious wife. Her husband composed her life, and Lily was sure Mrs Donahue was afraid of Lily Malone even before she had met her.

However, she did not seem to be.

When Gordon introduced them, her face was warm and she offered such lavish compliments Lily looked at her in surprise.

Is she clever, or simple?

She's simple. Or with that hairstyle she'd be wearing different makeup. She's afraid to be beautiful.

Beauty, after all, was a responsibility. Beauty did attract men, and men were not always kindly disposed toward beautiful women. Pat Runkle, for one.

'Thank you, Mrs Donahue,' said Lily, and escaped as quickly as she could.

Some time later, half an hour, perhaps two hours, Lily noticed, against her will, that only two or three feet away in that room now so crowded it was almost impossible to move, Pat Runkle was standing in back of Barbara, almost close enough to touch her.

As Lily watched, he moved one step nearer, until his body pressed lightly against Barbara's. Nothing anyone could notice or, if they did, find surprising. They were all of them pressed together, front to front or back to back, and why they did not spread out through the big house was one of the mysteries which, before tonight, would not have occurred to her as mysterious.

Now, everything had become strange, portentous; there was some curious unreality about faces, voices, gestures, sounds, all of which seemed distant, and unnaturally close. A disaster might occur at any moment.

As Pat moved, Barbara caught her breath, and turned to him swiftly, her eyes bright and alert, looking at him with a smile such as Lily had never before seen on the face of Barbara Sloan:

Why, she's in love with him. The idiot.

Lily turned away quickly, and began to talk to An Lu-shan, who seemed flattered by this attention from the night's real celebrity, who had outshone the Emperor himself.

Without looking at them, she was aware that Barbara and Pat Runkle were making their way through the room, pausing here and there to pretend they were in no hurry. And presently they were gone – off to the Motel of the Golden Dragon.

It was nearly two o'clock when Valerie and Frederick and Lily arrived home, and after kissing them good night, a strange subdued good night considering that the occasion was judged to have been a triumph and Lily the most

.triumphant among them, Lily walked to her bedroom as if she knew exactly what she must do.

She went to her desk, and quickly wrote: BARBARA SLOAN, tore off the page; wrote PATRICK FRANCIS RUNKLE on the next page, tore that off, crumpled the pages and tossed them into a pottery bowl, struck a match, and set the paper on fire. It caught quickly, and an orange flame blazed up.

Watching it, Lily repeated Jade Ring's curse upon Mei Fei when news was brought that Mei Fei had spent the night in the Royal Bedchamber:

'*Therefore I hate you with an intense hatred and now make war against you! Fire! Take this letter into the Spirit World, so that Heaven and Earth shall know of my hate!*'

She watched the paper burn out, blackening slowly, until the flame ran along the edges and was gone. A thin line of sharp-smelling smoke streaked straight upward.

Lily shivered slightly, and folded her arms, enclosing herself. She jumped at the sound of a knock on the door.

She went to unlock the door and found Valerie.

Lily gestured. 'I just burned a note – from someone.'

Valerie looked at her politely but, Lily thought, the politeness was incredulous, and perhaps she thought the excitement of the evening, possibly the effects of so much praise coming after the months of savage concentration, had driven her niece distracted.

Lily's face was calm but her eyes glistened. She opened the door wider, so that Valerie could see the room was not on fire.

'Someone – I don't know who – handed it to me tonight.' She wondered why she felt the need for the lie.

Would Valerie have thought it so strange if she had told her she was practicing Chinese black magic? Very little surprised Valerie, who must have been born knowing the world was full of unpleasant surprises.

'I see,' said Valerie kindly. 'Good night – dear.'

Good night – dear?

Did she think her niece was out of her senses?

Lily smiled. 'Good night, Valerie.'

She closed the door, examined the remnants of paper to be certain there was no writing left unburned, and crumbled the ashes between her thumb and fingers.

The next day she called Gordon Donahue's office and asked to see him at four o'clock.

He began to object that at five she would be putting on her makeup, and then he said, 'Of course, Lily.' Evidently she sounded as desperately helpless as she felt.

'One or two things about the performance I'd like to talk to you about.'

She rehearsed the speech most of the day.

She said it one way while she was taking her ballet lesson. She said it another way while she was conjugating French verbs. And she said it several other ways while she was walking from the French teacher's house to the campus and climbing the stairs, reluctantly, to Donahue's office.

She was going to tell him she would not play Jade Ring ever again. He might give it to Barbara Sloan; or he might give it to her stand-in. He might cancel the play, and she thought that would be best of all. The play was cursed. The very idea of playing at being people who had been dead more than one thousand years was cursed.

He dismissed a student, a young man Lily did not know, when he saw her in the doorway, head slightly bowed, and the young man slipped by her sideways, as if passing a royal personage he must take care not to touch.

'Yes, Lily?' Gordon came toward her, a questioning and troubled expression on his face.

She took two or three steps into the room, started to speak, and began to cry. He closed the door, and she heard him turn the lock. She sat in the chair she had occupied during their long conferences.

'Lily – what's happened?' It was the same quiet, calm, concerned voice which had directed them during the past several months, through those scenes of jealousy, revenge, excessive love and excessive hate, all of it contagious.

She went on crying. 'I – I can't – Oh, I'm sorry. I'm sorry. Forgive me!' She sobbed until she began to choke, and once she glanced up to see him standing with the helpless worried look of a man who sees a woman crying but has no solution for stopping her, or even for easing whatever had caused the crying.

'Lily – darling—'

She did not at first notice that he had called her *darling*, but then took it for the same kind of concern Valerie had shown when she said: 'Good night, dear', a grown-up, trying to comfort a distraught child.

'I don't understand. Everything went so well last night—'

'Oh, no! I've wrecked your play! I've wrecked my life!' She heard the words with vague surprise:

Is it as bad as all that?

'Lily – Lily—'

He knelt before her on one knee. She let her hands fall to her lap and looked at him despairingly, her face not contorted by the steady streaming tears, but almost serene, although she gazed at him pleadingly, asking for his help, his kindness, his reassurances.

His hands touched her head, stroking lightly across the crown, and passed over her hair and along her neck. She grew very still, waiting, surprised by the pleasure, the conviction that here was love, help, a curative magic for whatever ailed her.

She waited, scarcely breathing, and while he stroked her hair again and again, passing his hands over her neck, over her breasts, she sat with eyes closed, lips parted, motionless.

She had not, she thought, come here to have him make love to her, yet now she waited for it to happen.

The room seemed remarkably still as he continued to stroke her hair, her shoulders; his hands covered her breasts, and she felt his mouth on one nipple, circling it delicately and passing to the other. His mouth closed over hers as her hands touched his head, that black hair she must have been longing to touch; and very easily, the sweater was off, the skirt off, and it was Gordon Donahue, not Ming Huang, who was admiring Jade Ring's breasts, a smile on his mouth, glancing quickly and questioningly at her.

More and more dazzled by pleasure, eager with desire, her legs separated slightly, then wide enough to admit him, and he was inside her easily as if he penetrated a flower, cautious for a moment, until at a sound of pleasure from her, he began to move, more quickly, holding her against him, his head beside hers, turning to kiss her mouth, moving slowly, then all at once, as her legs closed about his back, the movements thrust deeper and harder, and she heard her voice, begging him; there was a moment of exquisite tenderness, diffusing sensation throughout her belly, a few more moments of stillness as she held him fast, and she saw him looking at her, a faint questioning on his face.

'Oh, my darling – thank you, thank you—'

To Lily's surprise, as she stood up and stepped into her skirt, pulled the sweater over her head, and began combing her hair and smoothing powder over her face to obliterate the tear tracks, she laughed softly, a practiced woman of pleasure's laugh; Jade Ring's, it might have been. 'That's not why I came.' She glanced at him across the mirror, to find him standing, hands in his pockets, feet slightly spread, watching her intently, carefully, wonderingly. 'I think.' All at once she laughed, gaily this time:

He's cured me.

But of what?

A few minutes later they left his office and, Lily supposed, looked as decorous to the few professors and students who passed them as any couple might who had been lost at sea for several hours and were finally found, cast up to shore among the seaweed.

It was after five, time for the makeup session, but Lily said she would go home first, change her clothes – she gestured vaguely. They walked to his car, which they had done often these past several weeks, drove the few blocks in silence, and when Lily opened the car door she turned, thinking she must say something, but instead touched his hand briefly and got out. He smiled, nodding, as if at some unstated but well-understood agreement, and drove away.

A few days later, when *Jade Ring* had completed its triumphal week's progress and finals were about to begin, he sent her to his doctor. By then it was clear that something had begun which might last a long time.

Why it had not begun earlier surprised Lily, but seemed not to surprise him. He was a conservative man in his living and habits, however he took flight in his fancies of T'ang history, and if she had not cried it might not have begun at all. But the tears seemed to have broken some resistance in both of them.

Jade Ring played its last successful performance, and three days later Lily took her first final.

She had noticed that Barbara looked very happy for a few days, as if she thought this triumph would last forever: it was at least as good as having been elected Homecoming Queen.

But soon Pat was taking other girls to other parties, and Barbara looked anxious and avoided Lily. At any other time, Lily would have taken satisfaction in the powerful working of her evil charm, but in fact she forgot it.

During the two weeks of finals, the excitement of Senior Week, the campus broke up, people went in all directions, friends lost track of one another overnight, and sometimes never met again.

It was as if, at the end of each semester, a great city was deserted, abandoned because of a sudden plague, the inhabitants fleeing in disarray, some of them without waiting for news of the plague's development; others dilatory, waiting. But the city itself was chaotic, sad and rejoicing at once, for another generation had passed to its reward, graduation or failure, and presently a new generation would arrive, unknown faces and talents from unknown places. The campus streets were almost empty at seven-thirty.

'How strange it always seems,' Lily said late one

afternoon as she and Gordon left his office. 'I've seen it happen every year since I was five. We've always lived in that house, I've always come to the campus with my aunt and uncle. And it has always affected me the same way. It's sad, because nothing is ever put together again the way it was before. And it's a relief, because whatever it's been, there's some of it you're glad to know can never happen again.'

Barbara was gone. Gone.

The last time Lily had seen her had been in the auditorium, where the final for their art history class was held. But Barbara had been elusive ever since the night she had left Donahue's party with Patrick Runkle and, after attending the last formal DKE dance and two other parties with him, had evidently lost the favor of the Shining Emperor – who knew why? – and had been sent back to the Pepper Chamber.

But when Lily did not see Barbara and was told that Barbara had gone to visit relatives in Colorado, an unlikely place for Barbara to have relatives – at least, she had never mentioned them – Lily thought no more about Barbara. One day she would come back. Or she would not. They would be friends again. Or they would not.

Pat Runkle had also disappeared. But that was not surprising, since he lived in the southern part of the state.

A few days later Lily received a newspaper clipping from someone who did not sign a name, mailed from a town several hundred miles away, with the announcement that Patrick Francis Runkle had been married to Lydia St Denis of Pasadena on the twenty-eighth of June.

The bride had attended private schools in the east and in France and Switzerland. Her father was chairman of various boards, sundry banks, and in the photograph she was a pretty, aloof, dark-haired girl, dressed in a gown reported to have been designed by Worth for her great-grandmother, and she carried a bouquet of lilies of the valley and small white roses. Patrick Francis Runkle, in his morning coat, looked the proud young bridegroom, sickeningly handsome, perhaps even in love.

Lily threw the paper in the wastebasket. Patrick Runkle married!

She looked at herself in the mirror, as if reflecting upon one of the strangest events she could recall hearing about, and was more surprised than she would have been at the news of another war, or the burning of a great city. The mystery of such an event seemed far greater than she would have guessed it might, had it been predicted.

For, after all, why should not Patrick Runkle get married?

Perhaps he was just the type of man who got married most easily, since it would mean so little to him. He need not reflect upon the assumption of burdens, responsibilities. Or perhaps there was another Patrick Runkle – someone quite different from the Shining Emperor, president of the senior class, captain of the football team, lord of the Motel of the Golden Dragon.

Lily smiled a little, reflecting upon Jade Ring's final conclusion about her life in the Palace of the Golden Bells: *'And a moment which ought to have lasted forever has come and gone before I knew . . .'*

CHAPTER 12

A goddess. A queen. A *grande courtisane*. A classical actress.

Those were her choices: he might have been joking – except that Gordon Donahue did not make fun of anyone, certainly not Lily. These were the choices, he said, which gave a woman like Lily space for exploration.

Perhaps he had meant that Lily Malone had no real interest in exploring the outer islands of anthropology. Her explorations would have no meaning for her unless she went exploring in her own character and personality, searching there and in assumed personalities, for herself and her life.

Except, she thought, unluckily one did not discover life; one must invent it.

'Make up your mind,' he advised her. 'These are decisions to make early. You're nineteen.'

Nineteen?

How had that happened? All at once it seemed an advanced age, and yet greater age was advancing, remorselessly, until one day she would discover her allotment here had been used up. It would be time for her to take her leave of whatever she had contrived to be, to feel, to invent, to give:

Where did yesterday go?

Everyone she knew counted time in chronological sequence, hour by hour, day by day; a year had passed, and that was an event.

Lily knew the days, the years, as well as they did. Her memory for dates was keen to the point of being uncanny – but so was the sense that none of it had anything to do with time, or with living: living took place by feeling, not by minutes or hours or years. A second might endure until the Last Judgment; and a year had never happened at all: the two years of Jack Davidson. The eternity of her discovery – in the act of peeling the mask from Barbara-Mei Fei's face – of her future self.

Yet she had pushed the future self aside and returned to the self she had had before that world was made: the self which wanted to please Valerie and Frederick, repay them for having devoted much of their lives for fifteen years to her nourishment and training.

Work in the graduate department of anthropology was engrossing, demanding, and she thought it was making her sick, a literal sickness, but not a definable one.

Books and lists, tests and papers, hours in class, hours in the library; and the lessons in ballet, voice, horseback riding, swimming, French, Spanish. She had no spare minutes but those she spent with Gordon Donahue late in the afternoon in his office.

Lily had begun to suspect that Marian Donahue was the Mei Fei of her own Shining Emperor; timid and modest, even in bed. Or how could he take such continuous delight in Lily's body, exploring her with an intimacy and care which would not have occurred with Jack Davidson, and which Patrick Runkle had not had time for in that one experience she could not obliterate.

Lily was pliant and enthusiastic, immodest, engrossed in her new experiences and sensations, which nearly compensated her for the hours in the classrooms and library.

Sometimes he talked to her before he made love to her; sometimes later when he often drove her home. Not every time, however, for they had agreed without words that this relationship, however serious, was separate from the rest of their lives.

After two or three months, sometime late in the summer, he said that he loved her, and Lily surprised herself by replying that she loved him. The word, at that moment, lost its tyranny. It became a word, not quite as any other word, but it was no longer talismanic.

They had not gone from there to talk about the future, or how long this love might last. They said nothing about his wife, who either suspected her husband was in love with Lily Malone or did not, but who evidently had the optimism of wives whose husbands fell in love with other women: it would be brief. It was not of any real meaning. The girl was young, she was beautiful, she was restless. He would come back to his home.

Occasionally Lily passed Marian on the campus. They smiled, spoke pleasantly, but did not pause to talk.

Lily knew what she was thinking, by observing her face in the quick passing, and she knew she was fearful: suppose this obviously determined young woman should decide she wanted to marry Gordon Donahue? Yes, she was afraid of her, and that pleased Lily a little. She had never frightened a grown woman before.

Still, if Mrs Donahue knew how little eager Lily Malone was to marry her husband – or any man – she might be no happier at this temporary loss, but she would be less apprehensive:

Dear Mrs Donahue, I don't want him to keep. I only want him for now. He's all you have, or ever will have – and I have a life to look forward to. You've made your choice, and you made it permanently. My mistakes will be more serious, but I'll be able to undo them when I want to. She added, for luck: *I hope.*

'You're twenty,' he reminded her on her birthday, just after he had given her a little statue, three inches high, apple-green jade polished smooth as silk, the Goddess of Mercy, Kuan-Yin – and she was thinking she would keep it with her, wherever she went, and speak Jade Ring's prayer and make Jade Ring's obeisance, each time she faced an audience for the first time, quite as Jade Ring had made obeisance before she went into the Post House, supposedly to be strangled by the Eunuch: one fate seemed not much worse than another.

She was sitting on his desk, and she had been combing her hair, looking in the mirror, always a little surprised by the change in her face after they made love. 'I know.'

She put the goddess in the leather envelope inside her notebook. She sighed, as if the notion of being twenty bored her.

And so it did.

Almost everything, it seemed, but those moments when their bodies closed together and the incredible pleasures began, everything else, since her great acclaim as Jade Ring, had bored her a little.

At least, she called it boredom, but kept it as a shameful secret:

What of it – that we are alone?

What of it – that the stars flow farther into space each instant?

What of it – that our lives happen once, and vanish in a flash?

What of it – that everything matters – but nothing matters very much?

But that was not the litany she had sung to herself as she had run up the stairs to Gordon Donahue's office that first afternoon – how many light-years ago?

When it suited her, when it was one of the *Days of*

Destiny, she forgot that nothing mattered very much. If she had tried to remind herself – to quiet the nervousness, to rid herself of the panic-stricken feeling that this one moment was the only moment which ever would have meaning of any knd – what then?

What would become of her?

Nothing would become of her.

What had become of Barbara?

What had become of other girls she had known?

Nothing.

And as for Barbara – no letters had arrived. Nothing to tell her where her former friend was or what life she was living.

Jack Davidson was an engineer now, she had heard, married to the girl he had walked about the campus with for two years. And, no doubt, forty or fifty years from now, it would be difficult to separate one from another the various elements which had gone to form the compost heap of Jack Davidson's life.

What became of people became of them in their imaginations, most of all in their feelings. And that was why she knew that this boredom was no boredom but a sickness.

Gordon Donahue was an evasion, a simple test substituted for a more difficult test – the test of herself against not one man who loved her for the accidents that made her beautiful to feel and look at and make love to, but the test of that self against all those others:

The enemy, as she perceived them.

Where had it come from? This distrust of the world's good will?

She could not imagine why she had proudly announced to Michael that one day she would be a great actress. Only to distract his attention from the chemistry set?

Of course not.

Her play, *Adventure*, the great adventure of the ninth year of her life: Antoinette, that *femme fatale*, ruthless, determined, ambitious. This eight-year-old vixen had taken the neighborhood grown-ups by surprise, not being what they would have expected of Valerie and Frederick's little niece.

That might have been when she had made her decision to dedicate her life to acting, as to any religious order. Then had come her disastrous appearance as the second lead in *Bitter Sweet*.

Once the humiliation of performing without complete control of the project had been made clear, she put the ambition aside. She would be better off as an anthropologist than playing second lead in *Bitter Sweet*.

She might have thought no more about it. But then Gordon Donahue had arrived and attracted attention even in the crowds which swarmed the campus streets; perhaps because his face seemed to reflect a secret humor – and it was that look of knowing a secret which attracted Lily.

Now, when he reminded her that she was twenty, she grew morose, and thought it an advanced age for a woman who wanted to be an actress: too late, right this moment.

'You're waiting for someone to make up your mind.'

'I suppose. After all—' She looked at him appealingly, so that he would tell her she could not go, he could not be without her. 'If I go to this acting school you talk about, if it turns out that I can't learn to act—'

'You can.' He was so confident she wished it were Gordon Donahue who must move into the position of vulnerability. 'But you must learn the techniques. They aren't easy. They aren't natural. What are you afraid of, Lily?'

She strolled barefoot about the room, wearing her pleated white silk skirt and sleeveless pink cashmere sweater, then returned to stand before him. His hands closed around her buttocks and drew her close. 'Leaving you?' It did not feel quite true as she said it – yet it was at least partly true.

'Oh, Lily – Lily, darling—' He was sober, moved, and suddenly ashamed. 'I have nothing to give you, except what you have – my love. The only thing you'll value one day that I want to give you is the will to try. You can come back – go on with your studies. You have money?'

'Our parents left five thousand a year each to Michael and me until we're twenty-one. Then seven thousand a year for another ten years. Valerie and Frederick have never used it. It's invested in interest-bearing bonds.' She smiled, slightly ironical. 'I'm a rich woman, for my age.'

Lily looked at him. *Why do we fear what we most want?*

He had never guessed she was suffering from a sickness she could not describe, or define.

There were no symptoms. She looked like a flourishing young tree. She had the health of spring, the freshness and vivacity of all growing creatures. Her laughter was real, and so were her tears.

Only something inside seemed to have failed. As if, in mysterious fashion, she had agreed with her unknown self not to take any of this too seriously; not to believe, for fear of being disappointed; not to love too deeply, for fear of being overwhelmed, or perhaps abandoned.

By whom?

Certainly not by this man, whose intensity increased, and who did, she never doubted, love her. Even after she had followed his advice, gone away to try her luck in that alien world she dreaded, he would love her still.

It was the first relationship with an outsider, outside the magic circle of her family, which she could imagine as permanent. He had, she thought, by his care, his concentration, opened her, perhaps a little prematurely, as a flower might be opened by a dedicated gardener.

Driving along the dark campus, late in the fall, nearly a year and a half after she had graduated, he said: 'You could have a remarkable career as a tragic actress. I doubt if comedy is your métier.'

She laughed softly. 'So do I.'

'You affect others deeply by what you do on the stage. That's a great power – and it can be a benevolent one. The power to open the imagination. Most people know nothing of their feelings. They live, so far as they live at all, vicariously. Acting is not a frivolous profession, Lily.'

'It may not be frivolous, or it may be no more frivolous than anything else – but it's a hell of a lot more terrifying.'

Once entered upon, there was no further decision to be made.

And the rewards?

What, exactly?

Returning from the headhunters, if she did, she might write a book, and great credit would be given for the hardships she had endured to procure that modicum of knowledge. True knowledge or false knowledge – who was to know for sure?

Yet, was there anyone in a theater audience, however vicariously he might be living his own existence, who did not know, with an absolute certainty, when he was presented with the truth of a feeling and when he was given the lie of a feeling?

'Are you so afraid of failure?'

Now it was December. Almost time for the Christmas reunion. He had not turned on the light in his office, and at five-thirty it was nearly dark, lighted dimly from a building across the street. There she sat, naked, on his desk.

'Of course.' She extended her legs, so that her toes touched the floor. 'I'm afraid, because I'm serious. How could you pretend to be someone else if you weren't serious?'

'Confidence will come – when you test yourself against the others. If I'm wrong, I can't help you, I know that. But I'm not often wrong about talent.' He laughed, somewhat embarrassed by the bold statement, and combed his hair with his fingers. 'Make up your mind. These decisions must be made early – or not at all.'

She smiled at him, a strange smile, something new. 'A goddess is overthrown by a new religion. A queen may be killed, by her king, or her people. A *grande courtisane* – like other women – grows old. And an actress eventually loses her public to a rival. She smiled and shrugged and opened her hands: 'You see? It's over before you begin.'

All these distant, unimaginable disasters. Yet, of course, they would come one day.

He seized her hands and held them fast: '*Jump! said the*

*philosopher. Jump off the housetop. The whole gist of the
problem lies in that . . .'*

CHAPTER 13

'History,' Arlette told Anthony much later, 'is made on
only certain days of our lives: the *Days of Destiny*.'

She knew which days they were, for her. She knew
what some of them must be for him, but she could not
know all of them. Anthony, like Arlette, saved more of
himself than he gave away, even to her, even by the time
she took him into her confidence about those *Days of
Destiny*.

Still, that must have been one of them, perhaps one of
the few they shared.

When they were introduced he looked at her with the
quick interest of a man meeting a beautiful woman for the
first time. She had smiled, holding out her hand, as if to
a stranger. He shook it peremptorily, his eyes narrowing,
as if to make certain he saw whom he thought he saw.

'Arlette Morgan?' he repeated, his voice low, even
though no one stood nearby. Perhaps he thought she had
some secret he must not give away. 'Lily Malone?'

Lily drew her hand away. 'Well, yes.'

Arlette Morgan was new to her – just a little more than
two years old. It did not even now seem completely her
own. Yet it was her own, since Morgan had belonged to
her mother and Arlette was a family relic, a great-
grandmother; perhaps a great-aunt.

'What a surprise.' He was smiling, amused, admiring,
and she thought a little condescending. She opened her
eyes wide in mock surprise.

'Why, Pat Runkle!' She laughed gaily.

'Sh! Anthony De Forest, for God's sake. I'll remember
your name – you remember mine.' He continued to
observe her carefully. 'How long has it been?'

Arlette replied promptly. 'Three years and six months. I thought you'd be a tycoon by now.'

He was still studying her, as if she had changed radically in three years and a half. Perhaps she had. She had no idea how much was left of Lily Malone.

She had gone to strange cities alone. She had traveled alone. She had crossed the ocean and lived in a strange country alone; for although she had an aunt and uncle who were living in London, she had not stayed with them. She had found places to live alone.

It was true she had been protected in these journeys more than she liked to admit. Gordon Donahue had been in England for six months, studying the traditions of Elizabethan theatrical production for a new book, and through him she had been introduced to an acting school and a Shakespearean coach, neither of whom she had liked. And Michael had been there, having graduated from the University of Chicago and gone to study biochemistry at Cambridge.

Even so, she was essentially alone, as Valerie had warned her when Lily had made the announcement: anthropology was not to be the staging area for her life, after all.

'You've won,' she had told Gordon with a slight smile, intended to conceal the bitterness and resentment that he had at last forced her to make the decision and set a date for carrying it into effect: on January twenty-eighth, she was to leave for Chicago, for a brief visit to her aunt and uncle, her brother, her cousins; then to New York, to find an apartment, and for a few months join a drama school which Donahue had arranged for her to attend; in May she would meet him in London.

Even so, she was convinced she had been alone, but not lonely. She had not been alone, without money, without relatives, without comfort for the several injuries suffered by her vanity, as other girls she had met were alone.

She had dreaded giving the news to Valerie and Frederick, not because they would blame her, but because they would not.

'I wanted so much to please you,' Lily said when she went to Valerie's study.

'My dear, I've never pretended to myself – and I hope not to you – that I'm your mother. I've never believed the individual has much real choice about his life, but perhaps I've been wrong.' Lily stood before her, feet together, hands clasped, head bowed slightly. 'You will be obliged to become completely self-reliant, Lily. That's not very much advice to give, but it's all I have. An actress – is always alone. There is no one to share, in any deep sense, your good moments, and no one to blame for your bad moments.'

The world Lily was proposing to enter was as alien to Valerie as if her niece had proposed to enter a convent. The individual, in Valerie's belief, belonged, blood and sinew, brain and muscle, to the world of those who had less luck.

Yet it was Valerie who had taught Lily to discipline herself for whatever she undertook, without stopping on that one fatal day to ask if this was the day she would prefer not to exert that discipline. In Valerie's opinion – and in Lily's – there were no such days: the first was the last.

Valerie had told her: 'We have acquired discipline only when the idea of discpline has become meaningless.'

Talking to Frederick was easier. He nodded, took her hand, and said: 'The fact is we can do only one serious thing in our lifetimes. Everything else is a hobby. If this is what you want to do, make everything in your life a part of this one choice.'

'I will.'

Frederick's desk, like Valerie's, was covered with papers, papers which accumulated each day as if by magic, were disposed of by magic; papers of students; notes for lectures; pages from a book he was working on. As the years went by, Frederick Morgan had become one of the academic world's authorities on the lives of the ordinary people of medieval England.

Who was to prevent him from being all those men?

And no doubt he had been. Of what other use was his knowledge of the Middle Ages if he needed it only to pass it on to others?

Just as Lily Malone had played Jade Ring so that she might become, for a brief time, another woman, in another world: one lifetime only was a cheat. It was the individual's task to discover ways to circumvent the shabby plan contained in the terms of the universe, stars in their spaces, atoms in their places.

'This life,' Frederick said, indicating the world of the University, 'might become a jail to you, in time. It does, even for those of us who like it.'

'For you, Frederick?'

'Sometimes. Still – well, Lily, there's another world. Several other worlds. And I think you have the explorer's temperament.' He looked at her sadly. 'Your mother did. Your father too. I've so often wondered what they would have made of the world if they'd had more time to examine it.'

'Oh!'

Frederick put his arms about her. 'I'm sorry, darling. Forgive me.'

Death did not return those it had claimed, only because they were still loved and needed. She found no essential distinction between past and present, or even past and present and future. There was only a continuum of experience; light came and went, darkness came and went. But the past never became the past.

'Someday – I may stop expecting them.'

'You may not. Some people have the capacity to forget, and others seem to lack it entirely. Be grateful for your memory – even when it's most painful. You'll need it one day.'

It had become evident to the bold adventuress Lily Malone, now become Arlette Morgan, that she did need her memory; all of it.

She needed everything she remembered, and everything she thought she had forgotten. Observation and experience and memory – these were of as much value to her now and future self as her beautiful face, her graceful, round, and attenuated body, her voice, which took easily to more difficult training, and her capacity for persistence, which above all was the only gift worth having.

The girls she had met during those two years in Chicago and London and New York, in directors' offices, teachers' offices, photographers' offices, agents' offices, thought she was lucky. She was unfairly good-looking; she had too easy a way of conveying sensuality without whorishness. What they did not notice was her persistence. She never mentioned it, and they did not suspect it.

They recognized, some of them, that this was the atomization of a star in the making, the fine particles which flowed more and more steadily together, which might one day, before their eyes, form itself into a glittering globe of light.

They saw it happen, from time to time – a young girl here, a young man there – who burst suddenly out of their enclosed circle. It always seemed to happen as if some supernatural force had touched them. Where had that star been before? The same person they had known; then someone else entirely, gone from them, leaving behind no secret formula; leaving them to discover the formula – if there was one.

'How great!'

'And overnight!'

'What luck, to have the star get sick!'

'How long will it last?'

'Remember Norma Lamont?'

'One day – her name up there—'

'And then—'

'An overdose . . .'

These sudden ascents and descents, luck and disaster intermingled, made them wonder who would be next.

For as long as Lily could remember, she had seen her friends and acquaintances drifting into irrevocable situations, without having made a decision of any kind. They had let the days run like a river, while they floated,

Ophelia-like, upon its surface, hands folded across their breasts, hair streaming like marsh grass:

They have no idea what they're doing, she told herself in horrified wonder. *They let it happen – they simply let it happen. And before they've begun to live, their lives are over, finished.*

The nearest she had come to experiencing any such disaster had been her encounter with Pat Runkle. And so, at the sight of him looking down at her with his black eyes interested and speculative, she raised her chin and smiled Jade Ring's bewitching smile:

Never forget. Never forgive.

He had not become a tycoon, after all. Another family rebellion.

'I started in that direction,' he told her. 'I went to Harvard for a year – business school. Then Korea— What have you been doing, Lily? I never expected—'

'You never expected to see me again. Of course not.'

He smiled. The smile was the same smile, although the effect had intensified. Or, at least, she was surprised to find her cherished hatred had vanished into a nostalgia for a life they had once shared: the shining Emperor; the Supreme One; the Palace of the Golden Bells. Mei Fei-Barbara. Nothing was said about her. The patina of the past had washed over the hatred, softening it – not entirely. There was still a sense of resistance and distrust.

'*Predestined enemies will always meet in some narrow alleyway,*' she reminded him.

His face became serious, and to Arlette's surprise, she was baffled. Anthony De Forest seemed a new version of Patrick Runkle, and whatever fascinations he had once used had now been polished, honed, improved, until there seemed no way of evading him.

'You're more beautiful,' he said soberly, no trace of Pat Runkle's ironic smile. This Anthony De Forest had lost Pat Runkle's carelessness with the feelings of others. 'Where have you been?'

'Chicago. England, for a few months. Here.'

'I've thought of you, Lily – quite often. Does that surprise you?'

'It does.'

'You still hold a grudge against me?'

'You gave me no choice. I hold that against you.'

'Or you gave me no choice?' He gestured. 'Well – forgive me. I wanted you. That's all.' His eyes narrowed. 'Are you married?'

He glanced at the narrow jade ring on the fourth finger of her left hand, Gordon Donahue's gift to her when she had left for New York. She had worn it on her right hand until she had returned from London. Now it was on her left hand.

'I'm in love with someone,' she told the young actors she met. Or: 'I'm married. It wouldn't be fair.' There was little they could say to that, for it covered all the territory they might have tried to usurp.

To Anthony, she said, 'It's a charm against the night goblins. No, I'm not married. But you are.'

He laughed. 'How did you know that?'

'Someone sent me a clipping. She's very pretty,' she added, improving Jade Ring's smile so that the jealousy did not show through.

'She's very beautiful. We have two children – a boy and a girl. The girl's not quite a year old.'

'How well managed.'

The boy and girl made her angry. The beautiful rich wife made her angry, for the clipping had been explicit: The St Denises were at least as rich as the Runkles; they had been rich for the proper three generations. Even the marriage made her angry.

This was not Patrick Runkle. This was not Ming Huang. This was a stranger: Anthony De Forest.

The temporary illusion of meeting a part of the past which folded itself upon the present became indistinguishable from it, was gone. She held out her hand. 'I'm glad to have seen you again,' and her tone added that she would not be glad to see him again.

'Where are you going?'

'I came here to read for a part. My drama coach wanted me to. And, anyway, the show is going to Chicago. I'm staying in New York, whatever happens. And you're Romeo.' Reason enough.

'I'm Romeo. It's the first good chance I've had, even if it is a road company. I hope to Christ I don't fuck it up – or I'm finished.'

'Finished?'

His face changed, a face fit for Othello. 'I made a bargain with myself when I came back from Korea: three years to find out if I wanted to be an actor. Or could be an actor. Two and a half years will be gone by the end of this year, when the tour ends. You understand that? You've got some such schedule?'

'No.' No secrets were to be exchanged; no common or different plans explored. 'Just to study.'

He looked skeptical, but politely declined, as Anthony De Forest, to say what Pat Runkle would have said: She was lying, and he knew it.

He was examining her again, and as his concentration intensified it became a physical force. She felt herself losing Arlette Morgan. Lily Malone came swimming to the surface. If he had not made love to her, she believed she would never had thought of him again; but the body remembered what she wanted to forget.

'Where do you live?'

'On Seventy-second, between Park and Lexington.'

'Alone?'

She smiled, letting him know he would not be invited there. He was a treacherous guest, who helped himself to his hostess's larder without invitation or so much as asking if he might. 'Yes. Alone.'

'Have dinner with me.'

CHAPTER 14

'How did you decide on Arlette Morgan?'

He seemed honestly concerned to know her reason, but Arlette hesitated to give it, not sure she could trust him with even so small a secret. Yet this man seemed almost the mirror image of Pat Runkle. Or Pat Runkle had been the mirror image of the man who had been Anthony De Forest all along.

'Gordon Donahue told me that Lily Malone was a name for the contemporary theater, but not for a classical actress.'

'He was right. Yes – even then you were extraordinarily serious. Did you know that? I think – I've sometimes thought – that may be why I did what I did that night.'

'Without so much as a *Please, Ma'am*?'

'You wanted it.'

'Yes.' *Beyond reason*. She shook her head. 'I don't know why.' It seemed, even to Lily, somewhat curious that she should pretend not to know why when the evidence was there three feet from her.

They sat opposite each other in an Italian restaurant a few blocks from the hall where the auditions had been held.

It was, she supposed, Pat Runkle's notion – if not Anthony De Forest's – that by easing her from the rehearsal hall into a restaurant, then into a taxi and uptown to her apartment, he would presently find himself in bed with her, and resolve the question as to why he had wanted her enough to have used no more ceremony than if she had been a beautiful stranger, met in a strange land, where none of the shibboleths of sexual politeness prevailed.

But, Lily assured herself, surprisingly at ease as they began to eat – that reliable ceremony for turning strangers into momentary friends – this time she would surprise him.

And where was that wife, whom Arlette could only imagine wearing her great-grandmother's lace wedding gown? Where were the two children – which no doubt Pat Runkle had pounced upon in the hospital with the crazy delight of the average man discovering little yelling images of himself, miracles of gratified egotism?

What were they doing, the three of them, while Patrick Runkle busied himself with becoming Anthony De Forest? Hostages to fortune, so it was said, and yet Anthony De Forest seemed to have given no more hostages to fortune than had Patrick Runkle. He was free, so far as Lily could tell, of everything but ambition, his own intense self-awareness – generator of that fascination which would be a large part of his ability to capture audiences.

Its source, she guessed, was an egotism which created the insatiable need for charmed victims, as a heathen god must have its blood sacrifices.

'Is it true,' he asked, glancing at the jade ring, 'that you and Donahue are lovers?' Anthony's eyes had lighted up, suddenly bright with suspicion, envy – or was he acting? She acted so continuously, it was difficult to believe other people did not do the same.

'Yes. We are.'

'Are you in love with him?'

'Of course. Do you think I sleep with everyone?'

'Are you going to be married?'

'We've never talked about it.'

She was slowly pleating a drinking straw. Lily did not often let herself fall into these nervous habits, and Arlette Morgan would never have done it. Yet here she was, looking across the table at Patrick Runkle, talking about the past – as Gordon Donahue seemed to be – and he had put her at a disadvantage. 'I'm not going to get married.'

He smiled; an old tale, heard too often. 'Never?'

'It's too much trouble getting divorced. My friends say so.'

He laughed. 'Are you trying to impress me, Lily? Grown-up, sophisticated, cynical.'

'I haven't been cynical since I was fifteen.'

They looked at each other silently, Arlette smiling with determination the bewitching smile. 'I'm sorry,' he said. 'I was trying to put you at a disadvantage. I don't know why.' He glanced around, asking for the check. 'Must we sit here?'

Arlette's apartment was on the sixth floor of an early nineteen-thirties building, with an elegant lobby, an elegant doorman, and white-gloved elevator operators. So much for his expectation that she must be living in a brownstone walk-up, like several girls she knew at the Downtown Drama School. Not Lily Malone. And not Arlette Morgan.

The three-room apartment had a large living room, with a fireplace, where she promptly touched a match to the wood. There was a small bedroom, a small bathroom, and a small kitchen.

The entire apartment, floors, walls – but for one bedroom wall covered with a mirror for practice sessions of Yoga and ballet exercises, calisthenics, and private rehearsals after her lessons with Alicia Fiedler – was painted white, walls, ceilings, floors. There was a glass-topped desk before a living-room window, which over-looked a tall building, and a courtyard planted with a few straggling trees. The overstuffed sofa and armchairs were upholstered with white sailcloth, made with zippers, to be cleaned whenever she thought they needed it; quite often, since she maintained Valerie's housekeeping stan-dards.

On the floor and on the chairs were cushions covered with purple, lavender, bright red, colors Lily Malone had long ago discovered were becoming to her golden-blonde hair – once the hairdresser mixed the formula to her satisfaction, both of them elated as medieval alchemists happening upon the philosopher's stone.

On the wall were large paintings, careless, enthusiastic, boldly colored, rimmed in narrow strips of black wood, signed A.M. When she tired of one, or someone admired it, she gave it away and painted another in the class she attended on Saturday mornings – except when Gordon Donahue was there.

She bought flowers every week: white daisies for the bedroom, where the double bed had a spread of white seersucker, covered with a cream-colored lace tablecloth Valerie had inherited but never used. A tall palm sought what light it could find in the living-room window, and in the bedroom a bamboo touched the ceiling with its yellow-tipped leaves. When she could get them she had a bowl of anemones on the white-painted coffee table in the living-room; sometimes purple lilacs in the spring, white peonies in the summer.

She was not there often, only to sleep, bathe, make up her face, change her clothes. She was proceeding from class to class, very much as she had done since she had first gone to live with Valerie and Frederick. The habit of learning, practicing, was evidently indelibly impressed on her brain cells, her muscular structure and nerve endings.

Anthony politely admired the apartment for its freshness, its California indifference to the realities of New York, its practicality for an undomesticated young woman. *Charming*, he said, and smiled.

Arlette gestured, asking him to sit down, waited until he had selected an armchair near the windows, and sat at a distance on the white sofa, dressed in what had become her invariable costume for classes of all kinds: black sweater, black skirt, black tights, black dancing pumps with grosgrain bows. Over it, on this cold January night, she had worn her one winter coat, heavy wool, black on one side, bright red inside, which she might wear either way. She did not have many clothes, and did not need them.

She looked at him with a slight inquiring smile:
Remember, Arlette, you're not Lily Malone any more.

It was necessary to keep that in mind, for there he was, handsome as a leopard, waiting – she thought – for something; whatever it might be such creatures waited for as they sat and reflected.

Without those usual props of strangers – cigarettes and a drink – it seemed they became increasingly strange the longer they were together. It was as if Ming Huang, Jade Ring, their college feud, their one experience of love-making, their shared history, had happened to other people, in another age, a different country.

And as she smiled at him, she began to feel that now it was Anthony De Forest who was uneasy, watching her intently.

He was wondering, of course, how long he must wait: *A long time. You'll never catch me off guard again.*

If he had the patience for a contest, then she would win it. Anthony De Forest, if he was willing to give her a choice, must prepare himself to sit there as long as he chose and then go home.

Or had he a home in the city? Had he left his family in California? She could see no evidences that he had begun to succumb to the entropy of marriage.

They talked about the past few years, without either of them committing themselves: England. London. Dona-hue's Shakespearean studies. Her dislike of English actors, English teachers, English climate. As for Anthony, he was perhaps not a complete Anglophile, but he declared a liking she thought suitable to Patrick Runkle. Even Anthony De Forest.

He had given no explanation of how he had happened upon such a name. And then all at once he said she was wondering about it, and so he would tell her.

'The guy was a nineteenth-century actor in London. He had changed his name from Brian Mulligan.' Anthony laughed softly, and Arlette smiled, as if this were a delightful secret he had shared with her.

'I won't tell anyone.'

'For Christ's sake, don't.'

He looked slightly alarmed, and slightly angry. His face had changed swiftly, and she realized what she had known since their years together during the T'ang

Dynasty; Anthony's face was, all the time and under every circumstance, an actor's face, mobile, flexible, registering emotions from second to second, seemingly without awareness, and with little change of expression. As quickly as it had appeared, the look of anger was gone. 'I'm sorry. I know you wouldn't.'

'I had no idea you ever apologized, Anthony.'

'I don't. Or I should say I didn't. Four years ago.' The mobile face was serious and reflective. 'But then I'm not the guy I used to be.' He laughed. 'Maybe I never was. Maybe I was a figment of Pat Runkle's imagination.'

He considered this possibility, and then Arlette laughed, a new laugh to him, recently discovered during a session of rehearsing Rosalind with Alicia Fiedler, a long, song-filled, seductive laugh. Here was an improved Jade Ring, the ruthlessness concealed by the bewitching smile, charming manner, the elegant courtesan's ability to please.

'And so you were in Korea.'

This was news. But then, everything about him was news, since that day of graduation, when she had seen him at a distance, in the cap and gown, holding the diploma, class president and football star, being photographed and interviewed. And the clipping with its picture of the bride and groom.

After that, she had supposed he had vanished forever – to wherever the inconvenient people in her life, Barbara Sloane, Pat Runkle, vanished.

'I was in Korea.' He was silent, and she waited. '*Korea.*' He spoke as if the word itself might explain any change of plan, change of heart, change of identity.

Perhaps it did.

But Anthony De Forest showed no disposition to discuss what had happened to Patrick Runkle in Korea. None of the men she had known talked about their experiences during wartime. The young actors were silent. Even Gordon Donahue had nothing to tell her of his two and a half years in the Pacific during the Second World War. War was a man's secret.

'I wouldn't have been drafted,' he said, as if he were talking of buying a pair of shoes. 'But there it was. The mountain at dead center. I wanted to find out if I could climb it.' He looked at her somberly, as if to tell her that was all she would ever know of Patrick Francis Runkle and Korea.

He mentioned two more words, code words, perhaps, in whatever had served to transfer Pat Runkle into Anthony De Forest: *Inchon. Chosin.* He continued to watch her with the same somber, thoughtful expression, and had evidently sunk down into some deep inner well, left her there, watching him, waiting for him to return to the surface, if he ever did.

Now that she could look at him, she found herself increasingly conscious of the need for possession and being possessed, the abandonment of Arlette Morgan, who might never again coalesce into her former dimensions. She marveled that she did not get up and go to him, but continued to sit where she was:

I must not have him. He would leave me again.

Sensuality was a lotus land for Lily Malone and Arlette Morgan; the garden of sensual delights had more certain pleasures and rewards than any present or future ambition.

When he spoke, in that same low, thoughtful, concerned tone, she was startled, as if she had forgotten he might speak again. 'The war wasn't worth a damn – it wasn't worth killing one man for.' He stared at her somberly. 'No damn war is.'

'No.'

Inchon, Chosin.

That's what happened to Pat Runkle.

She was thinking of what she had read about the *shaman*, the Asiatic priest or magician, who divined the hidden by his power, controlled the events of his own life and others, who compelled the spirits to obey him. That was the secret Pat Runkle had discovered during those months of cold and fear, loneliness, self-exile. And that was the power which would be at his command when he took the stage.

'And so you're in love with Gordon Donahue.'

'Gordon has done everything for me.' She sounded as she meant to: young and idealistic, in love with an older man. 'He makes all my decisions. It was Gordon who made me go to England. It was Gordon who made me come to New York to study. He introduces me to people I need to know, directors and teachers of all kinds. He arranged to get me enrolled at the Downtown Drama School – they have a waiting list. He's wise and good and kind.'

So much for you, Pat Runkle. No one will ever describe you as wise and good and kind.

All at once he stood up. 'Good night.' He walked to the door. Her speech about Gordon Donahue had convinced him. She followed him.

He looked at her for a moment, intently. At last he smiled, touched her face, and was gone. Lily shut the door, locked it slowly, and leaned against it, staring at the floor. Her eyes opened a little wider, then closed:

Good night. Just like that. Good night.

But why?

CHAPTER 15

Arlette's life with Gordon Donahue seemed to exist in and of itself. He was one man, alone with her. That same man occasionally took her to meet some of his professional friends, at their houses, a restaurant or supper party after they had been to the theater. She liked to think there was no other Gordon Donahue.

And, when he left, she discovered that wherever she looked, about the apartment, along the streets where they had walked, there were transparent photographs of them before her eyes.

There were other traces about the apartment, which sometimes she did not notice for a week or two, and then, growing lonely, she became aware that in the closet hung one of his bathrobes, a suit, several ties. The jade ring was on her left hand. And on her dressing table, the moment she entered the apartment and removed it from her handbag, stood the statue of Kuan-Yin, whose smile baffled all Arlette's efforts to imitate it: that smile of profound wisdom, of compassion, of perfect understanding; the smile which was subtle, seductive, without sensuality.

Gordon, Arlette believed, was the one significant man of her lifetime. He loved her, no doubt better than she loved him, and he was interested in her as a gardener was interested in tending his favorite rose tree.

He paid attention to everything she did, and one day when she began absent-mindedly to sing in the bathtub: '*I never will marry, or be no man's wife. The shells in the ocean shall be my deathbed*—' he had appeared in the doorway, looking alarmed.

'Lily! I don't like that – please don't sing it.'

'My old song? You don't like it? Why?'

'It – doesn't suit you.'

She shrugged, wondering if she should tell him that the song stated for her the only real question anyone was required to face:

When, and how, do I die?

No. Gordon had enough of her secrets.

Perhaps he did not like to hear that she would never marry?

But they both knew she would never marry him, and she was relieved to have fallen in love with a man who would not want to marry her. She was also relieved that it was not his way to tell her domestic news – to talk of his son's growth, or what it meant to him; or, for that matter, what little Mrs Donahue meant to him.

So far as she knew, there was no domestic news.

If Marian was happy, that was no business of Arlette's. If she was jealous, that did not concern Arlette, either. Mrs Donahue might, so far as Arlette ever thought of her, be only an imaginary character. If she had not met

134

her, she would scarcely have been able to believe she was real.

Now here she was in New York, being ushered into Alicia Fiedler's apartment, while Gordon Donahue was at this minute lecturing to his students on Shakespeare's tragic women.

Once the butler had taken her bright red wool coat with its black moleskin lining, she walked into the vast dim drawing room, wearing a sleeveless red dress, her latest costume for all special occasions.

While she waited she strolled about, examining the photographs massed on two or three dozen tables.

The ceiling was fifteen feet high, the room appeared the size of an auditorium, and it was expensively furnished with Victorian furniture, black teak, inlaid mother-of-pearl, tufted sofas with rows of fringe, a crystal chandelier. On the tables she examined photographs of Alicia Allerton as Rebecca West, Alicia Allerton as Juliet, as Medea, as Electra, as Candida. Alicia Allerton had been a great actress, but more impressive to Arlette, she had been a fearless one, and judging by the authority of the photographs, had conquered each challenge as it came her way: her life's *corrida* had been triumphantly celebrated.

Above the fireplace hung a life-size portrait of Alicia Allerton as Rosalind, wearing a peaked hat with a green feather and green tights which displayed her fine legs. The Forest of Arden was painted on a curtain, and one foot rested upon a papier-mâché tree stump, her arm across her knee, as she smiled directly at Arlette, a smile so candid, so fresh, so self-confident that Arlette was taken aback:

I could never learn that.

Alicia Allerton's life was dedicated now to the creation of new Juliets, new Rosalinds, and new Orlandos, new Romeos. Her gift as a teacher had proved as rare as her gift as an actress. She could make men and women of children; produce depths of emotion where only tics had been evident. What could not be learned from Alicia Fiedler could not be learned.

Was it possible, she wondered, that occasionally someone was born without fear – and that person was Alicia Fiedler? Arlette did not believe it. Fear was the common condition.

'That was done a very long time ago.'

A voice tolled like a bell, sounding softly, as in the distance, sending reverberations which caused Arlette to spin around, looking for its source.

There stood Alicia, in the doorway of the dining room, and possibly she had been standing there for some time, studying Arlette studying Rosalind.

'I'm sorry,' murmured Arlette, as if she had no right to look at the portrait.

There, finally, was the famous lady herself, Alicia Allerton, looking young, flexible, alert, at once authoritative and gentle, not broken by whatever it was which broke most men and women, but most especially women, Arlette thought, by the time they were Alicia Fiedler's age: fifty-two, Gordon Donahue had said.

She moved forward with a flowing motion, smiling, and held out her hand. Arlette took it eagerly, and found it warm, firm. Alicia knew what she wanted others to think of her, how they were to accept her, and she knew how to make them do it:

That's what she must teach me—

Arlette fell into one of her infrequent spells of profound envy. For here was a woman who had learned everything which she had yet to learn, who had conquered the doubts and misgivings and faults she had still to discover. Here was a woman who knew herself, and therefore knew others.

Arlette wished she had not come, and began to consider how she could best escape.

'I'm not sure I have any talent, Mrs Fiedler. Perhaps it was a mistake for Professor Donahue—' Alicia was smiling, a look of patient irony, and Arlette added pleadingly: 'I'm afraid of you, Mrs Fiedler. You know everything. I know nothing. I'm not what Professor Donahue thinks I am,' she added sorrowfully.

Alicia seated herself at one corner of a long sofa and gestured toward an armchair. 'Whenever one person fears another, the entire relationship is in danger.' Alicia was silent, watching her.

Alicia was not much more than five feet tall, Arlette guessed, slender and erect. Her light blonde hair, an ash blonde which might have been natural, was dressed high, softly waved, a curling wisp escaping in front of each ear and at the nape of her neck. She wore a simple elegantly cut black dress – nothing but black since her husband's death, so Gordon Donahue had said – and a wedding ring. He had been the one man she had ever seriously loved: a famous composer, Elia Fiedler, twenty years older than she. It was not long after his death that she surprised her friends by retiring to become a teacher.

She was rumored to have been married previously to a stockbroker and a tractor manufacturer, both of whom had died and left her so much money that she was believed to be worth somewhere between twenty millions and fifty millions. Alicia, Gordon had said, was one of the world's wise women, wise enough never to have talked about herself. Her life had entered the realm of mythology before she was twenty-five, and by then she had been a star for ten years.

'There's only one of her,' Gordon had said. 'You must meet her, for that reason alone.'

She owned a famous jewel collection, perhaps gifts from her first two husbands, or from her lovers. She was a *grande dame*, Arlette decided, the first she had met. She laughed like a girl, smiled like a sphinx, and gestured like a Javanese dancer.

'She has endless endurance, endless patience, with a student she respects,' Gordon had advised her. 'But none at all for those she doesn't.'

It was time to begin her litany, stop wasting the great lady's time. Established actors were cooling their heels, perhaps in some anteroom where she imagined them sitting in rows. Arlette Morgan must speak her piece and depart.

'Tell me whatever you want to about yourself. As little or as much as you choose. If you prefer, tell me nothing at all.'

Arlette glanced down at her hands, quietly folded, as if she had a captured bird which she did not want anyone to guess was there. Perhaps the captured bird was her heart, which she hoped would be still, so that she could talk.

She had planned a speech, but now it was gone. 'I'm not sure I can learn to act. If I can't, I'll quit – I don't believe it's necessary to get one idea and cling to it forever.' She leaned forward slightly, looking intently at Alicia. 'The truth is – I'm terrified of acting.' She glanced down at her cupped hands, opened them, and the bird was no longer there. Her heart had apparently flown its refuge, gone back to where it belonged.

'You're terrified?' asked Alicia, as if Arlette had admitted that she had forgotten to order the groceries.

'Yes. I'm afraid of trying to act, and I'm afraid of not trying to act.'

'Everyone is.'

'Other times I think I have more ability than anyone who's acting professionally today. Some of the best actors look ridiculous to me.'

'They do to everyone – who has the courage to say so.'

'I'm afraid,' concluded Arlette.

Why had she not come in and announced that she was afraid of nothing and no one, had perfect confidence in her abilities and her capacity for development? Too late. She had told the truth, even though she knew it was often a mistake. Particularly with strangers.

'Now,' said Alicia, 'I'd like to have you read a little—' Arlette's eyes opened wide. Terror showed on her face, in the swiftness with which she sat forward in her chair. 'I'm more interested in what you can do than in what you think you can do. There's usually little correlation.'

Alicia got up and left the room as Arlette watched

anxiously, wondering what trick she meant to play on her.

Arlette decided that Alicia's real purpose in leaving had been to give her the opportunity to make her escape.

But if that was why Alicia had left the room, Arlette was still there when she returned with two typewritten pages, one of which she gave to Arlette.

'Read this. I'll read the Nurse.'

Juliet, and the Nurse, after Romeo has left. Juliet, no longer a virgin, Juliet, unwittingly preparing herself and her lover to die. She had played it several times in class; innumerable times before the bedroom mirror.

She looked at Alicia in dismay. 'But I could never play Juliet. I think she's a damned fool.'

Alicia laughed, a soft sound which at once restored Arlette's confidence. 'If you become an actress, you can't play only your twins. Don't bother with gestures. Just read the lines.'

Alicia began to read the Nurse's part: '*I think you are happy in this second match . . .*' She spoke in her natural voice, continuing the speech: '*Your first is dead; or 'twere as good as he were, As living here, and you no use of him.*'

'*Speakest thou from thy heart?*' Arlette heard her own voice, coming from some distant planet.

Alicia continued, not glancing up: '*From my soul too, Or else beshrew them both.*'

'*Amen!*' Arlette remained silent, continuing to study the paper, even though there were no other typed lines.

'Good.'

Arlette looked up, incredulous. 'But I only read a few words!'

'You read only one word that interested me: *Amen!*'

Amida Buddha! thought Arlette with awed incomprehension.

Only one word: Amen!

Alicia stood up. 'Juliet lets the Nurse know, at that moment, that she's a little girl no longer. She's become a woman. That's the way you read it.'

Arlette got up slowly. Had she read it as if she knew

that Juliet had become a woman? Had she known that was the moment – or was it an accident which had happened once, never to be repeated?

'Come on Thursday afternoon, at four-thirty, if that's convenient.'

'Oh, Mrs Fiedler – of course it's—'

Alicia was crossing the room, Arlette walking beside her, although reluctantly, for she was by no means eager to leave this bright moment when it seemed to her for the first time since that performance of Antoinette in *Adventure* that she could become an actress – perhaps had become an actress without realizing what was happening.

Like falling in love: the moment could never be rediscovered.

'We'll work twice a week. One hour and a half each session.'

Alicia held out her hand and Arlette grasped it with both her own, but when she began to thank her, Alicia Fiedler smiled, nodding, and the butler appeared magically.

Alicia had made a similarly magical disappearance through another door into another darkly lighted room, and Arlette ran down the hall, down the stairs, since the elevator was intolerably slow for her spirits, and started off in she had no idea which direction. As she went she looked up at the sky. It was one of those cold winter days when the sky could be seen, still blue in the late afternoon, and there was a small new moon:

Amen! Amen! Amen!

She went into a drugstore, intending to call Gordon Donahue at his office, but came out again. *I'll call him when I get home – no – I'll wait until he calls and surprise him.*

She walked along, smiling:

Amida Buddha. Amen! Amen! Amen . . .

CHAPTER 16

They had agreed, the three of them, when they first began
to trust one another, that while it was possible to recognize
a genius on-stage, it was not possible to describe one.

But it was possible to tell actors who were serious from
those who merely hoped for success, but not at the
sacrifice of their indulgences, supposed harmless, until
they found themselves in their late twenties or early
thirties all at once less sparkling, less resilient, less in
command of themselves.

Those were the actors who forgot that an actor's
physical equipment, strength, grace, coordination, speaking voice, laugh, was as important to him as the engine of
a racing car.

And so Arlette and Eva and Minerva made a list, their
private manifesto, of one hundred vows:

*Never go to bed without washing your face and teeth, even if
you're dying.*

Get on the scale every day. If you've gained a pound, lose it.

Work.

Never be satisfied.

No cigarettes, coffee, alcohol, pills, except vitamins.

Never feel sorry for yourself.

*Put on makeup and do your hair as soon as you get up, even
if you're going to spend the day alone.*

*Look at yourself naked, front, back, sideways, every day, in
a full-length mirror in a savage light.*

*Don't get tired. Keep your body strong enough to endure
fatigue.*

Work.

Their rules were Spartan and unforgiving, but for one
recommended luxury:

*Lovemaking is good for you. Good for your health, good for
your skin and eyes and hair and disposition. Good for pleasure,
good for happiness.* Lovemaking – preferably with love, or

its illusion – was the panacea for almost anything but a train wreck.

In this one area only, they did not discuss one another's solutions.

Eva French was married, and had been since shortly after her debut two years before, to a young lawyer, Stephen Nash. Minerva Grey was in love with one of the students at the Downtown Drama School, Max Gilmore. He was enough older to have seen service in the Second World War, and he had come to acting after leaving medical school.

According to their code, since Arlette had nothing to tell them about one or more lovers, they did not ask. Still, she had the gleaming skin, the clear glowing eyes, the gay and confident manner of a woman well loved by someone, someone not inconsequential. And she did wear a ring on her left hand.

'We must never break one – single – rule,' said Minerva, her green eyes dark with intensity.

'We must be ruthless with ourselves.' Eva was small and dainty, blonde and blue-eyed, still more or less a debutante, in Arlette's opinion.

Minerva was voluptuous, with large breasts, long dark red hair – a color she admitted she had not yet solved; sometimes too orange, other times too bronze. Arlette thought there was a little too much of everything about Minerva, a tree in need of pruning. Minerva scattered her abundant resources everywhere, smiles, glances, extravagant gestures. She was a tumbleweed in a gale.

Arlette had discovered several secrets they had not yet found: she never permitted one feature to detract from any other. Everything must be in harmony – and so she created an impression of disconcerting beauty which required study.

Minerva and Eva turned to Arlette, waiting for her to sum up the situation. She did: 'All life is a struggle against gravity.'

Eva sighed, despondent at twenty. 'I know. The face,

the boobs, the behind – the works. It drags at you every second—'

'When you're lying down?' asked Minerva hopefully.

'Don't lie down,' said Arlette. 'Unless you're asleep or making love. Stand on your head for five minutes if you begin to think that way.'

Nothing was more obvious to their sharp scrutiny than a professional actor who had infringed one of those rules. A few times, and they could see it. A habit, and everyone could see it.

Acting was not only the discipline of learning to act, speak, move, convey emotion by voice and gesture and facial expression.

Acting was the food you ate, the water you drank, the alertness of your attention to the world and your experiences; it was your memory, your capacity unconsciously to connect one seemingly unrelated episode to another. It was each smallest nuance, motion, change of tone, which composed the whole.

When they went to a play because they wanted to study a particular performer, they talked at supper about what was good, more about what was bad, which they could see but the audience could not: this actress was drinking; that one was taking Benzedrine and sleeping pills; another was not exercising enough.

'Once you're born, you're on your own.'

'Never blame anyone else – even when they deserve it.'

'Almost every woman over thirty-five has let her face set like plaster of paris.'

Thirty-five was a long time away – but they did not intend to find one day that the years had gone and they had brought on themselves that same look of sadness, bitterness, or a hard defiant gaiety.

Eva was fond of recounting tales of actors, five years ago, ten years ago, about whom she had heard or read, and the dismal courses their careers had taken.

Eva's nature was optimistic, whimsically humorous, and yet the misfortunes of others seemed to encourage her as to her present and future. 'A young actor comes along and takes off like that!' Eva's arm described a comet's flight. 'Everyone is amazed. He's the greatest. And then—' One hand described a sudden explosion; fission had taken place; the comet is no more. 'It's all over.' She smiled. 'Early success destroys them.'

'But *success is bitter when it is slow in coming*,' Arlette said.

Eva and Minerva smiled with wondering admiration. These Chinese quotations, never identified, had convinced them she was too wise for her years not to be an old spirit.

And so she was, thought Arlette. Jade Ring possessed her still; the Chinese poets and philosophers Donahue had quoted were as present to her mind as the newspaper she had read that morning.

Eva repeated the line thoughtfully. 'Marvelous.'

Minerva looked like a morose gypsy, pondering her own fortune. 'I've thought it a million times.'

'Careful. *Thoughts are things*.'

Minerva laughed merrily. It was a charming laugh, a watery sound, promising warmth and enthusiasm to the man who caught her interest; and it was full of more female wisdom than Minerva seemed to possess. 'If only they were.'

Of course, Minerva was not a Buddhist.

Still, even after Arlette had been studying – without mentioning it to anyone but Gordon – for more than two years with Alicia Fiedler, she had not had one professional role. Neither had Eva French nor Minerva Grey. They knew everything, but so far their knowledge had not found a part for them on a real stage.

This troubled Gordon, who urged her to go to more auditions, see more directors, and Arlette said she would, she would, she would when she was sure she was ready.

'But we can't be sure of anything, Lily, until we've done it. Even then, we can't be very sure. One day you will get a part – afterward, the others will be easy.'

'Easy?'

'Easier.'

144

Arlette did not like lies, even when they were protective lies. She wanted the truth, sweet or bitter – and it was her belief that the truth was most often bitter.

This was the Lily Malone who baffled even Valerie and Frederick, who could trace its thread through the years, growing longer, emptier, as the hope of the little girl slowly gave way, leaving her with the bleak future where no fine dreams came true – unless, perhaps, by some accident.

When she made a plan – and she made a plan for each hour, each day, each week, even each year, and then proceeded to work her way down the list, one by one, hour by hour, year by year – each time the plan was fulfilled, there was the same sense of disbelieving astonishment:

The plan had gone according to plan.

A giant cat's cradle was the way she saw the universe, and anyone might snap a thread at any moment, whether from carelessness, mischievousness, malice; whether by pure cruel intention – or equally cruel inattention.

Nevertheless, neither Minerva nor Eva, nor any of her new friends or acquaintances, guessed that these thoughts were in the mind of Arlette Morgan, whose semblance of gaiety and triumph baffled everyone who knew her, as it had baffled Lily Malone's friends.

Without a single appearance on the professional stage, she had confidently announced to Alicia that there were four parts she would never play: Joan of Arc, Elizabeth I, Norah, Portia.

At the moment, speaking with an access of hubris, after an hour and a half of studying six lines from *Othello*, and about to bid Alicia good-bye, she felt that all these parts were hers for the asking.

Alicia looked at her, smiled a little, a smile of subtle irony, to Arlette's dismay, and nodded to signal good-bye. Arlette walked out and started slowly along the street. confused, unhappy, yearning to go back and explain – what?

A few days later, Alicia ended their session by giving her an unsealed envelope. 'Don't be late.'

Alicia disappeared before Arlette could open the envelope, see that the address was a rehearsal hall. The hour conflicted with her speech lesson, and the name was that of a director who had formed a new repertory company, intended to produce the classics, three or four or five a year – a hazardous experiment which had all the young actors in a frenzy of ambition and determination.

All but Arlette.

She had remained aloof. No such company existed in New York. No such company could prosper in New York – or on the road tours which were part of its program. And, if it did, the director was too domineering. She had not met him, but she had heard about him:

Jerry Hoffman.

But she dared not go to Alicia and admit she had lost the envelope in a taxi, or forgotten to look at it until it was too late.

There she sat, far back in the rehearsal hall, away from the others, some of them no doubt from the Downtown Drama School, or other classes she had attended. She hoped not to be seen:

Alone, Arlette.

Valerie had said it first, and Lily Malone had thought about it, decided it was true, but it made no difference. She had spent much time alone by preference and habit.

Now, it was a different aloneness. The idea seemed extraordinarily pathetic. How could she have gotten into such a predicament?

She had followed the path Alicia had marked out for her, arriving early and introducing herself to a man who looked at her quickly and critically, as if he had seen too many beautiful young women who wanted to read for him. Still, this one came from Alicia Fiedler, and that apparently had some effect on him.

'Glad to see you, Miss Morgan. I'll get to you when I can.'

Lily sat for more than two hours, hoping that if he did

146

not glance back there he would forget her even if she had come from Alicia Fiedler.

There were hard chairs and hard lights in the small circle opened for the auditioners; no curtains, no props. Nothing but the script.

Jerry Hoffman was a famous director, and the fact that he had undertaken this new project, a development from an older repertory company which had played its greatest successes on the road during the past four years, was probably what had brought together this unusual assembly of students and actors of some experience, even if there were no stars visible. Nadine Logan was the star of his former productions, but she had gone to have a baby, make a movie, and take a year's leave of absence from the theater.

'Good,' Minerva had observed, as if nothing had stood in her way but Nadine Logan.

It was said to be a necessary, if not necessarily pleasant, experience to work with Mr Hoffman. He did not try to seduce the actresses. He did not try to seduce the actors, either. He took the theater to be a serious place and treated it seriously. He looked for his diversions elsewhere, and it was possible that his young wife, a former actress, and his two children diverted him enough when he was at leisure – if he ever was.

He did not smile at his actors, but for a perfunctory grimace, to indicate there was no hostility, no approval to be deciphered from whatever he had decided: thumbs up or thumbs down. He was patient. He listened intently. He was polite. He gave them no instructions during these readings, and apparently took it for granted no one would be foolish enough to read for him who had not had some years of training, if not experience before an audience.

'You're as prepared as you'll ever be,' Alicia had told her. 'This side of the footlights. Classes are helpful, but only for a while. They begin to seem real.'

Even school, once, had been promised to her as real life. But in time, that must be abandoned, as outgrown, and another real life found, in Chicago and London and New York.

Now, it seemed, that was not real life, either. Real life, apparently, was a mirage, steadily receding.

Alicia did admit to having experienced stage fright, severe to mild fits, some only disagreeable, others nearly incapacitating – yet she spoke of this hazard of the occupation as if it were no more than a cold or case of flu.

'Remember, it's a good symptom. You can't have stage fright when you're not on the stage.'

'I can. I've had it for years.'

To her relief, she was not called that day, and she escaped by a side exit, to avoid Jerry Hoffman and any reminder of Alicia Fiedler's note, and made a call to Alicia from a pay booth. It was six-thirty, and Alicia's last class was over.

'I don't think he wants to hear me. I think he lets me sit there to oblige you.'

'You don't know what Jerry Hoffman's reasons are or aren't, and neither do I. He'll call you. He told me he would.'

And so, it seemed, she was no different from the girls she criticized. She wanted to be an actress who had slipped past those barriers. She wanted to have the next three or four years of her life done with.

She was there the next day and she studied each actor who stepped into that unflattering spotlight Jerry Hoffman had arranged, apparently to discover how resilient they were about adapting themselves to disagreeable and unexpected conditions – the ordinary lot of the actor's life, to be sure.

Jerry Hoffman obviously thought it necessary to find out at the beginning if, placed in a situation which would search them out ruthlessly, they would be able to summon that basic egotism they were going to need if they could prove of any use.

She sat bolt upright, then leaned forward as a new actor approached that perilous lighted circle.

Each time an actor completed his reading, he gave an

anxious and stricken or sometimes defiant glance at Jerry Hoffman. Each time the same thing happened: the actor stood a moment, looking as if he had entered the Hall of Judgment, where he confronted Osiris and the scale which held, upon one balance a feather and on the other the heart of the actor. Each of them, Lily perceived, was reciting some version of that ancient Egyptian prayer: *O my heart, rise not up against me.*

Jerry Hoffman looked at the actor, eyes narrowed to fix by concentration the actor's appearance, his reading, his voice. Then he nodded.

'Thank you.'

The supplicant, as if stricken by an arrow, nodded in reply, looking curiously ashamed, and walked out of that lighted area, where he made a retreat as quick and anxious as if he had been given leave to depart a battlefield.

Lily's heart, seemingly transfixed during those few seconds, began to beat hard and fast. Mr Hoffman might call on her next and, if he did, she would not be able to get up, walk to the lighted circle, find the page, or force any word from her mouth.

When he called someone else, her fears subsided, and she became as concentrated upon the next actor as if she were not Arlette Morgan but Jerry Hoffman, prepared to pick apart the candidate: voice, stance, inflections.

Then she was less concerned with the suffering of the actor than with his presence on the stage, his capacity to forget his own personality, forsake it to become that other: Baptista, Bianca, Gremio, Petruchio, Biondello, Katharina, or some miscellaneous Lord, Widow, Huntsman, Servant, Tailor, Haberdasher.

She would not have hired one of them if she had been in Jerry Hoffman's position, and she began to perceive that they knew no more than she did, and most of them knew much less.

CHAPTER 17

Jerry Hoffman's manner was soft. His voice was soft. His appearance was by no means soft, but his gray eyes shone with a brilliance that seemed to indicate compassion for one of the fallen among his chosen few.

'He's not destructive,' Alicia Fiedler told Arlette. 'But he does occasionally destroy. More or less by accident.' Alicia smiled and shrugged: the flaw was in the original material, too easily broken through.

After all, Arlette thought, Alicia could smile and Alicia could shrug. Alicia had survived any such possibilities. No one could destroy Alicia Fiedler. Only death would put an end to her. But she could not be destroyed. She had proved her strength to herself and to the world, and now she was free to enjoy this luxury, the greatest any human might experience, but for love.

Arlette had no such silk velvet sofa covered with brocaded cushions, no such Oriental delight of the emotions.

The world of the future was to her bleak, unadorned, unpeopled, but for a few she knew would always be there – Gordon, Valerie, Frederick, Michael, Alicia Fiedler? Without them, she saw herself upon an empty stage, no other actors, no script, no play, no dialogue, no audience, no costume, no makeup, no director, no idea of what she was doing there, why she had come, how it happened the once confident Lily Malone should have turned into this forlorn young woman.

Alone, Arlette. Less easy than she had supposed.

Alicia Fiedler's calm statement that Jerry Hoffman was not destructive, but that he did occasionally destroy, pierced her, penetrating like the point of a very fine invisible dagger.

If he sometimes destroyed, then Arlette Morgan would be one of his inadvertent victims. Lily Malone did not always feel so strong as she pretended, and Arlette Morgan almost never felt as strong as Lily Malone had felt on any ordinary day of her life.

The strength of untried youth, Arlette suspected, was a mirage shown to each of us when we are young – a phantom moving forward and away, vanishing, reappearing, beckoning. What was it? And what was it trying to say?

'If he isn't cruel, I can get along with him.'

'He isn't cruel.'

And so it proved. Jerry Hoffman was not cruel, although some of the actors fell apart anyway and could not be rescued.

They became emergency cases, and must be sent somewhere for remedial attention. Others took their places.

But once this select few had begun to work together, there were no further disasters. It was as if he had discovered the weaknesses in those who were going to disintegrate, and like a magician, had made contact with them at some vital point – without a word, without a touch – and they were gone.

The others, grateful for what he forced them to display of themselves, however painful that display was, went on with their work.

Jerry Hoffman kept no pets among his cast, for that would have set them at one another's throats.

'It's hard enough, under the best of circumstances, to act as tamer to a crew of actors – and the youngest and least experienced are the hardest to handle,' Alicia had remarked when Arlette came, breathless from running and excitement, exultant, dazzled with future visions of a stage no longer bare: people, sets, costumes, her entire future life seemed previsioned by having been given a part in this play.

And, she told Alicia, almost shyly, at the end of that first day of rehearsal – which had proved no rehearsal at all, only an hour during which Jerry Hoffman had talked to them, casually as if they were old friends, about what he expected of this project – afterward, as she was leaving, he had attracted her attention by a brief look, and summoned her with a nod.

'Never forget, Miss Morgan, what it was that tamed her.'

Arlette replied promptly, glad to show him she was an apt pupil. 'His lecture on the virtues of abstinence.' He was still smiling, and that encouraged her. 'That's why her lecture to Bianca and the Widow is ironic: Pretend to give him what he wants, she tells them – that's the way to get what you want.'

The few words grew as she got into a cab and set off for Alicia's, and by the time she arrived a symphony had fulfilled itself from them, a symphony of triumph, celebrating her future and final triumph over Anthony De Forest, who had arrived in her life once more, this time incarnated as Petruchio.

They began, that first day, by being extraordinarily polite, shaking hands, this first time in over a year, while he had been touring the country in a Chicago company's production as Romeo – as if only the night before they had had dinner at the Italian restaurant, returned to her apartment to sit warily watching one another, and after an eternity, he had left.

'I'm glad to see you again, Miss Morgan.'

'Again?' inquired Minerva when he walked away.

Minerva, Eva – Arlette: together in the first professional project any of them had appeared in:

Yes, it's fate. We're friends for life – or enemies. We'll see.

Minerva was the Widow, a part Arlette thought she had won by her watery laugh, since the part gave her little other occupation. Eva was Bianca.

Arlette glanced quickly at Minerva, her conspirator, with Eva, against all other actresses, against false lures of laziness, one extra pound, one missed class in voice control, ballet exercises, Yoga, movement. Minerva, she decided, with her dark red-brown hair which reached to her waist, a predatory look in her green eyes, had some qualities she had overlooked before. Minerva was perhaps no more scrupulous than she was.

'We met at some cocktail party – I think.'

'You think?' asked Eva. 'You met him – and you don't remember where?'

Eva was not so entirely trustworthy, either. Eva, with her increasingly elegant silver-blonde hair, her delicate face and body, her gaiety and vivacity.

And when Anthony stopped Arlette as she was going down the hallway toward the exit after the third day of rehearsal, when they had read their lines with stoical meaninglessness, as if each were determined to outdo the others in concealing his skills, Minerva entered the hallway, saw them, and disappeared as if she had forgotten something:

The bitch is waiting for me to leave.

She looked at Anthony with a polite smile. 'Yes?'

'You're pleased by our change in status, aren't you? I'm not Ming Huang – and you're not the Emperor's favorite concubine—'

'No, you're not Ming Huang—' The change in their positions was more agreeable to her than seemed logical.

'I'm just an ordinary Elizabethan schmuck trying to marry a rich wife and keep her from cutting his balls off. That suits you better.' He was smiling more broadly. But the smile was a clear signal of warning.

Minerva was approaching them again, carrying her coat negligently by one finger, holding it slightly away from her body, so that her breasts quivered in the thin white wool sweater. She smiled at Arlette as she passed.

Anthony, who had been looking at Arlette, glanced around quickly, alert and questioning. He smiled, and stepped politely aside to let Arlette pass him.

Arlette went out, turned, and walked swiftly toward Sixth Avenue:

What difference does it make? What difference—

She repeated the question several times, and so prevented herself from turning to see if Anthony had caught up with Minerva.

Nevertheless, at home she sat at her glass-topped desk, wrote on a sheet of white paper: MINERVA GREY, and slipped the sealed envelope into her dressing-table drawer.

After that day, neither Minerva nor Eva paid particular attention to Anthony De Forest, beyond an occasional expression of admiration for his looks, his slowly unfolding Petruchio, and Arlette decided that either the hex had done its work or his wife and the two children were in town and he was showing them a portrait of marital fidelity.

She had felt herself reduced to a field mouse in despair of the reaping machine the first day she read for Jerry Hoffman. Nothing would ever come of it – that was her consolation.

Anthony De Forest's name appearing after Petruchio, when the cast was posted, had given her a curiously sick sense of shock, for she had not heard him read – although it was true she had not attended the first two days of auditions – and had supposed that he would disappear back to his father's board rooms and never emerge again, unless to offer her congratulations in his humble way on the night she performed Lady Macbeth to an audience shouting *bravo*.

'Hoffman expects Katharina,' Anthony advised Arlette when she had the part sealed in a contract, 'to have the energy of a charge of dynamite, the malice of a witch, the cleverness of a sphinx, the grace of a wild doe, and the beauty of a man's imagination. So he said, after a couple of drinks.' Anthony smiled, and before he could ask if all this was in her repertoire, she walked away:

One of these days, Anthony—

After all, there it was in the script. Act II, Scene 1: *She strikes him*.

Nevertheless, the memory had woven itself into her flesh. Four years and a half had not obliterated it, as they had obliterated Jack Davidson and – she could foresee – future years might obliterate Gordon Donahue.

The memory of the flesh was treacherous, choosing and discarding of its own will. The body's owner had no

154

choice about what the body would remember, incorporate into cells and tissues, blood, bones, muscle, what would become permanent, ineradicable.

'*He's wise,*' said Petruchio's man, Grumio, early in the play, when the others were convinced he must be daft to undertake so formidable a task as the training of Katharina, even if she was rich and beautiful.

Jerry Hoffman began his preparations at a slow tempo, reading and rereading, permitting few gestures, few actions, making no demand for facial expressions, not even any emphasis upon what their voices must convey. He let them feel themselves into their parts, discovering who they were from one day's rehearsal to the next.

He never subjected an actor to sarcasm before other actors, and was known to believe that if a man had any hope of training a thoroughbred he did not begin by breaking his spirit. He gave them one sacred pronouncement: *Flower.* They flowered under his attentions, or they became faded flowers with a faded flower's destiny.

If they were strong and vital, wise enough to know that not even Jerry Hoffman knew everything, they flourished, they put forth new leaves, fresh green slips which unfurled, and went on to accomplish whatever had been the innate limit of their capacity to grow.

It was Jerry Hoffman's belief that each actor had his own destiny to fulfill, and he was never to be coerced beyond the potential.

A tree, however encouraged, did not shift its character to become a lion. Nor could a lion be encouraged into becoming a rose bush. Still, he worked upon his actors as a catalytic agent; and they were either perpetually grateful to him or they blamed him for the destruction of their careers.

Later in the rehearsal schedule, it was said, he became like a madman at the pipe organ, pulling out all the stops at once, whipping his actors into a frenzy, speeding up the action until they were dizzy, dragging emotion from them until they were exhausted. Then all at once he let go

– left them to play the parts as they could, in costume for the first time.

If they had not struck a balance by then, he had little more to offer them.

And, since the fable was that Jerry Hoffman did not fail, the responsibility in the end became their own. After that he sent them on their way: first to New Haven, for this play. Then, if the omens were propitious, off on a tour which would take them to every town in the country, it seemed. They were themselves no longer, but had become Petruchio and Katharina, Bianca and Lucentio, Baptista and Grumio and Gremio and the Widow.

Each day, on her way to the rehearsal hall, Arlette prepared herself by reciting:

Never forget. Never forgive.

Anthony, it seemed, realized this.

Two weeks after rehearsals had begun he came to sit beside her in one of the chairs arranged in the area blocked out as the stage, toward the back of the hall, in semidarkness.

Although they were the stars, they had long periods of waiting while rich men were disguising themselves as scholars to woo Bianca, or Grumio was describing the church ceremony between his master and the terrible termagant.

Anthony crossed one ankle over his foreleg, folded his arms, and watched intently while Bianca flirted with her favorite suitor. They sat in silence for three or four minutes, Arlette angrily aware that her heart was beating faster and the skin had chilled over her breasts.

'You still dislike me, Arlette,' he said at last. No one was nearby, but Jerry Hoffman insisted upon strict silence during rehearsals, and so he leaned nearer and spoke in a whisper. She continued to watch Bianca. He waited a moment. 'It was a thousand years ago.'

She smiled. 'What was a thousand years ago?'

Presently he walked away, and did not try to talk to her again offstage.

However, they met each day in mortal combat, and

156

Arlette looked forward to the day when they would begin to act their parts with all the vehemence of Shakespearean comedy – which Jerry Hoffman talked to them about occasionally, but so far had not permitted them to express, except by a kind of shorthand, evidently convinced that once they had acquired the feelings of the character, the gestures and aggressive style of walking, the bravado would come of itself.

On that day, she would have an opportunity it seemed she had been hoping for for as long as she could remember. She would slap Pat Runkle. It seemed to her a kind of comic good luck which only the malicious gods could have provided.

There it was, clear as a mountain lake:

She strikes him.

Of course, she was also obliged to kiss him, but she would find a way to kiss him with her back to the audience.

The day came steadily nearer, as Jerry Hoffman began to intensify their behavior with one another, even their feelings toward one another.

'It's his way of working,' Alicia Fiedler said. 'He works them into a state of near hysteria – lets them come unraveled before one another – and him. And then all at once he begins to pull the threads together: a little less from you, here – a little more from you, there.'

Filled with the buoyant prospect of her great scene, Arlette waited for the first day of dress rehearsal, when she would indeed be Katharina, no longer Arlette Morgan – and therefore entitled to Katharina's temper, Katharina's shrewishness, Katharina's violence.

One day at Alicia's she declared: 'There are some scenes I can't wait for.' She looked at Alicia in dismay.

Arlette had begun to suspect that Alicia Fiedler was also a mind reader, and now she proved it.

'Katharina slapping Petruchio?'

Arlette lowered her eyes, caught in the act, and ashamed. 'Why, I don't know – I—' The lie was no help.

Instead, she smiled at Alicia, a helpless little smile, to indicate innocence.

So far as Alicia Fiedler knew, she and Anthony De Forest had never met before they had been assigned those two parts. At least, she did not know unless Gordon Donahue had told her of *Jade Ring*.

CHAPTER 18

Alicia had some advice the day before the first dress rehearsal: 'It's what you think about that makes the difference, Arlette. If an actor has the capacity for intense concentration, if you can imagine how it feels to lose a child, even though you've never had a child, you can convince an audience of anything. Most actors fail to concentrate – they fall to daydreaming, a few seconds, which they imagine won't be noticed. But they've lost the audience. Worse, they've lost themselves. Two seconds can destroy a performance. Remember that, if you don't remember another thing I've told you these past two years.'

'Two years? My God. Two years and two months. Yes.'

With that realization, sobering as a bucket of ice water full in the face, she approached her moment of triumph with a deadly concentration, speaking her lines with such vindictive force that Anthony looked surprised.

But then, this was the rehearsal where they were to *forget themselves to be themselves*, as Jerry Hoffman had reminded them.

Everything before had been preparation for this rehearsal. Nothing was to go wrong, and if it did, they would put it straight, once and for all.

They were in costume and full makeup for the first time, and it was notorious in Jerry's productions that before a dress rehearsal the players were never in complete control of their parts. Then all at once they became the characters they were to play.

Before the rehearsal began they strutted about the stage, the women's red and yellow and blue stockings showing beneath the ankle-length skirts; ropes of pearls and chains fixed to their waists with great pins; the looped ribbons on their sleeves gave every gesture a grandiloquence never seen in rehearsal.

The Widow wore a widow's cap and veil, and a high-necked black gown, even though Minerva had pleaded with Jerry Hoffman to let her show more of her breasts.

Bianca was in a modest sky-blue satin gown with a white lace ruff, as became the hypocritical favorite daughter. Katharina was in bright red velvet, cut as low as Jerry Hoffman would allow, with flounced sleeves and a train she had learned to maneuver like a dancing bird.

'Not too low,' Jerry Hoffman had warned at the first fitting. 'After all, Katharina is a shrew, not a whore.'

'A shrew is just the woman to enjoy being provocative.'

'We might all enjoy it,' said Minerva virtuously, 'but the play's the thing.'

'Hear, hear,' muttered Baptista.

Arlette stood with Eva and Minerva at one side of the stage as Anthony arrived, exactly on time. As she watched, astonished, this Elizabethan braggart strode onstage in breeches and doublet, sword at his side, plumed hat on his head, a close-trimmed black beard Jerry Hoffman had added that morning.

'He's beautiful,' whispered Minerva.

'He's dazzling,' Eva agreed.

Arlette kept silent, then all at once sailed forth to do battle with this dazzling Petruchio, this Anthony De Forest, this Pat Runkle, this bane of her existence.

'*Good morrow, Kate.*' He greeted her pleasantly, surprised to see her arriving as if for a tournament.

'*They call me Katharine that do talk of me,*' Arlette replied in a cold even tone.

Petruchio slightly raised his eyebrows and surveyed her from the top of her head to her square-toed red velvet shoes, whereupon they pitched into their quarrel with fierce eagerness.

Petruchio was good-natured for a time, but stubborn, while Katharina became more angry as the quarrel continued, and began to flex her fingers with anticipatory nervousness. She was breathing fast, her eyes had narrowed, and as they traded puns on buzzards and wasps, bearing and childbearing, Katharina approached him slowly.

They had not rehearsed this slow approach, and it gave a slightly eerie effect, as of a hunter moving toward its quarry. Petruchio stood his ground, unintimidated by the flexing fingers, the increasing menace in the voice. He was smiling slightly, as if this virago were a new amusement.

Then, weary of the contest, he turned away. '*Come, come, you wasp; i'faith, you are too angry.*'

'*If I be waspish,*' she said with a venom which made the others more alert, '*—best beware my sting.*'

'*My remedy is then, to pluck it out.*' He was still merry and gay, impertinent with the confidence of his good looks and vitality.

'*Ay, if the fool could find where it lies.*'

All at once, Petruchio caught her excitement, her eager hostility. He snapped back, no longer the bored, tolerant gentleman, willing to endure more than a little of his future wife's viciousness, since she came with a good price on her head. He raised his voice, and Anthony's voice was powerful, grown stronger and more authoritative. '*Who knows not where a wasp doth wear his sting? In his tail.*'

'*In his tongue!*' she cried, frantic with the conviction of having been insulted not by Petruchio, but by Pat Runkle.

'*Whose tongue?*' shouted Petruchio.

'*Yours, if you talk of tails; and so farewell.*'

She turned, swirling the train and deftly kicking it aside, then stopped, rigid, as he inquired in a tone of sardonic amusement: '*What, with my tongue in your tail?*' She stood staring at him. '*Good Kate; I am a gentleman.*'

She took a quick step toward him, drawing back her hand as if she held a whip. '*That I'll try!*'

She swung her arm with all the force of her body. Anthony seized her wrist and held it as if he had caught a bird on the wing, glaring at her, still holding her while she struggled to get free.

The others watched silently, enthralled by this show of hatred between Petruchio and Katharina. '*I swear,*' he told her between his teeth, '*I'll cuff you, if you strike again.*' He let her go so abruptly she took one backward staggering step.

'Well!' That was Jerry Hoffman, not far away; but they were still engrossed in each other.

'Don't do that again,' Anthony muttered; his face was malevolent.

The others seemed not sure whether they should go on with the rehearsal or wait to see what Jerry Hoffman was going to make of this deviation from tradition. Surely this was the first Petruchio to defend himself and threaten his leading lady with vengeance if she followed stage directions.

Jerry Hoffman, smiling a little, nodded at Anthony. 'I've wondered for years why some Petruchio didn't have the guts to defend himself. No offense, Miss Morgan.'

'Of course,' agreed Baptista. 'I've played Petruchio. Why the hell didn't I think of it?'

'What kind of Petruchio would let her slap him?' demanded the Widow.

'It's out of character with everything else he does,' said his loyal man, Grumio.

Arlette stood motionless, concentrated on forcing herself to keep her expression tranquil.

'You understand that, Miss Morgan?' Jerry Hoffman's voice was reasonable. How could she not?

Arlette nodded, but felt her face growing hot. She had made the amateur's blunder, letting her feelings triumph over her character. She had lost herself, and – as had happened the moment she had bent over Barbara Sloan to peel away Mei Fei's mask – the floor had begun to shift beneath her feet and her head seemed so full of blood it would burst.

She must do something immediately, or she would have lost them all.

Moments passed, seconds, minutes or hours, for all she knew, as she became aware of an intent, amused, increasingly impatient aura.

All at once it appeared – a conquering intuition: Jade Ring's dazzling smile, which not one of them but Pat Runkle had seen before. To all the others it was Arlette Morgan, upon whose beautiful face there shone with miraculous suddenness a smile of such bewitching charm they were taken aback.

'I'm sorry.' She spoke directly to Anthony, who recognized the smile, no doubt about that, but was as surprised by its appearance as any of them.

The others visibly relaxed, smiling understandingly; it might have happened to any one of them. Had not actors mortally stabbed one another on the stage?

She turned, still smiling, to Jerry Hoffman. 'Perhaps I should play Katharina like a lady,' she suggested with sweet logic. 'Cuff him lightly.'

Anthony gave a brusque laugh. 'A lady does no cuffing.'

'Shall we go on?' asked Jerry Hoffman. 'Let it stay as Mr De Forest played it. Audiences will understand that better – and if they don't, the hell with them. It's Petruchio, that's for sure.' He signaled them to continue.

Surprised by her quickness, Arlette took up her lines, speaking to Petruchio with tart impudence, a trace of humor in it now, and that seemed also to surprise Anthony and the others.

Here was an actress who did not become the character until she was wearing the costume, makeup, hairstyle, jewelry. All at once she had put on a hundred nuances of expression, voice tones, movements of body and hands – the character was drawn out of her, like pith from a reed, fresh, green, whole, removed from its chalice intact and unexpected. Arlette Morgan had all at once given way to Katharina.

162

Leaving the theater, Arlette ran to a drugstore and called Alicia Fiedler, asking if she might talk to her for a few minutes after dinner. To her surprise, since it had never happened before, Alicia said that she was through work for the day, and invited her to dinner.

Arlette arrived a little early. She had not gone home, but to a bookstore, where she glanced through several books, scarcely seeing the print, wondering how she had let herself be cheated of that great opportunity to slap Pat Runkle. Now she had missed the chance once and for all. She bought three books and set out for Alicia's, announcing when Alicia entered the room, in tones of tragic declamation: 'They wouldn't let me slap him!'

'Who wouldn't let you slap him?'

'Everyone! Anthony, Jerry Hoffman, all the rest of the cast. Everyone agreed that I can't slap him – ever!'

Alicia was not smiling, but she seemed to be taking care not to smile, and Arlette, thinking that now all the world was against her, extended both hands in pleading despair. 'The first time in four hundred years—'

She continued to hope that one day she would flash her hand through his guard and slap him across the jaw. The conviction made her eyes shine with excitement and seemed to communicate itself to the other members of the cast, who took as much interest in the contest as if they had bets on it. Perhaps they did.

But each time, Anthony's hand seized her wrist as easily as if a butterfly had come wafting in his direction.

The day of the last rehearsal, before the beginning of the last act, Jerry Hoffman was talking privately to Baptista and Lucentio, and Arlette saw Anthony standing at one side of the stage, legs apart, arms folded across his chest, head lowered, apparently sunk deep into one of those morasses which engulfed him from time to time.

She looked at him, wondering what dark mysteries he was pondering, what magician's secrets he was rehearsing. For there seemed to be about Anthony De Forest certain qualities much intensified during the past years – qualities of power and some unshakable dignity, qualities of magic and charlatanism; she could never believe there was not in Anthony De Forest some element of treachery, some compromise with the devil.

Where else had he acquired the good looks, the magnificent body, the evocative voice, the quality which drew people to him, men as well as women, whenever he wanted them, with scarcely an indication to summon them by?

He was, she had jealously concluded, a wizard, a creature from another time and another world – and in a sense she was afraid of him. Which made her all the more inclined to step up to him with a pert and sassy face, as he stood there, seemingly immune to sound, sight, surroundings.

'Anthony?'

He glanced at her swiftly, angrily, as if she had interrupted some deep communion within himself. Then, quickly, he smiled. 'Arlette?' He became polite, attentive.

'Just the same,' she told him softly, 'I'll do it one day.'

'Are you still thinking about that? It's been decided. What difference does it make? It wasn't logical as it was written. Shakespeare is by no means logical – most of the time he's illogical. That's the ambivalence we admire so much.'

'I'm not interested in logic or illogic.'

'You just want to win. Is that it?'

'One day – I – will – slap – you—'

They looked at each other, Anthony's face so serious that hers became as serious. 'For both our sakes,' he said slowly, 'I hope you never do.'

Everything that happened seemed to give Anthony an advantage and put her at a disadvantage.

Toward the end of the play, when Petruchio demands that his reformed shrew kiss him, Arlette stepped up to him quickly, with a charming smile, prepared by some weeks of reflection and planning, bent down as he lounged in his chair, one leg thrown over the side, placed her palms upon his face, her back to the audience, and made the sound of kissing without touching him.

'*Noblesse oblige,*' she whispered.

Anthony gave a short burst of surprised laughter, but had nothing to say.

Jerry Hoffman, however, knew that Katharina had not kissed her Petruchio, and at the end of the rehearsal he stopped her on her way to the dressing room, summoning her to his desk, where she stood before him in that last-act gown, yellow satin with white lace sleeves garnished with yellow satin loops. He looked up from the notes he had been writing.

'Miss Morgan, I won't ask you why you have so many difficulties playing with Mr De Forest. So long as it doesn't interfere with the final performance, it's none of my business. But I hope it's your intention, when the time comes, to kiss him. It's only a wifely kiss, after all. I can't imagine any possible danger.' He smiled ironically.

Arlette clasped her hands. 'Oh, Mr Hoffman, I must tell you something.' She lowered her eyes, struggling to find words for this confession. 'This is difficult for me to say—' The words came out in a rush. 'I'm in love with another man. Really in love. It's a peculiarity of mine.'

'I see,' said Mr Hoffman. 'Well, that's not unusual.'

'But you don't understand. I can't kiss another man. And the audience will never know the difference. It's only two people who've married for money.' On sudden inspiration, she added: 'Anyway – if I can't slap him, why should I have to kiss him?'

Now what the hell made me say that?

CHAPTER 19

It's almost over. Nothing can go wrong now.

It was the first night in New Haven, and she stood as she had during rehearsals, bent over him, her back to the audience. As she made the sound of a kiss she was disconcerted to see Anthony's black eyes beneath her as he lolled in the chair glittering with a wicked challenge. She moved quickly away.

Even so, Petruchio was going to demand another kiss; but not for a few minutes.

She was too much aware of Alicia's advice about concentrating to dare wonder what she might do if Anthony took a notion to behave badly onstage.

She became engrossed in her combat with the Widow and Bianca, teaching them to be good wives out of Kate's new store of knowledge of the art and pleasures of wifery, insulting the Widow with splendid disdain, ordering the two women about with bravado and a gala spirit, as of a woman not so much tamed as having turned her wild energies in another direction; she was clearly a Katharina who had won her man as much as he had tamed her.

'*And place your hands below your husband's foot,*' she advised Bianca and the Widow, smiling with sly mockery. '*In token of which duty, if he please, My hand is ready, may it do him ease.*'

She concluded her sermon with a gay flourish, swirled her train, and started off the stage. But she stopped short at sound of Petruchio's loud voice, and turned slowly, as if with suspicion of what all this mock subservience would come to.

Petruchio still lounged in his chair, one leg cocked over the arm, and gave a sweeping gesture, shouting: '*Why, there's a wench! Come on, and kiss me, Kate.*'

She hesitated, then went to him, sailing high upon an in-rolling breaker of triumph and unspent energy, for the long speech seemed to have prepared her to play the entire performance over again.

She bent across him, giving the audience that impertinent view of her back, only to be seized by Anthony and dragged swiftly forward, until she lay across his legs and her head hung over the side of the chair, out of view of the audience. Anthony's eyes gleamed as he placed his mouth over hers, and in helpless astonishment she felt the sharp pain of his bite.

With a warning glance, he released her, tossed her

upright from the helpless position he had forced her into, and started offstage, holding her by one wrist and striding at a pace which made her run to keep from being pulled off her feet. Somehow, she had forgotten what Lily Malone had known about Pat Runkle: he was a superb athlete, and he was not a gentleman. Whatever the game, he would win it!'

'Come, Kate, we'll to bed!'

Running after him as he dragged her along, grinning wickedly at his friends, Arlette remembered to cast a backward glance of mock fear and lustful anticipation at the envious Widow and Bianca as he hauled her offstage, shouting to make himself heard above the beginning applause: ' *'Twas I won the wager, though . . .'*

All at once Katharina was Arlette again.

She pulled her hand so forcibly he let her go.

He quickly returned to the stage, obviously expecting her to run beseechingly after him, as they had rehearsed it. Instead she stood there, deciding that if she was struck dead she would not join that Petruchio and bow to the applause of those idiots who had no idea their Petruchio was an impostor.

But someone took forcible hold of her shoulders and she heard Jerry Hoffman's voice: 'Get on out there, god damn you!'

She ran out, bowed quickly, showing them Jade Ring's smile, and earned herself more applause by flashing that smile at Petruchio and then escaping from him off the other side of the stage. This time it was Petruchio who shrugged and gave a smile of mock resignation.

Arlette dashed into the dressing room, closed the door and locked it. She stood against it, breathing as if she had got into the wrong element and her lungs could make no use of whatever surrounded her.

She sat with her back to the mirror, her head bent to her knees.

Her mouth was dry, and she felt a chill sweat over her body. Her ears rang, and as she sat, hearing the applause as from some great distance, it was difficult to distinguish what was the sound of clapping hands, what was the singing blood against her eardrums:

That's it. That's what it sounds like.

A real audience was making that noise, not teachers and parents and other students.

And for all the rest of my life that is what I'll be listening for—

This sound, full of terror and exaltation, this sound would be her only real communication with the world outside her body.

She gave a start of horror, for above the applause, above the singing of the blood, a low beating roar as of an ocean swirling through her head, there were sharp loud raps at the door.

'Arlette! Arlette, for Christ's sake! Open up!'

It was Jerry Hoffman, looking at her as if she had gone mad, Jerry Hoffman, who had never called her anything but Miss Morgan, who now said: 'Get your ass out there. What the hell do you think this is – kindergarten?' He gave her a sharp push, and she staggered before him.

'Was I terrible?'

'You've done it – now get back out there!'

With no realization of how she ran, propelled by Jerry Hoffman's hands on her shoulders, she arrived onstage and stood among the others, all but the major characters having left by now, and the returned prodigal was given a welcoming burst of applause. She took Anthony's offered hand as he turned to her, bowing.

He turned again to the audience, inclining his head, the same resistant acknowledgment he had given as the Shining Emperor.

All at once Arlette was fully alive after what seemed an eternity of semiconsciousness. She bowed from the waist, deeply. Jade Ring's bow, and her hair fell forward, nearly touching the floor. Then as she straightened and flung her head backward, the hair settled about her head and shoulders in a golden-blonde mass, and she smiled at the audience, surprised to find she could see them, the first several rows, and that their faces were friendly.

Just when she had begun to enjoy it, the curtain came down, and this time it stayed down.

She stood a moment, expecting something more to happen, still facing the audience but seeing only the curtain. She was aware of the others kissing one another in hysterical excitement, and then there was Alicia, smiling, taking her hand.

'I'm so pleased,' Alicia said softly. 'So pleased.'

Arlette looked at her questioningly: *Is she really pleased?*

She saw, dimly, that Anthony was approaching them, looking straight at her, and she ran, darting around Minerva, who was crying in the arms of Lucentio. Eva French was kissing them one after the other, a bee with a gardenful of work to be done. Jerry Hoffman held Alicia in a lover's embrace.

In the dressing room, Arlette hung her costume on a hook, kicked off the yellow satin shoes, pulled off the yellow silk tights, and stepped into her black skirt, pulling on the black sweater, ran to the exit, putting on her coat, and dashed up the street like someone about to jump off a bridge, determined to give busybodies no chance to interfere.

In the hotel room, she sat on the edge of the bed and looked at the telephone.

She had promised to call Gordon Donahue if things went well, and he was waiting in his office. She picked up the telephone, heard the hotel operator's voice, and said: 'I'm sorry. It's a mistake.'

'She went into the bathroom and leaned close to the mirror, examining her lower lip. There was no blood, only a purple mark as she rolled her lip downward with her fingertip.

She wrung her hands savagely, as if she were strangling him.

She applied lipstick, and was glad to see the mark had become invisible, like everything else Anthony De Forest or Pat Runkle had done to her.

No one could see the devastation: he had set fire to the forest, and no one ever discovered the culprit. He tore up feelings and sensitivities, caused sorrow and humiliation, exerted revenge – for what? Because he knew she hated him?

She stood in the bedroom, staring at the carpet, surprised by the intensity of rage.

Why, after all?

The injury was nothing – a reminder she must not try to trick him, playing with those mock kisses, planning to slap him hard enough to knock spots before his eyes.

Why should Anthony De Forest know her so well when she kept telling herself they had scarcely met? Yet he did, and she knew him better than she knew Gordon Donahue.

There was a soft tap at the door, and without hesitating, her eyes wild, convinced it would be Anthony De Forest, she flung it open and saw Alicia Fiedler's surprised face.

They looked at each other as if each had encountered a dangerous stranger. And they began to laugh.

'Have you called Gordon? Why aren't you dressed? The party's under way – there are a hundred people there at least – hurry, Arlette. Get dressed. I'll call Gordon.'

Alicia tossed aside her long black broadtail coat and sat on the bed in her black silk evening gown, with a strand of marquise diamonds worn as if they were something she had won in a lottery.

As Arlette hesitated, not certain if she should rebel, make a fool of herself on the first great triumphant night of her life, sulk here in her tent alone, Alicia began to talk to Gordon and gave Arlette a casual dismissing wave of her hand.

Arlette started the water running in the tub, so that she could not hear what Alicia was saying. She began to renew her makeup, glad there was someone here to make her behave sensibly. She would hate one day to remember that on this night of all nights she had shown the worst of Arlette Morgan to all those people – whoever they might be – who composed the only world she would know from this day forward.

Jerry Hoffman was giving the party in a suite of four rooms in the hotel, and Arlette moved through them in her mauve silk jersey evening gown, cut to leave one shoulder bare, to fit as if it had been molded on her body, for the shirred seam down one side drew fine pleats across her breasts and hips and thighs.

She was introduced to people she had never seen, embraced by members of the cast as if she had returned from a long and hazardous journey – something they could understand well enough. All the while she smiled as if the smile were a permanent fixture, as she intended it to be, whatever came. No more rude surprises for that night.

She felt that she was famous, the world was her prize, and she was sorry she had not let Gordon Donahue come to share it. Except that she had pictured something quite different, perhaps a mass exit by the audience, hissing, booing; these possibilities had terrified her for weeks.

Now there was a conviction of success, as if she could never fail in anything – all fears obliterated.

Without so much as a glass of champagne, she circled the rooms, feeling herself bewitched, bewitching everyone who looked at her. Fame was becoming to her. And it made her attractive to others, who would not leave her alone, but returned again and again: the other actors; Jerry Hoffman; people who wanted to meet her:

What was I afraid of? It was so easy, after all.

It was impossible to be sure if she had been right to worry about every smallest detail, every potential mishap, whether to herself or any of the others. Whether it had perhaps been by means of her superstitions and hobgoblins, her fetishes – her prayer to Kuan-Yin just before she left the dressing room for her first entrance; Lily Morgan Malone's pearl necklace about Katharina's neck – perhaps even with all that help, it was Arlette Morgan who had brought the play to its glowing life.

'Arlette, I'd like to have you meet my wife.'

Arlette heard his voice – and then she turned, glancing swiftly, as if for a mortal enemy in hiding, who stood directly before her. She shook hands with Lydia De Forest.

Lydia smiled, without animation. 'I've heard so much about you from Anthony.'

To Arlette's disbelieving surprise, Anthony's smile was full of affectionate pride, and this pride and affection were directed toward Arlette – or Katharina?

He lowered his voice, as if to tell her a secret. 'You carried us all—'

Arlette laughed, disconcerted, since she had been hating him. A true professional, he valued the performance above the performer, and the production above his own achievement.

He was not jealous of her success, of the compliments, and this, from Anthony De Forest, caught her off guard. It was as if they had never met before, never quarreled, never made love, and he was the businessman he had intended to be, flattered to be talking familiarly to an actress, even if she was young and inexperienced, appearing in New Haven, at that.

Whoever this Anthony De Forest might be, she could not imagine.

Still, she felt no skepticism in him, at that moment. The compliments, the intoxication of the actors and their friends gathered to participate in what seemed a confused but delicious festival taking place at the bottom of the sea, caused Arlette to find it not only easy but entirely natural that she should be a recently crowned queen and they her subjects, hysterical with gratitude.

There was an uncanny quality about this moment, a timelessness, something which seemed never to have begun and was never to end, and which seemed to be happening with such intensity that all noise, all color, all emotion had heightened to a pitch which would have made her cringe if this were ordinary life – if there was such a thing any longer.

She smiled at Anthony to thank him, and perhaps there was something more than Jade Ring's enchantment in the smile, for, as if she had been tapped warningly on the shoulder, she glanced at Lydia and found her watching her with the careful speculative expression of a beautiful woman appraising another, and was struck by an exultant discovery:

She's jealous.

Then she remembered that of course Lydia was jealous of her — Lydia was jealous of everyone, having been married to Pat Runkle for almost five years.

Arlette had hoped not to meet her, not have anyone point out a young woman and say: *There she is. That's Lydia De Forest. That's his wife.*

They stood looking at each other, for Anthony was talking to Jerry Hoffman and Alicia and Jerry's wife.

Lydia was a little taller than she, one of the contemporary style of young woman, sleek, thin, with shining black hair, parted on one side and combed diagonally across her forehead. Her eyes were blue. She smiled slightly, as if she found the world perpetually amusing:

I hate her.

There was no choice; she had hated her since the day she had seen her wedding photograph, wearing her inherited lace gown, carrying a bouquet of white roses.

Arlette turned away, nodding, murmuring that she was glad to have met her; and as she turned, Lydia's blue eyes watched her from their corners, shining, cold, perhaps warning her not to lay hands on Anthony.

'You didn't like my wife?' Anthony asked her, some time later, and by then Arlette had almost forgotten she had met her.

Arlette looked at Anthony, her face so guileless that he gave her a wry smile. 'She's very beautiful.'

Anthony was studying her seriously. 'I'm leaving, Arlette. This is my endurance for parties — I haven't the patience for too many people. Good night.' He took a step away, then turned. 'Arlette — you can act.'

CHAPTER 20

Gordon Donahue saw the play later on, but she did not invite him backstage, and still had some reluctance about letting Eva French and Minerva Grey and the other actors know he was the man she had hinted about. Gordon was a celebrity to them; they had studied his books, his reviews, and would study the review he intended to write of this performance.

Or was it Anthony she did not want to see Gordon Donahue?

She delayed each suggestion Gordon made to visit her on tour, until they arrived in Chicago.

Once the decision was made, she was eager to introduce him to Minerva and Eva, Grumio and Gremio, Baptista and Lucentio, for they were integrated into her life by now – all of them but Anthony – and she wanted them to be impressed and envious.

There he was, the mystery lover, flesh and blood; rather tall, a little stooped about the shoulders, with a courtly elegance, combing his black hair with narrow long fingers as he talked to them, smiling a brilliant, quick, charming smile. Watching him, Arlette was struck with a pride and love she had nearly forgotten in her absorption with Katharina and her life in Padua, her contests with Petruchio.

She summoned him away, touching his arm, smiling at the others, and as they started toward the exit, hoped she had succeeded in spiriting him away before Anthony could appear.

But there he was at the end of the hall, near the exit, still in costume and full makeup, unrecognizable to Gordon, she was sure, and perhaps they could whisk by before he saw them.

This would not have happened if Lydia had had the common sense to accompany him once they left New

Haven. But no, not Lydia, as Eva and Minerva had predicted. Lydia would go back to Pasadena with the children, and take her chances on her husband's fidelity, rather than follow him from Philadelphia to Pittsburgh to Milwaukee, staying in hotels she would detest, eating food she would not tolerate.

It was not easy to imagine Anthony married; and he gave no indication of having bartered away freedom, the life that late he led, only for the social politeness of having married the proper girl at the proper time and produced the proper number of children. What he did in his spare time, they could not imagine. He was not often seen, except at the theater.

'He talks on the telephone,' Eva advised them. 'Most of the time he's talking to Hollywood or New York. Business,' said Eva mysteriously.

'Business?'

'And he reads – scripts.'

'How do you like that?' asked Minerva.

Why were they not reading scripts?

No one sent them scripts, was the answer.

There he stood, in his striped hose and doublet, thumbs hooked into his jeweled belt, absorbed in conversation with Baptista.

Yet Gordon recognized him. 'Pat Runkle?'

Arlette smiled ironically. 'Himself.'

'I'll be damned.' He had evidently known all along who was masquerading as Anthony De Forest, or he would never have perceived Pat Runkle hidden behind Petruchio's beard, his black wig, the massive elegance of his Elizabethan costume. Quickly, he approached Anthony, extending his hand. 'Gordon Donahue. Congratulations!'

'Donahue! For Christ's sake—' He glanced at Arlette and back to Gordon. Anthony was pretending too.

They shook hands, the oldest, dearest friends, meeting by chance after years of having searched the world over. Arlette looked at them with infuriated disgust at the hypocrisy which governed men in one another's company.

'I'll be damned.' Anthony displayed an enthusiasm so

palpably false Arlette longed to nudge him and say it was no use, he was transparent as chiffon. 'Hey, I read your last book . . .'

And so they went on, while Arlette glanced here and there, then took out a mirror and studied her eye makeup.

'Great job,' Anthony was saying. 'Great – I mean it.' He seemed, for Anthony, almost obsequious.

Donahue nodded, gracious, smiling shyly. He seemed quite taken aback at the news that Jerry Hoffman had made his cast read his three published books. Arlette had told him so, but evidently he found it necessary to lie about this tribute.

'We all read them, didn't we, Arlette?'

'Of course.'

Arlette had long ago concluded that if Anthony De Forest became the great star he intended to become, since it was impossible for Anthony to imagine himself occupying a middle position anywhere, then it would be because of his effect on women.

Yet he had learned the more difficult task of not antagonizing men.

Men, she thought, were hopelessly obtuse in their judgment of another man, and before a man could recognize his rival, he must be a caricature of Don Juan himself.

Other men preferred to think well of Anthony De Forest.

Now Anthony was talking in confidential tones to Gordon Donahue, while Arlette thought of male vanity, male ambition, male pride, male hypocrisy. Nevertheless, she was aware that what Anthony was saying about Gordon's books was both sensible and sensitive.

Gordon was listening in his unfailing polite manner. He would be polite, thought Arlette, if it were announced the ship was sinking, the building about to blow up, a Red Alert had been called. Finally, he turned to Arlette, as if to ask if she was happy, or would she prefer to be somewhere else.

'Jesus, I'm sorry. You're in a hurry, and I've kept you—'

'Not at all, Anthony,' Gordon protested. 'Authors are vain, and they don't often have the opportunity to enjoy vanity. Well—'

'So long, Arlette,' said Anthony, smiling at her charmingly. 'See you.' He turned and they started toward the exit. All at once he called: 'Maybe we can have lunch tomorrow?'

'Maybe,' replied Arlette before Gordon could accept.

'He's changed,' Gordon said reflectively.

She and Gordon sat opposite each other in a Chinese restaurant.

Anthony De Forest had contrived to interest Gordon, too. He was her rival, it seemed, everywhere with everyone and all the time. 'We've all changed.' She shrugged. 'You. Me. After all, five years is a long time.'

She thought there was a slight guilt in his eyes now, and that the mention of five years – the period of time they had been lovers – troubled him, as if she had meant it as an accusation.

'Pat Runkle,' he said seriously, 'did not seem likely to become the man I saw tonight. Not in five years. Not ever.'

'Korea.'

'Oh?'

Arlette looked at him steadily. *He's worried. He thinks we may be having an affair.*

He must have known for a long time that Anthony De Forest was his former student, Pat Runkle, yet Anthony De Forest had not become a reality to him until tonight. That must mean that Gordon, seemingly mired in compliments over his work, had been studying Anthony's face, just as he now studied Arlette.

Gordon had not intended to fall in love with her. That had been accidental. But there had been nothing accidental about the years since. He was perhaps wondering for the first time if she might have been expecting that one day he would marry her.

When they had finished dinner he continued to sit, looking at her attentively. Arlette became aware of herself as she looked to him, agreeably aware that even to Gordon, as to other men, she had acquired a kind of beauty which was an unfair advantage to take of the world. For she was reticent and aloof, and her bewitching smile led only to disappointment for the men who were surprised by its sudden dazzle. Whether or not she meant to be cruel was not clear, even to her. She meant to be desired, that was clear.

'Arlette—'

'Yes?' She spoke carefully, for he was about to say something which was important to him. She had a horrified premonition that he was about to propose marriage.

'I don't think you're the kind of woman who should spend her entire life with one man—'

Surprised by the difference between what she had been anticipating and what she had heard, she laughed.

'And I think you may have spent enough of it with me.'

My God. He's a mind reader, too.

He saw something, something, when he looked at Anthony and me – he saw something that isn't there . . .

'Let's not talk any more, Gordon. Let's go to bed.'

He had nothing to say on the drive back to the hotel, but there was a strange look, an unease, something different from any expression she had seen before, somber, sorrowful. Even the quick smile he gave her as they entered the hotel lobby did not change that.

Arlette walked beside him, filled with wonderment and disbelief:

He meant it. He didn't say it so I'd disagree. He meant it.

As they reached the elevators, Anthony crossed their path as if he were dashing away from a policeman, registered astonishment at this new coincidence, and paused, seizing Gordon's hand and shaking it. 'I forgot to buy a paper. Just came down—' He indicated the paper under his arm, then smiled broadly, as if the lie were so outrageous no one was expected to believe it. 'Good night! Have breakfast with me at one—' He went on his way.

Anthony wanted to observe the relationship between them, and like any challenging man, he wanted to test himself against Donahue. Anthony De Forest seemed unlikely, Arlette thought, to buy a suit, read a book, hail a taxi, without putting himself against some ever present real or imaginary antagonist. Combat was in his nature, as tenderness, concern, cherishing, were in Gordon's.

When he and Gordon had spent two hours next day dueling in the dining room of the Palmer House, ignoring Arlette, so intent they had become upon discussing every point in Donahue's books, as well as several he had not made, she excused herself. They quickly rose to a half-standing position, sat down again, and the last she saw of them they were deep in serious talk.

She went to her room, combed her hair, questioned her makeup and touched it here and there with traces of color, looked at herself carefully in the long bathroom mirror, moved her arms like a Balinese dancer, asking herself all the while what these damn-fool men thought they were accomplishing.

When she returned, smiling slightly, ironically, Gordon leaped up to move her chair, outwitting Anthony in that maneuver at least, and their conversation resumed.

She turned her attention upon Gordon, studied his wide forehead, the way his black hair grew over his temples, the straight line of his nose, somewhat thin; studied his mouth, not so full as Anthony's, nor so ruthless, nor so flagrantly sensual.

Then she studied Anthony, first his hands, the few brisk black hairs upon the backs of his fingers, the broad powerful palms and fingers long as a musician's.

The duel had gone on for two hours and a half, when all at once Gordon looked at his watch, announced that his plane left in an hour, and Arlette jumped up. Anthony quickly stood, summoning the waiter, gesturing away

Gordon's wallet, thanking him profusely for his help and encouragement, and did not glance at Arlette:

Which of you won?

Arlette had no idea and, she guessed, neither did Gordon Donahue nor Anthony De Forest.

On the drive to the airport, Arlette began to talk of where the play was going next, removing the schedule from her handbag and reading it to him, determined to prevent him from referring to Anthony or his earlier statement that she had spent enough of her life with him.

She walked with him to the departure area and all at once they faced each other. They fell silent, and after a few moments, Arlette was crying. The tears ran smoothly, and she made no sound. He gave her his handkerchief, kissed her, patted her shoulder, but had nothing to say until the plane was announced.

All at once he smiled nervously, kissed her once more, ran his hand through his hair, saying he would call tomorrow, and was lost among the other passengers.

It seemed that perhaps she would never see him again.

CHAPTER 21

Later, they could not remember the name of the city.

It had not been Boston, Philadelphia, Detroit. Too late in the tour for any of those.

It was not easy to be sure, from one day to the next, whether they were in Kansas City or had left the week before. The map had become confused in their minds, an unfinished jigsaw puzzle, and Portland might be only a few miles from Indianapolis.

One thing was clear: Jerry Hoffman had recently staged one of his guerrilla raids, shaking them out of a complacency few of them felt.

He appeared from time to time, unannounced, to watch a performance from the back of the theater before he came

180

to tell them what had gone wrong, whereupon a rehearsal would be called for the next morning.

The tour – even after several months, two weeks here, a few days for travel, moving equipment, a gypsy caravan by now – the tour was not theirs, but still Jerry Hoffman's.

It was his reputation, not theirs, that was being built, or damaged.

Actors became lazy as a show went on, he had warned them. They imagined everything had reached perfection. Lucentio was caught glancing idly out at the audience. Gremio missed a cue. Baptista forgot two lines and went on as confidently as if he had spoken them.

Anthony De Forest was found to be in character. So was Arlette Morgan.

They glanced at each other, exchanging the slight smiles of two successful conspirators. And all at once Arlette was aware of a warmth in her feeling for Anthony, a forgiving affection. They were the stars, and they were helping each other. A camaraderie had unexpectedly grown between them.

All their unusual antagonisms resolved in the final kiss Petruchio claimed each night.

For a time she had dreaded the kiss; then she began to look forward to it, as if it were an extension of the kiss he had given her long ago, and possibly forgotten, while she remembered its effect with uncanny sensitivity.

There was something in Anthony for her to fear.

Almost everything he did, whether onstage or on the few occasions they met in a restaurant, a hotel lobby, passed on the street during the long walks the actors subjected themselves to, not to lose their physical tone on this endless voyage, made her increasingly suspicious, and one day she realized that, yes, she had appointed herself detective of Anthony De Forest's character.

But she was not the only one. So had the others, for he seemed to have acquired, before their eyes but without their comprehension, the actor's authority, with a sureness and swiftness the others could not match. This made them even less sure of themselves.

They suggested that perhaps he had been born with some secret they would never discover – since it was no more and no less than the secret of his vital energy, which upon the stage became a palpable force, as if he reached out his fist, seized a handful of strings to which the audience sat passively attached, and dragged them to him.

When the play had been run through, Jerry Hoffman spoke to her quietly. 'Remember, Arlette.' He was pleased with an actor when he used the first name. 'Katharina really does want to slap him.'

She looked at him accusingly.

She felt he had taken away her pride in her ability at having remained afloat all this time, never sinking out of Katharina's character, never losing the play's remorseless internal synchronization.

'A comedy is not a tragedy,' he had repeated during the rehearsals whenever one of them fell a beat or two behind that swift tempo he set.

'I'm not allowed to slap him, Mr Hoffman,' Arlette replied, smiling with anger.

'But that doesn't mean you don't want to.'

That's what he saw. I've let that son of a bitch scare me, and it shows.

'It seems so hopeless.' There was a murmur of laughter, telling her they knew how little chance she had against him. 'He's so quick.' She did not like the sound of that.

Jerry Hoffman took pity on her, letting her walk away and lose herself among the other actors while he went on to bring up lines and scenes which required immediate rehearsal.

'Anthony, begin with: *Verona, for a while I take my leave—*'

He glanced around, discovered Arlette where she was hiding, behind Minerva and Baptista. 'We'll come back to that again.'

And when they did, as she passed Jerry Hoffman, on her way toward Anthony with a grim determination, he stopped her. 'Take it back to here—' He flung his arm back and slashed the air with all his strength. 'Maybe you can surprise him.' He added: 'He may not be as quick as you think.'

Oh, but he is. You don't know him like I do.

Arlette set her teeth, blotting out all immediate eyesight which would make Anthony's face too clear as she approached, narrowing her eyes so that he became an unknown antagonist, a problem to solve, a face she must slap for the good of her entire future.

She was convinced that every one of them, Jerry Hoffman, Anthony, would never respect her if she failed in this task. So simple, so easy, so absurd. Women did it every day.

Then why could not Anthony De Forest accept this slap in the spirit of male indifference to female impulsiveness?

By now she was so angry she had decided that if Anthony grabbed her wrist again she would find a lethal weapon – somewhere among the props – and kill him. Any punishment was preferable to dishonor.

'Good Kate; I am a gentleman.'

'That I'll try!'

She was surprised to hear her voice shout more frantically than ever before, then drew back her arm until it almost threw her off balance, and swept it forward. Midway, her wrist was caught, deftly, delicately, and he smiled, almost apologetically, not at Arlette but at Jerry Hoffman.

'It's automatic—' He released her.

'You see?' she said pleadingly.

'But the swing was a good one – with all the determination anyone could want.'

'Oh, there was determination,' said Arlette bitterly.

'Keep the shout. It's the shout of a frustrated woman if I've ever heard one. I wish we'd thought of it long ago.'

Arlette retired to the back of the theater and sat in raging silence while Bianca began to play the spinet under the instruction of her disguised fiancé. She was so absorbed in her humiliation she did not see Anthony until he spoke.

'Arlette,' he said softly, 'for Christ's sake, I don't know what you want me to do. You'd like to kill me, I think.

Does that mean I must let you do it – to prove Petruchio's a gentleman?'

He took her hand, very gently, stroking it, while Arlette sat bolt upright, refusing to look at him:

He's a sorcerer, a wizard. A warlock. Look out for him. He's up to something.

She pulled her hand away, as if he had taken unlawful possession of it, and ran down the aisle, hearing a soft laugh, although he did not move until Jerry Hoffman pronounced the rehearsal complete.

She saw him walking down the aisle, slowly, toward the stage, and ran to get her coat, as if his approach were a mortal danger:

Not me. Not again. Oh, no, you don't.

But if he was plotting against her, there was no further evidence.

Except onstage, she did not see him, or only in the distance, waiting for an airplane; standing in line to register when they arrived at a new hotel; in the lobby talking to two of three of the cast. And they had no further meetings until they reached – what town was it?

She had left the hotel one Sunday morning early, intending to eat breakfast, since the dining room was not open, and then return to spend the day as she always did on a Sunday: reading, exercising, grooming herself, washing her hair, manicuring her nails, for she had no trust in such services west of Fifth Avenue.

She left the usual notice that only long-distance calls might be put through. No gossiping on Sundays with Eva or Minerva; no lunches or bicycle rides with one of the men. Sunday was the day she restored the energy she felt herself spending during the week. She had a conviction that energy was a hydraulic system, a mechanism to be used to its fullest capacity, and periodically repaired.

The weather was cold again.

She was still wearing her favorite red wool dress, sleeveless so that it was comfortable in the summer, and today she wore the flared red coat with its black moleskin lining.

After she had walked several blocks she went into a diner to eat breakfast, conscientiously assuring herself it was as important to know about diners, as it was to know the difference between upstage and downstage.

Then she walked for blocks and blocks, counting out three miles as she circled back toward the hotel.

The town was quiet, most of the population not yet on their way to church. Arlette had found herself baffled by any town which had fewer than a million inhabitants. She could not imagine who lived there, what they did, and although she observed them carefully, they remained as indecipherable as beings from another time, another world.

The Flowery Middle Kingdom was far more real, far more comprehensible.

Des Moines? Denver? Kansas City?

These were puzzles greater than the puzzle of the dragon which appeared upon the mountaintop one morning, opposite Ming Huang's palace, and was diagnosed by the Taoist priest to be a rival monarch. All that was easy to comprehend.

But where were the dragons on mountaintops, and where were the golden palaces; where were the artists who could paint upon a wall and vanish into that painting, never to be seen again? The commonplaces of the Flowery Middle Kingdom were nowhere in evidence in this town on this Sunday morning. And when Anthony's voice spoke, just a few paces behind her, she stopped as if she had been struck between the shoulder blades.

'Arlette—'

She turned slowly. 'What?'

They stood observing each other carefully, until Arlette glanced away, confused by his nearness, perhaps even more by the burden of having spent so much time thinking of him, for the accumulation of memories and speculation had become a guilt, heavy and resented.

How had he changed their relationship? She had no

idea, and even less idea of what, exactly, he had changed it to.

They had conscientiously ignored each other, except when they played a scene together, and then with explosive suddenness she was in possession of great energy, a ferocity and forcefulness which came of itself, and from nowhere. Or it came from him, from some command he gave, in some secret language, understood by her body.

He was carrying a newspaper under one arm, and he wore what he usually did since they had started on this tour – dark gray slacks, a black turtleneck sweater, a tweed jacket. Whenever she had seen him in dinner clothes or a dark suit it was a transformation. But so was it a transformation when he became Petruchio, in gaudy Elizabethan costume and maliciously shaped black beard and curled wig.

Anthony was able to transform his clothes, rather than being transformed by them.

'I found a copy of last week's *Times*,' he told her, as if he had discovered a rare jewel, so far from Byzantium. He smiled confidingly, nothing about him to suspect, and started walking toward the hotel.

As they walked, Anthony began to talk. And Anthony was not talkative with anyone. Either he was trying to make himself agreeable or he was as nervous as she was.

He talked about the town. He talked about the play. He asked if she had heard from Donahue recently. He talked about Donahue's books, and said he disagreed with some of his interpretation of *Macbeth*, adding, 'Of course, that's a long way off.'

'What's a long way off?'

Arlette was outraged he should find fault with Gordon's interpretation of *Macbeth*. What did he know about *Macbeth*, compared to Gordon?

'*Macbeth*,' said Anthony reasonably. He smiled, and she was convinced he knew she was having trouble breathing and that her muscles had had a sudden poison shot into them, causing them to begin to dissolve. She wondered if she would be able to walk back to the hotel. 'You're not expecting we'll hit New York and be offered *Macbeth*, are you?' He laughed triumphantly. Even disappointment he seemed prepared to turn to victory.

They saw no one from the company as they crossed the hotel lobby. One elevator stood open and Arlette got in, followed by Anthony; she gave the operator her floor number. Anthony remained silent.

Arlette stepped out, Anthony followed her, and at her door held out his hand with the confidence of a man expecting the key to be given him. She placed it on his palm, and they entered the room. Anthony took her coat, hung it in the small closet, removed his jacket and hung it there. He smiled at her questioningly.

Arlette shrugged, opened her hands in a slight gesture: *Here we are*, and went to close the door into the bathroom, glad the maid had been there to make up the bed.

Anthony had put the paper on the coffee table and was now examining, as in an art gallery, the prints on the wall, eighteenth-century ladies and their gallants, picnicking beneath trees; one of Van Gogh's sunflowers, dangerously alive, sinister flowers speaking of sinister forces let loose in the world and perhaps loose in this room as well.

Arlette remembered her responsibilities as hostess. 'Breakfast?'

'I've had breakfast, thanks.' Anthony peered more closely at the sunflower.

'Tea?'

'Great,' said Anthony with no enthusiasm, and as she ordered he sat on the sofa and began to take the paper apart. She sat down and he inquired, with the first self-consciousness she had seen, which section she preferred.

'Whatever you don't want.'

They had reached an impasse of politeness, and avoided looking at each other, industriously turning through the paper, until finally Arlette selected the magazine section and Anthony the editorial section. They exchanged smiles at the accomplishment of this diplomatic triumph and began to read with intense concentration, until the doorbell rang and Anthony rushed to open it, seized the tray from the waiter and paid him, and set the tea on the table.

Anthony returned immediately to his reading while she poured tea, using all the delicate ceremony of Jade Ring pouring tea for Ming Huang.

'Thank you.' Anthony picked up the cup, found the tea hot, and set it down again, shaking the paper vigorously. Arlette glanced at him. Yes, he was uneasy, and the disadvantage had made him surly:

He's afraid of me.

She looked at the paper, and when she glanced sideways again, found his shining black eyes watching her, alert, suspicious, intent, and fierce. He returned immediately to the paper, and Arlette took in a deep breath:

Or is he afraid of me?

She drank the cup of tea, then got up and went to the window, bending forward and leaning on the sill. She remained there, pretending to be fascinated by the Sunday strollers who had finally come out of hiding, aware of exactly how she looked to him, that the position made her waist smaller, her hips rounder. Anthony spoke sharply.

'Arlette – stop that!'

She turned and leaned back, hands balanced on either side. 'Stop – what?'

He began shaking the paper again, as if he had a troublesome dog by the scruff of the neck. 'Stop wandering around. Sit down and read.'

Happy to know she had him on the defensive, concerned to present his version of the better side of Anthony De Forest, she grew bold and impudent, eager to make him suffer for this belated assumption of virtue. She sat on the sofa as he tossed away the editorial page and picked up the front news section. 'Hmm—' he observed.

He gave her another glance and nodded toward the papers, indicating that her share of the bargain was to read, too. Why should he barricade himself behind the New York *Times* while she sat with arms raised and hands clasped behind her head, legs curled upon the sofa, her body languid and easy?

She smiled, a friendly, polite smile, as if to say that while he was reading she was meditating, and each might do what was most congenial. Several minutes passed in silence, as Arlette glanced about the room, looked at him, and at last said: '*Predestined enemies will always meet in some narrow alleyway.*'

Anthony flung that section aside and seized another. 'The predestined enemy, you remember, was not Ming Huang – but Mei Fei.'

'Does that spoil the truth?'

CHAPTER 22

'The truth, Arlette? Do you think because a Chinese said it a thousand years ago, it must be the truth?'

She found herself studying him more closely than she had ever dared, looking at him as if he were any object of great artistic value. The beauty was everywhere: the blackness of his hair, its crisp texture and pattern of growth; the ease of body; his hands, with their extraordinary long fingers, taut and hard, two of them slightly bent from a football accident. The real charm was a felt emanation, an alert waiting strength, of confidence in skills proved too often ever to be questioned.

His voice, perhaps the most powerful equipment he had as an actor, able to fill a theater with its resonance, or be heard when spoken little above a whisper: '*Kiss me, Kate,*' had poured into her the past few months with sensual pleasure.

It evoked whatever he wanted it to evoke, or evoked whatever there was in her, waiting for him – waiting for his voice, his hands moving over her, waiting for him to be inside her.

She moved abruptly backward. All at once she had

remembered the possession would be brief; she would lose him again.

For the first time, she had discovered the possibility of a permanent need. She did not believe in it, yet she must have foreseen what she had not been aware of knowing – that her desire to possess a man could, if she was not careful, control her life: one way or another, one day or another, she would lose him.

Better never to have the experience at all, she had decided. Better to love someone she did not need in that sense – who, perhaps, needed to possess her more? Gordon Donahue? Better to keep free of what promised future pain, sure anxiety. Even if she did not lose him to another woman, living every day with the knowledge that sooner or later one of them must die, leave the other.

Only in fairy tales – such as her parents' life sometimes seemed to have been – did lovers die at the same moment. In real life, there was always one left alone:

Alone, Arlette?

After real love?

Anthony moved, but not toward her. He sat forward, knees spread, arms resting on his thighs, hands lightly clasped, hanging between his legs. It was a posture he often took at rehearsals, when he studied the floor, listening to Jerry Hoffman.

'I think I'm in love with you.' He spoke with such solemnity that Arlette gave a low sound of surprise, neither a laugh nor a protest of disbelief, and he glared at her, blaming her for his predicament – if in fact he was in the predicament, since he seemed not sure. 'I think I always have been.'

'Always, Anthony?' Her voice was light, unbelieving. She knew she was smiling and tried not to, but the smile was persistent. 'While I've been hating you?'

Now, there was a triumph great enough for her greed:

Of course, he's lying. We both are.

Once she had accepted the idea that either she did or might as well love Gordon Donahue, she had come to accept the idea that sensual love was all there was to the world. She enshrined love, she bowed to it; she was so skeptical of it that she believed it did not come once in a lifetime, but that nevertheless there was only one search worth making.

Fame was good. Success was better than failure. Money was more convenient than poverty. Beauty was an asset for what she wanted. But love was the real adventure, the one risk greater than the risk of life itself.

'Like hell you have,' he told her, but that did not seem to interest him at this moment. 'I said *always*, didn't I? Well, I'll admit it's hard to remember. You're never sure what you felt, and what you later think you must have felt.' He glanced at her, then fixed his attention on the floor again. 'Something in my feeling about you has always been strange – and the very least they say about love is that it's strange.' He gave her a quick glance, a slight questioning smile.

'Is it?'

'Maybe not to a woman. It may be their natural element. It sure as hell isn't mine.'

Arlette drew slightly away, taking notice of the warning. But she continued to watch him with that yearning which grew steadily more painful. It made no difference what he said. He loved her or he did not. It would happen in exactly the same way.

Not looking at her, he inquired, with deep seriousness: 'Have you any idea how much time and thought and conniving, spying, questioning of bellhops and elevator operators, bribing desk clerks and waiters, went into my grand scheme to see you alone?' He smiled, but not at her. 'I've been stalking you for a long time. A long time. But you were always hidden, or with your chaperones – Eva and Minerva.'

Arlette laughed softly. It was true. She had contrived to be inaccessible, not only to him.

He looked unhappy and angry, although now the anger was not directed at her. His eyes narrowed, his face became jealously suspicious. 'You love Donahue?'

'Of course.'

'Or you're grateful to him?'

'Both.'

'That's not love. After that lunch in Chicago, I knew you weren't in love with him.'

Arlette walked a few steps away. 'I know if it's love or not.'

He looked surprised, then all at once he laughed. He stood up.

He held out his hand, and she hesitated. Then – since there was a little distance between them – she stepped forward and put her hand in his. With his other hand he clasped her about the neck, sliding his fingers into her hair, taking hold of her as if this were a rehearsed performance, a ritualistic dance, for it seemed they had performed exactly these steps, these gestures, accompanied by the same serious, questioning, wondering expressions many times before:

It's happened the same way – but when?

Each night, on the stage, Petruchio seized Katharina, as if not convinced she would not try to avoid him. But then it happened at so fast a tempo even the memory of it had changed, the experience was a familiar but different one.

They held each other as if they were in danger of being swept apart, and the embrace grew harder, until she felt herself lapse into a state in which every sensation had been miraculously heightened, as if her flesh had grown too sensitive, too responsive, and pleasure too close to pain.

Her dress fell on the floor and she stepped out of her shoes, impatient with this paraphernalia, which should disappear when it was not needed.

His hands held her face, examining her with rapt attention, as if he had never seen her clearly before, and his expression was unguarded, showing her a face she had never imagined might belong to him, wild, anxious, with some curious new quality – as if he were grief-stricken, suffering from some real but unidentifiable sorrow.

In bed, the boundary of bones and flesh dissolved as they came together, hands moving to discover new lands, new fields of wild grasses. Her legs locked around him, her arms clasped his back as he moved slowly, testing this new environment. His eyes were closed and she closed her own, hard, then harder, until behind her lids there spread a brilliant glow.

All at once the content of her body dissolved to the limits of her bones, disintegrating to some sound of distant soft cries. He lay without moving, while she listened, as to a seashell, to the pulsing of her blood, the curious humming in her ears, marveling that she could no longer distinguish her body from his, although she could feel the throbbing of blood in their thighs, beneath their navels, inside her belly, where from time to time she felt the beating pulse of his penis, another species of time, counted by pulsations, by a burst of violent energy, as an eternity revolved in rare pleasures, following the moving wake of his slower thrusts, diminishing occasionally to a period of bodily stillness and silence, when her arms were no longer able to hold him and she lay with eyes closed, gazing inside herself to some distance where all life began and ended; they had dropped through some rupture in the seamless universe to enter a different time and place, where nothing existed as it had on earth.

Stuporous, she drifted through the realms of time not experienced or guessed at; saw them floating through some night of stars and blackness. It had, she supposed, happened through a surfeit of sensation, creating an incapacity to absorb further sensations, which had seemed to have turned the familiar universe inside out, turned her body inside out, exposing raw nerve endings, flowing blood, throbbing through throat and breasts, thighs and legs.

Beside her, his eyes were closed, one arm circled her waist:

The end of the world. That's what it was.

She found a wondering pleasure in the discovery. Dams had burst, mountains eroded, rivers boiled away:

Everything is dead – only we are alive.

They awoke at the same moment, looking at each other

in momentary bewilderment, and he leaned over to kiss her. 'This is how the world began.' He was smiling.

He learned the same thing I did, only the opposite.

His face was serious as he watched her, perplexed, considering – what problems? Hers? His own? Lydia? His children?

This is how the world began.

Whose world, Anthony? Ours?

But she said nothing, and when at last he moved she let him go, closing her eyes. She opened them and found him lying on his back, one arm across his forehead, staring at the ceiling, as in deep perplexity, trying, it seemed, to solve an insoluble riddle.

Some period of time passed, several minutes, an hour, and whenever she glanced sideways she found him in the same position, his face profoundly serious, still trying to solve the insoluble problem.

All at once, pitying him, and unwilling to say that whatever it was it would never be solved, problems never were solved, not the troublesome ones, only the easy ones, she kissed him lightly. He looked at her and smiled, then closed his eyes as they lay side by side, motionless.

With a sense of sad dismay, but a sure knowledge, she understood what was troubling him:

He's no more mine than he was before.

She was fully conscious again, enough to be aware of some surprise at how automatically they had formed the intimacy of lovers, rare and precious, not depending only upon fitting one body into another, producing sensations enough to produce one vast final sensation.

It depended upon – what?

Some species of miracle she could not describe or identify. It existed immediately, as if it must have been between them years ago: the reason, perhaps, why he had driven her home without a word, his face fierce, as if he might lose himself in an outburst of rage:

Well, why not?

To fall in love was a fearsome business, better avoided. Finally, they had not been able to avoid it.

Here it was, the naturalness of two people who had achieved trust and intimacy at one stride into unself-conscious pleasure – only after years of an intimacy unknown to either of them, ripening, preparing for the moment when the ripeness should burst free from where it had been contained, so as not to disturb their ordinary lives, their self-absorbed ambitions.

But she did not think of Gordon Donahue, or she thought of him briefly, closed her eyes, as if to cast a spell which would abolish him.

She thought of Lydia – upon whom she had marked her hex, written LYDIA ST DENIS upon a sheet of paper, sealed it in an envelope the day she had first read of their marriage. For good measure, she cast Lydia out of their lives again; that was what preoccupied the man beside her, concerned about the consequences of what he had done.

This man was someone other than Pat Runkle. An Anthony De Forest she had not guessed at.

She might have fallen asleep again, for what she heard next was the ringing of the telephone, waking her with a start. She was holding Anthony's arm as he reached to pick it up.

'Anthony!'

The telephone continued ringing. He sat up, looking at her curiously, with slight amusement. 'I was going to give it to you.'

The telephone went on clamoring. Gordon Donahue evidently thought she was in the bathtub, or involved in some complex Yoga posture, and would answer if he waited.

Arlette got up, turning her back to avoid Anthony's smile. 'You've got to talk to him sometime.'

'Not with you here.'

She went into the bathroom, started the bath water, and all at once there was the abrupt release from its insistent clangor, a shock of relief. She stepped into the tub and slid down, letting herself be covered by foamy bath salts, closing her eyes against the feelings of danger and damage, the physical weakness and tender vulnerability.

To her relief and surprise, her body had looked, before she immersed it in this foaming blanket, just as she remembered it; and so it must have succeeded in reassembling its dissolved bones and membranes; the melted flesh had flowed like lava back into its former mold.

'I ordered lunch.' She opened her eyes and Anthony stood naked in the doorway, smiling at her confidingly. Whatever the devastation, whatever those attacks upon the order of nature might have been, all had been miraculously restored. 'It's two-thirty.'

'At night?'

'Afternoon. Steak, rare. Salad. Tea. Grapes and apples. Port Salut.' His diet was as Spartan as her own, and for the same reason. Acting, like love, required a strong body, a powerful will, a maniacal discipline; or, like love, it never reached its outermost limits.

By the time the waiter arrived, Arlette had made the bed and retired into the bathroom, while Anthony, drying himself from the shower, advanced to the door with a towel wrapped around his waist.

'He'll think we've been reading the fucking paper,' he assured her.

CHAPTER 23

As they ate she talked gaily, about whatever seemed certain not to disturb him. Men were skittish, easily alarmed, especially after lovemaking, when they seemed to expect some unusual and unfair demand would be made upon them:

Give me your soul.

While she talked, Anthony smiled occasionally, nodded, but had little to say. He had last eaten, he told her, at six-thirty that morning – several months ago.

Arlette did not mention Lydia. She did not speak of his

196

children. She did not talk about Gordon Donahue. She did not talk of her future plans – for in fact she had none, only to go back to New York after the tour ended in San Francisco, resume her studies, and hope to find other work without a heartbreaking time of waiting.

They had talked so little, giving each other neither hints, instructions, nor demands, she decided perhaps there was no reason for people who loved each other to talk very much. Words almost always turned out to tell someone either more than they wanted to hear or not enough:

We have better ways of saying what we mean.

That was not necessarily true either, only because she wanted to believe it. These past hours had melted the core of their lives, a stream of molten lead poured through a snowbank, leaving no trace of its passage, only the open space, wide and deep and perpetually unexplainable to outsiders.

Even so, those recent experiences might not mean what they had seemed to. For there was about this long day something of the unnatural intensity of a dream.

. The telephone started to ring – as she had been expecting, for it was her custom and Gordon's to talk every Sunday. That Sunday call had been the beginning of the week for them, and had acquired ritualistic significance.

Anthony started to get up, glanced at her as she gave a sound of protest, sat down and resumed eating. But now he looked angry.

They sat in silence as it rang, and Arlette began her Patience Count:

Pearls. Ivory. Emerald. Opal. Amethyst. Topaz. Coral. Leopard.

She kept her eyes lowered, then glanced up and found him watching her, serious, disapproving.

Did he think she was cruel: that one day it might be Anthony himself calling, helpless to force her to answer – and another man would be with her? The chances, she thought, looking solemnly across at him, were that he did not trust her any better than she trusted him. They were both prepared for disappointment: today or tomorrow. No degree of pleasure could save them from their fears of each other.

'Are you never going to answer it?'

'Not with you here.'

She was thinking, with one of the few attacks of guilt she had experienced, that Gordon had spent the day in his office; or he had gone there in the morning and then returned:

This is the way the world ends, Gordon. Your world and mine.

They sat, waiting for it to stop. But this telephone was more stubborn than the last, determined to coerce her to its will, however long it might take.

Arlette lowered her head, unwilling to see his expression. 'How could I talk to him with you here?'

He got up, throwing off the towel and stepping into his slacks. Arlette watched him, as astonished as she had been the night he had driven her back to Valerie and Frederick's house, saying not a word, glaring at the road.

He was pulling the sweater over his head, and at that moment the telephone fell silent. They looked at it as if expecting something more, then at each other, and Anthony flung away the sweater.

'He's not a stupid man, Anthony. He would know—'

'Of course. Of course.'

He was going to leave her. He had picked up the sweater again, and was drawing it on slowly. He put on his socks, thrust his feet into the moccasins, and took his coat from the closet.

He would leave her, go to his own room, and she would lose him.

And if he did, the loss would be permanent, signifying that his obsession had been cured by a simple homeopathic remedy. He could now go his way, freed of the need which had driven him to stalk her about these towns, questioning bellboys and elevator operators.

A sick apprehension passed through her as he stood,

hand on the knob, his back to her. It was possible that he supposed she wanted him to leave, so that she could call Gordon; but if that was what he was capable of thinking, now, then she was willing to take the chance of silence:

Fate comes when it will.

He turned slowly, and his face was miraculously tender. Silence and motionlessness had effected the miracle? *The power of action which is actionless?*

But then, he did not know how well prepared she was to be alone.

He had no way of knowing, from the little she had told him of why she had grown up in Valerie and Frederick's care, that she had no belief in permanence, that the earliest lesson she had learned was that life was not to be trusted; happiness could not be depended upon, and those you loved and needed most would be lost to you.

What difference, then, if he disappeared, too?

He walked back, slowly, intently serious, and she stood, as if to meet a newcomer. 'Yes?'

His hand touched her shoulder caressingly, but the caress was casual, as if he were thinking about something else. 'Tomorrow's Monday.' He glanced at his watch. 'It's nearly four.'

She smiled, nodding. No argument there.

'You have—' He was not looking directly at her, but had begun to examine her shoulders, pushing aside the white silk robe, a man examining a piece of sculpture. 'You have plans for tonight, do you? Dinner with Minerva and Eva?'

'No. No plans.'

She went on smiling, slightly, letting him arrive at his decision. Arlette prided herself on her pragmatism. A bird in the hand was the only worthwhile bird in the forest:

Take the present, Arlette, before it's disappeared into the past. You won't be back, remember that—

'Can I stay with you?' She was surprised to realize he had been as apprehensive as she.

'Please stay with me!'

199

After all, she might have been one of those girls who worried about waiters, desk clerks, elevator operators, her friends, who had not seen them all day – when ordinarily on a Sunday members of the cast passed one another in hotel lobbies and on the street, coming or going on a variety of errands.

'Sit down, Arlette. I want to talk to you.'

She went promptly to sit on the sofa, kneeling to face him, palms upon her knees, and observed him watchfully as he sat at the other end.

'I didn't join the rest of you at dinner last night.'

Did he think that would surprise her?

The company had fallen into a habit, soon after they left New York, of having dinner together on Saturday night, although every other night they went their own ways.

'I'd like to tell you why.'

Arlette grew wary.

He was going to tell her something incredibly foolish: Lydia was pregnant; one of his children was sick. Any man with a family led a precarious existence, in constant danger of having his allure as a lover betrayed by one or another of the absurdities of domestic life.

He was going to tell her something she did not want to hear, the seriousness of his expression indicated that. And he would tell it for his conscience's sake, even if she asked him not to. Another proof that Pat Runkle no longer existed, had been abandoned somewhere along the Chosin Reservoir.

'Yes?'

'I was reading a script. Rereading it, for the fourth or fifth time.' He smiled a little.

Arlette sat straighter. 'Oh?' This was a far more interesting piece of news than she had been expecting, even though they had all heard of those scripts. 'A script?'

Even now, when she had supposed herself sunk out of view of every reality but Anthony and the past few hours, a script did not sound unimportant. It was the one thing in life she wanted.

'A movie script of *Jane Eyre*. You won't approve of that, I know.'

The young actors were scornful of movies, describing an actor they disliked by saying, 'He might do in the movies.' They had never said that about Anthony De Forest, whose native turf seemed the stage, as another man's was the floor of the stock exchange or the operating room of a hospital.

Arlette was trying to look as if *movie script* was not the dirtiest word she had ever heard. 'I see.'

'It's well done, I think. A guy named Jim Lennox.'

'I've heard of him.'

'The director is Andrew Thyssen, and the producers are General Film Associates. Thyssen controls it.'

'But those are all very good people, Anthony,' said Arlette consolingly, marveling at how she, whether as Lily Malone or Arlette Morgan, had never envied anyone but Anthony. Yet she did, and a pricking thorn of despair had begun to cause her pain. She was losing him as he talked. 'They will spend money on it?'

'About three million, my agent thinks.'

'Your agent,' murmured Arlette. 'I don't have an agent.'

She was ashamed of having said it, so self-concerned at a moment when he was telling her something which must be of importance to him.

He laughed, the tolerant laughter of a man interrupted by a disappointed child. 'Do you want mine? I know he'd take you. Art Friedman.'

'I've heard of him.'

Yes, she had heard of Art Friedman. He was famous for the number of his successful clients. Indeed, he had no other kind. They were either successful when he accepted them, they became successful after he undertook their guidance – or they were Art Friedman's clients no longer.

She felt betrayed. All these things had been going on, Anthony had been in the process of changing his life while they had been playing Petruchio and Kate, in Des Moines and Kansas City and Chicago and Buffalo and

God knew where else. All the while he had been stalking her, he had been stalking his own future, too.

'The movie will be made in Hollywood—'

'Hollywood,' repeated Arlette, as if she had never heard of it.

'And a couple of months in England. If they bring it in on schedule.' Anthony was watching her with a shrewd, slightly suspicious questioning. He shrugged. His tale was told. 'That's all. I wanted you to know about it.'

Arlette studied him for some time, thoughtfully, but it seemed her mind-reading abilities had failed. She could not tell what he was thinking, what he was feeling. She bowed her head.

Anthony sat silent a few moments, and then got up, wheeled the table into the hallway, and closed the door. When he turned, they looked at each other carefully, and it seemed the information had reconstructed the past years, obliterating the few hours which had passed since they had met on the street this morning:

What right have I to an opinion about what he's going to do – what his life will be? None.

Lovemaking was not a system of barter. Lovemaking existed for its own sake. It belonged to the moment; it had no past, no future, except as the future might occur without manipulation.

That was what she had told Jack Davidson, and Gordon Donahue. And that was what she believed. Nevertheless, she felt that today Anthony had done her serious, unjustifiable injury, even if she could not identify its nature.

'A matter of a few months, maybe six or so. I don't intend to stay with pictures. But I want to find out if I can do it. And, to be truthful, it may give me more clout.'

'Of course,' murmured Arlette, ashamed to find she was no longer the rational woman, convinced of each human being's right to independence and autonomy; all her favorite beliefs. 'I think it's wonderful.'

'Like hell you do. You think I'm a bloody opportunist.' He came toward her, smiling.

She looked at him seriously as he stood beside where

she knelt on the sofa. By some effort of will, a force she had been able to count upon to save her from unbearable suffering, the paralysis of fear – that force was summoned and, like a well-trained genie, it came:

The miracle of good feeling toward him. The ill will she had begun to feel against herself for her envy – that ugliness was gone:

Of course I'm glad. What was I expecting him to do?

She took an oath:

Whatever else, I'll never ask him any damn-fool questions.

Take the present before it's disappeared into the past.

Here it was, Anthony holding her, beginning to feel more at ease, although for a few moments his body remained slightly resistant, as if to demand that she say now whatever she was going to say – or forever hold her peace.

I'll forever hold my peace.

I hope.

PART II

1954

CHAPTER 24

'Serious love is dangerous to a serious actress.' That had been Alicia Fiedler's advice two years ago, and so it was plain she did not consider Arlette's love for Gordon Donahue as seriously distracting. 'There's no time for an actress to sit moping when something goes wrong, and something always goes wrong when feelings are serious. Remember, Arlette: when eight-forty comes, love goes.' Alicia gestured. 'Men handle it better. But then, men live outside themselves – even the introspective ones.'

Alicia had been right, Arlette decided, as the hours passed.

Sunday night was gone. Monday morning they awoke to bright sunlight, for they had forgotten to pull the shades. Anthony had awakened first and again lay on his back, one arm across his forehead, eyes narrowed in concentration as he gazed at the ceiling.

Thinking – what?

His face was somber, and she remained motionless, watching him with that sense of wonderment at the luck of bone structure, the width and shape of black eyebrows, the form of his nose; the curved underlip, feeling a painful admiration and love, and a terror of the day she must lose him:

What will happen after the world has ended?

She remembered, as if it had happened years before, that sometime during the night she had heard her voice, rising slowly and softly, as he lay briefly still. Her voice had risen slowly, steadily, until it became a sound of wailing, a forlorn keening, as at a wake or some unknown religious rite, as the sensations increased, drawing the taut nerves tighter, drawing blood vessels into a throbbing knot. The wailing grew higher, and at last, as if all the network of her body had come unknotted, the wail paused, slid slowly down the scale, and resolved in low sobs.

That was the first time, lying still and reflective, when she had remembered Alicia's warning. And she thought of it again as she waited for him to discover she was awake.

At last he turned, and smiled.

'Arlette, Arlette—' He got out of bed quickly, fully restored by sleep – how many hours of it they could not guess. 'What shall we eat?'

They looked at the clock and found they had nearly ten hours until they must be at the theater, since it was the habit of both of them to arrive no later than five, not only to allow time for makeup, getting into costumes, but also time to return to sixteenth-century Padua.

Anthony ordered breakfast while Arlette went to bathe, wondering if, when the curtain rose, she would be able to follow Alicia's advice.

She listened to his program for the day.

It took into consideration both their needs, from that moment until time for them to leave for the theater:

And after that? After that, Anthony? Will you be here with me?

His program had been outlined only to the moment the curtain went up. Perhaps he was wondering, too, if they were disciplined enough to play Kate and Petruchio, uninfluenced by Anthony De Forest and Arlette Morgan.

Anthony's program began promptly when breakfast was over. He kissed her, told her to get dressed, and said he would be back in fifteen minutes. He was going to shave and change his clothes.

And telephone?

He was out the door.

Looking at the closed door, Arlette had an ominous conviction that it would never open again, not to admit Anthony De Forest. That was his way of escaping – sure, swift, unceremonious, with a proper excuse. That always had been his way of escaping, so she had heard, when she was Jade Ring and he the Shining Emperor.

She worked carefully on her makeup, watching the clock: fifteen minutes. Was it necessary to spend fifteen minutes shaving and changing his clothes – only to put on something that looked like what he had been wearing?

Disappointed by this new Arlette, she decided, when he had been gone for seventeen minutes that he had, indeed, escaped. The key turned in the lock and Anthony was back. She stood, naked, holding brushes, makeup sticks, pencils, and smiled at him in the mirror, a conspiratorial smile of welcome home; but then, she had known all along he would come.

He put a shaving kit on the bathroom chair, handed her a bouquet of pink roses, explaining that the town and season offered no pink peonies, and leaned against the doorjamb, watching her and smiling as she went about throwing away a vase of wilted flowers, arranging the fresh ones.

'I went to get the local paper – that's all I could find – and the flowers, and ran into Lucentio and Gremio, on their morning march.'

'What did they say?'

' "Hello." I looked at them. "Hi," I told them.'

Arlette laughed with pride and relief that he was not going to pretend. She moved toward him.

'Look out. We'll never start on that walk. Put something on.'

Arlette stood before him, face delicately colored and defined, hair looking as if it had been done by a professional. She wore her sleeveless red dress and black pumps, and Anthony held the coat:

Even if we never saw each other again, we'll never know each other any better than we do right now.

That was bravado, and pathetic as well. She was ashamed of her diminished self-confidence.

'Five miles. Okay?'

'Okay.'

'Arlette—'

'Yes?'

'This won't bother you? Coming and going together.

The hotel staff. The other guys. Your friends Minerva and Eva?'

Arlette laughed softly.

No damn-fool answers, either.

They saw no one they knew going through the lobby, but when they had walked at that brisk military pace some three miles, they met Baptista and Grumio, striding along at the same rate, coming in their direction. They hailed each other as if months had passed since their last meeting, and stopped to talk, unusually jovial as they discussed the fine day, the good audience Saturday night.

Neither Baptista nor Grumio seemed surprised. They displayed no sly understanding amusement, and then Anthony casually slipped one arm about Arlette's shoulder. 'Another two miles?'

They waved good-bye, voyagers departing for distant ports, and who knew when they would meet again?

Even in that brief meeting, the few words, was the unspoken recognition that those two nations, Morgan and De Forest, formerly at war, had signed a peace treaty. By the time they arrived at the theater tonight, the news would be general, though mentioned by no one.

That was a part of what she had loved from the beginning: the camaraderie, strong even when envy and jealousy and competitiveness distilled its essence. They were loyal, and forgetful; disloyal, and affectionate; envious, and proud of one another's achievements. They were open, alert, intense, keenly alive. And she had felt that at last she had found the country she could accept as her own. Here was the flag she could salute, the loyalty she could give without irony.

The fear of walking onstage to confront Petruchio and finding she had been unable to put on Katharina with Katharina's bold red dress caught her in the stomach as they were about to leave for the theater.

'What if we can't do it the same way any more?'

'Do what the same way any more?'

'What if we can't be Katharina? Petruchio?'

'Forget this—' He gestured toward the room behind

210

them. 'Just forget it. It never happened. Forget it until eleven o'clock – then remember it again.'

They had become more professional these past several months than she had guessed. Katharina was Katharina, not Arlette Morgan. And Petruchio was Petruchio, not Anthony De Forest.

Time did pass, after all.

For several days it seemed not to. It seemed she could preserve them as they were, in this miraculous cocoon of warmth, desire, joyousness.

For three weeks and a half they were together twenty-four hours a day, separated only by their dressing rooms or Anthony's occasional forays in search of flowers or fruits. They ate together, slept together, took daily five-mile hikes, striding along at a well-timed military pace, synchronized in Anthony's head once and forever.

While she made up her face he read to her; or they read in silence, giving each other opportunity for the introspection which was needful to both of them. But they exchanged no gifts about the nature of this introspection – leaving each other those secrets. They made love, sometimes briefly, sometimes until they were exhausted.

Arlette tried to convince herself that twenty-seven days were all there was to marriage.

Then, although she pretended it would come some other day, some other morning, or perhaps never, Anthony made his casual announcement: 'Lydia's getting in on the ten thirty-eight. I'm going to pick her up. The kids aren't coming.'

Arlette had supposed she had prepared herself for the news, however it was brought, by Anthony, or by another – Minerva Grey or Eva French. Possibly by seeing him with Lydia in the lobby.

However it would happen, she was ready.

Somewhere in that part of Arlette Morgan which was first and foremost Lily Malone, she had an ally who could protect her.

For Lily Malone understood very clearly what Arlette Morgan had not. Lily Malone, after all, had never been in an earthquake where her only companion was a man; she had never experienced a storm at sea, a forest fire, a hurricane of hysterical emotion, and so Lily Malone knew that to survive such events of nature it was necessary only to seal them off, into a separate chamber, closed with an unbreakable lock.

Anthony looked across the breakfast table, serious, apologetic. They had not talked about the fact that this was coming, the future arriving one day soon in the form of Lydia, beautiful, with her cool blue eyes, her expensive clothes and well-trained voice; her possessiveness too arrogant for demonstration. Lydia had two children, demonstration enough.

He seemed disconcerted by the smile, the silence. 'She wanted to see how the production had changed.'

'Of course.'

Anthony kissed her quickly, and left the room. 'See you,' he said.

The door closed behind Anthony after his brusque announcement – brusque with self-consciousness and, she thought, fear – that ancient masculine fear of an hysterical or accusing woman. A jealous or angry Arlette might be quite a different woman from the one he late had known.

She looked at the closed door as if it had a message written upon it in some foreign but not indecipherable language: the message dealt with the subject of love and Lily Malone; love and Arlette Morgan.

And the message was written by Arlette to herself, and therefore inaccessible to decoding by other archaeologists of the heart, students of the multiple leaves of the brain:

I can fall apart, cry all day, tell myself life is over.

That was one way, and perhaps not the worst way, either:

Or I can exercise, practice my voice lessons. I can finish reading the galleys of Gordon's new book.

The decision made, everything followed in precise order:

She wheeled the breakfast table into the hall. She hung

the *Do Not Disturb* sign on the door, made up the bed, threw her robe off, and set the timer for one hour.

She began by standing on her head, convinced there was almost nothing which could go wrong in the life of a healthy person which could not be put into perspective by five minutes standing on the head. . . .

CHAPTER 25

'*See you.*'

Yes, Anthony. You will.

He would see her at the theater. He would see her after this last performance of the tour, in San Francisco at the party Gordon Donahue was giving for the cast and some old friends.

What old friends? Arlette had wondered.

During the two weeks they had been there, with interviews and photographs in every newspaper, the theater filled each night, she had not one telephone call nor one note from any of her school friends. Nothing from Marjorie. Nothing from Barbara. Nothing from Jack Davidson.

Were they afraid of her? Thinking, perhaps, that she was a celebrity who would not acknowledge them?

Had they forgotten her – as she had forgotten them? Still, not to hear or have one note – had left a baffled feeling of hurt and bewilderment.

That, and Anthony's almost furtive departure, made her determined not only to play the best Katharina of the tour, but to be prepared for this party. She did not intend ever again to let herself be taken by surprise, as she had been in New Haven. Alicia was not there to rescue her again.

All at once, that safe world Anthony had created had broken apart. A tree, living and growing, had been killed. Whatever she tried to do to distract her attention, she felt herself to have been wounded, left raw, as if her skin had been peeled away.

She went on: one half hour of calisthenics, taught her by a gymnastics instructor who had apparently thought she wanted to join a circus.

Finally she threw herself on the sofa and began to laugh, with a freedom which astonished her. The laughter brought relief, as if she had narrowly escaped some desperate situation, some unknown but terrible danger.

The danger was Anthony.

For Anthony would go about his life exactly as he had planned it – and Anthony was not only spontaneous, reckless, impulsive; he was also a planner, with a cautious but profound belief in his destiny. He would become Rochester, dour and handsome, petrifying Jane Eyre into dithering admiration; after that, autograph collectors would chase him down the street. Yet he would continue to be Anthony De Forest.

If he had stayed with her – however he contrived to get rid of Lydia – in time he would have usurped not only her body and emotions, but her ambitions, perhaps even found a way to steal her talents – although even Arlette, in her iconoclastic fury, could not overlook the fact that it was Anthony who seemed to have the greater talent, and need not steal such goods from others.

She began to recite the Second Player's speech.

'It was a custom of the nineteenth-century actors,' Alicia had said during one of their early lessons. 'Recite it every day – from now until the end of your life. It is one of the greatest intricacies of the English language – few actors are equal to it. Let nothing interfere.'

She never had, until these past weeks.

Perhaps she had been embarrassed to have Anthony hear her recite it – fearing that he might listen politely, hearing all the flaws, but sparing her the humiliation of letting her guess he heard them?

In the midst of her recitation, the telephone rang. Arlette went on, but thinking perhaps it was Gordon,

Valerie or Frederick, even Barbara Sloan, she picked it up.

'Arlette?' She hated herself and she hated him.

'Yes?'

'I'm calling from a booth. I came out to get some—' Anthony hesitated, perhaps wondering what a bellboy could not have been sent for. 'Flowers.'

'A phone booth?' She began to laugh, and as he repeated her name pleadingly, she continued to laugh with ironic hilarity. 'Flowers! Oh, Anthony!'

'I'll see you tonight,' he said, and hung up. Arlette put the telephone back, smiled reflectively, then began to recite the Second Player's speech again, beginning at the first line.

The rest of the day followed her usual routine: Balinese hand exercises and dance steps; washing her hair and rolling it up, drying it quickly and brushing it; bathing. At three-thirty she ate steak and a salad of raw vegetables, tea, and a pint of milk. One more cup of tea before she left for the theater, and then nothing until after the performance.

Alicia had warned her that hunger, a little hunger, sharpened the mind, braced the body tone.

All the while, moving slowly through the carefully choreographed ritual, Arlette continued to polish her script for Gordon Donahue's party.

That was the real challenge; not Katharina, which she had played two hundred times, but Arlette Morgan, star of the production, star of future productions – a demanding part she had been writing for several weeks, working on the script secretly, visualizing it, memorizing her lines and the lines of all the other actors – while perhaps Anthony had supposed she was concentrating upon buffing her fingernails.

The script had been clear for at least a month; from time to time she applied new touches.

When she was ready to leave for the theater at five-thirty – later than usual, to avoid the possibility of meeting Anthony in the lobby – the script was so well prepared she was eager to be done with Katharina and go on to the important task, which she intended to use as prophecy: it was to show her the design of Arlette Morgan's future life.

Her own lines were set, requiring only minor changes as surprises occurred. The lines of other leading members of the cast were written: Gordon's, Anthony's, Lydia's, Minerva's, Eva's, Valerie's, Frederick's; all the actors of the caravan. They might speak them verbatim; they might change them extemporaneously; they might forget them. No matter. Their lines were of little consequence compared to her own.

She knew what she would do, how she would behave, how she would look, smile, move; whom she would kiss. No matter how many lines the others might forget or how many cues they might miss, she would continue imperturbably to play the part written by Arlette Morgan for Arlette Morgan, no more dismayed than she had been during the performance of her production, *Adventure*, when every character but Antoinette had made one blunder after another.

She knew exactly how the performance would play.

The rooms would be crowded, one hundred or more people jammed into a three-room hotel suite, drinking and eating from the buffet table, laughing hilariously in one another's faces, talking too loudly in futile hope of being heard when no one was listening.

Glasses would be broken. Canapés would be dropped and ground into the carpet. Vases of flowers would be overturned. Drinks would be spilled over dinner jackets and on evening dresses by loosening fingers. Exaggerated apologies would be made. Anger would be concealed and grand disdain for such trifles would be indicated. Smiles would freeze, throats grow tense.

Most of the cast, whether those from the caravan or outsiders, were spear carriers in Arlette's script. But those were some of the most important parts, whether they knew it or not. For in escaping to talk to a spear carrier, Arlette could avoid a character who had misread his cue.

And the main characters would inevitably miss their cues, read the wrong lines, engage themselves in the wrong business.

Through all this, she foresaw that Gordon Donahue would be bewildered by her high-spirited arrogant charm. Anthony would not believe this was any woman he had seen before. Lydia would be astonished by the glitter, the radiance.

But first, she must play Katharina with so perfect a concentration that she would not become fully aware of Petruchio as Anthony De Forest, and when they had changed their costumes for evening clothes, she would set out with Eva and Minerva, Lucentio and Gremio and Grumio, Arlette making sure they did not arrive until the rooms were half filled.

Then she was prepared to enter like a flame, smiling Jade Ring's bewitching smile, unaware of herself as anyone but her character in her script, unafraid, confident, gay, self-contained, joyous, kind. She meant to cast Donahue's entire audience into her spell, scatter over them the bewilderment of beauty seen as in the fiery descent of a Fourth of July display.

Once, as she stood waiting for her next cue, she heard Anthony's voice in her ear and felt the light pressure of his body against her back. She moved away, smiling sweetly across her shoulder, placing one finger to her lips.

Even Petruchio's kiss did not disconcert her, neither the first one nor the second; she closed her eyes and convinced herself he was Anthony De Forest's standby.

She dawdled in the dressing room, while Minerva and Eva ran in and out, announcing that everyone had left, everyone was waiting, and at last they got into a taxi, Arlette riding in silence, saving her energy for the moment when she swept into the room to be immediately embraced by little Mrs Donahue; and by means of some magic internal switch, Arlette would turn herself into the star of the evening.

Marian's admiration, the pride in her smile, was not in Arlette's script. That made no difference. Across his wife's

217

shoulder Arlette saw Gordon's face, anxious, and the look of pain in his eyes. For a moment, knowing she had irretrievably injured this man who had loved her with generosity and kindness, she began to lose hold of her script. The star was in danger of fading before her performance had properly begun.

To distract herself from that pang of guilt, she looked down at Mrs Donahue and smiled at her with a charm so forceful as to be almost intimidating.

'We're so proud of you, Lily — Arlette. Excuse me. All of us. But Gordon in particular. I believe he thinks he invented you.'

'I think he did.'

The line was not in the script, but guilt and gratitude had made her forget what lines she had written to deliver to Marian Donahue. During the moment they stood together, Arlette was thinking that Marian looked five years older and yet exactly the same, in the way of women like Marian Donahue.

Marian had perceived that her studious, thoughtful husband would not permanently interest a girl like Lily Malone, too beautiful, too restless and ambitious, for a quiet man like Gordon. And although it had taken a while, finally she had been right.

Gordon, perhaps relieved by the picture of mutual devotion the two women presented, moved forward to embrace her, carefully, as if he was not sure whether he should be the exuberant professor displaying his prize pupil, the deferential admirer, or the man who loved a woman and knew she no longer loved him.

Arlette moved from Gordon's arms, looking him straight in the eyes for one questioning moment, to Frederick, who held her close, telling her he was proud of her; to Valerie, who smiled and spoke the lines Arlette had assigned to her.

Arlette hoped not to see Anthony and Lydia. But she was ready for them.

Quite late, they did arrive. Or of course they might have been there for some time before Arlette, moving so quickly, talking with such vivacity and gaiety to everyone who crossed her path, whether she knew them or not, was surprised to find Lydia standing before her, smiling – Lydia, aloof and beautiful in her green chiffon dress with a gardenia pinned at one side of her black hair.

'I'm Lydia De Forest. We met some time ago. I want to tell you how much I admired your performance – how it's grown since New Haven!'

'You're so kind.'

Arlette turned to one of the spear carriers and was dependably whisked away.

In the doorway, talking to Jerry Hoffman – he might have come with the De Forests – stood Anthony. Both men were looking at her and, she knew, talking about her. Without indicating she had seen them, Arlette turned so that her back was to them, and began talking to two professors, who said she had been in their classes and she had performed beyond—

A man's arms – not Anthony's – encircled her waist from the back and held her fast, talking in her ear, that urgent, intense voice of Jerry Hoffman's. 'Arlette, I can't get over it! That was one of the best Katharinas I've ever seen! For Christ's sake, what's happened since Chicago?'

He turned her around, holding her face between his hands, studying her. He was elated, in love with all his players – an emotion known to overcome him at the last performance of any successful engagement, when he no longer feared that something might happen to destroy his work.

Arlette kept her smile, although she became uneasily aware that Anthony was making his way slowly toward them, watching her steadily. She was caught off guard, forgot her script, and glanced at Anthony.

Jerry read the glance easily. 'Oh.'

Arlette's eyes lowered, ashamed she had lost control of her part.

Anthony was a few feet away, approaching them with the slow prowling walk of a determined man.

The flash of embarrassment over, the bewitching smile

219

returned, and Arlette left Jerry, murmuring something he could not understand.

She kept her back to Anthony and he came no nearer.

She talked to other spear carriers. She felt, once again, swept up, onward upon her self-created flame, and then – when her gaiety seemed to have reached its farthest boundary – her eyes searched the room at a glance, grown so noisy it was impossible to hear individual voices, and so crowded it was nearly impossible for anyone but Arlette to keep moving.

A thought not in the script took her by surprise:

What difference does this make? We'll all be dead someday.

She experienced no horror at the treacherous reminder, no bitterness – only an uncanny wonderment. Then it was gone.

At one time she realized, with relief, that Anthony and Lydia had left – and she had not spoken to him. She had heard, from someone, sometime during the night, that the De Forests were leaving the next morning, and so she did not go downstairs until noon, when she encountered Minerva in the lobby.

They talked about the party for several minutes.

'They're gone,' Minerva said at last, as if she knew that was what Arlette wanted to ask. She looked guilty, perhaps thinking Arlette might blame her for carrying news of disaster, and it occurred to Arlette that during these past months she and Minerva and Eva had become durable friends.

This was a friendship to last, a thing all three of them needed.

She and Minerva decided to take a brief walk. By evening all of them would have gone their separate ways, most of them back to New York. All but Arlette, who was to spend a week with Valerie and Frederick.

The omens, she had decided, when she awakened in the morning, had been good ones. The stick-throwing had proved a success. She had learned how to behave like a star.

That part of the job, at least, was done.

CHAPTER 26

In January, Arlette was again studying with Alicia, taking classes at the Downtown Drama School, and had begun to wonder if there had ever been a *Taming of the Shrew*.

Minerva had lost Max Gilmore to Jennifer Knight during the long tour. Otherwise, there they were, exactly as before, Eva, Grumio, Lucentio, Gremio, Baptista – meeting in rehearsal clothes, at auditions, during intermissions at theaters where they had gone to see a new production, such as they had left so recently.

None of them mentioned Anthony De Forest; his picture had been turned to the wall. No amnesty, no mercy. Treason was punishable by forgetfulness.

Walking toward Alicia's one afternoon, she stopped:
What went wrong?

Nothing had gone wrong, of course. Nothing had gone wrong with her that had not gone wrong with Minerva and Eva, Lucentio and Gremio, all of them but Anthony De Forest. And he had gone astray in a different direction.

'What are you going to do, Arlette?' Alicia asked when Arlette appeared for her first lesson since the caravan had set off, each bravely convinced they would be welcomed back with contracts, scripts, more offers than they knew what to do with. Their scrapbooks overflowed with flattering reviews, flattering photographs, most of them taken before they had left New York, flattering interviews with tame provincial interviewers.

Arlette was taken aback, supposing Alicia must be referring to Anthony. It was impossible she would not have heard of them, for Alicia knew everything that happened in their world. And Jerry had read the news in Arlette's quick glance at Anthony.

But then she realized that was not what Alicia was talking about.

Her students' love affairs did not concern her. They

were part of the stuff of a personality; they nourished it, or withered it, but Alicia could work only with what they gave her.

'Study. Work. What else can I do?' She glanced away, ashamed.

'Films don't interest you?'

'Of course not.' It was true. Unlike Anthony, she had no interest in discovering if she could climb that mountain. 'But – I haven't had any offers.'

'You could have. I'm sure of that. There are actors who believe a film is the only real immortality – it goes into a can and is there to be reheated, year after year.'

'I want to act. Here.'

And why was she not being given the opportunity?

She had been training – four or five years, depending on whether she counted England; she had had experience with audiences. The audiences had not cured the stage fright, but she had been able to face them every night, the only one of the cast except Anthony who had not lost one or two performances to a headache or case of flu.

She had even had her heart broken: a broken heart, the open door of the emotions.

When Lily Malone was seventeen, she had thought she would never be blessed by that experience of blasted romantic love. How was she to experience the agonies of unhappy love when she got tired of her admirers before they were tired of her?

Later, she had stopped thinking of it as a necessary part of her theatrical equipment: she had no hope that Gordon Donahue would break her heart, either. She loved him, but Donahue was not a man for breaking hearts. It was his deep concern to harm no one. He did not wish for it or seek it, but Arlette had known from the first day he made love to her that in time it would be Gordon who would suffer.

Then Anthony fell in love with her, and fell out again when it became inconvenient, and that had struck her with the force of a blow she had thought might kill her.

She had watched the door when he had left that morning:

Is that the sound of a breaking heart?

She had listened attentively, but either it happened in silence or she had been too distraught to hear it. All the same, it had happened – and its effects were as unmistakable as any other break in the system of the self.

Even that, however, was evidently not visible: this new Arlette, wounded, sorrowing, with her knowledge of love and hate. Jerry Hoffman seemed not to have noticed it. Nor Alicia. Not even Minerva or Eva had indicated that she was, at last, equipped for the tragic theater.

She felt resentful that Anthony should have harmed her, and the harm had no beneficial effects. For Anthony had suddenly, unexpectedly, treacherously, from his own need, revealed to her another world, profound, deep as the past, dark as a night without a moon, terrifying as the foreknowledge of death.

What exactly his crime against her had been she was not sure.

He had called from the Los Angeles airport – she guessed – since the call came a little before twelve-thirty. She had returned from her walk with Minerva, packed her suitcases, and was waiting for Gordon, who was to drive her to Valerie and Frederick's.

'Mr De Forest calling, Miss Morgan.'

There he was, and Lydia was standing about while he went off to a telephone booth with the excuse that he must notify his agent of something important.

'I'm not here. I just left.'

She hung up and stood motionless, wrapping her arms about herself, shivering slightly, convinced she had won a victory.

Anthony was not the man to be disconcerted by her refusal to talk to him. Indeed, she saw him shrugging in that occasional gesture, smiling a little, then walking out to join Lydia as if he had been quite successful in his conference with his agent.

When the operator called to tell her Mr Donahue was

waiting, she said: 'Please ask Mr Donahue to come up. I've not finished packing.'

Arlette had spent some time thinking about this.

Gordon had known, ever since their duel at the Palmer House, that she was in love with Anthony, and she had read that knowledge in his expression the night before.

Much as she despised the idea of ever acting from motives of conscience, nevertheless today she asked herself a point-blank question:

What am I to do about Gordon?

Ask him to come up, of course. And leave the rest to him.

Gordon came to the telephone. 'Yes, Arlette?' Perhaps he was expecting to hear that Anthony was with her; she was not going to Valerie and Frederick's after all.

'Wouldn't you like to come up? I'm not quite—'

He replied quickly. 'We'd better shove off. They're having some people in at four to meet you. And dinner at my house is at seven-thirty. I'll get the bellboy.'

So.

Conscience had a usefulness, after all. At least, if you were dealing with someone who had a conscience of his own.

'What are you going to do, Arlette?'

At the end of March, the question was no more resolved than it had been in early January. Arlette had begun to think that Alicia Fiedler was expecting her to apologize for wasting her time.

And then Alicia invited her to dinner. 'Only a few people, some you know. Don't dress. Seven forty-five.'

That posed a series of problems. Dinner, why? Alicia never did anything without a reason. And a dinner at Alicia's – she had had dinner only twice at Alicia's, the two of them – this was an occasion.

Don't dress, she decided, meant: *Look your best. Don't pay any attention to what the other women have on. Come prepared to obliterate them.*

Alicia did not waste time with people who came to chat idly and eat the food for which her cook was famous. When she asked people to her house, they were expected to come at their best. There they were, the women dressed, as Arlette had foreseen, the men in dark suits, and Arlette in the yellow silk jersey evening gown which had made a star of her at Gordon Donahue's closing-night party.

The guest list was not easy to decipher: Sy Harman and Jonathan Morris, the producers of Hoffman-Repertory. Arlette had met them during the time they had rehearsed and performed in New York before they set out for the provinces. These two men, congenial in manner, inoffensive in appearance, seemed to her to belong to a dark and mysterious world. They were producers, and producers ruled the stage – they provided financing.

Putting a play on the stage, Jerry Hoffman had told her, was in the mind of a producer like sending a seventeenth-century galleon laden with gold homeward bound to Spain. The return on the investment of time and blood and treasure might be great. More likely the ship would be scuttled, the treasure lost by ill winds, a bungling captain, a mutinous crew, a clever pirate.

The pirate might appear in many guises. Even directors were suspected by producers of piratical inclinations; not to mention the stars, the stagehands, and the members of the musicians' union.

That superstition accounted for the guest Arlette was least happy to see, Jennifer Knight.

Jennifer Knight was not only the girl who had stolen Max Gilmore from Minerva and married him while Minerva was touring the country. That was the least of Jennifer's crimes, even in Minerva's opinion. Jennifer was, at the moment, an actress cherished by the fickle public.

Arlette had met her, and had seen her perform in *Hedda Gabler*, her only performance from the classical repertoire. Her other plays had been modern. Two comedies, and one which had been called a tragedy: the two main characters were in the end declared insane.

Now, this young woman, as Arlette studied her, warmly congratulating her that she was to play Juliet in the new Hoffman-Repertory production, appeared to have certain fatal flaws.

Her eyes were blue, but not blue enough. Her smile was mechanical. Her body moved cautiously, which meant that her discipline was inadequate. She was pretty, oh, yes, thought Arlette, she was pretty. But where was the quality which, when Juliet pronounced that fatal word, *Amen*, would make it clear that Juliet was no longer a child but had, bursting open with the unexpectedness of a moonflower, become a woman?

'I liked your Katharina,' Jennifer said to her across the table, speaking in the low husky voice which had some evident allure, even if Arlette detected that its placement was dangerously wrong.

'Really?' Arlette seemed to marvel at such kindness. 'I liked your Tiffany.'

'Oh? That was so simple, really.'

'Was it?'

Max Gilmore, who perhaps could perceive the elaborate politeness which was Arlette's mask of sarcasm, spoke: 'How is Mr De Forest?'

Jerry Hoffman gave Arlette no time to worry about answering that one. 'Anthony is doing a hell of a job with Rochester. I talked to Thyssen the other day.'

Arlette left, shaking hands with Alicia and giving her a sad, if not quite accusatory little smile, wondering why Alicia should have invited her.

Jerry Hoffman, whose wife had not been there, took Arlette home in a taxi. She glanced at him, wondering what to say to the great man, but he seemed, as he usually did when not immediately involved with work, absorbed and distracted and somewhat uneasy. They said nothing, for Arlette was afraid that if she said anything, it might be wrong, and then he would never let her read for him again. Her self-confidence was unreliable these days.

He spoke of the news of the day, the bad news of the day, since there was no other. He complimented her again on Katharina, but with the air of a man who was trying to remember something, and not remembering very well.

He was probably so absorbed in his new project that he had forgotten how she had played Katharina.

Arlette sat in silence, recognizing that – but for love – there was nothing else to think seriously about in life for people of their kind: work was the world.

But Jerry Hoffman, she guessed, did not think about love, and thought about lovemaking only a few minutes before he did it, and for less than a few minutes afterward. As for love itself, she was sure he would not tolerate it.

'Here I am, Jerry,' said Arlette softly, so as not to disturb him. He sprang from his reverie, jumped out, and held the door. Arlette paused, smiling.

'Good night, darling,' he told her, and was back in the cab.

Arlette walked to the elevator, and when she entered the apartment was still repeating:

Good night, darling; good night, darling . . .

Sailing upon this evidence of progress in Jerry Hoffman's estimation, Arlette was all the more despondent when Alicia told her he had called to suggest that Arlette might be a good possibility for Jennifer Knight's standby.

'Standby?' repeated Arlette, as if at some unknown word. 'Was he ashamed to ask me himself?'

Something had gone radically wrong with Lily Malone or her incarnation-to-be, Arlette Morgan. Her life had fallen upon evil days, she thought, and sat down, gazing away from Alicia in a morbid despair:

This is the chill and lonely hour.

Alicia smiled gently. 'It doesn't happen quite that fast, Arlette.'

But Arlette was thinking about Anthony. She was thinking of Jennifer Knight and other actors and actresses. She would be twenty-five in June – an advanced age, surely, for a standby.

'Sometimes it does.'

'Jennifer Knight is an irresponsible young woman. She's had several successes, but never one where she didn't come apart. If you take this, however much it hurts your pride, you'll have a chance to play Juliet one day or another. I know Jennifer, and she's convinced the gods are out to get her – and whoever believes that is right.' Alicia smiled. 'What shall I tell Jerry? Or would you rather talk to him?'

'I talk to him? What about? I'll take it. And if this bitch doesn't—'

JENNIFER KNIGHT.

She wrote the name carefully, in large letters, and folded the page, sealed the envelope, and dropped it into the drawer to which she consigned enemies and rivals.

'Remember,' Alicia had said, 'this is an art form, we like to think. But it is also a business, and to run a business requires money. Jennifer Knight's name is worth money. For how much longer—' Alicia shrugged. 'Jennifer is not strong enough for the talent she has. Talent without the strength of the devil is useless.'

CHAPTER 27

'Juliet,' she said scornfully to Alicia, 'not fourteen yet, and ready to die for love.'

The work must be done as if it would be Arlette Morgan, not Jennifer Knight, who would play that part for three months.

'Fourteen is probably the only time when such a notion might seem logical,' Alicia reminded her.

'Of course,' Arlette agreed, and concentrated upon the script, not liking such comments even from Alicia; too close for comfort. 'Who else would do such a damn-fool thing?'

She had not told Alicia what she hoped to make of Juliet, if once she got the opportunity.

Her Juliet would be no child-woman, victim of circumstances, but the victim of her own violent nature. It was not the feuds of the Montagues and Capulets which would kill Arlette's Juliet and her Romeo. It was Juliet herself – sensual, impatient, greedy, savage, and dazzled by death, talking of death from the play's beginning until its end, as if that had been her goal all along.

Now and then she read something in a newspaper or magazine about Anthony. Press agents put out photographs of the filming, and one Sunday morning she saw a large photograph of Anthony, dressed as Rochester, smiling down at the little governess, Larka Haverill, gazing up at him with what Arlette thought was more than professional adoration.

The part was obviously a good one for him: *the black Scotch Irishman will have his day*. In the photographs he looked what she had always believed him to be – a magician, a demiurge, who had lingered on since the days before the Christians invaded the green pagan islands.

He called her three times from Los Angeles, and during each conversation she had let him talk, saying almost nothing, pleased to hear him sound increasingly uneasy. As revenge went, it was not very satisfactory, but it was better than no revenge at all.

Why do we remember so much and forget so little?

She had forgotten nothing, forgiven nothing.

Memories were companions. Memories were friends and enemies. Memories were the only sure signal that you had been alive and were still alive. When experiences were forgotten, there was no ruined city to excavate; no earlier lives to be reconstructed; no other selves to remake and reinvent. There was no China and no Elizabethan England, no Ming Huang, no Jade Ring, no Petruchio, no Katharina. No Juliet.

There was only the blank present, dead one inch beneath the surface; no shards could be discovered there from which to reconstruct ancient civilizations, unknown individualities.

One Sunday morning, when rehearsals had been under way for almost four weeks, Anthony called, taking her by surprise, for she had convinced herself the last conversation was the last they would ever have.

'I've called you a dozen times these past three weeks.' He sounded accusatory.

'I'm not here often.'

She felt her face grow hot, convinced he had called to remind her that while he was becoming a star, photographed at openings and restaurants – while he was becoming *Anthony De Forest* – she was preparing to stand by for Jennifer Knight.

'You've got a part, I hear.' His voice was almost humble.

'I'm going to be standby for Jennifer Knight's Juliet.' Her voice had a sweetness from which she had, by miraculous effort, been able to squeeze the bitterness. 'I'm sure you won't think much of it.'

'I do think much of it, Arlette. It's a much bigger production than we had. And – well, the bitch is always getting laryngitis.'

She laughed delightedly, surprising herself again. Perhaps he did, in his fashion, wish her well.

The laughter was momentarily joyous, but it seemed perhaps too reminiscent of other shared laughter, for it stopped suddenly. There was silence.

'Good-bye, Anthony. Don't call me again. Thank you.'

She quietly replaced the telephone and stood, smiling reflectively in the mirror:

I was, by Christ, able to do it. How?
And there's nothing he can hate me for.

Jack Davidson.

Gordon Donahue.

Anthony De Forest.

She had left them no ugly images. No hysterical pleadings; no snide sarcasms; no inane questions they could amuse themselves by recalling.

She had left each of them a magical bouquet, fragrant and imperishable, quite a surprise.

That was another revenge, a triumph of a kind. Better, at least, than what most women left: a boxful of scorpions to be opened at peril of being stung to death by ugly memories.

Once the play opened to better than average reviews, and the public had decided in its favor, or in Jennifer

Knight's favor, Arlette sat every night in the balcony seat assigned to her, so intensely concentrating upon Jennifer Knight's reading of Juliet's lines, she was unaware that others also sat in the audience.

For those two and a half hours she was not Arlette Morgan but a presence, watchful, critical – honorably critical, she hoped – learning from this other woman when she thought there was something to learn; rejecting most of what she did.

She sat there once with Alicia, and forgot her – until the end. She did not emerge from her state of mesmerization during the intermission, which passed without any sense of time, as she reflected upon how Jennifer had read this line and how she had moved across the stage; how she had leaned down, touched Romeo's face. All of it wrong or inadequate.

She sat there another night with Minerva Grey, who had done some television commercials, and so had acquired a quick celebrity as the girl in the Silk Shampoo ad; for forty seconds Minerva smiled at the camera, whipped her head about so that her hair, the color now of polished mahogany, undulated like a matador's cape, smiled again, this time into the eyes of a young man, whose lapel she touched with her long fingers, their red nails sharp as a mandarin's.

Minerva enjoyed her ability to convey so much sensuality in forty seconds. Men wrote her love letters and several asked to meet her, while some women demanded that she be removed from the commercial. But this little conquest left her dissatisfied. Eva French had a part in a contemporary play, a part which she referred to as her 'feather-duster' part, although she played a young prostitute and had eight lines to speak.

They met at classes. They had lunch together. And they were alternately gloomy and full of enthusiasm for the bright future. Their experience of traveling with the caravan, which by now seemed to have lasted several years, had given them a comradeship she had never felt for any of her school friends.

They understood each other as if they were compatriots meeting in a foreign country, where no one else spoke their language. Most of the other actresses were willing to accept fatalistically that they might become famous or they might not. Arlette and Eva and Minerva had long ago repudiated fate, which they thought was on no one's side. Fate was fate, perhaps – but it could be altered by the individual will.

Minerva fought a running battle with Jennifer throughout the performance, and when they went to dinner, declared: '*You* would never play Juliet like that!'

'I hope not,' said Arlette, and her eyes were bright with hatred and jealousy, although her face remained tranquil. 'I only hope I get to play her at all. The damn bitch has been sick in every other part – but so far she hasn't had one thing wrong with her.'

'She fainted one night playing Norah. But then she came to and went on. She had an abortion, and the understudy played the part for a whole week.' Minerva looked as optimistic as if this sequence of events were certain to be repeated. Arlette smiled.

Immediately she was ashamed of herself, wishing for her rival to slip on a banana peel. It was not a good omen for Arlette Morgan to share Minerva's malice.

Lucky people had no need of such cruelty. Arlette was superstitious that the misfortunes she wished on others would, like a badly aimed boomerang, return and knock her dead.

Jennifer Knight continued in blooming health, performing Juliet with a delicacy which enchanted the audiences, although Arlette did not think delicacy was what had killed either Romeo or Juliet. They were dead not of romantic yearning love, but of the passion and terror of its loss – they were dead of Juliet's barbaric impulsiveness.

Once, she was startled and embarrassed to find Jerry Hoffman in the seat beside her. She had no idea if he had been there all along or had only that moment sat down, as the play was nearing its end. He smiled at her, almost shyly, when she glanced at him, guilty as if she had been caught where she had no right to be.

Arlette promptly immersed herself again in the performance, and did not emerge until Juliet stood before them, bowing. Then, slowly, she turned to Jerry and found him watching her with an inquisitive smile.

'What do you think of her?'

People were moving around them, but they sat, Arlette looking intently at that face which changed so quickly and subtly he might appear to be several different men in the space of a few minutes. Whatever he thought registered on his face – but the thoughts were complex hieroglyphs.

'I think she's marvelous.' Arlette displayed Jade Ring's smile. Jerry Hoffman continued to look at her, slightly smiling. Skeptical? 'Don't you?'

'I think she's adequate. I wouldn't have cast her, but the producers are convinced she's magic. The public loves her. For the time being.'

For the time being?

It must mean something, for Jerry never said anything unless he meant to deliver a message. Something, surely, was about to happen. And Arlette, meeting the Nurse one day, asked her what she thought of Jennifer Knight's performance.

The Nurse, old as she appeared in the play, offstage was as free in her movements, as charming and commanding as Alicia Fiedler, whose friend she was. Other women, Arlette thought, grew old and smileless, their faces set. But actresses, obliged to remember twenty-four hours a day the discipline of their craft, remained alert, mobile, interested in the world, interesting to the world.

'She's getting more nervous with every performance. That's the way it began with *Hedda Gabler*. Each night, more and more stage fright. And then: "*Yes, you must put some more wood in the stove. I am shivering.*" ' The Nurse shivered. 'So help me, with those lines she lost her voice. She began to shiver, and when she tried to speak—' The Nurse opened her mouth, moved her lips, uttered an

233

unintelligible croak, and all at once gave a burst of derisive laughter. 'Just like that. She was finished.'

The next night, Juliet's voice began to fail her.

In Act IV, when Juliet had been left alone by her mother and the Nurse, and must contemplate taking the potion which was to leave her in a semblance of death until Romeo returned, Juliet's voice faltered.

She began bravely, addressing her departed mother and the Nurse: '*Farewell! God knows when we shall meet again. I have a faint cold fear—*'

Her voice stopped. She might have suffered these horrors too often these past weeks. Whatever it was, she spoke her lines in a strange new voice, quavering, and Arlette leaned forward, fists clenched.

'*My dismal scene I needs must act alone. . . .*'

Her voice broke. Arlette, eyes glittering with concentration, grasped the balcony rail.

Jennifer's face was pleading, but the plea was not addressed to the pathos of Juliet's life and her bravery in trying to rescue her love for Romeo. '*Shall I not then be stifled in the vault . . .*'

The sounds had become guttural, and she had skipped several lines.

Arlette felt as if a rock had dropped through her stomach, she waited, to discover if Jennifer's croak had been only a temporary hoarseness.

The audience began to grow uneasy, for the sight of an actress losing control of herself onstage produced a strange and contagious fear.

Juliet continued, but her voice grew fainter, sounding across the theater like a tortured animal, a mere whisper, broken now and then by a terrifying croak: '*Alack, alack, is it not like that I . . .*'

Arlette was ready to cry, out of terror for the girl, for herself, for gratitude or exultation, wild victory. Juliet finished her lines in a whisper: '*. . . madly play . . . dash out my desp'rate brains? . . . Romeo . . . I drink . . .*'

The curtain came together, ending the fourth act, and Arlette sat immobilized, waiting. They would call for her now – or Juliet would recover her voice during the time she had free in the next act. She looked around, but saw no signals given, no fires set atop the hillsides to summon her to glory or defeat. Only the restless, murmuring, shocked and, it seemed, grieving audience.

The actress had died in their presence, and before her time, before Juliet was to die. The curtain rose swiftly. The action went on, and evidently, somewhere backstage, Jennifer was convincing herself, and possibly Jerry Hoffman, who had been there more often the past week, that she would finish the play:

She can't do it.

Arlette sat back, hands folded in her lap, waiting.

CHAPTER 28

Arlette had been up since six o'clock, following her usual routine and assuring herself this was a Sunday like any other Sunday. Nothing out of the ordinary had happened, nothing very different from deciding to jump off the Brooklyn Bridge or swim in Maine waters in December: a major decision, perhaps, but if you survived, you had something unusual as a lifetime souvenir. Her two performances the day before seemed equally desperate.

The important thing was to keep going, Yoga to ballet barre to Second Player's speech to voice exercises to calisthenics.

At ten the telephone rang and she sprang up from where she had sat reading the Sunday papers on the living-room floor, dashed into the bedroom, and paused to draw a deep slow breath before she answered.

It was Alicia. 'They're good, Arlette! They're superb!'

Arlette hesitated, afraid of so much good luck. First, that she had notices, then that they were good.

She had done Juliet that Saturday two times, the matinee and the evening performance, but it had become one performance to her by now. And she could remember almost nothing of what had happened: she had played the part through, that much was evident. And she had stood before the curtain, bowing low so that her hair fell forward and touched the floor.

What else had she done?

Someone must tell her – someone who was not a reviewer. Someone she knew and trusted.

She remained silent and Alicia spoke her name in a tone of alarm, as if she thought she might have fainted. Reviews and actresses had a strange association, strange and traditional, like that of the virgin with the unicorn, the beauty with the beast.

'You say they're good, Alicia?'

'Arlette!' Alicia protested, although of course she knew what Arlette's trouble was: the fear of success. 'You've read them?'

'Yes,' said Arlette softly, wondering if now she would suffer the fate she had wished on Jennifer Knight. She made an effort to speak in her normal tone, and was surprised when her voice came forth strong and clear. 'I've read them.'

I've memorized them, Alicia. For Christ's sake.

Alicia read: ' "*This Juliet is a dream of fair women—*" '

'How nice.'

' "*Her demeanor is natural . . . her feeling intense . . . every action seems spontaneous.*" Arlette, do you realize that nobody has played Juliet with spontaneity in twenty years?' (The twenty years, perhaps, since Alicia Allerton had last played her.)

'They're all so nice.' Try as she might, she could not prevent herself from sounding like a little girl who has done as she was told and is being praised for it. Where had the other Arlette gone – the Arlette who had expected that if such luck, such reward for her evil intentions, should come her way she would take it as her due?

' "*When registering violent emotion, she does not distort her face—*" '

'I hope not,' said Arlette meekly.

When Alicia hung up, the telephone rang again. 'Everyone's been calling me! Everyone!' It was Minerva. 'Arlette, I'm so proud of you!' Minerva began to cry.

Arlette was trying not to cry herself – for in fact the situation seemed to her more sorrowful than joyous. All these people were pleased for her, glad that one of their own, someone they had traveled with and been tired and hopeful and despairing with, had now the sudden acclaim they all wanted – if only for one night.

One of them had to be the first kernel in the hopper to pop, and while they had expected it would be Anthony De Forest, he had left them.

Arlette sat on the bed and listened to Minerva:

How incredible! I'm more pleased for them than for myself.

She laughed aloud, the rich, warm, flowing laugh which Baptista had told her would make a man fall in love with her even if she were not beautiful.

'What the hell are you laughing about? This is the greatest day of your life!'

'It may be,' Arlette agreed softly. 'Nothing like it may ever happen to me again.'

Eva was the next to call, and once more Arlette heard with astonishment the honest pleasure her friends found in her playing a difficult part and playing it well.

'You're a star! You'll never be anything else again!'

'Oh, Eva!' Arlette protested seriously. 'Please don't say that. It may have been only good luck. I can't remember a god damn thing.'

'Arlette – you did it for all of us!'

'I knew you were there. I would have hated like hell to let you down. It sounds corny. It's only a play,' Arlette said gently, hoping to take away a part of the curse of this hubris.

'Only our whole lives!'

'I know,' Arlette murmured consolingly. 'I know.'

Eva hung up, weeping, and Arlette began to cry.

After several minutes she went to rinse her face, comb her hair, and gaze accusingly into the mirror, asking how it was that Lily Malone should be crying when she had

237

played Juliet and, it seemed, played her well; played her, perhaps, with the ferocity she had felt.

However little she could remember, Arlette knew at least that she had stepped onto the stage with her heart full of the savagery of her own Juliet, a savagery concealed by her composed brilliant expression; and it might be she had given the audience an unexpected Juliet: nice girls, after all, did not die for love.

Neither does anyone else.

Arlette picked up the telephone to hear Gordon Donahue's voice.

'Alicia just read the reviews to me—'

Arlette began to cry again. 'Oh, Gordon! I wish you'd been here! It's the only time I'll be able to do it. I can't even remember what I did—'

Gordon's voice was comforting. He talked as he had during the years when they had been lovers, while Arlette, soothed by her confidence in him, stopped crying, listened, and began to wonder what had made her hysterical in the first place.

In the past she had been grateful, and sometimes resentful of what he had done to help her. Now she saw him sitting in his office, smiling as he talked, combing his black hair with his fingers, and an ease flowed through her, as if a soothing magical fluid were being poured into her veins. Gordon Donahue was, after all, the man who had insisted that Lily Malone become Arlette Morgan.

'Do you know where I'd be today, Gordon, if it weren't for you?'

'You might be exactly where you are.'

'If you hadn't given Jade Ring to me instead of to Barbara Sloan – I'd be in Borneo!'

They began to laugh, as they had laughed on the Sundays when they had slept late and made love, ate breakfast and talked, gone walking and stopped at the museums to visit their favorite pictures, linger about the cases of T'ang ceramics, as if they were relics from the attic of a recently deceased maiden aunt.

'If Miss Knight doesn't recover too fast, I'll try to get back there—'

'Oh, Gordon, I do love you—'

She stopped, afraid he might have misunderstood the kind of love she was talking about.

'I love you, Arlette. I always will.'

'We've been good for each other, for a long time.' The doorbell rang, a brief hesitant ring. 'Good-bye—'

The bell rang again, several quick impatient rings, and she hung up, as if this must be a summons to heaven or to hell. She ran out of the bedroom, then stopped.

No one rang her doorbell unless they had been announced by the doorman. Whoever it was had been recognized.

She peered through the peephole, but the distortion made it impossible to be sure if that was Jerry Hoffman or a florist's delivery man. She opened it, and Jerry handed her a bouquet of two dozen white roses, enveloped in green florist's paper, looking at her with a shy smile. 'Hi – I brought these.'

'Come in.' He hesitated and she grabbed his arm as the telephone began to ring, then ran out, carrying the flowers. She snatched up the telephone, cried, 'I'm not here!' and put it on the bed, disconnected.

She went back to the living room, still carrying the bouquet, and smiled at him, remembering that she was wearing the white silk robe, not very securely fastened. She went into the kitchen, pulling the sash into a tighter knot, and began to arrange the flowers. Jerry Hoffman had never been there before, and it seemed that someone she did not know had arrived.

'I'll make tea,' she told him as he appeared in the kitchen doorway, smiling as he watched her, the thoughtful, concerned, sorrowful smile she had sometimes seen while he watched a rehearsal. Arlette did not imagine she could read Jerry Hoffman's mind, generally agreed to be sealed like a walnut – full of meat, no doubt, but closed fast against curious outsiders.

'I shouldn't have come bursting in like this, but I kept

trying to call and the bloody line was busy. I wanted to give you something—' He gestured toward the flowers. 'They're for the way you played it. Thanks.' He had disappeared from the doorway. 'See you tomorrow.' She ran after him into the living room.

'But please have a drink, or tea, or something to eat?'

The door was open, and if he moved at his usual rate, in another moment he would be gone.

He hesitated and, taking that for a good sign, she ran back, no more aware of what she was doing than he seemed to be, returned with the vase and set it on a low table, then rushed out again, telling him to shut the door and sit down. She was back presently with two glasses of iced tea.

Jerry drank the tea at a gulp, remarking that it was very hot outside, and Arlette watched him, thinking that here was another species of fate: he had not been able to reach her by telephone, and so he had come. She had been there, not at Alicia's or having a lunch of celebration with Minerva and Eva. And she was wearing that white silk robe, which concealed only enough for the sake of nominal modesty.

No doubt there was a prophecy in the making here – if she could keep Jerry Hoffman from slipping away from her. Today she was full of triumph. Tomorrow the gods might change their minds.

'I'd better be on my way. Got to take the kids to the park.' He smiled. 'Married man, paterfamilias—'

He started for the door, and again she intercepted him.

They stood looking at each other for several moments, until slowly there appeared on his face that look of surprised pain she recognized as the look of a man who felt himself betrayed into a woman's sexual power.

'What's the trouble, Arlette?' His voice was low, encouraging, concerned. He was looking at her seriously, and the expression of painful desire had disappeared in the professional concern for the next night's performance.

'Do you think they felt sorry for me? Having to take Jennifer's place?'

Jerry laughed sharply. 'Arlette, you know critics aren't sorry for anyone. I was at the hospital this morning, by the way. She still can't talk. The doctor says it's nothing serious.' He smiled. 'It never is anything serious with Jennifer. Just enough to give her a few days or a couple of weeks to hide – from whatever the hell she's hiding from.'

All at once Arlette felt quite superior to Jennifer Knight. She knew about fear; she knew about terror, and was not hiding. When the time had come – however terrified – she had walked onto the stage.

'If she has to hide, why did she try to act in the first place?'

Jerry gave a sharp impatient laugh. 'Why, Arlette? Why doesn't someone pick out exactly what will make him happy every moment of his life – and then do it?'

She looked at him carefully. He was angry. Only because of what she had said about Jennifer? Or because of what he was thinking about her?

Perhaps he was thinking – as actors complained some directors did think – that the actor was his puppet.

But that was not what they said about Jerry Hoffman. He was thought almost unique in believing that actors were human, that they felt pain, wept tears, loved and were loved, and might be struck dead by a glancing blow which someone less vulnerable would not notice.

'Even so,' she said very softly, staring past him, 'I must try to do it again tomorrow night, and maybe several more nights. Until she comes back.'

'You will.'

She glanced at him doubtfully. His face was somber as they looked at each other, asking the same question, finding the same answer. His hands slipped beneath the robe, pushing it slowly down her arms until it came apart and fell to the floor. 'I've been thinking about this for a long time,' he told her gravely. 'I swore to Christ I wasn't going to do it.' His mouth touched hers. 'But I am. I am—'

CHAPTER 29

It was men who were the keepers of secrets, and it was men who knew what knowledge was – if there was such a thing.

The search had gone on, one way or another, for as long as Arlette could remember: the secret of how her own life had begun; the fluid seed of the young man who had been her father; only she and Michael were left to testify for him.

Frederick had given her secrets, woven into the web of her nerves. He had shown her the world as it looked to him, and that was how much of it now looked to her.

Jack Davidson had been expected to give her more than he was able to give, although at first she had felt a mystical conviction of having achieved some final knowledge.

You haven't answered my question.

What was the question?

Michael, she had supposed, now, at twenty-two, soon to become an associate professor of microbiology, might answer that question one day, if she asked him often enough. She asked him again, when he came to see her Juliet and they went to supper.

'Do you know yet, Michael? What is it – that secret you're after?'

Michael always smiled as the question was asked each time they met. 'No, Arlette. I suppose we are looking for some moment when life might have begun. Of course, even if we think we find it, we can never be sure. It may be only one way it could have happened, out of millions. We can never retrace the steps. They've been obliterated by the processes of life developing itself. We search as much for the excitement of the search as for the hope of discovery.'

The same reason she had for acting.

Yet it seemed that whenever she fell in love, this time

it would reveal the ultimate secret. Her search was not so long a one or so ambitious as Michael's.

She wanted only the secret of that one man, the center of his individuality. She expected he would reveal it inadvertently, since no man would give away the secret of his individuality if he knew he was doing it.

There had been times, with Anthony, when the discovery seemed to have been made in some clear moment of exquisite pleasure. But like the occasional dream which seemed to be making some profound statement, that secret was gone before the return to complete consciousness.

Still, if it was to be found anywhere, it would be found in those minutes of unity, when her senses drove her into tormented excitement, as if each nerve ending were being coerced into streaming delight:

I swore to Christ I wasn't going to do it. But I am. I am—

Jerry made love the way he directed a play: he controlled the experience by some undefinable means.

He moved so quickly, throwing aside his clothes, she did not know if he had stopped kissing her to take them off, and he was inside her, directing her feelings and movements with all the authority he brought to directing any complex dramatic orchestration of emotion and behavior.

As with his actors, he began by taking her captive. She looked up at him briefly, surprised by the suddenness and completeness of intimacy, and closed her eyes. His movements began a remorseless acceleration which carried her with him, as he carried his actors from one level to another, lifting their confidence to a higher pitch, gradually but steadily quickening the pace of excitement, demanding from her greater effort, greater energy, forcing her to conform to the rhythm he set until she was clenching her fists in despair of matching his demands.

He acquired that dominance which he acquired over each member of the cast, giving them a conviction of strength and capability they had never suspected, and then all at once – with a few swift-spoken words of warning –

he moved at a pace she could no longer sustain, and then lay still upon her while she held him fast, reflecting with a vague distant curiosity that, yes, lovemaking and life were the same.

At last Jerry sat up, arms clasped about his knees, his forehead resting against his hands. His body was more muscular than she had expected – when he was dressed he appeared quite slender – and his skin glistened. He sat motionless for some time, while she watched him.

She began to feel a sense of strangeness. This man who had been inside her now seemed formidable, intimidating. She closed her eyes and presently heard him get up and begin to dress.

She felt his hand on her breast and looked at him. He knelt on one knee and kissed her gently. 'Thank you. You're as beautiful as I thought – good-bye.'

He was out the door before she could answer – and, anyway, she had no answer.

She began to distrust him almost immediately. And when she saw him the next night, as she entered the theater – for apparently he felt it necessary to be there now that a new actress had usurped his earlier Juliet's place – she avoided passing him.

She went into Jennifer's dressing room, which had been assigned to her, although she did not want it, for Jennifer's clothes hung there, Jennifer's cosmetics were scattered upon the long table, Jennifer's telegrams were stuck in the mirror, and Jennifer's strong gardenia perfume was in the air.

Arlette had at first been pleased to be given the star's dressing room, but now she felt like an intruder.

Someone, Jennifer Knight, had just left in great haste, although her dresser had hung her clothes on the rack and emptied the wastebasket.

She carefully avoided examining Jennifer's cosmetics, costumes, wigs – and told herself they were not there.

Yet she was grateful for the privacy of Jennifer Knight's room, since no one was chattering, no one was obtruding another demanding personality, and she began, very slowly, to enter into what she must concentrate upon for the next two hours – an effort which seemed hopeless.

Suddenly, she sank into an element different as water from air. She had drowned Arlette.

The nervousness began to clutch at her stomach, her body began to quiver, and she could quiet her hands only by staring at herself, demanding why Arlette was such a coward:

What are you afraid of?

She had Juliet's life and death to endure – not her own.

She came out of the dressing room when a light knock let her know she had two minutes, and stood watching the action, thinking that to the audience the stage must look as if it were populated by the world's most self-confident people – speaking their lines clearly, never forgetting a word, killing each other, fighting, falling in love, drinking dangerous potions, defying parents, performing with aplomb all the most difficult chores of living. While, backstage, some were brooding in silence, others pacing in silence, glancing suspiciously about, eyes strangely fixed or wildly shining, as if one had entered a ward for the criminally insane.

Arlette did not look at Jerry and hoped he had not seen her. For if he spoke her name, she would be carried off in collapse – and who the hell would play Juliet?

And presently she heard herself speaking in a low urgent voice to the Nurse:

'Go, ask his name – if he be married,
My grave is like to be my wedding bed.'

Arlette Morgan had disappeared – until at last she snatched Romeo's dagger and stabbed herself, saying in a voice of passionate ferocity: *'This is thy sheath . . . let me die,'* and fell upon the body of Romeo with such relief she wished it were true.

She stood with the others in front of the curtain, not sure if her ears were ringing with that curious distant clangor which now and then came over her onstage, or if it was applause.

She bowed deeply, then gave her body a backward

sweep, stood erect, and gazed out into the auditorium, her face serious, accepting their praise but not treating it lightly, as Jennifer Knight did – for Jennifer could not resist smiling, as if the play had been a game.

She came off the stage feeling that vast relief which spread through her when any performance was over.

She went into Jennifer's dressing room, locked the door, and for reasons not very clear, dawdled about changing her clothes and removing some of the stage makeup. She was expecting that when at last she came out, Jerry Hoffman would be gone.

At last she opened the door and looked out. There was no one in sight. She started down the hallway which led to the rear exit, almost at a run, and was stopped at the door by Jerry Hoffman.

'Jerry!' She looked at him as if this theater was the last place where she would have expected to find him. In fact, it was. It was his habit to disappear before the curtain had come down for the last time.

Now he opened the door, and as she stepped into the street he gave a piercing whistle, gesturing for her to get into the cab. 'I was beginning to think you'd climbed out a window.' He gave her address to the driver.

This Jerry Hoffman – this man of mystery to his company, his friends, perhaps to his wife and children, himself, too – did not act upon the random impulses which took others in charge, made them say and do foolish regrettable things.

Now Jerry looked straight ahead as they rambled through the theater traffic, making their way toward the East Side, and seemed to be thinking about some abstract problem. After a time he took her hand, stroking it gently.

'I suppose you know why I waited for you.' Jerry Hoffman told his actors what he wanted and why, and he was proceeding to do the same with her.

'You wanted to talk to me?'

'I wanted to talk to you, all right. I wanted to explain a couple of things.' Arlette laughed, and he glanced at her, smiling wryly. 'I know. Who explains? I do. I always explain what I mean, what I want, how I think it can be done by a certain actor, and how close I think they can come to it. What were you expecting me to do tonight?'

'I wasn't expecting anything. I was worrying about what I would do.'

'Good,' he said, as if she had got that answer right and now he could proceed to the next one: if she knew where the continent of Australia was located, they could go on to speak of Tasmania.

And so he did, except that Tasmania proved a territory more surprising than she had expected.

'I'm not going to fall in love with you.'

'All right, Jerry.'

He looked at her with a trace of anger, but then held her hand harder, kissed her fingertips, and looked ahead through the traffic, his eyes slightly narrowed. 'This won't last long. A few weeks. A few months.' He shrugged. 'I'm serious about you. I'm serious about everything – that's my problem. But I've got some saving grace of self-protection. Am I clear?'

Jerry Hoffman was as explicit in directing his life as he was in directing his actors. He stated the problem – and the solution – at one and the same time.

'Yes, Jerry. You're clear.'

He was silent another few minutes. 'You played a Juliet I've never seen before: a savage, outside the norms of her family, and even her society. And she is cruel – she kills them both. Not entirely by the accident of hard luck. You saw it that way, and you played it that way – and you had never told me that if Jennifer Knight's hex gave you the chance, that's the way you would do it.'

'Everything else I'd seen looked a little wrong. All the classes. But I might have copied Jennifer.'

Jerry laughed aloud, joyously. Among his other surprises, he had a habit of returning abruptly, if momentarily, to his very young manhood. 'What a Lady Macbeth you'll make someday!'

She started as if he had spoken some unimaginable profanity. 'Jerry! Don't even think about it!'

At her apartment house, Jerry paid the driver without a questioning glance at her, and as she unlocked the door to her apartment, said: 'I won't stay long.'

Jerry never did stay long, as it turned out.

He had no interest in converting a rampant affair into a mock-domestic drama, complete with playing in the bathtub, sharing breakfast; he never made love to her in bed, as if that might too forcibly remind him of the monotony of the marital domain. He made love on the sofa, on the floor, on a chair, naked or almost fully clothed, quickly or lingeringly, only once, or two or three times – and a few minutes after it was finally over, he left. Still, she never felt that now she no longer interested him and so he was going. He left because this was only a part of their lives.

Two weeks to the day after she had lost her voice, Jennifer Knight returned to the cast, with a welcome as if she had risen from the dead.

That, thought Arlette bitterly, watching the hysterical demonstration, was the treachery of this world. They were not pretending – they were glad she was back. Just as, two weeks ago, when Jennifer had suffered an attack of laryngitis, they had been glad of that.

An actor, she decided, if chemically analyzed, would be found to be two parts quicksilver, one part commercial diamond.

Arlette, who had felt she had been living in a whirling kaleidoscope, retired to her balcony seat and knew her triumph had ended. It was Jennifer's tradition to interrupt a show only once. Twice, she no doubt understood, would be once too often.

Arlette sat, more critical than ever of Jennifer's perform-ance, feeling defeated and abandoned, even though no one treated her any differently. It was obvious that her playing of Juliet in the way she had played it had changed their opinion of her. So far as they were concerned, she was not quite a star, but that was where she was going.

'And now?' she asked Jerry. 'Do I at least get to keep the slipper?'

CHAPTER 30

Even when she had not talked to him for more than four months, and even though she was in love – however they avoided the word – with Jerry Hoffman, Arlette was still trying to balance the ledger against Anthony De Forest.

It had become a hobby, and she worked on it at odd moments: riding in a taxi; glancing through the morning paper; while she washed her hair or made up her face. Whenever she was not entirely engrossed in what she was doing, she found herself picking up this piecework and adding a few negative touches.

Anthony was an easy subject for her denigration. Anthony was ruthless. Anthony was competitive, determined to turn all attention, all emotion, all excitement upon himself. He was not interested in means, but in ends. He was ambitious beyond the bounds of common decency, and she felt he meant to gobble up the theater entire and digest it.

With all this, the wonder was she had ever imagined she was in love with him. But Anthony was not, after all, so easy to forget.

Now and then she heard or read about *Jane Eyre*. He was said to have picked up the knack of underacting for the camera as readily as he had been able to demonstrate the greater stress required for a character onstage.

Evidently Anthony's Scotch-Irish handsomeness, slightly hostile, his smile, dazzling but never reassuring, the suggestion that he was mettlesome as a blooded stallion, had inspired his producers and press agents with hope that here they had a new variety of movie idol, one who was Hollywood-proof.

What was more, he had the appropriate wife, since she was not like other movie stars' wives: a remote young woman, serenely patient with photographers, who conveyed the impression that she was not interested in this prank of her husband's.

There were photographs of their houses: her family's house, his family's house, their own house, all in Pasadena. No flight to Bel Air for the De Forests. They could stay where they had been put by birth.

In several photographs he was dressed as Rochester, an even more becoming era for him than Elizabethan England, staring sullenly at the little governess.

Yes, it was all there. The selfishness, the exaggerated sense of individuality, the anarchic indifference to others' needs and wishes, as well as the zest, the flourishing health, the temptation presented by an unusually pure form of male beauty. What was good about him he owed to luck; what was bad was his own choice.

At last she decided the ledger could not be balanced. Time would have to do the job. Time, and her own work.

Early one morning, as she was about to leave for her first class, she picked up the telephone. 'Yes?' No one called at that hour. Certainly not Jerry.

'Hi.'

'Hi *who*?' She was angry, less with him than with herself.

'Arlette, for Christ's sake.'

'Why – Anthony.'

They had seen each other last nearly one year ago, and there was no more to be said than *Hi.*

'I'm in New York.'

He was in New York. What of that? 'New York?' Someplace she had not heard of.

'We've finished the picture. It's being edited.'

'What was it like?' Arlette inquired, and was sorry to hear a wistful note in her voice.

'Bleak moors, torrential rains, winds whipping up our clothes and tearing off our wigs. The melancholy of the lonely heath. The house in flames and Rochester dashing in to save his mad wife – afraid she might escape and turn up again someday.'

Arlette was silent. He had despised it, or wanted her to think he had. 'Has it been what you wanted?' To her surprise, the interest was real, the concern was honest. The intimacy was there. He might have walked out of the hotel room, glancing back with that curious smile, on his way to meet Lydia at the airport, only a few minutes before.

'I found out I could do it, if that's what you mean.'

'Do you like it? The working part, at least?'

'Not particularly. There's a hell of a lot of boredom, and a hell of a lot more shit – but after it's over, the public knows you. They see to that, all right. I think – I hope – it may make coming back here easier and quicker.'

'I hope it does, Anthony.'

Arlette was aware of a shrinking of her pride, as if, during the month they had spent together, she had inadvertently sacrificed to Anthony some part of her confidence; worst of all, she had sacrificed something of her belief in her destiny. Now, it was only Anthony De Forest who seemed one of those rare creatures equipped at birth with a destiny – an appointment with a Fate meant for no one but him.

'Arlette – I want to see you.'

'What for?'

There was a brief silence, and then a soft, slightly embarrassed laugh. 'I want to see you. Any time you're free. I want to talk to you about your Juliet – I hear you were great. Whenever you like. I'll pick you up and we can have lunch or dinner. I want to see you.' The last sentence was not spoken by a friend from out of town. There was some desperation in it, and some fear.

'I have no time, Anthony.'

'As I've told you, Arlette, Thyssen is here. I'm leaving with him tomorrow. The bloody picture has to be edited. He's doing me a favor. Tomorrow morning at eleven-thirty we—' He paused, and when she said nothing, added: 'Tell me when I can see you.'

All at once Arlette was in a great hurry to hang up, run out of the house, to be at her calisthenics class, where no thinking was possible.

'You can't see me at all, today or any other day.'

There was a silence, which she sensed as a literal weight. 'That's it?'

'That's it. Good-bye.'

They hung up, apparently at the same moment. She ran out of the apartment, putting on her coat in the elevator, talking to the operator with unusual vivacity and concern about the weather: very cold, very windy; really? Snow maybe.

Once in the cab she grew unexpectedly quiet and peaceful, as if some great battle had ended.

Then, looking out the window as they rattled along, she was surprised it had ended so easily, so painlessly:

Who were the strugglers, what war did they wage?

And, a little sadly, she thought of the bitterness she had felt toward Anthony, who had given her so much pleasure, more than she had imagined possible; and perhaps, had given her love with it.

The next morning she threw out the newspaper without opening it, afraid of finding his picture, even more afraid of finding Lydia's picture, with him and the children. That had happened several times by now, and she had come to dread being taken by surprise.

She returned to the apartment at nine o'clock, after having dinner with Alicia, and neither during the class nor at dinner was there any mention that Anthony had been in town. He must, of course, have seen Alicia or talked to her, and during the day Arlette had heard there had been photographs of Anthony and Lydia and the children, standing on the plane steps, waving good-bye to friends and admirers.

A florist's box was given her as she came in. There were two dozen dark red peonies, flower of the Middle Kingdom, symbol of everlasting love. She found a card: 'Arlette. Anthony.'

There was a letter in the mail the next morning which contained a business card:

ARTHUR FRIEDMAN ASSOCIATES
Dear Miss Morgan: I would appreciate an opportunity to talk with you. My secretary will call. Arthur Friedman.

Now, who had arranged that?
She never found out, for she did not ask any likely suspects and no one told her.

Alicia Fiedler? Alicia had mentioned him, calling him the best agent in town, which had made him the only agent in town.

Jerry Hoffman? Jerry had told her she needed an agent, but she must not take any agent at all; only Arthur Friedman. Agents, he had assured her, were to an actor a permanent alliance; and while love affairs and husbands and wives might come and go, an effective agent went on forever.

Had the suggestion come from Gordon?

Anthony? Arthur Friedman was Anthony's agent. But if it was Anthony, why now?

They had been waiting, one or all of them, for something: Juliet, perhaps.

Fate comes when it will, Arlette reminded herself on the way to Mr Friedman's office, in the elevator en route to the thirty-second floor.

She stepped out, and with Jade Ring's bewitching smile, flowers added to embroidery, softly gave her name to the receptionist who sat at a large desk, behind which hung a large Miro.

Arlette waited, nervous one moment and confident the next, reminding herself that she must be serene, smiling. However he may have gotten her address and her unlisted number, he was Arthur Friedman Associates.

But once she was in his presence, shaking his hand, taking the chair he indicated, she found herself confused not only by Arthur Friedman but by his surroundings: areas of polished wood, sofas and chairs upholstered in brown suede, a desk almost bare but for one implement of his trade, a telephone with what appeared to be dozens of flashing lights, which he ignored; several contemporary paintings, some by artists unknown to her. Whatever she had expected a famous agent to be, Mr Friedman, who was forty years old, was it.

'I liked your Juliet,' he told her, and smiled vaguely, placing his fingertips together to form a temple. She was not certain if he was being polite or if he had seen in it what Jerry Hoffman and Alicia Fiedler had seen. But then she reminded herself that Arthur Friedman was not an actor — he was not inside that world in which they depended upon one another for confidence and support. He was a tradesman, a barterer.

'Thank you.'

'I've talked to a few people about you.'

'Oh?' asked Arlette, her voice rising like a flute.

'That's not a very reliable guide,' he added. 'I prefer to follow my own instincts.'

Well, of course. Why not? A man in his position could tell a young woman in her position that he was where he was because he followed his nose, his astrologer, or the advice of an old maiden aunt. However he did it, he did it.

Arlette waited for what he had to say about his instincts. If he was the agent he was reported to be, the flattery of young actresses would only seem silly to him.

'I saw you twice. The first time I was quite taken aback. It was a Juliet I'd never seen before. I went the second time because I wanted to be sure you were doing it intentionally.'

Arlette laughed, a full free laugh, the laugh of a young high-spirited girl with a woman's sensual wisdom, and then looked at him soberly, waiting.

'It was intentional,' he told her.

'Of course.'

'You have the ability to concentrate.'

'Yes.'

'You have the will to work.' She nodded. 'That's not quite the same thing as a willingness to work. Many

254

actors are willing to work, but the real will for it is not there.'

'I know.'

'You obviously take nothing for granted, since you paid little attention to the usual concept of Juliet, and so you must have an inquiring habit of mind. A valuable thing for an actor.'

'I hope so.'

'Miss Morgan, I'm going to send you a script. It's a contemporary comedy – the theater isn't all blood and sorrow – and I like it. If you do, the director will give you an audition.'

Arlette left the office in a stupor, after shaking Mr Friedman's hand and thanking him, then stopped when she was outside the building and drew several deep breaths which brought her senses back from wherever they had wandered to.

She took out her appointment book: *11:00 AM: VOICE.*

The manuscript arrived the next day and she sat down to read it without taking her coat off until, after two hours, she had finished it and began it again, noticed the room had become warm, and threw the coat on the floor.

It was called *A Night and a Day*, and she had met the playwright several times. He had married one of the girls from the Downtown Drama School, a girl she and Eva and Minerva had thought showed some of the same promise they believed themselves to have: Margo Blake.

John Powell had had a play produced two and a half years before, *Summer Bouquet*, which they had gone to see for Margo's sake.

The play was nostalgic: a sixteen-year-old boy, spending a summer as a waiter at a mountain resort; a beautiful, spoiled young girl; disapproving rich parents; unconsummated love; loss and – thereby – learning.

It had been a play of moods, the playwright's own, she supposed, remembrance of times past, and although it had had an affecting tenderness, it seemed like something which either had or should have happened to every member of the audience. It had lacked the resonance which might have made them lonely for their own youth, rather than merely sympathetic with two pretty but not wildly determined young people. Obstacles defeated them too easily, and this had made the audience uneasy; it was their history, too.

The obvious good will of the playwright and his deep feeling for the young boy and girl had gotten him several good reviews, but the audience had not been singed by the experience, and the play had run only a few weeks.

She began the manuscript expecting this would be another, slightly older, slightly less autobiographical version of the same play – untraced by any of the cruel insights which came of themselves to people who kept their eyes and hearts alert.

But *A Night and a Day* was a play of a different kind, with such different characters, so much malice and irony, humor and good-natured cynicism, that either Mr Powell had changed greatly or he now knew other people from those who had inhabited his boyhood.

This play had only two characters: a young woman in her middle twenties; a man in his middle forties.

The man, Alicia had told her, was to be played by Jeffrey Brooke.

Jeffrey Brooke was a golden opportunity for any actress of any age. No matter what the play, Jeffrey Brooke would make it succeed, if there was an inkling of success in it. And Jeffrey Brooke would not have agreed to do it if there was not.

Arlette had seen him in several movies, and when Barbara Sloan was fifteen, he had been her ideal man. (He had continued to be, until Pat Runkle appeared on the campus in their junior year.)

But Jeffrey Brooke was more than a handsome movie star. He could also command a stage, and he was of an age where his command had reached its full maturity. He could carry, it was said, any vehicle, as well as weaker actors and actresses; Jeffrey Brooke was described as if he might be a superior drayman.

Whatever else, she decided, the young Mr Powell of *Summer Bouquet* had turned into quite a different kind of playwright, whether because he had become wise in the ways of the public or because youthful nostalgia was like fog in the early morning – not much sunlight was needed to disperse it. His first play, she supposed, was a bouquet Mr Powell had never picked, but only fantasized as an outsider, from the real perils and excitements of being young.

But *A Night and a Day* was witty and sardonic, a little cruel, and uncompromisingly comic: life was comedy, sex was comedy, love was comedy. The human being was comedy: body, heart, behavior. There was no trace of bitterness.

'Whatever happened to John Powell?' Arlette asked Alicia the next afternoon. 'Marrying Margo Blake and having that kid couldn't have changed him this much.'

Alicia laughed, that low delicious laugh from her acting life. 'Maybe it did. But that's unkind to Margo. Something happens to all of us in three years.'

CHAPTER 31

Arlette arrived at the appointed time. Ten-thirty on a Saturday morning, unhappy at the prospect of this private screening Jerry Hoffman had arranged, so that she and Alicia, the other members of the caravan, along with two of Anthony's lawyers, Arthur Friedman, and three of his subagents, could see *Jane Eyre* before the Hollywood premiere one week from then.

'I'll let you know,' Jerry had said, leaving her apartment.

He came to her when he could find time, and when she could find time, and just now it was more difficult for him than it was for her. He was rehearsing Nadine Logan in

Candida, and Arlette had several months to wait until Jeffrey Brooke had finished his film.

She often doubted it was a real script, that it had a producer and a director, and that one day she would step onto the stage in the double role of Elizabeth Doyle-Gloriana and try her luck at not being swallowed whole by Jeffrey Brooke.

She and Alicia had gone on with their usual studies in the classic repertoire, and Arlette was ashamed that Jerry Hoffman was now directing another actress.

Sometimes, it seemed, Jerry was ashamed of it, too; or he was, at least, unaccountably surly. Perhaps he was in love with her; or perhaps he suspected she thought she should have had the part of Candida, even though she had no interest in playing it, now or ever.

This won't last long, he had said. *A few weeks or months.*

Now it had lasted seven months. The time must be almost up, she supposed, and she never saw him without some apprehension that this time, he would advise her, was the last time. He had never spent the night with her, and had assured her that among the other defects of marriage was the incessant presence of the other; the failure, slow but inevitable and terrible, of any capacity for surprise.

And Jerry had an unspoken but strong jealousy of Anthony; perhaps that was why he was determined to have her sit through the screening at his side.

'I've heard it's good,' Jerry said when she protested that she was not interested. He looked at her shrewdly, and Arlette, who had been sitting on the floor while they drank tea and ate cold chicken and black bread, stood up quickly, a tray in either hand, and disappeared into the kitchen. 'I've heard he's good.'

Arlette stood in the doorway. 'Is he?'

Jerry got to his feet, agile as a cat, snatched up the sheepskin-lined canvas coat which, it seemed, was his only coat, since he wore it over slacks and a sweater when it was snowing; he wore it when it was raining; and he wore it over his dinner jacket when he was obliged to dress in one.

His hand was on the knob, and she ran to touch his face, kiss him before he was gone. Once Jerry decided it was time to go, he might have been a man leaving a burning building. But something had been left unsaid which he must have meant to say.

'You may not believe this, Arlette – but so help me, Christ, you're the first woman I've ever worked with that I've made love to.' He smiled, as if the admission embarrassed him. 'It gets everything screwed up.' He kissed her. 'I'll let you know.'

Arlette was alarmed. 'Let me know when you'll call me?'

'No, baby. When I can arrange the screening. Okay?' He smiled, the slightly mocking smile which appeared now and then, and was on his way down the hall.

They had never talked about Anthony, but for some casual exchanges on what the newspapers and magazines and the professional grapevine reported. But there it was, and she knew it shamed him. Jealousy came too close to possessive love for Jerry Hoffman's comfort.

She closed the door:

He'll leave me one day. But he'll never take from me the right to ask for his help when I need it.

For as long as they lived, they would inhabit this special small world; they would never be far from each other. And it was that future which Jerry would preserve for them.

He tried to reason away Arlette's regret that she had committed herself to a contemporary comedy – the part of Elizabeth Doyle, ambitious editor in a publishing house, whose new telephone number had belonged to a call girl named Gloriana:

Gloriana who? she asked herself. *Gloriana, that's all. What the hell needs to go with Gloriana?*

She had been eager, after the contract was signed, to begin work with Alicia. But after a few explorations it was clear she was convinced if she played this part it might destroy her future as a classical actress.

The first day she and Alicia had met to consider the possibilities, she had entered Alicia's apartment in high spirits, buoyed by the euphoria of her recently signed contract, her acquisition not only of a part opposite Jeffrey Brooke, but of Arthur Friedman as her agent. The world must be good to have provided all this in only a few weeks.

She stood beside the fireplace and waited for Alicia to make her entrance. Alicia always made an entrance, and it was an impressive and instructive thing to see. Alicia's entrances had been another component of her fame, and there were actors who talked about them still. Alicia entered at times under full sail; at other times she entered gently, in thought at least as deep as Hamlet's; yet other times she approached in dignified hauteur, as if the rabble must be cleared to make way for her.

'Do you like the part, now that you've had time to think about it?'

Any new part was a difficult task for an actress as inexperienced as Arlette. A play others had seen, discussed, performed, had come to inhabit the universe, as if the air contained these spirits of the human imagination. But a new play had projected no spirits as yet. It was still inert matter.

Arlette opened her hands in a tragic gesture, a queen whose kingdom had been lost. But she spoke in a normal tone. 'I don't want to play a girl who has never even thought of killing herself – or someone else.'

Alicia had warned her, before she signed the contract, that she must not even consider the part if she was going to be supercilious. And Arlette was being supercilious.

'How do you know she hasn't?' Alicia asked. 'Because it isn't on page twenty-three?'

As Arlette reflected on her troubles, she folded her hands, crossed her ankles, and tried to think of a suitable way to explain that this play was too trivial for her. She ought to be studying, studying, studying, until the great part came along. Finally she said it.

'Comes along – how, Arlette? Someone must have seen you, must have heard of you from others who have. Juliet is not a permanent stamp in their minds. This world you've chosen has a short memory.'

'Oh, yes. It does.'

'Now – is there anything about her that interests you?'

'Not that I know of,' said Arlette, aloof and resistant.

'Then we won't discuss it until you find something. It's there. You're not looking in the right places, and I'm not going to point them out.'

By the time for the preview of *Jane Eyre*, Arlette still had not found anything to present to Alicia about Elizabeth Doyle or her alter ego, Gloriana. Perhaps her trouble, she admitted to herself, was that she continued to measure her small accomplishments against Anthony's large ones. And so she arrived in the projection room hopeful that the film would be at the least tiresome; Anthony might be stiff, unused to the medium.

Jerry nodded casually and gestured her to a seat beside Minerva. Arlette glanced around, finding that most of the audience was the caravan, together for the first time since they had drifted their separate ways; gathered from their various projects to see what the deserter had done with his time.

After a few minutes they had taken their seats and the projection room went dark. Arlette was relieved to find Jerry beside her, as if he would help her survive seeing Anthony on the screen.

The music began, suddenly and very loud, a melody of wild storms, tensions, tenderness, anxiety – a movie theme meant for popular success – and there he was: black eyes glancing here and there, as in some angry futile search; his face filled almost the entire screen. There was a general catch of breath, and they fell silent. He was still one of them, at least so far as they were concerned.

After the first few minutes, Minerva murmured, 'Jesus, he's good,' and Arlette felt a swelling in her throat of pride and gratitude, for alongside the mean-spirited Arlette, there was another Arlette, who wanted him to astound them all.

Even so, she found it difficult to concentrate upon the way the novel had been reworked; the costumes and sets; the cutting – for she was concentrating on Rochester, trying to determine if he had made love to Larka Haverill.

When Rochester's horse slipped on the ice and he fell, Arlette involuntarily caught her breath. And when Rochester gloomily told Jane: '*Remorse is the poison of life,*' Arlette advised him: *I'm glad you've found that out.*

When Rochester took Jane to walk in the garden and told her she must leave Thornfield, Arlette was surprised to see that he looked at Jane with that same challenging and guilty expression his face had shown the morning he had left for the airport, remarking: *See you.*

And when Jane – in childbed, wan and triumphant – turned back the coverlet to show him his infant son, Anthony took up the baby and held him with an easy authority which made her press her fist to her mouth:

Yes, he's a good father – he knows how to handle a child . . .

When the lights came up, there were tears in her eyes, and she looked quickly away from Jerry. There was a burst of excited applause, heads turning, faces smiling, as if to congratulate one another upon their own Petruchio having so distinguished himself.

Minerva kissed her cheek and disappeared, without a word. Arlette, after a long moment while she sat in silence, found Jerry watching her. He raised his eyebrows questioningly, and she nodded. She could think of nothing to say.

The others were filing out, talking, still of the film, although they were beginning to go back to their own concerns: auditions, new parts, openings, rehearsals. At the door, Arlette and Jerry paused to speak to Grumio.

The film had, no doubt, a strange effect, casting a bewitchment in and of itself, not contrived from their memories of the caravan days. Grumio made a face, turning his mouth down, shrugging. It was his indication that his master, Petruchio, was a strange man, a difficult man, but – as he had early advised them when Petruchio arrived in Padua – *a wise man.*

'Well?' asked Jerry.

'Just for a riband to stick in his coat,' said Grumio.

'Or an Oscar to put on his shelf,' replied Arlette. She smiled at them, but Jerry was watching her with dour suspicion.

By the time they reached the street, the caravan had disappeared among the hurrying pedestrians, become, like them, specters, ghosts, the disembodied spirits of New York streets, never seen, never clearly felt or experienced, unless they did something extraordinary, fell beneath a taxi, got stabbed by a passerby. And Grumio disappeared as quickly.

Jerry and Arlette stood facing each other questioningly; both of them looked baffled, resentful, it seemed, not only of Anthony De Forest but of each other.

'When's your next class?'

'Ballet. Two o'clock.'

They went into a nearby restaurant, Jerry ordered hot bean soup for both of them, and while they waited, Arlette pretended to glance about as if she found the patrons remarkably interesting. Jerry looked at her skeptically.

'Jerry?' she inquired at last.

'How the hell do I know what you're thinking?' he demanded.

To Arlette's dismay, her eyes filled with tears.

He stared at her suspiciously, for he knew she could cry whenever the character she was playing called for it.

'I'm thinking about you, Jerry,' she said softly. She began eating the hot thick soup.

Tears were running slowly down her face, which no doubt made it seem all the more like acting to him: Juliet, waiting for Romeo. Katharina, learning patience from her savage husband.

'Like hell you are.' Jerry refused to look at her; the tears might be real or might be faked, but they troubled him, and when they parted outside the restaurant, he did not say good-bye.

Candida was to open three nights later, and Arlette was not surprised that he did not call. And that, she thought, might mean this was the time he had warned her about: the day when Jerry Hoffman decided it was best for Jerry Hoffman not to see her alone again.

Two weeks later there was an announcement in *Variety* that Anthony De Forest had signed a contract to play *Jude the Obscure*, in a film which would be made in England. Sue Bridehead would be played by Larka Haverill, and Susan Miller would play Arabella. But that was not what was most interesting: the director and producer would be Charles Granville. Arlette dropped the paper on the floor of the taxi and sighed as if she had read her death sentence.

Jerry Hoffman called that night, speaking as confidently as if there had been no quarrel, and when Arlette began to congratulate him on *Candida*, he laughed, a sound of secretive triumph, and asked her: 'Have you tried thinking of Elizabeth Doyle as a domineering, charming, vengeful, sensual bitch?'

Arlette listened, repeating Elizabeth-Gloriana's characteristics to herself. 'Why, that's it. Of course. Why didn't—'

'Elizabeth is a call girl by choice. For one night. For revenge on her lover – petty revenge. And maybe she's been wondering about it all along – women do, I've heard.'

They began to laugh, and the quarrel was over. For a few months longer, Arlette guessed. A reprieve. Perhaps until he had seen her through Elizabeth-Gloriana.

'What's her specialty?' Arlette demanded quickly, hoping to get this crucial bit of information before Jerry refused ever again to discuss it.

'Whose specialty?'

'Gloriana's. These guys are so crazy to see her. Robert Dudley comes all the way from the Coast. She must have a specialty of some kind.'

Jerry was silent, and Arlette waited eagerly. If she could only discover what Gloriana's specialty was, perhaps she would have the fatal clue as to how she must be played. But then he laughed again, a brief laugh, ironic and a little cruel. 'What's yours?'

CHAPTER 32

She began to write notes to herself about Elizabeth Doyle-Gloriana. She read them and scratched them out.

What was Gloriana's specialty – since every call girl, she supposed, must have a specialty:

What's yours?

Mine?

Concentration. Concentration that flatters the hell out of them. Responsiveness.

And the mystical faith that here was life's meaning, however temporary, the only reality destined to become, so quickly, one more illusion:

If that's her secret, there's no way I can convey it, not even if Jeffrey Brooke screwed Gloriana onstage. I'll have to find some way to look as if Elizabeth knows all this as well as Gloriana does.

'You're complicating it unnecessarily, Arlette,' Alicia told her. 'That may be a good thing, later on – but right now, you must make up your mind about Elizabeth and Gloriana.'

'I never expected to play in a contemporary comedy.'

But then, she had never expected that Anthony De Forest would be a star – quite possibly soon to be known all over the world – while she would be cast in a modern comedy by an unknown playwright, opposite an actor so skillful he would obliterate her as surely as if the electricians were to keep her in total darkness and Jeffrey Brooke in a flaring aurora borealis.

More and more she felt this was the wrong play at the wrong time of her life. Three years ago she would have been delighted. But that was before Katharina and Petruchio; that was before Jennifer Knight's laryngitis.

'*Nothing in your life will ever be the same again.*'

So Jerry had told her when he had left her apartment the night before the cast – Arlette Morgan and Jeffrey Brooke – the playwright, the director, the stage manager, were to assemble for a first meeting.

She repeated that to herself when she was introduced to the director, Thomas Marvell, a nervous, serious man. His youth and shyness gave her courage, and feeling herself a seasoned professional, she shook his hand and found it cold and the palm damp.

'Good morning, Miss Morgan. I've been looking forward to meeting you.'

Arlette smiled at him mysteriously, but did not return the compliment.

Here she was, alone with these men – the star of the show had not yet arrived – and she wanted to impress them immediately with her confidence, her fearlessness.

The only one who was not a stranger was John Powell.

John Powell was charming, and the charm seemed unself-conscious. He was tall and slender. He was only three years older than Arlette, but he seemed to have grown up since she had seen him last. His eyes were blue and the expression keen, with an eager alertness, and his light brown hair had a slight wave. He put on horn-rimmed glasses when he became uneasy, and took them off and slipped them into his coat pocket when the nervous qualm had passed.

'Thank you, Miss Morgan, for accepting this part. After I saw your Juliet, I wanted you so much.' He looked slightly disconcerted. Arlette did not smile, or only enough to let him know she was not unaware of these intrusions from the unconscious into the minds of young men so well brought up as John Powell was said to be. 'My wife,' he added, eager to repair the damage, 'made the suggestion.' That also seemed to trouble him, and he put his glasses on. 'Women, of course—'

'Intuition,' said Arlette reassuringly.

He seemed grateful. 'Of course. Juliet and Gloriana – two more different women—'

The leading man arrived, and without his presence being announced, that intuition of which they had been talking announced him to them.

Jeffrey Brooke came striding toward them, tanned, smiling, and looking to Arlette, who had seen him on the stage and screen, amazingly like Jeffrey Brooke. He advanced with the light tread of a trained athlete, or actor, and without being introduced, shook Arlette's hand, smiling at her insistently. Arlette felt slightly dizzy.

'Miss Morgan.' Even his normal voice was an actor's voice, for it had become so familiar it seemed less a voice than an object. 'Miss Morgan, I have been wanting to meet you ever since I saw your Juliet. We will make this play a great success.' He seemed to have no doubts, and now Arlette understood that the real director was Jeffrey Brooke. She felt easier. 'Gloriana has a great many potentialities for a beautiful woman with your vitality. But I'm sure you know her very well by now.'

'I'm afraid I don't.'

The three men laughed, as if exchanging news that she was clever, witty, beautiful, and without doubt she was joking. Of course she understood Gloriana, and Elizabeth Doyle. What was there to understand, after all? The play was essentially a simple one, as John Powell quickly advised them. The problem was to make it seem more complicated.

Not sure if she had been joking, Jeffrey Brooke leaned nearer, and as the screen image she had seen so often approached, Arlette instinctively drew back, quite as if he had leaned forth from the screen and might topple out of the frame like some great stone idol, knocking her flat.

'You're studying with Alicia Fiedler?'

'Yes.'

'Well, then.' He glanced at the others. How could anything go wrong where Alicia Fiedler was in charge?

'Shall we begin?' asked Mr Marvell, evidently thinking the time had come to assert his authority, if he was to have any to assert, and they sat down and began to talk. At least, Jeffrey Brooke began to talk.

'This play will be an absolute failure – for me,' Arlette told Jerry gloomily when they had been in rehearsal for two weeks.

'Jeff Brooke's not invincible,' he had assured her. 'No actor is when there's a beautiful woman on the same stage. Later, you may wish people would think less about the way you look.' He had smiled, a strange smile, almost contrite. 'But they never will. They never will.'

She and Jerry sat on the floor, where it seemed they spent most of their time together, and drank tea. He had come at eight o'clock, because she must be at the rehearsal hall at eleven, and the bright hot August day filled the room with sunlight. She was silent, staring at him morbidly. 'No matter what I do, he will have the stage to himself.'

She got up and went into the bedroom to dress. Jerry followed her – the only time he entered the bedroom – to sit in a chair and watch her put her clothes on. When she took them off, there was no time for observations, only the haste which overcame Jerry and, by contagion, Arlette, when the possibility of lovemaking was there.

'Will he?'

'Of course. Well, they say that the plays actors enjoy during rehearsal always fail. And we're certainly not enjoying this one. At least, half of us aren't.' She turned to him, fully dressed in one minute: black tights, black linen skirt, sleeveless black silk sweater, black pumps. She picked up the black leather handbag which contained everything she might need for a trip around the world or, at least, around New York for one day. She stood looking down at him, unhappy and convinced of future defeat.

As they walked through the apartment and out the door, down the elevator and the length of the long lobby, then stepped outside into the heavy beating heat, Jerry talked to her quietly. 'You can learn from Jeff Brooke if you'll stop thinking this whole deal is beneath you. It's too early for you to have such delusions. Later, you won't need them. The public tolerates the kind of work you want to do for the sake of its vanity, not because Broadway wants *Macbeth* and *Lear*. Producers regard such plays as a dose of physic, given the public to clear out its system, so it can go back to the kind of nourishment it likes. If you can't play a sharp contemporary comedy, then you sure can't play a complicated in-joke written four hundred years ago.' All at once Jerry laughed. 'You need a little larceny in your soul, Arlette.'

'What for?'

'For the occasions when you can use it.' He kissed her lightly. 'Here.' He put a card into her hand. 'Meet me tomorrow after rehearsal – six o'clock.' And he was off, dashing up the street, while Arlette got into a cab and studied the address – in the East Seventies, between Madison and Park – as attentively as if there, in code, was all her future success or failure.

He was waiting outside the four-story red brick house, surrounded by an ornate late-Victorian black iron fence, with black shutters and a black lacquered door.

'Where *are* we?'

Jerry smiled, pleased with his stratagem. 'Be patient.'

A butler admitted them to a dark entrance hall, furnished, so far as Arlette could see, with handsome antiques, the taste of a slightly eccentric but self-confident collector. They were led into the drawing room, its green velvet curtains drawn, leaving it dimly lighted by a few bulbs in wall sconces. The room was crowded with furniture, most of it eighteenth-century English, but no portraits, no photographs, nothing to give away the private life of the lady of the house.

'Darling!'

Arlette turned swiftly. Jerry was embracing, closely but carefully, a woman as tall as he, whose dark brown hair fell almost to her knees, and who wore a long-trained black lace gown with ruffles about the low neckline – a nineteenth-century costume to be worn by a member of the aristocracy receiving informally.

Jerry made the introductions. 'Mrs O'Neil, Miss Morgan.' Arlette stepped obediently forward, shook the lady's hand, and found herself slightly intimidated, as if she had happened into a strange land, ruled by a strange queen.

'What will you have?' asked Mrs O'Neil, and smiled.

The voice, smile, composure, beauty – although the lights were low, and so the beauty was evidently not what it had once been – all this meant that he had brought her to meet some *grande dame* of the theater.

But who was she?

The butler was dismissed with a light gesture, and they sat down. Jerry and Mrs O'Neil began to talk, with the animation and warmth of old friends who had not seen each other for some time. She was obviously several years older than Jerry, and yet Jerry knew everyone she mentioned, people whose names Arlette did not recognize, or recalled from newspapers and magazines she had read in school.

They might have been talking in a foreign language, but Arlette listened with polite interest and tried to guess why Jerry had brought her here, and why she could not place this Mrs O'Neil, who had the look and manner of someone who had been famous for a long time and had not forgotten it.

She was no longer on the stage, but perhaps as compensation she continued to play her roles in her own home, with friends for audience.

Jerry wanted something from Mrs O'Neil; Mrs O'Neil knew what it was and he was paying for it in advance with this elaborate display of interest in Mrs O'Neil.

For Arlette had never heard Jerry discuss retired or dead actors, or the past. Even yesterday's news did not interest him. Jerry did not step in the same river twice. Yet for fifteen minutes he had been in deep conference with Mrs O'Neil, both of them laughing – often mockingly – over old friends and old times.

'Didn't you know what happened to *her?*' asked Mrs

O'Neil in a tone of such malicious glee that Arlette listened alertly, wondering what could possibly have happened to *her*, whoever she was. 'She was bitten by a pet poodle and died of hydrophobia.'

Mrs O'Neil laughed, as Arlette caught her breath in horrified sympathy, and Jerry shook his head, marveling at the mischief fate could work.

At that moment a man came in, walking briskly, a man several years younger than Mrs O'Neil, so excessively handsome that Arlette's eyes opened wide. He was accompanied by two black poodles, and he approached Mrs O'Neil deferentially, kissing her cheek. He shook Jerry's hand, then shook Arlette's hand and smiled with the businesslike charm of a retired actor. Asking their forgiveness, he left the room.

'My husband,' Mrs O'Neil explained to Arlette. 'Isn't he beautiful?' She turned to Jerry. 'Now, darling – what, exactly, do you want?'

'I want you to teach Miss Morgan how to take off her clothes.'

Mrs O'Neil looked at Arlette, while Jerry explained Miss Morgan's problem as an actress who must contend with Jeffrey Brooke alone on a stage without being crumpled like tissue paper. 'She's a deft and ironic comedian,' he added.

'That's not enough to compete with Jeff Brooke,' said Mrs O'Neil. 'He's a deft and ironic comedian himself. It's been his business for twenty-five years.'

'She has only one chance of taking at least a part of the show away from him.'

'My dear, please stand up.'

Arlette stood, turned at Mrs O'Neil's direction, walked when she was told to, turned more swiftly, sat down quickly, crossed her legs, stretched her arms above her head, flung her hair so that it swirled across her face, arched her throat and laughed, and forgot Mrs O'Neil's instructing voice in the sheer pleasure of performing and knowing that she was performing with verve, delicacy, provocation.

271

It was a capsule performance of Gloriana, her private Gloriana, not the Gloriana she had displayed in rehearsal, where Jeffrey Brooke would immediately perceive what she meant to do and find a way around it.

She had discovered this trait of his quite early, when she first began to have some sense of the two women, Elizabeth and Gloriana.

'Hmm,' he had said.

Whereupon Arlette had promptly begun to diminish Gloriana's allure. She would surprise him with it on opening night – for if he saw it during rehearsals he would convince Marvell, perhaps John Powell, that she must play a more subdued Gloriana. Her lines might be rewritten, her stage business curtailed.

He had shown unusual interest in the wardrobe fittings, observing that the black evening dress was cut too low, both in front and in back. It had, after all, come from Elizabeth Doyle's wardrobe, not Gloriana's.

'Miss Morgan, if I may express an opinion—'

'Of course, of course! Please do!'

'People think they own a beautiful woman when they've seen most of her body. For your own sake, as a future tragedienne—'

There was no way to argue with such a man. Arlette accepted every suggestion and thanked him. Later she took the dress to her dressmaker and had it sewn to suit Jeffrey Brooke, but sewn so that on opening night a pair of manicure scissors would make of it the dress she was convinced Elizabeth Doyle would have worn for such an ironic-romantic encounter.

Even so, that small plan did not go far toward solving her essential problem, which was Jeffrey Brooke's formidable capacity to seduce an audience.

When Arlette had completed her series of maneuvers, Mrs O'Neil nodded approvingly. 'She can do it easily. She has the quality.' She turned to Arlette. 'My dear – your friend, and mine, has described the scene which concerns you. He wants you to know how to take off your clothes in exactly fifty seconds.'

Jerry smiled at Arlette. 'Mrs O'Neil has had experience in this field. There is a difference—'

'I'm not modest, Jerry.' Mrs O'Neil spoke directly to Arlette. 'My dear, I'm an artist. I haven't been on the stage for sixteen years, but I have never forgotten my training. For many years I was the world's most famous artist in this field.' She smiled, as if tolerant of the past, refusing it the homage bitterness. 'One day,' she said gently, 'I looked at my behind in the mirror and saw that it was beginning to look like the rind of a cantaloupe. I'd depended on lighting for flattery – not concealment. I decided to quit.'

'I see,' said Arlette solemnly, wondering if Mrs O'Neil was teasing her, or if perhaps the lady was not only eccentric but slightly deranged. But Mrs O'Neil's face was serious, and so was Jerry's.

'Jerry has explained that in this scene you will be wearing a black evening gown with nothing under it—'

'A nude body-stocking,' said Jerry quickly.

'You will be wearing nothing under the dress but a black garter belt and black stockings. In fifty seconds this comes off, and you are tying the belt of a white silk robe, without the audience having seen as much of you as they think they have. It's all illusion, Miss Morgan, the art of striptease. And it *is* an art.'

Well!

All at once Arlette was astonished at her own stupidity. Why had she not realized that this elegant woman was not an actress – not what she thought of as an actress? She was beautiful. If she had been on the legitimate stage, she would still be there.

'What do you have on?'

'Tights. These are rehearsal clothes.'

'Darling' – Mrs O'Neil spoke to Jerry – 'will you ring and ask the butler to bring a garter belt?'

Mrs O'Neil's elegance, Arlette decided, was somewhat precarious, but after all, Jerry had brought her here to learn from an expert how to perform one of the most delicate and, so far, elusive bits in the play. If she did it

273

well enough, with grace, boldness, and modesty, the play was hers; at least, that much of it was.

When Jerry left the room, Mrs O'Neil smiled at Arlette. 'In one hour I will make a professional of you. You must remember only one thing when the time comes.'

'Yes?' Arlette was as eager to learn Mrs O'Neil's professional secrets as she was to learn those of Alicia Fiedler.

'We,' said Mrs O'Neil, delicately indicating Arlette, then herself, 'we are the artists. They – are the voyeurs.' Her contempt for the audience was awesome. 'You must never forget to despise them. But smile, smile, smile every moment. The joke's on them.' And once again, as Jerry returned, bearing the garter belt upon his forefinger, there came that remarkable rippling waterfall of laughter.

When they left, an hour and a half later, Arlette's skin was wet, her hair and scalp were moist, for the work was hard, as hard as her calisthenics, and Mrs O'Neil was a demanding taskmaster – but she knew how to take her clothes off in fifty seconds and wrap herself in a robe without having displayed more of her body than her plans for the future would permit.

At the drawing-room door, Mrs O'Neil and Jerry embraced again.

'Thank you, darling.'

She shook Arlette's hand. 'You could become a great artist.'

Arlette smiled kindly, but all at once her ferocious pride in the future she expected reasserted itself. She had learned the trick; the trick was valuable. But it was, after all, a trick.

Jerry and Arlette set off in search of a taxi. 'But who is she, Jerry?' Arlette pleaded, running to keep up with him, for Jerry was on his way somewhere, and Jerry was late. 'I know she's famous. But who?'

'You didn't guess? She's Della Dorne.'

'Della Dorne! Of course! Of course!'

Jerry opened the cab door, leaned in to kiss her good-

bye, and said: 'Now you've got it.' He shut the door, gave
the driver her address, and waved good night.

CHAPTER 33

Now she had the magic formula, the one sure way to back
Jeffrey Brooke into a dark corner on opening night.

But after another week of rehearsals, she was less sure.

Jeffrey Brooke was one of the world's charming men.
He had studied the art most of his life, for he had begun
to act in his native London at sixteen, had been a leading
man by the time he was twenty, and played his first
starring part one year later.

By reason of his dozens of films and plays, he was
familiar enough to seem to any audience an old friend of
the family – who would, luckily, never come to visit
because he was too busy being charming for a living.

He had been married four times, and he had two
children, and all this enhanced his reputation for charm,
for Jeffrey Brooke conducted his family life with the same
easy manner he stamped upon each part. Easy or difficult,
when Jeffrey Brooke did it, it looked easy, except to other
actors.

The theater would be filled to capacity, for Jeffrey
Brooke's opening nights were stylish events, and Arlette
foresaw that – take off her clothes in fifty seconds or two
minutes – Jeffrey Brooke would absorb her spotlight.
She wondered if there was ever a time, asleep, making
love, reading, when he left off being Jeffrey Brooke.

Had Jeffrey Brooke ever gazed accusingly at Jeffrey
Brooke in the mirror as he put on his makeup, thinking:
Why are we never as beautiful as we wish to be? Unlikely.

What he thought mystified her. He might be thinking
anything, so highly polished was the façade, so blinding
the refraction. He might be very clever, or he might be
very stupid. But of one thing she was convinced: like all

men who impressed her for one reason or another, he had his secret, and she began to covet that secret.

'He is so experienced,' Arlette told Alicia.

'I know Jeffrey quite well. He is, in fact, a kind man. Naturally, he's competitive. He'll take the show away from you – he expects to. He thinks it belongs to him and, Arlette, you know that it does.'

'I've made a mistake.'

'You seem to spend most of your time thinking about what Jeffrey Brooke is doing. Think about yourself.'

Arlette walked swiftly along the street, repeating: *Think about yourself*, as she often repeated Alicia's parting words, trying to discover in them what step she must take next to keep her appointment with that destiny waiting for Arlette Morgan.

Not more than twenty minutes before the end of the play, Arlette took her clothes off with deftness and a slight ironic hauteur. Jeffrey Brooke's eyes widened, since this was not the way she had removed her clothes during last night's dress rehearsal, and she smiled at him that dazzling smile he had never seen before, Gloriana wearing a transparent white silk robe and slowly tying the fringed sash.

The audience began to applaud, then to whistle, feet were stamping, and for several seconds the show was effectively stopped, even though Jeffrey Brooke approached her quickly and with more stealthy determination than he had rehearsed.

The play continued, while Arlette told herself she would remember that moment as long as she lived: she had stolen the spotlight from Jeffrey Brooke, and the realization gave some heightened recklessness to everything she did from then until the end, when Jeffrey, having bedded Gloriana in a brief blackout, kissed her good-bye, and she closed the door and gave a triumphant leap which carried her a third of the way across the stage.

Again the businesslike editor, she sat down, dialed a number and gave instructions to disconnect her telephone.

She picked up another telephone: '*Take my name off the door. I'm moving tomorrow.*' She pitched the Ben Franklin glasses across the room, stretched her arms over her head so the wide sleeves of the robe fell back to her shoulders, stretched her legs straight, and when the telephone began to ring, seized it and shouted: '*I'm not here!*' a line John Powell had added at her suggestion.

As the curtain came down she sprang to her feet and slipped through it to confront the audience before Jeffrey could appear. That was contrary to their rehearsed curtain call, but since she was sure to be brought to account for her sins, no further niceties concerned her.

She was smiling Elizabeth-Gloriana's wicked smile, and when Jeffrey Brooke seized her hand they bowed to each other.

Before the director could rush forward to drag her off the stage, before John Powell could protest she had turned his elegant call girl into a strumpet, before Jerry Hoffman could declare this was the end of her once and for all – she bowed low, threw her head back and had once again that euphoric sense of having dominated her world.

She ran off the stage in the opposite direction from where she had seen Marvell and John Powell waiting, sped swiftly past the stagehands, exchanged smiles with the musicians as she flashed by them, threading through the props and ropes, taking the steps two at a time to her dressing room, and found the dresser frowning, her face troubled.

'Wait,' said Arlette, with no idea of what she was to wait for, only to keep her from prophesying disaster. Arlette leaned against the door, smiling as if at the recognition of some wonderful secret she would never share with anyone.

Whatever might come of her insurrection, the applause, the whistles, the laughter of approving conspiracy, were more than compensation for the glancing blow she had dealt Jeffrey Brooke's ego.

She was twenty-four years younger than he. And he must have been wondering for a long time when something like this would happen – not, perhaps, so traumatically; not at the hands of a girl who had seemed docile, under his control and direction, awed by playing opposite him. Until, from nowhere, there had sprung a young lioness:

I've done it. And I can do it any time I like, with any part I get.

Jerry had been right. For if she had not tried her confidence first in this comedy, she might never have acquired the courage to try it in a play which intimidated her.

There was a sharp rap at the door and Arlette jumped, placed her forefinger to her lips, and went to sit at her dressing table, gazing into the mirror, wondering who that was she saw, with such big eyes, baffled, frightened; that white face.

The rap came again, and Jerry's voice shouted her name.

The door opened. Jerry dashed in and kissed her. Jeffrey Brooke pulled her to her feet and whirled her around the room, as he had whirled Gloriana around the stage in a mock waltz, declaring: 'By God, Arlette, that was a *tour de force!*'

John Powell had come in, followed by Margo; Eva French kissed her; Minerva embraced her; Alicia put her arms about her. In a moment the room was crowded. Only Della Dorne was noticeably absent.

'You're not angry?' she asked Jeffrey Brooke in a whisper.

'My dear, it was superb. Very few actresses would have dared do that to me.'

'I was so afraid of not seeming to be there at all.'

The reviews were better than she had hoped for, and Arlette found she had become a minor celebrity. As she left the theater she was handed slips of paper by young boys and girls who looked remarkably stupid to her, but to whom she nevertheless felt a keen warm gratitude:

People that age always look stupid. Or did we?

Well, it made no difference if they looked stupid or

were stupid. They wanted her autograph and she gave it graciously, asking for each name, then writing carefully: *To Margaret Reynolds, with all best wishes, Arlette Morgan.*

A few weeks later she was scribbling only her name, the smile was perfunctory, and she wished this younger generation were busy at home with stamps or erector sets.

Each night she found herself anticipating her great scene while she parried Jeffrey Brooke with the wry nonsensical dialogue between this unlikely pair who had come together on one of those life rafts which float upon varying levels of every apartment house in New York.

'*But who are you? Now that you've talked my secretary into letting you come here,*' Elizabeth Doyle asked him.

'*I'm Robert Dudley, Gloriana. Surely you haven't forgotten?*'

'*You seem to have forgotten me, Mr Dudley – if that is your name.*'

'*You've changed, Gloriana. Something about you is different.*'

She leaned across the sofa, toward the audience, forcing Robert Dudley either to turn away from the audience to peer into Gloriana's eyes and her low-cut dress or ignore her.

'*I've dyed my hair and I'm wearing contact lenses.*'

From time to time, Arlette surprised him, curious to see how inventive she was now that she and this Elizabeth-Gloriana were at least nodding acquaintances, perhaps even more curious to see how thin a veneer was Jeffrey Brooke's charm. But she never caught him off guard. Whatever she did to him, he repaid her within a minute or two, and her one triumph remained the fifty seconds of taking her clothes off.

Some actresses, immediately they achieved this much success, began to imagine the success had made them fragile, and so they spent the day resting for the night's ordeal. Arlette thought it was much too early for that, and indeed she felt stronger and more energetic than ever before.

She continued as many classes as she could, and studied with Alicia twice a week. Alicia had not scolded her, to Arlette's surprise, but seemed amused and pleased that her student had found her own way to stop a show, make an audience aware of her.

'Wherever did you learn it?' Alicia asked, recognizing that this was professional undressing, quite beyond the dexterity or grace of the most accomplished amateur.

Jerry had warned Arlette to tell no one this secret, for it would pique Mrs O'Neil's considerable vanity to have it known that what she could no longer display with the confidence of years before she must now teach to a newcomer.

'I went to some shows.'

Alicia smiled. 'I doubt I could have done it so well, even when I was the age to try.'

That was the compliment that counted.

Now that she was no longer Katharina, but had become the season's most spectacular young actress, Arlette was convinced by Art Friedman that it was her duty to give a few interviews, but almost immediately she began to hate any interviewer who walked into Art Friedman's office. She gazed upon him with brooding suspicion.

'What are your hobbies, Miss Morgan?'

'Hobbies?'

'What do you do with your leisure time?'

'I have no leisure time.'

That was true. Arlette was convinced that now she was beginning to learn her trade, she did not intend like other young actresses to pay attention to her public, be seen in fashionable restaurants, attend cocktail parties.

'You're a celebrity, Arlette,' Minerva told her. 'Aren't you going to act like one?'

Arlette smiled. 'With this one little play?' She was still snobbish about John Powell's play, and supposed she always would be. 'I'm a working woman, with more work to do than ever.'

Arthur Friedman, who kept a clipping service on each of his clients, filing everything pertaining to any one of them with as great care as if he would one day be called upon to answer to the Bureau of Internal Revenue, the FBI, or the Passport Bureau about them, showed her clippings which had appeared in newspapers all over the country: 'Sensation of Broadway Fall Season'; 'Professor's Daughter Stops Broadway Show'; 'Phi Beta Kappa Girl Gives Strippers a Lesson,' and various encomiums which caused Arlette to wake at three in the morning, asking herself how it was possible that her greed for success had let her make such a fool of herself.

Arthur Friedman gave a wave of his hand and laughed. 'Why, Arlette, you don't know what a lucky girl you are.' It was said that clients knew the relationship was permanent when Arthur Friedman began to call them by their first names. 'This is the kind of publicity young actresses pay for.'

'Not if they hope to be taken seriously. I've wrecked my life. The very first chance I got to destroy myself – I took it.'

'Perhaps you think you'd be better off still taking lessons, lessons, lessons? And never be seen anywhere at all until you appear as Lady Macbeth? There are plenty of reasons to go to the theater besides feeling supercilious. There is entertainment, fantasy, visual delight, for instance. You've given them that.'

'Never again,' said Arlette gloomily.

'You won't have to do it again.'

'No one will give me a chance to do anything else. It's all over.'

Arlette gazed at the carpet, thinking she had been scornful of Anthony, with his *Jane Eyre* and *Jude the Obscure* – which were being spoken of in the trade as among the best films of the past several years.

'Don't worry about it, Arlette. You made Gloriana a very elegant call girl. The kind that only exists in the imagination of the guy at the other end of the telephone.'

CHAPTER 34

She had seen Jerry infrequently during the past several months, since the night of the private showing of *Jude the Obscure*, when he had unexpectedly made his expected announcement. But not before he had made love to her, three times, for luck, she supposed; or perhaps because he was angry enough to hope he might dominate her.

'The premiere will be in Hollywood on the thirtieth, just in time to be eligible for the Oscar, and no doubt they'll get it,' Jerry said.

Wearing the white silk robe and seated on the floor with her knees drawn up, Arlette stared across the room at the fire, and thought bitterly of the Anthony she had seen on the screen a few hours before:

Jude Fawley making love to Arabella; drunkenly reciting the Nicene Creed in Latin; feeding hot soup to Sue, while she sat drying her hair, dressed in his Sunday suit, looking like a drowned scarecrow.

Charles Granville gave his actors no advantages they could not discover for themselves. His pictures had some quality of cruelty in them, and the cruelty was said to emanate from Granville.

In Anthony's case, the two men had been a fair match, and the picture was somber and powerful, without the romantic beauty which had made *Jane Eyre* a lady's treat. If they found Anthony De Forest attractive as Jude, then they must be able to find attractive the hardness of male character, and it seemed that in the process Jude Fawley had emerged from his Victorian shell as ruthless and confused as any sensual idealist of any era.

Anthony was now a celebrity on quite a different scale from Arlette, although her fame had seemed burdensome enough and she had complained to Alicia a few months before: 'They won't leave me alone.'

Alicia had smiled, perhaps thinking that soon they would. 'Don't be too accessible, Arlette.'

'I don't think I have been.'

'Publicity is an albatross. As long as it hasn't been published, it isn't true. Once it's in print, then – true or false – it hangs around your neck forever.'

Anthony's albatross was invisible. Perhaps he had strangled the bird.

Yet Anthony De Forest was known to people everywhere who had never met him, never seen him on the stage or in either movie. He was said to be good copy, partly because he had little to say. The more famous he became, the better-looking he was or seemed to be. It might even be true, Arlette thought, that success itself bestowed an aura which made its owner more attractive to men and women alike.

'He came to see me when he was here,' Jerry told her, in a voice so somber that if Arlette had glanced at him she would have known better than to answer carelessly.

'Who did?'

'Who the hell do you think? De Forest. Who were we talking about?'

Jerry was on his feet, with that spring which signaled that in less than a minute he would be gone. But this time, he stood with his feet apart, hands in his pockets, and looked down at her.

It was the first time he had mentioned Anthony for almost a year, since the private screening of *Jane Eyre*, and Arlette had supposed the jealousy was gone.

Anthony had been in Hollywood. Anthony had been in England. Anthony had been in all the newspapers and magazines with his beautiful wife, his beautiful children, his beautiful house, and all the other beautiful things which belonged to Anthony De Forest, who seemed to acquire beautiful possessions by some magnetic attraction. Like attracts like.

'And,' said Jerry, 'he saw you.'

'Me?' Arlette looked up at him, her voice so light it seemed to float in the air like an echo.

283

'But you didn't mention it.'

Suddenly angry, Arlette smiled Jade Ring's smile, and continued to sit with arms folded around her knees, looking into the fire. 'I didn't see him, Jerry.' Jerry was silent, and since Jerry preferred to say what he had to say without odd silences, discreet innuendoes, the silence was ominous. 'I've been faithful to you.'

Jerry gave a sharp laugh. 'We never talked about that.'

'But I have been.'

They had made no declarations, exchanged no promises, and yet without looking at him again Arlette was convinced that if she could not preserve now and for the future Jerry Hoffman's male conviction that she had taken him, and his body, seriously, she would have lost something quite different from what she would have lost in any other man.

'I want you to believe me, Jerry,' she told him quietly. 'If you don't believe that – then you'll suspect me of other things, too.'

Jerry had been on his way to the door, picking up the sheepskin-lined coat, and he spun around with the fierce swiftness he might have liked to see from some of his actors. 'What might I suspect you of, Arlette?'

'Maybe of wanting something from you?'

He came back slowly, and when she still refused to look at him he squatted on his heels, his face level with hers, touched her chin, and after a moment she looked at him, with a face more accusing than his own. He was jealous, and that was painful to him; but his jealousy had made him petty, and it was Jerry Hoffman who was at a disadvantage.

He touched her face, stroking one forefinger along the side of her cheek and beneath her lower lip. 'I'm a bastard, you know, in my own way. I think I've begun to be afraid of you.'

'What an idea.' She glanced at him quickly, saw that it was true, and looked away again.

'Why not? There's nothing more terrifying than a woman you want to make love to every day.' He touched her hair, and Arlette read in the touch that this was the last time they would be together as lovers. 'We'll be working together again – and I'll have to make the decision. This got started, I forget how. What the hell difference does it make? But if we keep it up long enough, I won't know what I'm doing when the time comes. Do you think it's possible for a director to separate his objectivity from his prick?' Jerry nodded. 'It's too easy to turn it into a Pygmalion-Galatea thing when the director is screwing his star.' He stood up. Arlette looked at him; Jerry nodded, the brief nod he often gave as he left, which implied more than his invariable salute? 'Thanks. I'll see you.'

But it was three months before he saw her, and on this day Anthony De Forest was there, Minerva was there, Eva French was there, Max Gilmore was there. Several other members of the caravan were there. And Jerry now began to talk to them about their new project, just going into rehearsal.

'This guy is a maniac, we may as well agree about that right now, because if it's played any other way, it makes even less sense. How else can he believe those inept lies, fall into a fit that leaves him senseless, strangle the only woman he loves, and rave on about his pathetic condition for another twenty minutes? Granted – he's crazy as a jaybird. But then, a lot of us are.'

Arlette smiled slightly. While Jerry talked she concentrated on the tabletop, and the sound of his voice.

Anthony wore a solemn expression, befitting one who must one day not far distant undertake to portray this maniac without making him ridiculous.

But then, jealousy, perhaps, had never troubled Anthony. He had spent his life creating jealousy in others, and that may have been an effective lightning rod. If he had any jealous misgivings about what she had been doing these past two years, there had been nothing to indicate it when he had approached her earlier, holding out his hand.

'Why, hello, Anthony. Congratulations.'

He had looked at her seriously, then slowly smiled, as if they had parted friends and lovers, and met in the same spirit. Arlette stared at him, the hatred seeming to chill, harden inside her; and all at once Anthony spoke rapidly, in a voice scarcely above a whisper, since the other members of this large cast were standing about as if gathered for a cocktail party. 'What the hell did you expect me to do? Lydia knew nothing about you. Should I have told her to take a cab from the airport?'

'I didn't expect anything, Anthony. Did you think I did?'

'I know you did.'

The others were shuffling chairs, taking their places at the table, and they stood so intensely concentrated upon each other the world had vanished.

She walked away and took her chair. A moment later he sat across from her at the long table, Jerry Hoffman at its head, perhaps as umpire.

But it was not likely Anthony was at all concerned about how she had spent the two years, or whether she had fallen in love with some lover, or even how many she might have had.

Two, that was all.

Jerry Hoffman and, somewhat to her surprise, Jeffrey Brooke.

But that had been in the nature of an accident, perhaps an inevitable accident, once they had entered into a contest to discover who could be more charming. It had heightened the relationship between Gloriana and Robert Dudley, gave a piquancy to the relationship between Elizabeth Doyle and Robert Dudley, pleased the audience, and delighted John Powell, who said the play improved with time, where most comedies, after a few weeks, lost their snap and sparkle.

The contest of charm became so successful, and eventually so exciting, that a few days after Jerry had declared himself out of her life, Jeffrey Brooke saw her home after the Saturday night performance and did not leave until it was time to go to the theater on Monday.

It may not be love, Arlette reflected, somewhat morosely, *but I need it anyway. And what woman wouldn't give up all hope of a sable coat to have Jeffrey Brooke as her lover?*

When Jeffrey left for London, three days after the play had closed, he said with an air of gallant sacrifice: 'We won't make heavy weather of saying good-bye. Will we?'

He had sent quite an assortment of parting gifts to her apartment earlier in the day. There was a pot of green speckled orchids, and it stood on the low table, where she had also placed the tin of beluga Malossol caviar on a silver plate with mother-of-pearl spoons and knives, and a bottle of Dom Perignon in the silver bucket it had arrived in with two champagne glasses.

Jeffrey knew that Arlette did not drink, had no silver buckets, no champagne glasses or mother-of-pearl knives, but that was what the occasion called for and so there it was.

'One glass, my dear,' explained Jeffrey as he went to the kitchen and expertly removed the cork. 'We've much to toast each other for – haven't we?' His smile was tender, nostalgic even before they had said good-bye. He was as well prepared for this part as for any other.

Arlette sipped the champagne cautiously, and looked across the room, thinking of Jerry Hoffman and Arlette; of Arlette and Anthony De Forest.

'Yes,' she agreed. 'We do. Most love affairs are sad, or pointless. My friends seem to have the pointless kind. I have the sad ones.' She smiled. 'Thank you for not making me sad.'

Jeffrey covered her hand gently. 'Let me, if I may, tell you something. Don't care whether love is sad or pointless, or whatever else it may be. Just experience it. Let it go, if you must – or if it must. But don't refuse it. Don't refuse any experience that won't irreparably harm you. The first thing to remember is that you're an actress. The second is that you're a woman. One day you'll be a very great actress. I've thought that only three times before.' He nodded. 'I've been right.'

Arlette was astonished to discover the tenderness, the generosity beneath that charm – which she had sometimes suspected was only a trick. So they parted gaily, promising to see each other in the spring, to write now and then; to remember now and then. She concluded it was impossible for her to have an affair with a man without falling in love with him to some degree. The pleasure, the intimacy, were more powerful, even after a short time, than seemed possible when she began, blithely thinking: *This won't do me any harm – it may even do some good.*

She felt a sense of loss, an expectation of hearing his voice on the telephone, and was unreasonably pleased when his first letter arrived – until she read it.

Jeffrey Brooke was obviously wise and experienced as a lover, and the note he wrote might have been written to an adolescent fan, so devoted he felt obliged to make some polite reply. She tossed it into the fireplace, and smiled as she turned over the silver box which had accompanied it, shaped like a heart, with someone's initials inscribed a century before, asking herself:

Why is pleasure brief and quickly forgotten – and pain lasts forever?

Within a month, she could not remember what pleasure she had found in Jeffrey Brooke's lovemaking, yet the pain Anthony had caused her was as clear and savage as it had been two years ago.

As they began to rehearse, she discovered that Arlette was there on the stage each day. It was Desdemona who was not.

And as she began to feel that the absence of Desdemona was puzzling the other actors, she talked to Alicia. 'I've turned into Lot's wife.'

She thought it would be a relief if Jerry Hoffman took her aside, talked to her gently – and she guessed it might not have been easy for Jerry to persuade Sy Harman and Jonathan Morris to take a chance on her – and suggest

288

that perhaps she needed more time, more study, another Elizabeth-Gloriana.

Alicia was watching her, and Arlette grew uneasy, for she thought that probably Alicia knew her secrets.

And evidently Alicia decided that if Desdemona was to be saved – at least for Arlette Morgan – it was time to break her self-imposed rule never to discuss her students' personal lives. 'What are you looking back at, exactly?'

'I'm sure you know, Alicia.'

'I'm sorry, Arlette, of course. But it hasn't killed you yet, and it won't. *Men have died from time to time and worms have eaten them – but not for love.*'

'Oh, it isn't love that's bothering me.'

'What, then?'

'Hate. I can't play Desdemona to a man I hate.'

'Why not?' Alicia paused, while Arlette studied her interlaced fingers. 'It's a kind of stage fright, nothing more serious. Except that for the time being, Anthony is your entire audience. But you must remember, he isn't, really. Anthony is thinking about himself – and about Othello.'

CHAPTER 35

Arlette knew what Jerry Hoffman expected of his actors for this *Othello*, but to give him the Desdemona he waited for had proved impossible.

She was somewhere, no doubt, but Arlette could not discover her, and without her Jerry could not produce an *Othello* with the capacity to disturb, provoke, demonstrate hidden and repudiated feelings in actors and audience alike.

There was, Arlette thought, in Jerry Hoffman a fierce puritanical need for conversion: a conversion of actors and audience to his belief that there were few choices in life, and most of these were made unconsciously, or by others – yet the consequences of these choices must not only be endured, but experienced to their full and final dissolution. Between life and the theater he drew no distinction.

There was no great play ever written, he had assured her, which did not contain the possibility of converting the viewer. He might have entered the theater to acquire a little culture for the good of his soul, or vanity, Jerry had told her bitterly. 'But when I'm through with him, that's not the way he leaves.' He had glanced suspiciously at her, to see how she responded to this Jerry Hoffman. 'That sounds bloody egotistical, but I can't do it alone. The people I work with have got to want the same thing, without needing to talk about it. If you talk about shaking the guts out of the audience, you make actors nervous. No one, no matter how self-confident he imagines he is, thinks he's able to do that. Instead you create an atmosphere whereby the company slowly, imperceptibly, begins to shake the guts out of one another. Finally, if the music gets loud enough, everyone in the theater can hear it. If the ceiling finally caves in, if the audience goes out, making their way through the shambles without noticing it – you've got a performance worth having done.'

Now, if only he hadn't told me that.

During the first two weeks the play began to take form, as if Jerry had changed them into malleable creatures, instilling them with his comprehension of Iago and Emilia, Cassio and Bianca.

If Jerry Hoffman was even aware of himself as a man separate and apart from the Jerry Hoffman who was their director, there was no way for them to detect it. He abandoned himself, as if he sloughed off clothes and skin, tossed them into a heap, and mingled among his actors, coaxing, encouraging, never demonstrating, slowly evoking what they were to be.

Even now, he had turned Max Gilmore into an Iago of such malice and savagery that Minerva said to Arlette: 'I understand how the need to kill a man you live with could become stronger than love ever was.' Minerva's Emilia to Max Gilmore's Iago had seemed to some of them a possibly dangerous casting experiment. Old love could never be relied upon to have consumed itself entirely during its lifetime.

But Desdemona still had not put in an appearance.

This Desdemona, whom it seemed she knew so well, even the day she had auditioned for Jerry, had not reappeared. For Othello had not challenged her, and would not until Jerry signaled them to bring the whole play to life.

This process was quite different from what Jerry had used to force them into coherence in *The Taming of the Shrew*. For these rehearsals proceeded slowly, seemingly with less demand being made upon each of them at any given time, because, as Arlette perceived, these were vast and final passions. However Anthony might quarrel with the stupidity of characters getting themselves into such ridiculous plights, there they were, and their lives were in forfeit. So were the lives of those who undertook to play them.

What Jerry Hoffman had contrived to do, with delicacy and infinite patience, was to build a tension which became increasingly difficult to endure. Anything, by now, would relieve it. If he had shouted at them to murder one another, Arlette had visions of a mass carnage.

She was more resentful of Anthony than ever, more convinced that he had never worked as she had worked: he had imposed his own concept – Ming Huang, Petruchio, Rochester, Jude, Othello. Anthony was a sorcerer, just as Othello was accused of being a sorcerer in procuring Desdemona's love by the tales of his hardships.

One day, Jerry would begin, as if tenderly at work on mummies embalmed three thousand years, to remove the wrappings and set them free.

The sooner the better.

During the first four weeks she and Anthony did not speak directly to each other – only through the speeches between Othello and Desdemona, while they tested each other, waiting.

Othello was to make her fall in love with him, to love her, doubt her, murder her, still loving her. At the end, she thought, there would be little left of either of them. The play would destroy the entire cast by its power, its cruelty, the emotional stupidity of its characters. Jerry Hoffman would be the only survivor.

She walked into Alicia's apartment at the end of a Friday rehearsal with her eyes brilliantly shining, in a state of exultation so great she seemed a woman eager to welcome her executioner.

'Tomorrow,' she said. 'He'll begin tomorrow.'

'He's said so?'

'I know it.'

Arlette and Anthony met the next morning as they arrived at the rehearsal hall on a day of heavy rain, so heavy that Arlette held the umbrella low over her head, and when a man's hand reached to take it from her at the door she glanced up, smiling spontaneously, and saw Anthony's grave face.

He knew Arlette's superstitions included the weather. Bad weather might equally signal a bad omen or a good one, a bad day or a good day, failure or success, happiness or sorrow. It was all a matter of knowing how to read the auguries, and during the three and a half weeks they had spent together she had given him each day's prediction, a bulletin delivered casually at the breakfast table.

Anthony took her coat, hung it on a hook, and questioned her with mock seriousness: 'Meteorologist – what of the day?'

Arlette laughed, Anthony smiled, and they were suddenly pleased with each other. With Anthony beside her, the two years disappeared into some irrecoverable limbo. He was smiling, he was warm, and the warmth seemed to flow through her, restoring her confidence, even her self-respect. She was astonished at her eagerness to accept whatever he chose to give.

They entered the stage area of the rehearsal hall and, yes, Jerry was there, far in the back, talking to Sy Harman and Jonathan Morris, the two producers and angels for the company, who had been at no previous rehearsals.

'Ah,' said Arlette softly.

'It looks that way, doesn't it?'

'I knew it. I knew it.' Her heart was pounding with that sickness called stage fright; her eyes were wide open, staring at some unseen terror.

'When you woke up and saw it was raining?' Anthony smiled. 'I want to talk to you, Arlette. May I?'

There was no doubt that Anthony wanted something, and wanted it as desperately as he had once wanted to make love to her – although it was not lovemaking he was thinking of today. His face had a hardness, there was an occasional twitch along his jawline, and those signs were clearly legible.

He led her to a far corner, nodding as they passed some of the arriving actors; there was a hush among them today, a premonition of crisis.

Arlette sat, and he took a chair, brought it near hers, and leaned forward. For a moment they looked at each other, as if each were taking full recognition of something seen long ago, and perhaps half forgotten in the multitude of other objects.

'Trust me, Arlette.'

She looked at him serenely. 'Yes?'

'I'm not at all sure how you intend to play Desdemona. You haven't given many clues so far.'

'Desdemona is submissive. She is in love with this man for reasons which aren't clear to me.'

'They aren't clear to you?'

'She admires his courage. She pities his past suffering. Are the reasons for love ever clear, Anthony?'

'You're god damn right they're clear. You've heard Jerry say this is a play about sensuality as much as it's about envy and jealousy, power and revenge.' Anthony moved a little nearer, and Arlette had the alarmed sense of being engulfed by him, as if a wave had risen and overthrown her. 'You agree with that – don't you?'

'Yes,' she said quietly, and the fear and hostility were gone. 'I do believe it. But Desdemona is essentially a passive woman. She lets it happen to her.'

'She's not dealing with a fourteen-year-old boy.'

Arlette felt her face grow hot. She quickly looked toward Jerry and the two men.

'Listen to me, Arlette – forget Anthony De Forest exists, or ever existed. Respond to Othello – not to me.'

'I'll try.'

The part, after all, was not one she could dominate. Desdemona dominated no one. Desdemona, even when she seemed most fortunate, was a victim.

'There's one more thing, Arlette. The love scenes are, in a real sense, the most important part of the action. Nothing else would have occurred but for this man's need for this particular woman, and hers for him.'

'Of course.'

'We can't play these scenes by me turning you away from the audience. The audience must see what Desdemona does not say.'

'I know that.'

'Desdemona's love is chaste.' He was watching her carefully, as if she might betray something he could not afford to miss. 'She is faithful by nature. But Desdemona is sensual.'

'I know.' She was surprised by the smile on his face, appearing so slowly she did not immediately recognize it as a smile.

'And remember one thing more—'

'One thing more, Anthony?'

'When he goes to murder her, he kisses her first.'

'So the script says.'

'But what he does, of course, is fuck her.'

'That's impossible—'

'Impossible onstage. Not impossible up here.' He tapped his forehead.

'He wakes her.'

'She is pretending to sleep.' He glanced down the hall. Jerry Hoffman was standing up. He left the two men and started slowly forward. There was a sense of apprehension among the actors. Anthony turned back swiftly. 'Listen to me – a woman who thought his pleasure might save her life could pretend to sleep.' Arlette glanced at him. 'There's always some murder in love, Arlette.'

'I know that, too.'

Jerry stood before them, and every actor had turned toward him.

Arlette and Anthony walked forward to join the others, standing side by side, as if – without words of admission – they had agreed.

'No scripts today.' A few actors, shamefaced at being caught in possession of objects damaging to their professional standing, disposed of them.

'Everyone ready?' He gave a gesture, simple, decisive. 'Then let it go.' He pointed a forefinger directly at Iago and sat down, folding his arms.

They spread out swiftly, as if this moment had been choreographed and rehearsed, the actors who would not appear until later scattering to the far sides of the stage.

Roderigo and Iago walked upon the stage, and the others watched, silent, for fear of breaking the spell. Arlette became aware of Anthony, standing just behind her.

Iago was bellowing beneath Brabantio's window: '*An old black ram is tupping your white ewe!*'

She stood motionless, undistracted by the feeling of quickening desire, following the action with a strange fixed clarity she had never felt before: all this had to do with her – Desdemona. Everything in the play had to do with Desdemona. The power of passivity struck her as formidable, setting into motion chaos, evil, murder.

Anthony moved past the other actors and walked onto the stage with Iago and their several attendants, while Arlette, suddenly terrified, waited for the first sound of his voice. It came, clear, resonant. Othello's command: "*'Tis better as it is.*'

She drew in a deep slow breath. After that she was able to give her entire attention to Iago and Othello.

When Othello answered Brabantio's ravings humbly: '*It is most true; true, I have married her . . .*' Arlette listened as if expecting to hear something more: *I have married her . . .*

Arlette took a few forward steps, Iago beside her, as they prepared to enter the stage.

'She lov'd me for the dangers I had pass'd;
And I lov'd her that she did pity them . . .'

She continued walking slowly forward, looking directly at Anthony. She heard a slight intake of breath – she had surprised the others, too – and her feeling of love and devotion for the Moor, her husband, seemed to flow from Desdemona, a mystical reverence, as she dropped to one knee before her father.

'I am hitherto your daughter: but here's my husband . . .'

CHAPTER 36

A few days before opening night, they moved from the rehearsal hall to the theater.

In the advertisements, Anthony's name was above *Othello.* Hers was below. That was the contract she had signed, and Broadway contracts, like the ancient Chinese concept of Fate, could be altered only by the will of heaven. So far, heaven had not spoken on the subject, nor had the Shining Emperor. Why should he? She would not be Desdemona at all, but for Anthony's suggestion to Jerry Hoffman; or Jerry's to him.

Two weeks ago there had been misgivings, as Jerry had later told her, as to whether she could sink herself deep enough into the part of Desdemona. But after that first full rehearsal, there had been no question in anyone's mind.

What had made the change?

Jerry had nothing to say about that.

She was not sure she knew, either, but it had not been the love scenes, which had begun, with that rehearsal, to become scenes of passion and eagerness, despair and longing, from the first kiss to the last embrace given by the dying Moor to his dead wife.

Minerva had asked her, 'Are you sure you know how those scenes look out there?'

'I've got a good idea.'

Jerry Hoffman had early informed them this was a play about a man's lust for one woman. 'And lust is a form of insanity.'

Arlette had wondered, even before Minerva asked, how those scenes might look to outsiders. The first kiss, Othello's greeting to his wife upon her arrival in Cyprus, was easy to imagine as the audience would see it: Desdemona moving quickly forward, reaching out to him, and Othello turning to stride toward her, hold her close with one hand clasping her hair to draw her head backward, giving her a kiss of rejoicing, expectation of pleasures soon to be renewed. Even in that least demonstrative kiss there was violence and need.

And when presently they left the stage, Desdemona ahead of him, whirling her long skirts – once she had long skirts – Othello following with the predatory step of a man stalking not his wife but his soul's prey, the audience would not question whether this simple, impulsive, ferocious, doting, credulous, brave man would kill a woman he loved to such a degree of distraction if she betrayed his exaggerated concept of his honor.

The bed, once they moved it onstage for the final rehearsals, was two feet from the floor, the headboard raised until Desdemona was almost in a seated position. In the final act at that first rehearsal Arlette surprised them by moving restlessly in her sleep – while the Moor stood looking down at her – flinging one arm across the edge of the bed, and with one leg doubled beneath her, she looked like the ecstasy-stricken woman of Fuseli's *Nightmare*.

The movement was accomplished with a quick natural simplicity, and presented a Desdemona unresigned to her death. His distraction of jealousy became immediately more reasonable, and when he bent across her body, Arlette looked up and saw Anthony's eyes watching her.

'Just don't get any closer,' she heard Jerry murmur to Anthony, 'or it'll be all over.'

'It was your idea that he fucks her.'

'It was my idea that *Othello* fucks *Desdemona*, not Arlette.'

Minerva was indignant. 'Listen to them.'

'Minerva,' Arlette said gently, 'if that scene is under-played, there goes the tragedy. You're left with the story of a simpleton with a mean friend and a dumb wife.'

She sounded brave, but at the end of each rehearsal she was glad to be dead, to have a few minutes of quiet, while Othello raved on and, at last, lay fallen upon her.

It gave her time to reconstruct Arlette Morgan out of the shambles made of her by Desdemona and Othello – before she must stand, walk forward beside Anthony to the edge of the stage, where, day by day, that audience could be seen by Arlette as a band of Indians creeping steadily nearer.

Soon they would be no apparitions, but paying custom-ers sitting there, tomahawks at the ready.

There was no sentimentality in Jerry Hoffman's view of this play. There was little pity, whatever Othello might think about it. Their world was dark, brilliant, intense, alight with evil and uncomprehending love. The sets were simple, the costumes handsome, their colors black, white, yellow, mauve, vermilion and ruby red. When Desde-mona appeared in one color, it dominated the stage. Bianca and Emilia wore one of the other colors, in a subdued tone. Desdemona's hair was lightened to look like gold; gold powder would be shaken onto it. The production was stark in its lighting, extreme in tenderness as in cruelty, in beauty as in ugliness.

For Arlette, the crucial day in her relationship with the cast, with Anthony and Jerry Hoffman, the crucial day for her future in this nation, had been the first time Othello slapped Desdemona.

Nothing had been said about the slap as an actual blow, but enough of the cast had been in the production of *The*

298

Taming of the Shrew to remember the difficulties over Katharina slapping Petruchio.

There was no case to be made for Desdemona pleading that she did not deserve to be slapped, and Arlette waited, passive, so far as anyone could tell.

No one had ever slapped her, and a feeling of shame came over her each time she thought of it.

She tried to convince herself she should be able to accept it as a piece of play-acting – but that was not the kind of production Jerry Hoffman directed. There was no play-acting. There was his own uncompromising idea of the illusion beyond reality. The slap, the greedy love-making. Othello's despairing rage before his suicide, could only be shown ruthlessly.

The days passed, while she anticipated the slap and grew to hate Anthony and Jerry Hoffman, herself, and the entire cast.

Then it happened and, in a flash, was over – sharp and unexpected – for all that she knew exactly when it was to come, for all that she had watched, with mesmerized fascination, each time Anthony's hand had drawn sugges-tively back, then dropped to his side.

Now, without warning, he lashed out so quickly she felt the blow without seeing it, across her cheek and jaw, so that her eyes closed and when she opened them were full of tears, as the script directed.

She looked at him, tears streaking down her face. Anthony glared at her, ready to defend his right to what he had done.

She became aware of silence, a waiting, and then she heard her voice, soft, gentle, a bewildered protestation of Desdemona's innocence: '*I have not deserved this.*'

The words were spoken simply, from Desdemona's honest bewilderment, and to Arlette's astonishment there was a burst of applause, and Anthony's arms were around her, stroking her hair. 'Forgive me.'

She glanced at him, slightly smiling, the tears still running down her face. He stepped away. The cast returned to its earlier intense solemnity, and Emilia's arm encircled Desdemona's waist as they walked off the stage:

This must be the greatest day of my life.

I never thought I could do it.

She felt that some perpetual if unknown fear had been obliterated, freeing her – for future work; even for her future life.

No one mentioned the slap, or their relief that she had played it as Desdemona, not reverting to Arlette Morgan; neither did they mention Anthony's lover's concern, which did not prevent him from slapping her at each subsequent rehearsal. And each time, with perfect reliability, tears filled her eyes, and she was still crying when she left the stage.

The slap was sharp and stinging, but it was not the slap of a man in a jealous rage against a woman he intends to kill. Arlette did not think about that, assuring herself that the worst had been done.

The morning of the full costume and makeup rehearsal, Jerry came to her dressing room to inspect the nightgown. He had asked Alicia to be there, to give her opinion on the entire production, and when he entered Arlette's dressing room she turned to him eagerly. She liked the white silk nightgown, with its deep border of lace, its loose sleeves gathered at the wrist, and best of all she liked the low-cut neckline.

'Too low,' said Jerry. 'Hoist it up.'

'It's a nightgown, Jerry.'

'Never mind what the hell it is. I wouldn't let Bianca wear that nightgown. We want the critics to keep their minds – and their reviews – on the performance. Higher,' he repeated sharply to the fitter.

He asked Alicia two or three questions, he approved the nightgown at last, and all at once he turned to Arlette with an angry expression.

'I hate like hell to say this, Arlette.'

'Say it anyway, Jerry.'

She was convinced nothing could be worse than this

crisis of the nightgown, for there would be no such pranks as she had played on Jeffrey Brooke.

Jerry looked unhappy, and although she thought Jerry usually was unhappy, with whatever fox gnawed at his vitals, it was not often detectable.

He stood behind her, looking at her in the mirror, their eyes searching, possibly remembering something of what each had searched for in the other when they had been lovers. 'That's a rehearsal slap, you understand. Not much more than a love tap.'

'Love tap?'

'Not quite a love tap, Jerry,' said Alicia.

'Keep quiet, Alicia.' The rudeness was so unusual that the voices of the women stopped and the fitter sat back on her heels, placing no more pins in the hem of the nightgown. 'I'm sorry. But beginning tomorrow, that bloody dress rehearsal and every performance – it's going to be a hard slap.'

Arlette looked away, closing her eyes, feeling the slap, trying to absorb it, wondering if she would be able to accept it, or if she would forget Desdemona, the play, her temper. He looked at her carefully, shrewdly.

'All right?'

'All right.'

Jerry kissed her. 'Thanks. Well, Alicia—'

He turned, as if now the day's important business had been accomplished and it was time to be on his way to wherever he was going next. There was no rehearsal today, only the final fittings, the nervous preparations of the actors to come to terms within themselves for the *corrida*.

There was a knock and Jerry opened the door; an actor's dressing room, the actor's home, was his home, too.

'Mr De Forest would like to see you, sir. The costume for the last act.'

Jerry was gone.

All at once Arlette was effusive with her compliments to the designer, who soon disappeared at a summons from Jerry; her compliments to the dressmaker and the fitter, had them convinced that Miss Morgan was the least temperamental actress they had ever worked with, ready to be knocked dead if the play required it.

The fittings were finished, and while Alicia talked to the dressmaker, an old friend, Arlette stepped behind the screen, handed the nightgown to the fitter, and came out wearing the white silk robe with its fringed sash.

The robe would not last much longer, but she refused to have it replaced or accept the copy she had worn in *A Night and a Day*. That would be accepting a fake painting or any other forgery.

Jerry rapped at the door and opened it. 'Here's your Othello.'

Standing in the doorway, smiling a little, as if to apologize for the intrusion into this room filled with women going about women's preparations, Anthony was dressed as the Moor of Venice, black velvet doublet, black velvet hose, sword at his side, and a wide black velvet mantle hung by gold chains from his shoulders. His face was stained dark brown, there was a short black beard along his jaw, and his black hair was cut shorter.

He spoke to Arlette with ironic humor. 'I thought you'd better know what I'm going to look like tomorrow. Fierce enough for a murderer?'

'Gorgeous, Anthony,' said Alicia.

Jerry's eyes glittered with triumph: the nightgown victory; the acceptance of a harder slap; the Moor as he had never looked before. 'I only hope the audience can keep its mind on the play.'

Arlette burst into a laugh of pure joyousness and, quite impulsively, approached Anthony, stroking one hand delicately along his sleeve, the exact gesture Desdemona used at the first meeting. The designer, the dressmaker, the fitter had gone, and Jerry spoke to Alicia, who kissed Arlette, smiled at Anthony, and left the room.

'But I thought we were having lunch,' Arlette protested to Alicia.

'I have a lesson at two. It's late.'

The door closed and Arlette looked at Anthony, apprehensive and uneasy. Who was this stranger? What had he come for? She backed away two steps, then stopped.

After all, it was Anthony, and he was smiling. But that was who she was afraid of. Not Othello.

His clothes came off by stage magic, and as he came nearer Arlette watched him suspiciously.

He turned quickly, locked the door, took hold of her shoulder, and she sat on the chaise longue. He knelt beside her, and with the quick movement of Desdemona she fell into the posture of acceptance and self-abandonment; he entered her smoothly, easily, stirring a feeling which seemed never to have left her, only to have waited for this moment. Her legs encircled his back, arms holding him fast. She gave a soft cry, whether of joy or resentment that he had so easily captured her again she could not tell.

As he moved swiftly, not looking at her but pressing his head against her shoulder, she began to cry with terror and relief, and at last, with an infinite tenderness, he kissed her, as if to reassure her. The kiss was soft, quickly brushing, and he said something unintelligible, forcing deeper and deeper into her, until her body seemed to melt, spreading outward like a skein tautly stretched, released, then drawing farther apart. Vaguely she heard her voice, pleading softly; Anthony fell motionless, silent for several moments, but did not leave her.

When he moved away, looking at her, there was a slight questioning smile. She wondered at the smile, unable to translate it, that smile which appeared after he had made love to her, asking a question; a smile of success and gratitude. She closed her eyes.

'Sweet as summer—' he said softly. 'You're as sweet as summer, Arlette.'

CHAPTER 37

Alicia had described fame to Arlette two years ago, when Jennifer Knight recovered from laryngitis and took Juliet away from her.

'This is an omen,' Arlette had said. 'It means I will never—'

She stopped, not wanting Alicia to hear her state her ambitions so bluntly. She insisted that work was all that interested her. Fame or success – what were they? Work was its own reward.

Alicia did not ask Arlette what she meant. Instead, Alicia explained it to Arlette.

'Fame is one of the paradoxes,' she said gently. 'If you want it, you think it will never come – you will die unnoticed. Then, if it does come, it's impossible to lose. It will be part of you for as long as you live.' Alicia paused. 'Sometimes, long after.'

Arlette smiled sadly. 'But that doesn't concern us.'

Anthony and Arlette had left the theater nearly four hours after he had come to her dressing room, without having said a word about Othello, Desdemona, dress rehearsals, Jerry Hoffman, or Lydia.

He hailed a taxi, nodded as if to remind her of something, and as it drove off, signaled one for himself. She did not look back, and told herself she must forget him again: Anthony was gone, back to whatever life he had with Lydia.

Lydia.

She took out a mirror and looked at herself carefully.

Lydia would be an easier woman to defeat than she had thought: Lydia was self-centered. Lydia had not learned yet what Lily Malone had known as a young girl – false pride sickens the spirit.

She got out of the cab and walked swiftly through the lobby: *I'll never ask him why he married Lydia, or if he loves her.* She stepped into the elevator and searched for her keys. *I'll never ask him one bloody question.*

She went to consult with the oracle in the mirror over the fireplace.

Questions would do no good. Anthony was not a man who gave whatever he gave because he had been asked for it. Coercion was futile where Anthony was concerned. Anthony was sufficient unto himself.

She did not see him the next day until they met, onstage, in the first act of the full dress rehearsal. And then he was Othello, no longer Anthony De Forest, and for the first time she felt completely immersed in Desdemona, moving toward him in her heavy white silk gown, embroidered with pearls and gold thread, smiling, holding her hands toward him.

Earlier in the day she had been convinced that some enormous failure was waiting for her: she would trip over the long-trained gown. She would be distracted by memories of Anthony's lovemaking and forget that he was Othello.

He looked at her quickly, as if to warn her that this was the significant moment for both of them, and the fears were gone. His quick glance acted as a miraculous cure.

She was alert, intent, and when he slapped her, a hard blow, she cried real tears, so blinded by them that Emilia was obliged to lead her from the stage. In the wings the tears vanished and she turned with a radiant smile to the makeup man, powdering her face, telling herself that no other actress cried like that: real tears – but without the facial distortion which made real tears ugly to watch.

She saw no one when the rehearsal was over. Jerry Hoffman had disappeared, she heard one of the actors say, as they were forming for curtain calls. Anthony had left the stage in the opposite direction. And Arlette hid in her locked dressing room, waiting until the theater was cleared before she ventured out, ran down the hallway, and hailed a cab. She had seen no one. No one had seen her. That seemed a sign of good luck.

'Don't study your scripts tonight or tomorrow,' Jerry

had warned them. 'Don't think about anything. Sleep. Take a walk. Listen to music.'

Anthony telephoned at eleven o'clock the next morning, as she sat reading the galleys of Gordon Donahue's latest book, *The Restoration Comedy*, which he had sent with a letter explaining that she ought to play Millamant one day.

'Arlette?'

'Did I do something wrong yesterday?'

'You were fine. I'm at Sixty-ninth and Lexington. Can I see you?'

'What?'

Anthony hung up and Arlette ran into the bathroom to comb her hair, and ran out again, for the doorbell sounded so quickly he must have come at a run. She looked at him apprehensively. Something had gone wrong, something she had not noticed yesterday. But Anthony was smiling, he threw off his raincoat, held her close and began to kiss her, and took her to bed without a word:

Has he come because he wants me – or because he thinks this is the best way to make him forget what's going to happen tonight?

Then she no longer cared why he had come, whether from need, from love, from a determination to control her. The pleasure, with its intervals of such intensity she felt consciousness slipping away, the violence and tenderness, did make her forget the great occasion, and the stage seemed on another planet.

When finally he told her it was time to go, she must sleep an hour before she left for the theater, Arlette held out one hand in a pleading childlike gesture, but then smiled quickly, and realized she was still afraid of making him angry. Anthony might not want her to love him too much; possibly he wanted her not to love him at all.

'I love you.' She had been wanting to say it, and she had been reluctant to say it, and so she drew in a quick breath and said it softly.

Anthony had been out of bed for less than a minute, and now he was dressed, standing looking down at her.

He was silent, watching her with a curious look of reflection, perhaps some little suspicion. He bent and kissed her. 'I love you. Don't get up.'

It was, she thought, a confession of which he was ashamed, and perhaps he had felt obliged to say it only so that she would not have the question in her mind tonight; Desdemona must know she was loved, all too well.

Whatever questions were in her mind, once she stepped upon the stage they were gone. The time Anthony had spent with her that afternoon had become some imaginary experience from the distant past.

The opening-night party was given by the two producers, convinced at last that their venture upon the high seas of Jerry Hoffman's ambitions had been a sensible money-making proposition, and Arlette arrived at the suite at the Plaza with Jerry Hoffman.

She wore a low-cut velvet dress the color of a ripe mango, and at the door she discarded the velvet coat with its thin rim of white ermine collar, entering like an exiled queen returned to her grateful people. No more Jennifer Knights in her future, she was convinced of that.

She moved about the rooms, vanished from one to another, appeared and disappeared, swept along on that hypnotic tide she had learned years ago to ride from far out in to shore without teetering even once.

She was charming, she smiled, she laughed, she exchanged embraces and kisses, or the pretense of kisses, and before she had been there ten minutes knew they were convinced, company and producers and guests, of what it was usually necessary to wait to find out: the reviews would be favorable, and some would be more than that.

All at once she was surprised out of her trance by Anthony standing in her path. 'You haven't spoken to Lydia.'

She looked at him, wondering at this information. 'Or Lydia hasn't spoken to me?'

Anthony was disconcerted, and this was so rare that she took it as a sign he knew she had become a star with that night's performance. She had impressed him. She could not have been more elated, or more brutally triumphant.

'Be generous,' he said.

Arlette looked beyond him, smiling at a stranger. She glanced back at Anthony and quoted Jade Ring's words to Mei Fei: '*Two women who love the same man are not often good friends.*'

She turned away, with a sliding glance, to greet an unknown admirer whom she had summoned from across the room and who was now holding her hand, looking at her with the worshipful expression she realized she had been seeking all her life. It was more likely to prove habit-forming than she would have imagined. Even more surprising, it was worth what it had cost:

But how sweet it is, sweet as summer.

You're cruel, Arlette, she admitted when she realized, later that night, that Anthony and Lydia had gone.

She was seated on a sofa beside Jerry, who was talking to several young actors gathered about him on the floor, eager to catch a few words of advice when he seemed in a mood to remain still a few minutes.

Jerry's wife had divorced him not long ago, a little-publicized Mexican divorce; not only Louise but his children had become an inconvenience to his work. And when Arlette had asked if he meant to marry again he had looked at her with incredulous disbelief. 'What the fuck for?'

Arlette had studied him carefully, wondering what he had against marriage; for marriage was on her mind nowadays, marriage pro or con.

Perhaps her old song was true for her now as it had been for Lily Malone. And the bitterness which Jerry clearly felt for the eleven years of his marriage was unrelieved by his two children, for his devotion to them was real but desultory. Too much time with them was too much time deducted from Hoffman-Repertory.

Once upon a time, so she had heard, Jerry Hoffman and Louise Durant had studied acting at the same school, and Jerry had spent almost two years convincing her to marry him. Louise was young; she was almost beautiful; she was ambitious, and her coaches thought she had talent.

They must have felt, Louise and Jerry, for a time at least, that excitement about each other which she and Anthony exchanged, even when they were quarreling silently about Arlette's refusal to speak to Lydia, now that she had the upper hand in this nation of theirs.

And suppose she got her wish? Suppose Anthony left Lydia and his two children? Suppose Anthony married her?

One day, that longing – intolerably painful after even a day apart – would disappear.

She looked intently at Jerry, still talking to the students, and thought of herself and Anthony: two empty shells, clacking up against each other now and then. The sap would fail the tree at its roots.

When the papers arrived, Arlette and Jerry, as if by some unspoken agreement, contrived to escape the young actors and find a room where there were few guests.

Arlette could hear, nearby, Minerva and Eva reading the reviews aloud to each other, and she interpreted them from the sounds of their voices and their laughter: Eva's like a Chinese bell chime; Minerva's watery laugh, low, suggestive. They practiced their craft, as she did, twenty-four hours a day.

'It's a crock,' said Jerry. 'Don't let it get to you. Whatever they say.'

'I won't,' Arlette promised, and thought she meant it, but when Eva approached them and began to read aloud, Arlette listened with a wistful smile, wondering how much she dared believe.

'. . . *that tender beauty – perilous magical attribute* . . .'

Eva was ecstatic over her friend's success, the next best thing to her own, and a lucky omen. 'Imagine,' whispered Eva, shaking her head so that the short silvery-blonde curls bounced. '*Perilous!* Oh, what I would give to be perilous!'

Arlette laughed. 'What *I* would give.'

She glanced sideways at Jerry, catching the ironic,

brooding expression, for it was Arlette he was studying, not the reviews, and perhaps wondering if the star would presently obscure the actress. For when he could maneuver her away from Eva and Minerva and the others, he began to talk to her, standing her in a corner against the windows, planting himself before her so that she was all but hidden from searchers.

'This isn't what counts in your life. What counts,' he told her, with a solemnity unusual even for Jerry, 'is the internal crisis.' He formed one hand into a bowl. 'Don't let it overflow, spill out of you. It's so valuable, Arlette – that vulnerability you have, wherever it came from. However it happened. If you only knew.'

'But I don't know,' Arlette objected, lying. 'I've never thought of myself as vulnerable.'

'It comes straight across the footlights. Men fall in love with you for it – even when they think it's your beauty and sexuality. And women forgive you, because they recognize it. Something very painful went into the forming of it. But not lately.'

'No. Not lately. It happened when the world began.'

CHAPTER 38

A few months later, Anthony was awarded an Oscar, accepted for him by James Lennox, who had written the script for *Jude the Obscure*, and Arlette and Alicia watched the ceremonies on a television set Jerry Hoffman had sent to her dressing room.

The rumors had been heard for several months, but there it was. 'Something for the man who has everything else,' she remarked to Alicia, asking herself what good it did to work as if her life depended upon it. The magic had been given to Anthony.

To make it worse, Anthony said nothing about the award. Perhaps his secret was that whatever part he was playing obliterated all others; they became black holes in his life. After Anthony had received it, Jerry was perhaps concerned his actors would become overconfident, for he stopped Arlette as she came off the stage after the last curtain call and pointed a finger at her in her white silk nightgown, recently arisen from her death-bed. 'Don't ever become satisfied!'

Arlette gave a start of mock alarm and laughed. 'I'm not. I won't. I change her a little every night.'

'I know. I haven't missed it. And go on changing Desdemona – and Arlette Morgan. There's no other hope for any of us. Change. That's all there is.'

Alicia agreed. 'When a personality sets – it's dead. Life has been lived. Change, until the last moment of your life. Now – what shall we change today?'

Alicia had given Arlette fewer compliments than anyone but Jerry. Or Anthony. And since the opening of *Othello* Alicia had only one piece of advice. 'Don't start acting like a celebrity. Envy is dangerous – like breathing carbon monoxide.'

'Oh,' said Arlette wisely, 'I know, I know.'

She had made the mistake of granting one interview, in a burst of euphoric affection for the wide world, the morning after the reviews. The reporter came to her dressing room. 'It was very easy for you, Miss Morgan, wasn't it?'

'Easy?' asked Arlette hurt, and then angry. She smiled at him. 'I have always worked very hard.' She offered him tea, demure as a geisha, but that did not placate him.

'But you never had to struggle for anything, did you? It all came your way.'

'I have always worked very hard,' she repeated softly, and then repeated it again.

Gordon Donahue had told her this long ago. 'They will love you, and hate you. It's difficult to say which you will find more unpleasant.' He had smiled and combed his hair with his fingers, that gesture she saw each time she thought of him, and she thought of him often, for in a sense he had formed her life.

'Let Art Friedman deal with reporters,' Alicia told her

after that first interview appeared. 'You're rehearsing. You're at this class or that class. Modesty is the price you pay for success.'

'It's not a high price.'

'Anthony likes to ride forth to meet them in mortal combat, pennants flying. Let him. Anthony has no stake in modesty. Anthony is a man, and the less humility he shows them the more deference they'll show him. Anyway, Anthony doesn't trust anyone, and that's his protection.'

Arlette wondered if Alicia had heard gossip: the hours he left her dressing room, late at night, putting her into a cab, taking another.

Anthony was a magician at heart. He liked to accomplish his effects suddenly, dramatically, unexpectedly. Anthony was an athlete and an actor, and those were sorcerer's trades. But whether or not Anthony had any surprise in preparation, Arlette could not guess.

When his picture appeared in the paper, negligently holding the Oscar, there was Lydia. Other pictures showed Lydia and the two children. And whenever Arlette found one, she tore it into shreds.

She found herself suspicious of almost everything nowadays, and might have taken refuge in her apartment and never ventured out to find whether the world was mocking her, but for her responsibility to Desdemona.

Once the New York engagement ended in mid-August, the company would set out on a tour of ten cities, which would not end until the middle of January, and then, Arlette was sure, she would have him to herself again. That was a long time to wait, and of course there was the possibility that Lydia might decide to accompany the caravan.

That seemed unlikely. For it was to be seen on Lydia's face that she took everything for granted. If Lydia confronted any questions in her suite at the Hotel Pierre, Anthony's clothes hung in the closet, Anthony's hairbrushes were in the bathroom, and Anthony himself was there – although at intervals which must have begun to seem odd, even to Lydia.

Lydia was protected by too much self-confidence, too little capacity to imagine that her world, like others, was a fragile one, susceptible to instant or slow destruction. Lydia had no doubt heard of such accidents in people's lives – perhaps even in the life of someone she knew or had met. But they did not happen to Lydia:

Lydia didn't know about you then, Anthony had told Arlette. *She knows about you now*.

But what does she know?

She had made her vow and clung to it with monastic fervor. It was all that saved her from some absurd or disgraceful behavior.

And she could imagine many kinds of disgraceful behavior: begging Anthony to marry her was one. A wilder scheme: a meeting with Lydia.

She had held several imaginary conversations with Lydia, and riding in taxis was one of the most treacherous occupations for her nowadays. Invariably she became engaged with Lydia in some foolish and self-defeating dialogue:

Why do you want him? You know he loves me.

We have children. Why should I hurt them – for you?

Some of the dialogue reminded Arlette of Jade Ring and Mei Fei, quarreling over the Shining Emperor. Jade Ring had solved the problem by giving instructions to have Mei Fei killed should she ever again leave the Pepper Chamber.

Ah, well, things were simpler then, Arlette reflected, with some amusement, but more bitterness.

For Anthony came to her apartment one day and not another; sometimes not for two days. Each time, she would be sure she would never see him alone again: he had promised Lydia to send Jade Ring to the Pepper Chamber.

Must I die – for you? Mei Fei had asked when Jade Ring and the Eunuch had taken her into the Post House.

This would be Lydia's reasoning. Rejection was a form of death:

And here I am, for the first time in my life, I could be rejected any day. I would never believe in myself again.

She did not doubt Anthony knew she wanted to marry him.

She saw this certain knowledge, sometimes in his eyes, watching her, intense and full of light. She saw it in his face, serious, slightly suspicious.

'Love is not fun,' he said when they were preparing to leave her dressing room, at almost one o'clock. He had started to open the door and then paused, to look at her grimly, blaming her. 'Fucking may be good sport – if the woman accepts it that way. But love – no, love is the end of the world.'

Once, Anthony, you said: 'This is the way the world began.'

Anthony was disturbed. His anger came in flashes, and usually disappeared before anyone but Arlette was aware of it. His disturbances were evidenced by an increasing quietness, a preoccupation which left those around him wondering where he had gone and what he was doing.

If she was thinking he was disturbed because he did not know what proper solution to make of this volatile chemical atmosphere – too volatile to be held for long in suspension – he pretended, instead, to be disturbed by the extraordinary success they were having. *Othello* was not only sold out every night, but most of the time one hundred people stood for nearly three hours.

He quoted *Jade Ring* to her while he sat staring into the burning fireplace on a cold spring night, raining and windy. He had come to her apartment after the theater. He sat on the sofa, in the position she so often pictured him in, knees spread wide, arms resting on his thighs, his large, long-fingered, graceful hands falling loosely between them. Anthony, the thinker.

Arlette would have supposed it was a night for celebration – at least on her part, even though she dared not show it, not until she knew how it had come about.

She had arrived at the theater to find Jerry Hoffman

waiting for her, his face lighted with an unusual excitement, a slight smile. She stopped, looking at him questioningly.

Something had pleased him immeasurably. Something perhaps he thought she knew about? But what?

'Jerry . . . ?' she asked very softly, for fear of disturbing the delicate balance of excitement and joy registered on his face.

Jerry summoned her to follow him, adding that she was to put her raincoat on, and he took an umbrella, raised it, and she walked beside him around the corner. He stopped, indicating the marquee:

ANTHONY DE FOREST   ARLETTE MORGAN
OTHELLO

Arlette started forward, bumped into someone, and Jerry grabbed her arm. 'It's prettier from a distance—'

She stopped, clasping the coat to her throat, shivering. 'Anthony's name first!' She was horrified by the spontaneous child's protest of disappointment at not having the entire pie for herself.

She turned, laughing apologetically, Jerry gave her a whack on the buttocks, and they went back into the theater. 'Ungrateful bitch.'

Once inside, she grabbed Jerry, held him fast, and kissed him. 'Thank you, thank you!'

'Not me. It wasn't my decision. It was – a lot of guys'.'

Now here sat Anthony, looking morose, staring at the fire, and he had neither kissed her nor run his hands quickly over her body, as he usually did the moment they met.

'I saw your name,' he said. 'I'm glad they gave it to you.'

'They? Not you?'

'I'm not the producers, the director, the board. Everyone wanted it. The show belongs as much to you as to me – maybe more to you. That's not what acting means to me. You're as important to my being Othello as I am to your being Desdemona. We play one part – just two different people.'

He is going to marry me. He's made the decision, but he's waiting for something.

'Just remember, Arlette – the road gets steeper from here on.'

'I know.'

He gave a slight wry smile, not a usual one for him, and this time he quoted not Ming Huang, but the Emperor's adopted Tartar son, An Lu-shan:

'Comes recognition, comes fame,
Comes bale and woe . . .'

CHAPTER 39

When Anthony warned her about the photographs of the house in Pasadena, taken for a magazine when he had returned from making *Jude* in England a year ago, she promised, 'I won't look at them.'

But when the day came she stopped at a newsstand, bought the magazine, and ruffled through the pages four times before she slowed down enough to see it.

There was the house. There was the swimming pool and tennis court, the greenhouses and rose garden. The furniture was handsome, the library filled with real books and paintings of unusual quality.

Everything about the house enraged Arlette, for it made impossible her fantasy that Anthony was not married – Anthony *was* married; Anthony had a wife and two children, dogs and horses, swimming pool and tennis court and all the paraphernalia of a rich man's respectable home life.

Arlette threw the magazine into the first trash basket she passed.

All her love, which had seemed to go racing through her veins when she awakened that morning, remembering

only what her body remembered of their lovemaking the
night before, had made her get up and look out at another
hot day as if it were weather fit for a poet's song.

Now that love turned to hate and a fury so intense that
a red sun exploded upon her inward vision, giving her a
moment's fear she might be losing her mind.

She felt more sympathy with Othello than she had ever
felt for Desdemona. Desdemona was killed, and the
suffering was brief, but Othello had been condemned to
the torture of jealousy:

There's some murder in love, Arlette.

Yes. Anthony, there is. There is.

She decided she would not appear for the photographs
scheduled to be taken the next day by a national picture
magazine, publicity recommended by Art Friedman.

'Don't talk to them,' Alicia had said. 'They'll find a
way to make you commit yourself to something you
won't recognize.'

'Never imagine that because a cameraman seems at a
safe distance, he is,' Jerry Hoffman had warned. 'Don't
forget those telescopic lenses.'

All that advice – for nothing:

What a surprise when I'm not there tomorrow morning.

She was almost gleeful at the prospect of their conster-
nation – the telephone calls, perhaps a police warrant:

Find her, wherever she is.

They would have to use her understudy.

But this idea of the understudy grew increasingly
menacing as the day went by, and Arlette was at the
theater at eight-thirty Sunday morning, stage makeup on,
in costume for the first shots, Desdemona's bright yellow
silk gown with its burden of black jet embroidery, smiling
and shaking hands with the photographer and his three
assistants when Anthony appeared, in costume, exactly at
nine.

Arlette did not glance around, but went on smiling Jade
Ring's smile at the photographer, and neither heard
Anthony or saw him until he was taking her into his arms
and kissing her before the photographer was ready.

'Sorry, Mr De Forest. I missed that. Once more – if you please.'

They made love for the cameraman, amid Jerry's constant interruptions and directions. Then Othello strangled her until Arlette grasped his hands, afraid he might kill her. Anthony drew back swiftly, his eyes glittering.

When they stopped to rest, to give Jerry an opportunity to move the photographer and his assistants off the stage, Anthony stood before her, his back to the others. 'Stop being a damned fool.'

Arlette's eyes opened wide, her mouth opened, and all at once Anthony stepped to one side, presenting the photographer with a full view of Arlette, and delivered that sharp, stinging slap. A light flashed at a distance, and Anthony turned and gave the photographer a brisk congratulatory gesture.

'That's the only one,' he told the photographer, and for once Anthony smiled charmingly. 'I promised her.' He turned to Arlette. 'I thought it was best to take you by surprise.'

The photographer came running forward, like a man standing at the window who sees a falling body go by. He climbed onto the stage and Arlette went on weeping for Desdemona's humiliation, undisturbed by the camera five inches from her face. The chance to cry for a legitimate reason was so welcome that before she was able to stop he had taken three or four dozen pictures.

'There's not another actress who cries as Miss Morgan does,' Jerry gravely informed the photographer. 'Exactly on cue, and always looking beautiful.'

They were photographing the city's two favorite lovers, but they were also, she thought, taking pictures for the future of Arlette Morgan and Anthony De Forest: news was expected.

Jerry announced that if they did not have their story by now, they would never have it. 'I don't want you to kill them. I need them tomorrow night.'

Arlette thanked the photographer, disappeared without a glance at Jerry or Anthony, sat at her dressing table, and began to cry again. When she was able to stop crying she looked into the mirror and saw an Arlette who did look tired, who did look miserably unhappy, whose makeup was streaked, and who was, so far as she was concerned, not Arlette Morgan at all.

A despondent young woman, a stranger – or perhaps, after all, the person who lived inside her; Arlette's other self, the spirit which had preceded her into this world and would precede her out of it:

I am a haunted house.

Finally she was dressed, the new dress she had bought to replace the favorite red dress and coat she had worn – but for her rehearsal sweaters and skirts – ever since her first interview with Alicia Fiedler, five and a half years ago.

The red had been her symbol for the conquest of fears and sorrows.

This dress, not very different, sleeveless, with a flared skirt, thin cashmere so light it might have been silk, was the color of a yellow jonquil, the color of triumph, as she had meant it to be when she had had it made during the rehearsals for *Othello*.

She felt that the phoenix had earned new plumage by that time.

She glanced once more around the dressing room. Gordon's little statue of Kuan-Yin was in her handbag. The photographs of Michael, of Gordon Donahue, of Valerie and Frederick, the photograph of her parents standing beside a windy lake, all in their accustomed places. She unlocked the door and started down the hallway.

At the exit she found Anthony seated on the night watchman's chair, tipped back against the wall, reading a newspaper in that dim light, or pretending to.

She turned as if to go back to her dressing room. Anthony threw the paper aside, and she heard a sharp laugh. 'Come here, Arlette. I'm going with you.'

'You are?'

She approached him and all at once, as if banishing a

cobweb which had appeared in a green forest, smiled: *I love you.*

He looked serious, but he laughed, more naturally this time, then took firm hold of her arm. Anthony knew she had spent the day trying to punish him.

In the cab he sat so close that she was crushed into the corner. Either that was more anger or the love scenes had caused him the same kind of pain they had caused her, as if blood and muscles had coalesced, come together in a hard obdurate knot, demanding release.

'Do you think they got what they wanted?'

'I think they got a hell of a lot more than they expected.' He was silent a few moments. 'Arlette, you gave me a bad time today. If I didn't love you—'

'I was—' She hesitated, and then, deciding that confession was good for the soul, said humbly, 'I was unprofessional.'

Anthony gave a burst of laughter.

Yes, he was laughing at her. 'All right,' she amended. 'I was an unprofessional bitch.'

'You were. I know why – not that that's any bloody excuse.'

'I will never,' said Arlette solemnly, 'never again permit my private feelings to interfere with my professional responsibilities.'

'You'd better not. Or you won't have any professional responsibilities.'

When the photographs appeared, they were in Boston, the first stop of the tour, and Lydia was in Pasadena: the children were in school.

Jerry Hoffman had assured them he would get an advance copy to them, if he had to bring it himself. The pictures, he said, were beautiful and terrifying.

'Do you think he's exaggerating?' Arlette asked.

'Jerry doesn't exaggerate. He's too good a pessimist.'

He looked at her with a shrewd curiosity. Each day for several days he had disappeared from time to time: his Hollywood agent, he explained, from Art Friedman's Hollywood branch; his accountant; Jim Brown, or another lawyer. These people seemed to be following him about the country.

He left her to guess:

Is Lydia pleading? Is Lydia making threats? Is Lydia talking about the children?

She could not guess, and he did not tell her.

When, at last, the magician produced his miracle – if he did – he would do so without having let the audience in on his secrets.

He came to her hotel room one night after one o'clock, after leaving the theater to meet his tax lawyer, so he said, and woke her, touching her shoulder gently.

He held the magazine before her, opened to the page before their article began, and flipped it over slowly.

Arlette sat up, wide awake, and they studied the five pages in silence. There was Anthony's slap, and the picture covered the entire page, showing only their heads and shoulders. There were two full-length pictures, Desdemona running toward Othello, and this one had been taken facing Anthony, showing his face alight with the look of a man surprised by the sight of a woman he loves distractedly. There was Desdemona in bed, with Othello's body covering hers, their faces concealed in the embrace. There was another full page of their faces, her mouth apart and his closing over it.

'My God! Is that what we've been doing every night in front of people?'

There was a final picture, Othello strangling Desdemona, with the look of an ancient priest sacrificing upon the high altar, a look of holy savagery; Desdemona's face showed an expression of martyred ecstasy, a willingness to die, purified, released.

Anthony tossed the magazine aside. 'There it is.'

'Yes,' Arlette whispered, horrified to think she had given so much of herself away to anyone who bought that magazine. The next moment the triumphant thought came:

This will be what makes the difference.

Lydia's suffering – if Lydia permitted herself to suffer

– meant nothing; Arlette was concerned with her own suffering.

If he loved her, what did he intend to do? If he did not love her, what would she do? Arlette had forsaken all effort to protect herself. What good was self-defense when he came to her night after night, creating new sensations and pleasures, then slept beside her, sometimes making love to her in the morning before they were quite awake. He had come to her the first night they had left New York, as if that was what they both expected, now that they were free again.

Free for how long?

Five months? And then another parting – which, this time, would surely kill her:

Lydia took the chances any woman takes when she married a man other women will never leave alone. And I took that chance when I fell in love with him.

Anthony continued his frequent disappearances, after the evening performance, or in midmorning.

The caravan moved from Boston to Philadelphia to Pittsburgh to Detroit. Late in October, while they were playing in Chicago, Arlette saw Michael, for the first time in more than a year.

She went to visit him at the University laboratory, the world he lived in, that world beyond the microscope, the world more surmised than known: the secrets which separated the living organisms from the nonliving.

Here was the world of real mysteries. Her own world, of which she was otherwise inordinately proud, was a world of sham, of illusions and the pretense of significance.

'I envy you, Michael. I think I envied you that Christmas – when I saw how much you loved those strange bottles and colored water. I knew you had found a world you could live in – and so I told you I had, too.'

'And you have. That must be a satisfaction.'

'I'm never satisfied.'

Michael put his hands in the pockets of his laboratory coat and gazed reflectively at the floor. All at once he looked up. 'Now that you mention it, neither am I. I just don't think about it. Come – let's celebrate. Let's go to the museum—'

The coat was thrown aside, and they were on their way, running along the street hand in hand. Anthony had disappeared at noon, without so much as a note, and she would not see him until she went to the theater.

In the museum, moving slowly from picture to picture, pausing in silence, Arlette asked: 'But there is, somewhere, a secret, a code of some kind, at the very center of life? Isn't there?'

'Not all of us are so sure there is a secret, or if there is, that we will find it. Why this need for final secrets, Arlette?'

'Maybe because I think then I will know why it happened.'

They walked on slowly. 'You refuse to accept the idea that perhaps there is no reason. For anything.'

'You spend your life trying to find it.'

'Of course,' Michael said gently. 'I must spend my life doing something.'

It was time for her to leave for the theater – and Anthony, back from wherever he had been.

She was never concerned that he might be with another woman, or even that he might be with Lydia. Something in him nowadays, or something in her need, had obliterated the earlier distrust.

That time had gone by; another period of their lives was in the making:

What song did the sirens sing?

'And suppose,' she suggested to Michael, 'that we were one day to understand the universe – whatever it may be – and found it had no value of any kind?'

'That's possible. Some of us study the microcosm, some of us study the macrocosm. And several of us think there's no great difference between them. Perhaps no final difference at all.'

'And some of us study only what's here.' She touched her temple. 'And here.' She touched her left breast.

323

'You're the romantics.' He kissed her good-bye; the caravan was leaving town tomorrow morning. 'I'll be in New York not long after you get back. See you then.'

'Be happy, Michael. Be happy with Doris.'

Doris was the daughter of a family friend in Chicago, who had known Michael through college. He would marry this young woman he loved, on November second, less than a week from that day. But she could not attend the wedding – she would be being strangled in St Louis. St Louis? She took out her calendar. One city, in time, became every city. Yes, St Louis.

CHAPTER 40

How had Lydia been persuaded to let him go?

Arlette could not imagine, and Anthony offered no explanations.

It was possible they had agreed to a divorce without ever talking about it. Perhaps they had simply let their lawyers talk about it instead.

He came into the bedroom, waking Arlette from a sleep so deep she seemed to have been swimming through dark waters, to hear him explaining that he was sorry to be late, he had been in another hotel for the past three hours, talking on the telephone to Lydia, in Mexico—

Mexico. Lydia. The words left her momentarily unable to speak.

Still wearing his raincoat, Anthony sat on the bed facing her. When she continued to look at him doubtfully, he reached out, touching her shoulder, and all the while watched her questioningly, suspiciously.

It occurred to Arlette that even at this moment he was wishing he could return to the past, undo what he had done.

'The decree was final today. There's a little town near here – Jim Brown has found a justice of the peace. We'll use our own names. No publicity that way, for the time being. We'll be married on Sunday, if you like.' He was staring at her angrily, and all at once grasped her chin and jaw in one hand, pressing his fingers hard into the flesh:

He hates me – for the trouble I've caused him. For Lydia, and his children, his parents . . .

All at once she was frightened, longing to get away from his insistent stare, the pressure of his fingers.

'Anthony!'

He released her and moved back, glancing away, his face turning darker. 'I'm sorry.' His expression was still full of suspicion. 'You *do* want to marry me?'

'Of course!' Distractedly she got out of bed, as if escaping from a mortal danger. She turned her back and covered her face with her hands.

Proposals, she had heard, were never proposals; only a random statement, residue of love and hate, error and accident, decision and indecision – all this produced a scene which was inevitably pathetic and harrowing:

Like marriage itself.

At the moment, she did not want to marry him, and wished she had not willed it so fiercely that, without a word, without a question, she had nevertheless brought it about.

Or was he marrying not the Lily Malone whose name would be on the license, not Arlette Morgan – but a compound female: Jade Ring and Juliet, Katharina and Desdemona and Elizabeth Doyle-Gloriana, and – one day – Millamant, perhaps Hedda Gabler, Cleopatra, Rosalind, Lady Macbeth.

Lady Macbeth.

Arlette raised her head swiftly at that treacherous thought. She turned slowly and found him standing, raincoat thrown aside and hands in his pockets, head lowered, watching her. The proposal had seemingly become a contest for power.

These disappearances of the past few weeks, telephone calls taken in the adjoining bedroom, the comings and goings at odd hours. All with the intent of persuading Lydia to divorce him before there was publicity, humiliating for Lydia, if not for him and Arlette, since actors were believed to be wanderers over the social landscape.

As Arlette wrote the scripts of his dialogues with Lydia on the nights while she waited, half asleep, for him to come back, she had not honestly believed that one day it would happen.

Yet what alternatives were left? Was it to be expected that while they traveled together, lived together and – it was now obvious – would appear together in one play after another, Lydia would continue her role of elegant unconcerned wife?

Another woman had married Lydia's husband without having taken the trouble of filing necessary documents.

Anthony did not look anxious, or pleading. He looked angry, as if he had brought a child a very expensive gift, troublesome to find, and the child did not understand its value.

'But I don't know why she gave you up.'

'You don't know Lydia.'

She knew well enough. Lydia had had no choice.

Anthony raised his voice, the tone Othello used, harsh, commanding, when he asks Desdemona if she is a strumpet. 'Don't talk to me about it again – ever!' After a few moments he crossed the room, turned, and spoke in a quiet even tone: 'If you ever leave me, for any god damn fucking reason whatever, I swear to Christ I'll kill you.'

Recognizing the truth when she heard it, Arlette sat down on the bed as if she had been given a blow. She looked at him, smiling tentatively, and in another moment the smile shone with the full radiance of Jade Ring's smile. 'Anthony, please believe me, I've never had a nicer proposal.' He smiled, but the smile was reluctant, and Arlette felt sudden pity, since whatever this had cost him in pain and conscience, whatever the loss of his children meant, he would never tell her. 'Forgive me.'

'I don't believe in marriage – neither do you. But I love you. I've never believed in that, either. Our old friend

Ming Huang said it: *"The greatest disaster of a man's life — one from which not even emperors or dragons are immune . . ."* '

He was smiling, and she understood that the anger was finished, the resentment against himself and her for what he had done was over. Anthony did not reconsider the past: once done, he had no more to say.

I'll learn from him. I'll learn to forget — some things, at least.

But her fears continued.

One day we will begin to grow old.

One day — one of us must die first . . .

They were almost silent as they got ready for the drive to the town forty miles away, where arrangements had been made for Lily Malone and Patrick Francis Runkle to be married at the home of a justice of the peace, at five-thirty on that warm late-October afternoon.

Arlette wore the jonquil-yellow dress, and she was slipping into the coat, mauve wool, lined with pale-yellow-dyed moleskin. Anthony stood knotting a tie over his white shirt, an unusual concession to the solemnity of the occasion. And both of them seemed unable to think of much to say.

Minerva had told her, a few days after she had married Frank Courtney: 'The time when you feel as if you've never seen the guy before is that terrible hour or two before the ceremony.'

Perhaps it was a general condition. The fear of getting what you wanted most. Life had no pure moments; each arrived with its own corruption.

She approached him timidly. 'I love you, Anthony. I'll always love you.'

He smiled. 'Will you? Let's hope so. We may be lucky, and we may not. But don't ever forget — that's not all there is to this.'

Surprised by the brusqueness, hurt that he had seen fit to issue one more warning of dire consequences, she said softly, 'Most people stop loving each other — I've heard. And we've known each other nearly ten years.'

'Ten years, by the calendar. How long?'

'I don't know how long. Before our parents met. Where were we then?'

All at once, in a sudden access of contrition or love, he caught hold of her and kissed her. 'Now, let's go. And why don't we just say nothing more until it's over with.'

'I never expected that it would actually happen.'

Now why did I say that?

'Neither did I. But it has.'

She said little until they reached the town – only talked about the clouds, the sunny day, the beautiful countryside, so near the big ugly city, the warmth, the turning leaves.

She thought about Lydia, and she thought Lydia was her own victim. Lydia had not been able to keep her husband from falling in love with another woman; and once he did, Lydia had refused to believe that serious love sometimes had serious consequences. She had imagined that Anthony was less Anthony De Forest than he was Patrick Runkle, and so had failed to see that another world from the one he had been born to was the entire globe itself to him now.

She felt no guilt about Lydia, and little about the children. Guilt, she thought, was the most sordid vice of all. Guilt repaired nothing, mended no hearts, stitched together no torn feelings.

During the reading of the brief ceremony, Arlette gazed solemnly at the justice of the peace without seeing what he looked like.

She heard a man's voice talking, distantly; she heard her voice and Anthony's reply. Then all at once she was alert again, smiling, shaking hands with the justice of the peace and the two witnesses. She wore the platinum thread tied in a miniature bowknot, and Anthony – after a momentary hesitation of surprise – wore the wide gold band she had offered him.

The secrecy over this ceremony, since they were going to remove the rings and not wear them until the announcement, some time after the road tour had ended, Arlette took to be a concession to Lydia's pride, while the marriage, done so quickly, had been for Arlette, because he knew she was afraid that Lydia would appear again.

'It may be a marriage to us,' Anthony told her, once they were driving back. 'But when Jerry and Alicia and Art Friedman and Sy Harman and the rest of the Hoffman-Repertory hear about it – it'll be a merger!'

Arlette laughed joyously, as if they had made a successful raid on a bank and were now off to enjoy the plunder without any of those hazards a movie script would have put in their way.

Anthony told her that when the announcement of their marriage was made, she could have another ring, whatever she chose. That one, he explained, had been produced by tying a thread around her finger while she was asleep, then sending it to James Brown, who had dispatched one of his lawyers with the finished ring to Chicago.

'I wasn't sleeping.'

'Then you weren't surprised.'

'Oh, yes. I was surprised. I still am.'

Anthony's ring was a gold band, half an inch wide, and the reason for its width became clear when he took it off, once they were in the hotel, and studied the inscription which circled around inside it: '*Lest you and I who love should wake some morning strangers and enemies in an alien world, far off . . .*'

He held the ring between his thumb and forefinger, beneath a lighted lamp, squinting slightly to read the print, turning it, reading it again, and at last glancing at her with a slight smile. 'Elizabeth to Essex.'

'Maxwell Anderson,' she agreed.

'You didn't have this made after I told you about the divorce?'

'I had it made in New York, before we left.'

Anthony's eyes narrowed thoughtfully, examining it again. 'You were sure of what I would do.'

'I wasn't sure. I was going to give it to you after the last performance.'

'I see.' He slid the ring back onto his finger. 'And

whichever way it went – you thought that was a sentiment appropriate to the occasion.'

'I suppose I did.' She looked at him earnestly. 'Or why would I have had it made?'

She expected to discover his secrets without asking what they were.

She looked at him reading the Sunday papers, seated naked before a window in the hotel room – somewhere, after they had left St Louis – Des Moines, Seattle, Portland? The cities were even less individual to her now; a hotel room, a bed, a dressing room, a stage, a taxi cab, an airport.

She lay in bed watching him. The sunlight through the window polished his hair and skin. This was present and future, so far as she was concerned. But not to Anthony.

Anthony had plans, evidently plans enough to fill the future, however long it might prove to be. 'There's only one reason for acting: you believe the theater gives people a sense of their long history, and their possible future, if they don't fuck it up. You have an audience—' Anthony leaned forward, elbow on his knee, and doubled his fist. 'You have an audience, sitting there half dead. If the actor's any good, he's going to bring them at least partly to life. And that's a gain. It may not last long, or it may last longer than we think. I've never been sure that any authentic experience, in a theater, a museum, listening to music, reading a poem, is that momentary. Somehow or other, like everything else, it gets woven into the guy who sees or hears it. However lethargic the son of a bitch may be.'

Anthony loved and hated the audience.

But Anthony did not regard himself as a star, alone on the stage but for some human props. He was a fragment of a whole, and when he hated the audience it was for their reluctance to be brought fully into the performance. He hated them when they curled into themselves, and his acting was enhanced to a ferocity, challenging them to let themselves be invaded, swarmed over, terrorized, seduced. Anthony's relationship with the audience was as passionate as his relationship with her, and the same end was sought: their mutual temporary oblivion.

Jerry called from time to time, and when he did they discussed the production he wanted to do next year: *The Way of the World.*

'It's the right balance,' Anthony told Arlette. 'After what you've done, and the pictures I've done – that's logical for the next one. But not too soon. The public will gobble you alive; once it's got a taste for your flesh. One a year, that's it. The rest of the time – work.'

'You'll need work for this one,' Jerry had warned them. 'A Restoration comedy will bore the shit out of an audience unless it goes off in their faces like a round of buckshot.'

Arlette laughed, delighted by these two men, so serious about their professions they thought in terms of murdering the audience, shooting a round of buckshot into its face to keep it alert; who talked in terms of rape, lust, murder, rage, passion – and balance. Always they came back to balance; the right mix.

Jerry surprised them by appearing for the last performance in San Francisco, although they did not see him until he arrived at Gordon Donahue's hotel suite, where she sat with Valerie and Frederick in a far corner of the room.

'You've become a very good actress, Lily. A very moving actress.'

Arlette looked at Valerie. 'But it's not what you wanted—'

Valerie smiled. 'Perhaps I wanted for you what I once wanted for myself.'

'Your influences—'

'My contributions have meant very little. I'm the true believer who is no longer quite certain what he believes. Frederick is luckier – the Middle Ages will always be there. There was such a time, it's a matter of how one interprets it. The theories I've studied change and change, and are perhaps meaningless.'

'They weren't meaningless to me.'

She wanted to cry, but that would spoil Gordon's party, so filled with lively, noisy, gaily talking young men and women, and a few not so young. The triumph of this night, her marriage to Anthony, seemed remote from this man and woman, of whom she did not think often, or even call often.

For all the good I've been to them – I might have been their own child, she thought bitterly.

Anthony, seeing her in distress, came to sit facing Frederick, and Valerie and Frederick and Anthony fell into sober discussion of the current political situation, a safe subject.

Jerry Hoffman's theories of shaking the guts out of the audience, Arlette reflected, would not have seemed a valid social project to Valerie and Frederick. For once their guts had been shaken, Valerie and Frederick would have pointed out, the audience must return to that other world in need of a much more profound shaking.

When Valerie and Frederick left, it was Gordon and Arlette who walked with them to the elevator, and when the doors had closed, Arlette murmured, 'How strange.'

She glanced at Gordon, who was watching her as he did whenever they were unlikely to be watched by others; and the memories he had kept well burnished showed in his eyes. Anthony, she guessed, had decided to tell Gordon they were married, as he had decided to tell Jerry Hoffman.

'You're happy now?'

'Oh, Gordon – he's my life. Is that ridiculous?' She stopped, shocked at the self-centered cruelty. But before she could apologize, make it worse, Gordon kissed her lightly, and she went swiftly ahead of him.

Late at night, when everyone had gone but Jerry and Gordon and Marian, they began to talk of *The Way of the World*.

'It's too long for a contemporary audience,' Jerry said. 'It needs cutting. I've been doing some work on it.' He glanced from Anthony to Arlette. 'You'll do it?'

'If we all decide to.' Arlette glanced at Anthony.

'Millamant's laugh—' Gordon smiled. 'That's what this play hasn't had for a long time.'

'That conspiratorial laugh.' Jerry was smiling reflectively.

'Mine?' Arlette asked innocently.

'Of course,' said Anthony. 'No other woman laughs like you do.'

CHAPTER 41

When they arrived in Venice, Arlette discovered that years ago Anthony had spent considerable time in Europe. He had not thought of mentioning it, as, of course, he had not thought to mention hundreds or thousands of things he had done and seen and thought about.

These were parts of him she could never know, any more than he could rediscover Lily Malone as she had been before – or even after – he had known her: the Lily Malone who had loved Gordon Donahue; the Arlette Morgan who had loved Jerry Hoffman; who had played for a few weeks at loving Jeffrey Brooke.

When Anthony had been between ten and fifteen, his parents had made annual excursions to Europe, dispatching him and his younger sister, Felicia, in the company of a tutor, through every museum, church, significant village or city, on the Continent. His sixteenth year he had spent in Switzerland, a strict school he remembered with loathing and gratitude for its discipline.

Like early events in the life of Lily Malone, this had become such ancient history that he mentioned it only when he recognized a painting or remembered some famous monument. Or when Arlette complimented him on his French, a little jealous, since it was better than hers.

And how had he come to spend the last two years of college at a state university? He left her to guess at that: perhaps to discover if the environment where he had lived

333

so far was, after all, as natural to him as if he had been borne into its inland sea.

The reason, she supposed, was not different from the force which had propelled him to Korea later; then out of Harvard Business School and into the theater. Anthony took life with zest and curiosity, confidence and unspoken respect for every person he met – at least until he had made a decision about them.

The day they arrived in Venice, they slipped the rings on each other's fingers again, standing before the window over the Grand Canal, heads together to observe this solemn mysterious ritual.

Despite their happiness, there had been a strangeness and solemnity between them these past three months, as if each were still apprehensive.

She had at last begun to believe he needed her as much as she needed him – a need woven by their lovemaking, laughter, the intimacy which at times obliterated even the sense of time past, which was finally what kept people separate: not the fragile contraptions of tissue and bones. All that could be penetrated by an act of powerful will and desire. But the past, the unshared and unshareable past, the minutes and hours and days spent apart, was the final unbreakable barrier.

Lydia was now a part of that past – known only to him.

In a year or two, she would forget Lydia St Denis had ever existed.

Lydia would have vanished among the People Who No Longer Count.

Her awareness of what people said behind their words and thought behind their smiles was keen. When it struck forcibly, she closed the lid of the oyster shell and went to work on the pearl, fashioning it around the grain which had swept in upon that tide of treachery and sorrow which Michael had warned her she must accept as a part of life's senselessness. It was Michael who told her not to concentrate so much attention upon the manufacture and polishing of that pearl:

But suppose I had no pearl – what would I do when the world becomes intolerable?

For even Anthony had not erased those memories of early loss. She had supposed that one great love might replace the earlier love. But the difference between them was too great: what she had lost as a child could not be recovered by an adult love of passion, joy, and excitement.

Since that grief was permanent, she told herself the superstition might be true, that every actor of consequence was victim of a slow poison which, as arsenic was said to do, brightened for a time the senses of one who took only a little, not enough to kill.

Anthony talked to her about his plans for their future, and the plans, eliminating their past lives with one sweep of the eraser across a densely inscribed blackboard, had obviously been some years in the making.

When they were in bed, or investigating museums and palaces, at theaters or the opera, eating in grand or simple restaurants, he outlined a program so concise and logical that she listened in amazement:

One play or motion picture a year.

One more road tour – perhaps *As You Like It*.

Macbeth, yes, *Macbeth*, one of these days. If they meant to take their work seriously and expected others to take them seriously. The question about *Macbeth* was not if but when.

Arlette hated the sound of *Macbeth*, and got a sick feeling when she thought of it; she resolved not to think of it. Perhaps it would never come. Perhaps they could plan and plan and plan until—

But Anthony did not make plans for the sake of amusing himself.

Soon it was clear that all these plans had been discussed, with Jerry and the Hoffman board, and a variety of lawyers, accountants, writers. Yes, writers. John Powell might be persuaded, indeed was almost persuaded, to do a screenplay about Emma Hamilton and Lord Nelson, a picture she could scarcely be too snobbish to appear in.

'Movies are as necessary as the classics, Arlette. When

we get back, I'm going to arrange a screen test for you. It's arranged,' he amended. 'If it turns out the way we expect – I'm sure Powell will do the script. Margo likes money, and the more kids they have, the more she likes it.'

Hedda Gabler was in the near future. Perhaps in two years. So was *Henry IV*, Part I, for Anthony. Alternating weeks for that combination. They would sometimes play together. They would sometimes play apart. They would be the De Forests. They would also be Arlette Morgan and Anthony De Forest:

Hedda Gabler. She's killed better actresses than I am.

Looking at him, admiring that remarkable face with a longing which even the distance of the dinner table turned into a wasteland she could never cross to reach him – she sometimes fell to thinking of him with bitterness:

He married me because I can do the one thing he really respects. I can make people feel what I want them to feel. I can take on the big challenges – more and more of them, and that's what life is to him. (One corrida *after another.) If I'm not as good as he is yet, I will be – one day. I know it. He knows it. He married me to complete his plans.*

Anthony reached across the table, not so great a distance, after all, to cover her hand with his. The decision for him, however long it had taken to reach it, was a closed circle.

'Anthony, this will take six or seven years. We haven't begun to learn what we need to know to do these parts.'

'Six or seven years is not a long time, Arlette.'

The plans included town and country houses, four or five cars, furniture, paintings, servants, secretaries. Anthony never referred to his money, although he had money; how much, he did not say. She had comparatively little, which always before had seemed to her riches enough.

Once the announcement of their marriage had been made by Art Friedman's office, Arlette refused to read the newspapers he sent.

But Anthony scrutinized them with the same care she

had seen him give to stock-market reports, business and financial sections. And Arlette found this was no desultory interest. Anthony was a shrewd and cautious businessman, who had no doubt learned much because of his father's money and his own inheritance, and had since taken it up with the fervor of a ballistics expert.

He had a sophisticated taste in antiques and paintings, china and silver – all of it abandoned to Lydia, she guessed, since he was now buying enough to furnish a house which seemed to Arlette bigger than they needed, even though he spoke of the little house he had put a broker to search out in the East Sixties or Seventies.

'Six or seven years—' she repeated doubtfully.

'Maybe eight. Maybe nine. Whatever it takes.'

'Then?'

'Then there will be other plans. We're not talking about a hobby.'

Anthony, she had long since determined, was at least as clever as she was – a thing she had never expected to discover. Perhaps he was more clever.

They smiled at each other, silently asking if it was time to leave, go back to the hotel, make love again.

The fury of sensuality, which she had thought could offer no more surprises between them, had proved, once they were left alone, to be more greedy, tormenting, painful than before. Whatever had not been explored had been explored now, and with a ruthless thoroughness which, often enough, left her distraught, perhaps momentarily insane.

The days were chilly, it rained often, and Arlette wore her new favorite costume, her wedding dress, as she thought of it. Anthony, in slacks and turtleneck sweater, wore a raincoat, whether it rained or not.

Wherever they went they were watched, greeted, shyly and often wistfully. Some few American tourists recognized Anthony, but Anthony did not recognize them and no one tried to talk to them. They moved in their own trancelike environment, arms touching for continuous reassurance. She smiled at the children and greeted them softly, speaking the few Italian words she knew. So they explored Venice, the city of soft trembling colors, half sunk in water.

Given a choice, Arlette would have chosen never to go back to those plans which waited: the discipline, the studies, the terrors of every night she must appear onstage. Not Anthony, however. This was a time for them to involve themselves in each other, blood and sinew, once and for all; a time, she thought, which he intended would weld them through common sensuality, so that those future plans would be the more effective.

'What if we find out we've felt everything it's possible to feel? There's an end, somewhere, even to the universe.'

'Is there?' Anthony looked amused. 'We never will.'

'My friends say—'

'Other people don't break through these walls—' His hand moved across her breasts and belly. 'Blood and bones intimidate them. They forget they're an illusion.' He turned away. 'And even so, no one knows what love is.'

'I do,' said Arlette bravely. 'It's the way I feel about you.'

'No one knows. They feel something, they can't understand it, they give it a name.' He shrugged, and laughed softly. 'It's a good enough name, but it has no god damn meaning.' He moved away. 'Get up – get up and do something. Get dressed – there's a future somewhere. It's on the calendar, June thirtieth, five forty-seven PM, London to Idlewild – that's where the future begins. Get up, I warn you, or I'll eat you for dinner.' He nodded. 'Don't smile. Love is a cannibal, along with his other crimes.'

Arlette was out of bed and dashed by him to the bathroom, beginning to splash about in the shower.

It took them by surprise, how quickly they went from the edge of unconsciousness, a dreaming state of stupefied half-awareness, to a sudden reawakening, an alertness to the reflections glancing upon the walls and ceiling from the canal, the flowers in vases, the clothes they had thrown aside, the disarrayed bed of the hour of siesta – and all at once it seemed they were no longer in danger of dying from this powerful medicine of lust, but were vigorous and gay, and nearly wild with happiness.

They avoided reporters until they arrived in London, and there, Anthony told her, it would no longer be practical. He had worked in England and intended to work there again, and had developed some cautious respect for the malice of the British press.

And when they got off the plane, a bouquet of red roses was forced into her hands, detestable with the mauve coat, but Anthony muttered at her to accept it and smile, smile. 'No matter what happens, keep the smile in place. I'll talk.'

Arlette was glad to hear that one of them would talk, since she would not, even if Anthony remained silent.

Lights flashed and a babble of voices went off simultaneously.

Arlette listened, bemused by Anthony's skill in dealing with these people he despised as a group and never considered as individuals. He was aloof, and he was charming.

He smiled, now and then, at the women, that smile she had once thought of as his yin-yang mirror, which, flashed in the eyes of the enemy, would hopelessly confuse him. He did not smile at the men, since the yin-yang mirror was of no use against a male adversary. And, in a few minutes, they had agreed that the Americans were tired, they must be given a few hours to rest. They let them go.

'Oh,' whispered Arlette when they sat in the limousine Anthony's British agent had sent. Her hands were cold, her face was white, but she smiled, waving her fingers at the photographers gathered outside, very much in the style of British royalty. 'It's degrading.'

'We'll never do much of it, I promise you. They're remarkably democratic, these reporters. They'll screw anyone at all. That's why I wanted to get the technicalities out of the way as quickly as possible.'

339

Arlette smiled, relieved and amused that Anthony, talking about their love, about Lydia's humiliation, his children, what must have been the disbelieving astonishment of his family and friends, referred to those thousand pains as 'the technicalities.' Anthony was a man of passion, but not sentimentality. Whatever caused him pain he did not mention. She might guess, but she would never get his confirmation.

Once again Anthony made himself charming to the thirty or forty reporters who appeared at their door at five o'clock.

He referred, gently and vaguely, to his children – somewhat like Macduff, she thought; and who could question a father's tender concern for his pretty ones?

He referred to Miss Morgan, his wife, seated beside him, a shy and sensitive artist, innocent of any responsibility for the 'circumstances.'

Arlette, a hesitant smile upon her mouth, an expression she had perfected long ago as having value under certain conditions, none of them on the stage, did indeed look as if she would not be capable of even knowing there had been 'circumstances' which had ended in her becoming Mrs Anthony De Forest.

The reporters left, more subdued than when they had arrived. Anthony closed the door and stood with his back against it, his face grim, reflective, angry.

'Well.' Arlette went to look in the mirror, to discover what effect this gang rape had had on her looks. None at all. She smiled at Arlette, not the sweet and tentative smile with which she had intercepted each curious, suspicious reporter's glance.

Yes, I'm a star – and I like that part of it.

CHAPTER 42

Arlette stood at the bottom of the broken steps, looking up at the old Long Island farmhouse, uninhabited for many years. The real-estate woman had warned her.

'Yes – this is a haunted house,' Arlette agreed.

'Then you don't want to go in?' Mrs Melrose, who had been sorting among her keys, turned away.

'But I do want to go in. That's why we came here.'

Half an hour before, she had sat in the small office, identifying herself as Lily Malone, a poet and writer in need of privacy and seclusion, escape from the sordidness one hundred and ten miles away on the island of Manhattan.

'Something isolated, a hundred years old: two hundred would be better. Five or ten acres, enough to grow whatever grows out here.' Mrs Melrose had smiled sympathetically, for Arlette's poet was pure and heroic, prepared to live in a ramshackle haunted house, only for the sake of the muse inhabiting the wind and the nearby salt spray and ocean surf.

She had driven out in the Mercedes-Benz which Anthony had acquired, along with the sought-for house on East Sixty-second Street, between Park and Lexington. She had come alone because Anthony was in Texas, looking at property with Jim Brown and two of his investment advisers.

The town house had immediately been put under supervision of an architect and decorator, and Anthony had explained: 'All we want is a place to live in which we can enjoy – and forget. The first one may as well be the last.'

'It may as well,' she agreed.

Looking for houses, buying houses, remaking houses, was not a project Arlette could imagine wanting to do more than once.

And this haunted house, far enough away from the city and the towns where Anthony's friends might want to envelop them, was the city's necessary antidote: a place to study, exercise, breathe fresh air, swim in salt water, walk and ride horseback, and keep themselves in the physical condition necessary if they were to carry out even a part of Anthony's plan.

Here was the house, and if it was haunted, so much the better.

It was near the end of the island, and almost hidden from the road, but for its shingled roof, or what was left of it. They drove along a rutted roadway toward the ocean, and got out to survey the house, covered also with silver-gray shingles, the shingles covered by rose vines which, Mrs Melrose said, bloomed with hundreds of old-fashioned blowsy pink roses for a few days every summer.

'Good.' The roses would be more valuable since they must plan for them, enjoy them, and remember them the rest of the year.

What Arlette saw, but did not describe to Mrs Melrose, was the house as it would be after one year or ten years, and for as long as either she or Anthony was alive. It would be a very different house, still covered with silver-gray shingles; the pale pink roses still blooming. But there would be nothing else Mrs Melrose would recognize.

'I'll like it here,' said the unworldly poet to Mrs Melrose.

'You haven't seen the ocean – or the cliffs— Let me show you other houses—'

'The other houses won't be haunted. Or I won't believe they are.'

That was the kind of reasoning Mrs Melrose understood, for such details made a house happy or unhappy, and that the house was haunted was an unarguable reason. At least it sounded haunted as they walked about. The floorboards creaked, mice skittered in the walls, the narrow staircase moved menacingly beneath their feet – and there, from the second-floor bedroom, was the ocean, gray and ominous on this August day which had begun so brilliantly only a few hours ago. Even the grayness pleased the poet.

'Yes, yes, that's the way it should be.'

The house Arlette could see, as she walked to the edge of the bluff, which dropped fifty or seventy feet down to a sandy beach, was a gray shingled house much bigger, with large rooms, three or four fireplaces, and season by season, year by year, a garden planted, a small greenhouse built.

The house, Arlette thought, would be a good companion to Anthony and to her – a trustworthy friend.

An architect was hired, a different kind of architect from the one planning their town house, and presently carpenters were at work.

Arlette had always thought of living expenses as something to trim narrowly, to use her inheritance carefully, since there was no way of guessing how long it must be made to last. But Anthony, with the generosity of a man who never imagined money could disappear, or perhaps the generosity of his own nature, paid for houses and cars, furniture and paintings, and Arlette had responsibility only for her clothes, since she insisted she must have responsibility for something.

As the antiques they had bought in Europe arrived and were restored, they began to replace the furniture in their hotel suite until their New York house was completed. And when Anthony's belongings came from Pasadena, she found he had an extensive and handsome wardrobe.

He also had four or five thousand books, and Arlette was embarrassed by the mere three hundred sent from her apartment.

She had use now only for the few articles of clothing she owned, the photographs which went wherever she did, and the envelopes she had taken from the desk drawer one day when she went alone to visit her old apartment and found it small, surprisingly lonely, for all its gay colors, and the plants, which had died under the super-intendent's care.

She left quickly, taking the envelopes like some shameful or sacred documents, for the little apartment represented everything which had evaporated from her life since she had married Anthony: in only ten months the past was gone.

She awoke each morning with a fulfillment of gratitude, experiencing her first conviction that long-lasting happiness – not transient joy or excitement – was a possibility.

All the more reason why those sealed envelopes were an embarrassment.

Alone in the hotel, she looked at them, a thick handful, white, pale yellow, pale gray, none with her address, for it was not Arlette's habit to tell that much about herself to the outside world.

She held them to the light, but the envelopes had been well selected – no light shone through them. She tried to remember when she had used that paper, whose name that blank envelope might contain:

Why was I afraid of them? Have they failed? Have they disappeared from my life?

She could be certain of only two names: Barbara Sloan and Pat Runkle.

She thought of destroying the envelopes, forgetting all the past with a gesture, but some superstition prevented that.

The envelopes were sealed as irrevocably as the records of the Spanish Inquisition after one of the accused had been sent to the stake.

She put them in a drawer of a fine eighteenth-century Chinoiserie cabinet Anthony had bought in London as a birthday present: silver gilt, embossed with dragons and peonies, containing dozens of drawers, some secret ones she had discovered, with a key which she put on her chain and about which Anthony knew nothing:

So much for them. At least, while they're there, they can't cause any trouble.

As for everything else in the apartment, she left it for the young actress who played the part of Betty in *The Way of the World*, a waiting girl in a chocolate house, who was not even listed in the cast by name.

The girl had inquired about an apartment she might rent. She had asked Minerva, who was playing Mrs Marwood, with Eva as Mrs Fainall, and they suggested to Arlette that the girl might lease it, since Arlette did not want a stranger moving into an apartment she had lived in. This girl was a stranger, but since she had passed through Jerry Hoffman's radar screen she was not entirely strange.

Arlette approached the girl after rehearsal one day, and for the first time it occurred to her that she was now a star without question, and that that stardom carried with it not only privileges, but the capacity to hurt others without intention.

'Miss Crane.' Arlette spoke in her warmest tone, very softly, since the girl looked frightened. 'Have you a moment?'

The girl was moderately pretty, with pale blue eyes and carrot-red hair, and a thin flat-chested body. She made a serviceable Betty, but Arlette thought that would likely be the end of her, unless she could learn to act well enough to compensate for a number of deficiencies.

'Oh, Miss Morgan—'

Arlette looked at her in disbelief, carefully concealed by a reassuring smile:

Was I ever that scared? Would I have let someone see it if I were?

'Someone told me you were looking for an apartment. I have one with a lease that runs another seven months—'

Arlette went on to explain that she would sublease the apartment, and that Miss Crane might have the furniture for nothing. The girl listened as if Arlette had said she was giving up the part of Millimant because Jerry Hoffman had decided Deborah Crane could do it better.

The girl was frightened and grateful, but Arlette noticed something more. She was watching her with calculation, trying to understand why Arlette was Millamant while she was to play the chocolate-house serving girl; why Arlette was a renowned beauty and she was one more

345

moderately attractive actress; why Arlette had married Anthony De Forest, who had loved her enough to give up another beautiful woman and his children.

'Never trust a young admirer,' Alicia had advised her when she had gone for her first lesson after their return from Europe. 'Remember they want to be you without the trouble you've taken to become yourself.' Arlette understood that Alicia gave this warning from her own experience. 'Be polite, but have nothing to do with them. The trustworthy world gets smaller, Arlette. There will be fewer and fewer people you can trust. You know most of them right now.'

Now here stood this twenty-one-year-old girl. Arlette gave her a few seconds to thank her for the apartment. 'My secretary, Miss Richardson, will call you when my personal things are out – it will be a day or two—' And she escaped from the grateful beneficiary.

All she had wanted to do was get rid of what she no longer needed. She had begun the transaction with some vague notion of being given credit for generosity where none was due and had ended with an odd feeling that this young actress, Deborah Crane, from this moment until the end of her life, would be Arlette Morgan's enemy.

However, the girl talked much of the generous Miss Morgan, as good as she was beautiful, and Arlette found she had established a reputation for largesse she had no intention of continuing. Then she forgot Deborah Crane. She had another young woman to worry about: Mrs Millamant.

Having conquered several fractious female parts, Katharina and Juliet and Jade Ring and Desdemona and Elizabeth-Gloriana, she had hoped that from now on she would fill several notebooks with conclusions and speculations, and proceed in businesslike fashion to present the character at its most vital individual peak. The worst must be over.

Between the time they had discussed *The Way of the World* in San Francisco and the time they went into rehearsal, months after Arlette and Anthony had returned from Europe and begun to settle the mechanics of their future lives, the play had come to seem inevitable as any other fate.

Jerry had cut the play radically, to give zest and speed. After all, Congreve was not Shakespeare, and *The Way of the World* was not sacred ground.

Jerry had taken her aside, near the end of the first week, to ask her to describe Millamant to him. The heightening of tone, expression, gesture, not to farce but to the comedy which recognized that the way of the world in the seventeenth century was no different than it was today – this would be easy to accomplish. That world was an alien world, more distant and more exotic than Othello's Venice or Petruchio's Padua.

'She wants him,' said Arlette.

'There's something she wants more.'

'She doesn't want to lose herself.'

'That's right. And one is not more important than the other.'

But that was not what she had thought about Millamant the night before, when Anthony had come into the bedroom to find Arlette, still in the black rehearsal sweater and skirt, lying on the chaise longue in the dark.

Anthony approached her slowly and she looked up at him, smiling a little.

'What went wrong? Something I didn't see?'

'Something you didn't see.'

He turned on the lights and sat beside her. 'What in Christ's name was it?'

'Mrs Millamant. Did you see her today?'

'No, truthfully. But Mirabell wasn't there either.'

She continued to look at him, thinking it would make little difference if Mirabell never made an appearance, either during rehearsals or during the run of the play. It would be all the same. For Anthony had the capacity to bring out in every actress, and most of the women in the audience, some female hungriness: the nun locked up too long; the spinster by accident. Sleeping beauties woke up suddenly in Anthony's presence, and Cinderellas would not leave at midnight.

'I don't like Millamant,' said Arlette with that resistant sullenness she developed against each new character. 'I don't understand a woman whose worst fear is being gypped out of her estate in case her aunt disinherits her or gets married. Why not play her like a whore, trying to make the best bargain she can for her tail?'

'Because her inheritance is not all she's concerned about. Those people gave away no more of their secrets than we do. She's terrified of losing something. But it isn't money.'

Arlette smiled slowly, reaching out to touch his chest, placing her widespread fingers flat against it. 'She's terrified of Mirabell. She's terrified she may not be able to make him stay in love with her once she gets him.'

I know all about that myself.

She had not admitted that fear of losing him to anyone, not Eva or Minerva, not Alicia; although perhaps Alicia knew it anyway.

For the first day she had gone to Alicia's apartment after they had returned from Europe, she had impulsively embraced Alicia and then, to her dismay, had given an unexpected sob.

She smiled quickly. 'I think this is the first time I've really believed that we're married. I kept thinking that somehow, someway – I've even dreamed it, lying beside him—'

'We never expect to get the one thing we want most.'

'I always did.'

'There were things you took care not to want most.'

Of course. I took care not to want Anthony – for a long, long time.

'Now,' said Alicia, 'you have him. And you always will. Anthony is a serious man.' She looked at Arlette thoughtfully. 'What does Millamant mean to you?'

She means one more incarnation – one more offering – one more life that might have been lived.

348

'I've never seen it performed,' she said cautiously. 'Is it effective?'

'It needs a great deal of style and confidence, and tremendous energy from everyone. It's an extremely difficult production.'

'But their intrigues are silly, and intrigue is one of life's serious businesses. All living is a conspiracy.' Arlette laughed, that conspiratorial laugh – the one laugh she had not cultivated.

Anthony would provide the fastidious Mrs Millamant with another sort of Mirabell. His native intensity, the pervasive suggestion of ferocity, would convert even seventeenth-century brocades and full-bottomed wigs into a species of ironic commentary on this gentleman who was half a pirate, entirely convincing when he coolly warned Petulant that he would *cut your throat, some time or other . . .*

CHAPTER 43

Arlette's Millamant developed day by day and week by week, summoned out of hiding by Anthony's sensual Mirabell, who talked of breeding with such intensity, so undeniable a need for this woman, that all at once Millamant turned away after a long session of bantering, declaring she would have nothing more to do with him.

Then she spoke softly, as to herself: '*Well, if he should not make a good husband, I am a lost thing – for I find I love him violently.*' Millamant's face was thoughtful and sad, a little frightened, and tears formed in her eyes as she raised the imaginary mask on its ivory stick to conceal them. At this moment Millamant's character changed once and for all.

There, finally, was Arlette's secret:
Why had she given it away?
Perhaps because she could not play Millamant to

Anthony's demanding Mirabell another day without those tears, gift of submission to Mirabell.

There was a general pause of surprise, and Jerry called out from midway back in the auditorium: 'Beautiful! For Christ's sake, don't lose it.'

Anthony came nearer, looking at her seriously, as if the moment had affected him not as Mirabell, who might not prove a good husband, but as Anthony De Forest, who if he did not prove a good husband might destroy this woman, who was less defiant, less independent, than either Mrs Millamant or Arlette Morgan.

'Why not before?' Anthony asked her later, in the dressing room. 'It sums up the play. Until then, it was too bloody seventeenth century. Now it speaks out for its own time and every other.'

'I have to have something no one knows about – something to get me out on that stage the first night. I'll have to find something else.'

On opening night, Millamant swept the stage with her train, her hair high and curled over a comb, black patches on her face, entering with all the bravado of a flamenco dancer, eyes flashing, smile flashing, using her fan like a pair of castanets, and felt a sense of rising excitement and pleasure in the audience, that forming delight which was a wave running toward them as they moved about in a choreography of rapid pacing, stopping, turning, a very clear but swift-spoken dialogue, the entire cast glittering with satin and gold brocade, diamond necklaces, and canes sure to conceal swords.

Lighting played across them in a continuously changing chiaroscuro, and when Mirabell exclaimed: '*Here she comes i' faith full sail, with her fan spread and streamers out . . .*' there was a burst of applause.

And when Millamant, at last, in a voice of provocative desperation, demanded: '*Why doesn't the man take me? Would you have me give myself to you over again?*' Anthony moved so swiftly that one hand was about her waist, fingers spread to touch one breast.

'*Ay,*' said Mirabell with a somber face. '*I would have

you over and over again. I would have you as often as I possibly can.' They looked at each other with the seriousness of two people who could not wait much longer. *'Well, heaven grant I love you not too well, that's all my fear.'* There was the dread of every man who finds himself deep in love and no help in sight.

Even as the last few words were being spoken by Lady Wishfort and Fainall, the audience was applauding, and behind the curtain Arlette and Anthony exchanged quick glances, knowing they had beckoned them into their fantastic stylish little world. The curtain shot up, for Jerry was determined not to slow the pace of curtains, bows, smiles, even Arlette's raised arm, quick signal of conspiracy between actors and audience, witch or queen, exchanging secret knowledge with true believers.

Now, we're married, Arlette assured herself as Anthony propelled her through the other players, saying as she passed: 'Thank you, thank you, you were all so wonderful. Thank God, it wasn't a tragedy!'

They arrived at Alicia Fiedler's party late, for they were unable to leave, heartlessly abandoning Millamant and Mirabell to their unconsummated desire.

Now here she was, a new species of flora, a woman in full bloom, never so beautiful before, and perhaps never to be as beautiful in the same luxuriant glistening way again.

Arlette had the enduring beauty which would last her a lifetime, however long she might live. But at that moment, sailing among them like Millamant herself, all but naked from the waist up in a yellow silk jersey dress, its weighted skirt swirling around her feet like eddying water, two long strings of diamonds falling from each ear to her shoulders – Anthony's gift, the first real jewelry she had owned – she was aware of herself as she was aware of herself only on the stage.

She knew what she was doing, heard what she was saying, watched herself kissing Alicia and Jerry, Eva and Minerva, Max Gilmore and John Powell, two or three dozen people who either were, or seemed to be, her dearest friends, whether or not she would recognize them tomorrow.

And all the while she was aware of someone else, who guided and maneuvered her, told her what to say, whom to kiss, when to laugh, which laugh, when to smile, which smile. There was the awareness that if ever in her life there might be a few hours of triumph and power, this was that time.

Later – yes, whatever came later would be different, if only because this had happened.

Eventually Arlette found herself talking to John Powell, who recently had become one of the directors of the Hoffman-Repertory.

His most recent play, produced a year and a half before, a play about the discovery of DNA-RNA, a somber and ironic comedy of rivalry among scientists popularly imagined to pass through life in white laboratory coats, walking a plateau of detached wisdom, had been more successful than anyone had expected of so serious a play.

Double, Double had given him the austere reputation he had sardonically fastened upon his scientists, and critics had taken credit for his 'growth,' as if they had pruned, watered, and force-fed the plant named John Powell until it ceased to languish in the denitrated soil of youthful nostalgia and impertinent sophistication and produced that outsize blossom.

While he had been writing and researching the play, he had asked to meet Michael, and had spent much time in his laboratory, traveling with him to the seminars and conferences with which scientists occupied themselves, engaging in new feuds and settling old grudges.

'You were the most delightful Millamant I've seen.'

He was looking at her intently, and Arlette realized it was only a deepening of the way he had always looked at her: *When I saw you play Juliet, I wanted you so much.* He had meant what he said, even if he had not meant to say it.

Now he took the horn-rimmed glasses from his pocket

and put them on, perhaps the better to study her: arms, breasts, nipples, visible against the silk jersey, mouth and teeth, hair and eyes. He seemed to be taking an inventory which would be available whenever he chose to re-examine it.

A little surprised, she realized that John Powell was in love with her, and perhaps he had always been in love with her, but she had been too occupied to notice it. Tonight, however, being both Millamant and Arlette seemed to heighten her response to everything: talk and laughter, music from somewhere, arguments and embraces, swirling around them.

'One day, Arlette, I want to write a play for you.'

I should tell him not to look at me that way, not to expect anything.

But neither Arlette nor Millamant was prepared to relinquish admiration. The pleasure of John Powell's admiration was keen and flattering, as another man's might not have been; and soon it would evaporate, like the spirit of Millamant herself. She continued to smile at him with a seductive encouragement she could not diminish.

'Did you hear what I said?'

'That you want to write a play. For me?'

'You – and a few others, of course. But it would be your play. One day, that's what I want to give you, when I've had more experience.'

John Powell, you must be more careful . . .

'You're one of the country's best playwrights today.'

'I'm not ready to work on it. If it happens—'

All at once there was Anthony, one arm about her waist, and she turned to him with a quick smile:

He's jealous.

'Will you do it with me?' John asked, having nodded a brief greeting to Anthony.

There was another of those ambiguous sentences he either could not prevent or possibly used as a means of telling her what could not otherwise be said.

'Let's wait, shall we?'

That was as ambiguous to John Powell and Anthony as anything John had said, and she deftly uncurled herself from Anthony's encircling arm and was away, joining a group of members of the cast – all of them talking louder and with greater excitement as the time for the morning papers approached.

Arlette moved from one person to another, one group to another, pretending to carry on conversations and listen to others, sustained neither by food nor champagne, but by some artificial atmosphere, graceful and buoyant.

Quite unexpectedly, Deborah Crane was before her. Arlette started to move around her, annoyed to see this girl whom she had, quite negligently, befriended and then forgotten.

No sooner had she given her permission to inherit her lease, sit on her sofas and chairs, sleep in her bed – although she had removed all linens, anything which could be regarded as having any personal connection with her – once having done her good deed, Arlette began to wish she had let the apartment to someone she would never meet.

Now here stood Deborah Crane in her path, smiling, almost slyly, Arlette realized with sudden anger.

Arlette smiled, Jade Ring's smile, and would have gone on by, but Miss Crane's voice rose to a plaintive note: 'Oh, Miss Morgan, I've tried so often to thank you. You can't imagine what it means to me, living where you lived, surrounded by your possessions—'

The earlier humility had been a pose. She was not afraid of Arlette, she was not in awe of her, she was not grateful to her: she was beginning to compete with her.

The girl was even less attractive than she had seemed at a glance. Freckles the size of sequins spotted her face and neck and shoulders. She had red eyelashes covered at the tips with black mascara, and a little nose. Her body was more or less concealed in an inexpensive dress, and either she did not like her body or did not know what to put on it.

All at once Arlette smiled at her, and having decided

that her best weapon was an old one, she resorted to a politeness so effusive the adversary was invariably made to feel guilty – for reasons uncertain.

'Miss Crane, what could I have done with it? I thought it might help you – you know what it is, looking for a place to live in New York.' Arlette glanced sideways, as if in dismay at the prospect of looking for a place to live in New York. 'I'm glad you can make use of it.'

Miss Crane's pale blue eyes were wide with astonishment to hear this great star speaking swiftly in her famous musically low voice. Arlette stopped in midsentence and turned, touched Jerry Hoffman's arm as he was going by, and walked away with him.

Arlette did not think of Deborah Crane again, or see her. Lily Malone had known long ago how not to see people she did not want to see, and had passed that information along to her successor, Arlette. With a flash of her yin-yang mirror, she put them out of commission.

But she did remember Deborah Crane later that night, the moment she and Anthony walked into their apartment. And when Anthony had gone into the bathroom, Arlette opened the Chinoiserie cabinet, swiftly wrote DEBORAH CRANE across a sheet of paper, folded it, and placed the sealed envelope in the hidden drawer, returning the key to her evening bag. So much for Deborah Crane.

CHAPTER 44

'You begin by hating every new character. Day by day and week by week you fight them off. And then, no one knows when or why it will happen – you give in. You become that other woman. Now, Arlette, why the hell do you waste all that time?' Jerry's gray eyes were troubled.

'Why can't I be more like Anthony?'

Anthony fell into his part, a man stepping into an open manhole, the moment he set foot in the theater – while

Arlette had to wait. During rehearsals, she underplayed each part, until the first dress rehearsal; more often until opening night.

From the beginning, Anthony had an awareness of what he was doing onstage, how he sounded speaking those lines, how he looked, his movements and gestures, how much authenticity he was able at any moment to give to his part, and how much he would expect later to drag out of his guts, as Jerry put it.

He learned quickly: the walk of a new character, the intonations of that character's voice, the way to wear the clothes that would be required, the use of the accoutrements the set would have.

Arlette must make long preparations in silence, within herself, speaking in rehearsal in a low voice, as if she endured some literal bondage and could not set herself free.

'That's not what I mean, Arlette.'

'That's all I can do, Jerry,' she told him, so earnestly, so solemnly, that he caught her in his arms and kissed her, but not on her mouth. 'Jerry, it's not so easy to give yourself – transfer yourself to someone else, without even a promissory note.' They laughed, that laugh which happened between them now and then, the laugh of former lovers with good memories.

'You know Hedda Gabler by now. Who is she?'

Arlette hesitated. '*Part of us all hates life, and some are completely against it.*'

'That's it. Now – do it.'

'I'll do what I can. Don't you trust me?'

'I love you. Sure, I trust you.'

The more often she appeared in a successful production, the more impossible it was to imagine exactly what she had contributed, what Alicia and Jerry Hoffman had contributed, what was due to the play itself, the other actors, the set designer, the stage-hands, the musicians playing poker.

How was she to know which of these people, including Arlette Morgan, had made her a star?

Now that she did not have Anthony on the stage with her, she began to regard him with some of the earlier distrust and envy, carefully concealed.

'It's the right time for us to play in separate productions,' Anthony had told her carefully and gently.

Anthony was safe with his Prince of Wales. Shakespeare was never dated, Shakespeare's characters were never dated. Whatever they did, however preposterous, was taken for granted by audience and actors alike, for they were embedded in a people's history.

And Anthony was a facsimile of Prince Hal, taking his young manhood and his present self and capturing them in one time unit. If he was ever to play it at all, this was the time. Another year, and Prince Hal would no longer be attractive to him. He would prefer a more challenging *corrida*. The part was too easy for him even now.

Anthony believed in the men he played with a passion as intense as the passion he brought to lovemaking. Dominance was his goal, whatever he was doing; and once accomplished, he looked for the next challenger.

For some years Anthony had been casting oblique glances in Macbeth's direction. She supposed he was waiting for her to catch up with him.

Hamlet did not rouse his aggressions for conquest, even though it was obligatory that he play Hamlet someday if he intended to claim title to being one of the great English-speaking actors of his generation. Even now, Ophelia would offer no great difficulties for Arlette. But Anthony's remarks about Hamlet seemed to refer to a young man to whom he had taken a profound dislike.

Anthony's rehearsals had begun two weeks earlier, and they progressed like a southern spring, while hers remained locked in northern winter.

Neither watched the other's rehearsals, but they met at the end of the rehearsal day and drove home together, in that limousine which Conrad, their chauffeur-butler, ferried about town.

'I hope we never do this again,' Arlette said late one night.

They had moved into the house on Sixty-second Street three months before. Now, with Irma and Conrad to run it, Arlette's new secretary, Edna Frazier, to oversee the nuisances of her life, it seemed they might have been living there for several years.

'We have to, Arlette. If we played every production together, we'd both lose by it. We don't act because we love each other. It's what we do with our lives.'

They rode in silence a few minutes, Anthony staring ahead, frowning upon some inward scene. At last he muttered: *'Who, I rob? I a thief? Not I, by my faith.'*

If Conrad thought that a strange statement, he did not seem to, and by now perhaps supposed these occasional disjointed sentences spoken by Mr and Mrs De Forest were ordinary actors' talk.

Anthony glanced at her. 'He's a good Falstaff, you know, god damn good.'

Arlette followed the rules and asked him no questions. Presently Anthony remarked: *'I will redeem all this on Percy's head.'* He gave Arlette a savage glance. 'Gilmore's the son of a bitch I'm worried about. He gets better with each part. Hotspur. He expects it to set him up for life. He's got some of the great dialogue, and he's in dead earnest. I think he'd like to kill me.'

'And you'd like to kill him.'

Anthony gave a short hard laugh. 'Like to? I will.' He fell into another silence. *'Fare thee well, great heart!'* he spoke softly, musingly, perhaps reminiscing, and when they got out of the car, Anthony looked suddenly into her face, for her eyes glistened with tears. 'Arlette – darling—'

'You're very good, Anthony.'

'If I could multiply you by fourteen hundred, three weeks from now . . .'

But it would no more be possible for him to think of

her while he was onstage than it would be possible for her, one week from that opening night of Prince Hal's, to remember him. She would not even be clearly aware of Eva French, her friend, but only of Mrs Elvsted, her enemy.

One morning, after Anthony had left, Arlette sat in their bedroom on the second floor, drinking tea while she turned the pages of the *Times*. She paused briefly at the society section, for something about the photograph of a young woman, smiling straight at the camera with an almost professional composure, seemed familiar. Beside her stood a handsome, white-haired man, smiling as if he had been told to:

Hedda Gabler.

She turned the page.

'Miss Frazier,' she said an hour later, as they drove to her first class. 'I meant to read something in the paper this morning and forgot.'

During the summer, her secretary, Caroline Richardson, had married and retired, and Edna Frazier, a year older than Arlette, had replaced her.

Miss Frazier was only moderately pretty, although Arlette had taught her to make up her face and arrange her hair, and she dressed well, in clothes which never wrinkled, however long she wore them.

Edna Frazier had been born in Philadelphia, of a family with money enough to finance her debut, which she had refused, choosing to spend a year in Europe instead, traveling and studying, apparently studying whether or not to break her engagement, for that was what she had done when she returned. That was all Arlette knew about Edna Frazier, but for her excellent secretarial training. But Arlette had looked closely at her a few times and diagnosed her case as one of perpetual virginity, literal or not. It seemed to Arlette she would not be likely to lose this superior secretary to marriage.

Miss Frazier promptly produced the New York *Times,* the *Wall Street Journal,* and *Variety* from her attaché case. Arlette thought that if asked, Miss Frazier could produce from that same attaché case a white peacock or a silver lamé gown.

Arlette turned quickly to the society section and carefully studied the photograph she had labeled Hedda Gabler.

Certain faces, seen passing rapidly but picked out from a crowded street, might offer her a clue. The clues to a character were everywhere: they came in swarms, whispering, urging, reminding, suggesting: *She would look something like that. She is cold. She laughs without humor, only mockery.*

She found each day something new to impress upon that character, to coerce her to continued growth. For characters often reached a certain level of development and remained there, unless they were forced to completeness. That was the art which lay beneath the art.

A new part had always been – and so it remained for as long as she played it – a plunge off the edge of the time she lived in.

She had glimpsed a photograph which had reminded her of Hedda Gabler, forgotten it, and an hour later remembered the caption:

LYDIA DE FOREST MARRIES RICHARD MARTIN LENNOX

I'll be damned.

If Anthony had known this was about to happen, he had not mentioned it.

Richard Martin Lennox also lived in Pasadena, and no doubt Lydia had known him most of her life.

He was respectably widowed, his freedom to marry Lydia having come by an act of God, no doubt an acceptable working of fate in the opinion of Lydia's family, possibly of Lydia herself. His schools were listed, as were the boards on which her served; his clubs; his three grown children, with their husbands and wives; his church affiliation; his membership in a brokerage firm. Judging from all this, he was about twenty or twenty-five years older than Lydia.

Lydia did not concern her any longer. But Lydia did

concern Hedda Gabler: Richard Martin Lennox would have been the perfect husband for Hedda. He could have saved her from having married the plodding scholar, meek and mild, George Tesman:

What luck. Just what I needed. And just when I needed it.

Anthony came into the dressing room that night, his rehearsal having followed hers, to find Arlette reading a biography of Ibsen.

He had played the end of the great battle scene, Hotspur's death, and his face was wet with sweat. He looked like a man still in the fury of battle. He stopped in the doorway as she glanced at him in the mirror, as astonished as if he had never seen her before – the automatic response to real life. All at once he smiled.

'Yes, I saw it,' he said, although the paper was not in sight. 'It's a good thing – a relief.' He watched her in the mirror. 'You understand?'

Arlette nodded. A divorced husband or wife was no doubt a sword of Damocles, a reminder of promises made and broken, and the thread of guilt was a fine one.

'What's more,' said Anthony, 'he's loaded. That's what Lydia needs.'

I was right. Of course it was what she needed: Lydia-Hedda.

All that had been left of Anthony's eight-and-a-half-year marriage to Lydia, when the shipment arrived, had been his cameras and dark-room equipment, his books, his large wardrobe. No picture of the children was enclosed.

She began to forgive Hedda her trespasses, her weaknesses and failures, and slowly acquired for her a not entirely benign compassion. Once that quality began to appear the character betrayed a reluctant tenderness, which other actresses had not given her.

While the hungry sensualist which Arlette perceived, gave to Hedda, in some explicit or suggestive way, the menace and intent of a caged animal, moving restlessly about the stage, cocking her pistols, laughing mockingly at the Judge's alarm, standing beside Mrs Elvsted and threatening to tear her hair from her head, a line she spoke with such ferocity Eva French looked up in pleading alarm.

Day by day, the members of the cast began to respond as if some uncanny presence had appeared in their midst, a woman ironically placed out of her natural time sequence, and Arlette sensed that she was slowly drawing them to her, dominating them more forcibly than she had dominated a play before.

When the first dress-rehearsal run-through was completed, she was surprised to find herself exhausted as she had not been years ago, when everything had terrified her. The exhaustion, perhaps the surprise, was that she had done this without Anthony's help; without Anthony having once seen what she was doing.

During the past several weeks they had avoided talking about Prince Hal or Hedda, as if they were dealing with emotions so delicately balanced that one word might shatter the other's characterization, as if a finely wrought glass object, still in the hands of the blower, had been tried too far and had burst into fragments.

Wearing a short curly blonde wig, big tinted glasses, and a sweater and skirt, Arlette was going to the opening of *Henry IV*, Part I, with Alicia, sitting midway back in the theater, where Anthony could not see her if he tried.

Arlette and Anthony ate supper at four o'clock, at a table set in the bedroom; for the dining room, even with two such quiet and reticent people as Irma and Conrad, seemed too exposed a place for the meal taken before a first night.

The dinner passed in silence. Arlette kept careful watch over Anthony, to determine if he wanted to talk, but he seemed not to know she was there.

He stared beyond her, out the darkening windows, eyes slightly narrowed, eating slowly. He was in England, five hundred years ago, more or less, and there he was amusing himself at rough tricks with Falstaff, ridiculing him; bidding him farewell as he lay pretending to be dead on the battlefield; complimenting Hotspur's character before killing him— The dinner ended and Anthony got up, started toward the door, and then turned.

'Excuse me.'

Let him go softly—

Anthony left the room. Arlette closed her eyes, reciting Jade Ring's prayer to the Goddess of Mercy, Kuan-Yin, and looked up in surprise to find Anthony bending to kiss her, whispering, 'See you later.'

He was gone as if he had to catch a commuters' train, and Arlette sat still, but did not follow him or look out the window when she heard the car draw away from the curb. It seemed he was going a long journey from her, and might never return.

And so it proved to be, that journey of Prince Hal's, while she sat watching him proceed from the youthful spirited reckless Prince to the man who took with casual acceptance the report of his old friend Falstaff's death.

There was a slight gasp, as of shock and disapproval, as the Prince stood over Falstaff: *'Poor Jack, farewell. I could have spared a better man.'* And he swiftly left the stage; on to the next meeting with the rebels.

The murmur, without audible words, terrified Arlette for a moment, and she glanced about for signs of a rebel uprising against this heartless Prince.

But in a moment they had accepted what Anthony had told them: in the Prince's mind, he was at that moment more in command of the king he was one day destined to become than ever before – aware at last that kings made sacrifices, whether of their own wishes and needs, their armies, their wives or lovers, their friends.

CHAPTER 45

In London, during the costume fittings for the Nelson-Hamilton film, the makeup and hairstyle experiments, Anthony had found a portrait painter he considered respectable to paint Arlette in the white silk robe before it must at last be discarded.

By now it looked as if it would momentarily dissolve, but she refused to have it copied.

'You know why, Anthony.'

'I know.' The lovemaking, the disappointments, the anger and excitement, the loss and the return, the minutes before they set out for the town where they exchanged rings; the thread with its miniature bowknot; the wide gold band with its warning. 'But we have all that anyway—'

'Another robe wouldn't have it.'

And so he decided to have Arlette painted inside these memories. The portrait, he explained to the artist, was to hang in their bedroom.

They went to his studio, Arlette in the new costume which had at last replaced her jonquil-yellow dress and mauve coat. Her day clothes were more or less similar, and this dress was also a simple one of fine cashmere, sleeveless and white. The coat was cut like the other, flaring from narrow shoulders, white cashmere lined with black broadtail. The clothes she wore at night were her fantasies.

The painter looked at Arlette with surprise; surprise, perhaps, at finding she was not an imaginary woman.

As Arlette believed all Englishmen were, he was tall and thin, with high prominent cheekbones and a long bony nose.

'What do you plan to wear, Mrs De Forest?'

'A worn-out bathrobe.' She took it from her handbag.

'I see.' He observed it a moment. 'Perhaps you would prefer I paint the garment as it was?'

'By no means,' said Anthony. 'Its present condition is part of its charm.'

Arlette thought that perhaps he would solve all difficulties by using what she thought of as his English-fog style, misty from a distance; meticulously worked in a near *trompe l'oeil* upon inspection.

'Paint what you see,' Anthony told him. 'A beautiful

woman. There won't be time for many sittings. We begin work in two weeks.'

Arlette visited him a few times.

She undressed in the little bedroom, stepped out to stand facing him, hands at her sides, bare feet together, straight but at ease. With scarcely more than a nod of salutation between them, he was at work on his picture, while Arlette worked on her pearl, thinking of the film to come, the difficult scenes, the dialogue she wanted John Powell to rescue from Charles Granville. For Granville was known to hire the most expensive writer he could find and then rewrite the script.

At the end of a Granville picture, it was said, everyone's pocket had been picked, his emotions wrung and left out to dry until some stray breeze carried their desiccated fragments away.

'He's cannibal,' one of Anthony's English actor friends warned them.

'I know this cannibal. He found me too tough for his stewpot once.'

Arlette had met Granville on his trips to New York, but then she had been sure she would never make a film and had observed him with benevolent indifference – fierce reputation, gentian-blue eyes and all.

Granville was forty-one years old and unmarried. He had spent six years in the Royal Air Force, part of the time making movies, had flown bomber missions enough to have his quota of decorations, and had been wounded, not seriously. For almost ten years he had been recognized as one of the best producer-directors in the world.

His reviews had been those of angry critics, adoring critics, bewildered critics – but his pictures were successful, if not always clearly understood, and possibly the enigma was one of his most potent resources.

He had made movies like *Jude the Obscure*; he had made farces, sardonic and cruel; long intricate mysteries, also sardonic. He was famous, demanding, and had a sharp mocking sense of humor.

To be directed by Charles Granville was an honor quite

equal to being directed by Jerry Hoffman. And while thousands of people saw Jerry Hoffman's work, millions would see Granville's.

Arlette was still scornful at the prospect of being seen by millions of people. The screen test had shown her that she gave more of herself to the camera than she meant to. Or the camera took more than she meant to give it.

On the stage she gave everything within her power to each part she played; but she felt protected by the physical distance separating her from the audience, and by the fact that when it was over she might run and hide in her dressing room.

But the motion pictures would turn her inside out; strip off her skin; pare her to the bone. Leave her not only naked, but dissected, an object of sadistic curiosity.

Anthony said that this self-indulgent fearfulness was not only unhealthy but bad for her work.

'Part of your job is to give yourself away. Drag out your guts, as Jerry says, trail them around for everyone to slobber over.'

'I never meant to be a movie star,' said Arlette, aloof and smiling with anger.

'Then you might better have married that guy Jack Richardson, Davidson, whatever the hell his name was, and had four kids.'

Intimidated not only by Anthony but by the thought of being directed by that tall, thin, elegant Englishman, with his impatience, his endless patience – an eerie combination, but her own, as well as Anthony's and Jerry Hoffman's – Arlette had no more to say about her misgivings.

To Arlette the ephemeral nature of performing in a play was a great part of the theater's charm, just as the ephemeral nature of the act of love was a great part of its charm, however greedy love seemed for eternity.

It would end, it would ebb, the sensations would fade, slowly, the more slowly the more intensely experienced. Yet eventually it was gone, and could be recaptured only by repeating the performance. Like love, it was never quite the same twice. Each performance, each encounter in love, differed from every other; both experiences partook of her panmysticism, her conviction of a world without end or beginning.

A motion picture was a fixed entity. It was cut, edited, trimmed, spliced. Tricks were played upon actors, script-writers, musicians; all with the end in view of playing a final trick upon the audience – presenting an image so vast, so engulfing, that it sat in helpless captivity.

By contrast, Arlette thought this medium would be closer to what she had been criticized for during rehearsals – underplaying. The slightest nuance would be gobbled up by the camera, caught in lights and from angles in which she had no participation, and translated into someone quite different from Arlette Morgan.

John Powell had arrived before they did and had spent several weeks in conference with Granville, who was less careful of the people he worked with than Jerry Hoffman, who prevailed without the bloody encounters which were notorious upon Granville's sets: women stars screaming at him; men stars challenging him to fistfights; extras turning sullen and uncooperative; writers hurling the script at him.

However, he accomplished what he wanted and had no qualms about how it was done. An actress who hated him might give a better performance than one who sat placidly doing needlepoint while she waited for a scene to begin.

He whirled them about, apparently convinced nothing ever came of letting an actor fall into a stupor, supposing he could leap from lethargy across the emotional chasm to fury, lust, wild energy, sorrow, joy. He kept his sets at a high uneasy pitch from the day's beginning to its end, and while some of his actors loathed him when the picture was finished, and swore they would never work for him again, others found themselves exhilarated, expanded into a new awareness, as by some powerful drug.

The difficulty was that the explanation was perhaps in the drug itself – Charles Granville. The sense of having traveled vast distances beyond their normal selves was

367

only an illusion which would not outlast the daily relationship with Charles Granville. In the end, it seemed that what he took from all but the most capable was their life's blood. They donated it to him as if they had come to a philanthropic institution.

'The son of a bitch will wring you out like that,' one of Granville's earlier victims warned them, and made a quick gesture, wringing a large towel, leaving not a drop.

'He didn't give me any particular trouble.'

'He knows you don't need money – and even before *Jude* you had what most of us are still not sure of: Fame, money, knowing how to act – discipline is what he values.'

'So do we,' said Arlette.

'The truth is, he's a prick.'

'Maybe so,' Anthony agreed. 'But what the hell difference does it make? I can be one myself, without any trouble at all.'

They laughed, and the ogre, wherever he might be – lurking about a cutting room; tearing up sheets of costume sketches; shouting for his secretary, who was invariably discovered beside him; taking an actor aside for one of those talks, from which the actor often emerged with eyeballs red with rage and went into the next scene in a blind fury which, miraculously, produced the result Granville had wanted – the ogre seemed less fearsome; for the moment.

'You survived him once,' their friend said. 'Maybe you can again.'

'Can I?' inquired Arlette, so beguilingly the young actor seemed struck dumb by this American beauty, an exotic imported species.

'He deals with women a little differently. He rapes them to get what he wants.'

'Really?' said Arlette, innocently wondering.

'Not necessarily with his dong,' Anthony explained. 'Though that's his preference.'

Arlette wondered how Charles Granville would go about raping her into performing Lady Hamilton according to his wishes, particularly since she knew exactly how she meant to play her. The movie character, after all, had no weeks of rehearsal in which to develop. She must know who Emma Hamilton was the first day she faced a camera.

Granville's concern, he explained during one of those dinners in their hotel suite, was not with the British Empire or its fate in the late eighteenth century; not with the love affair between a national hero and a girl of the streets; not with battles, except as they were incidental to the absurdity of human nature – his concern was with stripping away skin and bones from his actors and, while they sat watching, from his audience.

Jude the Obscure had been cruel and brutal and, for the most part, ugly but for the impossibility of making Anthony look ugly; yet his good looks had made Jude's misfortunes that much more obscene.

It was Arlette's responsibility, Granville advised her, to create an Emma so seductive that England's hero would lose not only his wits, but his position.

'That will be easy for you,' he said when Anthony left to take an overseas call. 'Emma is not one of those sinister women who may or may not exist, but who have always existed in the imaginations of men.' He looked straight at her, and she was sure an electric light had gone on behind those very blue eyes; for there was in them now the intensity of a hynotist's gaze, an accomplishment of which many of his actors accused him. 'You, Miss Morgan, are the kind of woman who has, historically, caused men to disrupt their normal routines.'

Arlette laughed. The formality of the speech was incongruous with the intensity of the gaze, and evidently he realized it, for he laughed or pretended to.

'I'm not afraid of him,' Arlette announced bravely when Granville had gone.

'He hasn't Jerry's conscience about human vulnerability. He takes vulnerability and uses it to make the actor more vulnerable. You may think he won't be able to get through your defenses, but he will,' Anthony assured her.

'Well? I was scared out of my wits by Jerry Hoffman. And by Art Friedman – and Alicia. By you, too, for years—'

Anthony looked serious, and was evidently ashamed that once upon a time he had set out to scare her. 'You were too beautiful. I had to do something.'

CHAPTER 46

The projection room was filled at eleven o'clock.

After the greetings, they quickly settled down to see the final form of *The Two of Them* before its opening in New York and London.

Arlette had made the picture without complaining about the physical and emotional hardships of working not only under the primitive conditions of small Mediterranean towns and a half-deserted island, but under the more difficult conditions set by Charles Granville, who was doubtfully sane of mind or sound of reason during the interminable filming of the picture.

'Never again,' she had told Anthony when the last day of filming came to an end. 'Fuck the bloody movies.'

She was in a fury, but bade everyone – even Granville – good-bye with her most charming smile and light kisses. She left them with her reputation intact as the most thoughtful, cooperative, uncomplaining star they had ever worked with, except for Anthony, who seemed not even to need self-control, so completely he was in command of himself.

Arlette sat between Jerry Hoffman and Anthony, and as the room went dark and a blare of music sounded, she slipped her hand into Anthony's. This picture was important to them, not for money, but their shared history. Many of the others had been together in *The Taming of the Shrew*, some in *Othello*, and several were to appear in *As You Like It*, when the time came for that. There were no outsiders, no members of the press. It was a family reunion.

John Powell and Margo sat in back of them, and Arlette was almost as much concerned for what John would find in this movie, which had once existed only in his imagination, as for what she and Anthony would discover.

'Don't leave out the Battle of Trafalgar,' Charles Granville had told John two years ago. 'And don't eliminate Sir William Hamilton, even though he's useless. Do anything else you like. We want a viable motion picture, not a history lesson.' There were, he had added, few history lessons to be found in history books. 'It's all fiction. You're on your own.'

But that was not the way it had been, once work on the picture began. Daily conferences between John Powell and Charles Granville became the rule; conferences long and private, apparently bitter.

Granville complained to Anthony that Powell was egotistical, convinced his word was sacred writ itself. And Powell told Arlette that the son of a bitch was leeching the blood out of his script. 'Christ knows what we'll wind up with.'

Now, they would see.

What had become of the close-ups, the long shots, repeated twenty or thirty times; the canned food served on the more inaccessible Mediterranean locations; the insect bites, heat, fatigue, interminable hours, the filming at whatever time of day or night Granville thought the light was what he needed. Then there were the battles with the French, during one of which Anthony had been struck by a carelessly wielded sword and required a blood transfusion, an accident Arlette did not hear of until several days later, for they had been working on different locations and Granville kept the news from her, since it might interfere with Emma's lighthearted scenes with the Queen of Naples.

The tents for dressing rooms and sleeping quarters were crowded together into a small slum, leaving them without reliable privacy. The curious country people followed them about, giggling, pointing, approaching to stare at Arlette's hair, her low-cut gowns, talking among themselves as if she were a dummy. Fortunately, only Charles Granville and Anthony understood part of what they were saying.

'Nothing, Arlette,' Anthony blandly assured her. 'The women wish they looked like you – though they're not sure you're real. The men would like to fuck you. The children want to touch your hair and feel your skin. It's all complimentary.'

'Don't let them near me. I'll have hysterics.'

Now that it was over, she thought of it sometimes as a prolonged nightmare, and sometimes as a wild comedy.

Was there any possibility Granville had contrived to bring anything coherent out of that continuous chaos, the madness of fatigue and the tension of tired and ill-fed men and women? What of the feuds and the brief violent love affairs; the sense of being isolated from the world, perhaps forever?

Even Arlette was caught with a momentarily disconsolate look, sitting motionless and silent, because she was tired of flailing at insects. He had sat in a camp chair beside her, quiet, sympathetic, and she listened like a sullen child as Granville described the final film.

'It's beauty will surprise you. Your own beauty will surprise you. If there's one thing I know how to do, it's photograph a beautiful woman, and there's nothing about you which doesn't photograph well, to my knowledge.'

Arlette glanced venomously at him, then recalled Jade Ring's bewitching smile.

'Thank you.'

There had been nothing else between them so nearly friendly and, it was said, Charles Granville did not believe in friendliness with his actors; it interfered with the authority he considered essential to the Commander in Chief.

The music played a martial blast, then a tender melody wove into it, usurping it as the credits passed across the screen against a background of Mediterranean islands, moist green English countryside, warships in battle formation, Lord Nelson standing peering through a telescope, his tight breeches immaculately white, then a moment later splashed with blood. Emma's face filled the screen at last with a look of longing, sorrow, and a soft sweet smile which brought spontaneous applause.

Arlette held Anthony's hand tighter and she felt as if her heart had expanded, surprised, disbelieving that she had ever looked like that – delicate, vulnerable, yet still with the quality of sensuality which made it evident that this love affair was a memorable one.

The credits passed swiftly, and the film was under way, beginning at a different place, with a slow, pompous court scene when Horatio Nelson, wearing the uniform of a British admiral at the end of the eighteenth century, one eye covered by a black patch, was presented to the King to be knighted.

The brilliantly colored costumes of the women as Nelson passed along the line of lords and courtiers formed at either side of the throne room, advancing slowly, never taking his gaze from his monarch; the expression of admiration on the women's faces – all had been swept together and fused into a triumph of British power and glory which took even this American audience by surprise.

Arlette released Anthony's hand and moved forward in her seat, caught up by the vast screen as if she had entered a dream in her own mind, was witnessing scenes in which she had never participated.

Yet she recalled in bits and pieces the many disagreeable experiences from which Granville had contrived this film:

She had been thrown by a horse. She fell into a river fully clothed, to emerge, dragged out by technicians and cameramen, with her muslin dress plastered to her body. She sat immobile, ignoring the insects while her face was made up for the sixth time that day. She played through the childbirth scene again, twenty midwives hidden behind cameras and microphones, and Charles Granville hovering about as if he would presently deliver a real baby

– for her pangs had seemed no acting, and by the end of the day she had exhausted herself and the others.

Now, where was all that?

The picture proved quite unrecognizable as it passed from scene to scene, with those quick cuts into action and out again which were one of Granville's trademarks, taking up a scene not at the beginning, but somewhere in the midst of a ball at the Royal Palace at Naples, where Nelson and Emma, Lady Hamilton, wife of the British Ambassador, first met; beginning a battle scene in the middle of the battle, even though he had shot film enough to make a three-hour movie of Lord Nelson's victories and defeats at sea; a scene in a hospital, where quarts of sheep's blood had been poured over men dying on bloody mattresses, while Nelson's arm was amputated. That scene began with Nelson's face in agony, and concluded with a scene of butchery so graphic that Arlette gave an outcry. She had not been on the set the day it was filmed, and was entirely unprepared for Anthony's agonized face and the scene's weird cruelty.

When had Granville done that?

It was as if he had worked treacherously in secret, for so the film seemed to have been made. It was as if neither she nor Anthony had participated in it, as if the six months in the Mediterranean and English countryside had taken place only in her imagination.

Yet here it was, eerie, beautiful, sensual, a man's quest for power, an Englishman's passion for his country, at the cost of his eye, his arm, the loss of his life, and a woman's passion for a man. This Emma Hamilton had been the mistress of other men, casually acquiescent, until Lord Nelson had demonstrated her capacity for self-immolation.

Granville, Arlette suspected, had perceived this quality in her relationship with Anthony, and had contrived to get it on film, so that what had been carefully performed in the camera's eye emerged upon the screen as little more controlled than if they had been alone on one of those hot nights, or during the two hours the cast and crew were

374

allowed to eat lunch and rest in their tents – escaping the worst of the sun.

And what had he made of the moment when Emma, strolling a precarious footbridge over an English stream, carrying fresh grasses and vines torn loose from the bank, had all at once and by accident – for it was not in the script, nor, she thought, in the diabolical mind of Charles Granville – plunged with the breaking bridge into the river and sank several feet almost before she knew what had happened; early nineteenth-century side curls, opened parasol, flower-embroidered gauze dress, and Emma Hamilton – all gone from sight.

She had emerged, struggling, aware of some vague gratitude that Valerie had insisted she become a good swimmer.

Abandoning parasol, Emma Hamilton, the movie, forgetting Arlette Morgan, a Shakespearean actress not to be publicly disconcerted, she began to swim desperately, only to be hauled out by three electricians, to be half carried, half dragged up the bank.

Anthony was not on the set that day; he was somewhere in the Mediterranean, with the fleet the studio had built and which he had come to regard as Anthony De Forest's private navy.

Arlette saw Charles Granville running toward her with terror on his face, the terror not of a lover – the perhaps more powerful terror of a man afraid his star might drown midway through a picture.

The side curls were still there, hanging over her shoulders in loops; her dress was stuck to her body, and Arlette was naked as Primavera, with water lilies clinging to her neck and arms.

'Are you all right?'

Granville whipped off his jacket and tried to put it around her, but she refused it, laughing gaily, as if she enjoyed such surprises.

Waving to the crew, most of them at a distance, for she had traveled several yards downstream, Arlette said: 'I'll be back in half an hour. I'm sorry to hold up the shooting,' and she walked away, toward the portable bungalow where her makeup man, hairdresser, maid, and Edna Frazier waited.

As she went, moving quickly over the wet grass in her bare feet, the silk slippers having gone downstream with the parasol, she heard Charles Granville speak to his chief cameraman: 'Did you get it?'

In a sudden fury, Arlette was ready to accuse him of having done it intentionally and threaten him with Anthony's vengeance. But Anthony was her husband, not her father; there were no duels being fought over a naked woman, or even a half-drowned woman, and anyway, she was quite pleased by her gallant behavior; swimming, not swallowing water, coming out of it as if the fall had been rehearsed.

'I got it – but we can't use it.'

Arlette walked into the dressing room, passing the silent committee of welcome, and gave them a brief wave. 'The water's chilly this morning.'

What could he have made of that? Nothing, however resourceful Charles Granville might be.

Yet he did find a use for it, although her half-drowned self was scarcely recognizable to Arlette when her face appeared, taking up most of the screen, caught by the telephoto lens of the same cameraman who had warned him there was nothing they dared use of the naked Lady Hamilton.

Once again, she had the uncanny sense that the face on the screen was not her own, the voice was not her own, and the scenes, as they passed in rapid montage, had never been filmed at all. The sense of mystery, of weirdness, the uncanny feeling that she was observing the life of a woman, perhaps herself in a different incarnation, became increasingly acute.

But when Emma lay in childbirth, Arlette recalled the filming with perfect clarity, for it had taken the entire day – another day when Anthony was not in England, but off fighting one of Nelson's battles, as Nelson had been the day his daughter was born. Only Emma's elderly husband had paced the hallways, knowing the child was not his own.

They used a bedroom in the house Granville had rented, for he had wanted the sense of overcrowding, women bustling about.

While she struggled upon the bed, Granville and his technicians hovered nearby, the microphone placed to catch the sound of her breathing, as of an animal in pain, soft moans and outcries of terror.

This had lasted through the day, for he had begged her not to eat lunch, not break the spell; the birth was coming nearer, nearer. Arlette at last began to feel that she must produce from this real pain a real baby, and that Charles Granville would bring it out of her body.

Late in the day she began to fear that she was in danger of losing control of herself, while he urged and pleaded for more effort, more suffering, and the cameras wheeled overhead. At last she covered her face with her hands and was horrified to hear herself sobbing.

'Let me go! I can't stand this any longer!' She came out of the trance abruptly and sat up, looking dazedly around. 'Oh, forgive me,' she implored them – midwives, the black-coated doctor, Charles Granville, electricians and cameramen. 'Something happened – let's begin again—'

She fell back, deeply ashamed, determined to show them she knew how to have a baby. But most of the lights went out, and to her astonishment Charles Granville, for all the world like a relieved, grateful husband, sat beside her holding her hand. 'It's all over. You can rest now.'

She looked at him, baffled, closed her eyes, and tears appeared beneath her lashes. Someone – Charles Granville, she was surprised to find – blotted them gently with a handkerchief. When she opened her eyes, the room was empty but for Granville and the maid, who stood beside her. Arlette smiled at her sadly.

'Thank you,' she heard herself saying to the woman, although she had not been aware of her since early morning, when, in a fresh white muslin and lace nightgown, Emma had gotten into bed to deliver a child. Nelson's? Anthony's? Granville's?

Charles Granville pressed her hand briefly. 'It was a fearful way to do it – but nothing else would have worked so well. I'm sorry if I've made you hysterical.'

'Oh,' protested Arlette in that same strange voice, 'I'm not hysterical. I feel fine. Can I have something to eat?'

Watching the sequence, which lasted only three or four minutes, Arlette grew dizzy, and was astonished to see, flashing by so swiftly they were scarcely visible, several close-ups taken when she had fallen from the bridge and emerged, wet, laughing, she had supposed, out of her attempt at gallant acceptance.

Even there Granville had discovered a few frames when she had first come to the surface, gasping, terrified, and had laced them into Emma's fantasies of pain and fear, a woman who felt herself drowning, whether in the rushing water or in giving birth.

'Oh,' whispered Arlette furiously. 'The son of a bitch!'

'Be quiet,' Anthony warned.

After all, he had never been told, because Arlette refused to complain or to describe Granville's trickery, of the lights, the endless rehearsals, as she had supposed them to be. To Anthony it was a miraculous performance of pain and determination, which Arlette had produced out of her own abilities.

Jerry Hoffman took her hand and held it hard, in silent congratulation. Arlette sat back, relieved the scene was over, for it was Granville's peculiar ability to produce something artificial which seemed more real than reality.

CHAPTER 47

Granville's conviction was that all real love stories had more of terror than of tenderness, more of fear and distrust than of faith, more of sorrow even in their ecstasy. He had taken the myth of romantic love, demonstrated by Nelson and the one woman he had loved, and portrayed it as an hallucinated state, fierce and joyous, too desperate an undertaking for any but the hardiest, most devil-haunted mortals.

The film might have been pretty; it might have been sad and saddening; it might have sparkled with a light and golden gaiety. It did all of that. But primarily it was Granville's grim vision of the Romantic Era, which took everything more seriously than it deserved; or perhaps, took everything only as seriously as it deserved, since life itself was a forlorn catastrophe.

That did away with the prettiness, the sweet yearning of Emma's fate, following the pacing of Lord Nelson's funeral cortege; it changed the seductive smile she gave him which sent them in search of a shelter for making love.

The love scenes, the angry kisses, Emma's face, betrayed the same anguish of the beginning of the childbirth scene. One had been linked – for all the very different scenes filtered between them – to the other.

Arlette was astonished to find that in a movie with its two stars under rigid contracts, he had nevertheless contrived to show a man and a woman making love, despairing that they could not fulfill the need for a union of near-religious ecstasy.

This was another betrayal. For she had supposed she and Anthony controlled those scenes, at least. Instead, their sensuality had been surrendered to the camera, and however Granville had cut and spliced these various scenes, he had produced one, before Lord Nelson sailed for Trafalgar and death, at which Arlette stared in wonder, convinced her love for Anthony had been stripped of its privacy forever.

But Anthony, when she glanced at him, was observing the workmanship, hers, his own, Granville's, the photographer's. The method by which it had been accomplished did not concern him.

Whatever his methods, Charles Granville had produced something that seemed, even in Arlette, very close to an inner truth, though he may have wandered from the original to invent a new one. He had, after all, chosen two actors whose professional lives had been spent in learning to portray that sense of wildness and insanity of human existence which was Charles Granville's *artistic code*, as he called it in a moment of candor.

He had said this only to Arlette and Anthony, who had been taken aback by this unusual confidence, and even more by the reference to something he regarded as a private and somewhat shameful secret: an *artistic code*, after all, was not the kind of indulgence to which a man like Charles Granville should confess. Any more than Anthony De Forest would.

Still, something had prompted it, and Arlette knew what it was.

It had happened after three or four weeks of living in the tent city on a half-deserted island off Sicily, and it happened after one more of those accidents to which the picture seemed prone.

Arlette had gone through life never expecting to fall, never to get sick, never to be physically humiliated. Yet as the picture continued, it happened repeatedly. Not only to Arlette.

The actors discussed it, and decided that although there might be reason to think the film was jinxed, it was in fact the locations, the circumstances of the shooting, the peculiar angles demanded.

One brilliant sunny day, Emma Hamilton and Nelson were riding horseback at a gallop, Emma in a black velvet riding habit. They set out gaily – this scene was from an early part of their love story, and would appear in the film as Nelson's startled, sorrowful recognition that a flirtation had become serious.

Ahead of them in a jeep, with three cameramen, rode Charles Granville. Two other camera-laden jeeps rode behind them, and two on either side, in the distance.

Emma was laughing; Lord Nelson watching her, seriously.

So swiftly that Arlette felt only a crashing blow, as if an

iron door had slammed into her, she found herself on the ground, having instinctively covered her head with both hands, face down and flat on her stomach. Her horse had stumbled, or shied at some small animal.

The jeeps came up beside them, men shouting, horns blowing. Anthony was kneeling beside her, then Granville, but Arlette lay still and silent, not unconscious, her hands exploring the grass to discover where she was, surprised to find it was grass and hard earth beneath her, not a soft bed. She was trying to determine if her nose was bleeding, if any bones were broken, and she was pervaded by that limitless indifference she had always supposed must precede death.

After a few moments, she felt herself being gently turned over, to lie upon her back, and smiled up at Anthony and Granville, until a sharp pain struck her ankle. Anthony held her in his arms. Granville was shouting for one of the jeeps to bring the nurse and doctor.

'I'm all right.' She looked at Anthony. 'But why did I fall? I thought I could stay on a horse whatever happened.'

The doctor arrived; the crew gathered around; Granville banished the cameramen. Once it was established that no bones had been broken, she was sent away in a jeep to spend the day in her tent, resting.

'What an idea. I'll be ready by two o'clock.'

Partway down the hill, she turned and waved, gaily smiling.

Later Anthony came into the tent to find her in her sleeveless yellow silk jersey robe, lying on the camp cot, while the doctor taped her ankle. 'Luckily,' he advised Anthony, 'she's a good rider. The art of riding is knowing how to fall without getting stepped on or breaking your neck.' Anthony smiled grimly.

The doctor advised two aspirins, a pillow beneath her feet, and no walking until tomorrow. 'Suppose we let her rest,' Anthony told him. 'I'll call for the nurse, if she's needed.'

The tent was cleared – hairdresser, doctor, nurse,

makeup man had vanished. 'That's the end of that scene,' Anthony assured her. 'This island is pockmarked with rabbit holes. He's going to cut in a scene with you on the ground and me – well, I suppose he's wondering whether Lord Nelson takes advantage of the lady's accident—' They smiled, quite as if they had planned the episode to give them a little time alone.

There was a light rap at the wooden doorframe. 'Would you like to have lunch, sir?'

'Spam?'

'I think so, sir. I can't tell by the look of it.'

'I'm not hungry,' Arlette said.

'Tell the cook to shove it,' Anthony advised the waiter.

'As you say, sir.'

In a moment Anthony, still in Admiral Nelson's immaculate white breeches with their concealed zipper, sat on a camp stool, and Arlette, throwing off her robe, lowered herself onto him, raised her legs bent at the knees to encircle his back, arms clasped around his shoulders. She gave an inadvertent soft sound of pleasure, then was immediately silent, for they could hear the voices of actors, coming from lunch to spend the siesta in their tents.

Silently, eagerly, they moved together, her head thrown backward, eyes closed upon a brilliant white light behind her eyelids, the moment when all worlds became one and the inside of her body a warm flowing sea.

There was a soft tap upon the wooden frame of the square screen in the canvas door, and she looked straight into the startled face of Charles Granville, who swiftly drew the curtain back across the opening. Anthony moved, and Arlette held him fast. 'Don't stop – it wasn't here—'

All at once his body shuddered, and there was again the mutual gratitude, the kisses, gentle and consoling, as if each would sustain the other, act as guide back to the land they had left those minutes before.

If was after dinner when, Arlette guessed, prompted by the need to exchange his accidental glimpse of private love with a confession of his own, Charles Granville talked briefly about his *artistic code* – to catch on film that wildness and insanity of human existence – and before they could reply, hastily excused himself and disappeared; as if he had committed an unexpected, unforgivable blunder.

Anthony's face was vaguely surprised and reflective.

Arlette smiled a little, not looking at Anthony:

And so Granville's as scared as any of us.

Slowly, the company's size diminished. When they left the Mediterranean, the big battle scenes had been shot, and several hundred extras were gone. There remained, for some later date, other battle scenes; but these required few extras, for they were the crucial close-ups of Nelson's disasters, the blinding of one eye, the amputation of his arm, his death at Trafalgar.

The clashes between the navies had been put on film, once and for all. So had the ballroom scenes in the Sicilian town they had used as the Naples of the late eighteenth century, as well as Emma's scenes with the Queen of Naples.

By the time they were back in England at the Hamilton estate, where crews had been shooting several thousand feet of English countryside in rain and fair weather – green and lush and wet with spring; flowering extravagantly in midsummer; beginning to sink under autumn's slow assault, so initially beguiling; gray and morbid in winter – there were only two dozen actors left, and nearly as many cameramen and technicians.

'He must know,' Arlette said to John Powell, 'that without us – you and Anthony and me – his bloody technicians could shoot their heads off and no one would go near the theater.'

'They're part of Granville's sense of omnipotence.'

She and Powell had taken particular exception to Granville's methods of rewriting scripts and shooting a film.

Anthony passed them, kissing her briefly, and went on his way, to stand in the distance talking to Granville.

Arlette looked at him for a moment, contemplatively, before she glanced back and found Powell watching her. He was envious of Anthony because she loved Anthony in the unquestioning, concentrated, worshipful way she did – a girl's adoration of the campus hero; a woman's admiration of a brilliantly successful man; a sensualist's gratitude to a man who never failed her.

As she looked at him, Powell quickly took the horn-rimmed glasses from his coat pocket and put them on. But she had seen in his face that they were a little cruel, she and Anthony, in their solidarity, their essential indifference to everything beyond their special world.

She felt an impulse to touch him reassuringly, for during the years since she had auditioned for Elizabeth-Gloriana, they had become friends who trusted each other, and they often discussed the world and its ways. John had more patience for these speculations than Anthony.

As John Powell grew older, he became better-looking. He had been very young when they had first met, a not quite finished intimation of a man. He was very different now. Still quiet, still thoughtful, still devoutly engrossed in his work, he had now the confidence that had come with his success.

Family duties and responsibilities bored him – just as they had eventually bored Jerry Hoffman.

As the actors left, Arlette began to feel that vague sorrow which had come at the end of every semester, when all at once the campus began to look deserted.

Every parting seemed to her a final one.

Yet again and again, she had been reassured that it did not necessarily happen this way: Anthony had gone to Sicily, and no sooner had she borne Nelson's child than he was back. John Powell disappeared, and reappeared. Edna Frazier came and went every few weeks.

She had lost few people, after that early loss. People were not so easy to lose. It happened only now and then . . .

384

But once, it had obliterated all the world, and the blackness in her vision had never cleared.

Whenever other members of the cast had run their course in the schedule, Arlette made certain that she saw them, to thank them, kiss them, shake their hands. She was aware that a part of her was acting and a part of her was telling the truth. Part of her was sorry to have them go, as if the loss would be serious, and part of her was admiring this generous, untemperamental actress, Arlette Morgan.

The actors were often moved to tears by their emotionalism as she provoked it, assuring her that she and Mr De Forest were the finest people they had worked with – the only stars who did not think themselves superior to ordinary actors.

If they only knew . . . reflected Arlette, and kissed them again.

They had come near the end of the filming, and Arlette was standing, early one morning, dressed in one of Emma Hamilton's low-cut gauze gowns, talking continuously but not paying much attention to what she was saying: 'Oh, thank you, thank you – you've been so kind. We'll never forget it. We'll meet again, maybe soon—'

Arlette watched them go, then found that while Anthony had gone to dress for the next scene, Charles Granville stood nearby, and had been watching her.

'You need to love people.'

Arlette, still not free of the spell she had cast over the departing actors and herself, admitted: 'I love them – and, yes, I need them.'

Granville was silent, somber, gazing at his shoes. All at once he looked at her with those astonishing blue eyes. 'Very dangerous.' He turned quickly and went into the house.

Arlette and Granville had not become friends. Watching him go, she was not sure if she had written his name on a slip of paper, sealed it in an envelope, and put it away to be discovered when they returned to New York. If she had, then it went into the secret drawer. He belonged among those who would bear watching.

He seemed to have felt no temptation to set up a contest with Anthony: director vs. star – apparently thinking at best, he would spoil the picture; at worst, he might be made a fool. Trying to push Anthony farther could accomplish nothing – except perhaps to start a fire in the grass.

Yet Arlette had thought he was resentful of her until the afternoon he had accidentally moved aside the small curtain of their tent door.

She had tried to imagine what he had seen in that brief moment: the camp stool was placed so that it was Arlette who faced the door, Arlette naked, arms holding Anthony, head thrown back and knees spread wide.

And her face? What did she look like when Anthony had driven her half insane? Pleasure, she had decided, was the least of it between them. It had begun to seem even possible that as the feelings intensified, the very nature of the feelings altered into something foreboding final disaster.

Arlette had sent word to Granville that she would be ready to go back to work at two o'clock, bruised ankle or not, and when she walked toward him, wearing the black velvet riding habit, the black shining boots, carrying a small riding crop which she flicked with a delicate menacing gesture, she gave him a challenging gaze, and was pleased when he glanced away, embarrassed. Then she was near him and he looked up, questioningly.

If she told Anthony he had seen them, it would make the rest of the filming impossible: two men with that image between them. Arlette smiled, and then added to the smile a straight look of reassurance:

Don't worry. I haven't – and I won't.

After that, he showed her a rather curious but distinct gallantry.

And perhaps that was why when they came at last to the one scene she and Powell wanted changed, he was willing to listen to her reasons.

Anthony was away, shooting Nelson's death for the fourth time.

It seemed that no matter how often he died, Anthony persisted in looking like a live man. The vitality could not be extinguished, not by his acting talents, by makeup, by grim determination. They would try again.

Granville's parting advice was: 'For Christ's sake, De Forest, stop thinking, can't you? For fifty seconds?'

'Tell me how,' said Anthony, somewhat surly. Nelson's death was real to him, he told Arlette. 'The son of a bitch thinks it's my responsibility to kill myself.'

During his absence, they spent most of the time filming Emma walking the grounds of the Hamilton estate, a lonely woman waiting for her lover; playing with the pretty three-year-old daughter, Horatia, until at last the day for filming Emma's first knowledge of Lord Nelson's death arrived – those few feet of film Arlette dreaded more than any other. The childbirth scene, long finished, seemed by now only a simple episode.

But for a woman to hear of the death of the man she loved – the one man she had loved?

She felt as helpless at the thought of trying to play this scene as if she had never taken an acting lesson or set foot on a stage or stepped before a camera. Whatever she was to say or do, it was not what Granville had rewritten into Powell's script; and the arguments over those changes had become increasingly bitter.

CHAPTER 48

She had brooded over those lines ever since John Powell showed her the changed script, and they looked at each other incredulously. Powell had discussed it with Granville from time to time, but sadly assured her that Charles was not a man to win an argument with, for his mind was set in concrete.

Emma was to meet the emissaries, come to inform her

of Nelson's death, walking out onto the terrace when they were announced.

The ranking officer, a vice admiral who had been with them during the early happy days, riding the Sicilian countryside, attending the court balls in Naples, the *fêtes champêtres* on the little islands, was to stride forward with a grave face: *'Your Ladyship, I come upon the most sorrowful duty of my lifetime—'*

Granville expected Emma to reply: *'You're going to tell me he is dead.'*

The Vice Admiral would go down on one knee before her, bowing his head. *'Your Ladyship – he is dead.'*

Emma would reply with whatever degree of resignation she thought appropriate. *'I know. I knew it when it happened.'*

From time to time Arlette inquired of Powell: 'Is he reasonable?' He was not, and the day was there. 'I'll do it that way today,' she told Powell. 'Tomorrow—'

She was convinced Granville did not yet believe she knew as much about acting as he knew about directing. He still, it seemed, distrusted her beauty, even though he had insisted upon an Emma Hamilton of great beauty; the picture would otherwise have no credibility. Beauty, vulnerability, sensuality: he had summed up his requirements.

And his camera had taken every advantage of her hazel eyes, which might occasionally be caught in a light with flakes of yellow gold in the irises, her slightly arched eyebrows, her narrow nose, not too small, the full lower lip and V-indented upper lip; the dazzling smile she could produce in the midst of tears or anger. He photographed her breasts as carefully as if he planned to have them cast in bronze. Her neck seemed to fascinate his camera, for it was long but not taut, and the hair grew upon the nape in the triangular design Japanese printmakers admired in their own women.

By then there were left only his most favored technicians and cameramen. As well as Arlette's maid, hairdresser, and makeup man. The waiters brought their meals to

388

their suites on the third floor, which had been set aside for Arlette and Anthony, John Powell, and Charles Granville. Edna Frazier was there, and mail arrived daily from New York. Anthony's secretary, Eugene Cartwright, had gone to observe Lord Nelson's final death scene.

After Anthony's return, they would be free men and women again, no longer Lady Hamilton, Lord Nelson, or a playwright turned scriptwriter.

Arlette did the scene as Granville wanted it. She was so cooperative she stopped in midsentence, telling the cameramen, the technicians, most especially Charles Granville, that they must forgive her, she was not getting it right, there was a lack of depth, of sincerity in her voice – she could hear it.

'Not at all, not at all.'

Charles Granville, who took pride in never losing his temper, had come near to losing it. Still, he agreed she might try again. Once more, only *once* more – this from Charles Granville, who would photograph a scene from dawn until midnight, however inconsequential it might be.

At the end of the day, Granville declared the scene completed to his satisfaction. John Powell had disappeared, but Arlette flashed a general smile and went up the stairs with Edna Frazier, to read letters from Alicia and Jerry, Minerva and Eva. She had hoped that Anthony might return. But he did not, and there were few communications from the isolated island where he had gone to die again for England and Charles Granville.

Granville's room was three doors down the hallway, and Granville was punctual in his habits. Every morning he took breakfast in his room and set out at seven o'clock for a brisk hour's walk, pondering the day's plans, she supposed.

This morning, at the bottom of the staircase, he found Emma Hamilton seated on a sofa, made up for the camera, her hair in ringlet side curls, head tilted forward, as in submission. She was dressed in a transparent white gown with its embroidery of flowers and a wide blue sash under her breasts.

She sprang up eagerly, asking if she might walk with him, for she had spent most of the night trying to imagine what she had done wrong and how she might correct it.

'The grass is wet. Your shoes are silk.' His eyes narrowed, and he studied her, as for a camera angle he had not used. 'Let's go in here.' He indicated the library, and she walked ahead. 'What is it?'

'She wouldn't have said that.'

'I think she would.'

Arlette smiled, sorry to disagree. 'No.'

She was determined to leave Charles Granville, tomorrow, or whenever they finished this argument, with her farewell bouquet of magical flowers, no thistles among them to prick his nose or fingers. But her concern was this scene, and her concept of Emma Hamilton as a woman in love with a great man – a love which had worked its wonders upon Emma's naturally rowdy, promiscuous nature. Or at least it had in John Powell's script, which was all the history that concerned them.

'What else would she say? She had sensed it. Any woman would.' He turned to leave, then swung back, glaring. 'Why can't you see that?'

She was silent a moment. 'Because – you don't know it when someone you love dies.'

'I think she would.'

'No. You don't know when it happens – believe me.'

The scene was shot before lunchtime. The Vice Admiral delivered his message. Emma looked at him, solemnly, and then very slowly, with a ballet dancer's grace and sureness, fell forward and was caught in his arms. She did not speak.

They played it through four times, evidently to satisfy Granville's compulsion that the first time was never right. Then he nodded at her with such grim solemnity that Arlette went upstairs to her bedroom, sat before the mirror, and studied Emma's face, Arlette's face, the face of Lily Morgan Malone: *No, you don't know it . . . .*

Anthony arrived in the late afternoon.

The house would be emptied tomorrow morning. Cars were arriving to drive the remaining members of the cast and crew to London, and by some general consensus, unspoken, they were to have dinner in their rooms; no gala farewells after this movie.

Only Anthony was still triumphant, still Lord Nelson, dead or alive; still Anthony De Forest.

Charles Granville seemed sunk in despondency for the first time in six months.

Late in the afternoon, Arlette opened the door to a light knocking, to find John Powell there, just as Granville went by on his way to his room, giving them a brusque nod.

'Come in, John. Anthony's asleep – he hadn't slept for twenty-eight hours. Unless he kills you, Granville doesn't think he has a picture.'

Anthony's clothes were being packed and the furniture was covered with her dresses and skirts and sweaters. She indicated a chair and John sat down, then hastily put on his glasses. 'I'm leaving early tomorrow morning – we'll see each other on the plane – but I wanted to thank you. I don't know how you changed his mind, but you did.'

'I don't know whether or not I changed his mind. He has both versions – we'll see which he uses.'

Anthony opened the door and gestured a greeting at Powell, who got up quickly. 'Sit down, sit down. Let's have tea. What the hell time is it?'

John Powell was on his way out the door, and Arlette smiled and closed it, telling herself not to think of Powell's misfortune. He was in love with her. Well – so were other men. And grown men should not fall inconveniently in love when there were so many convenient women about.

The next morning, as the cars were being loaded, Arlette kissed and thanked everyone indiscriminately. Whatever it was, whoever they were, she bade them farewell as if this were the world's end, the ark was being loaded, the rains would begin momentarily, and God knew when or if they would meet again.

As Arlette was again giving her grand performance, Anthony and Charles Granville stood talking soberly, seriously.

The cars were driving off. Their assigned chauffeur was waiting at the door of their limousine. Edna Frazier sat making notes.

Arlette passed Anthony, walking toward the car, on her way to say good-bye to Charles Granville. Smiling Jade Ring's bewitching smile, she held out her hand – and if Granville noticed that she had kissed everyone else, even an electrician or two, and was only going to shake his hand, he did not seem surprised.

He shook her hand, quickly, with more warmth than she had expected. 'You're a fine actress, Miss Morgan.'

'Thank you.' She smiled. 'Good-bye.'

Charles Granville's eyes turned that famous gentian blue, and he smiled in return – his smiles were rare, bestowed as favors earned, not for the sake of displaying charm. He did not care whether he was charming or not.

'Not good-bye,' he said, so gently that again she was surprised to discover there was another Charles Granville, a Charles Granville hiding behind the director who was evidently a live human being; partly alive, at least. 'We'll be meeting again. It's in the nature of this business.'

Arlette got into the car and Granville gave Anthony a parting salute as they started away. Presently, driving his own car, the top down, the back seat piled with suitcases, he passed them at seventy miles an hour and disappeared, on his way to his country house.

Someone would be waiting for him . . .

The announcement of Nelson's death, appearing in the form she had hoped for, was not the last scene in the picture. The last scene had been shot long ago, in London, when Emma's face was glimpsed briefly, the small sad face of an anonymous woman in the vast crowds which watched the passing of the Admiral's funeral cortege to Westminster Abbey.

The script did not carry Emma beyond that, and neither Granville nor Powell had thought anything more was needed to indicate Emma's eventual loneliness and poverty, and early death, neglected by the nation for whom her lover had worked miracles of war, asking at his death that Lady Hamilton be provided for.

That scene, taken so long ago she had almost forgotten it – until it came forth there in the projection room, Emma's face emerging for a moment in one vast close-up which appeared and disappeared, as if a ghost had passed above the crowds of mourners, then returned to the smallness and anonymity to which Nelson's death had reduced her – that scene, at the end of the film, caused a general catching of breath, a low whispered murmur moved through the room, and faded into absolute silence before the awesome music of the Death March.

The picture ended with the booming of the drums of death, the slowly passing cortege with its glossy black horses, its magnificently robed statesmen in official carriages, the sovereign languidly raising one hand in salutation, and that momentary focus upon the questioning, baffled face of Emma, Lady Hamilton, seeming to ask why the universe had been arranged to so little purpose for the good of human beings: Why must they exist at all, under the conditions allotted them?

The music of the Death March faded slowly, until it throbbed like the pulsing blood in the ears. Emma Hamilton's face filled the screen, then disappeared; the music trembled into silence as the cortege moved onward – a ghostly cortege, which had perhaps never passed through London or history at all.

The projection room fell into silence for several moments. Lights went on, and Arlette said sullenly to Anthony: 'He's stolen our souls.'

People were milling about, talking, beginning to approach them. Minerva was crying, presently she was sobbing. Alicia's eyes were bright as Arlette caught her glance.

'Of course,' said Anthony. 'That's why he's good.'

Beginning to respond to the faces and voices crowding nearer, Arlette heard Jerry whisper, 'Jesus.' But he did not look at her, and Arlette closed her eyes briefly, shocked by the sorrow she felt, for Emma Hamilton, for everyone there in the projection room, for the insoluble riddle of whether or not life was worth what it cost to live it.

She thought of Charles Granville with resentful bitterness. He had taken too much from them, only to make a picture. He had, indeed, stolen their souls, to create Emma Hamilton and Lord Nelson:

As if souls are so easily replaced at whatever commissary stocks them.

CHAPTER 49

A sealed envelope, reasonably certain to contain a sheet of paper with CHARLES GRANVILLE written on it, went into the Chinoiserie cabinet in her bedroom, and she tried to forget she would see him again, although the date for the New York premiere had been set – the end of January, two months after the preview.

'Maybe he won't come,' she told Anthony.

'He will. Don't think about it. It's a long way off. You have enough to occupy you.'

Anthony smiled, not very joyously. For the fatal decision had been taken not long after their return from London. The Hoffman-Repertory directors had offered them the parts of Macbeth and Lady Macbeth. The contract was signed, and study had begun, and neither of them had any sense of triumph; only a dismal conviction that no good could ever come of such hubris:

It's too soon.

But she did not say it, not to Anthony, not to Jerry, not to the board members, not even to Alicia, although when she went for her first lesson after signing the contracts she began not with her usual fault-finding with the character, but by finding fault with her own character.

'This requires qualities I don't have and cannot pretend

to have,' she said. 'Now, what the hell are we going to do about that?'

'Lady Macbeth requires qualities no one has.'

Alicia had played a famous Lady Macbeth twice in her life, with almost ten years between the productions, and Arlette had met several actors who remembered both performances vividly. But they had had no help to give either.

'*That most terrible test of any genius,*' Arlette quoted gloomily.

'She is,' Alicia agreed. 'Lady Macbeth is one of the great theatrical enigmas. No actress feels she can play it. But slowly, as you work, you will begin to discover that hidden in the writing of the part itself are the coded instructions for playing it. You'll find them. They're there, I promise you.'

'I wish Jerry had thought of something else.'

'He thinks you're both ready. You're essentially a tragic actress, Arlette. Lady Hamilton may have been a bravura part to play, but the picture can never pretend to be more than elegant melodrama. You can play comedy with great style, but tragedy is where your best work will be done. It's your secret – I don't want to know where it comes from.'

'Neither do I.'

She seldom thought of her old prophecy, made to Michael: *I want to die young, to be buried in an unknown place, and to be forgotten.*

How old was I when I said that?

Twenty?

Twenty-one. I was in Chicago, on my way to New York and London – scared silly.

She could see them, coming out of the Chicago Art Institute and standing on the steps in the winter cold, the wind blowing hard off Lake Michigan, talking about a cup of tea, when all at once she had said this. It had struck him like a blow.

It had seemed a premonition of something inescapable, a certain knowledge. But how had such knowledge come?

From dwelling. Michael told her, upon the past: from never forgetting, never forgiving. 'Does it make so much difference – a few years, more or less? It's a hoax, any way you look at it.'

'A hoax?' She glanced at him sideways, suspiciously.

Michael had laughed suddenly, as he did sometimes, as if he had discovered a joke so immense, so formidable, that laughter was his only defense against it. 'You don't think any of this has any meaning, do you? Still—' Michael spread his hands. 'Here we are – for a time. And if we're lucky, we get to choose what we'll have for breakfast.'

'And that's all?'

'It's a better bargain than most of the world's been given – from the beginning.'

Remembering that day, flashing into her mind as Alicia talked quietly about Lady Macbeth's possibilities and challenges, Arlette thought with intense bitterness of the death of the first Lily Malone:

I would never have become an actress. I had to find a way to complete her life with other lives.

'Now's the time, Anthony,' Jerry Hoffman had said, one evening after dinner at Montauk. They had been back from England less than a month, and Alicia and Jerry had come to spend the weekend at the house of the heroic poetess, now so transformed that neither poetess nor Mrs Melrose – nor the ghost itself – could have recognized it.

Arlette had glanced quickly, apprehensively, at Anthony just as his eyes flickered away from her. Consultations between them were complete without words, and although Jerry had not mentioned *Macbeth*, all of them knew what he meant.

Arlette and Anthony had left the city almost immediately after their return from England, to rest and regain their health, for Arlette was convinced Granville had all but destroyed their stamina. They had been riding, walking on the beach, reading plays, and occasionally talking about what might happen next. They were unhappily aware that the next decision would be a crucial one.

Arlette, Jerry seemed to think, could play Lady Macbeth as well as she had Hedda Gabler.

'The ladies aren't much alike.'

'You can do it,' said Jerry confidently, with that casual way he had of encouraging his actors, something in his glance and voice which could convince them they could step nimbly across red-hot coals, or let themselves be sawed in two, all with less trepidation than an ordinary actor playing a one-line part.

'We'll see,' said Arlette skeptically. And Anthony said nothing.

During the next few months they worked separately on their parts, but never discussed them.

From time to time Granville called from London, and even after the preview said that he was still editing; he would be editing until opening night. The finished picture would be better than what they had seen.

Anthony hung up and laughed. 'Bullshit. On the other hand – he just may be right.'

What they had seen in the projection room might look quite different in the theater itself. Of course, if might also look much worse.

What fish were in his net?

She had never attended a film premiere, but had heard horrifying tales of streamers of light invading the night sky, hostile crowds, groping hands, jeering voices, police barricades, lines of black limousines, flashbulbs going off six inches away.

'Yes,' Jerry told her dolefully. 'It's all true. That's what it's like.'

Jerry did not believe in such a shivaree over a motion picture, or even a play.

The night came and went sooner than she expected. Her recollections were vague, but triumphant.

Anthony had praised her effusively, and left on the dressing table his gift: a waist-length strand of square-cut yellow sapphires, with thirteen round-cut diamonds among them – one for each letter of her name.

She had worn it with a pale yellow silk crepe dress, cut low in front, with a halter neck which left her back uncovered, and a skirt that swirled below her hips to the floor. Over it was a long sleeveless white ermine coat. The golden hair and Jade Ring's dazzling smile did away with the hostile crowds as if she had passed among them by some magical process, moving swiftly, lightly, the smile never flickering – her yin-yang mirror.

If she did not look at them, only smiled remorselessly, she reasoned they could do no harm.

Perhaps the strategy was successful, or perhaps she could have passed through the *cordon sanitaire* and into the theater without molestation anyway. When the movie ended, Jerry Hoffman conducted her and Anthony and Alicia out another door, where no crowds waited, and they arrived at Granville's party before he did.

The movie was apparently going to be so great a success that she was ready to forgive him his tyrannies, for it moved at the pace of all Charles Granville's movies, swift as a summer storm, striking everything in its path with a sense of wonder at this unexpected power, and left them as if released by spontaneous sensual fulfillment, experienced with surprised gratitude.

Granville arrived and came over promptly to kiss her. She looked at him in brief astonishment, for she had supposed the entire project had taken place in an atmosphere of deep antagonism – Granville determined to dominate her, Arlette determined not to let him. Now, this same Granville gazed at her with his eyes turned deep gentian, and she smiled at him impudently, knowing what was on his mind.

'We'll make another picture one day,' he was saying. 'Better than this. After all, if we hadn't mangled the story we wouldn't have made a romance out of the two of them – his lordship and her ladyship – a scruffy pair, however you look at it. That's why I insisted on Powell for the script, and you and your husband for the leads.'

'Oh?'

Charles Granville had planned, Charles Granville had decided, Charles Granville insisted. And presently there they were – being bitten by insects, stifling in the hot Mediterranean summer, eating canned meat and canned string beans, drinking canned tea, sleeping on cots, falling into rivers.

'But I don't like making movies.'

'Like them or not, they are a necessary part of an actor's work. The stage alone won't make you famous – and the stage, as you know, becomes a memory very quickly.'

'Hi!' It was a female voice, low, determinedly sensual. 'Remember me?'

The young woman smiled at Charles Granville, ran her long-fingered hand possessively down his coat sleeve, and as he left them Arlette discovered the question had been addressed to her. The woman was still there, still smiling with a look of gay challenge.

'*Don't* you remember me?'

Arlette started to move away. But then her habit of using elaborate politeness as a form of sarcasm asserted itself. 'After such a long time?' Jade Ring was smiling at the young woman. 'But how nice to see you again.'

'Miss Morgan,' said the dear old acquaintance, 'you don't remember me at all. I'm Deborah Crane.'

'I know.' She turned to leave.

Who the hell is Deborah Crane?

But there was something about the girl's bizarre appearance, something about her artificially low voice, something about her air of a high school girl with a secret she would not tell, which made Arlette hesitate. At that moment Eva French, perhaps sensing a friend in need, arrived, blonde-silver hair, gleaming with freshness. Eva, beside whom this Deborah Crane appeared gauche, blatant, too intense.

At that moment Arlette remembered Deborah Crane:

Even safely sealed in the Chinoiserie cabinet, they sometimes reemerged.

Arlette had never been sure why this girl annoyed her.

Perhaps she was annoyed because Deborah had lived where she had lived, and the girl seemed to imagine she had absorbed something which made her comparable to Arlette Morgan. Arlette could read her undisguised envy – the ruling passion of the human race, she had concluded.

Deborah had spent the two years and a half since they had met in a strenuous attempt to redesign herself. Whatever had been amiss had been augmented or changed. There were no spaces between her front teeth, and all of them were gleaming white. Her body was thin, but her breasts were like cantaloupes. The strapless purple satin dress seemed to have been glued to her skin, for when Deborah moved, the dress moved with her. The carrot-red hair was strawberry blonde, brushed in a mass of short ringlets. Freckles had disappeared, and her skin was as white and chinalike as Eva's. Her pale blue eyes with their contact lenses were now a clear green.

Was she pretty, or was she ugly?

Only a man would know, Arlette decided.

Whatever she was, she gave Arlette some weird sense of foreboding, for her green gaze never wavered and her smile seemed almost taunting, as if she knew something Arlette would not want her to know.

Was she Charles Granville's temporary involvement? Did she know about the episode when Granville had turned back the tent curtain to see Arlette spread across Anthony's thighs?

'Do you like my dress?' Deborah asked in that husky voice which had been lowered an octave, sure to ruin it in five years. 'I read somewhere this is your color.'

Arlette turned, relieved to find John Powell nearby.

'It looks like hell with her red hair,' whispered Eva.

Eva and Arlette exchanged smiles, and Arlette did not see Deborah again until much later.

Then, as Charles Granville was bidding his guests good night, there was Deborah beside him, smug and possessive as if the sphinx had contrived to attach herself to Oedipus.

'Good night, Miss Morgan,' said Deborah. 'I liked your Emma Hamilton. I really did.'

Two envelopes, Arlette decided, were probably no more effective than one; and it would be the start of an inconvenient practice, trying to remember who was already there and who should be put there again.

Three weeks after they had begun to rehearse *Macbeth*, Anthony told her that he was going to cancel their contracts, pay back the investors, and they would go to Europe for a few weeks.

'This Macbeth of mine,' he said, 'is a bombastic idiot. Not only is he a bungler in committing murder, he has always been a bungler. He is a stupid man. Of course,' Anthony added with deep bitterness, 'all Shakespearean tragic heroes are stupid. The trick of playing them lies in making them seem victims of fate, and not victims of their own stupidity.'

Arlette was silent. She did not agree that Anthony's Macbeth was a bungler, much less a bombastic idiot. That was not the way they got along. One such agreement, and they would never be able to perform together again.

PART III

1962

CHAPTER 50

To be an icon was flattering, but it was also to be a man crossing very thin ice on very thin-bladed skates.

The meeting of the Hoffman-Repertory board proceeded: minutes were read, expenditures, income, box-office receipts, taxes, plans for the next year.

Seated between Jerry Hoffman and John Powell, Arlette thought of other things while she waited for Anthony to drop the hand grenade among them.

She had come from a class with Alicia, during which she had worked as if the play would open on schedule, and wore her black rehearsal skirt and sweater, by now a fetish, not only for her but for the entire company. Thrown over the chair back was Anthony's most recent birthday present, a sable coat – an extraordinary fact of life it had seemed when she had discovered it, unwrapped, as all Anthony's presents were, on a chaise longue. Fur coats, evidently in Anthony's theory of gifts, were suitable for birthday or Christmas presents; jewelry was for openings or the completion of a film. At first the coat had seemed too precious ever to consider wearing, but now it had become a casual friend and accompanied her everywhere when she was not in evening dress.

Anthony's face, as she listened to the statistics, gave her no indication of what he was thinking, and her only concern was not to cry when he made his announcement.

For Anthony to be prepared to admit to failure seemed to her something in the nature of an elemental catastrophe. He had been convinced that *Macbeth* was his most fateful encounter, the part he must play before he could call himself an actor.

Until then, he had kept some superstition that he had been lucky. He, Jerry Hoffman, the producers he had had in the three movies, either by shrewdness or chance he –

and they – had chosen parts he was equipped to perform as if they were written for him.

The business of the meeting was nearly over, and as her heart began to beat with sickening anticipation, she turned her attention to Jerry and studied his hands, those finely made hands, appropriate for a painter, a brain surgeon, a great lover. Perhaps it had been her diagnostic analysis of what Jerry Hoffman's hands said about Jerry Hoffman as a lover which had caused her to fall in love with him.

It had been no fault of Jerry's hands, and no fault of Jerry's, that the affair lasted only a year and a half. In a sense, it was not over yet. A kind of love, a devoted concern, continued to replenish their relationship, and perhaps made it possible for him to direct her with fewer explanations.

Love, she was thinking, hoping that someone would discover several pages of forgotten minutes to read, *is the only thing that never entirely disappears*.

Love – and, maybe, youth? The conviction of it, the sense of it. They must be with you until you die.

So far as Jerry Hoffman was concerned, beautiful women were a source of great pleasure, but they signified little in contrast to the one thing which engrossed his life. 'Never again, Arlette,' he told her, a year after his pride had put them apart. 'Love is the curse of the working man.'

Then in the midst of this reverie, she heard Anthony's voice begin to speak. Calmly he explained, with all the detailed care of a corporation president, that he was paying them back the costs of the rehearsal time, the rent, the actors' time, the work done by the set and the costume designers, and in fact, he was not ready for *Macbeth*.

'My Macbeth's a bumbling oaf,' he advised them.

There was a general uneasy movement, a moment of embarrassment and incredulity:

Is he doing this for me? He thinks I can't play Lady Macbeth?

'I'll be a son of a bitch if I'll do something I know right now in my gut I can't do. This guy's got to be played three times life size or he's a clown – and I can't do it yet. Someday – I hope—'

The silence continued. All at once Jerry spread his hands. 'Okay, Anthony. We'll take your word for it.'

'We're going to England, maybe Scotland,' Anthony smiled, somewhat grimly. 'We'll be back at the beginning of June.'

Anthony had not glanced at her, and Arlette took this to be a warning that she was not to cry and make a fool of him. She looked at her hands, folded in her lap, and the others began to talk about the next production – the De Forests' next production, she was astonished to hear, for she had supposed this would destroy them once and for all with Hoffman-Repertory, perhaps even with all theater.

They discussed several possibilities, but Arlette continued to look at her hands, lightly lacing the fingers, until she heard some words which caused her to look up in pleased wonder: *As You Like It.*

'Do *you* like it, Arlette?' Jerry asked.

'I like it!' She smiled, relieved of Lady Macbeth, of all the dreads which had surrounded that doomed woman, at least for a year or two – possibly forever. 'Do you like it?' She leaned forward, looking down the table at Anthony for the first time since they had left home that morning.

'I do.'

'And,' said Sy Harman, 'the public will like it. Thank God, we've found a legitimate excuse to show Arlette's marvelous legs.'

Which, of course, had been covered by floor-length skirts ever since her escapade as Elizabeth-Gloriana.

Rehearsals were set to begin on September fourth, and the time had come to discuss the announcements of the play and actors which would take *Macbeth*'s place. Arlette and Anthony got up to leave, moving around the table, shaking hands, Arlette glancing only briefly into each face.

Anthony smiled as he went, nodding, clasping a shoulder, for all the world a political candidate defeated by the narrowest margin, a good sport, a good winner and a good loser, that unheard-of phenomenon.

He had obviously thought this decision through so thoroughly that when the time came, he was in control of Anthony De Forest. No danger of his shaman letting him down in a crisis. Indeed, it was difficult to catch Anthony in a crisis – he seemed to have prepared himself long ago for all life's surprises.

While to Arlette, everything was a surprise, and all she had with which to meet these emergencies, which arrived as dust was said to arrive upon earth from outer space, falling steadily, was her natural resiliency; most of all, her fatalism:

This is the way I knew it would happen, someday, sooner or later.

Each shock seemed about to rob her of life itself by its force and savagery. That was what came first. Then – the acceptance.

In a minute or two, she had accepted Anthony's decision, as she had not when he had told her about it privately.

They had reached the door, and Anthony turned. 'I'm sorry as hell, you know that. Maybe – if you still want me to try it – in another year, or two.'

Arlette was about to leave without a word. Then all at once she turned and extended one hand. 'We will do *Macbeth* one day – won't we?'

In Scotland, Arlette made a conscientious effort to explore whatever might linger on there from the ninth or tenth century, and Anthony, whether to humor her, or battling a despair he would not talk about, agreed as she assured him it was impossible to be too wet, too cold, too hungry, too tired, in these highlands. She smelled air and leaves and damp forests, examined with her fingers old stones.

When Anthony got up early to shoot or fish, she went with him, and whether any of this brought them nearer to Macbeth's wild nature than they had been, they left

Scotland feeling they had been cleansed at some spa of their imagination. The unhealthy fears and doubts they had ingested with their experience of *Macbeth* had disappeared.

'Now,' said Anthony, filled with the joyousness of an athlete who has recovered prime physical fitness after a slight, debilitating illness, 'back to work.'

When rehearsals began in New York, Arlette was as happy as if she had left her home, wandered far and wide, and returned to find the house had become an enchanted castle in her absence.

The actors, the sessions with Alicia, the first meeting with Jerry Hoffman to discuss the general concept of the play, the costume fittings, all seemed new and yet as old as her own life, and precious beyond counting.

For Rosalind was gay. Even when she moped with love for Orlando, Rosalind knew she would have him one day, when the playwright got around to untangling his carefully tangled skeins. This play was a kind of game, and she became convinced they were living in Shakespeare's *golden world*.

Still, this did not mean that Rosalind's confidence and laughter, her impudence or sighs, could be played as a game. She worked with Alicia to summon forth Rosalind as seriously as she had worked to discover Desdemona or Juliet or Millamant.

It was not easy to find Rosalind's exact form, her expressions and tones and gestures, her quick responses and whimsical changes from light to dark. But it was not impossible, either. Rosalind had come to her at the right time of her life, not too early and not too late: and one day during the fifth week of rehearsal she stepped upon the stage of the theater into which they had moved the day before and encountered someone she knew vaguely who all at once turned into Rosalind. There she was.

The next challenge promised to be more difficult. When the play had ended its four months in New York, it was going to tour – the last tour ever in their lives, Anthony vowed, but a necessary one, a road-show antidote to *The Two of Them*, which was playing all over the world. The tour would end in Los Angeles.

Los Angeles.

'Oh?' asked Arlette when she read the schedule, as if that was a city unheard of by her or anyone else. 'Los Angeles?' She glanced at Anthony. 'You're sure?'

'Quite sure.'

'I see.'

Anthony was silent, studying the schedule. 'You don't want to meet them?'

'But of course I do! After all these years!' *Careful, Arlette.* 'Why, of course.' *I thought they never wanted to meet me. Why now, after so long?* She smiled, touching his hand. 'I do, Anthony. I thought—'

'Never mind. They want to meet you. They're looking forward to it. I hope you are.'

'Oh, yes. I am.'

And his children? Was he to see them? Had he seen them since they had married? Had Lydia let him visit them when she stopped in New York – or was their father just a man whose pictures they saw only in newspapers or on the screen?

She had no idea.

She had never asked about them, and had come to prefer that his parents, his sister and his children, his aunts and uncles and cousins, did not concern her. They were somewhere in the world, they went about their daily lives, they loved him, most likely, they missed him, probably – but Arlette had never had any feeling that they were real people to her.

There was, perhaps, something a little strange in this indifference. Possibly she resented the fact that he had a father and a mother. Perhaps it was too painful for her to think about what he might represent to them, the two people whose love had begotten him, and what she owed them for this man who encompassed her emotional life.

Arlette was not sure of her reasons, but she was sure that she was unhappy at the prospect of meeting them,

and so she decided to play a part for them, not Arlette
Morgan, apprehensive at meeting these stylish in-laws,
but some other Arlette Morgan who was not Desdemona
or Hedda or Rosalind.

'Who do you want me to be?'

Anthony looked at her in wondering perplexity. All at
once he laughed. 'You decide.'

'They're your parents.'

'Well? You're my wife.'

That made the decision for her. She knew who she
would be.

Not Anthony's wife – or only partly Anthony's wife.
She would be the niece of Valerie and Frederick Morgan.
Professor Morgan, esoterically famous for his historical
works on the English Middle Ages; Valerie, with a more
than local celebrity as an authority on the more advanced
theories of child psychology. She would be the sister of
Michael Malone, a molecular biologist, who was no
longer regarded as a child prodigy but had become an
authentic genius in the opinion of that small world which
shared his interests.

She would meet the Runkle family as Lily Malone –
someone she often thought she could no longer remember.

But Lily Malone would come back to her at the
appropriate moment, just as Rosalind would come when
she was needed.

CHAPTER 51

Her first meeting with Anthony's parents was after the
last performance of *As You Like It*, when she and Anthony
arrived at their own suite in the Bel Air Hotel:

*First, I'll be Arlette Morgan, just to let them see who he's
married.*

That would be after they had seen that he was married
to Rosalind; they might also have seen him more or less
married to Lady Hamilton.

Wherever they had gone, crossing the country, newspapers and billboards announced *The Two of Them*, into which Granville had distilled his *artistic code*: up to the permissible limits of violence, sexual excitement, bloodshed, childbirth agonies, rioting in Naples, hanging of aristocrats in the streets. Charles Granville had turned an ugly episode into a fantasy of great love, great patriotism, great men and women.

These two wives of Anthony's – Emma Hamilton and Rosalind – along with whatever they had heard of other alliances, might have led them to expect almost anything.

For a minute or two, Arlette decided to give them her portrayal of Arlette Morgan, star.

Then, before the effulgence dimmed their eyesight, she would turn into Lily Malone, niece of Valerie and Frederick Morgan. Those performances should carry her through not only the first meeting at the Bel Air Hotel, but also the dinner party at the Runkles' Pasadena home for other relatives and family friends the next night.

She entered a step ahead of Anthony, floating in on her own swift-moving cloud of mauve chiffon, long-sleeved, high-necked, swirling skirt, with Anthony's gift at her ears – tiny strands of pearls, each finished with a different stone; a ruby, an emerald, a diamond, a sapphire, the earrings twirling like a gathering of fireflies, flashing their signals on and off.

She walked in smiling, and the smile showed them that this was the beauty who had been worth the first divorce in the Runkle family; this was the famous actress, murmuring softly in reply to Anthony's introductions.

Once that was over, Arlette abandoned Arlette Morgan and turned into Lily Malone; and later she had little recollection of the Runkles.

The house was no surprise to Arlette – although it would have been to Lily Malone. This was where Anthony had grown up, and she found it quite fitting he should have grown up in such a place, among such people.

They were worldly. They had been everywhere they wanted to go, not once, but several times. They had met everyone they thought of consequence. They were unpretentious, but by no means simple. They were confident and assured, like Anthony. And when he was among them, he seemed to become like them.

Next night she was Lily Malone from the beginning, remorselessly beautiful in a long white chiffon evening gown, strapless and molded over her breasts, falling in a caryatid's folds to the floor, with diamonds at her ears.

She knew when she was charming people, whether a theater filled with critical first-nighters, a crew of cameramen and technicians, a hairdresser, a friend, a fan, a lover. And she also knew how to govern the charm, the smile, the voice, tuning these attributes as precisely as the pilot of a transoceanic jet tuned his dials. She charmed them not only because it was her responsibility to Anthony; it was her responsibility to Arlette.

This world, Anthony's early world, was a lost one to her, and although she maintained her tender manner to the end of the evening, she soon began to wish it were finished.

'Well—' she said when they got into the limousine Anthony's father had provided to drive them back to Bel Air. 'That's over.'

It sounded so blunt – as if just this once, out of a lifetime, was she expected to perform this chore. Having said it, she decided not to apologize, and after a brief silence, Anthony evidently did not expect her to.

If Anthony saw his children during those two days, he did not mention it; perhaps he thought it would trouble her to hear about it.

The possibility troubled her not at all, since she had taken care not to remember how old they were, and had quite succeeded in convincing herself they were of no more interest to Anthony than were Jerry Hoffman's children to Jerry, or John Powell's to him.

'I love them, of course,' John had remarked to Arlette, one day the summer before at Montauk, when there was a picnic on the beach and, off in the distance, the Powell children and the caretaker's children were playing.

'They're my flesh and blood, and man's primitive and an egoist. There they are – some part of me – some part I dispensed with on some day or night I don't remember. What do the Greeks say? *Children are memories.* I wonder.'

Anthony, she thought, probably loved his children in much the same partly guilty way, and would have spent little more time with them if he had not divorced Lydia. Lydia would not have been willing to accept his devotion to his work in the theater. Arlette was his work in the theater.

And that had been Anthony's argument – Alicia's, Jerry Hoffman's, even John Powell's – when, at a board of directors' meeting while they were planning the Hoffman-Repertory schedule for the following year, Arlette had said she was going to London and study while Anthony performed Hamlet with The King's Players.

This came as a surprise to Anthony, who had looked at her as if she had announced that she had decided she would become an anthropologist after all and pass her days considering taro planting and the uses and abuses of nail cuttings.

The discussion was not a long one, for the idea was ridiculous, and she knew it as well as they did; it was decided she would remain in New York – Ophelia having been lost to her as a challenge years ago – and take on a real challenge: Beatrice Cenci, with Max Gilmore as Beatrice's incestuous father, in Shelley's poetic version, considered impossible to stage.

Even so, nothing reconciled her to the fact that she and Anthony must look forward, at the year's end, to spending six months apart: the world would die, the seasons fall into disrepair, the flowers and leaves wither.

Anthony knew nothing of this.

Time had a different meaning for him. Time was his work.

'It'll be gone before we know it,' he assured her when the meeting ended and she had signed the contract for *The Cenci.* Contracts had been signed by both of them for the year after – *Macbeth*, at last.

'But it will be gone, Anthony—'

Did Anthony know anything about that?

No. Why should he? He's never lost anyone. Never finally, forever and ever, lost all he loved, at one time.

Anthony had accepted the situation as an inevitable part of the architecture of their professional lives: Hamlet for him; Beatrice Cenci for her. Then *Macbeth* together. It had to him the quality of a well-composed picture, a felicitous phrase of music.

'We can telephone.'

Where was the comfort in that?

Time had nothing to do with clocks, punctual as she was.

There were clocks, but they were not the clocks other people imagined told them time was passing. Real clocks were the pulsing blood; the seeming eternal closeness at the beginning of making love, which ended some time later in a sense of loss, as if it had never happened.

The fact that six months could pass very rapidly was easily demonstrated. They returned to New York from Los Angeles, went to Montauk, and spent the summer and fall and early winter there and in New York; and presently she was driving with him to the airport:

No damn-fool questions and no tears.

Anthony admired her ability to cry when the script required it and to cry however the script required, but when she cried as Arlette, he was uneasy, even a little angry.

It would surprise Anthony – who had perhaps suspected that she resented him for having agreed to such a plan – to know that now she was telling herself that in the end it would make no difference:

Six months is only six months.

'I'll come back when your show opens,' he said all at once.

Arlette glanced at him reprovingly. He knew she would refuse such an offer, and he should not have made it. 'Your contract doesn't permit it. We knew that when it was signed.'

They were silent.

Arlette spoke softly. The airport lights were ahead. 'You'll never see my Beatrice – whatever I make of her – and I'll never see your Hamlet. That part of our lives will always be missing.' She was silent again. The car stopped and Conrad opened the door. 'Even if you could come back,' she said, speaking quickly, 'that would make the rest of it worse.'

The door opened, the interior filled with light, and Anthony looked at her as if she had slapped him. He stepped out, extending his hand, and they walked into the terminal.

'Terminals, terminals,' Arlette whispered angrily. She was holding his arm.

His baggage had gone ahead with Eugene Cartwright, and they walked to the entrance of the customs office. All at once he seized her with all the despairing love of Nelson about to sail for Trafalgar and kissed her as if they were alone. The kiss, she began to hope, would never end. Then he turned, smiled, gave her a brief wave, and disappeared.

Arlette waited, thinking he might reappear, but at last started running down the corridors, unconcerned if people saw her crying.

She had prepared herself with three large calendars, a page for each month. One hung on the wall in her bathroom in the town house. One hung in the bathroom at Montauk. One was to hang in her dressing room when rehearsals started for *The Cenci*. Beside each, on a colored silk cord, hung a crayon, red, green, purple, tied to the nail with a bowknot, like her wedding ring.

Anthony telephoned, according to their plan, when she returned from Alicia's the next night. *The Cenci* was going into rehearsal in a week, but Anthony had waited to go to London until the last moment, and went directly to rehearsal when he arrived.

She did not ask if he missed her; it was in his voice.

He talked urgently, nervously, as if he hoped to distract

416

her by talking about Hamlet. 'I hate everything about him—' Arlette laughed, for his voice was full of anger at this character he had always detested who yet stood there in his path, foursquare. 'We're like two greased wrestlers having it out in an ice rink.'

That was his contribution. What was hers?

'I saw Alicia. My God, this is a hard part. You tell me! Was it her innocence – or her guilt?'

He said nothing for a few moments, then asked, quietly: 'Which is it for you?'

Arlette gave a moan, desperate as anything she might expect from Beatrice after her father's first visit.

'It must be both!'

The distance has made strangers of us in a day – what will it be in six months?

'I've got to go, Arlette—'

'I'm glad you called, Anthony.'

'You are?' he asked politely. 'I'll call the first chance – be happy, darling.'

'Oh, I am.'

They hung up without saying good-bye, and Arlette sat at the dressing table and looked at herself in the mirror.

Anthony, with his sometimes dark, sometimes brilliantly joyous, intense nature, had given himself and everything he owned to her. He was more concerned in the success of her professional life than she was; or he was equally concerned.

Of course, he must also have known that if their marriage had turned out another way – as it might have, since most marriages did – Arlette would have retreated to her green and private land, and he might never have been able to find her again. At least, he would not find the Arlette he was looking for.

And it was on behalf of what Anthony wanted for her, as much as what she wanted for Arlette, that she began immediately to search for this Beatrice Cenci, wherever she had hidden herself during the four hundred years which separated her from Arlette Morgan. She must be somewhere. She must be someone.

It occurred to her to ask John Powell. John Powell, she found, had accumulated considerable wisdom as the years went by.

This Beatrice Cenci seemed to her, because of the odd sort of play it was, poetic and lurid, beautiful and grotesque, tender and vicious, describing a world which had existed once and which she must contrive to enter – this play, this Beatrice, had brought into being a surprising facet of her own ambition.

She was determined to play Beatrice as she had never played another part, to take the potentialities she would discover, and justify her own interpretation, to show that there was a darkness in the brightest beings; a fascination of innocence with evil.

CHAPTER 52

Arlette suspected that Jerry was wondering what had intrigued him about *The Cenci*, unless it had been what usually intrigued Jerry: he admired a play. Then he wanted to see a production of it he could admire, and there was only one way to be sure of that: he must direct it himself.

'It's more or less,' he had told her when she had asked how it was possible to know when she had found Katharina, 'like trying to capture a ghost. You'd think you'd never know whether you've caught it or not—' He smiled, nodding wisely. 'But you know.' He seized one out of the air and held it tight. 'You know when you've got it.'

Arlette was surprised to find that eager excited anticipation she had felt when she and Anthony had set out together for the first day of discussion of any new production.

She liked to imagine that she would casually throw away six months to be with Anthony. But it would be absurd for her to behave like Margo Blake when she was Arlette Morgan.

There had been nothing easy about becoming Arlette Morgan.

And there was no question that in Anthony's grand design, *The Cenci*, dark and fearsome as Jerry Hoffman would make it, was a startling contrast to Rosalind with her *golden world* – and Lady Macbeth was waiting.

Jerry was pacing about, hands in his pockets, as she approached. He spun around and caught hold of her. 'Have you got it?' He made the gesture, swiping at the air, closing the character's ghost in his fist. Arlette smiled and shook her head. 'You will.'

Eva arrived as blithely as if for a party. This was Eva's way of preparing herself for the work ahead: pretend it was going to be fun, an adventure. She cast Arlette a swift pleading agonized glance, then smiled brightly again.

Eva and Arlette began to talk, while the others arrived, avoiding mention of the play, for Jerry forbade the cast to discuss it.

But Arlette had consulted John Powell when she saw him at Montauk.

'I think it's a mad idea of Jerry's,' she said. 'What can I make of this horrible woman?'

John laughed, clasping her briefly about the shoulders, and the laughter, free and spontaneous, and the embrace, was surprising. For John was a sober man, careful not to step farther than some line drawn upon his life's floor plan by his own hand. How long ago?

'This isn't a play about incest. It's about—' She looked at him imploringly. 'What the hell is the god damn thing about?'

John put on his glasses and looked at the sand. 'Let me see if I can remember some lines I read about those people—' He was silent, casting about in his memory like a fly-fisherman who knew the exact location where the trout might be hiding. 'Something like this: *Is there a beauty in the knowledge of evil . . . Is the beauty in the face of Beatrice Cenci from her innocence – or her guilt?*'

Arlette's face glowed with the rapturous expression of a woman surprised by love or gratitude, and then they became aware that above them on the bluff Eva was calling their names. Arlette and John continued to look at each other, two philosophers, astounded, disbelieving that after long years they had made the discovery.

Eva's news was that Anthony was calling from London, and without another word or a backward glance, Arlette had gone running up the steps to where Eva had parked, and as they drove off she forgot even to glance back at John.

Now, at the rehearsal, Arlette sat beside Jerry Hoffman, where today there were only the major members of the cast: Arlette, Max Gilmore, Eva, and the actors who would play two of Cenci's sons, the two assassins, Cardinal Camillo, and Orsino. The miscellaneous pages, waiting women, noblemen, judges, guards, banquet guests, and the crowd which was to populate this Rome of the sixteenth century were not yet present.

Jerry was carefully drawing a Chinese pagoda, and seemed to have become somewhat embarrassed by her presence, as he did from time to time.

Now, perhaps he was glad and a little guilty that Anthony was in London and he had her to himself again, even though he knew that her feeling for Anthony was in the nature of a primitive's fidelity to his fetish: once forsaken, everything was lost. The curse of the fetish would demolish the spoiler.

Scripts lay on the table. After a few moments Jerry glanced up, narrowed his eyes, and told them: 'This is an impossible play.' (So had *Othello* been an impossible play.) Indeed, Jerry's stated preference was for the impossible plays – the others were not worth the trouble it took to stage them. 'The audience will be off balance, slightly hysterical, once it realizes what's going on, and it won't take much to tip it over the edge into farce. Irony is no use to this play. It will wreck it.'

They waited silently, and Arlette, signaled by that system which told one person he was being studied by another, glanced at Max Gilmore and found him watching her intently – asking himself the question she had asked herself:

Could she be the woman for whom Cenci would commit his last uncommitted crime?

She and Max Gilmore had known each other for several years. Max had been in love with Minerva, but not enough to keep him from marrying Jennifer Knight. He had divorced Jennifer after two or three years and married a nonprofessional woman, by whom he had two sons. Max did not seem well suited to domestic life, and he had divorced that wife two years ago.

He had appeared in several productions at the Hoffman-Repertory: with Arlette in *Hedda Gabler*, with Anthony as Hotspur – a Hotspur Anthony had several times remarked was the most troublesome opponent he had encountered. As Iago he had been a curious mixture of evil and physical attractiveness, which made even the malice in his character a species of fascination.

'He's the best supporting actor we've got,' Anthony had said, after Max's Hotspur had threatened to upstage his Prince Hal. '*What can he want more but the kingdom?*'

Even so, Anthony and Max Gilmore showed each other the camaraderie of rivalrous men who respected each other's capacities, and Max often spent weekends at Montauk, bringing along his current infatuation.

Max was not so tall as Anthony, nor as handsome, but his shoulders were broad, his body muscular, and his black hair and intent black eyes made him arresting to look at. He had studied medicine, but then refused to complete his internship because surgery disgusted him, after which he had spent two years in the Army and been wounded in battle in France. All this had given Art Friedman a happy opportunity. Max Gilmore was not only one of his most cherished clients, he was one of his most satisfactory celebrities: flamboyant enough to be interesting; serious enough to be even more than that.

Now, as he lighted his pipe and gazed thoughtfully at his daughter Beatrice, there seemed no reason he could not play the part of a man self-described as without fear or remorse, hoping to live to enjoy *strength, wealth, pride, and lust.*

The Cenci history was at odds with the play, and Jerry inquired if they meant to play it from a sixteenth-century or a twentieth-century point of view: 'Are we with the guy, or not?'

'Even in the sixteenth century, there were enough people against him to murder him.'

'Not until he was forty-nine years old and had committed most crimes so far invented. All evil men have admirers—'

Shelley had chosen to treat the Cenci family as one of rare and unique horror in a world and time which dealt in horror as common commerce of the day.

'Whatever else,' said Max, 'I hope we won't play it from a nineteenth-century point of view. That would kill it. Shelley has this man describe himself as a sadist of no remorse, a connoisseur of physical torture.' Max, thought Arlette, was possibly relishing the opportunity to play this deep-dyed villain. 'Now,' asked Max, with a slight mocking smile, 'am I still up to all that?' Max was forty-two, in radiant health, and such crimes well might whet his appetite.

They laughed, and began to feel more comfortable. They would play it seriously; but if they began in dead earnestness to discuss the performance of a play which was, for all its graphic horrors, sentimental and bathetic, they would never arrive at any semblance of tragedy.

'And Beatrice?' inquired Jerry.

'Beatrice?' She looked at him quickly. 'Oh. Yes. Beatrice—' She studied the table. 'Beatrice is fierce, confident, bold, brave. She is not the daughter of a man who has broken her will, as Shelley has written her. It would be absurd to try to make her a victim. When she comes in half mad after he has raped her – I suppose we have to agree it was rape – she hasn't a bruise. But she describes her eyes as full of blood and imagines, or pretends to, that she's in a madhouse and her stepmother is her nurse.'

Arlette glanced at Jerry with a skeptical smile. 'What about that?'

'What about it?'

'Whose word do we take? Shelley says she's a victim. Beatrice, in Shelley's own lines, refutes that. And she lived in that isolated castle with her father and stepmother and one brother for three years. The fact is that she had a baby and tried to conceal the birth. Beatrice, I think, can't be played as an innocent.'

'It's up to you to decide who she was,' Jerry reminded her.

'I know.'

She must play Beatrice. That was the contract she had signed. But beyond her disbelief in Beatrice's victimization, she confronted impenetrable walls, doorless, windowless, behind which lay the degree of Beatrice's innocence or guilt.

'Maybe he drugged her,' said Eva, concerned for her stepdaughter's honor.

'He told her he was coming to her chamber after midnight,' the actor playing Orsino reminded her.

'He lost his nerve the first night,' Jerry said. 'He's terrified of her – the only person he's ever known who isn't afraid of him.'

All at once Max spoke out in a strong voice: '*Fair and yet terrible!*' Cenci was talking to his daughter. '*I know a charm shall make thee meek and tame* . . .' Arlette felt a slight dizziness, as Beatrice said she felt when she came from the chamber the next morning. 'This guy knows women – and apparently, he knows what he can do to them.'

Arlette had concluded that once Max Gilmore got into the part and they began to play Francesco and Beatrice, he would give her a worthy antagonist: this father and daughter behaved like demented lovers.

'We might keep one thing in mind,' Jerry told them. 'Shelley was primarily interested in the relationship between the oppressor and the oppressed. He thought he'd found a prime example in the Cenci family.'

'He may have thought so,' said Arlette, who had begun

423

to feel herself sliding into Beatrice, seeing the world through Beatrice's eyes, wondering how much of the madness was feigned to conceal her guilt. 'But what he's written is a love story.'

'You think there's no point playing it as it is written because he's written a lie?'

Max said: '*What has passed has made me bold, her fearful.* He sends her to her chamber, and admits to himself that his plan amazes him. But once it's done— *How the delighted spirit pants for joy.*'

Arlette was looking at him steadily, thinking of the scenes which were not in the play, that shadow-play which, in every part she had performed, composed as much of her final definition of the character, or more, than anything in the script: the girl in her room, waiting. The father entering. Her resistance, or acquiescence. Her hysterical terror and real or feigned madness the next morning. '*I slide giddily as the world reels . . .*' she had told her stepmother.

Whatever her response had been, pleasure or disgust, whether she had felt enveloped by a *clinging, black, contaminating mist,* her father's body, how was it possible to reconcile the hysteria with the fearless mocking girl?

Girls like that, thought Arlette, are not raped by men they know. And if he had threatened her, it had not prevented her from telling her stepmother immediately what had happened.

The history of Francesco and Beatrice Cenci remained essentially unknown, and even Beatrice's celebrated portrait was argued by scholars to be that of another woman. But whether it was her portrait or not, Beatrice's beauty had been notorious, and that made the problem more difficult. It suggested the possibility that this aristocratic outlaw of the senses, Francesco Cenci, had been the victim of an uncontrolled man's desire for the one thing the world denied him. If his daughter had been an ordinary girl, no temptation to Cenci or anyone else, he would have left her alone.

The pathos was not only in Beatrice's portrait, true or

false, but in what was known of the year she later spent in prison – strong enough to endure torture without confessing; and strong enough to help her stepmother and brother to die with whatever dignity had been left them.

They talked through the day, and at the end had decided only that tomorrow morning, Beatrice innocent or Beatrice guilty, they would begin to read their lines.

As they left the table, Max spoke in a clear distinct voice: '. . . *her bright loveliness* . . .' Arlette stood listening intently, and seemed, as Cenci had said, capable of illumining this dark world: '*Those love-enkindled lips*—' The words came in the midst of a curse against Beatrice for her curses upon him, curses spoken after he had left her *vanquished and faint*, yet obviously not defeated. 'Does he sound like a man who got nothing back?'

They started out, and Arlette and Max fell into step as if they had become partners or conspirators – two people who must solve the same riddle. As he shook her hand, telling her that he was flattered to have been chosen to work with her – even on this impossible project – he added: '*My heart is beating with the expectation of horrid joy.*'

Between the theater and her house Arlette's courage disappeared. She ran up to the bedroom and dialed Gordon Donahue's office.

It was late afternoon there. He would be interviewing students.

Hearing her voice calling his name despairingly, he demanded: 'What is it? Excuse me a moment—' There was a brief silence while he ushered a student out of the room. 'What's happened, darling?'

'Gordon, *you* tell me! We've been talking about Beatrice Cenci all day – oh, please tell me! Was it her innocence – or her guilt?'

He said nothing for a few moments, then asked, quietly: 'Which is it for you?'

'It must be both!'

CHAPTER 53

To be invited to one of Alicia Fiedler's Sunday breakfasts, as she called them, though the hours were from one to four, the draperies were pulled and the dining room and drawing room lighted by candles, was regarded as an honor. These breakfasts were held once a month, every month of the year. To be asked was evidence of having reached a position in that small nation of the theater where application for citizenship had been taken notice of by the authorities.

Arlette's first invitation had come years ago, long before Eva or Minerva had been asked. It had been for the Sunday after her two weeks as Juliet, and Arlette had gone in a state of fear not very different from the feeling she had each night before her first entrance.

She had heard about these breakfasts ever since she had first heard of Alicia. They were spoken of discreetly, as if the guests composed a sacred secret society.

She became almost immediately aware that this would remain one of the great embarrassments of her life. Not because anything embarrassing happened, but because she had never before felt so unnecessary to the occasion, which did not need her, and which made small ceremony over her presence.

In spite of her recent success as Juliet, most of the guests either did not recognize her or did not consider it necessary to recognize her.

The great buffet in the dining room was a subject for artistic contemplation; it looked as if several seventeenth-century Dutch still lifes had been laid end to end.

Small tables stood about, but many of the guests preferred to stand, drinking their breakfast; others sat on sofas or on the floor, but Arlette had been afraid to sit for fear of finding herself alone.

At last, and she kept furtive watch on the time, the

prescribed hour and a half was over, although people were still arriving – there were between forty and sixty guests on any given Sunday – and Arlette humbly thanked Alicia and escaped into the street, where she began to run as fast as she could.

She had kept the secret of her fear, and prayed she would be asked again, vowing that one day, one day, she would enter like a true denizen of this forest. The forest itself was not at fault: it was Arlette who had been a stranger in the forest.

On the day after the last performance of *The Cenci*, Arlette arrived at Alicia's at one-thirty, having come from two hours of Yoga instruction.

She was dressed in black skirt, black sweater, black tights, black flat-heeled pumps, but now the platinum bowknotted thread was on her left hand, and around her neck the carved ivory roses Anthony had sent by Eugene Cartwright on the night *The Cenci* opened.

She ran gaily up the steps of the apartment house, glad to be done with Beatrice. After the first two months, she was able to throw off the spell almost immediately – although sometimes, later in the night, Beatrice returned.

For it could have become a way of life – that strange girl, part heroine, part child, part fierce full-grown woman, might have usurped her own personality as no other character had done.

Entering the apartment house, Arlette unexpectedly remembered the first invitation, swept backward on one of those treacherous riptides in her memory:

That was a long time ago. And, yes, I would do it again. All of it.

It was July twenty-first, and the next-to-last X had been made on two calendars last night, after Anthony had called to say they were still working on Granville's filming of the stage production for television – it was five o'clock in the morning. His plane would leave at eleven that night, and she would meet him at the airport the next morning.

The six months were gone.

She entered Alicia's drawing room with her swift fluent walk, buoyant from the exercises, flashing Jade Ring's bewitching smile wherever she looked, formally kissed the air beside Alicia's face, and went to study the opulent buffet.

She moved restlessly about, sat at a table to eat for a few minutes, talking to Eva and Minerva and Eva's husband.

Minerva, unluckily, had fallen in love with Andrew Thyssen three years before, when she was making a film based on Powell's *A Night and a Day*.

With that one picture, Minerva had joined Arlette as a star, if not one of quite the same luminous density.

She had been reluctant to play a part she superstitiously thought Arlette had patented, but she had surprised them, with her gypsy-like challenging pride and her strangely self-contained, almost forbidding elegance, by showing herself a deft comedienne. She had played a very different Elizabeth-Gloriana from Arlette's, and was promptly offered another movie contract, whereupon she broke her oath to make one picture and no more.

Arlette laughed. 'But don't forget the Plan.'

Their Plan had not departed far from its original rough sketch; they were all three famous and rich enough, as such things went in their world – not, of course, in the world Anthony had grown up in, where fame was to be avoided and money not to be counted.

This Sunday, Arlette was the unofficial guest of honor. It was never very clear whether or not there was a guest of honor and, if so, if anyone but the guest of honor knew who it was. But today the signs were plain: the entire cast of *The Cenci* was present.

They talked for a few moments of Arlette's performance as Beatrice, or at least Minerva and Eva talked about it. Arlette still could not explain where she had found Beatrice, how she had conjured her out of the air, for assuredly she was made of nothing else.

Presently Arlette was talking to Jeffrey Brooke, back from another performance in England. That Jeffrey

Brooke with whom it seemed impossible to believe she had once been in bed. 'My dear.' He kissed her face. 'Superb. I saw it last night.'

Arlette smiled at the young men and women who had played servants and pages to the Cenci family and to the Cardinal, as if they were her dearest friends, thanked them for all they had contributed, then left them – dazzled by this brush with fame and beauty.

It was difficult for her to be still, and her stomach was turning nervously, a sign of unusually severe stage fright. The prospect of seeing Anthony after more than six months did terrify her.

'It was five in the morning and Granville had kept them working all night on the television version,' she told Alicia, as if this were an unsurpassed example of man's inhumanity. 'Anthony wanted the experience of trying TV, but he's promised – never again. As for me, I won't act for an audience that can't get its ass out of the house and just sits there, turning dials and pushing buttons. Oh, no!'

Then she was seated beside Jerry Hoffman. 'He's leaving tonight at eleven. Oh, Jerry, it's been so long!'

A slight change passed over Jerry's face, something like hurt and envy, and Arlette quickly grasped his hand. As if ashamed of having been understood, Jerry gave her one of those quick side-glancing smiles. 'It was good for the superstructure, but hard on the workmen. That's modern architecture.'

Arlette looked dreamily around the room, seeing these men and women she knew so well as if through a haze, far away; even those next twenty-one hours seemed unbelievably long, a period she might not be able to endure.

Jerry asked, a little ironically, what she thought of his new girl. 'The blonde in the blue jeans and transparent white sweater.'

His new girl, as Arlette knew, was the current magazine fashion model, tall, extraordinarily thin, with blonde hair, polished and gleaming, falling straight to her hips; and the white silk sweater displayed the breasts of a twelve-year-old girl with nipples like small corks. She could be photographed, it was said, from any angle, and she could wear anything or nothing with elegance. Her name was Sarita Stanhope.

'Very beautiful,' said Arlette, wondering if she was beautiful, or only vain enough and aggressive enough to make people accept her as she presented herself: a strange but challengingly desirable woman.

Since his divorce, Jerry had spent a few months at a time with a number of currently fashionable beauties, all of them outside his world. Jerry was sensual, Jerry was impatient, Jerry did not tolerate prudery, and so Arlette supposed the girl gave him something which pleased him.

'So far,' said Jerry, looking at the girl standing there with her wide beautiful smile, listening, or pretending to listen, 'I haven't tried talking to her.' Jerry's eyes were slightly narrowed as he watched her. 'Guess what – she wants to act.' He smiled at Arlette and shrugged.

Arlette burst into a merry laugh, stood up and kissed him, saying she must go.

Why so early? She was the guest of honor. It was only three-thirty.

Why? Well, because she must. She was too nervous to stay in one place any longer.

She left as she had arrived, distributing kisses and smiles, handshakes and compliments, her face brilliant with excitement.

Coming in the door as Arlette was going out was Max Gilmore, and he kissed her on the mouth – all fear of seeming the incestuous father was gone – and introduced her to another wife he had acquired recently: Susie Allen, several years younger than he and not as successful.

This was Conrad's day off, and Arlette had driven the Mercedes herself, which she did only when she expected little traffic.

But on this day either the traffic in the Park made the trip seem interminable or five minutes had become interminable. There was no reason to hurry.

After all, just so much time must pass; she could not set

the clock ahead and expect the world to obey it. Yet the excitement increased steadily, and would surely become unbearable before he arrived.

Now that she was at liberty, free of Beatrice – Arlette Morgan once again, an unoccupied country for the first time in six months – she floundered: no rigid schedule to help her through these next hours. Time suddenly expanded, a vast empty wallet.

She found a parking space three doors down the street – Conrad would put the car in the garage when he came back. She ran up the steps, giving a gasp of surprise as Irma opened the door.

'Irma! I thought you and Conrad had gone to a movie – is everything all right?'

'Of course, madam. We went to the movie, and we're back. I don't recommend it. Mr De Forest called a little less than an hour ago—'

'Is he here?' cried Arlette, wondering who this hysterical woman was who had taken charge of her.

'No, madam. He called to say that Mr Granville wants them to work tonight—'

'Tonight!' Arlette's voice was tragic, incredulous, and her face suggested some new horror perpetrated in the household of the Cenci. 'But he's taking the eleven o'clock.'

Irma continued calmly to deliver her message, and Arlette was relieved that she did not look at her as if she had lost her wits. 'And so he will arrive on Tuesday morning – on the eleven-thirty flight.'

'Thank you, Irma.'

Arlette ran up to the bedroom, rapidly calculated the time, and put in a call to Anthony's hotel. If he was not there, she would break their rule and call the theater. She must hear his voice, or lose her mind. She waited impatiently, all the more mystified by this Arlette with her premonitions of disaster, catastrophe, some irrevocable destruction.

'Hello—' It was Anthony's voice.

'Anthony!' She was as relieved as if she had only a

moment ago received notice of his death. 'I can't believe it—'

'You can't believe what? Didn't Irma give you my message? Granville doesn't like some—'

'Another day!' cried Arlette. 'Another eternity!'

'Arlette, for Christ's sake, what's wrong with you? Another day, that's all. It's part of the deal. I can't leave until—'

'Anthony – Anthony – listen to me. I'm going to the airport right now. I can get a plane tonight, and we'll spend two or three weeks—'

'Arlette!' He spoke sharply. 'You sound hysterical.'

Another voice, a woman's voice, was heard over Anthony's:

'For God's sake, darling – what in the hell—'

The woman's voice, that artificially lowered voice of Deborah Crane, broke off with a gasp.

Arlette sat down:

I will never be happy again.

The thought was fixed, one of the eternal laws of the universe, and it struck her like the first knowledge that one day she must die.

During that silence of three or four seconds, she realized that she had not quite consciously been expecting this. Not because of Anthony: because she had read it on Deborah Crane's face, perhaps the first day Deborah had thanked her for the lease of the apartment.

Yes, it had been there, legible enough, and Arlette had read it, but then hidden it and pretended it had been her own imagination which had produced that cruel image. Of what consequence was Deborah Crane in her life?

After a few seconds, Anthony spoke again, his voice anxious and strained: 'Arlette—'

She placed the telephone in its receiver, hearing him say once again, pleadingly, 'Arlette—'

CHAPTER 54

She went swiftly but softly down the stairs, a thief sneaking out of her own house. The telephone was ringing again in the bedroom; it was still ringing as Arlette closed the front door and dashed to her parked car.

She set out in the quiet hot Sunday afternoon streets, and without any thought of where she meant to go, turned toward the Midtown Tunnel.

That this unexplained departure would seem curious to Irma and Conrad was less consequential than the dreadful possibility that if she had talked to Irma, made up a lie to explain where she was going, she would begin to cry.

The secret she took out of the house seemed so shameful she was terrified that anyone might suspect its existence.

She drove on, and now had a clear vision of their house in Montauk, where no one would disturb her, where the caretaker-farmer and his wife would not come – once they saw her car – unless she telephoned; where, in fact, she could hide.

The outgoing Sunday evening traffic was light and she drove fast, glad to have the speed of the car to concentrate on, to keep her from thinking that now the end of the world had come, on schedule or off, she could not be sure, since she had been expecting it for a long time. Everything certain and reliable now seemed never to have existed at all.

I still have something left. But what?

An Lu-shan reminded her: *'Fame is the only treasure that endures.'*

Perhaps. Alicia thought so. Anthony thought so. Jerry Hoffman thought so. It was possible that even Arlette thought so.

She passed cars, driving carefully, swerving around them, and all the while it seemed that this great surprise was not a surprise: *This is the way I knew it would happen, someday, sooner or later.*

She smiled, thinking of how Lily Malone had wanted to have her heart broken so that she might become a great actress:

Well – it wasn't necessary after all.

For almost sixteen years she had been expecting that – as Jade Ring had tried to persuade Ming Huang to have Mei Fei killed, for her own good – one day she, too, would have absorbed all the good fortune of which her nature was capable. She would be killed; if not literally, then in some worse way: In a sudden seizure of joy, which she thought might prove unendurable; in Anthony's arms – she had been wondering:

When will my life end?

Now, at least, I can stop wondering. I know the answer. I know the date. I know the time, to the minute.

But neither Lily Malone nor Arlette Morgan had believed in permanence. The earliest lesson she had learned was that life was not to be trusted; happiness was not to be depended upon; the people you loved and needed most would one day be lost to you:

For God's sake, darling – what in the hell—

The artificially lowered voice, speaking in its artificially elegant accent, telling her the news. Arlette laughed aloud.

Jade Ring's uncle reminded her: '*Heaven will put her at your mercy one day.*'

Just now, of course, Deborah was at Anthony's mercy, and that might be a worse fate. Anthony did not respond kindly to those who made Anthony De Forest feel like a fool. And that was the least of the punishment he must be enduring. She saw Deborah, putting her clothes on, leaving the hotel suite, trying to think of something to say. But Deborah was neither clever enough nor sensitive enough to say good-bye to an angry man who might want to kill her. Deborah would have left the hotel without a word, only a few tears she would no doubt consider appropriate as her contribution to the damage she had done.

Of course, neither Deborah nor Anthony knew just how much damage had been done.

Had there been other Deborah Cranes? She had thought jealousy beneath her as an idea; impossible as reality. Now – had the cause for it been there all along?

Pretend he doesn't exist. Pretend he's someone you've only heard about.

She set herself the task of reciting every speech of every character in *Jade Ring*. If she could remember that, then she had kept some of her wits. The hurricane had not blown straight through her skull, obliterating the essential personality.

She began with the morning Audience Chamber of the Shining Emperor, Ming Huang's courtiers shouting the toast raised only to an emperor: *'Ten thousand years! Live ten thousand years!'*

Ming Huang strode onstage and they knocked their heads upon the floor.

But Ming Huang was a treacherous monarch: all at once he turned into Patrick Runkle, standing beside her on a hillside above the campus. In the windshield she saw her reflection vaguely, the late sunlight striking across it, and through the windshield Patrick Runkle stared straight at her.

She ignored him and proceeded with the play.

The Emperor spoke to his Taoist Priest: *'Tell me what you make of this: early this morning I saw across the water a rosy cloud—'*

Barbara Sloan's face appeared beside her own in the reflection from the windshield: Lily Malone and Barbara, standing side by side in the Women's Room, combing their hair, glancing at each other and back to themselves:

Is she prettier? Am I? Which of us will be chosen?

As if switching to a different television channel or radio station, Arlette declared a blackout on *Jade Ring*. Every line was too dense with memories.

She searched for something which had nothing to do

435

with Anthony, and chose *Hedda Gabler*. Furthermore, Hedda was safe from love and safe from the harm love could do. It was Hedda who was destructive of those who loved her.

As the car raced along, passing through the small towns, out toward the end of the island, Hedda Gabler's life marched before her.

Arlette made a bet with herself that she could play it through and time it to kill Hedda at the moment she turned off the highway onto the road which led to their house.

Her Hedda Gabler had been a creature of guile and treachery, despising the life she found herself condemned to, longing for the world to which she would never belong.

Hedda cocked the pistol and aimed it through the opened windows: '*I'm going to shoot you, Judge Brack.*' She laughed, Arlette's laugh of mocking conspiracy.

For all its ferocity, the play proved to have an oddly soothing effect as it performed itself before her, needing rapt attention to reproduce itself gesture for gesture, tone for tone.

As the car approached the house, she slowed down; then, with a decision she might have made subconsciously when she heard Deborah's voice, she drove by.

Six miles farther on she swung into the semicircular driveway of John Powell's house, brightly lighted, as if a party were in progress – one of Margo's innumerable parties; not likely, since John was going into rehearsal in less than two weeks with a new play called *A String of Pearls*.

Margo was there, or Margo was not there:
If it happens . . .
Arlette tossed the keys into her bag, stepped out of the car and closed the door softly, ran up the steps. She paused:
If it happens – at least I'll know I can live without Anthony.
Angry at her cowardice – for the idea of another man making love to her had transformed her into a virgin more

apprehensive than Lily Malone had ever been – she rang the bell once, quickly, lightly, and there was no answer: *Maybe someone's with him.* Arlette smiled, telling herself she was not to begin seeing naked women under the bed of every married man she knew. One for today was enough.

She rapped, softly, then a little more loudly, and John opened the door, looking at her in astonishment. Quickly she raised her head and smiled.

He caught hold of her arm, drawing her toward him, and for a moment she was slightly resistant. If this was what he had been expecting for several years, then she must make him understand that either he would not get what he wanted or he must spend time enough to convince both of them it had happened by accident:

That's the important thing about this night – for both of us. If he can help me at all, he must never think that's what I came here for—

'Darling – come in. Margo and the kids went back this afternoon so I can finish this bloody thing. What are you doing out here? Is Anthony back?'

John wore blue denims and a blue and white striped T-shirt, his feet were bare, and apparently he had not shaved that day: John, who seemed to have come into the world perfectly groomed, permanently fastidious.

Arlette moved across the room, almost warily, noticing the desk covered with typewritten pages, the notebooks. Slowly she put down her handbag, and stood with hands clasped before her.

'Anthony will be back Tuesday morning. I had to get out of the city, I had to get away from Beatrice. I just stopped to say hello. I won't interfere with your work.'

John gave a quick joyous laugh and came toward her again. Yes, he thought that was what she had come for, and he was not prepared to postpone this pleasure he had lived with in his imagination ever since, she supposed, he had seen Gloriana take off her black silk dress and turn to the audience wearing a white robe, slowly knotting the sash as she looked at Robert Dudley.

Still, if she was not actively resistant, or modestly reluctant, she would never get from him what she needed more than his lovemaking — his love and gratitude. If he guessed she had come because she was hurt, she would lose both: John and her own pride, which she had come to recover.

There was probably no situation she could not handle as an extemporized play — once she knew what character she was playing.

She was not playing Mrs De Forest. She was not playing the famous actress. She was not the casual neighbor, since this man had told her he was in love with her more than once. None of these parts were any help to her now:

I'm a scared woman. My life has dissolved, and I've come here to be rescued.

'Are you hungry?' John asked, sobered, it seemed, by her retreat across the room.

'I went to Alicia's breakfast. Jerry has a new girl — Sarita Stanhope. I think he likes her.' She smiled. 'Can we walk on the beach? I want to forget about Beatrice. 'Oh,' she confided as they went out to the wooden terrace and started down the stairway built against the cliff, 'that Beatrice Cenci. She was harder on me than any of them.'

John went ahead, and at the bottom he lightly touched both hands to her waist, kissed her, and would have drawn her closer, but she smiled, shaking her head, and they set off up the beach.

John did not know this script as she did: There was to be a walk on the beach, talking of his play, of Anthony's return, of Minerva's unhappy affair with Thyssen. There would be showers in separate bathrooms, since she would run too near the ocean in an exuberant moment. Then they would meet in the living room, Arlette wearing one of his — not Margo's — bathrobes.

That would be the time when he would miscalculate his lines again, supposing that since neither of them had on anything under the robes, she was ready for what logically came next.

But that was not the way the script read.

They would prepare dinner. John would grill steaks in the fireplace, as he often did, and she would tear up a salad of Andy Webb's special lettuce crop. They would eat, and talk, and when, finally, he made love to her – in the living room, on the sofa, or on the floor – he would suppose it had all happened by miraculous good luck.

'I couldn't wait to get out here and let the wind blow me to ribbons.' She ran near the water and, as John pulled her back, they were splashed from head to foot.

John had fallen silent, and she supposed he was suffering his own pain, not of loss, but of craving. She began to talk about *A String of Pearls*, of which she had read four drafts over the time he had worked on it. It was a play with two characters, but eight actors.

The characters had no names, only ages: the Old Man; the Old Woman. Their other selves were middle-aged, young, and children of twelve and thirteen, and all of them inhabited the stage together – strangers meeting and passing, sometimes failing to recognize an earlier self, or the earlier self of the other.

They had been married, the Old Man and Old Woman, for fifty years, and Arlette thought this possibility must exist in John's mind as a continuous premonitory nightmare. The play was bitter with hate and matured resentment; it was tender and sorrowful with early happiness and excited love.

'It's terrifying,' Arlette said. 'Do audiences want to. know that much about themselves?'

'That's not my business. My business is to write the only play I can write at a given time – and this is the only one I can write now.'

He stopped, catching her hand, and they stood close together as John's fingers touched the ivory roses, slipped beneath her sweater, and closed around her breasts.

This was not part of the script, and yet the pleasure, quick, intense, so that she wondered if she had all along obliterated this possibility between John and herself for the sake of Anthony and herself, threatened to demolish

439

the script; but this script was important for those future
scripts they would play.

'Please – let's go back?'

She moved, and he let his hand fall to his side. Contrite,
she slipped her arm about his waist, and they walked up
the staircase, silent.

The wind, the sudden collision with the Atlantic, the
run on the beach, John's touch, had left her exhilarated,
curiously happy, and she became so eager for the script to
run its course, reach its denouement, that she warned
herself she must not forget the future for the sake of
rushing into the present.

And John, it seemed, understood now that it was
Arlette's script, and Arlette's timing. Arlette would give
him the cues.

Arlette came out of the bathroom, where she had
washed away the salt and combed her hair, wearing a dark
red terry cloth robe of John's, to find John smoking a
cigarette, drinking Scotch, and wearing an identical robe.
Arlette clapped her hands, amused by the grown-ups in
their costumes.

John had picked up his cue, and as Arlette sat opposite
him, her bare feet touching the edge of the coffee table, he
offered his share of the dialogue which was to occupy
them for another hour or two, or for as long as they could
tolerate the increasing tension:

'I work on a five-year plan, give or take a few months.
Two years for a play, sometimes three. One for a movie.
A little time for the miscellaneous surprises. I like five
years as a unit – I know I can complete what I set out to
do. At least, I always have.'

All at once John was standing beside her, looking down
with an extraordinary seriousness, asking her how much
time must still run. His hand touched the side of her face,
and she pressed it lightly against her lips, then stood up.

'Let's get dinner.'

Evidently he trusted her not to tease him, or he was
apprehensive because of Anthony – or he was still some-

what afraid of that final abandonment of himself to a future he could not foresee.

In the kitchen they went about their tasks quickly and methodically, and when John mentioned Anthony, she gave a slight start, as if Anthony had entered the house to ask what was going on there in his absence.

'Anthony,' John told her, 'seems to work on a lifetime scale.'

John went into the living room to broil the steaks in the fireplace, and Arlette followed, carrying dishes, napkins, knives and forks.

'Anthony does not make mistakes,' she advised John without a trace of a smile, and set the coffee table – black-handled knives, red plates, red linen napkins. 'My plan has been only to try to learn to act before I die. And to read the Five Cartloads of Books.'

John had read *Jade Ring*, and quoted from it often, a secret language they shared. But then, so was it a secret language between her and Anthony. And Gordon Donahue. And Jerry Hoffman. A lovers' Esperanto?

John was concentrating on the steaks, turning them, his face serious, unhappy, and all at once she was ashamed. She went to kneel beside him.

'John? Do you want me?'

You've saved my life. I'll give you whatever you need . . .

CHAPTER 55

Two days later, Arlette walked slowly along the beach, pausing now and then to examine a shell, determining whether or not it was a worthy addition to the two in her hand. Earlier she had found a small purple feather and stuck it into the buttonhole of her flowered white linen blouse. The blue denim pants were wet, for now and then she ran into the water. She had left John's house at eleven-thirty on Monday morning. She had left him again at nine this morning, so that he might work, and returned to the haunted house, to practice her daily routine.

The telephone had rung once this morning, but she had not answered it.

If Anthony went to the house in New York, that was one solution.

If he came here, that was a different solution, or the beginning of one.

She had no speech to make: she had prepared nothing with which to greet him, if he came:

Take it one second at a time, one minute at a time, one day at a time: a flash, and all is over . . .

And whether he arrived or whether she never saw him again, it surprised her to find that Anthony De Forest could not now be summoned before her:

I lost a world the other day.

At eleven-thirty – if his plane was on schedule, and if Anthony was on that plane – he might call, or he might not. She did not want to be in the house, tortured by the chance that he might not call.

By assuring herself that Anthony De Forest was not real, she had achieved what struck her as an admirable serenity, almost sublime, in its way.

As if she had been assigned by a director the role of a thirteen-year-old, lingering briefly along that dreaming edge between girlhood and womanhood, Arlette walked slowly, trailing a strand of seaweed she had caught out of a low foaming wave.

She had brought nothing to eat, although she did not intend to return to the house—

Until when? Perhaps until it was dark.

And then what? That was too far in the future to think about.

Now, she guessed, it was about two-thirty. She had left her wristwatch on the desk with the garland of ivory roses, to do away with the temptation to try to imagine where Anthony was at a given moment.

When it might have been three-thirty, she started back. Even walking slowly, she had come a long way.

After about an hour, far down the beach she saw a man running toward her.

She walked even more slowly, wondering with deliberate naïveté if it might be John Powell, or Andy Webb. The man was shouting, but the distance was great, the ocean drowned out his voice.

The house was on fire?

She thought of other interesting possibilities.

At last she saw that it was Anthony, running fast, shouting her name.

All at once she felt a spasm of fear, as if he had come to do her some desperate injury, kill her, perhaps. She turned and began to run in the other direction, and ran until her heart was pounding and there was a pain in her left side. Each step became more difficult, and at last she slowed down, then stopped.

'Arlette! It's Anthony!'

She glanced around and he was much nearer. She could not yet see his face clearly, but it was Anthony's body, Anthony's black hair. He wore gray slacks and a sweater and was barefoot. As he came nearer she saw to her disbelieving astonishment that he was smiling.

All at once she removed the thin platinum thread with its bowknot from her finger and tossed it casually aside, into the water, not glancing around to watch it disappear.

In another few moments he was there, still with that smile of joyous greeting and renewal, as if this were the reunion they had been anticipating for six months. He was in front of her, opening his arms.

Arlette took a quick backward step, watching him with an unsmiling warning gaze.

He looked surprised, baffled, and his arms fell to his sides. 'Oh.'

She watched him as if suspicious this stranger might try to catch her off guard. But Anthony began to talk, eagerly, excitedly – peculiar in itself, for Anthony.

He doesn't know what's happened to us, thought Arlette. *He doesn't know at all.*

443

'Arlette, you had me scared pissless! Why wouldn't you answer?'

Arlette was smiling, a slight ironic smile, as if she were only vaguely interested in whatever they were talking about, while she warned herself that she must keep a broad distance between them, not let him break through and reach her, touch her in any way.

He went on talking, eager, determined to convince her. 'Finally, I called Irma, and she said you'd come in and gone upstairs and that was the last she'd seen of you. She rapped at the bedroom door, and when she went to look, the car was gone.' He seemed honestly bewildered. 'You'd left.'

'I'd left. Of course the car was gone. I took it.'

He seemed to be taking great care to explain to her some extraordinary events, of which she could have no knowledge. 'But that's not like you. I had Cartwright put in several calls while we were working. But each time he talked to Irma she hadn't heard from you. He called here half a dozen times that night. Finally, I told him to call the Webbs. By then it was midnight here, but they said they hadn't seen you and the car wasn't here. I was god damn near out of my mind. Jesus! You've never done anything like this before, Arlette!'

'What were you afraid of, Anthony?' she asked with that vague knowing smile, not Jade Ring's, not Arlette Morgan's, either; the smile of someone he had never known – that inquiring thirteen-year-old girl, Lily Malone, who had grown up asking questions, and would go on asking them as long as she lived. 'Did you think I'd kill myself?'

'No, of course I didn't think you'd kill yourself. Why should you? Oh, Arlette – I've been acting like a crazy man these last two days. I took a cab from Kennedy, I didn't want Conrad around. And here you are – and you're all right – you're all right—'

Yes, apparently he had been afraid she might do herself an injury. He must be feeling very guilty.

Once again he approached, trying to take her into his

arms, and again she took a backward step, eyes brightening dangerously, her face losing the wistful innocent smile. The young questioning girl disappeared.

Anthony's arms dropped to his sides; he gave a light sigh. He looked at her, narrowing his eyes, as he did when he had a deep problem to solve. 'Is that it?'

Arlette continued watching him with the same steady gaze. Presently Anthony frowned, and then, as if he had made a decision of great importance, began to talk swiftly. But there was a resentful savagery on his face and in his voice.

'I wasn't going to talk to you about this. I thought we shouldn't talk about it ever.' He paused, then spoke as if he could not get it said fast enough. 'I know what's on your mind. You're wondering how many times – how many other women. Listen to me, and believe what I'm telling you. I give you my word – there's been no other time since we married. That was it, just that once.'

'Just that once?' She nodded. 'Just that once.'

'Look here, Arlette, you're embarrassing the shit out of me, but I'll tell you about it, because God knows what your imagination will do otherwise. She thinks Granville will make her a star, with all his film and TV clout. Christ knows what she thinks. She's wrong. He doesn't pick actresses that way. And she's terrified of losing him. Apparently Granville's not an easy guy to hang onto. Anyway, the hell with that. I threw it in, in case you think she'll be following me over here. She won't, and I wouldn't see her if she did. This is what happened, and it's all that happened.' He bent a little nearer. 'What does that smile mean?'

'Was I smiling? I doubt it.'

'Listen to me! I was asleep – the son of a bitch had to give us a few hours to sleep now and then – and she showed up, knocked on the door until she woke me and I opened it. I didn't know who the hell she was, handkerchief over her hair, dark glasses, and I was about to shut the door when she began to cry and took off the glasses and said I must help her. She rambled on about

Granville. Could she trust him, would he keep his promise – that crap—'

Arlette clapped her hands, a child whose adult entertainer has reached the crucial point of his story and she had guessed the ending. 'And then she unzipped the dress – and guess what she had on!'

'Where'd you get that idea?'

'Not from doing it myself. That corny trick went out in the forties.' Arlette shook her head, wonderingly. 'And it worked, didn't it?'

'It didn't work. I screwed her, and that's all there was or will be to that. Arlette, we're not going to talk about this any more.'

'I didn't ask you one bloody question.'

Anthony looked at her intently. He was clearly and honestly surprised by the fury hidden within that smile. 'Arlette—' One hand reached out, pleadingly, but Arlette took a backward step.

'You don't know me, Anthony. You don't know me at all.'

'It was so meaningless.' He laughed quietly, shaking his head.

'Meaningless.' She turned her back, ashamed. 'That makes it worse.'

'It meant nothing. Nothing. Less – if that's possible.'

He put his hands gently on her shoulders and turned her to face him. She was smiling again. 'Once, Anthony? Or a thousand times? What does it matter?'

'You think it makes no difference?'

'Of course it makes no difference.'

'Oh, Arlette—'

'You think I'll forget about it – that everything will be the same. After I got over my hurt feelings.' She looked at him curiously. 'Don't you?'

'I know you will. It's too god damn inconsequential even to discuss.' He made a quick angry gesture. 'Let's knock it off.' He took her left hand and pressed his thumb hard against the fourth finger. 'Where is it?'

She gestured toward the water, and they both glanced

out, as if there it would be, light, sparkling, returning on a wave. Anthony released her hand and glanced at the wide gold band on his left hand, its bitter prophecy carved inside. For the first time, there was keen hostile suspicion on his face. 'You've been waiting all along, haven't you – for me to do the one thing you wouldn't forgive?'

'Of course I haven't! I had it engraved so it would never happen. Don't you know it's the things you dread and fear most that don't happen?' She looked away.

'But nothing real did happen. It was – a kind of accident.'

'Accident.' Her skin grew moist, and there was a brief humming in her ears, an uncanny sense of being far from herself and far from where they stood. 'Of course,' she whispered, 'an accident.'

They started toward the house, and as they walked, silent for several minutes, Arlette looked at the sand, seeing her footprints coming from that direction, digging deeper as she had begun to run; and not far away Anthony's footprints had pounded into the sand.

Anthony stopped to pick up his shoes.

'I haven't decided what I'm going to do,' Arlette said.

She did not look at him, but he turned and caught her by the shoulders. It still surprised her when Anthony did not carefully check his physical strength. He was as strong, as quick, as he had been when they had first met: Lily Malone and Pat Runkle, the campus phenomenon, splendid to look at, arrogant, successful in everything he did, with his policy of one woman, one night.

'I have,' he said in a tone of calm practicality, all problems resolved.

Arlette looked at him, struck by a bitter resentment of the physical beauty of this man she had expected to love all her life, whom she would love no more. 'What?'

'Not a damn thing. Nothing. This has changed nothing.' They walked on. He looked angry, and his voice was hard. 'Do you think that what happened means anything to Jerry Hoffman or Art Friedman or Jim Brown or any of the other people we're under contract to? *Macbeth* goes into rehearsal next January – and that's it. Be as irrational as you must with me, but remember that you have responsibilities to other people – a hell of a lot of them.' He laughed sharply. '*You* don't know what you're going to do!' After a time he spoke softly: 'I love you.'

Arlette laughed, a quick, cruel laugh. But Anthony, whose pride was as alert as her own, and more easily triggered, ready to fire at the lightest touch, continued gravely, ignoring the laugh. 'I love you, and I need you. Our history is too long to pretend it never happened. It would be like disentangling our veins and arteries – we might be able to do it. But what would be left?'

Arlette answered with a sadness in her voice which surprised her. Where was the rage, the irretrievably broken pride in everything she valued? 'Your body had become a part of me.'

'Of course.'

Of course? Then why did you do it?

As they entered the house, Anthony set out for the kitchen. 'I haven't eaten since we left London. I'll see what's around.' Domestic. Tranquil. Confident. There was nothing which could ever disturb Anthony's confidence.

Nothing serious had happened. She would forget it presently.

And having explained that everything was as it had always been, he would have something to eat; then take a shower, since Anthony took showers as she did, a kind of medicine, two or three times a day; then he would sleep to restore his body.

Nothing had happened, because nothing had happened that meant anything to Anthony.

She crossed the living room with its painted black floor, spattered with spots of many colors. There was a big stone-faced fireplace. The white walls were almost covered with modern paintings, blank washes of color; large canvases striped or splashed with dots; others with swirls of twisting color like a nautch dancer's scarves.

The sofas were covered with coarse cotton in solid

448

primary colors, bright red, bright yellow, bright green, crowded with pillows. Low tables were piled with books and magazines; ashtrays stood in rows. No lamps were in sight, for the room was lighted by an intricate system of concealed lights installed by Jerry Hoffman's favorite lighting engineer.

We thought of everything. Yes, we did.

But why? Since this was going to happen one day, one way or another.

She started up the stairs.

Every chair, every table, every picture, had the past hidden in it.

And the past was never a quiet guest, never an undemanding spectator. The past waited patiently, with malice in its heart. The past, evidently, never overcame its resentment of having lived out its experience with you. The past was a genie of evil design.

In the bedroom, as she took her clothes off, Arlette was surprised to find she had in her shirt pocket the two shells she had picked up hours before, and she laid them carefully on the desk, removed the feather from her buttonhole and placed it between them, as if she were making a design of arcane significance.

Then, unexpectedly overcome by a sense of distance from herself and this moment, she studied the drawing she had made before she set out on her walk, surprised to find it still there: here was a drawing done by someone else – someone who had sketched it rapidly, left it, and walked some miles before Anthony had caught up with her.

The drawing was in black ink on a sheet of heavy white drawing paper; a big white daisy with a black center which occupied half the page. Throughout the center and covering the petals she had printed in letters almost too small to read: *I love to hate. I hate to love. I love to love. I hate to hate. I love to hate.* The center was black with the message.

She crumpled it slightly and tossed it toward the wastebasket, then walked into the dressing room with the intention of taking a shower, getting the sand off her feet, the sweat from the long walk on this hot day from her body, throwing her clothes aside. She stopped, curious at the sight of herself in the mirror, and approached it cautiously.

The face was serene, with a slight questioning smile: *Alone, Arlette?*

Anthony, it seemed, thought not. She was glad to see that the pain he had created had left no visible marks. Still, it had left questions:

When will my life begin again? She smiled at the mirror. *When will rivers run uphill?* the mirror replied.

The telephone rang and Arlette started as if a pistol had gone off nearby. She ran into the bathroom to answer before Anthony picked it up in the kitchen. Picking it up, she heard Anthony's voice: 'Hello.'

'Anthony?' It was John Powell. 'You're back?'

'I'm back. What did you want, John?'

'I'd like to talk to Arlette—'

'I'll be over in half an hour, John.' She hung up, then stood beside the bed, and once more had sunk into that inertia, the lethargy of hopelessness. She had been about to do something.

She glanced around suddenly when the door opened and closed, to find Anthony standing, looking at her. They watched each other silently for several moments.

Anthony would speak first, if she waited long enough, for inactivity was unendurable to Anthony. He could not wait for events to happen; if they were slow in coming he must create events. Good or bad – anything was preferable to waiting.

In a few seconds he did speak, slowly, thoughtfully, without anger, and Arlette listened, alert once again, that preternatural awareness which Anthony summoned by no more effort than it took him to exist. She had been certain almost the moment they met on the beach that Anthony knew she had been with John. After all, he knew her well enough to have guessed long before he saw her where she had been those two nights.

450

Yet, if the telephone had not rung at that moment, he would have gone the rest of his life without ever having mentioned it. Not because he was guilty about Deborah Crane. Only because he had decided, perhaps before he left London, that John Powell was of no more consequence in their lives than Deborah was:

And he'll never think anything else. I can't convince him. It would be like talking of ice to a butterfly.

'So that's why no one could find you Sunday night – and Margaret Webb thought you'd driven out on Monday morning.' He spoke slowly, thoughtfully, with no indication of anger or resentment. There it was. A simple statement of a simple fact.

But even if he had pieced together the puzzle of unanswered telephones, and even if he had thought himself prepared and resigned, when she continued to stare at him, her face impassive, a dark red color spread slowly beneath the tanned skin of his face and neck.

Yes, it hurts, doesn't it, Anthony?

He was walking slowly toward her, with no indication of threat or menace, but all at once she was convinced he would kill her – not by intent; it would be another accident. Anthony's temper had been his life's antagonist, and she knew what heavy battles he fought to control it. Athletics had been one release. The year in Korea. The parts he played, most of them turbulent men.

She ran across the room and took refuge on the other side of the bed. He stood still and smiled at her. 'Stop being childish, Arlette. You don't destroy years with a gesture—'

She backed away slowly, then sat on the deep windowsill, leaning lightly on her hands, scarcely aware that she was naked. She felt, at least, fully dressed in resentment, challenge, anger. And she smiled a little, to complete the costume.

She was prepared to wait as long as he chose:

Ask me anything—

He came no nearer. 'That was a mistake, Arlette. You've hurt the wrong man.'

She looked at the painted green floor with its transparent poppy wings, then glanced up quickly, with some notion she might surprise him. 'Maybe not. It saved my life.' That was unlikely. Not Arlette, who loved even the worst days of her life. 'And it's something he's wanted a long time.'

'I know.'

He moved toward her again and she remained motionless, watching him cautiously, although her earlier fear seemed ridiculous. Anthony would no sooner hurt her than he would kill himself.

The crumpled drawing caught his eye; he stopped and picked it up with that swift gracefulness which was still a fascination to her. He looked at it, slightly smiling: *Self-Destroying Daisy*. And so it was. He laid it on the desk top, smoothing it carefully with his hand.

He glanced at her, smiling curiously. 'You've done Powell more harm than you've done me. John's a serious guy. And he'll know – he knows right now – that you're not in love with him. Oh sure—' She had started to protest. 'You love him. But you love a lot of people, Arlette. You always have. Donahue. Jerry. Michael. Frederick.'

'I was serious.'

She was pleased to see she had provoked a glaze of pain in his eyes. But it did not last long. The determination to control was stronger than any injury she could do his pride.

'Okay, you were serious. I'm not sorry for Powell, for Christ's sake. But you should be a little careful about who gets knocked around while you're telling yourself that in ancient China revenge was a sacred duty.' He smiled again, a slight grimace. 'Sometimes I wish Donahue had written his play about anything but the T'ang Dynasty.'

'If I hadn't found it there, I'd have found it somewhere else.'

'Revenge isn't a god damn toy. It's a hand grenade. Well – that's it. You went there.'

He took a few steps nearer. Powell was of no more

consequence than Jack Davidson had been, that young man who had loved her before she had ever heard of Pat Runkle.

The steady intense concentration of his black eyes, the concentration gathering on his face as he moved nearer, had made her begin to feel the helpless drift of longing, even while she watched him, resentful that his physical beauty was a fatality in her life. The energy of pride had drained away, and she lifted one hand warningly – warning which of them?

Anthony stripped the sweater over his head and dropped it, stepped out of the slacks naked, and as she began to move away, a kind of trancelike movement, slow and uncertain, he had captured her, his hands cupped around her breasts, then quickly separating her thighs as he stood between them, and without knowing how it happened, the old habits, vehement as ever, had brought him inside her. She heard herself begin to cry, and the crying grew steadily more frantic, until that semblance of defeat came suddenly, with a shuddering collapse of her muscles, her arms fell to her sides, and he paused, but did not move away, waiting, while she began childishly wiping the tears with both hands, sure that everything inside her had been melted away, her life's history disappeared in those destroying moments.

Unexpectedly she looked at him, surprised by the seriousness of his face, the seriousness and hurt concern. With a great effort she spoke his name, as if she were trying to talk when coming out of anesthesia, then clasped him suddenly as he began to move again, slowly, watching her, moving deeper with greed and anger.

As he moved more swiftly she looked at him, then closed her eyes, trying again and again to tell him something of great importance.

'Don't talk.' He spoke reassuringly. 'Oh, Arlette – my darling—'

'Anthony, you—'

'Be quiet – quiet—'

Anthony, you hardly knew me . . .

453

She reread the reviews of *A String of Pearls* at the breakfast table the morning after it opened.

'I'm so relieved, so relieved,' Arlette told Anthony. 'It's a hard play, a very bitter play – people don't like to know how ugly life becomes as they grow old. Thank God, that's one thing I don't have to worry about,' she added, as gaily as if she had been given a pledge that other women might grow old, might stiffen their smiles and their muscles and their emotions, but she would not.

The premonitory menace of the words did not occur to her, and seemingly not to Anthony, and they set out for the rehearsal hall as if this were no grim day of work and frustration, but a day for a gallop over the moors, a long walk on the beach.

The same papers had carried the story that Deborah Crane was on her way to Hollywood, where she was to appear in a comedy-melodrama, *Silverheels*, a film about two sisters who had kept the most elegant whorehouse in St Louis at the end of the nineteenth century. But they said nothing about that.

It took Arlette a long time to become familiar with all those others, Macduff and Donalbain and Malcolm, even though she arrived on the first day knowing every character's lines as well as she knew her own.

It was only to Anthony that she responded with a semblance of her finished performance.

When she faced him onstage Deborah Crane had never existed.

And there were no other actors of significance. The play belonged to them – those others were necessary to fill in the edges. Arlette was far more indifferent to the other actors than they guessed, and far more indifferent than Anthony, who played with real concern for his relationships with the major players, Macduff in particular.

Anthony singled out his real enemy in each production, and apart from his concentration upon the character played by Arlette, he gave his strongest playing to the end of defeating the enemy, even though, in this play, the enemy would at last emerge carrying Macbeth's severed head.

No matter, was Anthony's conviction. He had stripped Macduff's hide off him long ago. That he, Macbeth, had been killed was the playwright's fault, none of his own.

'Who is he?' Alicia asked her when Arlette had gone for an early lesson because Jerry was working with the Witches and Macbeth and Banquo. From time to time Jerry took fragments of a play and went over it, hammering it into their brains like a man diligently hammering a skull with iron nails.

Alicia had asked the question before, but this time Arlette had an answer. 'Lady Macbeth is a Druidic priestess—'

'Ah?'

'You don't think so?'

'I do think so. Although I never played her that way.'

'She's primitive. She's cruel and fierce. She's sensually demanding. He murders as much for her as for himself. She wants to be queen. But if she looks and sounds like a power-driven harpy, the sleep-walking scene is gone before the play begins.' She added, rather gloomily: 'Now all that's left is – do it.'

During the costume fittings, she experienced a brief euphoria. The costumes would produce the character: the long-trained dresses, the long sleeves with pointed cuffs, the flat long-toed shoes. There, she could imagine, was Lady Macbeth herself.

Her costumes were all cut alike, fitting her body to below the waist, and were laced loosely over a white linen garment which showed as a lining of the bell-shaped sleeves.

In her first scene, Arlette's dress was a bright vermilion. This act was triumphant, and the gown's brilliant color made that statement. The second-act dress was black:

night and murder, that dress said. The third-act dress was purple, with its sleeves and train edged in ermine, and she wore a crown for the banqueting scene. She did not appear in the fourth act, which was Eva's, who, as Lady Macduff, must lose her children and her own life. And when Lady Macbeth appeared in the last act she wore a long white gown, nearly transparent, and she would walk the stage barefoot. That was the last anyone saw of Lady Macbeth, and Arlette meant they would not quickly forget her, once she had found her.

Jerry felt the essence of this production was the passionate aliveness of the characters. Whatever tragedy the audience might feel must derive from witnessing the destruction of vitality, energy, intensity, and, yes, love – by ambition, or self-punishment.

He made a brief speech the first day the cast was assembled. 'We're not trying to modernize the play. If anything, I hope we'll end with something which recedes into pre-Christianity. The morality is Shakespeare's – not yours or mine. Murder was the usual means to power in those days. Don't regard Macbeth as an unusual fiend. He was a guy on the make, and that was the way to make it. He wanted the throne of Scotland, and that was the way to get it.'

When she could find an hour or two, Arlette spent it with Alicia or her voice instructor. She was convinced Lady Macbeth needed higher notes than she could ordinarily command. A Druidic seeress, to give her speech that incantatory mesmerizing fervor, must use a few notes which were almost keened.

That was a surprise Arlette was keeping to herself, and there were some few others she had demonstrated only to Arlette Morgan, performing in the bedroom after Anthony had gone for an early lesson in broadsword fighting.

She thought he took great joy from the savagery of his battle with Macduff, and seeing the glitter in his eyes as he left her, she wondered if this play had stripped a thousand years of cruelly acquired civilization from all of them.

Jerry had performed his feat of slowly driving his cast to such a condition of excitement and distraction they seemed no longer twentieth-century actors. Step by step, he had driven them back into a darkness where neither good nor evil existed.

But where is she? I'm still looking. I've got to find her.

Each day she expected to be told by Jerry Hoffman that the board had decided she must be replaced. She was still terrified when she left, and sat in silence beside Anthony during their drive home.

One night, in a voice she scarcely recognized, she asked meekly: 'Anthony?'

Anthony was also given to long periods of silence during rehearsals, and evidently spent the time preparing himself for the next day, pruning and cutting away whatever he did not like of that day's work, watering and mulching the character to bring it into blossom next day.

Now he turned so quickly that his solicitude, his tender concern for her fears, made her wonder why she could not find a cure for her vindictiveness:

Never forget. Never forgive.

A good enough motto for Lily Malone. But for Arlette Morgan? Yet there it was, a corroding jealousy of that moment when it had been another women who had Anthony inside her.

'For love is strong as death, jealousy as cruel as the grave . . .'

She had not believed it. But it was true.

The bitterness was forgotten when she stood on the stage with him. For then she needed him for something which seemed of infinitely greater significance than love, or some random infidelity.

She needed him for his confidence, now that he had decided the time had come.

She thought perhaps the Anthony who had played Hamlet was not the same man who had gone to England. Hamlet, that character he had detested, seemed to have

457

given him greater freedom to be other characters, at still farther remove from Anthony De Forest.

If, thought Arlette, any of us actors are real. Or are we only manifestations of some universal human need to know – and be shown – life's fatal secrets?

'Anthony, do you think I'm sick?'

'Sick? What symptoms do you have? Is your throat sore?' His hand pressed her forehead, felt her pulse. 'When did it begin?'

'I don't know. Something's wrong.'

'But where? *Where?*' As they started up the steps of their house he had one arm around her, demanding, 'Where? Answer me!'

'Everywhere. All over. Maybe I should tell Jerry.'

Arlette went ahead of them into the small drawing room, dimly lighted, as if it were submerged in a mauve-colored inland sea, the mauve silk velvet carpets, the mauve silk draperies and upholstery of the furniture, the touches of gilt, the jade figures, the gleaming paintings, vases filled with white roses, this exquisite and intimate room through which they passed without more awareness than they had of the darkly lighted entrance of the rehearsal hall.

Anthony took her by the shoulders. He spoke in a low voice, his face angry. 'This is nonsense! You're not sick! You're afraid, that's all.'

'That's all?' she asked softly. 'All? I'd rather die than play it.'

Jerry seemed to think that if she would make her entrance with a flourish, it might cure her. But she would not do that, either.

'Why?' he asked her sorrowfully. 'Why, Arlette?'

They were sitting far back in the theater, watching the progress of the battle in the fifth act, where pandemonium had broken loose, and Anthony and Max Gilmore were lashing at each other with their air-drawn broadswords. 'If someone doesn't get hurt in this thing, I'll be astonished. Anthony really believes the battle must be real enough to be dangerous or they're cheating.' She looked at Jerry. 'Why won't I come on like Diana the huntress?'

'Something like that.'

'She's not exuberant when she first appears. She's stunned, she's thoughtful. A wish granted suddenly – takes time to absorb.'

John Powell, for example. John was not accustomed to the granting of his wish even now; each time she went to him, he was as surprised and grateful as he had been that first night, more than eight months ago.

Jerry got up and left her, walking to the front of the theater where the actors lay strewn about, dead and wounded, while Macduff, eyes gleaming with triumph and hate, held aloft the imaginary gargoyle of Macbeth's bloody severed head.

'Let's remember one thing,' Jerry was saying. 'These are not toys – and no convincing battle is fought without some degree of loss of consciousness.'

They were all feeling the increasing tension, and there was more than the usual number of bursts of ill temper, sarcasm, complaining, as the day came nearer. No one was satisfied with his costume, his armor, his battle equipment, the lighting, or the scenery. Only the words remained unchanged.

Then sometime during a morning rehearsal of the final week, Anthony seemed to suspect he was dealing with a Druidic priestess, a worker of evil magic, who craved his kingship for her own sake, not his.

This was no contemporary helpful middle-class political wife who caressed him as they talked about murder – but a reincarnation of some ancient forest deity.

'Where did you go, Arlette?' he asked her later.

Arlette glanced at him curiously. She had, in fact, gone to John Powell's office late the afternoon of the day before, and wondered if her disguise had been penetrated by some elevator operator or taxi driver.

That was not what he was talking about.

'Lady Macbeth is beginning to possess you.'

'Or I'm beginning to possess her.'

It was true. She was haunted by that other woman nowadays. There were traces of her in Arlette's hazel eyes, which changed under the spotlights to a color nearly as dark as Anthony's.

She had gone to rehearsal on that first day, feeling sick, her resources depleted, her pride obliterated by that husky voice coming to her from five thousand miles away, wondering if she could ever find the strength to play this part she had waited for ever since the idea of acting had first become serious to her.

But then she had told herself, as she listened to Jerry talking to the cast, her life's history was not to be seen by looking backward: history was the eternal present.

I've been sick before, she reminded herself.

She remembered the sickness, some strange indefinable sense of negativeness, a sudden chill fallen over her life, and seemingly over all the future. Somehow she had cured herself, and the sickness had not come back again – until she had made that call to London.

So small a coincidence for so large a blasted area of her destiny.

Unless Lady Macbeth could cure her.

The cure was to escape the sickness, leave it behind in the shell of its owner. Lily Malone or Arlette Morgan, and build a new healthy, strong, and vital individuality: let her sick self die. Bury her deep. And come to life again, a new incarnation.

She glanced at Anthony, staring ahead thoughtfully as they drove home through the heavy traffic, and asked him if he thought her hair was long enough. She had been letting it grow, and it was four or five inches below her shoulders.

He touched the ends tenderly. 'Beautiful—' he told her. 'You are – you really are, you know.'

He's forgotten the whole bloody thing. He's forgotten, and I'm condemned to this god damned everlasting memory . . . That voice.

The pain was keen and sharp as it had been at the

moment when Anthony's hand covered the telephone and she heard that life-cracking silence:

She'll never know what she did to me.

Arlette scarcely noticed that on opening night she had neither fears nor apprehensions.

She and Anthony dressed in silence, as if to speak would break some spell. Anthony's face was drawn into a concentrated tautness, his body muscles hardened, even when he was exerting no more effort than to apply his makeup, which, he and Jerry had agreed, was to look no more unusual than any ordinary stage makeup. No trace of the fiend in this Macbeth's appearance.

When Anthony started out the door without a word, Arlette sat and smiled in the mirror, as if this wordless departure had been anticipated.

He turned quickly, came back, kissed her mouth, murmuring: 'Remember,' and was gone to meet the Three Witches.

Even this caused no concern.

What was there, after all, which was of more consequence than her first performance in her own self-produced *Adventure*?

A play to be performed. A job – no better, and very little worse, than any other job.

She had dismissed her dresser and now she was pacing the dressing room. As she walked, something caught her eye, hanging on the wall at the far end among the framed mementos of other years: photographs of Michael, of Valerie and Frederick, of Gordon Donahue. The red-framed page with Jerry Hoffman's doodles made at the conference about *Hedda Gabler*. A clipping from the paper which had first carried the news of the marriage of Lily Malone to Patrick Francis Runkle. No family photographs for Anthony, but two pictures he had taken of Arlette, one in profile, one looking straight at him, with some complex impenetrable thought upon her perfectly spaced features.

And now: the *Self-Destroying Daisy*, rescued from the waste-basket, smoothed out, framed in white wood.

How had he happened to save that? It amused him? Not likely. He was teaching her a lesson? Anthony did not teach lessons, and did not want anyone teaching him lessons.

She left the picture of the daisy, for the flower was cruel and unforgiving, and its threatening message told her – and Anthony – more than either of them had any need to know.

There were three sharp raps at her dressing-room door. 'Two minutes, Miss Morgan, please.'

She was overcome by a petrifying terror.

She started toward the door, surprised to find she could walk. All at once she paused, turned to the dressing table, and bent one knee before Gordon Donahue's miniature statue of Kuan-Yin.

'Great mercy, great pity, save from sorrow, save from suffering.' She rose slowly. *'Amida, Buddha!'*

With a surge of confidence, she went out, took a folded letter from someone's hands, and walked onto the stage with a slow gliding movement which brought her around a fragment of one of the stone pillars, which Jerry had asked his set designer to give him by way of a castle.

Her slow entrance, head slightly bowed as she read the letter, affected the audience as if an electric current had passed through it: the gilt hair, the red dress showing her shoulders and breasts as she glided down the stage, reading so softly that after the surprised intake of breath, there came a profound silence. Whatever Lady Macbeths they had encountered before, this one was not a copy.

Her voice grew stronger as she read, and went winging across the theater in a tone of joyous triumph: *'Thane of Cawdor . . . Hail, king that shalt be . . .'*

She raised her head and gazed for a moment straight into the blurred mass of the galleries. All at once she laughed aloud, a laugh of savage mockery, Lady Macbeth summoning the ancient gods to witness the life to come, whatever it brought: triumph, futility, death. The laughter was that of a cruel and dominant spirit.

When she returned to normal speech there was that

intuitive awareness which came at certain moments during any production, letting her know the audience was attentive; prepared to submit because an imaginary woman had become more real to them than they were to one another.

Knowing that she held them now, she had no intention of letting them go until her part had been played through. She had left Arlette Morgan – somewhere. Here was Lady Macbeth, prepared to commit and endure the effects of real murders, real madness, real death.

'*Yet do I fear thy nature; It is too full of the milk of human kindness* . . .'

At the messenger's arrival to inform her that the King of Scotland would arrive that night, she cried: '*Thou'rt mad to say it!*'

She threw her head back, and the white throat presented a vulnerability; as if by that movement she strained to reach the gods: '*Come, you spirits* . . .' The voice pleaded with her demons, guardians, and potential destroyers of her life. '*Unsex me here* . . .'

After a pause, while Arlette summoned all her will to make her voice obey her, she heard the eerie wail of the Druidic priestess praying to her pagan gods, and knew its effect by the chill which passed over her breasts and arms.

Her hands took hold of the deep neckline to pull it apart, uncovering her breasts: '*Come to my woman's breasts* . . . *take my milk for gall* . . .'

Lady Macbeth was complete to them now as a passionate, violent woman, part deity, part demon. She had convinced them she was more of the supernatural world than the Witches themselves.

Macbeth strode toward her with the conqueror's energy, and she turned to him swiftly. This Lady Macbeth had a woman's hungry body, and her arms reached eagerly around him as he held her, one hand covering her breast, the other holding her buttocks.

They had decided there would be no 'suburban kiss,' as Arlette called it, quick and absent-minded; this kiss was greedy and prolonged.

For all her craving for power, she was eager to get him into bed, assuage her own need – and then attack the questions of war, of murder, kingships lost or stolen. But Macbeth, the ever impatient male, impatient for power first, love later, moved her away from him – not easily, for her arms clung; she released him reluctantly.

Now she began to talk to him of murder, in a manner not very different from her pleading for lovemaking. And once the king had almost finished supper and Macbeth confessed he was not capable of murder, she approached him furiously, cold and contemptuous.

In despair of overcoming his refusal to kill his king, she pretended a madonnalike tenderness, and her arms took the form of a woman holding a baby to her breast. *'I have given suck,'* she told him softly: *'and know how tender 'tis to love the babe that milks me . . .'*

She let her arms fall to her sides, disposing of child, maternity, tenderness. They studied each other, enemies and conspirators; Macbeth seemed mesmerized by the beauty of his wife, intimidated by her cruel courage.

Arlette ran to the dressing room, speaking to no one, afraid she might lose that Lady Macbeth, who by now seemed some alien spirit into whose body she had entered and who, at this moment, struggled to escape her possession. She dressed quickly, combed her hair back from her face with a gesture of both hands, and ran toward the stage, looking as if Lady Macbeth might have gone mad.

'What are they thinking out there?' she murmured, not glancing at Jerry. She did not hear his reply, if he made one.

This time she swept onto the stage, her voice low and fierce: *'That which hath made them drunk hath made me bold . . .'*

Dressing for the third act, in the purple gown, the murders done, the grooms smeared with blood, she looked at the mirror. Lady Macbeth gazed back at her, a Lady Macbeth wild, proud, cruel, still beautiful. But now it was the beauty of a murdering sorceress. She had contrived to strip away the centuries, setting Lady Macbeth back into the primitive forests, where the Druid priests imprisoned men in cages of green boughs and set them afire.

The play's acceleration, urging them along, forced them to exploits of energy never tried in rehearsal. They acted each upon the other. There seemed some general comprehension – although no one had lost a line or missed a cue – that nevertheless they were all insane.

During the fourth act – and she carefully avoided encountering Eva, as Lady Macduff, on her way to the stage – Arlette changed to the long white nightgown.

Tonight, it seemed, tranquillity was as lost to her as it was to Lady Macbeth, and she walked the floor of the dressing room, silently reciting each speech being spoken upon the stage. She was too distracted to stand in the wings, superstitiously afraid her presence might be a communicable disease which would cause one of the Witches to forget her dance steps, Macbeth to miss a cue. Lady Macbeth had indeed become a malign influence, making Arlette fearful of her power for evil.

As she walked back and forth, she began to tremble. Her leg muscles quivered. She stood still, commanding her muscles to relax. But still they shook.

'Two minutes, Miss Morgan, please.'

Arlette ran to the door and opened it. 'What did you say?'

He repeated the information, looking puzzled.

She slammed the door, then opened it again. 'Where's the bloody candle?'

'It's ready, Miss Morgan.'

'Go see that it's lighted.'

She shut the door quietly, closed her eyes a moment, and emerged, slowly, gliding along. She passed other actors and stagehands, but did not see them. She saw no one until she stood in the wings and looked out at the stage, suspiciously watching the Doctor and Waiting Gentlewoman, for it seemed they were not discussing the peculiar behavior of Lady Macbeth, but of Arlette Morgan, driven mad by this part:

'*When was it she last walked?*'

'*I have seen her rise from her bed, throw her nightgown upon her, unlock her closet, take forth paper, fold it, write upon it, read it, afterwards seal it . . .*'

All at once the inner trembling stopped and Arlette smiled, recognizing Lady Macbeth's bizarre behavior in her own: the sealed envelopes in the secret drawer of the silver-gilt cabinet.

Yes. They were talking about her.

A burning candle was put into her hand.

Arlette moved onto the stage, set the candle on one of the stone pillars, and began the process of washing her hands, slowly and gently at first, then more rapidly, until she gave once again that eerie wail of supplication – a faint echo of the first, a cry of plaintive despair.

'*One; two; why, then 'tis time to do't . . . Here's the smell of blood still . . .*'

She had decided long ago that this scene was hers – not the playwright's, not the director's, not the other actors' – Arlette Morgan's. She had no wish to show the audience how to feel, but had a sense of absolute indifference. Let them feel about Lady Macbeth as they might; pity, condemnation, hatred, sorrow. What difference did it make?

Lady Macbeth would soon be dead.

She took up the candle and slowly recrossed the stage, speaking quietly, as if telling a secret to herself. '*What's done cannot be undone: to bed, to bed, to bed.*'

Whether by luck, whether from his own problems with Macbeth, she did not see Anthony again until she went for the curtain call. She approached slowly, still in the nightdress, looking from one actor's face to another, only dimly aware of the applause behind the curtain. The faces, grim, still under the spell of their sufferings and sorrow, told her nothing.

When Anthony took her hand, his face was extraordinarily drawn and serious, and she saw that there was a gash across the right eyebrow, and a streak of blood ran from it.

'Oh!'

'Be quiet.'

The curtain lifted and Arlette bowed low, only slowly becoming aware that most of the audience had risen to its feet, applauding, and there was shouting among them. She looked at them, bewildered. The curtain came down and rose again. The applause went on, the bows went on. The minor actors had disappeared. Arlette and Anthony stood with Eva French and Max Gilmore, and then she and Anthony stood together.

The curtain went up, and this time she stood gazing at them with more curiosity than surprise, more defiance than gratitude.

You will never see me again. I can not do it.

The curtain came down, and Jerry Hoffman was embracing her. Surprised, Arlette smiled tenderly. 'Why, Jerry – you're here?'

At that he laughed, and then was shaking hands with Anthony, with Max, embracing Eva, and in the midst of all that demonstration Arlette ran to hide in the dressing room.

She closed the door and leaned against it, and a sense of relief washed over her, cleansing her of the night, of the terrors of attempting Lady Macbeth again.

Anthony pushed against the door with such force she stumbled and he caught her. 'It seems to have gone quite well,' he said, and Arlette gave a burst of laughter, wild with relief.

' "Gone quite well," Anthony!' The uncontrollable laughter surprised her, but there seemed no reason to try to stop it. 'How incredibly funny! "Gone quite well"—'

All at once Anthony relapsed into the character of Ming Huang, the defeated, dispossessed emperor: *'Heaven cannot be trusted. Kingship is easily lost.'*

Arlette's face grew serious. The laughter had not been real, even to her. 'No. Tomorrow night – there's that – isn't there?'

CHAPTER 57

'Are you tired, darling? Oh, can't we take off those terrible black goggles? You look beautiful without them.'

Arlette submitted. She was too exhausted to argue about the dark glasses, meant to conceal her fatigue after the night flight, or even to ask how he came to be there – Sir Charles Granville, who should have been in Dorset, overseeing whatever filming was in progress today:

Who is this man? He acts like my lover. I thought we were enemies.

Not in Sir Charles' opinion. He touched lightly the shadows beneath her eyes, at which Arlette took out a mirror: *I look like hell. Why did he come?*

'Shall we drive – it's four hours at this time of day, and you have a nice cottage, and a housekeeper. On our way I can tell you what's been done.'

No rest for the weary when Charles Granville was around. 'We may as well.'

At least he had not tried to coerce her into his helicopter, one of his several flying machines.

The car began to move through the traffic in the dense January fog, and this new Sir Charles Granville – less new, she suspected, for being Sir Charles than because he was alone with her and she was his leading lady, and this picture was of more than usual importance to him – began to talk beguilingly.

No, there were other reasons, too, for this royal treatment. He was in awe of actors who could act, who knew their craft to its finest dimensions. He was more in awe of her than she had ever been of him.

Anthony had kissed her good-bye the night before at Kennedy Airport. 'I love you,' he told her with intense seriousness. She had never again been able to tell Anthony she loved him – each time she thought she would, she could not, after all.

She had surprised him only twice in their history: the engraving inside his wedding ring; and her visit to John Powell after she had heard Deborah's voice.

'I'm going to miss you like hell.' She smiled at him sympathetically, and paused near that final barrier where she must leave him: Eustacia Vye for her; *Henry IV*, Part 2, for him.

'It's only a few months.'

He glanced away, then looked at her quickly, caught her arm as she started off, and kissed her once more.

Sir Charles – although he had not been Sir Charles yet – had come for the opening of *Macbeth* in New York. Arlette's contract with him had been signed and he was assembling his cast and laying out production costs, sets, filming background shots, preparing *The Return of the Native*, even while he was in the midst of editing his last film, which he described as a comedy of terrors.

She supposed he had come because he wanted to see what she had learned during the four years since *The Two of Them* was completed. He wanted to know what he could expect of her Eustacia Vye.

His appearance at the opening-night party of *Macbeth* ten months ago at Art Friedman's house had surprised her. There was a look on his face of pleasurable speculation: here was his Eustacia, better than even he had hoped for.

Friedman's house was furnished with eighteenth-century English furniture, Chinese and Persian rugs too valuable to step on, much less toss lighted cigarette butts on; crystal chandeliers and sconces burning candles. Here were all the trappings of an English gentleman of the past century surrounding Art Friedman and his wife, who had not become wholly accustomed to her husband's eminence. Where, she seemed to be wondering, had all these murky blue velvet draperies, these eighteenth-century landscape paintings, these large pieces of antique silver, bowls and tureens filled with yellow roses – where had they all come from?

For that matter, where had the guests come from?

Two hundred of them, at least. Most of them beautiful, men and women alike. And all of them in a seeming state of hysteria, kissing one another, darting here and there, each and every one filled with self-confidence, aggressive health, and the mysterious secret of maintaining an expression of joyous brilliance.

Arlette had met Mrs Friedman several times. And when she and Anthony entered Arlette went directly to her, embracing her and pressing her cheek against hers, thanking her for giving them such a beautiful, beautiful party. She held Mrs Friedman's little hand and smiled Jade Ring's smile.

She had done it on impulse, and was pleased to find it the most effective entrance she had ever made. Kind Miss Morgan, generous Arlette. Who else would have done it?

This, Arlette was convinced, had been the most important night of her life: past, present, or to come. She had played Lady Macbeth – whether to her own satisfaction she could not know – but, it seemed, to everyone else's.

There was only that one flaw: the sulky low voice; and her own memory, too accurate for comfort.

Deborah's voice or not, she was determined to think of this as the greatest event of all, and she was dressed for it: black velvet gown, fitted and falling straight to the floor, cut across one shoulder to a point low on the opposite breast. Wound three times around her neck was a strand of baroque pearls, the small figure of the Goddess of Mercy depending from the middle strand between her breasts – Anthony's present, discovered an hour before amid the jars and bottles on the dressing table.

Charles Granville approached and kissed her while she was still beaming upon little Mrs Friedman, wondering how to break the spell she had cast.

After that she forgot him, and a few days later came the news that he had received a knighthood, a prediction he had made privately to Anthony:

'It was your bloody Hamlet, De Forest. The *coup de grâce*, no doubt about it.'

Later in the evening Arlette found Anthony beside her,

470

his arm around her waist, casual and possessive, as he explained to John Powell, Gordon and Marian Donahue, what his wife had accomplished that night with her Lady Macbeth.

'It's a harder part than Macbeth – although I didn't think so before we tried it. Everything Macbeth does is what any guy would do, give him a few centuries' relief from civilization. Arlette – God knows how she's done it – goes back three thousand years with this woman.'

In fact, she did not know any more about how she had done it than he or anyone else did. These were mysteries she did not even try to clarify, for fear of losing that dark primeval world to which she must return each time she put on the red gown and looked into the mirror: for it was that first searching look which seemed the magic key, leading her into that other world of madness and crime and depthless sorrow. Whatever the part, she entered it through the looking glass.

Now, after four months of playing the Druidic priestess, after nearly seven months at Montauk and New York, she was riding beside Sir Charles on her way to meet Eustacia Vye.

At least, she supposed she would find her there, on Egdon Heath.

Summer scenes and early autumn and winter scenes which were either background shots or did not involve Eustacia had been filmed. Today, Charles explained, they were shooting – although Charles had misgivings that his assistant was capable of it – the Reddleman's van trundling along the rutted road, bearing the invisible Thomasin.

Two hours from London, Charles remarked soberly: 'Arlette – Eustacia must have black hair.'

'I know. The wigs are in my luggage. No doubt Edna has them unpacked. Seven. Not too ugly.'

'No problem?'

'No problem.'

Arlette had long ago given up trying to explain to her reasons for wanting to play a part looking a certain way.

'Good.' All at once he snapped his fingers, as if remembering something he had been searching for. 'How's Anthony?'

Arlette saw little of Egdon Heath as they rushed across it in Charles' black American limousine, the one big car in his fleet, which at Egdon Heath consisted of vans, trailers, station wagons, sound trucks, jeeps, golf carts with side curtains, for bad weather, though Sir Charles in good English fashion did not think weather was good or bad, but only suitable or not suitable for the scene he wanted to film that day. In which event he rearranged his shooting schedule, and the day's work began.

He proceeded as if neither God nor any actor's indisposition or temperament might interfere with that film which, Arlette had thought ever since she played Emma Hamilton, existed complete in Sir Charles' head before he shot the first frame.

Sir Charles went on location nowadays with the pomp of a medieval monarch traveling from castle to castle, but this contemporary monarch paid handsomely for what he used of the land and the people upon whom he descended.

Egdon Heath consisted of a vast expanse of moorland with inhabited cottages set at varying distances, for he had located a site not very different from what it had been one hundred years ago. Granville had bought some cottages, leased others, and signed more than one hundred members of the local community to serve as extras, and if their accents contrasted oddly with those of the other characters, that was expected: the villagers had no education; the leading characters had.

There were trailers, where some of the actors and technicians lived. There were floored tents for others. The cast came and went, depending on the phase of the story being filmed.

The moors extended over an apparently endless horizon, covered with furze. Small ugly ponies roamed the countryside. A perpetual haze covered the moors through the late fall and winter, giving them the unreal look of a landscape seen under water.

Charles had provided Arlette with a housekeeper-cook, Ann Parish, a village woman with a reputation as the best cook for miles around. No canned beans and canned meat on this location.

The cottage had been bought and remade into a complete house, in which Arlette would live, and where for the film Eustacia Vye would live with her grandfather.

Charles took her directly to Eustacia's house at the top of the highest hill in the area, introduced her to her housekeeper, kissed her as if she were a valuable object, and said he would call at noon the next day to take her to meet those members of the cast who played leading parts.

'In the meantime, don't think about it.'

'I don't believe I could.'

But after twelve hours of sleep she was alert again.

She knew how to recuperate in one day, rather than one week. She knew how to smile when she wanted to cry. She knew how to convince herself of the feelings she needed. She knew how to force Arlette to be happy even when she was sad. She was, she thought, as much the sum total of what she had learned not to do as she was the triumphant product of what she had learned to do.

She was determined now to live this experience as if it were a new green world to which she was being introduced and she herself had no history; had never met Anthony, never married him, never been damaged by him. This picture was to be the magic formula by which she would banish Deborah and her voice from Arlette Morgan's life, now and forever.

Arlette thought carefully about her introduction to the principal players, but decided that since they were probably expecting an overdressed star, glittering with arrogance and that peculiarly annoying American manner of having the world in thrall, she would surprise them. She did not expect a warm and admiring welcome.

She entered the main room of the reconstructed inn, The Quiet Woman, at twelve-fifteen – driven by Sir Charles in his jeep, wearing a yellow cashmere dress with

473

a flaring skirt, and over it a jonquil-yellow coat, lined with lavender.

The other actors sat at a long table, drinking tea from paper cups, for even this free-spending monarch had his small economies. They turned as the door opened, curious about this newcomer, Eustacia Vye, capable of disturbing all their lives, perhaps destroying some.

The faces were familiar, for she had spent a day with Anthony and Alicia in the projection room, watching clips of films. She was not meeting strangers. She had studied them attentively and felt she knew them better than they knew her, or ever would.

She dropped the coat onto a chair and walked forward. They stood up, as if a dignitary had entered, but Arlette understood that the dignitary was Sir Charles Granville. Their faces showed the suspicion and hostility she had expected: why could not he have chosen an English actress to play this most English heroine of the novelist's work?

They really hate all of us.

Okay. Arlette smiled demurely around the table. *Fuck you. You may never like me, but you'll bloody well respect me before this is over.*

CHAPTER 58

Arlette walked beside Charles Granville to where they stood at attention, awaiting the autocrat's bark, and Sir Charles presented her first to the famous middle-aged actress, a Dame of the British Empire, who was to play Clym Yeobright's mother.

The actress nodded brusquely. All at once transforming her face with Jade Ring's smile, Arlette walked around the table and shook Dame Ellen's hand, telling her how much she admired her work. Clym's mother seemed somewhat taken aback, but determined not to be taken in.

Undiscouraged, preserving her opinion of Englishmen,

she continued to smile bewitchingly, shook their hands warmly, and found some compliment for each of them as she continued around the table.

Robert Parker, who was to play her future husband, seemed suitably studious, idealistic, and just handsome enough for the part. He looked like her own picture of Clym Yeobright, Hardy's hero. The actor playing Damon Wildeve was a challengingly good-looking man, suited to play the ladies' man and engineer, who later turned innkeeper. He examined her carefully as they shook hands, with a knowing appreciation, and then straightened his face abruptly. Sir Charles was giving him a warning glance.

There was Thomasin, looking young and fresh and simple, quite a different girl from the one Arlette had seen in the projection room playing a Piccadilly whore with savage flair. Sir Charles had not made that picture, but it had given the girl a reputation as a serious actress.

She was introduced to the other actors, and lunch was served, Sir Charles seated beside Arlette. The others promptly set up a rapid-fire conversation, as if the picture had been finished long ago and they knew all the agony and all the humor. Arlette Morgan was an outsider now and – she suspected they were telling her – forever.

Arlette accepted it philosophically, reminding herself of the Taoist belief that *of the value of action which is actionless, very few are aware*.

She ate slowly, smiled occasionally, a tentative smile, since she was done with dazzling them out of their hostility, and beside her, Charles Granville ate in silence.

All at once he began to talk. His own bad manners he understood very well, and used them when he thought they would serve a purpose; but the bad manners of others to his Eustacia had enraged him, and he began to attack Robert Parker.

'How long have you been acting, Parker?' he demanded loudly, his voice full of menace and cruelty.

Parker was about thirty-five, Sir Charles ten years older, and Parker looked as if his father had struck him with a bootstrap. He paused, swallowed, and replied with the hopeful air of one who thought the question had been prompted by idle curiosity. There was silence, as if a river rushing noisily over a rocky bed had suddenly fallen into a still pool. 'I've been acting all my life, Sir Charles.'

'Answer the question.'

Arlette continued eating, glancing with innocent attention at Sir Charles and then at Robert Parker.

'I was first put on the stage at the age of five. My father was an actor of some note, perhaps you've heard of him . . .' Parker went on, outlining his dramatic schools, his first appearance at the age of nineteen in a leading role. He looked stricken and humiliated, as did the others. Sir Charles continued to eat, nodded occasionally, and signaled him to go on.

Arlette listened, astonished, thinking that an Englishman actually was something of a mad dog, equally willing to attack or be attacked by a stronger adversary.

All at once, as Parker looked increasingly anguished, Granville spoke to him in a slow steady voice. 'Very interesting. But the scene you played yesterday stank. It's got to be done again tomorrow. Ten o'clock.'

Briskly, Sir Charles turned to Arlette, and there was a smile on his face, but neither did Arlette trust his smile:

One word, just one word, you son of a bitch.

'Miss Morgan, I've been thinking you might prefer a double for the scene in the weir?'

This weir was a body of water, dammed to form a lake, which they had rebuilt and which was now – in storm conditions – as dangerous as it had been in 1850, the period of the novel.

'No,' said Arlette serenely, determined to prove that her near-drowning as Emma had not frightened her, 'I'll play it.'

'Come along, I'll show it to you. We may shoot it this next week, if a suitable storm comes up.'

She shook her coat and they were out the door, into the jeep, and he was bouncing it over the moors while Arlette held onto the overhead structure to keep from being thrown from her seat.

'I know that was a bloody thing to do, but it was better right then than later. I'm not a man noted for his conscience. In my business there's no time for such niceties. I'll treat myself to a conscience when I retire.'

'I could have handled them, after a few days.'

'Now you don't need to waste a few days. Here we are.'

He leaped out and she followed him. The weir was a small lake, with water pouring sluggishly over the dam, for there had been no recent heavy storms.

'There it is.'

Arlette looked at it, saw it as it would be during a great storm – the scene would be shot at night in a downpour – and it was Eustacia's part to fall in and be dragged out, dead. Arlette studied it, thought of the long full skirt, the entangling black wig, and shrugged.

'Of course, we'll have an ambulance and a doctor and nurse.'

'That's thoughtful of you, Charles.' She laughed gaily.

'We'll also have a couple of scuba divers.'

'By then, I'm afraid it wouldn't make much difference to me.'

'If you change your mind, let me know.'

'I won't change my mind.'

'I don't think you will. Now, may I have a look at the costumes and wigs?'

Sir Charles sat in the downstairs parlor, going over the next day's shooting schedule, while Arlette went upstairs to turn herself into Eustacia Vye.

Sir Charles had been very explicit about how he wanted her to look.

They were not the sort of dresses Arlette liked, but she hoped to overcome their drabness with makeup, Eustacia's blue-black hair, and her own vitality.

These were the dresses of an outwardly respectable young woman of vanity, but no great resources. They were of the period, copied exactly from plates in the

British Museum, and the colors were to blend with Egdon Heath and the techniques he intended to use: muted, softly focused, suffused with the mist and gloominess of the heath – except for the brilliantly colored 'mummer' scene and the 'gypsying.'

I'll have to dominate the hell out of these clothes, she had warned herself while they were being fitted.

She waited in the doorway until he glanced up. He peered at her, leaning tensely forward, told her to turn slowly, and was across the room and had her in his arms.

'You are Eustacia, by Christ – the way I've been seeing her! Arlette, my darling!' Nothing gave him more delight than being presented with the right material to work upon.

She went upstairs and came down, dressed and undressed, changed from one hairstyle to another, and for four hours she and Charles discussed each effect as seriously as if they had been discussing Rembrandt.

At last she reappeared in her black sweater and skirt, barefoot, and they sat down to talk over the general plan of the filming. The plan, unless the weather betrayed them, was to film the first scene tomorrow night, when bonfires were lighted along the hilltops, with Eustacia's bonfire a signal to Wildeve.

As Arlette walked with him to the door, Sir Charles turned, to look down at her from his extraordinary height, a question on his face.

Deborah Crane, she was convinced, had told Granville that she had slept with Anthony. And the possibility renewed her resentment against Anthony, which waxed and waned, but never disappeared. The one thing he could have done to estrange her, he had done – *more or less by accident*.

'Good night,' Charles told her.

She smiled and nodded.

He gave her a quick salute and went down the stairs the way he wanted his actors to run down staircases, as if they were on ice skates. 'Tomorrow at five?' He sounded almost supplicatory, and so he was not rebuffed. If it had been too easy, he would have been suspicious that she was getting even with someone, and that would not have flattered his pride.

It took them three nights, from five in the afternoon until three or four in the morning, to get the bonfire scene to his satisfaction.

Perhaps others could not see them, but no one questioned the colors seen by Sir Charles. For it was color, his subtle and unexpected use of it, the shadows he threw upon landscapes and bodies and faces, which made his pictures not only emotionally engrossing, but visually so pleasurable that people saw them several times.

Concentration, conviction, some inner vision, at once vague and clear; dozens and hundreds of minute faculties coalesced at some crucial moment, and the effect was there: he had the frames he had been searching for. She had the expression, the tone, the gesture he had known belonged to Eustacia.

For three nights the bonfires blazed along the crests of the hills, while Eustacia, in her black silk dress and swirling black cloak, paced back and forth, urging the boy Charles to keep the bonfire blazing, raised the Captain's telescope and trained it in the direction of The Quiet Woman, then took a brand from the fire and held it to the hourglass, finding the sand to have run through.

Her face, illuminated by the flames, brooded over the hourglass, and she at last dismissed the boy. The wind blew in heavy gusts each night, and Eustacia's black hair came loose from its knots and coils – loosened further by Granville's long fingers as he stepped forward just before the filming began and extracted, carefully, three pins.

'I'll look like a witch.'

'I hope so.'

Each night he began with the bonfires, the pacing, the blowing cloak with her hair coming undone, so that from time to time she seized it impatiently, and he asked her to leave it alone, gently explaining the best effects came by accident.

'Accident?'

But then, what did he know of accidents? A minor wound while he was flying for the R.A.F. That was the only accident anyone had ever heard of in Charles Granville's life.

For three nights Wildeve tossed the stone into the pond and emerged over the crest of the hill, a dark figure in silhouette. For three nights they quarreled over his abandonment of Eustacia to marry Thomasin.

On the third night Sir Charles interrupted the quarrel and told them to proceed with the love scene.

'What love scene?'

'He's going to kiss you. Remember, they've been lovers. She's not a virgin. Hardy didn't say so – but I say so. And so did Eustacia.'

'It wasn't in the script you gave me last night.'

'I changed it today.'

He gave a loud snap of his fingers which signified general silence, and Wildeve – quite a different man from the actor she had met at lunch – with his new black mustache and black hair, his elegant frock coat and checkered trousers, his look of breeding and insolence, pride and self-contempt oddly combined, appeared before her.

Without hesitation he began to kiss her, and one hand unbuttoned the bodice, slipping inside it to cover her breast. For a moment she was caught by the eager curiosity of sensual pleasure; but all at once she remembered Eustacia, and shoved hard against his chest: '*I won't give myself to you again!*'

That was what Hardy had Eustacia say during the quarrel; the kiss and unbuttoning of the dress were what Sir Charles said had been his real meaning.

One kiss did not gratify Sir Charles, and possibly not Wildeve. Arlette buttoned her dress, the makeup man performed some repairs, and Sir Charles came near to observe her. 'You look magnificent.' He was using few lights and the night was starless. 'This time' – he nodded to Wildeve – 'more warmth. And another couple of buttons.'

'Remember my contract.' Lady Macbeth, Mary Stuart to be, must not display too much naked skin.

Charles nodded to Wildeve. 'Remember her contract. He snapped his fingers.

The kiss was repeated, the camera moved closer, and Arlette found herself struggling with Wildeve, who was either enjoying this opportunity or had been advised by Sir Charles to get as much into the film as possible, and trust him to know what to cut.

'Better,' said Sir Charles. 'We'll try again. Remember, my dear, they were lovers. And she is in love with him, in her way.'

'But she does have too much false pride to let him know it.'

She let Wildeve kiss her, and perhaps he was skillful, perhaps she was susceptible, she grew somewhat dizzy until that warm caressing hand pinched her nipple and she shoved him away, closing her dress, speaking Eustacia's lines with fury.

'That'll do,' said Sir Charles.

'I didn't hurt you, Miss Morgan?'

'Don't apologize. If I'd been expecting it—'

She looked at Sir Charles, accusatory and a little sullen. Another of his treasured accidental effects. The strict Victorians, off guard. But of course, if he had told her what instructions he had given Wildeve, he would not have photographed a woman becoming helplessly responsive and then furious because she thinks she is being exploited.

Wildeve and Sir Charles waited until Arlette waved good night from Eustacia's doorway, and drove down the hill at Sir Charles' regular racing-car speed.

Arlette was alone in the house from the end of the day's work until eight in the morning, when Ann Parish came to prepare her breakfast. Sir Charles had asked if she wanted to have Mrs Parish stay overnight.

'I feel no hostility in this countryside. I love its wildness.'

481

Is that the reason I don't want her here at night? Of course not.

She wanted to be there alone. She also wanted the freedom not to be there alone, if it should happen that way; unplanned.

CHAPTER 59

Granville was so eager to film the weir scene it did not occur to him the storm might not arise when he expected it during the next few days. He was not concerned – although he often scanned the horizon and consulted the local weather authorities – for they needed clear weather to film Eustacia and Clym's ride home after their wedding ceremony.

The scene between Christian and Wildeve, her former lover, had been shot on several hot nights the summer before.

For this new scene neither Wildeve nor Christian was present – and Eustacia smiled her mysteriously conspiratorial smile directly into a camera set almost at ground level. Conspiracy with whom, against whom? Arlette and Granville had agreed that Eustacia should be a supernatural being, in conspiracy against all simple fallible humanity, personified by the two men she destroyed.

The director's reason for filming that scene before his eagerly awaited storm arose was that they had made only one green silk dress for her to be married and later drowned in, and it was necessary to get those few feet on film before the gown was ruined once and for all.

Once that midnight scene was done to his satisfaction, he promptly began to fret about the weather. Now, the storm was overdue.

Several times, after lunch, he asked Arlette to go with him to look at the weir. Perhaps there had been a storm, perhaps the stream had filled. They would gaze into it, Sir

Charles morosely commenting that no, the bloody thing had not risen.

One day Arlette gave a burst of mocking laughter. 'What's the hurry, Charles? You don't want to waste too much film on an actress who may have to be replaced?'

'Replaced? You?'

'If I drown.' She switched Eustacia's rust-colored skirt and smiled impudently. 'I won't drown. You remember Emma. I've taken swimming lessons since I was five. I can swim a quarter of a mile in twelve and a half minutes.'

'But, my dear, if you can swim that will spoil everything.'

The storms did not come in sufficient force to flood the weir, which was to be shot in great artificial flashes of lightning at the moment Eustacia fell into it. But Sir Charles made good use of the milder rains, for they were one of the main characters in the film.

'This picture,' he told Arlette, 'has two major characters, and neither of them is you, my dear. It may be far from Hardy's exact story, but the atmosphere is right. One – is Egdon Heath. The other – the weather. In this story, it isn't character which determines fate so much as it is the place, as Eustacia tells Wildeve, which has destroyed all of them. It's the place, and the weather, which kill Mrs Yeobright and creates hatred between Clym and Eustacia. It's the weather which kills Eustacia and Wildeve. Of course, all this is meant to represent fate on the grand scale. In my opinion, it's irony, not fate.'

'Any of it could have happened another way.'

'But for the weather. But for the heath. That's why this bloody weather is the first thing I think about in the morning and the last thing at night.'

They had rehearsed Clym's frantically shouted directions, the Reddleman's calmly spoken preparations. And should a storm of adequate ferocity strike the heath, they were prepared to arrive at the weir ten minutes after the air-raid sirens summoned them. Jeeps would be off to collect the actors and the paraphernalia, and the scene would be under way.

Eustacia was to fall, with an alarmed cry, into the weir, as a streak of lightning illuminated her, and sink from sight. She was to float, face down, while the cameras turned upon the Reddleman's activities to bring her out of the weir by means of a hooked pole caught in her belt, with Arlette's surreptitious help.

Months later, in a darkroom in London, Sir Charles would piece the puzzle together.

They went over it, usually after lunch, until Arlette began to dream of falling into the weir, of drowning, of storms and death, and was ready to pray for a real storm to suit her director.

While they waited, there were small bits and pieces to be filmed: Eustacia's face gazing ominously from the window of the house where she and Clym lived after their marriage. Eustacia's face in a variety of close-ups: ironic smiles; scorn, despair, anger, love and gaiety for her early happiness with Clym – and then Granville announced a surprise:

Most of them were given their first three-day holiday since filming had begun the summer before, and only Arlette and Clym, three cameramen, one of Sir Charles' secretaries, the makeup man and hairdresser and Arlette's maid, and four sound technicians remained, with the cook of The Quiet Woman.

No storm was forecast by the most esteemed of the native prophets.

'What are we going to do?' Robert Parker asked Arlette, and seemed apprehensive of Sir Charles' surprises, hatched in secrecy.

Arlette and Robert bade the others good-bye as they drove off, joyous at the unexpected holiday, then walked back to drink tea at The Quiet Woman.

There they found Granville deep in thought, and after a few moments he looked up, casually remarking: 'Now, to the wedding night.'

Robert and Arlette glanced at each other, as if to say of course they had known this all along.

This wedding night was more crucial to Sir Charles

than Egdon Heath or the weather – it was his emotional equivalent in the film for both. And she guessed he had not wanted to film it until Arlette and Robert Parker had played enough scenes together to be at least superficially acquainted.

Arlette was given her script for the following day. Very few words, as Sir Charles did not believe in dialogue during love scenes. She was told to be on location at Clym's house at ten in the morning.

The bedroom had blackout shades to simulate the midnight when they arrived, after passing Wildeve and Christian on the heath.

The small room had a four-poster double bed, and was dark but for one candle. Arlette, in a long white nightgown, her black hair wound in a loose coil, turned slowly for Granville's inspection, glanced suspiciously at the cameramen, and got into bed. Clym would enter in his nightshirt, but Sir Charles advised him the nightshirt would provoke laughter, and so he would not be seen getting into bed. Only Eustacia's face would reflect his approach, as she lay upon white embroidered pillows beneath a down quilt, looking at him with vague apprehension, and yet the eager expectation of an experienced woman. Clym's face, once he lay beside her, was to show distrust and fear of this demon-beauty he had married.

But it was Eustacia's face which interested Sir Charles. Clym's shoulders and back must do most of his acting for what was to become an increasingly violent scene.

Granville's instructions had been vague and given privately. To Arlette, he spoke as one dark conspirator to another. 'You're naked under that tent, aren't you?'

'Of course.'

'No screwing.'

'Jesus Christ, I'm not interested in screwing him.'

'You aren't at present. But I've put actors in bed before. Leave them long enough and the temptation becomes irresistible. But it wrecks everything. Anyway, never forget that the cameras miss nothing – the smallest change of expression – even of thought—'

Arlette gave a sorrowful little laugh. 'Charles – what the hell are you talking about?'

As the day went on, she found he had been more intuitive than she had supposed. Still, little happened, for he obliged them to repeat each smallest gesture, each smile – until by lunchtime Clym had not kissed Eustacia once, but her smile was changing, and no doubt by the time he had shot several hundred feet of film, Sir Charles would have the smile he wanted: a woman pleading for a man's body.

Arlette said she preferred to eat alone in that room, hoping to put aside whatever feelings had begun to distract her, and when Charles rapped at the door, asking if he could come in, she sighed. 'Of course.'

'Arlette, I know this is difficult. You're used to the stage—'

'I'm giving up too much of my privacy.'

'We all give up too much of our privacy in this business. We peel off our skins and dance around in our bones. That's what it's about. Stop worrying about your fucking contract. Trust me. If it doesn't suit the picture, I'll cut it. Get in bed.'

By the end of the day, Sir Charles sadly told them that although they had at last been permitted one tentative kiss, they must try again tomorrow.

'Try what again tomorrow?' Arlette demanded.

'Try to look like a couple making love for the first time. Every couple has to do it for the first time sometime. Stop thinking it's the nineteenth century – the basic equipment hasn't been recycled.'

Arlette, having convinced herself she could enjoy this – after all, the Hoffman-Repertory directors had final veto power – jumped into bed, pulled off the nightgown and threw it across the room. Clym-Parker was called in and found her, arms crossed behind her head, smiling at him.

At Granville's instructions he got into bed, removed his nightshirt, and tossed it aside and was – as perhaps Arlette's face registered – wearing trunks, which Sir Charles instructed him to remove.

The cameramen appeared, to find Clym and Arlette laughing, lying on opposite sides of the bed, their hands clasped outside the quilt, holding fast as if for salvation. Charles nodded at one of the cameramen, and there was the first scene, this laughter between Clym and Eustacia – a laughter which could only have come hours after the first explorations and culmination. A nice touch. Sir Charles assured them he would find a use for it. 'Now – to work.'

Parker's mouth closed eagerly over hers; the cameras were set so that only his back or profile was photographed, and Arlette closed her eyes, feeling his body move to cover hers. The kiss continued for what seemed to Arlette some interminable time before Sir Charles ordered: 'Cut.'

After a while, he left the room, saying he would make a telephone call, and in the meantime they were to extemporize.

Arlette moved away. 'We'll wait for him. This is his responsibility.'

Sir Charles returned to find Arlette in her nightgown, Yeobright in his nightshirt, sitting downstairs in the parlor with the cameramen, drinking tea and listening to the radio news: another war.

He smiled as if this was what he had expected. Perhaps he had realized that once such tensions had been established, an hour or two would only serve to increase the frustration.

They got into bed once again and this time, as Parker kissed her, there were no comments from Sir Charles. The scene proceeded according to instructions, Arlette's head turning with restless eagerness, her hands clasping his shoulders, the nails lightly indenting the flesh.

At last she threw her head back like a woman in crazed excitement, when she was in fact in a profound agony of desire for a man she did not know; her arms reached out desperately, clutching the posts of the headboard, and her body rose beneath him.

'Cut,' remarked Sir Charles. 'That's enough for today.'

'Today!' Arlette glared at him.

Sir Charles tossed the nightshirt to Parker – who looked haggard as any bridegroom after five hours of lovemaking; then he tossed the gøwn to Arlette, who gave him a glance of bitter resentment.

In the hallway, Parker touched her arm pleadingly and spoke to her in a whisper: 'Miss Morgan, if I have offended you, forgive me, for I knew not what the hell I was doing. Another half minute—'

'I know.'

In Eustacia's dressing room Arlette pulled off the nightgown, stepped into a red skirt, pulled on a red sweater, slipped on a pair of dark red leather moccasins, and throwing a sealskin-lined black leather coat over her shoulders, ran out and jumped into the jeep, where her driver waited to take her to the cottage. She was angry, more enraged with herself than with Sir Charles or Parker:

I'm not a professional. I shouldn't have felt anything.

She was so angry that when Sir Charles came dashing out, she looked at him with fury. He signaled the driver away, got into the seat, and set off up the hillside.

'Arlette – for God's sake – how else could I get it?'

'You got it, I hope. You made fools of both of us.'

She was out of the car and up the steps, when Granville took the key from her and unlocked the door. She ran in, trying to shut it in his face, but a slam with the flat of his hand pushed the door wide, and he walked in, locked it, and tossed the key onto a table.

Ann Parish had been instructed that Miss Morgan would eat lunch and dinner with the crew, and the house was empty.

Arlette ran upstairs, threw her coat on the bed, and sat down to look at herself in the mirror.

She was surprised to find, once she had removed Eustacia's black wig, that she looked more like Lily Malone – as she supposed Lily Malone might look by now – than Arlette Morgan:

Granville's changed me. But how did he do it?

And how long will it last?

Will I be myself tomorrow morning?

She stepped out of the moccasins and crossed the floor to look out the window. The jeep was still there; Sir Charles was in the living room, waiting for her.

She descended the staircase silently and stopped in the doorway. He sat writing on one of the legal pads he habitually carried. She folded her hands and stood motionless.

At last he looked up, and they studied each other warily from across the room.

'I'm sorry. I had no idea it would bother you so much.'

'You'd have done it anyway.'

'Of course. But nothing happened.'

'You mean he didn't fuck me? Maybe that's why we both feel like such idiots.'

'Never mind, it will wear off,' he told her soothingly. 'Shall I make tea for you?'

Arlette gave a burst of laughter, and all at once it seemed absurd that something so inconsequential as a simulated love scene could have made her so angry.

She walked toward him slowly, he tossed the note pad aside, and she stood between his legs. His hands went beneath her skirt, clasping her buttocks, and she stripped off the sweater, holding his head against her breasts, then knelt before him and parted her lips for his kiss. His hands moved over her breasts, and all at once she was lying on the floor, feet braced against his shoulders, and he was inside her with a deep swift movement which brought a cry of protest, turning to a soft sound of relieved delight.

CHAPTER 60

With Conrad driving, Arlette listened to Edna Frazier's schedule for what was left of the day. The plane had landed at five in the afternoon.

'Mr De Forest will be back in time for dinner. He and Mr Brown are on the six thirty-three.'

'Texas?'

Texas, Arizona; horse ranches, orange groves. When she and Granville arrived in London from Dorset she had talked to Edna in New York.

Once Anthony's *Henry IV* had finished its run in mid-August, Arlette sent word that she would be back in a few days, no use for him to make the trip; and so Anthony and Jim Brown, with their experts, had set out to inspect property, sell property, buy new property: clean, tidy tax shelters.

Arlette listened with a vague feeling that nothing Edna was saying had anything to do with her.

How long had she been away? A seeming eternity. How long had Granville been her lover? Five and a half months. How long had Eustacia Vye been her true self? That long and longer. And so these names, Mr De Forest, Mr Brown, Mr Hoffman, Mrs Fiedler, these names belonged to people she had once known, long ago.

The leaves along the highway were dark green, heavy with late summer, and the day was bright and hot – unusual weather, Edna Frazier assured her as Arlette adjusted the cuffs of her pink chiffon blouse.

Egdon Heath had been dim, misty in the mornings, and now Arlette was not certain if this weather was peculiar, or if that land over there was strange. She was not even certain how Arlette Morgan should behave now that she had returned to her native land, alien as any returned native.

How much had he changed her – that Englishman who had had her to himself for so long? Had he changed her at all? She could not guess – for while her memory retained, it seemed, everything, her feelings wrought a forced self-protective change upon those memories, wrapping them in some opaque covering, storing them away, out of immediate awareness.

Once, early in June, she had been awakened in Eustacia's bedroom by Sir Charles slowly stroking his hands over her body until she opened her eyes to find him, fully dressed, seated beside her.

He touched a light switch and she saw him smiling with a surprising tenderness, the tenderness which had been the biggest surprise she had discovered in Charles Granville as a man and lover.

She smiled, stretching her arms over her head, then curled her loosely clasped fingers around the back of his neck with that trustfulness which filled her when a man had lately made love to her.

'We forgot your secretary,' he told her.

Arlette had forgotten that she had been advised of Edna's *surprise visit* by cable, and had been looking forward to it. Tomorrow was her birthday, and even though Arlette was secretive about birthdays, the date as well as the year, she was pleased that Anthony planned small occasions for her wherever they were, together or apart.

Edna Frazier had arrived, bringing letters and presents from him.

'My secretary,' Arlette repeated softly to Charles.

'She sent word to us yesterday. Remember?' He was smiling, and perhaps mistook her engrossment with his lovemaking for the stuff of love itself. But he knew only the Arlette she let him know, who would disappear on the last day of filming, returning to her other life, her other selves, her one real world.

'She's waiting at The Quiet Woman. I've given her a room. I told her we were working all night and you'd be down in an hour or two.'

She had greeted Edna with a warm embrace, an effusive delight over the letters, the little presents from so many people who wrote that they missed her.

Granville had perceived that something had happened between her and Anthony since the filming of *The Two of Them* or she would not have taken him as her lover.

Arlette was convinced that not only did Sir Charles know something had happened, he also knew what had happened.

'You're not in love with Anthony in the same way you

were then,' he said one day, several weeks after the first night he had spent with her.

They were riding in the curtained jeep, on their way to photograph the scene where Eustacia sees Clym – nearly blind, working as a furzecutter, no sign left of the elegant young man who had returned to his native land from France.

'I love him,' Arlette said softly, but looked straight ahead. She was made up as Eustacia – thin black brows slanting slightly outward, dark brown irises, white skin and full red mouth, intricately coiled and braided black wig with loose tendrils along the sides of her face.

That first night they had spent together had no doubt been more surprising to her than to him, who had planned the opportunity, waited, and perceived unerringly the first moment when she was not only vulnerable, but eager. Since then, he had spent so much time with her, manipulated her body and emotions with such skill, that she sometimes grew suspicious this was one more technique to get the picture he wanted. Actors were the means for him, not the end.

And perhaps Arlette Morgan was the means toward producing a convincing Eustacia, a supernatural being, restless, sensual, dissatisfied with her lot among common mortals like Yeobright and Wildeve: a witch fallen into bad company with beings not her equal.

Arlette studied his techniques with serious interest. She watched him signaling the cameramen into their positions, checking the lenses, and more or less absentmindedly he said: 'Caravaggio – that's what I'm after in this one.'.

No other painter could so well convery the sense of menace, tension, the luxuriant overemotionalism which this movie required, at least as it was prefilmed in Granville's mind. Later, he told her each film he made was designed after a particular painter's color and style. Once upon a time, he admitted, he had meant to be a painter.

'I love Anthony,' she replied when he told her that

something had changed sometime during those years since they had first met in London and on several Mediterranean islands.

'You love him. Okay. I happen to be one of the few guys who knows that peculiar difference between what women mean by loving someone and being in love with them.'

'What gave you such a ridiculous idea? Because of us?' She smiled ironically. 'That doesn't prove anything. I've been away a long time. I'm susceptible.'

'You weren't. Not when I first met you. You weren't susceptible to anyone but Anthony. I think you hated me.'

'Oh, I did. You wanted me to, didn't you?'

'I did not!' He glanced at her sharply. 'You wouldn't have let this happen then. You were one of the few – maybe the only woman I've met who was unequivocally in love with one man. And you'd have waited this time, if it killed you—'

'Time does pass. People do change,' Arlette assured him serenely. 'Everything we think can never happen, happens anyway.'

If he mentions her name – so help me God, I'll kill him.

They had arrived at the location site. Charles smiled, clasped her hand, as if to assure her that was the end of the conversation, and so it proved to be.

Granville did not mention Deborah Crane even when the newspapers arrived reviewing *Silverheels*, bathing Deborah in adjectives describing her cat-green eyes, her white teeth, her blazing flawless skin, her magnificent breasts, her red-gold hair. *A triumphant woman, by any standards*, one critic declared in his impetuous enthusiasm.

Granville surprised her with one piece of news not long before she left.

Egdon Heath was in its pure greenery, with occasional blue skies, occasional yellow sunlight, and that was essential for Clym's proposal to Eustacia, giving the scene a lightness at sharp contrast with everything but the 'gypsying' and the 'mummers' scenes. A sense of springtime was necessary, fresh and clean in its lighting and color.

And it was necessary for the scene where Eustacia went to the village 'gypsying,' wanting to dance and be happy, but then, self-conscious and a stranger, walked on, encountering Wildeve on her return, whereupon they joined the dancing.

Their dance with the villagers took three days to film, in a scene which mounted in vivacity and abandon, Eustacia and Wildeve growing increasingly joyous and unself-conscious.

One early evening, at the end of the day's filming, with Arlette still Eustacia – her black wig tangled and caught with a few sprigs of flowers, a few bright ribbons, Charles drove to where he wanted to show her the afterrays of the sun from a low hillside.

The spell of the 'gypsying' was still on her; she was gay and happy.

'How I love this country!'

'That's because you can leave. Eustacia couldn't.'

He stopped the car and they got out, Arlette's flowered rosemadder dress billowing in the wind. 'I'm going to tell you something,' he said slowly. 'Something I'd promised myself I would never tell anyone.' Despite Granville's brusqueness, he hesitated.

Presently he continued, speaking quickly.

They had been on an island off Sicily. Emma Hamilton's horse had stepped in a hole and thrown her, and Arlette had gone back to her tent to have the doctor examine her ankle, to eat lunch, and to rest.

As Arlette listened, the hot day, the horrifying surprise of the fall, the pain, were almost as sharp as when it had happened.

She had returned to the tent, undressed, and put on her robe. The doctor had found her ankle bruised but otherwise sound, and Anthony had come in.

Sir Charles approached his secret.

He had come to their tent, thinking they were eating, had turned aside the tent flap as he knocked lightly, then he had seen Arlette astride Anthony, who sat on a camp stool, his back to the door.

'You looked straight at me,' Granville said. 'For just – that long.' He snapped his fingers.

'I did?' She glanced away, hoping he would not guess his great secret was no secret at all.

'Your face was rapturous as a saint's, and as wild – concentrated on sensation. I backed away, feeling as if I'd committed a crime. Maybe I had. Whatever else, I'm not a voyeur. I prefer to be in the middle of the action. I've never been able to forget your face at that moment – it became an obsession. It came into my mind at all the wrong times: that look of dazzled wonder. But more than anything else – it was the concentration, absolute and complete. It did something very strange to me.' He touched one of the ribbon loops in her hair. 'I'd have whacked you over the head that first night at Eustacia's house – if you'd given me any trouble.'

All at once he laughed, that mocking laugh she had heard now and then, usually when a scene went exactly as he wanted it, or when he was furious with an actor and might have liked to kill him – but instead suggested patiently that they begin again.

Arlette turned away. 'How strange. I had never thought of—'

'Me?'

She wanted to answer honestly, since physical intimacy was one of life's few serious experiences, with serious consequences, whatever happened. 'I thought of you. Of course. But – I never really thought of anyone but Anthony . . .'

CHAPTER 61

Arlette sat at her usual place in Art Friedman's office library, where Hoffman–Repertory held its board meetings.

Art Friedman now had a staff of nearly two hundred employees, fifty of them acting as agents: agents for playwrights; agents for movie scriptwriters; composers, television writers; agents for actors for film, television, and the theater; for singers in opera, concert, rock, and supper-club performers. His artists might live as they chose, but they must keep it out of the newspapers.

Divorces were permitted, but more than five marriages was questionable.

When it reached that point, Art Friedman advised his artists to forsake the idealism of matrimony. Alcoholism was bad form, drugs were worse, and jail sentences were sudden dismissal.

Even interviews, unless managed by the Friedman office, were discouraged. For many artists had the common failing of their breed: when a reporter seemed interested, they were likely to take off all their clothes at once.

To have been on his roster and then disappear from it was a worse fate than losing a beloved person, a beautiful body, or the good health which artists cherish.

This was what Anthony had explained to Arlette when she had said at Montauk she did not know what she would do about their marriage:

'Not a god damn thing. You don't throw away half a lifetime of work over some triviality.'

It was their work – that public seriousness about them as actors – which must be preserved: the less audiences knew the better.

Once the first anger had passed, she had seemed as affectionate, as responsive as before, and any other man would no doubt have believed she had forgiven him. Anthony knew her better. He had only not known her quite well enough.

Even during the months when she had experienced violent pleasures with Charles Granville, a sadness and loneliness for Anthony had caught her now and then. But there were other times, perhaps rising upon the crest of some overpowering excitement and pleasure, when there came the surprised conviction:

How easy it would be to forget him . . .

If she could forget him, that would be the revenge which would satisfy her best.

In her mind's clear picture, there he would stand, gazing with curiosity and surprise at the fresh bouquet she had placed in his hands the moment before she left him – that magical bouquet, the memories she had taken care not to damage.

When Edna Frazier had appeared at Egdon Heath, Arlette had opened Anthony's present and found an intricately carved bottle of antique white jade filled with her perfume, that potent mix of honey, roses, and jasmine.

She had retreated to one of the upstairs bedrooms, away from the festivities.

Charles Granville, the democratic Sir Charles, filming the Christmas 'mummers' scene in midsummer, had decked the halls of The Quiet Woman with holly and invited every member of the cast and crew, all the local extras, cooks, technicians, cameramen, wardrobe women and makeup men, to a feast of roast suckling pig and plum pudding.

They had eaten heartily, drunk strong English ale, danced to the native musicians' fiddles and horns, and were, after midnight, still disinclined to end the fiesta – an occasion which might last longer in local memories than even the drowning of Eustacia, an event for which they had gathered at the outer edges of their weir with its surrounding camera crews, the propmen and electricians, in the hope of seeing this Eustacia Vye, too, drown for her sins.

If that was what they hoped for, she disappointed them – but only after some terrifying moments of floundering beneath the weir's surface, flailing about in search of the Reddleman's pole.

And when at last the Reddleman had dragged her out by that pole hooked under her belt, she must have looked more drowned than alive, a triumph for the director and photographers, at least. She was carried swiftly to the ambulance, and Sir Charles Granville – as she found when at last she opened her eyes – knelt beside her looking like a man half mad with terror that he might have drowned his star.

She looked at him briefly, then closed her eyes, and it was a long while before she could find will and energy to speak.

'Did you get it in the can?' she whispered.

Charles, with a harsh sound, suspiciously like a sob, seized her hand and kissed it, stroking her forehead, nodding. But he did not say that if she had drowned in the spinning guts of the weir, it would have been her fault, not his, since he had several times begged her to use a double.

Later, Arlette remembered with wry amusement Valerie's advice: 'No serious event in life ever requires a game of tennis, golf, or bridge – unless you're a professional. But to swim and ride superbly – that can be your salvation.'

She later suspected it might have made him finally fall in love with her, a far more persuasive talent than any pleasures they had shared – that stubborn professional insistence to risk her own life, if that was in the script, but not to let someone else risk his because she was Arlette Morgan.

Anthony's box had brought the white jade bottle, with its delicately carved lotus leaves. It had brought letters from Jerry Hoffman and Gordon Donahue, Valerie and Frederick and Michael; Irma and Conrad; John Powell; letters and presents from Alicia and Minerva and Eva.

Perhaps, she thought, as she began to read Anthony's letter, this was the first letter he had written in longhand since he had gone to summer camp.

But the combination was more than she could tolerate: the experiences of the night before with Granville; Edna's arrival, reminding her of that other life, her real life; the jade bottle; the boisterous fake Christmas festivities, nevertheless invoking that saddest day of the year, the one holiday which sank her deep within herself, where she crouched alone in a dark grief for those two young people – their youth fixed for eternity, beautiful as chloroformed butterflies – who had died in the splintering of a windshield, that mirror in her mind which turned to diamond knives and razors.

She had not read a paragraph of the letter, written with love and whatever humility Anthony was able to command, when she was crying bitterly, lying on the floor in an upstairs bedroom:

Why is it so easy to be disillusioned and so hard to be grateful?

The day she got on the plane, Charles began to talk to her in a strange new voice as they approached the air terminal.

The glass partition between them and the chauffeur shot up, and Charles took her hand. This surprised her, even though they had gotten out of the same bed this morning.

There had been no farewell addresses.

There had been a general departure, actors and crew members leaving so swiftly it might have seemed to the natives an alert had gone out that another war had begun. The remnant of their prolonged encampment was being loaded into vans. The heath returned to its quiet, its autumn mist, and whatever memories its people chose to retain of this group of men and women who had appeared from another, unimaginable world.

Sir Charles had little to say about love, and Arlette nothing at all. There had been no promises; no thanks; no regrets that all good things must end.

Arlette was content to let it go at that. It had begun by some compulsion which caught both of them at the same time, and it ended because of the lives they had lived before and would now resume.

'If anything should happen between you and Anthony—'

'Nothing will.'

'If it does . . . You can act, Arlette. I admire that. You've got guts – maybe I admire that more. And so far as I can tell – though I'll admit it's a subject I'd never thought about before and can't say with any honesty I know what the hell it is – it seems to me that I love you.'

The limousine stopped, and as the chauffeur opened the door, they looked at each other. 'Thank you, Charles. Good-bye.'

'I'm coming to the gate with you. Anything's possible. Any time. For anyone.'

'No, Charles. Believe me. It isn't.'

She wondered, once she was on the plane, how she had been so sure of that. But when Anthony entered the house, eleven hours later, at the sight of him walking toward her slowly, she felt again that sense of shock at his physical beauty. It had struck her the first day she had seen him, and she was convinced that fatality would not end until her own life ended.

Even so, the bitterness was there as she waited, motionless, for him to reach her.

Why did you begin it, Anthony? Didn't you know the first mistake is always the last – when one person loves another the way I loved you?

Arlette could see in his eyes, blacker and more brilliant than usual, that change which signaled intense concentration and, quite often, the suspicions which Anthony entertained toward many people – but never before toward her. Was he thinking of Sir Charles, his friendly enemy, the very man to have attracted her with his authority, his fame, equal to her own, with its added flourish of his recent knighthood?

Concealing her own suspicions behind Jade Ring's smile, Arlette was wondering what women had been his solace these past eight months?

Women, not one woman.

No more ambitious actresses. Deborah Crane had taken him by surprise, but the surprise had also been fair warning. A marriage spoiled; Arlette's single-minded devotion to him demolished over an absurd young woman.

There were other kinds of women, much safer from

Anthony's point of view: the women he had known as Lydia's friends.

As the Hoffman-Repertory secretary read the minutes of the last meeting, Arlette listened with that system she had perfected by the time she was in grade school: she took in, like the oyster with its shell partly opened, the waves of seawater, extracted what would contribute to the construction of her pearl, and let the waves wash out again.

These minutes dealt with the receipts of the previous year; the cost of repairing the theater presently leased by Hoffman-Repertory, as opposed to the purchase of a new one.

She was immediately alert when the secretary read that it had been proposed at the last meeting that Hoffman-Repertory buy its own theater, refurbish it during the summer – and then Arlette went back to her reverie as the secretary read the expenditures for electrical work, new seats, improvement of dressing-room facilities.

She sat and looked across the table at Anthony, studying him as carefully as if she had never seen him before:

Where are the promises we did not keep, Anthony?

All at once, she was alert again.

The motion had been made and voted at the last meeting, and she was being asked for her vote. She quickly cast her vote to buy the theater. The secretary went on to ask if she voted for the otherwise unanimous agreement that the theater be named: Alicia Allerton.

'I do!' cried Arlette, for Anthony had kept this secret for her to learn today, and she jumped up, ran to Alicia, and embraced her. 'How wonderful, wonderful – oh, Alicia, I'm so happy!'

She laughed, brushing away tears. Jerry Hoffman came to put his arms around her, and the board meeting all at once was full of sentiment and tears, surreptitious and noisy, embraces and kisses. Even Art Friedman coughed discreetly and, thinking better of it, frowned.

The secretary, blandly aloof from these artistic displays,

began once again to read: ' "The last subject on the agenda is the character of Elizabeth the First in the fantasy scene of *Mary of Scots*, and who will play the part." '

'Elizabeth,' said Jerry Hoffman.

'Elizabeth,' said John Powell. 'Maybe it's a bad idea, but it's been done, by Schiller, for one.'

'It's a good idea,' declared Max Gilmore. 'It could have happened. It should have happened. Anyway, this is a play, a myth – not history.'

'Elizabeth,' said Art Friedman. 'Maybe there's no one who can be made to look the part – who's willing to act the part? We've auditioned – how many?'

'A four-minute scene.' Jerry Hoffman shrugged as if to ask who would want it.

There was another silence. Arlette smiled charmingly and folded her hands on the table. 'Deborah Crane?'

Anthony gave her a sharp incredulous glance.

Jerry Hoffman laughed aloud.

Max Gilmore began to light his pipe. 'That slut?'

John Powell looked at Arlette, his face curious and thoughtful, and put on his horn-rimmed glasses. 'Let's think about it.'

CHAPTER 62

Le Muguet was cool and dim in the October heat, with baskets of lilies of the valley on each table, and wallpaper which made a lacy spring forest on the walls, as Arlette entered.

Two or three times a year, she and Minerva and Eva had lunch at this restaurant as a kind of informal celebration on behalf of themselves.

Neither Minerva nor Eva had arrived, and she was shown to a table, where she sat thinking of the man she had seen, passing her swiftly not three minutes before, wondering if he might presently overtake Conrad's limousine and enter this restaurant.

These fantasies, which had become frequent, must signify something; yet an infatuation with an unknown man seemed absurd for Arlette Morgan – or Lily Malone. Was he the man she had seen on the plane?

During the weeks since she had returned from London she had found herself looking for him on the streets, going into a building, John Powell's office, Alicia's apartment, her own house.

Why? She had no idea.

Some expression in his eyes as he had smiled, listened to her tale of having lived and died in China twelve hundred years ago; the glint of the late afternoon sunlight through the plane window momentarily turning his eyes green as emeralds; some quiet in his body, some sense that while his muscles were still, his emotions were kept under perpetual surveillance.

But of course that man in the street had not been the same man. And, anyway, she knew there was no such thing in life as a coincidence whereby a man sat on an airplane, having accomplished whatever he meant to accomplish in China, and returned to pass her on the street in New York seven weeks later.

Not long ago, Michael had returned from China and they had had dinner in the garden behind the Sixty-second Street house; Anthony was away on one of his expeditions in search of real estate.

'And what is China like now?' she had asked, having paid it little attention during the past twelve hundred years.

She listened carefully as Michael told her of the gathering of scientists in Peking, the first of its kind ever held, where nearly one thousand men and women from all over the world had met to read papers, attend meetings, and contemplate a number of scientific revolutions presently in progress, of which most of the world's population remained unaware, supposing that only announced political revolutions were real.

She had found herself thinking of the man who had sat beside her a few weeks before on the plane, studying symbols and hieroglyphics all the way from London to New York.

Perhaps he had attended the same meeting. For what other reason would a man go to China nowadays? The T'ang Dynasty, after all, had ended more than a thousand years ago, and so far as Arlette was concerned, that was the only China worth visiting.

'Who was at the meeting? All kinds of people?'

Michael laughed. 'All kinds of scientists: biochemists, exobiologists, gas-dynamics physicists, radio astronomers, molecular biologists, molecular geneticists—' Michael smiled, inquiring if that was enough.

'Were there any from London?' His accent had been somewhere between Oxford and Harvard.

'Dozens, I suppose.'

'Anyone who looked as if he might be from Egypt?'

'There were people who looked like everyone you've ever seen.'

'Do you know them all?' The question was ridiculous. She would never discover the man's identity by asking Michael random questions.

'We're a rather inbred group, you know, each in his cubbyhole. These conferences may be a waste of time, but they give a great temporary euphoria – for a few days you honestly believe that all science is a web, however loosely stitched together, and that it can catch not only the tiniest submicroscopic particles, but the most expanded galaxies. The stimulation is incredible.'

No clues to be found that way.

Eva arrived at the restaurant and began talking about the hazards of the morning; the hairdresser late, the traffic unbearable, the fitter so stupid, the telephone call from Walter Hodges from Pittsburgh. A hopeful sign.

After two divorces, Eva was beginning to talk of future husbands not in terms of their positions or even their physical attractions, but of their Dun and Bradstreet ratings.

In another moment Minerva arrived and they began to study the menu, then promptly ordered the same thing:

cold consommé, cold salmon, Bibb lettuce, raspberries. The discipline had become so habitual they did not think about it.

The journey seemed long, when they looked back at it, but most of the time they preferred not to. The past, so far as they were concerned, might have happened to three other women.

'Successful people lose the past very quickly,' Arlette had remarked when Minerva had impatiently brushed aside some reference to the first play they had all appeared in for Hoffman-Repertory.

'Of course,' Minerva agreed. 'It's up to the failures to figure out what went wrong. We did everything right, didn't we?' She smiled wickedly.

Of course they had, or they would not be here today, looking as they did, dressed as they were, talking about the next play, the play or motion picture after the next.

If time troubled them, they did not talk about that.

The public, the public, they sometimes complained: the fly in the sweet-smelling ointment. The public would no longer go to see so-and-so. The directors and playwrights forgot her. The interviewers and photographers forgot her.

The crucial decision was when to disappear: before that public revenge had begun to set in. Before the ferocity of interest had begun to decline. Like any other love affair, it could be conducted successfully only if it ended a little prematurely.

Once the passion had been spent, no Prometheus could set fire to it again.

'It's not only our lives, it's our work,' Minerva said when they discussed a recent magazine article about the dead seriousness with which actors took their profession.

'And in our work, we're on our own. On our own. Of course, Arlette, you have Anthony.'

'I would have been a different kind of actress without Anthony. I might never have been any actress at all. I might have given up – like Margo. Remember?'

They laughed.

Those classes, those lessons, those tests of abilities they had not yet developed. Remember? It was like asking if you remembered your first day at school; your first love affair; your first formal dance.

This was the disarming Arlette, as she knew very well.

Arlette was the best actress of their early classes – perhaps the best anywhere. But Anthony, Anthony, Anthony was given all the credit – or enough of it to remove some of the curse of envy.

But between them, neither Arlette nor Anthony suffered illusions about who had helped whom. Without ability and the discipline they had developed together and separately, all the helpfulness in the world would not have turned them into the De Forests. They understood this, but neither made the mistake of saying it aloud, or by implication. That was a way, indeed, to kill the relationship with unkindness.

Pat Runkle, Anthony De Forest, whom she had loved and hated, suffered jealousy for and plotted revenge against. Anthony De Forest – from whom she had learned most of what she knew about love, and nearly all of what she knew about herself and men. Anthony had composed much of her life's content and form.

At that moment, she discovered the man she had seen on the street, seated across the room with another man, and they were holding an animated discussion – China, perhaps?

He glanced at her, either because he had noticed her before and wanted to look at a pretty woman again or he had recognized her as a celebrity; or she had attracted his attention by looking at him.

'Someone you know?' Minerva was almost as alert as she was.

'No. I thought he might be – an old friend.'

'He looks like someone,' said Eva.

They speculated, Minerva and Eva: Wasn't he a famous trial lawyer? No, a publisher? A professor of something esoteric? An archaeologist? A foreigner, a Frenchman, an Italian, a Spaniard? An Englishman?

'He's no one at all,' said Arlette, so firmly that they shrugged and lost interest in him, went on to talk about *Henry V* and *Mary of Scots*.

He was no one, because he was not the man who had been on his way home from China.

She was annoyed – not with this man, whoever he was – but with herself, because she could not stop looking for him, discovering resemblances where none existed.

Now, why was this?

Something was missing. Something she had failed to find or to be or to experience. Perhaps something was missing which she had had once and lost. And this man was expected – if she ever saw him again – to give her the answer, out of his store of hieroglyphics.

He read secret languages. His face looked as if he contained secrets. Men did know secrets – or was this her own fantasy?

She decided to find out what Minerva and Eva thought about it.

'Of course they know secrets,' Eva said. 'That's why we can never leave them alone.'

'They do,' Minerva said seriously. 'Oh, yes, they do.'

'Secrets we can never learn?'

'They don't have the same kind we do.'

They were silent, taking a few bites of the light lunch they had permitted themselves, and Arlette was amused, feeling a sudden bright affection as she watched them struggling with the conundrum.

That was the difference between women of their profession and women of other professions, or no profession at all. The lifelong discipline in charm had its way with them finally. It became impossible for them to be other than charming.

When they were angry, when they were jealous, when they were sick, when they were hurt, they went about the management of their emotions in a way quite different from other women. They eventually acquired Jade Ring's capacity for charm in a rage, charm at the moment of being sentenced to death. They never abandoned their own best versions of themselves.

'Still,' said Minerva, 'he looks as if we should know him.'

'You mean,' said Eva, 'he looks famous. But the world is full of famous people one never sees.'

Arlette laughed, that soft conspiratorial laugh, and perhaps it attracted his attention. He glanced across the room, and for a moment looked straight at her:

No. It's someone else.

'Good-bye, Mrs De Forest. And thank you. I enjoyed your performance – as always.'

She had heard that often enough.

But never before from a man who had looked as that one had; who, for several hours as they sat side by side on the airplane, had seemed to pay no attention to her, who had smiled tolerantly when she confided that she had lived and died in China twelve hundred years ago, and who had at the last moment smiled once again – a curious smile, for she remembered it clearly, although she believed that smiles almost never revealed character, but were used as masks. Most smiling, she thought, was only another form of lying. And she had studied smiles as tools of her trade.

Not this man's smile. For even though she had studied the smile from time to time during the past weeks, she was still not certain what it had said.

He had been telling her the truth when he said he had enjoyed her performances. She read on his face, saw in the long slender hands, with flat square-shaped nails, in the immaculate set of his coat on his shoulders, the black hair, not short or long, making no public declaration of profession or politics, that he was not in any sense a fan. He enjoyed a theatrical performance as he enjoyed a painting, a building, a concerto, a Chinese poem – impersonally but not unfeelingly.

He was protected by an impenetrable membrane of silence – that was why she had started talking to him. She wanted to hear what tones came from that silent being,

508

what accent he used, what part of the country or world had produced him.

Then, when he did speak, she heard the accent she and Anthony and Jerry and Eva and Alicia and Gordon Donahue and everyone else she knew had, who had trained the regionalisms out of their voices.

A few words, a slight smile, that flash of sunlight as the plane banked, which momentarily turned his gray eyes to emerald green; then back to the hieroglyphics again.

The past was all very well. Egyptian pharaohs and medieval scholars and Spanish grandees and a dozen other roles she could conjure him in. But what was he in the twentieth century?

'Where are you going?' asked Minerva. Lunch was over.

'I have my car.'

'So have I.'

'So have I.'

They got up to leave. They were going their separate ways — and they did not give up their secrets, either.

As Arlette walked out she noticed the man was gone. He had been the wrong man anyway, and she resolved never to think of him again.

It was profoundly humiliating that she should have thought of him at all.

Had there, perhaps, been something unusual about her that day which had caused her to distract herself by studying his face, noticing what he was reading; telling him the story of her life in China, when she had been the Supreme One?

It was all true enough, in its way — and so his smile had seemed to tell her:

I know. Of course you were. And now you're someone else. And in another time, another age, another country, you will be someone totally different. And perhaps we will meet then, too.

CHAPTER 63

'There's your little scene-stealer,' Eva whispered to Arlette as they took their places at the table.

There were more than thirty men and woman, twice as many men as women, since it was men who – one way or another – had decided Mary Stuart's life, and not her cousin Elizabeth Tudor.

Arlette sat next to Jerry, and Eva next to her. Max Gilmore sat opposite, smoking. And beside him was Clarissa Powell with her father. Margo took a chair in back of her six-year-old daughter.

Where the others were sitting, Arlette had not noticed. But at Eva's ominous words she glanced about, seeing no sign of Deborah Crane – who must have taken a seat on the same side of the table, at the other end. Hiding, perhaps.

'Where?' asked Arlette, and felt a slight wave of sickness flow over her.

Eva nodded toward Clarissa Powell.

Clarissa sat straight, looking intently at Jerry Hoffman. She was even prettier this year than last, when Arlette had first noticed her growing into a beautiful little girl, with blonde curls, eyes which steadily turned a deeper blue, and surprising dark eyelashes.

She looked much like pictures Arlette had seen of Lily Morgan when she was that age. But of course all pretty little girls did not grow into beautiful women, and this might be Clarissa Powell's moment of glory – when she stepped upon the stage seven weeks from that night, dressed in gold tissue, with silver shoes and stockings.

There, surrounded by a brief display of color, music, lavishly dressed adults, the little Queen of Scotland would be betrothed to her cousin Francis, future King of France: two minutes only for the scene.

A flash, and all is over – thought Arlette, looking

gravely at Clarissa, for it seemed the little girl's entire future career was summed up in that two-minute scene – just as that scene might also be the sum of the life of the adult Mary Stuart, flowering out of this promising bud, to die by the executioner's axe.

Jerry shuffled through sheets of yellow legal paper, covered with his handwriting and architectural drawings.

Arlette looked at Margo, who seemed as tensely nervous as if the part were her own. Her husband was concentrating on his own notes, embellished with complex geometrical designs.

'Margo's finally where she's always wanted to be,' Eva murmured.

'Only she isn't. Her daughter is.'

'It's all the same to Margo.'

John Powell's pageant-play of the life of Mary Stuart was complex. It was meant to grab the viewer by the scruff of the neck and hold him in slightly uncomfortable suspension from its opening scene of betrothal, on through the alarums and excursions of Mary's life, which did not once abate as John Powell had written it, until the morning of her death, after her imaginary interview with Elizabeth I.

Jerry had begun to talk about the prologue, and while Arlette listened she was thinking of Deborah Crane, approaching her earlier with those long legs in purple tights moving like a pair of scissors, red hair bouncing, breasts shaking.

Arlette had given her a long careful look, and in that moment saw the original Deborah Crane beneath the face people nowadays took for Deborah Crane. She saw the face before the teeth were capped, the freckles obliterated, the carrot-red hair dyed strawberry blonde, the nearly colorless blue eyes before the green contact lenses, the flat breasts before the silicone implants.

Arlette studied her, hoping to settle this problem of Deborah Crane once and for all. But as she looked at her the bitterness was strong as ever.

You. There was a sharp pain of incredulity. *You, of all people.*

It was Jerry's practice, with a long play, to read one act on each of the first three days.

Clarissa had nothing to say in the prologue, and she walked through the part, smiling benignly and with queenly dignity, followed by her four little attendants, placed her hand in that of her five-year-old cousin, and listened soberly to the Cardinal's reading of the betrothal. She then calmly, holding her betrothed by the hand, passed on across the stage. Her mother took her home – or to another class.

Each night Conrad was waiting to drive her home, but one night, as she came out the stage door, she found Deborah there, her purple sweater and tights covered by a mink coat.

Arlette saw someone, not clearly Deborah at that first moment, and started around her. Deborah caught her by the arm. 'Miss Morgan – please let me talk to you.'

The sidewalks were crowded, people rushed by, the racket of dinner-hour traffic surrounded them. Arlette started on as if she had mistaken her for a fan or some other nuisance.

'Please, Miss Morgan!'

People were beginning to glance around. New Yorkers, Arlette thought, were unnaturally curious when they should not be, and unnaturally indifferent when they should not be.

'Yes?' asked Arlette, and smiled, a vague but kindly smile, to put the hesitating passersby on notice that this was a friendly encounter.

Arlette had decided, the day she had seen Deborah at the first rehearsal, that her hatred was under no better control than on that afternoon when she had telephoned London.

If she looked at Deborah, there was danger.

If she heard her voice, reading the lines when that four-minute scene began, she must force herself to ignore the fact that it was Deborah Crane's voice speaking so reasonably to Mary Stuart, asking her to forswear all right to the throne of England.

After that first sinking stone had fallen to the bottom of her stomach, an early warning signal, she had read her lines with absolute conviction that it was not Deborah Crane's voice replying.

Now here was Deborah, clinging to her arm. Other actors were coming out, and were taking notice.

'Miss Morgan – ever since I heard about it, I've been trying to talk to you. I've called your house, but your secretary never calls back—' She flung her hands outward, a gesture so dramatic that Arlette looked at her with surprise and moved toward the car. 'Oh, Miss Morgan – how can I thank you?'

Arlette had a vision of getting into the car and, as the car moved away, pushing the electric button and shooting the window up, catching Deborah's fingers.

'You leased your apartment to me. You got the board of directors to give me this part – my greatest opportunity—'

'I?' Arlette smiled incredulously.

'But – I was told—'

'You were misinformed.'

The low voice grew more intense, and Arlette thought that here was Deborah Crane, giving the best performance of her life to an audience of one, and that one able to appreciate it only because of hatred.

'Please believe me, Miss Morgan – it wasn't his fault – it was mine—'

'Whatever are you talking about?'

Arlette got into the car, locked the door, and as Conrad started away from the curb Deborah began to rap at the window. 'Miss Morgan!'

They moved through the traffic.

Surprised to find herself quite calm now that she had met the enemy and defeated her, Arlette picked up another biography of Mary Stuart and began to read:

That is that.

She was right. Deborah did not try to talk to her again during rehearsals, and as the weeks passed Arlette was able to concentrate on Mary Stuart and Elizabeth Tudor, not Arlette Morgan and Deborah Crane.

She had promised herself not to set foot in the newly refurbished theater until the first dress rehearsal.

But it seemed that unless she saw the theater before opening night there might be other disasters. The horse was a problem anyway. It might fall as it galloped across the stage. Jerry had left the horse in the script, then taken it out – saying that *Mary of Scots* was not *Mazeppa*. But Arlette had begged him to leave Belinda in, a grand flourish to this play which must be vibrant and colorful as the flash of a hummingbird into a flower and out if it was to fulfill John's script.

She went to the Alicia Allerton Theater on a Saturday afternoon and she went alone, entering through the back, hearing the pounding of hammers, the whining of buzz saws, the shouts of what sounded like one hundred workmen, and made her way among them so quickly she was down into the auditorium before they knew the premises had been invaded.

She sat far in the back, and took in the theater as she took in a deep breath, absorbing it, feeling it, trying to sense if the theater's intentions were kindly or malicious.

Would it betray them, after all their hopes for it?

Would it welcome them on that first night?

The theater was Jerry Hoffman's more than the architect's, and it was warm and enveloping, not spare and modern.

The walls, the comfortable chairs, were upholstered in deep crimson. High on the walls were dim murals of six scenes from Hoffman-Repertory's most admired productions. From the ceiling hung an eighteenth-century crystal chandelier, which would hold pale pink bulbs, not pink enough to throw color over the audience, only enough to make them think they had never looked more attractive:

Yes, there's magic here.

She imagined the theater silent, the audience alert, and the crimson curtain with its twined initials, AA, worked in gold, snatched apart as if invisible fingers had reached to pick it up.

Emerging from the reverie, she glanced at her watch and ran out, back to the rehearsal hall.

Jerry had asked her to play the minor part of Katharine in *Henry V*. 'We can't have an opening night of the Alicia Allerton without you. It would hex us for life.'

It was her duty to play Katharine to Anthony's Henry V, for all their sakes.

The English king, changed wondrously since his roistering days as Prince of Wales – majesty put on him all at once – had come to take back to England what he considered his share of France. And the French princess, anticipating she would be considered rightful English property, was trying to learn a few words of English from her lady-in-waiting, Eva.

The others grew increasingly nervous, increasingly critical among themselves as Jerry cut and slashed the speeches of the rabble which followed Falstaff, and of Falstaff himself.

'Humor changes,' Jerry remarked philosophically, as he crossed another line of Falstaff's off the script.

'We'll be acting without ever having seen the bloody scenery in place.'

'I haven't the damnedest idea what's been cut and what hasn't.'

'I'm not sure I'm still in the fucking play.'

It was not even clear to Anthony and Arlette how their one scene would coalesce – or if it would.

They met on the stage of the Alicia Allerton on the opening night of *Henry V* to find the scenery miraculously in place, the lighting working its intricate complexities without error, the house crowded, and Arlette as Katharine and Anthony as the conquering English king standing in midstage while a look of bewilderment passed between them.

Arlette was surprised to see, during that brief moment,

Anthony's eyes pleading with her not to forsake him, to come with him, follow Henry's wooing, accept him, as he was, for what he was.

All at once she smiled at him, a radiant reassuring smile, which seemed to obliterate the past two and a half years, and before Anthony spoke his first lines to her, an expression of gratitude and relief passed over his face.

Henry's opening speech to Katharine, as they stood together, with Eva as chaperone and interpreter, was a long one, declaring that he could woo her by a soldier's arts, but he could not *look greenly*.

The French princess smiled at him with whimsical curiosity, tried to reply, and grew confused. All at once Arlette found herself helplessly dazzled by the physical beauty of this man who stood before her – not her husband, but a stranger, Henry Plantagenet, come to marry her: taking the princess, as he had told her father, in lieu of taking several more French towns.

As Anthony talked, pleading his cause – with Arlette, not with Katharine – his voice grew stronger, richer, full of a virile man's need for the beautiful woman who seemed a little frightened by his impetuous English soldier's style.

'*A good heart, Kate, is the sun and the moon—*' Arlette felt tears in her eyes, and her throat ached. '*Take me . . . take a soldier, take a king . . .*'

His hands reached toward her imploringly, and the king foundered upon the humility of male desire, seeking its release. She smiled, brushing the tears away, but turned aside from being kissed, appealing to Alice to explain that French princesses did not kiss before marriage; whereupon he took her in his arms and kissed her.

Arlette's arms went eagerly around him, she closed her eyes, and listened for the words which concluded the kiss: '*You have witchcraft in your lips, Kate . . .*'

Three minutes later, when the curtain came down and they paused before stepping forward with the rest of the cast, Anthony raised the hair from the back of her neck and touched his mouth there. 'I love you.'

The curtain went up and Arlette bent until her forehead touched her knees, then rose with a dancer's triumphant flourish, while Anthony bowed slightly, as to a gathering of casual friends. She was aware the audience had loved them unusually well tonight and, most of all, had been moved by the love scene, taking it for a real wooing; so it had been.

The opening-night party for the Alicia Allerton was to be given a week from that night, after *Mary of Scots* opened. Tonight there would be no general celebration.

Alicia and Jerry Hoffman, Eva French and Walter Hodges met them at the Sixty-second Street house, and they sat down to a supper of jellied chicken consommé and lobster soufflé with lobster sauce.

They talked quietly, subdued by the triumph of this uniquely triumphant play, aware that something unusual had happened tonight, yet uncertain of its components. They talked, instead, about the upholstery, the acoustics, and discussed improvements they would make. All the omens were favorable, they agreed.

Yet when Arlette awoke in the morning, the world seemed larger than she had supposed, darker than she had anticipated, and she herself more vulnerable than she would have guessed. Anthony moved beside her, turned over, and she curved her body around him, willing herself to fall asleep:

How much do you really forgive?

Do the feelings finally knit together – like injured tissue?

If it could happen, it would have happened last night.

When, in effect, as Henry V wooing Katharine of France, Anthony had carried her back to their first recognition of love – sometime when they had been playing that other Katharina and her determined Petruchio:

When will my life begin again?

CHAPTER 64

The great hall at Fotheringay Castle had been draped in black and crowded with black-robed nobles, as well as some few village people. And for all of them – minor actors, executioner, Eva French as Mary Seton, Arlette – it had proved a more unnerving experience than they had expected; time and reason suspended by some witchcraft not easy to shake off.

Mary Stuart stood motionless as two of her women removed the black velvet gown, the black velvet widow's cap with its flowing white lawn veil, and stood, surprisingly fragile and young, in her crimson velvet petticoat and red satin bodice, cut low so as not to interfere with the executioner's work.

She faced the audience, her face serene, with a smile which was not bitter or ironic, but movingly resigned, and stood patiently while the executioner took her jewelry, his fee for the task assigned him, begging her pardon for what he was about to do.

All the while Arlette was aware that the hush which had increased during the past several minutes grew steadily denser, thicker.

She remained motionless and silent while Mary Seton bound her eyes with a white kerchief, and slowly knelt upon the cushion before the black-draped block. She bowed her head: *'In te Domino confido, non confundar in aeternum . . .'*

She laid her head upon the block, and as the executioner raised his axe, a black velvet curtain dropped with the suddenness of a blow. As it touched the floor, the crashing sound of the axe was heard, the unmistakable splitting of a wooden block, and a gasp went through the theater like a soft wind.

The executioner's voice rang out: *'God save the Queen!'*

The red velvet curtain fell slowly across the black one, lowered by its gold silk cords with their heavy tassels.

Until the last curtain call, Arlette was as disturbed as the audience. She could sense the unusual seriousness of those before her, while her face showed none of Mary's tranquil courage, but a somber look of having suffered some deep inner shock, some severance of a vital cord at the severing of Mary Stuart's head. The queen's character had gained stronger possession of her as the performance progressed – until she had almost lost Arlette Morgan.

At the last curtain call, she brought Clarissa out again. Clarissa bowed solemnly, and her beauty and unawareness of Mary's future tragic life seemed to relieve all of them, audience and cast alike.

Clarissa looked up at Arlette with a serious questioning expression, and Arlette touched the girl's hair tenderly.

For the party after the opening, Arlette arrived at Jerry Hoffman's apartment wearing a triumphant dress to banish Mary Stuart's tragedy from all their thoughts – red chiffon, cut low and trailing the floor, sprinkled with red rhinestones, which made it impossible to tell what was dress and what was Arlette. From her ears to her shoulders hung Anthony's gift to Mary Stuart: earrings of twisted pearls and rubies.

Yet all that seemed not to have taken her mind off Mary Stuart, and her smile, as she talked to Michael about quasars and galaxies, had something in it of absent contemplation: four hundred years between them.

But she also had a sense of deliverance, a sense of keen refreshment – as if she had spent several days in the high mountains, among pines and clear water.

Elizabeth I, her old enemy, had been demolished.

Deborah Crane had looked remarkably ugly, her face a white mask, the skin stretched by tape until it was drawn and wrinkled, her forehead shaved two inches back from her hairline, a short curly red wig on her head. Her eyebrows were red-brown lines drawn in arcs over the pale blue eyes; her mouth was pulled taut and painted orange red.

She wore a farthingale so wide it gave her the look of a piece of furniture, and it teetered precariously, jutting out from her waist like two tables when she sat in the royal canopied chair.

During their four-minute scene, Arlette had proceeded daintily, lightly, charmingly to the destruction of Deborah Crane as a serious actress. She had killed Deborah Crane as literally as if she had killed her outright. The murder came to her as great relief, a purifying ritual.

Now, here she sat in Jerry's apartment beside her brother, talking to him with such seriousness it was a signal the queen must not be approached, and while they discussed galaxies and quasars, or while Michael discussed them and Arlette tried to imagine what he was talking about, she surveyed this new domain of Jerry Hoffman's, who since his divorce and until recently had been content to live in a three-room apartment not far from the rehearsal hall they most often used.

The new apartment was grand and imposing beyond anything she would have expected Jerry might permit himself to be talked into buying, much less living in.

The uncurtained windows were black with the night; they overlooked the East River on one side and, on the other, faced uptown, where millions of stars seemed to hang in other apartment buildings.

The rooms were furnished in black and white; some floors were painted white, some painted black; some walls painted white, some painted black. Zebra hides were scattered across the living-room floor, a herd of them, as Arlette calculated.

African, Melanesian, Alaskan carvings – real, old, valuable – some of them almost ceiling-high, stood in corners or doorways. Others, perched on pedestals of lucite or weathered wood, ranged along those walls not covered with vast canvases by the few contemporary artists Jerry liked. The statues, the carvings, the paintings, those were Jerry's contribution.

The glass and steel tables, so contemporary they had been completed only a few days before; the immense pieces of white leather-upholstered furniture, those were Sarita's.

Concealed lighting had been designed by Jerry's favorite lighting expert, and it cast a soft warming glow over what would otherwise have been intimidating.

What did Jerry Hoffman need sixteen rooms for?

He told Arlette he had no idea. It was something Sarita wanted, begged him for, and he had decided to find out whether or not he liked living like a rich man.

'Why not? Since you are one.'

'I haven't time for it. Being rich is a hobby. I've got no hobbies – except Sarita, I suppose.'

But that Sarita would ever become a permanent hobby, Jerry had told Arlette was unlikely – even though Sarita might have begun to hope that three years was a deposit on forever.

Deborah had not arrived, although it was nearly one-thirty, and perhaps she had lost courage. But not to come was the equivalent of committing suicide. The rules were strict: win or lose, triumph or disaster, gallantry must be displayed.

Now, feeling as light as if she could float, Arlette sat very straight, hands loosely folded on her lap, and went on to question Michael about the composition of a quasar, even though this was not his field of discipline by several millions of light-years.

'Quasars emit too much radiation to be stars, don't they?'

This line of questioning was familiar to him from their childhood – residue of the influence of Valerie and Frederick, who had assured her it was each individual's responsibility to construct his own world and universe, adding to its foundation increasing complexities, until the last day of life.

'It seems they do. At least, that's the current consensus.'

'Some catastrophe has changed them? But what is the catastrophe and why does it happen?'

'Lily, darling – do you expect all secrets will eventually

be solved – the microcosm and macrocosm split open like a pomegranate? I hope not. Where would the poetry go?'

'I hope not, too. But I read the other day that quasars may be exploding galaxies. Imagine such a thing. I can't. Can you?'

Arlette was talking as casually of space and eternity as if she had spent the evening watching someone else perform that extraordinarily demanding role:

Violent love scenes with Darnley and Bothwell. Cantering across the stage on Belinda at the head of her troops. Fending off the murderers of her Italian lover, while her husband held a weapon to her pregnant belly. Kidnapped in a wildly choreographed scene by men with hoods over their heads, to be raped in a remarkably literal demonstration by the Earl of Bothwell. Screamed at and called a whore by her own people. Shrieking out the window of one of her prisons at her tormentors, breasts almost naked, hair tangled.

Then miraculously recovering her dignity, her charm and beauty, to fight the lords and prelates with pride: *'Look to your consciences and remember that the theater of the world is wider than the realm of England.'*

If she wanted to talk of other universes now, then Michael was ready to oblige her.

'Like everything in astrophysics, there are several theories.'

'Give me one, Michael.'

Arlette was approaching nearer to telling him why this new and curious interest in other stars, other spaces. But she preferred to put off the confession, and felt some unexplainable reluctance to tell him she was not only trying to forget Mary Stuart:

'Dr Micah Benoni has recently been appointed to a professorship in astrophysics at the Institute for Advanced Studies . . .'

Three or four weeks ago she had been going quickly through the morning paper and paused at a photograph which arrested her attention – it was the photograph of an arresting face; the photograph of a familiar face.

A casual snapshot, but there was the same straight gaze,

the same concentrated expression, the same dark hair growing in a slight point over the wide forehead; a look of challenge, in curious combination with austere responsibility; a suggestion of recklessness – and the disciplined control she had sensed as she sat during the hours of flight, more or less continuously aware of this man's enormous patience and reserve.

Micah Benoni.

Not the man she had seen in the restaurant, or passed on the street.

She turned slightly toward Michael, about to make her full confession regarding quasars and galaxies, and then stopped abruptly, as if she had heard her name called in a strident voice. Yet there had been no voice above the general babble.

Nevertheless, there was Deborah Crane, just arriving.

Deborah's head was thrown back to display that white arching throat, one of her few natural attributes. There was a broad smile on the bright red mouth, and a look of confidence and conquest as she entered with the actor who had played Lord Darnley.

Deborah was wearing Russian broadtail pants, dyed deep purple, a pink sequin-covered blouse, and Elizabeth had been wiped off her face and Deborah Crane reapplied. A golden-red wig covered the shaved forehead, the green eyes flashed, and as Lord Darnley removed her purple broadtail cape, Deborah gave a gesture of casting it aside as if she never wanted to see it again.

The entrance was spectacular, or it would have been if anyone but Arlette had seen it.

Now Deborah was moving about, accepting kisses, stroking the backs of men's necks as she passed, leaning her breasts against their arms.

For two or three minutes Deborah walked quickly about, and it might have seemed to a stranger that here was the star of the show, until all at once the façade collapsed.

For Deborah encountered Jerry Hoffman and threw her arms about him as most of the guests watched with as much surprise as if a building had slowly crumbled, walls melting and dissolving.

For several moments Deborah embraced Jerry, holding him despairingly, while Jerry responded by folding his arms about her and patting her reassuringly. Still, it was not easy to play Deborah's uncle.

All at once she flung her head back, stared into his face, a silent laugh stretching her face. Then she was crying; in another moment she was sobbing.

Nervously, embarrassed, as if those who had been watching had witnessed some shameful deed, the conversation resumed its normal pitch, while Jerry walked slowly, with Deborah quite hysterical, out of the room.

'She's happy?' inquired Michael reflectively. 'Or she's sad? She's pleased – or she's mad?' Arlette smiled, but said nothing, and Michael evidently thought they might better return to their talk of quasars. 'Why the sudden interest, Lily?'

'In what?'

Deborah?

For as Deborah dissolved before her, Arlette had gone sailing out of the room and back to Fotheringay Castle, where less than three hours before she had demolished Elizabeth Tudor. She was thinking not of quasars and galaxies, but that for six nights a week for five months the same thing would happen. She could perceive a series of subtle tortures.

'Quasars. Exploding galaxies.'

Sailing back into Jerry Hoffman's apartment again, Arlette laughed gaily, too gaily for the question. She was laughing in triumph, but she could not tell Michael that, and now she saw Anthony making his way to them, being stopped at every step. His face, when he glanced away from whomever he was talking to and looked straight at her, was serious, almost menacing.

She got up, taking Michael's hand. 'Come – let's talk to Alicia and Max. He was incredible tonight, and I want to tell him so. I had no idea he could give off so much heat.'

Star talk again. What's come over me?

CHAPTER 65

Arlette contrived to keep a distance between her and Anthony.

She preferred to talk to Sarita Stanhope.

Sarita had been gliding barefoot among the guests in her white and silver lamé pajamas, opened to the waist in front, moving with her boneless grace, tall, thin, vaguely smiling, her long straight hair now several inches below her waist.

Sarita solemnly assured Arlette she had worked her tail off for six months to make the apartment everything Jerry would enjoy. She was very serious about what it had cost her in time, energy, trudging hour after hour with the decorator through artists' studios and little factories where modern furniture was made to order.

It was not easy to be sure if the apartment was a background for Jerry or for Sarita.

It was certainly not a background for the Jerry Hoffman Arlette had met thirteen years ago, when Anthony De Forest and Gordon Donahue had talked him into hiring an unknown young actress to play Katharina.

But Arlette had seen nothing of that Jerry Hoffman for several years, nor had he seen anything of the ambitious, determined, alert young woman who had been afraid of everyone in that nation where she felt doomed to be a permanent outsider.

Now – between them, and some few others – they owned the candy store, and everything in it. They might pick and choose among the sweets.

They could look at each other, she and Jerry Hoffman, on the rehearsal stage, at a board meeting, walking the beach at Montauk – and in a moment the present slid away, the past was there.

The exchange of a glance, a slight smile, and the past, like a piece of scenery on a track, slid off again. They stood in the present, with that long history to color each word, influence every feeling.

'You're an artist, Arlette,' Sarita was saying, 'a great, great artist. It's all I want, and I can't seem to find the Rosetta stone. Is there one?'

'Work. If there is one – that's it.'

'But I do work. I work my ass off. It isn't easy – always looking as if you're feeling great, bursting with vitamins and self-confidence when maybe you feel like dying instead.'

'I know, Sarita,' said Arlette, with that tender tone she used to conceal the fact that Sarita's problems seemed insignificant.

Somewhat unexpectedly, Jerry was there, returned from his errand with Deborah Crane, and Sarita slipped her arm through his and whispered in his ear – a habit, he had told Arlette, he could not break, and anyway, she never said anything but: 'I want you.'

'She should be looking for a husband,' said Jerry as Sarita glided away to greet some newcomers, and all at once his face had that brooding expression which came when he pondered subjects as disparate as Sarita's future, his neglect of his now grown children, or a scene which would not coalesce onstage as he saw it in his mind.

Where was she? That girl in her pink sequin blouse and purple broadtail pants? She had not been seen for the last hour. What had become of Elizabeth I?

Arlette did not ask Jerry, and Jerry went on talking about Sarita.

'She takes lessons, lessons, lessons. She can act like crazy for a still camera. But the feelings are phony – fashion feelings. She's got the stamina of a horse, though she may look like a pipe cleaner.'

He would keep her awhile longer, perhaps another year or two, until she found that husband she would need when she could no longer earn two hundred thousand dollars a year as a model. Sarita was self-indulgent as a cat, and Jerry had admitted he was not sure whether he was more an amusement for his cat than his cat was for him.

All at once, Jerry was through talking about Sarita. 'You know what I think about your performance tonight.'

'No, Jerry. I don't. You haven't told me.'

'You know, for Christ's sake. The best. But there's one thing – that girl—'

'Deborah?'

'Who else? She looks like she could swallow a keg of nails, but she's a cream puff. She's back there some-where—' Jerry seemed still unfamiliar with his apart-ment's rooms and corridors. 'I gave her a tranquilizer. She said she'd ruined the play. She was going to kill herself.'

'But she was doing so well in rehearsals. Alicia was quite encouraged.'

'There was nothing in any of the rehearsals to indicate you meant to play that scene the way you played it tonight.'

'I thought—'

'You thought.' He was not concerned about Deborah Crane, but about the balance of the play. His eyes were slightly narrowed and gleaming silver gray, an expression she saw only when he was angry, when the play would not move as he wanted it to, but which she had never seen directed at her. 'She can't take it. That's all. She'll conk out.'

'Elizabeth I does not conk out.'

'But Deborah Crane does.'

'The audience will be very much surprised.'

Jerry and Arlette began to laugh, and laughed so hilariously that John Powell approached them. 'Thank God, I finally found you laughing,' he told Arlette. 'I've been waiting to talk to you all night. But you looked so serious.'

Arlette laughed again, but this was a laugh of gleeful mockery. And even Jerry seemed relieved by John's appearance.

'Yes,' said Jerry. 'Her best performance. We were talking about it.'

All at once John lost his shyness, forgot Jerry, and

began talking to her like a lover. 'I can never thank you – you did more with it than I thought possible—'

'She did more than any of us thought possible. Arlette – you have some responsibility in this. Hiring that girl was your idea.'

Arlette turned to John. 'What did you think of Deborah's performance? It seems she thinks she's spoiled everything.'

'She didn't forget any lines.'

'John, for Christ's sake! Arlette did a great job. Okay. Why the hell shouldn't she? The play was written for her. And, yes – darling – you would have anyway. But this poor slob, this overstuffed Cornish hen, Deborah Crane, bloody well threw one of the most important scenes out of the window. She didn't play Elizabeth Tudor – she played a terrified amateur.'

'But she is,' said John gently, 'a terrified amateur. Alicia will work with her.'

'She won't improve if Arlette springs a surprise on her every night. That's hard for an experienced actor – it's murder for someone who should never have set foot on the stage in the first place.'

John looked puzzled. 'Are you concerned because Arlette came onstage from a different direction than she did in rehearsal?'

'She came up on the woman from backstage. And she came silently and stood there – so the audience began to watch her, waiting for what she was going to do next. Deborah didn't even know she was there. After all, she sits in that ridiculous dress with a canopy over her head and a curtain behind her. She's trapped.'

'Queens,' said Arlette reasonably, 'are always trapped.'

'Deborah knew what she was taking on,' John said.

The playwright, who wanted not only Arlette but Mary Stuart to emerge as victor, and the director, who wanted to keep the seamless fabric of his direction, without any amateur's collapse to rip it apart, seemed about to quarrel.

Arlette stood looking from one to the other with a

slight smile, as if she could not imagine what all this was about.

'Arlette,' said John, 'it was a brilliant concept. Mary Stuart had begged for that interview for more than twenty years. By the time she was granted it, she was a woman condemned to die.'

Arlette smiled gratefully. 'It only occurred to me as I went onstage: Mary Stuart would not have come like a supplicant. Mary knew she would be dead in a few days. Death, I've heard – the certain knowledge of near death – obliterates any desire to placate the living. They are not needed any more.'

Jerry was looking at them suspiciously, as if his playwright and friend, his star and former lover, still beloved, had entered a conspiracy to sabotage the one thing he loved better than either of them: the integrity and wholeness of any play directed by Jerry Hoffman.

'*Ah, so there you are—*'

Arlette had spoken softly as she stood behind Elizabeth's canopied chair.

Deborah Crane, in her farthingale, her tight-curled red wig, her stretched white mask, blue eyes darting anxiously from side to side, had given a yelp, clutching one hand to her throat, and made a bouncing leap out of the chair and back.

Arlette moved swiftly around and stood before her, slightly smiling. '*You've come – at last, at last—*'

The Queen of England recovered a semblance of composure. '*My sister – my cousin—*'

'*My enemy.*'

'You've been so kind,' Deborah said to her one day after rehearsal. 'I'm afraid of being on the same stage with you, but you've been so kind—'

'I want the play to be what John Powell and Jerry Hoffman expect of it. There's nothing personal in my kindness – as you call it.'

Arlette stood facing Queen Elizabeth seated on her rehearsal throne. She looked at her carefully, and read her mind. Deborah believed forgiveness had been granted.

But revenge concerned two people only – the offender and the avenger.

If anything else was destroyed, it was no longer revenge but vandalism.

At the first dress rehearsal, in Elizabeth's white mask, breasts pushed flat behind the stiff corset, Deborah had come onstage with the white satin farthingale pitching like a ship on a turbulent sea, interrupting the rehearsal to show them how ugly she looked.

'Have you ever seen anything more grotesque?' She turned for their inspection, smiling all the while.

'Very good, Joe,' Jerry Hoffman told the makeup man. 'It's a perfect likeness.'

'Thanks,' said Joe disconsolately. 'It wasn't easy.'

Deborah laughed, until Jerry reminded her: 'This is a dress rehearsal, Miss Crane.'

'Oh, I'm so sorry, so sorry—' She retreated behind the stone pillars of Fotheringay Castle.

The only part she had ever played with professional skill was the part of the new Deborah Crane. Arlette knew that whatever self-confidence she had would be gone after opening night. The sweetness of revenge was in her mouth like honey; conquest made her face gleam.

And so she took Deborah, Jerry Hoffman, John Powell, Anthony – in the audience with Minerva and Andrew Thyssen, Michael and Gordon Donahue – by surprise with her very different entrance and performance on opening night.

'*Ah, so there you are. You've come – at last—*'

'*I have tried to save you, Cousin!*' Deborah screamed. Her eyes were wild, and she turned this way and that, trying to bring Mary into her line of vision.

None of this had happened at rehearsal, and Deborah became more frantic until, at one moment, she seemed about to hoist herself out of the chair in order to find where her condemned prisoner was standing. The next moment Mary had glided into view again and stood facing her.

Between the last dress rehearsal and the opening night, Queen Elizabeth had met a new adversary.

After the final curtain, Anthony had come to her dressing room, kissed her, and placed the earrings in her hand, smiling, folding her fingers gently over them. No criticism, no hint that he disapproved of what she had done.

Her last speech to the Queen of England was delivered with her back to the audience, in a low steady voice which carried as if bells had been set ringing: *'In my end is my beginning. You are without children. And you are fifty years old. My son and his sons and grandsons will rule England, long after we two are dead.'* That speech, the tones of her voice, had perhaps prepared him to forgive her anything, for the silence through the audience had grown more intense, as if every word had been the tolling of the death bell; and Elizabeth's face had grown more blankly terrified as she gazed up at her accuser, possibly seeing in Mary Stuart's eyes the hatred the audience could not see. *'What?'* Mary had continued mockingly. *'Does that surprise you? You, my cousin – are mortal, too.'*

After a pause, Deborah gave her hoarse scream of reply, and the lights flashed out. The silence was absolute.

Now as Arlette and Jerry and John Powell stood talking in Jerry's drawing room, John told her: 'That was the way to do it, Arlette! You made her betray her guilt! It's so logical – why didn't I write it into the stage direction?'

Arlette smiled at him:

Because you don't hate Deborah Crane.

'Arlette,' said Jerry, 'is always logical.' Arlette looked at him quickly, and he put one arm about her and kissed her. 'Forgive me. I'm not concerned about that bitch in there. But she wants to quit before she has a nervous breakdown, so she says.' Jerry looked at her, and as Arlette looked steadily back at him, she knew he had discovered, by that divining rod he had for people's feelings and interactions, why Arlette had cracked apart the chalk-white mask of Elizabeth I. 'She doesn't blame you, Arlette. She thinks it's all her fault.'

'It is!' John, gentle, considerate, cooperative John Powell – *scarcely like a playwright*, Jerry had once said in wonderment, *more like a gentleman*. 'She should get the hell off the stage and stay off. After this run.'

'Your protégée,' Jerry said to Arlette, his fists in his trouser pockets, making him look like a street bully in a dinner jacket, 'wants to quit tonight. Tonight – do you understand? We don't have an understudy. We didn't think it worthwhile for such a small part—' He gave her a sinister glare. 'But I don't think she will. I've got her scared pissless – I hope.'

'How?'

'I told her that if she quit she'd never work on Broadway again.' Jerry hovered near Arlette, threateningly, while Arlette continued to watch him with the same wistful expression. 'I told her it wouldn't be because I'd blackball her, but because no one would ever trust her.'

'Jerry, Jerry – it wasn't as bad as you think, please believe me. It wasn't what you expected, but her response was truer than if she had played it the way it was rehearsed. Elizabeth felt guilty about those years in prison, signing the death warrant of her cousin. Elizabeth was suffering from severe guilt – I only made Deborah show that.'

CHAPTER 66

'Here they are!'

The waiters were carrying piles of newspapers, passing them out like canapés, while screams and shouts of excitement began, growing louder and more joyous as they read, some reading aloud, some beneath their breath, as in a church recital.

'We've done it!'

'We've done it! We've done it!'

There was never any doubt in a Hoffman-Repertory production about who the stars were, and yet, each time, not only the stars but every member of the company was convinced his effort had been the crucial piece in the vast complexity of a Jerry Hoffman puzzle. Without them the production would have failed to reach its fullest flowering.

Several reviews referred to Miss Crane's original interpretation of Elizabeth. But the review they most treasured when it was favorable, most detested when it was adverse, concluded: *She resembles a female version of one of Francis Bacon's agonized popes or business tycoons. It is an uncanny concept of the final triumph of Mary Stuart. Miss Crane is to be congratulated on a brilliant portrayal of a woman suffering the effects of remorse and guilt . . .*

Arlette read the reviews through. Margo threw her arms around her. 'Darling, he says it's the best performance you've given.' Others approached and kissed her. Arlette responded automatically, like a child accustomed to being kissed and fondled by adults because of its beauty and winsomeness, and all the while she was thinking: *Jesus Christ, I got away with it.*

She heard Jerry's voice, very near, and glanced across the paper to see the grim smile on his face. 'Those bastards are even more stupid than I thought they were.'

He started off at a sprint. Arlette looked after him wistfully:

Not one word about what they said about me . . .

Jerry moved like an athlete, rhythmically, with the sudden stops and starts of one who had spent high school and college years on basketball courts, and now he stopped as if a finger had been snapped directly before his face, spun around, and the next moment was giving Arlette a quick kiss.

'I've got to show this to Deborah – she'll go out of her mind. Forgive me. I guess I haven't gotten over you – maybe I never will—'

Arlette felt her heart begin to pound, too hard, too threatening for exhilaration, and was all at once in a hurry to escape.

She started across the room, circling around people when she could, accepting their kisses and embraces when she must, smiling all the while Jade Ring's smile, keeping it on her face with determination.

At any moment a shrieking hysterical Deborah would come running into the room and try to thank her. She might even burst into tears of grateful joy and throw her arms about her.

Anthony, she was vaguely aware, was still on her trail, slowly, following her at a distance, having problems of his own in freeing himself from the tentacles which encircled him, the mouths pressed to his face.

He had followed her all evening, keeping his distance only when she was talking to Jerry and John Powell, and she was afraid of what Anthony would say when, inevitably, he caught up with her.

He must be contemptuous of the tactics she had used. He might despise her for harboring such jealousy. She did not want to hear his voice or look into his face.

Near the foyer, she found the two men she had been seeking. 'Gordon! Michael! Let's leave. Let's go home – I can't stand this noise.'

They looked at her in dismayed surprise, which informed Arlette she had let go of Jade Ring's smile. She quickly replaced it. 'I'm not nervous – I'm not upset,' she assured them. 'It's just that – let's leave—'

'Arlette—'

That was Anthony's voice, and she stood quite still, the trumpet flower of her skirt still swirling with the abruptness of the pause.

'Yes?'

Michael saw something here between husband and wife, and went to join Gordon, who had put on his coat and was holding Arlette's.

Later – for it might have taken a little time for him to overcome those pictures of Mary Stuart enough so that beyond them he could see the terrified, frozen image of Deborah Crane – he had moved toward her, waiting for her; and now finally caught her.

He stood so close behind her she could feel his body lightly touching hers. 'Never forget. Never forgive,

Arlette?' She remained motionless, and presently he spoke in a tone of bewilderment and disgust: 'Sometimes I think a woman will take her desire for revenge with her to the grave.'

She turned slowly, anger in her eyes, although she was still smiling. 'Anthony – you don't know me.' Gordon held her coat and she slipped into it.

He snatched his coat from the rack and they were out the door – not a moment too soon, for they heard Deborah's voice, entering as if upon universal acclaim for having rescued the evening's performance.

'Oh, John—', That was Deborah, no doubt throwing her arms about his neck. 'John – darling! I didn't disgrace you, after all, did I?'

Anthony was gone the next morning when Arlette awoke at ten-thirty, and there was a note on his pillow:

'Off to bloody rehearsal. Gordon called at nine-thirty – taking eleven o'clock. You were magnificent. Will pick you up at the theater tonight. Minerva and Thyssen want us to have dinner with them.'

Arlette stretched in slow luxurious movements, and as she read the letter she remembered, with the lingering sensation of fullness in her belly, that Anthony had had nothing more to say last night about her vengefulness.

They had sat in the drawing room, eating little sandwiches and talking with Gordon and Michael – not about the play but about Gordon's most recent book and the senior class play, *The Duchess of Malfi*, the new theater which was being built on the campus, and about Michael's work in molecular biology.

It was two-thirty when they parted, Gordon to his hotel, Michael to his room on the third floor, promising to delay his flight to Chicago long enough to have breakfast with her. 'Call me when you're ready.'

'It won't be early. My one luxury is a quiet day after opening night.' This house, the cars, the furs, the Montauk house, the jewelry, the clothes, these were not luxuries, evidently. Only one quiet day out of a year counted itself a luxury.

Next morning, wearing a yellow pleated wool skirt and yellow sweater, Arlette called Irma and was told that Dr Malone was in the greenhouse.

The little greenhouse extended twelve square feet into the garden, the door opening into it from the dining room. Anthony had had it built as a surprise for her while she was in England, and ever since they had eaten there more often than in their bedroom or the dining room.

She and Michael sat opposite each other at the French iron garden table, covered with a long yellow cloth, and talked as if they had not met for several years.

Surrounded by banks of ferns spilling from standing planters and potted lilies being brought to proper condition for cutting, they ate scrambled eggs and Canadian bacon, drank orange juice and tea, and after a few minutes Arlette said: 'I read that book.'

By now she was almost intoxicated by the warm food, replenishing her energy. It seemed that whatever other people got from alcohol, she got from food, shooting its nourishment into the brain, giving her an almost immediate sensation of well-being, a near euphoria.

'What book?'

Michael's last book had been published two years ago, and she had questioned him about that several times.

'What the hell is it called?' She snapped her fingers and smiled triumphantly: '*Thermodynamic Stability of Relativistic Stellar Clusters.*' She looked soberly at Michael, who seemed surprised, then thoughtful, and all at once he gave a burst of laughter.

'Forgive me, Lily. It was – a surprise. So that's why you're so interested in quasars and exploding galaxies.' It sounded suspicious, even to her. Why the interest, indeed? 'Micah Benoni.' He reflected a little. All at once the greenhouse contained a visitor. An astrophysicist, of all unlikely intruders. 'What did you make of it?'

'Nothing. What did you?'

'I didn't read it. It's all any of us can do to keep up with what's going on in the immediate vicinity.'

The essential difference, she sometimes thought,

between herself and Michael was that Michael had become a philosopher, using his gifts objectively, while she had remained caught by the past. Time had not proved a cure for her grief, or anger.

Yes, since she seemed destined to play tragic women, she could give little of what she wanted most to give – the joyousness, the sweetness which showed so clearly in the photographs.

Michael's reparation had perhaps some obscure connection with his search for the why of being. While she had chosen, whether for her own sake or for the sake of the man and woman because of whom she existed, to offer a variety of fantasized experiences to replace that real life, abandoned in the midst of hope and laughter, a life not yet touched by the knowledge that all life failed with time, that living itself became the last heavy burden.

'One of these days,' Michael said, 'Benoni and I may come a little closer in our disciplines. He's been doing some interesting work in molecular astrophysics – and this is where our work might one day touch.'

'Bring him to dinner sometime.'

Michael smiled – that smile which was in a masculine way so close to Jade Ring's smile, except that he used it sparingly. His molecular experiments would not flourish any better under the influence of the smile than they did without it.

Her work demanded the smile, the blonde hair, the disciplined, strong, and delicate body, the flexible trained voice. Who knew which was most essential? All of it, no doubt.

'I warn you – he's a formidably serious man.'

'I'm formidably serious, myself.'

'I'll bring him one of these days. I think he may be in New Zealand now.' Michael was smiling, but the smile did not mock her – he was smiling with pleasure that in her new world she had kept so much of what Valerie and Frederick had given fifteen years to teaching her. Reading the smile, Arlette hoped she was not deceiving him.

537

Surely there was nothing beyond the wish to know about the quasars? Nothing of consequence, at least.

'Yes,' Michael added. 'He was at the Peking meeting, with a thousand others.'

'I knew it. I was sure of it,' she amended.

CHAPTER 67

Sir Charles Granville arrived the day before the premiere of *The Return of the Native*. The British contingent seemed to lack a girl for Charles, and that, Arlette supposed, was his signal their affair was not over.

Granville was not a man who liked to have more than one woman at a time. 'It takes the edge off,' he told her. 'Concentration. Concentration on only one thing while you're doing it. A film. A scene in a film. A meal to eat. A horse to ride. A woman to give pleasure to – there's no other way to get everything out of it.'

Now she was about to see what he had got out of her in creating Eustacia Vye.

The premiere of the film was on a Sunday night in April, some three weeks after the opening nights of *Henry V* and *Mary of Scots*.

'If only I could go in disguise,' she told Anthony.

She stepped naked into her dress made of mauve silk, thin as tissue and embroidered in threads of real silver, cut to the waist front and back. The skirt poured over her hips and thighs as if she had wrung it out in water, and it swayed slowly upon the floor, as if weighted. Around her neck was Anthony's present, a long necklace of amethysts, each the size of a robin's egg, strung on a thin white gold chain, a net of platinum enclosing each stone.

'What if I don't deserve it? Shouldn't you wait until after you've seen the picture? I can't remember it any more. I've been Mary Stuart since then.'

One incarnation obliterated another, at least temporarily.

Yet even after eighteen years, Arlette was surprised from time to time to feel once again that sense of horror and evil which had come over her at the moment she bent above Barbara-Mei Fei, to peel the serving girl's mask from Mei Fei's face and replace it with a mask of Jade Ring's face – then sent Mei Fei to die for her.

With uncanny intensity she remembered the horror she had felt at the taking of another woman's life, killing her to save Jade Ring. Jade Ring – but not, at that moment, Jade Ring. It was Lily Malone she was saving; it was Barbara Sloan she had killed with a literal certainty.

After Barbara's abrupt disappearance from the campus, Lily had wondered from time to time if in some mystical sense Barbara had accepted Mei Fei's death as her own: Jade Ring had killed her. She was gone.

Lily had not made too many inquiries about Barbara, and had tried to forget her as soon as possible. She had never been able to forget her entirely.

Possibly Barbara had died in fact. Or Barbara lived somewhere today, and perhaps knew that the woman who had murdered her was known as Arlette Morgan, having accumulated by now a long history of criminal deeds through her power of portraying tragic, ruthless, sensual women.

When they reached the theater, Arlette quickly crossed the open space, willing herself not to hear yells of adulation and hatred, and found the sanctuary of the lobby – crowded with people who were, many of them, as frightened as she was.

She glanced back, looking for Anthony, who had paused to shake Thyssen's hand, just as Deborah Crane stepped out of her hired limousine, followed by Darnley, very elegant in his dinner jacket and look of haughty boredom.

A yell went up, accompanied by catcalls and whistles. For Deborah had bent low as she emerged, and her breasts overflowed the deep neckline of the dress covered with purple sequins. When the scrap of green-dyed broadtail shawl which was her wrap fell off, Darnley caught it and tried to return it to her, but Deborah did not notice it as she proceeded, smiling at every photographer.

'I have always known better than to wear sequins,' murmured Eva.

Eva was standing beside Arlette – Eva with her silver-blonde hair, her small exquisite body, her clear face, scarcely changed since Arlette had first met her, except for the look of confident sophistication, the enhanced artistry of makeup – wearing a white chiffon gown strewn with silvery beads and a pair of emerald earrings from Walter Hodges, who was at last getting divorced to marry her.

Privately, Eva called Mr Hodges by the name of his company, Ameritex Cellulose International, and Arlette had difficulty thinking of him as other than Mr Ameritex.

'Walter Hodges,' Anthony was murmuring as they went into the theater. 'Walter Hodges.'

They moved swiftly down the aisle and took their seats, Jerry Hoffman and Sarita Stanhope on one side of Arlette – Charles Granville had not yet taken the seat on her right. Alicia sat on Charles' right, with Anthony next to her, and Minerva Grey and Thyssen were beside them.

There it was, the closed circle.

Arlette felt safe, and now she talked eagerly and gaily to people on every side, in front and in back, and was so occupied with her role of star that when Granville sat down and the next moment the theater went dark and the music began, a distant sound of an eerie flute, as of a shepherd wandering over Egdon Heath which showed behind the titles, with the Reddleman's florid red cart lurching along the rutted roadway, Arlette felt she had come to see a movie because a friend had asked her.

Eustacia had become someone she could no longer imagine.

Then there she was:

Eustacia Vye, with her black hair, her nearly black eyes, her white skin and expression of sullen provocation and defiance, staring directly at the audience for a long intimidating moment before she picked up the Captain's telescope and put it to her eye. Around the rims of the distant hills, bonfires were alight. The effect was of a Druidic ritual; the nineteenth century seemed to have receded to the time when unknown craftsmen planted the great stone circles.

Arlette was somewhat stupefied by this Eustacia; who did not look like her or sound like her. There was, instead of Arlette Morgan, the brooding face of a morbidly unhappy, yet wonderfully beautiful woman.

Who is she?

Had she looked like that only eight months ago?

Was it the photography with its strong chiaroscuro, broken suddenly by the vibrant colors of the mummers' scene, with Eustacia, dressed in the costume of a Turkish knight, dancing wildly and boldly at Clym Yeobright's Christmas party, unrecognizable through her mask of fluttering ribbons, dancing like a bacchante, not like Captain Vye's granddaughter.

Clym Yeobright followed her outside: '*You're a woman, aren't you?*' She was supposedly, one of the young village boys, and the mask of ribbon streamers concealed her face.

'*Yes.*'

There was a large close-up of Clym Yeobright's face, so much more intense, scholarly, serious, painfully sensitive than Arlette remembered Robert Parker's to have been. That was Granville, too. He took actors and transformed them, invented them for each new part.

'*What made you want to do this?*'

Eustacia turned her head away. '*To shake off depression.*'

She did, in fact, sound depressed.

She had been depressed, sad, convinced she would never recover the part of her relationship with Anthony which had been lost by that telephone call, quite as if she had been standing upon secure ground and discovered that a piece had broken away and she was alone on it, moving across a shallow tide, carrying her to some unknown land.

Granville had obviously understood that she was in a

condition of vulnerability; the perfect condition in which to give herself over to his direction of this tragic woman, whose tragedy was produced by her reckless longing for a life which did not exist.

The love scene between Clym and Eustacia began, and there was another surprise. For the two days she had spent naked in bed with Robert Parker, who had looked to her such an ineffectual Clym Yeobright, now appeared as a scene of a man and woman distraught with desire and pleasure, and Eustacia's face was transformed, showing an ecstatic wonderment and excitement. The movement of her hands, fingers spread across Parker's naked shoulders and back; the profile of his face, intent, bending to her mouth, his forehead dripping sweat, and then, so swift a flash she was not sure if she saw it or imagined it, her naked breasts before his body covered her again.

Arlette whispered to Granville. 'What about my contract?'

He was leaning forward as if he had never seen any of this before. Even after there were no more possible changes, Granville still looked for what was wrong, not what was right.

Eustacia, as Granville presented her, was the moving force: it was Eustacia who was fate. It was Eustacia who was her own destroyer and that of Clym and Mrs Yeobright and Wildeve. It was Eustacia who destroyed the illusions and happiness of her husband; the naïve joy of Thomasin, Wildeve's young wife. She had become, in Granville's camera, a woman whose effect was murderous; whose intent was blindly selfish.

He had begun with telling her that not Eustacia but weather and the heath were the main characters; he had produced a film in which Eustacia was more powerful than weather, heath, and all other characters combined.

'We are all enemies,' Granville had told her near the end of the filming. 'The universe is not evil. The universe is not evil or good. Man is the destroyer. One day, he will destroy himself. We may be here to see it.' He gave Arlette a sardonic smile, as if the prospect pleased him.

He had had nothing against Eustacia – she was not evil for being female. She was evil because she was stronger than those she encountered, and Granville did not believe the strong were to be trusted. 'Look at me,' he had suggested. 'Or Anthony. Even you, my darling.'

Near the end, as the audience had fallen into steadily deeper silence, as if Granville had hypnotized them, too, the bonfires were lighted once again along the hilltops of Egdon Heath, burning for miles in every direction, when all at once a heavy rain began and, slowly, the fires went out.

In her bedroom, Eustacia threw her cloak around her, moved softly down the stairs, and went out into the storm, to meet Wildeve at midnight, for their elopement to Budmouth – then to Paris, in her tenacious dream.

'I'll go anyway. I've made the decision – he'll be there—'

The film was nearly black, the music roared with the rain and wind; then softened to the shepherd's lonely plaintive flute. In a flash of lightning Eustacia passed some distance behind Wildeve's carriage and, the next moment, pitched forward into the heavy waves of the weir, giving a long-drawn scream as she fell.

It was Arlette, no question of that, for since she had insisted on playing the scene, Granville had used telephoto lenses which brought Arlette's face, showing real fear, to the surface of the water two or three times before she disappeared and Wildeve and Yeobright leaped in.

Remembering the terror, the water she had swallowed, the stomach pump, Arlette was grateful when Jerry Hoffman seized her hand and crushed it until she thought he would break bones, releasing the pressure only when Eustacia was dragged out – with another merciless telephoto shot of a nearly drowned Arlette, her mouth open, water pouring from her.

The scene was cut short, and she was lying on the bed in an upstairs chamber of The Quiet Woman, Wildeve beside her. Eustacia's face had now a tender smile, the first look of peaceful happiness it had shown; but Wildeve, in death, was grim and angry.

'You damn fool,' Jerry whispered furiously to Arlette. 'He should be killed.'

The camera drew nearer, concentrated upon Eustacia, her wet hair spread about her on the white quilt, and Yeobright's voice, out of camera range, spoke softly to the young servant boy who had adored her: *'She's very beautiful now, isn't she?'*

Granville had contrived to convey in those words that she was finally beautiful to Yeobright, absolved of her crimes, pure and blameless, because she could no longer threaten his timid approach to living: her death had canceled her life.

'That,' Granville had advised her, 'is how much the weak fear those who are stronger.'

The screen turned black, the rain continued; there was absolute silence as the music stopped abruptly, then a few more random notes from the flute, and Arlette leaned close to Granville. 'You son of a bitch!'

The lights went up, and after a stunned moment the audience stood applauding, and to Arlette's incredulous astonishment there were shouts and cheers.

Charles grabbed her wrist, drawing her to her feet as she confronted them, relieved to see so many familiar faces to reassure her, familiar faces still under Granville's spell, still stricken with the terror he had contrived to infuse into his picture:

Why, they don't hate it after all – they're knocked out—

Unsmiling – since why should Eustacia suddenly smile brightly when she lay dead beside her lover in that upstairs bedroom – Arlette merely bowed her head slightly, one time, then once again.

All the while the sense of wonder remained. They thought it was an interesting picture? They had been impressed by it? Perhaps by Eustacia?

But who had played Eustacia, and where was she?

Certainly not standing there, Granville still firmly holding her wrist.

One more ghost in the house, that's who she is.

CHAPTER 68

Four days later Charles Granville returned to England, and the last thing he said to her was: 'Someday, you and I will be married.'

Sir Charles had occupied the house of some friends who were evidently very rich – for it had five stories, twenty-four rooms, five servants who lived there, three cars – and who were conveniently abroad on the husband's business.

'International finance,' Jerry remarked at the party Charles gave for nearly four hundred people in this house after the premiere. Jerry plainly regarded international finance as a joke, or perhaps a lie Sir Charles had made up to conceal some sinister occupation on the part of a man rich enough to live among such furnishings, such paintings, and so casual as to lend it to a friend for a party.

Granville's way of being host was original. He was negligent about introductions, assuming them to be unnecessary.

He talked only to the people who interested him for business reasons, and ignored those he or his press agent had invited who meant nothing to him. He did not speak to Arlette, although he held a long private conversation with Anthony, perhaps on their proposed filming of *Wuthering Heights*, a subject they had discussed ever since they had made *Jude the Obscure*.

Perhaps the host's blithe indifference was an advantage, for the party seemed more spirited, pervaded by an aura of triumph, than the average successful opening night. But the house itself was a goad to gaiety, as were the food and the wines and champagnes and the women, beautifully and expensively dressed. There were so many flowers, so many waiters, such loud music, that it was difficult to be sure if this was a party in celebration of a motion picture or a party being filmed for a motion picture about life among the gay and rich and careless.

Granville seemed to have forgotten Arlette was there until she and Anthony started to leave, since she had to be at rehearsal at ten.

At the Alicia Allerton, as had been expected, Queen Mary's horse had fallen, despite its thick track of tanbark, and Arlette had nimbly leaped off, demonstrating such deft horsemanship it brought wild applause, and then gasps and even sobs, when the horse, after a long struggle, could not get up.

And so another scene must be substituted, and Jerry was in a surly mood. The horse had never pleased him, and his worst prediction had come to pass. John Powell was apologetic for having written the scene: the horse was his fault.

'I can handle it, John,' Jerry told him. 'We'll substitute a march.'

As Arlette reached the first landing, Anthony paused to talk to Jerry, and Granville came leaping down after her. 'I've been watching you all night – don't think I haven't.' He looked at her seriously, and the hard blue eyes turned that violet color which transmogrified Charles Granville from remorseless director to pleading lover. He glanced hastily up the staircase toward where Anthony stood. 'When?'

She shook her head quickly, but his tall thin body bent toward her, the director congratulating his star, whispering, 'I'll call you at nine. Anthony's off to early gymnastics.'

Arlette and Anthony were out the door. Arlette arguing mentally with Granville as she got into the car:

I will not. What am I to Granville, and what is Granville to me? Just because it happened – does it have to happen again?

He called promptly at nine. 'I'll be at the theater about two o'clock. I have some things to discuss – maybe a cut here or there—'

'You're damned right a cut here or there!'

546

'It's a subliminal shot. People will think they imagined it.'

'My contract—'

'We'll talk about it.'

Ever since the horse had fallen the night before last, she had begun to worry about the effect it would have, should Belinda have to be destroyed, upon Arlette Morgan's playing of Mary Stuart. There had been hallucinations of going onstage to boos and catcalls from the Humane Society.

Arlette telephoned her breakfast order to Irma, and went to the dressing room to make up for lost sleep with Yoga and ballet exercises and a long hot shower which she turned slowly colder, until she jumped and dried herself with joyous vigor.

She arrived at the theater at ten minutes before ten, telling Conrad the rehearsal might last most of the day and she would have an early supper in her dressing room. That did away with the car:

But why? I'm not going anywhere with Granville – whatever he thinks.

Arlette hastened along the dark empty hallway, softly singing that old song which, from time to time, surprised her by sounding in her ears, scarcely loud enough to hear:

> *'I never will marry,*
> *Nor be no man's wife . . .'*

The next words she heard were:

> *'The shells in the ocean*
> *Shall be my death-bed,*
> *And fish in deep water . . .'*

She stopped, looking at the floor, then ran on, tossed her coat over a chair, and went to the edge of the stage, where Jerry sat at the table placed there when there was new work to be done. His back was toward her and the table was covered with telegrams which he was reading with typical concentration. She approached softly, put both arms about his shoulders, and pressed her face against his.

'Trouble, Jerry? How's Belinda this morning?'

He looked up at her, and there was some anger in his eyes, that jealousy which occasionally flared after so many years.

Granville? The scene with Clym Yeobright? Deborah?

For her tormenting of Deborah each time with some new subtle surprise which struck Deborah mute by the pure hatred in Mary Stuart's eyes, could only have the reason it had.

'Look—'

He indicated the telegrams, and Arlette glanced through several. The massed Humane Societies of the United States of America had apparently learned of Belinda's fall, the injury to her leg; and her recovery or possible future death was being followed more carefully than bulletins on a presidential illness.

Reading them, Arlette reflected that had she not spent several hundred hours riding over every kind of terrain, she might have been killed or permanently disabled when the horse fell. She had saved herself – it was no lucky accident the horse had not crushed her.

'The Humane Society.' She looked at him wistfully. 'Isn't there a Human Society?'

Jerry went back to his reading. 'Not that I've heard of.' He swung about suddenly. 'Arlette – those were your tits Granville treated us to last night.'

'They were?' She was incredulous. 'He says it was subliminal – no one could be sure.'

'No one who wasn't looking for it. But a lot of guys were looking for it, and there'll be a lot more when it goes into general circulation. What did Anthony have to say?'

'Nothing.'

'He had something to say to me. And to Granville. So did I – so did Friedman, and Alicia. Not to mention—'

'Jerry, how could I know what they were getting?'

'It goes out! Granville's coming here this afternoon.'

'Either it was an accident—'

'Or he thought he could get away with it. Not with you, Arlette. You're our cherished darling. We'll protect you if you won't protect yourself. Lady Macbeth does not display her tits on a wide screen, or anywhere else in public. Now – about that fucking horse—'

As it happened, Jerry, who did not ordinarily concern himself with what went on outside Hoffman-Repertory, had more annoyances this morning than the fallen horse, Arlette's breasts spread across fifteen feet of screen, or even Arlette's stubborn persistence in tormenting Deborah Crane with a new version of Mary Stuart's hatred each night.

As Arlette and the others waited while Jerry discussed with Max Gilmore and thirty men how they would form the line of march without the galloping horse to lead them, Eva French took Arlette aside and told her of Deborah's latest plight.

Eva's face could look pure as an angel's, knowledgeable as a street waif's, and so she looked as she told Arlette that the night before Deborah had approached them, walking like an upright fish, wriggling in her tight purple-sequined dress.

'So long as you're with Hoffman-Repertory,' said Jerry, who never had been heard to criticize one actor in the hearing of another, 'don't appear in a get-up like that.'

Deborah had looked hurt, surprised, had peered down into the deep neckline where her breasts were crushed together, protesting, 'Arlette goes around half naked all the time—'

'Arlette looks elegant, whatever the hell she's got on!' And, as Deborah's chin began to quiver, Jerry patted her arm. 'Don't cry, baby. Don't, for Christ's sake, cry again.'

'But she did, all the same,' Eva concluded. 'I found her later in one of the bedrooms, trying to put her face together. She's got no guts. No guts.'

While Arlette and Eva whispered, the men marched about the stage in various formations: they sped across;

they straggled; they charged. They stayed offstage while Queen Mary dashed across alone – but it seemed a queen, even as played by Arlette, could not be an army. They tried so many different charges that when the errand boys arrived with sandwiches and coffee at one-thirty, everyone sat down, wheezing and sighing and cursing the horse, whose ultimate fate seemed not to move them as it did the Humane Society.

Charles Granville arrived promptly at two and went to talk to Jerry. Now and again, as they sat at Jerry's table, isolated as an island in mid-Atlantic, Arlette realized it was her breasts they were discussing.

Jerry sent his secretary to bring Arlette to the table, since she had turned away the moment Granville appeared.

'The scene's fixed,' Jerry informed her. 'I'll see it later. Go along – Granville wants to show it to you, and you can't spend the whole bloody day here. You'll never be able to play tonight.'

'But what am I to do? March? Run? Walk?'

'I'll let you know. Run, I think. But I may think again. See you,' he said to Granville. 'Tonight.'

Arlette stopped to pick up her coat and handbag and found Granville waiting, slightly smiling, beside his host's black Rolls Royce, which was upholstered with gray velvet.

'Too much,' murmured Arlette. 'Why can't people learn where to stop?'

The car's upholstery did not interest Sir Charles. 'Your scene is twelve frames shorter. You won't believe me, but I didn't try for that shot, it happened, and it was so beautiful I couldn't bring myself to cut it. But then, they may be right.'

'Of course they're right.' Arlette cast him an ominous glance: movies were one thing; Hoffman-Repertory was another. 'Hoffman-Repertory is taken seriously because it takes itself seriously.'

'A beautiful woman's breasts are not serious?'

'Only to a man who loves her. Civilization puts nasty thoughts into people's minds. Any actress who doesn't know that is going to be made a fool of – like Deborah Crane.'

She gave him a sideways glance, although even Arlette could not blame Granville for Deborah's visit to Anthony's hotel. And Granville, who combined British tact with British rudeness, as suited his purpose at the time, was looking straight ahead, not hearing Deborah's name.

'I know. Nakedness is not serious to most of the public. A pity. But the hell with it – it's the scene I wanted, anyway. Here we are.'

'Where's the projection room?' Arlette demanded as they entered the house. 'Your eyes are beautiful, Charles – your charm, when you uncork it, is champagne out of a shaken bottle. I do want to see what is still in the scene.'

'Don't you trust me?'

Arlette gave a burst of laughter, but there was the surprise of a warming in her belly, a quickened beating of her heart, and the memories, carefully filed under: *People Who No Longer Count*, now slowly magically unwrapped themselves, and the scenes ran ahead of her as they walked up the stairs:

The living room in Eustacia's house when he had first slid his hands beneath her sweater and pushed it up to study her breasts; the lovemaking, when an opportunity offered or could be invented, the night he had spent with her, leaving just before it began to grow light and returning with the news that it was her birthday, which they had forgotten, and Edna Frazier had arrived bearing gifts and a box of letters:

Yes, he knows what he's doing. How did I forget it?

He took her coat and threw it aside, and the butler appeared to ask if Sir Charles would like to have lunch served. Charles, ushering Arlette ahead of him upstairs, called: 'I'll ring. Thank you. What time do you eat before a performance?'

'Four o'clock.'

'Four o'clock. In the projection room, please. Something light. Tea.'

'So there is a projection room.'

'Arlette – you do think I'm a prick. Well, I am. Would you want to see the—'

Without finishing the question he ushered her into a very large bedroom, evidently the one he was occupying, for he pulled down the brocade spread, threw off his jacket, and moved toward her with his eyes bluer, deeper, intense with feeling.

She said nothing, and he did not speak again until, several minutes after he had finished and they lay quiet, peaceful, entangled, then slowly separating, reluctant to lose the intimacy of each other's bodies, he told her that it was nearly four o'clock.

Arlette jumped up as if she were about to be late for the most important event of her life – whatever that might prove to be, for she thought it had not happened yet – and ran into the bathroom to take a shower and repair her makeup.

She smiled tenderly as he emerged from the shower, drying that tall lean body and kissing her shoulder.

'Someday, Arlette, you and I will be married. The movies are your real métier. I have seven in mind—'

The softness did not leave her face, the gratitude evoked by the pleasure of knowing he gave her himself, that he had approached her with need and generosity.

She walked back to the bedroom.

They would be married? Charles Granville and Arlette Morgan? Did he imagine a combination such as the De Forests – success, love as it had once existed on her part and still did on his – could ever be broken? It had survived real dangers, though no doubt Granville regarded himself as a more real danger than Deborah Crane.

'What gave you such an idea?'

'Your acting,' Granville told her, with an air of such honest sobriety that she laughed aloud.

In one minute she was dressed and they were walking down the hallway to the projection room. 'That – and everything else,' he added.

Sir Charles was busy with the projection machine, and the table had been set for them to one side, teapot steaming, a little bouquet of pink roses at each place. Arlette took a chair in front of him.

The film began to run, showing several feet of black spaces as he swore softly, then stopped it. He worked a minute or two and the machine was whirring again, the sound had begun to crackle, preparatory to the music and the soft voices of Clym and Eustacia.

'Maybe even love,' he muttered. 'If I had any idea what the bloody word means – there! Watch! Here it is—'

The scene passed. Nothing seemed to have changed, yet Arlette's nipples were no longer visible. He shut the machine off.

'Satisfied?'

'Thank you.'

CHAPTER 69

Belinda survived the fall and was photographed in Central Park early one morning, looking fit and impertinent, as if she relished the trouble she had caused, with Arlette standing beside her stroking her mane and smiling, but warily alert lest Belinda take her revenge by lifting one delicate hoof and stamping it upon her foot.

On the last night she did not see Deborah after the final curtain.

She had told Edna Frazier, who had come to see her perform this favorite part one last time, to let her know when the cast had left.

'Everyone's gone,' Edna told her. 'Miss Crane last – she still had her makeup on, and she was crying.' Edna looked puzzled.

Arlette picked up the little goddess Kuan-Yin and put it in her handbag. Another curiosity: the jade goddess. put out every night and returned to her handbag at the end of each performance. The strand of pearls – worn only on first nights or the first day of filming. They were eternal mysteries – perhaps the real secret of her employer's talent, Edna sometimes thought.

Arlette understood that Deborah was crying because she knew that her chance for other parts with Jerry Hoffman or any producer of comparable prestige had been destroyed by some uncanny process she could not define.

Now it was over. The damage had been done. And once Arlette knew she had – in a quite real sense – murdered another woman, that no one could point with any certainty to the weapon, only the victim's dead reputation, she felt not entirely triumphant. Yet she did not feel sorry.

She looked at herself carefully, unconcerned by Edna's presence, and Edna was too discreet to watch her employer studying herself in a mirror.

Would I do it again? Arlette asked the Arlette who gazed seriously back at her: *You bloody well would, and you know it. She spoiled the best thing you ever had.*

'I'm ready, Edna. I'll drive you home.'

Late in the summer, Eva French married Mr Ameritex International in a pretty ceremony in Arlette and Anthony's garden.

The garden was copied from one she and Anthony had seen in Venice. The back of the house, too, was embraced by a densely growing wisteria, old and unruly, twined about the ornate black iron balustrade of the second-floor balcony, where today three violinists played. In one corner stood a Chinese cassia tree, with lighted candles attached to its branches for the festive occasion.

Eva looked remarkably fragile, in a pale yellow silk dress, carrying a little bouquet of yellow roses, and she had promised Arlette that this time she would be happy; she had what she had always wanted. She did not say just what it was.

Arlette kissed her tenderly and agreed that she would always be happy; but Minerva, accompanied by Andrew Thyssen, was not so optimistic.

'Why does she keep marrying civilians?' Minerva asked Arlette.

Thyssen would marry Minerva when he could discover a means of getting rid of his second wife without losing her share of her father's motion-picture company. So long as he remained married to Thea Barlow, he owned the company. But if he divorced Thea – there went Andrew Thyssen. Minerva was prepared to wait, for it seemed she loved him; and Minerva, like Arlette, refused to contemplate the possibility of not having one day what she most wanted.

Here were their friends – hand-picked, in a sense; fate-picked, in a truer sense.

Arlette felt the wedding as a surprisingly tender experience.

The garden was beautiful; the people were beautiful; she had made the arrangements for her friend herself. Watching these people of her world, Arlette had again and again the sense, which struck her with an uncanny chill, that all their lies were fragments of an unending play.

She had spent her life, it seemed, playing such scenes. And every relationship she had ever had, every love or suspicion, the few hates, the pleasures and fears, were parts of this lifelong performance.

Arlette was sometimes troubled by the envy aroused by the good fortune of the De Forests, for she yearned for a warm and trustworthy world – even while she did not believe such a world existed.

Yet none of this troubled Anthony. He had no need of a warm and trustworthy world, perhaps from his long habit of reading history, all periods of time, all nations, all rulers and politicians.

'*It's better to be envied than pitied,*' he assured her.

'Charles II.'

They were still whimsically competitive. But when outsiders tried to pry a wedge between them, to find some opening through which to slip a poisoned note or purloined handkerchief, they found the fortress impregnable.

And so would Nicola Tash, Anthony's next leading lady, the movie actress, lately becoming a star, who would play Nelly Flowers, gangster's wife and nightclub singer, to Anthony's Mike Chance, private-eye, CIA informer, hired assassin. This was Andrew Thyssen's bitter mixture for a movie to be called: *If I Should Die Before You Wake*. He meant to fashion a film which would prove eerily fascinating, as beautiful, he promised Arlette, as one of the cruel flowers she painted.

And, for once, Anthony would be a modern man in a modern world – tragic and comic, as the classic roles were not.

'It's Thyssen's theory,' he explained, 'that this guy is not a psychopath, he's entirely rational, aware of his one-man stand against the world. He's the post-hedonist. He's the symptom of a slow but final earthquake.' Anthony smiled sagely. 'Anyway, I can't go through my professional life waving broadswords and rapiers. There are other ways to kill a man. That's what tragedy is about, isn't it?'

'Blood,' said Arlette. 'Lots of good red blood. It should be sensational.'

She was smiling, and Anthony could read Arlette's one hundred smiles.

Anthony, who did not like her disapproval – and never asked for anyone's approval – looked at her with slight hostility. 'There's lots of good red blood in every fucking classic tragedy either of us has ever played. This movie will become, in Thyssen's hands, a classic of its genre.'

Before he left, promising to come back on weekends when he could, Anthony said: 'I love you.' He had said it frequently the last few days, evidently thinking to shame her into repeating the words. She promised herself that next time she would, but when he left her with a farewell salute at the airport, she had nothing to say:

No. We don't trust each other.

From time to time, restless during the winter and spring months, she drove to Montauk with Edna. She liked Edna's casual undemanding companionship, and she thought Edna needed the feeling that Miss Morgan needed her, to take dictation, make telephone calls, or read cues when she memorized a script.

Arlette drove the Mercedes, and if she was silent most of the time, or listened indifferently to a cassette, Edna was silent, too. There was no need to entertain Edna, and Arlette felt she could not summon the vitality ever again to present the Arlette Morgan she had created, part Lily Malone, part the Arlette Morgan who had wanted to become a star, part the Arlette Morgan who *was* a star.

It was gone, mysteriously vaporized – that treasure of energy. But she must, somehow, pretend to have it. Not one must guess what had happened, whatever it might be.

'I'll memorize the script Saturday and Sunday. Then I may feel a little better about it,' was all she could find by way of explanation. 'Something is wrong.'

There. It was true. But Edna would not imagine what was wrong, and would not ask. She would think it was something wrong with Marguerite Gautier, not something wrong with Arlette Morgan.

Edna went to examine the refrigerator, to see what Margaret Webb had brought over at Edna's telephone announcement, while Arlette went upstairs to the bedroom, where she dialed John Powell's office number.

'John?' she asked in a light timid voice, wondering who talked that way. Not Arlette. No one she knew.

John's voice was anxious and unhappy, knowing before she said it what she had to tell him. 'Are you all right?'

'I'm not coming tonight, John.' Nothing defiant, only an apologetic but irrefutable statement. 'I'm at Montauk – with Edna.'

There was a long pause. 'All right.' He was silent again. 'I'm sorry.' That was John: she was in the wrong, and he was sorry.

All at once, for no reason she could find, she had demolished the sense of conquest and pride she had given him with her sighs and incoherent murmurs.

'I'll call when I get back, John. In two or three days. Don't be disappointed. Please. Good night.'

She looked at the floor, wondering what condition she had left that particular magical bouquet in. But if it had been damaged a little, it could easily be repaired.

She sat on the bed, kicked off the black pumps, drew up her knees, and looked out into the black night over the ocean. A few stars shone, but the night was misty.

She sat motionless, stunned into a blank thoughtless despair, forgetting Edna was waiting for her. She hunched her knees closer, seeking comfort and loss of herself, that self which did not forget itself, even asleep; the self which tried to merge with another self.

She jumped up, looked into the mirror, wondering how much she had changed since that last sickness of doubt, long ago, when she had been young. Yet she looked young still, that thirty-seven-year-old Arlette, gazing questioningly back at her.

The past, the accumulated moments and hours of her life, falling softly around her, sifting through the air, increased her sense of bewilderment. For a moment she looked at herself seriously, trying to remember where she was.

Montauk:

The haunted house.

And a good place to be at that moment. But there was someone else?

She started to pass the mirror and stopped, confused to see a face of such sad seriousness:

Now what ails you, exactly? Tell me your story. No, don't bother. I have nothing to give to the lifelorn. Nothing at all.

She started slowly down the staircase. 'Edna, I'll be right down – the call took longer than I expected.'

She went back and stood before the mirror again, for the mirror had a faculty for extending time:

The best thing for a woman to be able to say about her life is that the men I've loved have loved me. And they have, they have. They still do. Anthony, too.

She went down the staircase and arrived smiling in the

kitchen, clasping her hands at the sight of the table set in Margaret Webb's abundant style: a salad of spinach and mushrooms; Brie and Camembert; strawberries; a small cold roast chicken; and a pot of tea Edna had brewed while Arlette was upstairs, mulling over her life.

But Edna could have discovered no trace of that disturbance now, as they sat, Arlette chatting merrily about the salt sea air, their plans for riding or walking tomorrow.

As Edna set out for the guesthouse, where she spent so much time that she kept a wardrobe there, Arlette was saying: 'We'll begin at two. I want to read the script in the morning – and I'll die if I don't ride for at least an hour.'

Michael called two days later, while she and Edna sat in the living room, Edna reading cues, Arlette closing her eyes to visualize the words on the page.

'Lily!' he shouted joyously.

'Michael, where are you?'

'I'll be in New York on Tuesday. Can I bring—'

'I can't understand you!'

'We're flying back – Benoni, the guy you asked me about. Dinner – Tuesday – maybe at your house? They're calling the plane—'

Arlette hung up and went back to the living room. 'My brother,' she said, and had composed her face. Just an ordinary family call.

Micah Benoni.

The man who had read pages of hieroglyphics all across the ocean. What did he look like?

He looked like an Egyptian pharaoh: tall, narrow, with a narrow high-bridged nose, a narrow ascetic face, a finely modeled sensual mouth, and eyes that turned from gray to green as the sunlight struck them. He looked remote and wisely humorous, ferociously proud, intimidatingly serious. Why not? He knew the world's secrets. Anyone who had written *Thermodynamic Stability of Relativistic Stellar Clusters* knew the secrets of the world, and more:

I have a few questions for him.

She went back to trying to remember what Marguerite Gautier had to say to General Duval when he came to ask her to leave his son alone so that his daughter could marry into a respectable family.

'That's the way they looked at things in those days,' said Arlette philosophically, for she had not been able to take Marguerite's problems with any proper seriousness.

She closed her eyes, pretending to concentrate on the lines, and saw instead the sudden green which shone in Micah Benoni's eyes when the plane banked.

'*General Duval, please believe that I would not hurt your daughter's chances for a respectable marriage.*'

She looked at Edna, who nodded to indicate the reading was correct.

'But of course she would. Lennox has got to find a way to make that clearly ironic. There has to be something left unexplained in this woman or she's not worth playing again.'

Edna underlined the offending passage, and they went on:

Micah Benoni.
Micah . . . Benoni . . .

CHAPTER 70

Two hours before the dinner party for her brother and Dr Benoni, Arlette found herself apprehensive at the prospect of entertaining this distinguished man, and forgot that for every thousand who had heard of Micah Benoni, millions had heard of Arlette Morgan.

The awe he inspired, she supposed, was because he came from another world and knew secrets such as Michael knew; or their opposite. Dr Malone and Dr Benoni examined two mutually exclusive yet possibly identical worlds.

Stored somewhere in that man's finely shaped head, if once she found the right questions to ask, was the answer to that one innermost secret she had hoped all her life to learn:

Whatever it may be, I'll recognize it when he tells me.

First I'll ask him – where does the beginning end and the end begin?

There may be quite a simple answer, if you have the equipment to calculate it.

Arlette was usually a carefree hostess, who left all arrangements to Edna Frazier, Irma and Conrad, and the gardener. The gardener supplied flowers from the greenhouse, and Edna kept fresh bouquets throughout the house, having learned long ago what flowers Arlette wanted and how they were to be arranged – as if they had not been arranged at all.

The menu was planned by Irma, the wines by Conrad and Edna – who had become a connoisseur of Anthony's cellar, installed to provide a proper environment for the precious wines Eugene Cartwright bought and catalogued, which Anthony and Arlette infrequently drank.

She strolled about the little drawing room, wondering how her house would look to Dr Benoni; or perhaps Dr Benoni was the kind of scientist whose mind was fixed upon such distant planets he did not notice his own.

Michael, who had come in while Arlette was at her class with Alicia, was sleeping, and Dr Benoni, Edna told her, would arrive at eight o'clock.

The dining-room doors were closed, and Arlette found Conrad setting the table and Edna putting place cards around. She watched them, clasping her hands admiringly at the arrangement of vermeil plates and candlesticks, heavy crystal goblets, gold and jade wine bowls, and yellow speckled lilies. Giving them a little signal of approval, she ran out and went dashing upstairs to dress, something very special for this special night:

How lucky that Anthony's with Thyssen.

She paused. *Why? This has nothing to do with Anthony. Nothing to do with Deborah's Voice, either.*

But the sound will be in my ears forever.

Deborah had made a recovery of sorts from the mauling

Mary Stuart had given her every night for five months. She had abandoned her ambition to be a classical actress and had decided to make practical use of the plastic surgery, the capped teeth, the dyed hair, the whitened skin, the green lenses, in more films and on television.

And so Deborah Crane departed from their lives, and only Arlette knew how much this timid, inconsequential young woman had taken:

My life, as it once was.

Which of us is guilty, Anthony?

She longed to tell him that carrying a grudge was a heavy burden in itself, and, she would be glad to set it down once and for all – if she could find a way to do it without losing her balance.

Even so, he completed her life.

It was because of Anthony that she was surprised, and apprehensive, about her interest in Dr Benoni. What was he expected to give her?

She knew people enough, had friends enough, admirers enough, magic helpers enough – she did not want or need anyone else in her life.

Then why was she frightened at the prospect of admitting a newcomer, an outsider, to that closed world?

Dressed for dinner, that hour-and-a-half-long project – during which she memorized lines, reflected on her former lives, trained different voice inflections, and above all, studied Arlette Morgan, criticizing her ruthlessly, lest some flaw slip by unnoticed, go uncorrected two days or two months, and finally become uncorrectable – she looked at the finished Arlette, trying to imagine what Dr Benoni would see.

She wore black chiffon pajamas, finely pleated. The neckline of the hip-length coat circled her throat with a double ruffle, and was fastened there with one button, so that what could be seen of Arlette's upper body depended upon how Arlette sat and moved and walked. She thought of clothes as she thought of costumes: something to manipulate and control. She looked like a woman bent on conquest.

But this had nothing to do, one way or the other, with Dr Micah Benoni, student of hieroglyphs and galaxies.

She had heard the doorbell ring twice, and as she smiled confidingly at the Arlette setting out to meet this man whose studies she had interrupted with her tale of having lived in China hundreds of years ago, she was still not sure if their meeting was coincidence, arranged by the meddlesome fates – or was it a coincidence arranged by Arlette Morgan?

She decided there was an honest fatalism in the meeting, since she would never have asked Michael to introduce her to Dr Benoni, nor ever noticed his photograph, had they not been seated, by computerized coincidence, side by side on the plane from London.

She paused in the upstairs hallway and listened to the voices: Michael and Alicia Fiedler; Eva and her new husband. No other voice.

The famous man had not arrived.

So much the better:

It's only because I've been thinking about him. If you think about something long enough, it begins to seem important – whether it is or not.

She went down and entered the drawing room with her typical quietness, appearing as if an apparition had materialized. Michael came to kiss her.

Micah Benoni was the last guest to arrive, at exactly two minutes after eight, and Arlette and Michael went to greet him.

The others were talking in the drawing room: Eva and Walter; Jeffrey Brooke and his fifth wife, Malvina, a widow who had inherited more money than Jeffrey had ever made, a woman about forty years old, intimidatingly chic, with a manner of tolerant amusement at these actors.

The other two guests were Mr and Mrs Brian O'Neil – once Della Dorne, a fact no one mentioned nowadays and which perhaps few remembered, who had taught Arlette to take off her clothes, discreetly and provocatively, in fifty seconds. That seemed to have happened in another country, another dimension of time. Yet during those years Della Dorne had disappeared and in Della's place was Rhoda O'Neil, a confident, humorous woman, admired even by the most serious members of her profession.

Michael introduced her to the scientist. 'My sister, Mrs De Forest. Dr Benoni.'

Arlette looked directly into Micah Benoni's eyes, found them gray as the ocean at Montauk on a winter day, and then he smiled, shaking her hand. 'Hello. We've met before.'

'I remember.'

She glanced at Michael, whose expression asked: *Then why the hell did you need me to introduce you?*

'In China,' Arlette agreed. 'Twelve hundred years ago. I was Yang Kuei-fei. And you—'

'I'm not sure.' He nodded, still polite, but putting a little distance between them: the Emperor, or the Tartar rebel? Perhaps neither choice pleased him. After all, the astronomers of ancient China had been highly esteemed.

This meeting, she decided as she introduced him, meant something different to each of them.

Had he come out of curiosity? Out of politeness to a colleague? To amuse himself in a new environment?

She sat at one end of the dinner table, with Dr Benoni at her right and Brian O'Neil at her left: Brian O'Neil was a self-sufficient man who would not expect the hostess to pet him. Michael sat at the opposite end, and there were enough people, enough coming and going with the serving courses, enough conversation on the current political troubles – a subject Arlette regarded as eminently suitable for table conversation, since everyone imagined he was discussing something important and became animated and wise – so there was little danger of angry clashes disturbing the general enjoyment.

They talked of the current war, of various political stupidities, and about the fall season. Soon they reached the subject of Arlette's *Lady of the Camellias* and Anthony's *Coriolanus*, whereupon Arlette casually described their schedule: Hollywood and Paris and the French country-side for her; London for Anthony.

She glanced at Micah Benoni to see whether he had recorded that information, covering the next thirteen months of her life, and guessed that he had – if only because he recorded all information, processed and retained it, or filed and discarded it.

Dr Benoni talked to Malvina Brooke, who had all at once displayed a new and serious nature, questioning him about China. Malvina, thought Arlette, was not so amused and ironic with Michael Malone and Dr Benoni as she was with her husband's theatrical friends, and so she let her monopolize him until he made the effort to free himself.

Malvina was interested in Dr Benoni – or was she interested in his experience in China? Arlette could not guess, for she thought of Malvina as cold and treacherous. A woman who had never worked was not a woman she trusted. 'A painted ship upon a painted ocean,' was Arlette's opinion of the Malvinas of the world.

Two or three times, in the midst of talking to Brian O'Neil about his and Rhoda's projected trip to India, Arlette glanced sideways and found Micah Benoni looking at her, although he seemed intent upon absorbing Malvina's reaction to the Cultural Revolution.

All at once conversation shifted and Malvina was forced to let go. He smiled at her, as if to say that was enough about China, and turned to Arlette.

'And so here we are—' She heard his voice with a wondering pleasure, admiring the easiness of tone, the pitch, low and warm, caressing as an actor's. 'And you're about to undergo another transformation – Marguerite Gautier.' He smiled. 'You like the idea?'

'By no means. But they thought I should do a romantic part. One part to make people sad and nostalgic without any idea why. Who is there but Marguerite?'

'They?'

'My advisers.'

There was more curiosity and admiration in the smile

than humor. There was, she saw, no humor at all. Yes, this was a formidably serious man. He was serious even when he was entertaining himself. 'You have many advisers?'

'Oh, yes, I have advisers of every kind: my agent, my lawyers, my accountant.' She spread her right hand, holding it toward him and ticking off the advisers upon one finger and another. 'My producers, my directors. My acting coach, Mrs Fiedler, talking to Michael. My secretary. My financial adviser — my husband's, really. My publicity director, who is opposed to publicity. My fellow members of the Hoffman-Repertory. My best friends — Eva French and Minerva Grey. My former drama professor, who got me interested in acting in the first place. And — my husband. That is my world.'

'I see. And you listen to all of them?' He was beginning to participate in the game. 'You follow their advice?'

'I listen.' Arlette paused and glanced at him quickly, taking him by surprise, for now he seemed disturbed by the face so near, inviting, lightly challenging, promising, revoking promises. She was preoccupied with trying to imagine how he made love, reflecting on her old superstition of sexual experience as prophecy. 'Either I follow their advice or they tell me what I've been thinking anyway.'

He laughed. 'Yes. That's it. I've seen you in three plays. You are a very great actress. At this moment, too.'

'Now? Oh, no. But which plays?' Arlette could not believe a man enraptured by stars of another order should have found time to see three of her plays.

'*Hedda Gabler. Macbeth. Mary of Scots.*'

He had seen her so recently? He had recognized her on the plane and wanted to see her act again?

'Thank you. I'm a little surprised.'

'No one else performs as you do. And no one performs that way at all without having made the decision quite alone. Not in your theater. Not in Michael's. Not in mine.'

She looked away, through the doors into the garden,

still vaguely light, the candle flames quivering on the cassia tree. 'No. That's true. Any hard profession must be loved or let alone.'

'There's a question I'd like to ask, if I may.'

'Of course.' It had been Arlette's intention to ask the questions, and few people found courage to question her nowadays. 'Tell me the essential qualities for an actor. Forgive my naïveté. But it's an unknown world to me.'

'And to me. But since there are actors who could not be anything else, then, yes, they must have qualities not so useful in other kinds of work. For me, I suppose it's freedom, spontaneity, fearlessness – in spite of the terror.' She smiled confidingly. 'And technique – of course.'

'Of course.'

She nodded. 'Like love.'

CHAPTER 71

The white camellias, in a wicker basket, were brought in by Edna as Arlette sat drinking tea in the greenhouse, waiting for Michael to finish a telephone call from Maura, whom he had married after his divorce three years ago – his research assistant and a profoundly serious young woman, quite Michael's type, Arlette thought.

'Miss Morgan, look!' Edna stood in the doorway, holding the basket in both hands. 'They just arrived—'

Arlette bent over them, taking care not to touch the transparent petals. 'Oh, they're beautiful, beautiful— Who sent them?'

She knew, but asked for politeness' sake.

'The card's there—' The envelope was fastened by a silver thread to the basket's handle, and Arlette untied it, glancing at the card only read the sender's name.

'There must be exactly one hundred, don't you think so?' Edna loved flowers, and the miracle of one hundred camellias delivered before breakfast made her eyes shine. Undoubtedly, no one had ever sent Edna Frazier one hundred white camellias before breakfast, or any other time. But neither had anyone sent such a gift to Arlette. 'Shall I count them?'

Arlette smiled. 'There might be only ninety-seven – and then where would we be? The florist – or the professor? Let's assume there are one hundred. Why not put them in the living room – on the table next to the window? Be sure to pull the curtains – and check the water—' So many instructions, all for the sake of postponing reading the card:

'. . . *quelque chose d'ardent et triste, quelque chose d'un peu vague, laissant carrière à la conjecture*—' Thank you. *Micah Benoni*.

Arlette studied the card, searching out clues from this quotation she recognized. He was born in France? He had lived there? Or had he merely a good memory, too?

He had told her he was an American citizen, but had not been born in this country; then the conversation had changed.

Michael came in and Arlette slipped the card inside its envelope.

'Maura had some questions about an experiment. Edna showed me the camellias—' Michael smiled. 'He liked you. Well, now you've met your astrophysicist – or met him again, it seems—'

'But why camellias?'

Conrad came to serve breakfast, and as they began to eat Michael laughed, seeing the innocent question on his sister's face.

'You were talking about Marguerite as if you'd sold your soul for an unsuitable price. Give her those qualities of your own, I suppose that's what he's telling you.'

'But it's a silly story – an affair between a gigolo *manqué* and an illiterate girl who dies.' Arlette was still gloomy over the prospect of becoming Marguerite Gautier.

'Don't reduce a part like that, Arlette. You might as well throw a violet into a crucible.'

'Oh, but I always do it. I begin by distrusting those women I play – and end by turning into them.'

Michael stood up. 'I've got to go. Benoni will be pacing up and down in front of the Plaza. He's an impatient guy who counts time by an atomic clock. I think there's just one thing that scares him – boredom. A few spare minutes where he can't begin to figure the distance from here to eternity. The secret of genius may be only an overwhelming fear of boredom. Combined, of course, with a lively thinking apparatus.'

'Like yours.'

They ran up the stairs and Michael stood in front of the mirror, knotting his tie. 'Me?'

Michael laughed, that joyous laugh, as if nothing had ever terrified him. Such a laugh could come only from an honest belief in life, an affirmation of the working of their weird natural universe, a drifting scrap of which housed them and their kind: the three-year difference in their ages, that explained it.

The shock had struck her full in the heart, across the throat, like the blow of a fist. Michael's advantage of having been born three years later had protected him.

She had tried many times to remember what she had been doing at the moment when their parents' world ended:

Five years old. Four o'clock in the afternoon.

She and Michael might have been playing with other children in the neighborhood. They might have been called indoors to have a midafternoon celebration of milk and graham crackers. She might have been asleep, the afternoon nap. She had never solved the puzzle.

'Genius,' she repeated skeptically. 'But is there such a thing?'

'Maybe the capacity to sift experience and learning so that it's accessible when you need it. That's why a guy like Benoni is believed, by a lot of his colleagues, to be a genius in his field. He studies a problem, for God knows how long, eons, light-years – then all at once he pounces.' Michael made a swift gesture of reaching out and retrieving some object from midair. 'When he does, he's either right – or he sets himself and the rest of them thinking along different lines. He's something of a maverick – he wants to know everything about everything, all across the board. That's why he's pacing up and down at this minute wondering where in hell is that son of a bitch Malone—'

Is that what he's thinking about?

There was not much time left. In one minute and a half, at the rate he was moving, Michael would be out the door.

'Have you ever met his wife?' He had not mentioned a wife, but she took for granted that he had one. Greatly preoccupied men were often too distracted by work to think of getting divorced. Their wives became part of the household furniture.

'Once. What's she like? She's a nice-looking woman, I guess. Her name's Reba,' he added, for whatever use that might be. 'Rebeccah.'

Michael took his jacket from the closet but did not put it on. The day was hot and promised to get hotter. He started out and Arlette ran beside him.

'He has children?'

'Three. Two boys and a girl. The girl's supposed to be something of a musical prodigy – piano. So was he, once, someone said. Sorry, darling – I've got to go. Send me your questionnaire; I'll do my best to fill it out.'

He kissed her, ran out, and got into the car.

Arlette waved as the car moved off, and went back to sniff carefully at the camellias, as if even a deep breath might demolish them:

Reba. A typical faculty wife.

Another little Mrs Donahue?

She went to get the card, although where she could put it for safekeeping she was not able to imagine. Certainly not in the secret drawer with the sealed envelopes. That drawer was filled with bad intent, black magic, whether it had worked or not, and she was afraid the effluvia might contaminate this message of admiration.

She solved the problem temporarily by slipping it into the handbag which would see her through the day. She looked into the mirror:

Reba Benoni. She shrugged: *A creatura superflua.*

That disposed of his wife, his three children, including the prodigy, whatever her name might be, and indeed the entire content of Micah Benoni's previous emotional and domestic life.

The camellias, like the sun stared at too directly or for too long, left their afterimage.

As they faded and Arlette reluctantly permitted Irma to throw them out, she could still see them, as if a white nimbus, glimmering with pale mysterious light, hovered over the table. For several days she was relieved to find the nimbus still there, if much fainter:

The ghost of a flower has a very short life. We can't expect too much of them.

One day it was gone, and that was the last she ever saw of the hundred camellias.

She told herself she must stop thinking of Micah Benoni and apply herself to the problems of Marguerite Gautier. After all, Marguerite had a serious problem: she was dying at the age of nineteen, and she knew it. Then why did Marguerite's death not seem tragic to her?

Still, she had contrived to discover in Marguerite something she kept secret from Anthony and Alicia. Marguerite had her own secret about herself and the life she lived; the men who paid her, and – Arlette thought – also Armand Duval.

After all, Marguerite admitted she had fallen in love with Armand because he was her only constant visitor while she lay sick, wondering if she would live to be twenty. And Armand was guileless, while she was wise with a wisdom she did not want, a sense of scorn and irony about the way she lived and the men who paid her; even about her own greed for luxury. Marguerite Gautier was a woman of the world, with a perpetual nostalgia for original innocence.

Armand was to be played by a recently popular actor, twenty-nine years old – the first leading man she had played opposite who was younger than she, and he had been selected partly because he had the right appearance for Arlette's Marguerite: he was tall, with dark waving hair, an artless smile, a handsome body trained by a series of roles in Westerns, and he had the bewildered look in his brown eyes of the kind of young man who might idealize a whore – provided she had become a fashionable courtesan.

He was the searcher for lost beauty, lost innocence, lost soul; the lure of what seemed to Arlette the Romantic Age's unhealthy preoccupation with the sickness of young and beautiful women – as if it was the fate they deserved for not having been born ugly.

Anthony returned from making his first modern film, and there were the summer months to spend between Montauk and their studies in the city. Their lives were planned, contracts signed, for two and a half years, and when she left for Los Angeles in early October, spend two months filming the small scenes which could be done on sets, he drove her to the airport, saying: 'This is the last separation. Everything else is going to be done in the same place at the same time.'

Arlette nodded: *He comes and he goes. Then I go. Then I come back. Then he goes. Then I go. And after that—*

'Thyssen's a slow worker,' Anthony warned her. 'Slow and thoughtful, and impossible to satisfy.'

Even so, Thyssen pampered his stars, as Anthony had also said. He proceeded upon some private theory that a star was different from other actors: they were stars.

In all details, minute and large, it was the stars who outwaited, outworked, outthought, outfelt, outmaneuvered, outcharmed the actors who were not and never would become stars.

'Evans is terrified of you,' Thyssen confided when he met Arlette at the airport and ushered her to the limousine, saying his chauffeur would return for her baggage. 'Cross-country flights are worse torture than anything you'll endure the next few months. I'm going to drive you to your house—' Arlette smiled, amused that Thyssen's guesthouse, recently Anthony's house, was now hers.

'And I'll leave you alone for twenty-four hours. Then we'll talk.'

'I'm not tired. Tell me about Evans.'

'You've never seen him?'

'I've seen him. I see every actor I'm going to play with. I see as much as I can sit through.'

'He's scared, poor bastard. A lot of movie actors are very brave when they're with other movie actors. But most of them go to pieces with someone who has played the writers they would never dare try – and there's a lot of Shakespeare in your background.' Thyssen laughed. 'He's even more afraid of Anthony. The love scenes will be difficult for him.'

'It's impossible,' she had told Thyssen during one summer weekend at Montauk, 'for a woman of Marguerite's cynicism to love Armand.'

Remembering their conversation, Arlette thought of Armand's innocence – or was it stupidity? She had told Thyssen, 'It's fantasy, on both sides. He sees her beauty and desirability to other men. And don't forget that for a healthy young man to love a girl who knows she will soon die requires at the least a peculiar disposition.' Arlette had smiled mockingly. 'No, this Armand is really nothing – nothing.' She gave the famous gesture, palm upward, a brief gentle flinging away of some offending object.

'Arlette, listen to me. I would not have undertaken this picture without you. You can make it seem tragic.'

'Arlette,' Anthony had said, 'could make *Little Bo Peep* seem tragic.'

'I'll try. Just so we never forget that this is not a movie about love. It's about money.' She quoted Prudence's caution to Armand: ' "*By the side of the ideal life is the material life.*" That's the way I'll play it. But I'll make her as charming and pathetic as possible. That's the best I can do for Marguerite Gautier.'

Arlette had sat through five of Grant Evans' movies in a projection room, enduring it as she did the waltz lessons, costume fittings, wig fittings, piano lessons, French lessons.

Grant Evans had starred in two Westerns, which Thyssen called 'palship' films; he had also played a morose, dreamy-eyed psychotic killer of beautiful women; and he had been most successful as a wanderer through the American wastelands, full of hatred and lust for the most unlikely females, searching and hiding, afraid of being sent to war, and killing himself finally to escape the fear which had grown unbearable.

This last had been considered a terrifying parable on the condition of American society at somewhat past midday of the century, and he had been nominated for an Oscar.

Now this brash young man, as he was described by his interviewers, was about to encounter his first formidable opponent; he was to waltz with her, kiss her, make love to her in the wild scenes which were the best explanation Jim Lennox, in his script taken from Dumas' novel, could find for an otherwise unlikely love affair. 'Maybe some people fit together better than others,' he had suggested one day at Montauk.

'Maybe?' Arlette had inquired.

'Maybe?' Minerva had repeated, giving her the dark mocking gypsy smile which she was preparing for a new production of *Blood Wedding*.

CHAPTER 72

'Trust me,' Thyssen reminded her before they began the scene of Marguerite in her transparent nightgown kneeling before her lover, the old Duke. 'This scene is important. It won't demean you.'

Lennox continued to demand an explanation of his own script. 'Is he impotent?'

Thyssen shrugged. 'She looks like his daughter. We've made that explicit. This is played as a stylized routine between them. Many people prefer their fantasies to real life. Real life is a risky business. Arlette will know how to look at him.'

'I know.'

So far as Arlette was concerned, whether or not Lennox knew it, he had defined Marguerite's character in that one scene with the old Duke, seated on a stool, Marguerite kneeling before him, looking up questioningly, knowingly, before she obediently bowed her head:

She feels nothing. She acts everything. Her great romance with Armand is as phony as this scene.

Thyssen had explained at the beginning why he had picked Grant Evans. 'He's one of the few film actors who's quite evidently masculine, in spite of that dreamy look he can turn off and on – and that will make it understandable that a woman of Marguerite's cynicism could believe she's found a man able to love her. And she's wise enough, and ill enough, and despondent enough to know that no man with any character would love her - but for the old Duke. And he loves his dead daughter. That's why those two scenes with the Duke are of such importance. When Armand falls in love with her, she knows that his adoration, absurd as it may seem, is for Marguerite Gautier.'

The 'royally beautiful' courtesan, publicly calm, proud, earned her diamonds, her fine house and furniture, by performing the role of a dead girl – the Duke's daughter.

The filming proceeded for several weeks, and unless Arlette looked at the calendar, she often forgot what day it was, how long she had been there.

'It's the face, of course,' Thyssen told her. 'That incredibly beautiful face, which gets more beautiful all the time. Why?'

He was tender and considerate with her, even talking to her sometimes in his restrained way about Minerva. She had called him last night, after the first performance of *Blood Wedding*, which they would see on their way to Paris, where the outdoor scenes, scenes at the opera and in the little village in the Midi – a substitute for Bougival – and the little burial ground would be filmed.

She and Thyssen were seated side by side while the technicians worked with lights and Grant Evans brooded in a remote situation, trying to think of something to cry about once the lights were adjusted.

'Look at poor Evans,' said Thyssen whimsically. 'He's been dreading this scene ever since he read the script.'

What had happened to Marguerite Gautier during those several weeks?

She had lived quite a full life, splintered into bits and pieces, as was the way of the lives of movie characters.

In a variety of magnificent gowns, intricate hairstyles, diamonds and pearls and rubies, she stepped from her coach and smiled at the young Count – her other most reliable source of income.

Marguerite had gone to the opera with her neighbor, the retired whore, Prudence. Long shots of these scenes would be filmed in Paris. In the meantime, the old Duke was entering the opera box at the end of the performance, stolid and dignified, with nothing on his mind but the care of this charming and very sick young woman. Marguerite smiled at him, glanced at Prudence, and walked out; similar scenes were repeated in a variety of costumes, although each scene would last a few seconds.

Armand and his friend Gaston had discussed the beautiful young woman who had disappeared for a year at the height of her glory and reappeared in the company of the old Duke. There were rumors of his daughter's death, of Marguerite's uncanny resemblance to the girl, and Armand, at least, was willing to believe that anyone as old as the Duke could have only a paternal sense of pity for this beautiful but doomed young girl.

Doomed by what?

That was not mentioned. 'This is not,' Arlette had insisted, 'about Louis Pasteur. It's about an expensive whore.'

There was a scene with Marguerite in a mauve taffeta evening gown, leaning across an outdoor balcony, a young man on either side, one of them talking to her urgently, while she ignored him and smiled, gazing abstractedly into space, not seeing Armand, who was watching her from across the street in the shadows of heavily leafed trees.

Armand in the shadows was a scene for Paris; but here Marguerite, slowly stripping the petals, one at a time, from her bouquet of camellias, would be used behind the credits, the petals falling faster and thicker as Marguerite, indifferent to the young man's pleading, picked clean her bouquet, while the petals turned into a snowstorm and fell not into the street, but upon a fresh mound in the burial ground, forming a blanket of camellias, beside which Armand knelt, his head bowed.

The scene took two days to film, because one or the other of the young men either forgot to look urgent, caught his coattails in the ornate railing, coughed, or committed some other sin which had Thyssen ready to dismiss them and call in two other nonentities.

'Give them a chance. They're nervous.'

It was Arlette's reputation, not lost even during her encounters with Elizabeth I, that she was one of the few stars who did not try to steal every scene – who helped young actors. That reputation was a valuable asset, a part of her doctrine of the infallibility of Arlette Morgan.

Again and again Thyssen returned to the single frame of Marguerite's face alone: vixenish as she talked to Prudence, calling her ugly names in French, demanding the immediate return of the jewels she had loaned her to wear to the opera. Another close-up showed Marguerite greedily counting the Duke's money after he had left. Another celebrated her mocking laugh, walking past Armand at the opera, saying: 'You're a child.'

Neither Thyssen nor Lennox wanted this *Lady of the Camellias* to be mistaken for a fragile flower, trampled ruthlessly by the feet of cruel men.

The flower was cruel itself, contemptuous of the passions she inspired, greed for the luxuries she had never expected to own. She had no code of ethics. She had only a sentimental affection for the Marguerite Gautier, who was doomed to die young and knew it – and it was out of this sentimental self-adoration that Arlette must contrive the sense of tragedy which would shake the audience in spite of itself.

There were close-ups of the old Duke's cold impassive public face; of his shamed, guilty, anguished private face, as greedy for his pleasures as Marguerite was for his money.

There were close-ups of Armand's face against sets of Paris, fragments which would be spliced in among full shots: Armand following Marguerite, who ignored him, recklessly gay once she had recovered enough to receive those admirers who kept her in a style which became her better than any of the other *demimondaines* of the moment.

And what had Marguerite to think of but moments?

'If this has a tragic core,' Thyssen told them, 'then it must be the appeal to the knowledge – so cowardly hidden in each of us – that we are mortal. Marguerite accepts her mortality. That gives her a dimension she does not have otherwise. That's the essence of Lennox's script, and that, my dear, is what you're playing.'

'There's no other way to play it. Whores are not, by tradition, tragic. It takes a great deal of superstructure to create that illusion.'

Lennox was offended. 'Marguerite is not an ordinary whore.'

'I'm trying my best to give that impression, Jim.'

'And you're doing it!' Grant Evans declared loyally, for Arlette had easily taken him into the palm of her hand, coaxed him into quiet acquiescence. She was helping him give a better performance than he knew how to give, and he was aware of it:

At least, he's a grateful amateur.

Little by little they nibbled at the scenes which could be made on indoor sets, corners of rooms, doorways of houses, parts of gardens.

The grand ballroom scene; the sweep of the filled opera house with a performance in progress; driving in the

Bois de Boulogne; the little country inn with its quiet stream and trees; the country house where Marguerite lived, first with the old Duke, then with the affable Armand – those scenes must be filmed in Paris and outside the city.

One day Armand told Marguerite – exquisitely dressed with a complex twist of hair upon the crown of her head and ringlets to her waist, idly twirling her bouquet: '*I love you as no woman was ever loved!*'

As he spoke the lines Arlette glanced at him briefly and savagely, and gave a soft despairing laugh. Abruptly she turned to Thyssen. 'I'm sorry – it was unintentional. But of course she knows better than to believe him. He's never said it before.'

'Perfect! It's – Marguerite!'

Still, it took the rest of the day before Grant Evans, exasperated, flushed, sweating, brought forth his news with sufficient conviction to satisfy Thyssen, while Arlette's despairing laugh never once changed. She had, it seemed, an endless supply of them.

'And there's still,' Grant muttered to Arlette when Thyssen dismissed them, 'that god damned crying scene. How will I do it?' He seemed ready to cry at that moment.

'If you don't – I'll make you cry.'

His kindly protectress. 'You – how?'

'An actor must be able to cry, Grand. Just as he must be able to walk and talk . . .'

All the while she was aware that something was wrong. Something she had expected had not happened.

Each night when Edna came to the studio in Thyssen's limousine and Arlette rode back with her to the guesthouse in Bel Air, hearing Edna's recital of the day's telephone calls, the letters from Alicia and Minerva and Eva, from the O'Neils in India, Arlette listened eagerly, convinced that this would be the day.

Sometimes Edna had dinner with her and went over the next day's lines, when there had been changes; sometimes Arlette let her off at her hotel and had dinner alone. Occasionally she had dinner with Thyssen, whose wife was in Europe and had been for as long as Arlette could remember. But here or abroad, she owned her father's stock; that stock which was Minerva Grey's enemy.

When Edna had completed her recital each night Arlette asked: 'And that's all?'

'That's all.'

Micah Benoni had gone to New Zealand again, perhaps?

To Chile?

To Puerto Rico?

Chasing telescopes about the world was his business. But he had not written one letter.

She had been explicit: he knew she was here alone. He had not failed to write because he had thought it might offend Anthony.

He did not write because – she could think of no *because*. He simply did not write.

Her real expectation, she became aware, was that if she saw him again he would cure her of what she thought of as her sickness of living, come back again after so many years. He knew the final secret core, stored away in each living cell, in every star.

That, of course, was why she had asked Michael to bring him to dinner: to be sure she had not invented him since that first meeting two years before; to sense his possible meaning for her by that intuition she relied upon as he relied upon computers and dish telescopes.

When they had met, just before they had gotten up from the table, she had asked him the question which had preoccupied her: 'I want to know – if you don't mind – what you were reading on the plane.'

He had smiled, and the smile was ironical, but saved by a tenderness of admiration. 'What I was reading two years ago?'

'Surely you remember.'

'Do I?'

They looked at each other carefully, and Arlette grew more uneasy, feeling that he was offering her some challenge she was not accustomed to and did not know how to play.

'I shouldn't have asked,' she told him, ashamed. 'Reading is a private matter, after all.'

'Not mine. Anyone's welcome to it. Let me try to remember.' He was, she knew, delicately mocking, pretending to try to remember. 'Oh, yes.' He looked at her steadily: '*A stranger came to me from a distant land and brought me a single scroll with writing on it. At the top of the scroll was written, "Do not forget." At the bottom was written, "Good-bye forever." *' He raised his eyebrows slightly, to ask if that satisfied her.

Arlette laughed, then turned away, suddenly self-conscious, feeling that he understood her too well.

She has spoken softly to Brian O'Neil, and as they left the table and started toward the garden, she glanced at Micah Benoni again and found him watching her, his face entirely serious, perhaps even a little sorry he had played a game with her.

A warning sounded somewhere, like the faint sound of the glass bells chiming from the cassia tree in the garden:

If I saw you a few times, I might fall in love with you.

CHAPTER 73

Armand returned in despair to his modest shabby quarters, remarkable contrast to Marguerite's lavishly furnished house with its massive mirrors, candles burning in crystal chandeliers, hangings of purple silk against which her white and mauve and yellow gowns shone like flowers in an evening garden, and walls hung with massive paintings – Boucher, Fragonard – at which she never glanced.

But she did not fail to pause before any mirror, as if her beauty surprised and reassured her. Then the expression changed, took on a brooding despair.

These small touches – not in the script, nor in Thyssen's

direction, but in Arlette's increasing empathy with a beautiful young woman who would live not as long as Lily Morgan Malone had – were creating a Marguerite who surprised the cast, the technicians, the designers, her fellow players.

She was becoming a figure of tragic implication, a Marguerite who was a complex creature, mingling whimsical cruelty, detestation of her way of life, vanity, resignation to the knowledge that she would live only a brief time on this earth she loved. She contrived to convey a young girl's yearning for a time before she could have prophesied that first she would spoil her life, and then lose it too early.

Grant Evans followed her in these developments, but did not keep pace with her. Each scene they played together cost Arlette all the energy she had to wring out of him something more than the imitation of acting; she guessed he was still afraid.

Perhaps it was because they had not yet played even one of their love scenes – to which he had frankly told her he was looking forward with dread and excitement. 'I hope I won't be afraid to kiss you – you must promise not to be angry. We're supposed to be wildly in love.'

Arlette laughed as they strolled toward their cars and the end of the day, still in costume. 'We'll be in bed – with nothing on.'

He turned to her with a look of disbelieving joy.

'Thyssen claims to get better results that way. And that's the way Granville directed Eustacia—'

'I was sure he was screwing you – forgive me!'

Arlette laughed:

He really is as simple as Armand.

This Grant Evans, blushing and looking at her with an expression of hungry expectation, was as much in awe of Arlette Morgan, or perhaps of Rosalind and Desdemona and Hedda Gabler and Lady Macbeth, as ever Armand Duval had been in awe of the most famous courtesan of Paris.

'I don't think they were in love, either of them,' Arlette

told him as she stopped beside the car, where Edna Frazier waited with the day's reports.

'But love is the motivation,' Evans protested, as if she might deprive him of the symbol he was depending upon to see him through.

'Money, not love,' said Arlette gently. 'And a few kinds of sex. It's gratitude on her part, for a man who has no more sense than to think he loves her – and awe on his. The most desired whore in Paris finds something special about his penis.' She laughed again. 'It would be a comedy – but for that clever idea about her early death.' She got into the car. 'Go home and think about crying tomorrow.'

'Oh, Jesus!'

Arlette was in good spirits, perhaps because each day she felt herself gaining control, not only over Marguerite, of whom she had so few hopes in the beginning, but of Armand Duval and the other members of the cast.

They drove off, leaving Grant to contemplate tomorrow's great challenge, those tears he must shed in abundance. Meanwhile Edna began her recital with the day's most important events: the reservations were made for her to leave at eight o'clock on Saturday morning to visit Valerie and Frederick. She would fly from there to New York on Sunday afternoon. Michael hoped to be in Los Angeles the day after tomorrow, perhaps with Maura, on their way to a symposium at La Jolla, and Edna had made his hotel arrangements and telegraphed him a copy of Arlette's schedule for the next four days. Dr Micah Benoni had called from Princeton—

'Dr Benoni?' She spoke carefully. 'What did he say?'

They arrived at the portable dressing room, and to keep Edna from noticing her excitement, she ran ahead into the separate partition, followed by the maid, to remove the complicated gown. She came back wearing a thin red cashmere robe with big square pockets, sleeveless and floor length, her new all-purpose robe, as she thought of it. She sat and looked into the mirror as the hairdresser began carefully removing combs, hairpins, braids and coils and ringlets, and watched Marguerite Gautier slowly reversing the morning's transformation.

Edna spoke calmly, and if she was aware of Arlette's excitement, seemed not to be. 'He said that if he remembered correctly you would be in New York from December second to the twenty-first. He will be there for a meeting on the eighteenth, and would like to have you go to dinner.'

She smiled. 'He remembered all that? How remarkable.'

'Dr Benoni is a mathematician.' Edna was polite, reserved, almost as if Arlette had invented her – as perhaps she had, by kindness, a large salary, and a carefully partitioned sharing in the superficial aspects of her life:

Did I tell him all that?

Of course I did. I told him where I would be for the next year. I told him where Anthony would be, too.

She sat silently, until the hairdresser had finished his work, listening to Edna Frazier read newspapers.

'Tell him the eighteenth will be fine. Tell him we'll dine at home – I detest restaurants. He'll understand that, won't he?'

Will he also understand I prefer to be alone with him?

Would she understand it herself? This man who had appeared in her life and disappeared, then appeared again – sent for, it was true, by the chance of Arlette having seen his photograph.

Destiny was at work here: she meant something to Dr Benoni. Dr Benoni meant something to her. A great deal – or very little – they would see about that:

Get your mind on your work, Arlette, she admonished herself, as she sat alone later, reading the next day's schedule at the table in the small dining room of Thyssen's guesthouse.

It was the great day for Grant Evans, perhaps even greater than the days when Armand and Marguerite were to make love – for if he could not cry convincingly, then all the passion he might summon to his love scenes would

584

be inconsequential. Money might be the theme of the story, but love was the bait.

'We might,' Lennox suggested, as Arlette and Lennox and Thyssen sat – Arlette in a yellow taffeta ballgown with another elaborate coiffure – while Grant Evans struggled with his soul and perhaps called upon his deity to send the tears he needed. 'We might shoot another angle – let him cover his face with his hands and sob. If he can sob.'

Thyssen looked vaguely angry, for the scene had been rehearsed for two hours, and not one tear could this Armand summon to his eye. 'The hell we will. The son of a bitch will cry. His other directors have been too easy on him. An Armand who can't cry is no Armand.'

So much for this Armand, if he could not – or would not – do his duty.

After all, this was a serious moment in Armand's life: he had seen Marguerite, who had sent him a note telling him she could not see him that night, enter her house with the young Count, and after waiting until four in the morning had gone home to write her – in a passion of tears – his farewell letter.

'All this,' Arlette remarked to Thyssen, while the lighting was adjusted around Armand who sat, humiliated, his back to them, his fist beating the desk as if he would break it. 'All this for a piece of tail.'

'My dear,' Thyssen gently reminded her. 'You must remember this was the *Romantic Agony*. A piece of tail was idealized into—'

'Yes?'

'Was idealized,' said Thyssen, and gave another direction to his lighting engineer. 'You know quite well, there are times when desire is enough.'

'Enough for pleasure. Not enough for sorrow.'

'But that's not the picture we're making.'

All at once Arlette got up, walked straight to Grant Evans, and dropped to one knee as he looked down at her in horrified astonishment.

'What happened?' he asked, and seemed dazed, lost in some distant place. 'Has he changed his mind? Did I cry?'

She spoke softly, willing him not to glance away, and held his hand until her nails bit into the palms, hard enough to focus his attention.

'Listen to me. Look at me.' He nodded, more or less stupefied by the morning's humiliation. 'Think,' she said, in the tones she had used in Lady Macbeth's sleepwalking scene – the tones of a woman long since dead to the world and to herself: 'Think that one day you will die. Think about it until you believe it. Will you die alone? What will you die from? Will you die loved – or will the world be glad to have you go? Think of that – see yourself – dead—' She rose slowly, continuing to stare down at him, her face somber, sentencing him to the lonely death she had described, leaving him no way to escape it. 'If you really think of that – you'll cry.'

His eyes filled with tears, and Arlette ran out of camera range, as Thyssen signaled the cameras and sound equipment into action.

Armand Duval was crying, his shoulders shaking, one fist pressed to his forehead, and he cried as if, once begun, he would never stop.

At one moment Thyssen glanced at Arlette, standing beside him, her face exultant. She might have been a witch, wild at the sight of a great storm at sea she had conjured.

Thyssen never asked what she had said, and once the day's shooting ended, Arlette ran, before Evans could thank or blame her, and jumped into the car, saying breathlessly to Edna, as if she had been thinking of nothing else all day: 'We'll have billi-bi, my favorite soup. And crown of lamb with Irma's buckwheat dressing. Bibb lettuce. A perfect Brie, with French bread – separate course. Irma's marvelous lemon soufflé with lemon sauce.' Gleefully, happy as a child, Arlette rubbed her palms together. 'The table in the greenhouse. You choose the wines – three.' She laughed. 'Neither of us drinks.'

'Neither you nor Dr Benoni?' Edna inquired tactfully,

since Arlette had said nothing of who this menu was intended to feed.

'Of course. And Edna – the white nephrite plates on the green organdy cloth with the apple-jade bowls for the soup and . . .'

Who was Marguerite Gautier? What was she? No one of interest to Arlette.

PART IV

1968

CHAPTER 74

Conrad gave the car keys to Arlette. She thanked him, without explaining why she wanted the Mercedes at eleven o'clock at night. She got in and handed the keys to Micah. 'Have you been checked out on this?'

'More or less. My daughter drives one.'

They started off, and Arlette was pleased to find he was a good driver, with a mathematician's precision of judgment. There would be little traffic out of town at that time on a Saturday night, and there had been no recent snows or rains, so the road would be fast.

'Only about two hours and a half,' she had said when she suggested they run out to Montauk. 'Just to see it before I go. I'll be gone almost seven months.' What could be more logical? When they would arrive, when they would return, none of that was mentioned. It was his decision, since she intended to leave the choice to him.

While Conrad was gone to bring the car she ran upstairs to get the floor-length sable coat, Anthony's Christmas present of the year before, and saw her face in the mirror gleaming with anticipatory excitement.

She ran down quickly, afraid he might try to escape in her absence.

Montauk, which she had mentioned as if the impulse surprised her, and been spoken of with tender nostalgia: the night was clear and bright, the ocean would be strong, the winds probably heavy. She had made it sound as if Montauk were the cherished home of her youth, her vanished dreams, all her happiest memories.

In a sense, it was. Much had been deposited there from earlier eras.

He was still in the drawing room, bent over to examine a twelfth-century bowl of carved green jade, dragons and lotus leaves writhing around it, flower and imaginary beast locked in perpetual embrace. She had always seen that in the bowl. He, it seemed, saw something else, for he turned as she came in.

'Chinese art is a sorrowful art.'

More or less. My daughter drives one.

She gave him a quick resentful glance.

Now, why did he bring that up? I didn't ask about his daughter.

She had asked Michael, however, when Michael and Maura came to see her at Thyssen's guesthouse. After dinner they talked of the meeting they were to attend, a meeting designed to convince the scientists to set up surveillance over themselves; Maura went to bed early.

All at once, Arlette leaned forward, eyes alight with no scientific curiosity. 'He's asked me to have dinner with him. On the eighteenth.'

'Thyssen?'

Arlette laughed. 'Benoni.' She extended one hand. 'Michael, tell me about him. Where did he come from? What are his children like?'

'I only remember the girl. Her name is Zarah, and she's called Sally.'

'Why did you remember her?'

'I suppose because she seemed quite beautiful. She has long black hair, below her waist, like all girls nowadays, and black eyes that slant a little. She looks like a young Nefertiti. And I heard her play the piano. Exquisite!'

Arlette did not like to hear of this Zarah, her slanted eyes or long black hair or exquisite piano playing. The kind of girl a father would love and spoil and regard as his most important contribution to the world.

Or did geniuses think of their children that way?

'I'm looking forward to seeing him.'

'You are?' inquired Michael, who never overstepped the bounds of family propriety. Even their work was discussed with tentative delicacy.

But Arlette was determined to talk about this new magician in her life. 'He knows secrets I don't know. Do you know what is the first question I'm going to ask him?' She seemed Lily Malone at that moment, pondering the next question she would put to Valerie or Frederick. 'When will all the stars have been counted? Will he know?'

They looked at each other, the years passing over them as if a low tide swept their feet as they walked the beach on one of those excursions at Montauk. He kissed her good night.

'If he tells you – promise to send me a telegram.'

'I have other questions, too – so many questions – surely he can answer some of them?'

The earnestness was so real, the desire to learn the secrets of Micah Benoni, that she had quite persuaded herself there was no other reason she wanted to see him. She glanced obliquely at Michael as they parted: had she convinced Michael? There was no way of knowing. Michael's face could be as uncommunicative as her own.

But certainly no expedition to Montauk was in her mind then, or when she dressed for dinner. Not, perhaps, until the moment when they returned to the drawing room and she looked at him, thinking: *So here we are, having come the long way, half around the world and back.*

When Conrad had called on the house telephone to let her know that Dr Benoni had arrived – exactly eight o'clock – she had looked at herself in the mirror to make sure, once more, that what she wore was becoming, that she looked the way she wanted to look for him.

Two hours for this production.

The evening pajamas were chaste, and alluring and elegant, carefully fitted to invite imagination and not gratify too much of it. A man was entitled to his imagination, she thought, until everything came off and he must face the facts as they were.

She arrived as she had upon the stage several hundred times, taking the audience by surprise even though they knew she was expected.

He was standing, dressed in a typical, so she thought, professor's gray tweed suit, although not at all like those of Professor Donahue. This man's clothes were expertly tailored, and expertly worn. He was studying the portrait above the fireplace of Lady Macbeth, her arms braced against the weight of the crown as she lowered it to her head, emerged in her gray-green dress from the Scottish mists.

She looked at him carefully, critically, to decide whether or not he belonged there, in this room – in her house, quite possibly in her life, as well.

The fire was burning, throwing strange shadows upon Lady Macbeth, giving her a look of one of the Witches, a dangerous species of witch, for this witch was beautiful, and ambition had not diminished her strong sensuality. It had rather added to it.

The room is becoming to him. The house is becoming to him.

This man had the elegance of his profession in his face and body – the lean spare beauty; the erect posture; the absolute stillness as he stood there: a carefully tuned instrument.

'Yes. Lady Macbeth. How I hated her.' Arlette spoke softly.

'Hated her as a character?'

'As a necessity. I had to play her. Conrad's getting something for you to drink?'

'No, thanks. Not just now.'

They sat down, not far apart, but not too near. Near enough to concentrate; not near enough to lose all sense of proportion.

'What made her a necessity?'

He was going to ask the questions again?

Well, no doubt she seemed to him as he did to her, some rare exotic creature, a bird of different plumage from any he had known; a woman who devoted her life to pretending to be other women.

'What made her a necessity?' She smiled. 'She was part of the plan. She had been, from the beginning. Anthony organizes our lives according to very long plans. She was always part of his biggest plan. He has smaller ones, too.' *Coriolanus*, which was preparing in England, was one of the smaller ones.

'I see,' said the professor seriously. Whether he was

594

serious, whether he was amused, she could not be sure. He might have been studying another page of hieroglyphics. 'Forgive me for asking questions, but you must understand, the nature of my profession is such that I can't imagine yours. I can't imagine, for example, where acting leaves off and real life begins.'

'Do you know where speculation leaves off and conviction begins?'

He laughed, and she listened to the laugh with that trained ear, a musician listening to well-played music. 'By no means. I'm not sure there's any real difference.'

Then, gently, she began to question him, to construct the outline of his life – since nothing more was possible between two people who had met so far along as they.

He showed no resistance to her questions, quick and deft, getting the simple facts first, before she went on to more subtle questions. And he replied casually, as if it were the life of another man, or the common run of lives – for astronomers, at least.

His father, Jacob, had had what Micah Benoni called a *knack for mathematics*, and that had served him well in the import-export business in those days when rapid mental calculation was a far greater asset than it would be today.

'My grandparents were born in Cairo, but they migrated to Spain early in the century. The persecution was becoming a little heavy. My parents met in Malaga, and that's where I was born. My younger brother and sister, too.'

'And so you are a Spanish grandee. As well as an Egyptian pharaoh.'

'I'm sorry?'

'It was my fantasy. I try to imagine where people lived, in other incarnations. You lived where I thought you did. Egypt. Spain.' She spread her hands, smiling. 'Aren't you amazed?' Amazed at her, she meant.

'I suppose I am. But then, you did play Lady Macbeth as a Druidic priestess, it seemed to me.'

'It seemed to me, too. I suppose the signals were clear

enough, if anyone out there happened to be listening. And you were. It's time for dinner.'

As Conrad served the billi-bi and the first wine, Micah Benoni seemed to think he had spent enough time telling of his life. Not Arlette, however.

'Between Malaga and here, you've been somewhere else. Where?'

'Paris. We went there when I was about ten. My sister and I went to school there – my brother had died in Malaga. I was at the Sorbonne when Hitler began to seem a potential force in Germany. My father had a curious sense of coming trouble, and so early in the thirties we went to Santiago for a year or so. Relatives. Then to Toronto. More relatives. Finally to New York.' He had gone to school at Columbia, then to M.I.T., and had taken further degrees in physics before he settled on astronomy and was appointed to a full professorship at the age of twenty-nine. 'It is,' he concluded, as if sorry he had not something more dramatic to offer, 'a typical middle-class Jewish background.'

'Typical.' She shook her head, smiling sadly. 'But you are all the things I've imagined you might be – in this century or some other – since that day we met on the plane.'

'You've thought about me? Why?'

'You've never thought about me?'

'Of course. But how could I not? Your photographs, new plays, new movies. You're in the air, you know.' He laughed softly. 'One breathes you in.'

'I thought about you,' Arlette said slowly, 'for quite a few reasons.'

Conrad arrived with the wine for the lamb, and that reminded Arlette of the untouched food on her plate. If it was true that falling in love takes your appetite, then she was in danger. Dr Benoni's appetite, however, seemed quite hearty, and he ate, although rather slowly, with concerned interest for Irma's subtle cookery. Nevertheless, he ate like a hungry man, not a stricken one.

Despite his father's success in each of the countries they

had thought for a time was home, a place to build and abide, Jacob Benoni had never put his own name on any of the companies he had developed and been obliged to abandon. And his last business, in New York, had been given a *nameless name*, as Micah said: Old Glory Importers–Exporters. Micah smiled ironically.

She felt a twinge of guilt. 'But perhaps he was serious? Perhaps he believed in us – in our promises?'

'He believed,' said Micah, 'in no one and in nothing. But I don't think he meant it as irony. It was not controversial.' He smiled again. 'Not then.'

'He believed,' repeated Arlette softly, wonderingly, 'in no one and nothing?'

'His family,' amended Micah.

'Himself?'

'Probably not. He had no time for introspection. He was a man in a hurry, always. He wanted to be able to move on at a moment's notice. He never lost the conviction that the world would turn against him, against us. The summons – someday would come.'

'How long ago did he die?'

'Nineteen years ago. I was thirty-three.'

'And famous. He couldn't hide his name any longer.' Arlette gave a quick sigh. 'It's a terrible story. I'm sorry I asked. Forgive me—'

'It's a very usual story. There are – several million such stories. It is a story of incredible good luck.' His hand closed over hers as it lay at the edge of the table, warm, firm, holding hers closely for a moment, then withdrawing as she glanced at him. 'You're easily hurt. Why?'

Arlette was silent, stunned by the question, since not even Anthony, not even Gordon Donahue or Jerry Hoffman or Alicia Fiedler, not Michael, the few people she thought knew her best, had ever asked it. Or, possibly, had not guessed it was still true.

Self-conscious, embarrassed, another sensation so new to her these past several years she had never expected to feel it again, she gave a quick sideways toss of her head – Lily Malone's gesture, not Arlette's – and smiled, but was aware that even the smile was apologetic, avoiding the unexpected intensity of those gray-green eyes looking at her. Into her, as it seemed:

Maybe I should never have invited a mathematician to dinner? They're not like we are.

Here, at her table, she sat beside an enigma.

His quietness made her somewhat uneasy, as if it signified some supernatural control. Or perhaps he was a man of such vast pride he tolerated no mistakes from himself in even the smallest gesture.

Nor from others?

'I thought about you,' she said, 'because I think something about everyone I see. That's my business.' He was smiling, either amused by her change of subject or possibly enjoying the fragrant lemon soufflé. 'The first thing an actor learns is to observe and remember everything. We feed on the world and, if we're good enough, the world feeds on us. It's a symbiotic relationship. An actor needs a great many devices of self-protection.'

'Of course.'

Of course what?

Well—

She went on. 'You've just told me about your family's travels – and it's what I imagined, except that I imagined them taking hundreds or thousands of years. That day on the plane, reading those hieroglyphs, from London to New York, with such concentration as I feel only when I'm studying a new script . . .'

'That's what I was doing, as it happens.'

'I thought you were the incarnation of an ancient Egyptian pharaoh—'

He laughed, and there was the easy sense of power returning. She began to be aware that he was thinking about making love to her, and this made her cautious.

Some lovemaking could be done casually between two people who found each other attractive. With others, it was a final fatal decision, a prediction of the loss of self. All would be put into jeopardy.

'An Egyptian pharaoh,' she repeated. 'Or a Spanish

grandee of the seventeenth century, dressed in black velvet, with a cloak thrown across his face.' She gave a gesture, flinging the cloak, and he laughed, but the laughter was subdued, waiting. The magic was working; the poppies of mesmerization were making him drowsy, malleable. 'A medieval monk, poring over illuminated manuscripts, deep in study of the Dark Ages which went before him – and—' She lifted her glass, and Jade Ring's smile appeared; flowers added to embroidery. 'It was all true.' She extended the glass. *'May you live ten thousand years!'*

He smiled, inclining his head as she drank the champagne and put down her glass, then raised his.

'L'chaim!'

CHAPTER 75

More or less – my daughter drives one.

There was the flash of jealousy. Michael had described the girl as a *young Nefertiti*. Arlette did not ask him about his daughter.

She folded the coat around her:

I'll pretend she doesn't exist, this Zarah – Sally – with her long black hair and her piano and her Mercedes.

She held all these treasures against her, for everything had been given her by him: the black hair, the love of music, the expensive car. No doubt he loved her. And a father's love for his daughter, when it was strong, was a more formidable rival than a man's love for his wife, if they had been married several years. But why, exactly, was she moping about who this unknown man, this Micah Benoni, had committed himself to when her own life was so full of commitments?

He had told her nothing more about his immediate family than their names and the fact that the girl was regarded as something of a prodigy – but prodigies developed early, and sometimes faded just as early. The older son, Jacob, was in graduate school at Columbia, taking his doctorate in physics; the younger one, Samuel, was in Harvard Law School. His wife's name was Reba – Rebeccah. That was all. He did not refer to them again.

He preferred, perhaps, to concentrate his formidable energies upon her? He was planning on making love to her and wondering how he should begin?

Who knows? After all, he's a mathematician.

'Why did it mean so much to you?'

He was driving fast, at a steady rate between seventy-five and eighty. The traffic was light, they passed few cars, most of them traveling toward town, and by that time they were fifty or sixty miles from New York.

The question startled her:

Why did that trouble me so much? That belongs to something I said before – but what? I've forgotten, but he hasn't. I've been thinking about other things.

They had been talking, for the past several miles, about Michael and Maura, about their work, for he believed, as they did, that eventually the link would appear which would affiliate his world of macrocosm with theirs of microcosm, showing them to be identical, or perhaps identical opposites: a far more interesting possibility.

She remembered that he had returned to a conversation she had broken by her suggestion that they *run out* to Montauk, as if suggesting they go for the late papers.

'You never wear a wedding ring?' he had asked as they went back to the drawing room after dinner. Conrad had poured coffee and brandy and left.

Arlette extended her left hand, and seemed slightly surprised to discover his observation was accurate.

Other people had said the same thing, and each time she pretended to be surprised. 'I forgot.'

Now, however, she smiled. 'No. I never do.'

'You never did? Or you never do?' He looked serious, concerned.

'I never do.'

'Your husband does. On the stage. In the movies. Whether the part calls for it or not.'

'Yes,' Arlette had agreed, and they had studied each other for some moments, looking for possibilities of faith, trust, disappointment. Arlette decided to take the chance. 'It happened when it was in London, playing Hamlet. I was here – Beatrice Cenci. We were looking forward, and dreading our contract to play *Macbeth* that fall. We'd never been separated so long before, and it almost killed me. I loved him – more than my life, if that's possible.'

This was a story she had not told before. Not to Michael. Not to Gordon Donahue or Jerry Hoffman or Alicia Fiedler or John Powell. Certainly not to Minerva Grey or Eva French.

Then why had she begun to explain herself to this man she did not know? But she went on.

'The time passed, so slowly. At the end, I thought I couldn't stand another day, and I called him in London.' She stopped. 'Somewhere, in the same room, there was a woman's voice. A woman I knew.'

The moment was so immediately painful that she stared across the room, trying to concentrate on a vase of white lilies, afraid she might cry, and of course think that ridiculous.

The mathematical odds, after all—

She glanced at him and smiled slightly.

But there was the keen remembered sense of life having stopped; and her feeling, hard and despairing, was clear as the moment she had heard Deborah's voice: *I'll never be happy again.*

All at once she got up, smiled down at Micah Benoni, and suggested they run out to Montauk before she must leave for France in three days; the last opportunity she would have.

She had told him everything she meant to tell him. Anything more, about Arlette Morgan or Lily Malone, and she would have given away her pearl.

They had turned the car radio on to get the latest war bulletin, and heard instead a sorrowful melody and a girl singing, a song too familiar to Arlette by now. She listened curiously as Nicola Tash's voice whispered that song from *If I Should Die Before You Wake:*

'*There are lies that have a tender meaning*
That the eyes of love alone can see —'

A tear fell and she brushed it away quickly, guiltily. 'I'm sorry.'

He switched the radio off. 'The music is a variation of "Kol Nidre." '

'I didn't recognize it.'

'It's been put through several contortions. Even so — there's no possibility of making a joyous song of it, is there?' She glanced sideways and he was smiling thoughtfully, as at some secret of his own. That was when he asked the question again:

'Why did it mean so much to you?'

He had the same kind of persistence she had.

'You don't know me.'

'No.' He seemed to take the statement as needing considerable thought, someday.

He was silent again, and evidently this man of silences had learned that if you were patient, if you waited, if you were confident in your own authority, sooner or later you would be answered.

Relieved to be able to talk at last about the grain of sand to someone who would never betray her confidence, she said: 'Anyone but me — oh, I suppose it would have hurt at first, maybe for a few weeks or months. What was unusual was what I — and Anthony — lost by it.' He said nothing. Arlette waited a moment, but once begun on this secret it had cost her much to keep, she went on. 'Since then, everything has been different.' She laughed softly. 'No one has ever noticed the difference.' To her surprise, she laughed gaily. 'Except Anthony, of course. And me. We've noticed the difference. But no one else.'

Now that she had told the story it seemed inconsequential, and she realized that even to her, it was. But that might have been because of the man she had told it to, who had in him that quiet which seemed capable of absorbing the troubles of others, dissolving them by some magical process, relieving them of the burden without, at the same time, making the burden his own.

They were passing swiftly along the familiar highway. Out here the night was cold and black, with few stars, and she was not certain how near they were to the house. Perhaps another fifty miles.

The subject was ended.

Yet he seemed puzzled, as if the unusualness of this story was not that it had happened, but that she had been damaged by it.

Had it told him too much about her vanity and egotism, taking what she wanted, being given what she wanted? Would he begin to envy her luck? And, since men often did, would he become resentful, jealous of her? Beauty was too much for most men. The habit of arrogance might make him distrust or dislike her.

She began to regret the story had been a simple infidelity, uncomplicated even by Anthony's attraction to the woman. Perhaps she should have embellished it. As it had happened, it would be tragic to no one but Arlette Morgan.

'I'm afraid I don't understand what you lost.' The subject was not ended, after all.

'Spontaneity, the most valuable part of love. Spontaneity you don't have to watch—' She talked rapidly, her voice taking on a tone of resentment, a soft unforgiving ferocity, as if Micah Benoni were to blame quite as much as Anthony.

He would have done the same thing. Love was one thing. Pleasure another. The two might, or might not, be coincidental – but the question should never be taken seriously:

It's the difference between being the invader and the invaded. That's what they can't understand.

'Don't tell me any more. It's making you unhappy. I had no right to ask. But everything about you seems important to me. Shall we stop talking?'

'No. I've lied about this in everything I've said and

603

done for four and a half years. I lost – and Anthony lost – the freedom we had with each other. Now, we're careful. We have to be. And then – vulnerability. That's gone. He can never hurt me again. And so whatever he does means less – or something different – than before. Maybe the only thing that hasn't changed is what happens when we're onstage, or in front of a camera.' She paused, slowly uncurling her fist inside the coat pocket. 'That's why we're still together. And we always will be.' She smiled reflectively. 'He loves me still.'

'Of course.'

They drove several miles farther. 'We're almost there. I'll tell you when to slow down.' To her horror, she gave a sob, and covered her face with her hands. 'It happened by accident. No reason for it – no meaning in it. An accident.'

She had told him at dinner, so briefly that he quickly retreated from the subject, that her parents had been killed: '*The dead have great power over the living.*' She quoted the Chinese proverb, marveling at how easily this man extracted her most sacred secrets.

Sitting beside her at the dinner table, answering her questions as if he would tell her anything she wanted to know – as only secretive people will when they find someone they trust, for whatever mysterious reasons might lie behind that trust. He had sat there, looking at her carefully:

How still he is. The stillness at the eye of the hurricane.

'They do,' he agreed. 'They do.'

She had smiled at him, a slight, tender sorrowful smile, the smile which, as she knew, could make any audience cry. It was not a smile of brave confrontation; the smile had a quality of resignation. A smile of sympathy, extended to other victims; a smile of wonder and acceptance – a smile which had appeared unbidden after years of contesting with the painful discovery.

'My life, I suppose, has been only an effort at reparation. They were – twenty-seven and twenty-nine. I've tried, in some way, to complete their lives—'

Now, glancing out the car window, Arlette saw the lights of the Webb house.

'We've passed it.'

Micah slowed the car quickly, swinging, it around with such speed that she pitched forward, and was held back by his arm reaching across her. The car stopped on the shoulder of the road, and shutting off the motor, he took her in his arms, placing her head gently against his chest, stroking her hair.

She went on crying, burrowing her head against him like a child seeking comfort, and had some vague realization she had not cried so fiercely since that first day when Frederick had told her after yet another question that her parents were not coming back, ever. She had given a cry of protest, and begun to run away from him. Frederick caught her, drew her to him, and began to stroke her hair.

As this man she scarcely knew was stroking her, tenderly, silently, kissing her wet eyelashes, her face, her mouth.

'Then there were a million diamonds, each sharp as a knife.' She paused, and he was silent, kissing her from time to time. 'It isn't true, of course. Or – I don't know if it's true. No one saw it happen – only later, when the three people who had been in the cars were dead.' She sat for several moments, scarcely aware of his slow caresses. 'Yes.' And then, with great effort: 'It's not good to sit here. A car can come from nowhere. The house is back there, on that side of the road—'

As he drove slowly, Arlette watched in the black night for the turning point, and directed him into the main driveway, toward the guesthouse. If they were going to make love, and they were, it would not be in the bed she shared with Anthony.

He shut off the engine. 'Forgive me. Questions are a weapon. I wanted to know too much about you.'

She drew slowly away. 'Please – come with me—'

She got out and ran toward the house, unlocked the door, and they went inside. The room was cold and dark, and smelled of the pine branches kept in vases during the winter months. Arlette touched the switch and the room bloomed with soft light.

They looked at each other in surprise.

As if to conceal some unexpected embarrassment, he knelt to start the fire; she flicked on the thermostat and drew the heavy white linen curtains which closed that room off from the world. The Webbs would see the light, but if they came to investigate they would recognize the car and go away.

Arlette turned the bolt on the door, then approached the fireplace where Micah stood squinting into the flames, no doubt wondering how he came to be here and what they were going to be to each other, not tonight only.

He turned slowly and looked questioningly at her.

CHAPTER 76

She woke up, thought for a few moments about where she was, then moved her arm across the bed and found it empty.

She remembered that she and Micah, sometime last night, had gone to bed in the yellow guest room, one of four – each furnished in its own color: yellow, red, green, white; each with its dressing room and bath. But now he heard no sound from the bathroom, and the door stood ajar.

She switched on the light beside the bed: twelve-thirty.

The information astonished her. Twelve-thirty in the morning? Twelve-thirty at night?

He had gone away – perhaps taken the station wagon?

She got out of bed and pulled the curtains to look at a blazing day, without sun, the sky white with the ocean's reflection.

She took a terry cloth robe from the closet, opened the bedroom door, and stopped, breathing in the smell of brewed coffee and sizzling steak. She leaned against the door, so relieved her muscles turned weak. So he had not decided that last night's illusions of discovery would not endure the morning's clear scrutiny.

Her reluctance to see him was puzzling. Ordinarily, she rushed forward, into the bad news, the good news, the painful discovery, the joyous moment – anything, so she would not be a coward. And even at the moment of forward impulse she knew she would never capture it: the *fata morgana* was her own namesake.

The living-room curtains had been pulled back, the cushions were on the sofas, and a bright new fire burned in the fireplace.

She hesitated, with the first sense of shyness about meeting a man by daylight she could remember, then went into the bathroom, turned on the lights, and leaned close to the mirror:

My God, Arlette. She gazed at herself in awe and disapproval. *You have been wiped out.*

The night's memories were emerging, a film developing slowly, showing her at first only the slightest trace, a little ghost of what was to emerge. She brushed her teeth, pulled on a shower cap, bathed quickly, and combed her hair. After another glance in the mirror she slipped on a white terry cloth robe and walked to the kitchen, to stand in the doorway watching him, smiling tenderly, relieved that he was still there:

Why, in the name of God, should he not be here?

This man was a force of nature, and to have been made love to by him seemed an experience from which she had been lucky to escape alive; he was primitive and, in a sense, dangerous. Their love had become a species of ancient ritual.

'What did the gods of Olympus see in mortal men and women?' she had asked him just before they went to sleep.

'Mortality.' He kissed her gently, and she could hear the smile in his voice.

Now, this man who remained the objective scientist, returning to his senses not ten minutes after he had seemingly lost them once and for all, stood there in a dark blue terry cloth robe – the same she had last seen on Thyssen over his swimming trunks – his back to her, adjusting the heat beneath the steaks.

She approached softly and slowly. They were steaks. They were cooking in butter. Now, surely, this man was none other than the magician Merlin himself – or perhaps he who could foretell what Merlin was to know, for he lived several hundred years before Merlin would be born.

'Micah—'

He turned, smiling, put his arms about her, then held her back and looked at her, as if for traces of the night.

'Where did you find the steaks?' He had invented them?

'They came out of the freezer – last night. When you went to take a shower. Don't you remember?'

'I didn't know where you'd gone.'

'I was getting my bearings in the wonderful little place we've found, and I began to think about breakfast. I took them out of the freezer. Have some orange juice.' He opened the refrigerator and handed her a glass of fresh orange juice.

'You cook? A hobby?' She shook her head, marveling.

'I have to do it right the first time. I haven't time for hobbies.'

He set the steaks off the flame and knelt on one knee, beside where she sat. 'No regrets?'

'I love you, Micah. Are you surprised? Don't answer – I know how men are about that word. But I know what I mean.'

'Don't tell me. I'll draw my own conclusions.'

The night before, he had made love to her with a quickness and energy which seemed like anger, and in two or three minutes it was over. He lay on the floor beside her, while Arlette closed her eyes, not surprised by the brevity. After all, that was what they had been thinking about while they talked of families and disappointments, his travels, Anthony and Deborah's Voice and Old Glory Importers-Exporters.

All that time they had been waiting for those few minutes.

Lying beside him, glancing up occasionally to find his eyes closed, while one hand slowly, steadily stroked her shoulder, she was wondering if she was here because she loved him. She was there, and so was he, for the experience of that quick eager forceful penetration, the few swift thrusts, the low sound he gave as his semen spurted into her.

Several minutes passed while she lay luxuriously content, warmed through, and then he bent above her, and began to explore her, touching with expert sensitivity, his palms and fingers leaving a trail of sensation as she felt herself sinking into a state of acquiescence.

His hands used her gently, his teeth bit carefully, tenderly, his hands caressed her belly, touching her thighs, maneuvering with skill, a rhythmical insistence, until all at once he was upon her, when she heard her voice, as in the far distance, in a low wailing song, a dirge, wordlessly pleading. Finally she lay, eyes closed, stupefied by the intensity of increasing sensation, making no effort to move, for his swiftness and changing rhythms made it impossible, and when at last he sank upon her, she clung to him, closing him fast inside her:

When was all that? A thousand years ago or more.

They had at last summoned consciousness enough to look at each other.

'Which bedroom shall we take? You choose.'

'The yellow one.' In the Flowery Middle Kingdom, yellow was the color of joy. Did he know that?

That was when Arlette went to wash her face, brush her hair, take a shower, make herself ready for him, and that was when he had gone to forage in the kitchen.

They had gone to bed without speaking again, turned out the light and lay, motionless, scarcely touching. There was the vague recollection of another kiss, and his voice saying softly: 'Sleep well.'

Now he knelt beside her on one knee, looking at her seriously:

In another minute, I'll want him again.

He read her mind, or the lifting of her hand to touch

his face, and stood up. 'Later.' For a moment, his eyes, in the white light filling the room, were that emerald green she had seen when the plane banked.

They had gone walking on the beach that first afternoon, once they had finished the breakfast of orange juice, rare sautéed steak with béarnaise sauce he conjured to her astonishment, manipulating eggs and butter, vinegar and blending machine like an alchemist – quite as she had pictured him, except that this medieval monk's robe was a dark blue terry cloth bathrobe, too short for him.

The sauce, prepared without any announcement of what he meant to do, and poured beside the steak in less than three minutes, was more awesome than if he had told her the age, history, past and future, of every planet in the Earth's universe.

For all that might or might not be true – but there was no question about the béarnaise sauce.

'I,' said Arlette, who had contributed nothing to the breakfast, 'could never make it without a recipe, and it would take twenty minutes.'

'I lived in France for eight years.' No credit for inconsequential achievements. He smiled, the tender smile which contrasted so strikingly with the fierce mesmerized expression which changed his face once he began the overtures of love.

'Let's walk on the beach and breathe,' said Arlette.

It seemed best to wait, force nothing, let two or three hours, longer perhaps, drive them together. Lovemaking, after all, required a tightrope walker's concentration, and never more so than with this man.

He searched the general closet, equipped with clothes for all sizes and occasions, and put on jeans, a black turtleneck sweater, black rubber fishing boots, a sheepskin-lined overcoat, and an astrakhan cap. And with that she recognized him for who he was: An Lu-shan, the rebel general, ringing Ch'ang-an with fire as his soldiers marched upon the capital.

At this first clear sight of An Lu-shan, she realized that

for two years she had anticipated this day when he would become her lover.

But this man was no destroyer.

He had no great hopes of the human condition, but as far as Dr Micah Benoni was concerned, he would give to the world the best of what he was and had. His work was based upon some combination of idealism and deep pessimism, not very different from her own.

Astrophysics, he had said, was one of the few sciences which, so far at least, had proved itself remarkably intractable to the immediate uses of the military, or even the big industries.

'Astronomy, I'm glad to say, requires more from the military and from industry than it gives back. We take their money. In return, we give them a poem. I don't know how long they'll consider it a fair exchange. But since they don't really know what the hell we're up to – they leave us more or less alone.'

They had descended the steep flight of steps and set off up the beach, in the direction opposite to where the Webbs lived.

The Webbs were the most discreet of caretakers, perhaps because they were in awe of their employers – a strange breed to them, people who dressed up and played at being other people, and who did not confine their acting to their public appearances. The De Forests and their flamboyant friends, riding, walking, gathering at late day, the women in bright long silk dresses or pajamas, the men in slacks and turtleneck sweaters, must have seemed anachronistic to the Webbs.

All that, of course, was a long time ago – last summer.

And as Arlette walked beside Micah, it seemed there might never again be any such summer. Or, if they were there again next summer, she would know the difference. The place would be haunted now by a new ghost; another permanent guest, whom she would encounter each time she came there.

They spoke little for the first few miles – only an occasional pointing to a bird overhead, or Arlette stooping once to pick up a water-worn smooth purple stone, which she slipped into the pocket of her coat.

'Every time I come here, I find one, and leave it. Alicia began the custom the first weekend the guesthouse was finished. She left a thin white stone, almost round, with a black crow's feather beside it. Margaret Webb showed it to me. The glass bowl on the coffee table is filled with stones we and our friends have found, beautiful enough to be precious.' Had he noticed it? There was another vase in the guesthouse living room, a pottery vase painted yellow and black, with a streak of red, stuffed with the feathers of every bird which migrated across the Point.

After that, Micah was on the alert for feathers and stones. His vision was sharp, and he made no false starts to pick up one which would not meet his exacting mathematician's sense of aesthetics.

Arlette wore bright red tights, a red turtleneck sweater and pleated skirt, knee-high black waterproof boots, and red wool coat lined with sealskin. Her head was covered with a knitted red stocking cap with a waist-long tail, tipped by a tassel like a brush.

Once, in the midst of a struggle which became a little ballet before she subdued the unruly tail, she found him watching her from the corners of his eyes, slightly smiling, as the antics of a very young girl:

No doubt the way he smiles at that Zarah – Sally.

Or even his wife?

No, not likely his wife. She was not new to him, and she probably thought her days of charming him with feminine artistry were done – if she was the kind of woman who had ever gone in for such things.

But then, life was a serious business to this husband; this man whose passions encompassed not only the universal void, but the mystery of pleasure in a woman's body, taken by him to impersonate a firmament, more accessible; if no less incomprehensible.

They started back.

She glanced sideways at An Lu-shan, since that was who he had turned out to be, An Lu-shan without his need for destruction. A Tartar, all the same. A man who looked civilized, but who was not. A man at war with his passion for work and his passion for passion itself:

He's brave. He's reckless. He's of yang. Like me: Jade Ring, first speculating on An Lu-shan:

Two days ago we were strangers.

Are we strangers still?

She glanced away, fearful he might find her looking at him and feel she was perhaps finding some fault with him:

Now it's all to be done again. Loss and recovery, losing and finding, world without end.

She tried to guess what he was thinking about.

That he had thrown away those hours for nothing but pleasure when he might have written a page or two of that new textbook?

Was he thinking that infidelity had some penalties attached to it even if it should never be discovered? Did he feel troubled about his wife? Or was this a pattern long ago accepted, one of the prices paid for having been married too many years?

Now he took a swift wide step, swooped down, and returned, displaying with a triumphant and questioning smile a feather, glossy blue and black.

Was it good enough?

To keep it safe he placed it in the inside pocket of his coat:

In four days I'll be Marguerite Gautier again.

'Why,' Micah had asked her when she spoke of Marguerite with a bitter little smile, 'did you agree to do it? It's troubled you from the beginning.'

'I'm playing Marguerite to prove I can play something other than Lady Macbeth.' She laughed maliciously. 'After all the years it took me to learn to play Lady Macbeth.'

'I see.' She glanced at him quickly, challengingly. Yes, he did see.

They entered the guesthouse, and all at once Arlette was aware they had returned as strangers; their presence in this isolated place made them both uneasy.

They hung up their coats and pulled off their wet boots, and Micah went to slip the blue and black feather into the vase, then knelt to rekindle the fire. Arlette gently deposited the purple stone in the glass jar, then sat on the floor beside Micah, who held his warm hand over her bare chilled toes.

All at once, searching for something to reassure herself that they knew each other, she asked: 'What does your name mean?'

A slight grimness came over his face. 'Micah,' he repeated, as if the name were not his own. 'Micah means: *Who is like God?*'

'And so you decided to become an astronomer. Benoni?'

He was silent several moments. 'Benoni means: *Son of my sorrow.*'

'Forgive me!'

'Why? He didn't give me the name – it's a surname. Although it's true, I wasn't born at the happiest time of my father's life.' He looked into the flames. 'But if there was a happy time for him, I never knew. He had occasional gaiety, unexpectedly. But I don't believe he thought in terms of happiness. Only of surviving, from one day or year to the next.'

'The names are beautiful. And they're your own. You didn't have to invent one to fit your profession.' She smiled, a little shy. 'Like me.'

He turned quickly, stroking her hair away from her face, shaking his head slowly. 'Arlette—'

'Where is the love before we've felt it? Do your stars answer such questions?'

When they left at five o'clock on Monday morning, they had not gone into the main house, nor did Arlette glance that way as they passed it:

Everything has changed.

The meaning of the house, too.

She knew nothing real had changed: Micah would hire a car and drive to Princeton, hoping to arrive in time for his one-o'clock class. And the next afternoon, at five-thirty, she would leave for France.

As for Micah, there was that same eternity of space to explore and explain.

'And so to France,' she announced. 'And then – Egypt.'

'Egypt?'

'The two Cleopatras. They're our next Hoffman-Repertory contract. And after that, if we like the script, *Wuthering Heights.*'

That, as you can see, Micah Benoni, is why Anthony and I will never be divorced. Being married to each other is an indispensable part of our work.

Of course, Micah had said nothing about marriage or divorce.

CHAPTER 77

Thyssen instructed her to retire to her Paris hotel for twenty-four hours to recuperate from the flight, after which the chauffeur would drive her to the location for the first outdoor scenes, to be shot between two and five in the morning.

The first morning: Marguerite in her blue coupé with two fine bay horses; Marguerite gay and vivacious. Another morning: Marguerite in black, her face veiled, sick, on her way to visit Armand. Another morning: Marguerite walking swiftly in the park, smiling. Late one night: Marguerite, returning from the opera in her white gown and red velvet ermine-lined cloak, with the old Duke:

At least, those god damn love scenes are over.

They had photographed a fragment of the ballroom scene in Los Angeles, the pitched battle between Marguerite and Armand's new mistress, Olympe, which was to become so humiliating to Marguerite that she would faint and be carried out.

Arlette at first declined to faint, explaining that no

woman fainted from hatred of a rival, and she knew that to be a fact. Finally she was persuaded to faint not out of hatred of Olympe, but because she was about to die.

Arlette quarreled like a termagant with Olympe, snatched at her hair and forced her to defend herself for fear Arlette would pull loose the elaborate coiffure. And when she fainted she fell with the ease and grace of a spent bird, and was picked up by two young men and carried away.

There was an outburst of applause and delighted laughter when Thyssen signaled the cameras to stop, and Arlette leaped nimbly free of her young men and executed the sweeping bow she made nightly upon the stage.

But in her hotel room – recuperating from the flight and the two and a half days she had spent with Micah Benoni – she was convinced she might, like Marguerite, be dying.

The fear was that Micah might have taken charge of that hidden territory where, like any craftsman, she concealed the equipment and necessities of her trade.

Those two and a half days they had been together seemed to have severed her past and present selves, and this might prove impossible to repair.

The moment of decision would come on Wednesday morning, when the camera turned upon her pathetic smile to Armand as she sat in the box in the opera house saying to him those words she had spoken seven weeks before in Los Angeles. '*You are twenty-six, Armand. I will never live to be so old. Have you thought of that?*' The smile had been tender and wistful and the more sorrowful because it was without bitterness or irony. It was not an easy smile to recapture on cue under the most favorable circumstances, and the circumstances no longer seemed favorable.

For this Micah Benoni, she suspected – when he had stepped out of the Mercedes at seven-thirty that Monday morning – had gone off with everything she had of value: he had taken with him her ability to bring all the disparate fears of acting under control. He alone knew whether Arlette Morgan was a fabrication of the many women she

616

had portrayed or whether the many women were fabrications of Arlette Morgan. She had never been sure how the formula was mixed, but it seemed that he was.

These were dangerous secrets to have meddled with, capable of putting her out of commission once and for all. Whereas his profession carried no personal dangers to him different from those to anyone else.

Only, so she had told Micah Benoni with great confidence, only the body and its sensations made a clearly definable entity: the soul – perhaps Micah could explain to her what that was?

She had asked the question impertinently and he had not answered, only smiled, admonishing her, perhaps, not to tamper with such serious matters. But surely he had taken hers with him:

Suppose I find I need it for Marguerite? Can he send it back – on a radio beam? Dr Benoni: Please return soul. Must have to finish this stupid picture.

The apprehension of having involuntarily surrendered her *taw*, her secret magic formula, to that stranger from a strange land had continued as she sat waiting for Thyssen to adjust his cameras.

Thyssen gave his salute, signal for work to begin, the extras fell quiet, Armand leaned nearer, and Arlette smiled at him with that wistful gallant tenderness which was an exact replica of the smile she had given him seven weeks ago: her fears of having been destroyed by falling in love with Micah Benoni disappeared.

Thyssen came to clasp her hand, kissing the fingertips, as he sometimes did when a scene pleased him.

'How did you do it? The same smile, that same miraculous heartbreaking smile—' Marguerite smiled at him brilliantly, full of confidence:

I'm safe. He didn't take anything away.

One morning Armand went skipping down the streets of Paris after his first night with Marguerite, bowing to old ladies and waving to passing carriages, throwing his hat in the air. He would, in the film, be skipping along the streets while Marguerite knelt before the old Duke, who sat with his back to the camera, fully dressed, having removed only his hat, set his cane aside, inspected his daughter's miniature, and summoned Marguerite.

'Poor Armand,' Arlette said to Thyssen. 'Love and business – love and business—'

The little house in Bougival had been transferred to a location in the South of France, so they need not wait for clear skies or weather warm enough for Marguerite to run about the garden in muslin gowns, chasing butterflies and gathering bouquets.

And once they were there, Arlette began to tell herself she had forgotten Micah Benoni, or would when it suited her purpose.

Yet each time she was called to the telephone, she went nervously, strangely frightened. It was either Anthony or it was Micah Benoni.

So far, only Anthony had called, and he had called only three times, for either he was in rehearsal or onstage, or she was on the set when he was free. Once they moved to Thyssen's artificial Bougival, it became almost impossible to place a call, and she was convinced she would not hear from either of them until they returned to Paris, in time for her to go to London to see a last performance of *Coriolanus*.

When she was summoned from the set of the country house, where Marguerite was entertaining her raucous, well-dressed women friends, to take a long-distance call, she ran to Thyssen's trailer, frantic with anxiety. She had felt so safe, and here was the intruder.

'Arlette!' Anthony's voice was joyous, relieved, yearning. 'I've had a hell of a time getting you! Darling – are you all right?'

Anthony? Who are you? I'm trying to remember.

All at once she laughed. 'I'm entertaining my friends, the best-paid whores in Paris. We're having caviar and pheasant and champagne and they're drunk, but of course I'm too discreet—'

'Arlette, I've figured a way to get there for a few hours this weekend.'

'A few hours, Anthony?'

Something had gone wrong, and what had gone wrong was Micah Benoni.

'It's been long, Arlette.'

'You wouldn't get here in time to turn around—'

We've had this conversation before.

But the last time I wanted to go to London.

There was a pause, and then Anthony's authoritative voice: 'I miss you.' He was silent a moment. 'Arlette, who is it you're getting revenge on now? Anthony De Forest or Arlette Morgan?'

'It's not revenge. No more, if it ever was. Anthony – please.'

She ran back to Marguerite's house, where the old Duke had been driving away her noisy friends, and Armand sat before the camera, watching an imaginary Marguerite, his face wistful and adoring. Even Armand knew paradise could not last forever.

'*A few days,*' Marguerite had told him. '*They're all that's left to us, Armand.*'

She had not received a letter from Micah, or a telephone call, although when he got out of the car he had said: 'I'll call you.'

After nearly six weeks, he had not.

And so she had convinced herself, or tried to, that he was a wise man, a sensible man, a man who knew when to stop and start over again. It would do them no good to meet: the De Forests were one nation indivisible, now and forever.

She went back to her argument with Thyssen about how she should play the scene after the old Duke had sent the whores away in their coupés, screeching and giggling and making impolite gestures.

Arlette wanted an impudent uncontrite Marguerite, prepared to sever her connections with the old Duke for the sake of a few weeks of Armand's uninterrupted lovemaking.

The next day, at six-thirty in the afternoon, Micah Menoni arrived unexpectedly at their out-of-the-way little Bougival.

Earlier, while she stood for her costume to be fastened, she had assured herself she would never see him, and that, furthermore, it made no difference.

Still, he arrived at the end of an unusually beautiful sun-filled day, as the sun left its red glow on the river.

Thyssen decided he had the definitive scene of bucolic love, Armand rowing all afternoon on the river's still green surface, Marguerite smiling at Armand, that tender, sorrowful smile, which all the same contrived to contain Marguerite's – and Arlette's – ironic understanding of the delusion of this love.

Arlette jumped up, and as Evans protested she was going to swamp the boat, leaped ashore and ran to the trailer dressing room, to take off the corseted dress before driving the three miles back to the inn.

Several members of the cast and crew had returned to Paris during the past few days. The schedule here was completed, but for the night of heavy rain, through which Armand must trudge the muddy road to Paris in search of Marguerite.

'If it doesn't rain by Monday, we'll go back and wait for rain there,' Thyssen told them.

In the trailer, Arlette sighed as the maid released her from the corset. There was a soft knock, and a woman's voice, which Arlette recognized as that of one of the maids at the inn.

'It's Céleste, Mademoiselle Morgan. The doctor is arrived. He is waiting.'

'There must be some mistake, Céleste. Speak to Monsieur Evans. He has a headache.' Arlette stepped into a pleated white silk skirt and sleeveless silk blouse, and opened the door.

'No, mademoiselle. Not Monsieur Evans. He said he would wait until you returned. He did not look like a man to come so far by mistake.'

'So far? How far? What's his name?'

620

'A strange name – a name—'

'Benoni? Dr Benoni?'

'That's it?'

'Where is he?'

'In the parlor at the inn, mademoiselle, writing on some yellow paper in a new language.'

Arlette and Céleste drove back to the inn, Arlette running in barefoot, to see Micah Benoni seated on a sofa, his back to her, dressed in black slacks and a black sweater, bent over the low coffee table, writing.

She approached him softly and stood motionless, waiting for him to sense her beside him.

After a moment he looked up alertly, then smiled, taking her hand as she bent to kiss him on the mouth. 'Micah—' she whispered. 'Micah Benoni. I thought I'd never see you again.'

He drew her down beside him, and she sat, chin on her fists, gazing into his eyes. 'Did you?' His voice was somewhat ironic. For the first time she knew what he was thinking. She could read his mind, after all. He had missed her. He had been unhappy, and now he was a little angry. 'I told you I'd call. It wasn't easy. Neither of us stays fixed for very long.'

Arlette saw Thyssen and Lennox come into the foyer off the parlor, and called out: 'Andrew – I want you to meet a friend of my brother's. He's on his way to—'

'Budapest,' said Micah, standing to shake hands with Thyssen.

'Mr Thyssen. Dr Benoni.'

Thyssen knew him, it seemed. 'Micah Benoni?' And Arlette remembered Minerva's amused remark that when Thyssen was not making love or making movies, he was reading the damnedest books: sociology, psychology, chemistry, physics. Eclectic scholarship was Thyssen's vocation: making money was his hobby.

'Dr Benoni's doing some interesting work in molecular astronomy,' Arlette announced, happy to remember having heard Michael say so. 'Dr Benoni and my brother often meet at conferences – or wherever scientists meet.'

She laughed from excitement, and Micah smiled at her *One lie is as good as another.*

Thyssen made his bow to Micah, kissed Arlette's cheek, and left, saying, 'Monday at noon. We'll shoot Armand's hysterical outburst again, unless it's raining. Then he can march.'

Arlette laughed with an irresponsible gaiety, surprised by the keen excitement and gratitude she felt at being in this man's presence.

They studied each other, smiling, irrationally happy. 'Come along,' said Micah.

'Where?'

'I have a car. There are places. Maybe,' he added, 'you'll need a pair of shoes.'

CHAPTER 78

Micah said when they set out, driving a car so small he was obliged to crouch over the wheel, that he was going to Budapest to attend a gathering of astronomers and astrophysicists. It was no lie he had told Thyssen, after all. That was how he came to be there, so far from anywhere he might have been expected to be: their imitation Bougival, somewhere in the middle of the nineteenth century.

'From here to Paris and then to Budapest,' Arlette repeated wonderingly. 'And you're to be there when?'

'Monday.'

She had run upstairs, slipped on a pair of yellow sandals, taken a yellow cashmere coat, and run back down again, carrying the bag which contained Marguerite's face and hair, complete. He tossed his papers into an attaché case, and they went out, Arlette all at once silent, confused and embarrassed, as they drove off.

She was wondering where he was taking her and why she was going. She had been so self-protectively sure of never seeing him again.

It had grown dark. She asked if he knew where he was; he did. She had overlooked those eight years in France.

The two days they spent together collapsed time as neutron stars collapsed, with a slow beginning, so to speak, depending upon how you were counting time, and then a swift inward falling of all energy – until, in a matter of earth-counted seconds, nothing was left.

'The logistics,' she whispered wonderingly.

She was trying to imagine how he would get from wherever they were to Budapest and appear there with a working brain. She laughed. *What a question to ask a mathematician.* She had asked with the same bewilderment how he had found where she was, driven there in time to drive to the inn at Saint Paul-de-Vence, and back to their Bougival in time for – it required at least a knowledge of three- or perhaps four-dimensional time.

On Monday morning she got out of the car a little distance from the inn, so that she might stroll in casually, encountering early risers with her story of a morning walk, and found there were logistics of her own to solve, simpler ones.

Thyssen had left a letter. It had rained and Evans had trudged up and down, up and down, and now was at the Plaza Athenée, sneezing and cursing Armand, Marguerite, the motion-picture business. Thyssen had gone the day before. He concluded:

And then, dear, since there's nothing left but outdoor scenes of the riot of women invading Marguerite's house for the auction after her burial, you may go to London. You see, I did arrange that you might see Coriolanus. *But please – come soon to New York. Devotedly, Andrew.*

He wanted her in New York to begin dubbing the French version: another two months gone from the summer and Montauk.

But if it was not done then, it could not be done at all. Other contracts, other responsibilities, waited to gobble her time and Anthony's.

Caesar and Cleopatra.

Anthony and Cleopatra.

Jerry Hoffman's great project, for which he had sent hundreds of sketches – costumes, wigs and jewelry, swatches of materials. These two elaborate productions went into rehearsal in February and would open in April: the young Cleopatra first, frivolous and savage, through whose veins flowed not blood but Nile water, but whose dynastic plans were bloody. This primitive young queen, who must be made both naïvely charming and terrifying, at last put on Caesar's knowledge, with his power.

On alternate weeks she would play the mature, lust-ridden treacherous older queen, who had killed herself not for love but pride. And these plays would run alternately for almost five months.

'By then,' Arlette had observed, foreseeing all that future two years before, when they sat at the board of directors' table and signed contracts, 'by then, we'll all be wiped out.'

Anthony laughed, unintimidated. Arlette glanced at him with some distrustful jealousy: *Somewhere, somehow, he's learned that when the time comes he'll be there.*

Yet – for all her fears and superstitions – she was there, too.

After leaving Bougival, she met Anthony in London, to see his praised *Coriolanus*.

She had called from Paris, and was surprised to hear Anthony's voice, warm and affectionate, joyful at the prospect of seeing her.

Why – he has no idea at all.

But how could he? Neither Thyssen nor anyone they knew had any interest in gossiping about the De Forests. The De Forests were of value to all of them. And Dr Benoni had his own kingdom to consider, as he had warned her.

'Love,' he had said almost immediately, as if to put her on notice should she prefer to go back to Bougival, 'love has always been a thing for me to avoid. Men or women who are serious about their work can't afford romantic love.' He gave her a quick, questioning, rueful smile, as if he had been determined to make the announcement but was not well pleased with Micah Benoni now that he had.

Arlette had asked him for nothing – and if he loved her it was because she existed and chance had betrayed them into crossing paths.

No sooner was it dark than he had driven off the highway, onto an unpaved road, which sent the little car bounding along its rutted tracks, stopped the car, opened the door on her side, pushed her backward and glided forcefully inside her, deep and swift, until finally she covered her eyes with her hands and brought her legs slowly together again.

'We're crazy,' she whispered as they waited to recover their wits, surrounded by the silence of a forest gone to rest for the night, only a stream running somewhere nearby. 'Who may find us?'

Several moments passed, and then he drew away, lifting her to stand beside him, his voice tender, soothing, his hands passing over her hair. 'I do love you, you know.'

She laughed softly, leaning against his chest, balancing for support on the uneven ground as she stepped into the skirt and buttoned the blouse. 'You must. We must. Either that or we're a couple of sex maniacs.'

He backed the car down the unpaved track and onto the main road. 'Saint Paul-de-Vence. Have you been there?'

'No.'

'It was the only place I could think of – private – and not too far away.'

During the two days they did not leave the hotel suite, sending for food when they were hungry. Now and then she inquired whether he thought there would be enough left of either of them by Monday morning to go back to their separate worlds and reconstruct their former selves: the actress and the genius.

Love, once the lovers were grown-up, was less welcome if it was serious. Yet she had not welcomed it when she was young, had she?

Late the second afternoon, she began to talk to him about the one secret she had left.

'Twice,' she said as they sat at a table next to the windows, overlooking the mountains, 'twice in my life I've been sick. Oh, I don't mean physically sick.' A gesture dismissed that. 'I think Valerie scared me into thinking only lazy children got sick. No – the other kind. The first time, I was nineteen. I looked in the mirror one day and could not find Lily Malone. The same face was there, but I – was not. I felt a terror of trying to stay alive long enough to find out whatever was still coming to me.' Micah watched her seriously, his eyes slightly narrowed, as if this secret hurt him. 'The other time—' She smiled a little. 'Well, of course you know when that was. Deborah. Deborah's voice. After that, I was so sick I thought I might die of it. Perhaps Anthony wouldn't let me. Or maybe I didn't want to just then. We were going into rehearsals for *Macbeth* – I couldn't die and leave *her* to someone else—' Arlette laughed.

Micah continued to watch her seriously and steadily, slowly tearing the rind from a soft-skinned orange and offering sections to her. 'Yes. It happens. We're all in danger of drowning in an inch of water.'

'Lady Macbeth didn't scare me. She took all of me, it seemed, but there was still something left, something which could never forget the sound of that voice. It kept playing in my head, sometimes very soft, sometimes loud. Like that!' She doubled her fist and opened the fingers wide, as if to explode the voice. 'Even so, I was sure that any moment – someday when I least expected it – there would be that flash of feeling. Pure happiness. Simple joy at being in the world. Do you know what I mean?'

She waited, for he was silent several moments. He shook his head. 'No. I'm sorry. I don't know. Oh yes – when I'm with you. Not otherwise. Now and then, during an experiment, when something unexpected happens. Totally unexpected. That's it.'

She went on. 'And then, I have no idea how long ago, one day I was horrified to realize that although apparently I seemed the same to everyone else, I'd lost not only the

626

capacity, but even the will for happiness. I gave up expecting anything more – ever.'

'And during this time you played Lady Macbeth, and Mary Stuart—'

She gave a soft laugh, as if to confide that she had fooled them. Friends. Strangers. Enemies – whoever they were. Audiences. They had never guessed what she was hiding. 'Eustacia Vye—' She looked at him, her head to one side. 'Has that ever happened to you?'

'It's happiness that surprises me.' He gestured, indicating her sitting there with her breasts naked, a white bath towel around her hips.

'But you would never have troubled to become who you are. You would never – make love the way you do.'

How he felt or had ever felt, or why – he did not propose to discuss it. But then, his profession kept him at several billion light-years from these subjective pains. He preferred to question her. 'You have it still? This – sickness, as you call it?'

She looked away. He had misunderstood, or was pretending to, the reason for her confession. 'How can I be sure?'

'Every now and then, Arlette, we meet a stranger who turns out to be ourselves.' He gave her a questioning smile.

'Yes. Then I met one more stranger – not myself. And that's made the difference.'

She had been looking out at the mountains, watching as they turned slowly majestically blue. All at once, with a swift movement of her head, she looked at him, eyes accusatory, as if demanding to know whether he was willing to accept this responsibility of her love.

She was surprised to find herself thinking for the first time in years of Lily Malone and Jack Davidson, sixteen and nineteen years old. They had made one great discovery together, and after a time parted. At least, she had parted from him:

That's the great advantage we have now.

She was thinking not only of herself and Micah, but of

627

herself and Anthony, herself and Minerva, Alicia, Gordon Donahue, Jerry Hoffman; those people who had been with her in the early days. As she thought of it:

To know not only who you are and where you are, but — where you've been. That's what we don't understand when we're as young as they were — Lily and Jack. They lived on the edges of unexperienced time — How could they know — anything?

Lily Malone and Jack Davidson. Two people she had known once, and could remember now only by a concentrated effort.

'Micah.' She spoke soberly, determined to convince him. 'I have always believed that unhappiness as a permanent condition is the one real sin against others. Most of the time my happiness has been real. Because of what happened to my parents — all my life there's been the need to triumph, one way or another. Happiness seemed the only reasonably sure way.' She was silent, watching him, studying his face, slowly being concealed by the settling darkness. 'I know that finally we lose. The question is — what you do until then.'

She could no longer see Micah's face clearly. There were shadows cast by the late sun falling across his cheekbone, lighting the high formal structure of his nose. After several moments he spoke quite practically. 'Yes, of course. That's the way it's been dealt.' His hand reached out, and he was standing beside her, then drawing her slowly upward by her forearms. 'There's some time left.'

CHAPTER 79

'The most alluring cruel young Cleopatra . . . the most sensual, strongest Queen of the Nile . . . a queen as we like to imagine one.'

Gordon Donahue looked at her as they stood on the stage of the Alicia Allerton, surrounded by the cast in Egyptian and Roman costumes, the guests in evening clothes, drinking from the goblets which had been used in the banqueting scenes.

Gordon's body was still slender, the shoulders a little more stooped, and he had the same gesture of combing his fingers quickly through the thick black hair as he talked to her. The charm which Lily Malone and Barbara Sloan had found potent enough to allure them into his first drama class twenty years ago had improved with the years; for during those years he had continued to polish his skills, publishing articles and books which had made him one of the country's most respected critics in his field.

Arlette looked at him silently, listening, smiling, as if she would reassure him, soothe that nervousness which attacked him each time he saw her perform:

Yes, it's quite easy for me to know why I was in love with you, Gordon – for how many years? How long ago?

Little Marian Donahue was somewhere on the stage, lost from Arlette's view amid the perhaps two hundred people Jerry Hoffman had assembled. Little Marian Donahue, who had greeted Arlette like a proud older sister when she had first appeared after the performance – sweeping through the closed curtains at the back of the stage like the resurrected Queen of the Nile herself. She had discovered Marian not far away, smiling that wistful tentative smile which had never changed, and all at once Arlette had put her arms around her, pressing her face to Marian's. 'Thank you for coming.'

Marian had not lasted the years as well as her husband, and looked as if she had been diminished by time. She did not look unhappy. She looked more like herself, and momentarily baffled by the attention of this actress who a week before had played the young Cleopatra with the high spirits and subtle cruelty of a young leopard. Anthony had been an elegant Roman Caesar, amused and bored by his dangerous unpredictable pet, who upon departing had left her an empire as a toy and the promise of a gift of great value: the most admired Roman of them all, Mark Antony.

Now, one week later, the charming young leopard had

played a Cleopatra transformed by age and power, a woman of solemn beauty and presence, acting with her Mark Antony a love defeated from within its own walled city.

When the curtain came down the last time, Jerry had stood with Arlette and Anthony, tears gleaming in his eyes. Only Anthony remained alert, intent, unchanged by the portrayal of his love, his pain, his joys and disgraces. Jerry embraced them one after the other.

'It could never be better than tonight.'

Half an hour later, with Anthony beside her. Arlette came through the curtains at the back of the stage, emerging with the bravura of a star of the highest magnitude, thrusting the curtain aside with one hand, standing motionless, secretively smiling, enveloped from neck to floor in Cleopatra's death robes, a floating circle of dark blue silk embroidered with stones of every color – the Egyptian night sky seen through a whirling kaleidoscope. She wore Cleopatra's black wig of state, which now had fastened at its center part a flawless white diamond Anthony had given her as they looked at each other in the dressing room:

Were you satisfied?

Was I good enough?

They said nothing aloud, both still afraid of the emotions, underplayed at every rehearsal, but played tonight with the mutual sense of one man and one woman representing the histories not of their own lives, but of their nations. There was no playfulness in this play, even when there was gaiety – for the gaiety held its premonition of disaster.

They had played it with bitter seriousness, as symbols of greatness in disarray.

When Cleopatra's voice rang out, sounding more like some newly invented musical instrument than a human voice: '*I have immortal longings in me . . . Husband, I come . . . I am fire and air; my other elements I give to baser life . . .*' there was a general quick intake of breath.

After that, as first Iras died, then Cleopatra and Charmian, admonishing the Roman with their Egyptian triumph, '*Ah, soldier!*' the audience was on its feet, applauding.

In another moment the cast, all but Antony and Cleopatra, stood before the curtains, bowing. There were three curtain calls before Arlette and Anthony appeared: Anthony's face, grim; Arlette's, serious and sorrowful as she made her deep bow of obeisance.

After three bows, three inclinations of Anthony's head, the curtain stayed down and the cast scattered, suddenly afraid of one another.

In their dressing room, as Arlette got into her evening dress – not one of Cleopatra's costumes – they had nothing to say. And when he stood behind her and fastened the diamond at the forehead parting of Cleopatra's wig, they looked at each other in the mirror and left all questions unasked.

Anthony had resumed Mark Antony's first-scene costume, the short soldier's tunic, and now he placed the cloak around her shoulders. She walked to the door, stopped, and turned to look up at him:

There's something I should say.

The two plays had said it all for both of them: their whole history had gone into those performances. There it was – the joyous playfulness of the young Cleopatra and her amused lover; the sorrow of the older Cleopatra and her Mark Antony:

What's left of us now to give away?

Arlette stepped through the curtains with Jade Ring's conquering smile on the night she had first been presented to the Shining Emperor, embracing Marian Donahue as if she had found her only friend, and Anthony relieved her of the enveloping cloak.

She was surrounded immediately, so caught up in the excitement over Cleopatra and Mark Antony that she forgot to look for Micah Benoni, who was to have come with Michael and Maura.

Micah Benoni, whom she had not seen since the morning he had left her at Thyssen's Bougival and set out for Budapest, where, he had said with a slight smile, he was going to meet with other astronomers in pursuit of the charm of the quark.

That had been June twenty-second. This was April twenty-ninth.

He could not write. He could not call, since there was no way of knowing when. And so he had asked her to call his office, and told her the hours he was likely to be there. Astronomers went hunting not only quarks but the stars themselves.

'Billions of years for a star,' she had said. 'A flash in darkness for us.'

Arlette had called him five times – it required a considerable calculation to be alone in the presence of a telephone with no teacher, no director, no husband, no secretary, no fitter, no wigmaker, at an hour when Dr Benoni would be free to receive a personal call.

But none of her calls turned out to be such a call.

They were both uneasy, confused. She sometimes thought she was calling a man who did not exist; or whom she had seen once on an airplane.

On these few occasions they talked of their work.

That was safe. Furthermore, it was all there was to talk about; it consumed their time. That work schedule, so neatly arranged, so strong, so binding, gave her an image of each of them in a cell, from which there would never be any possible escape.

Or, perhaps – as at Montauk and Vence – an occasional jailbreak, a day or two, and then they would be captured by responsibility, guilt about the expectations of others, plans for the present and future.

Yet these memories had gained their hold and seemed part of bones and blood and the mysterious soft internal organs of her belly – although, for all this physicality, she had been convinced of experiencing the first religious communion of her life. This frightened her, brought up the old superstitions, and provided some new ones.

That inherent splendor of being he gave her was surely not the work of a normal man. She began to tell herself there was something sinister there: what would cause any rational human to take such an impassioned interest in the stars; the empty – or, as he said – teeming spaces; the world's beginning and its end? No one, she decided, but a reincarnated warlock.

She smiled at these notions, once he was safely out of reach:

We met too late.

I wish we'd never met at all.

She looked around the stage.

Where is he?

And where were Michael and Maura?

Gordon Donahue was reminding her of the argument he had used to send her to New York: 'Now you've had them all – *actress, queen*, grande courtisane, *goddess*.' Cleopatra had closed the circle.

A man's arms seized her around the waist, and Michael kissed her face hard, while Arlette reached her free arm around Maura. Over Michael's shoulders, a few steps away and smiling seriously, she found him at last: the sorcerer, in black dinner jacket, the civilian's uniform.

She smiled, holding out her hand. He moved quickly to take it. Michael stepped aside. 'We've brought you a friend.'

'Yes.' The gift Caesar promised to send the young Cleopatra. 'You have. Hello. Welcome.'

'Very beautiful, both of them.' Micah moved nearer – Michael and Maura were talking to Jerry – and he looked at her with that steady intensity, ominous only when she was away from him. Now, the same expression looked like the concentration of a man in love, unable to conceal it, whose mind functioned with such intensity she listened for the soundless workings of some intricate technological device. 'The young girl – and the woman.'

'You saw the young Cleopatra, too?' asked Arlette, smiling Jade Ring's smile as the only reliable means to keep from trembling.

'Of course.'

633

'But you didn't come backstage—' She laughed, self-conscious.

Arlette saw Alicia Fiedler nearby, and introduced her to Micah, forgetting they had met the night of her dinner party for him.

Something, someone, must rescue her—

From what?

From her own feelings, and her fear that they must show as plainly on her face as on his. If he prevented her from acting, then someone – Anthony – would pass by, and all her hard work of hypocrisy would become a shambles, less easily overlooked by either of them than the sound of Deborah's voice.

Deborah was meaningless.

One glance at Micah Benoni, and Anthony would understand that this man could not be meaningless to any woman if he decided to take an interest in her.

Alicia was questioning him, and Arlette was glad when Sarita Stanhope came up, telling her how wonderful she was, how super, and then took her hand, whispering: 'Please let me talk to you. For a minute.'

She and Sarita passed slowly through the crowd, for she was constantly stopped, again engrossed in being the star, hoping that Micah Benoni was impressed by this world she moved in. Eyes watched as she passed. There she was, Queen of the Nile, Star of the East.

Far to one side of the stage, Arlette and Sarita found a space and Arlette looked at her questioningly.

Here was Sarita, with her straight blonde hair, dressed in orange-red chiffon, gazing at Arlette with tears in her eyes. 'You know, don't you?'

What Arlette knew was that Sarita had had the first shock of her twenty-six years: her perfume contract had not been picked up, and in the past two months she had appeared on the cover of only one high-fashion magazine.

Arlette knew a little more, and so she looked at Sarita sympathetically, feeling some curious pity for this girl who had fallen in love with Jerry Hoffman and was still in love with him; who was essentially too soft for the world she lived in, yet too vain to go back to wherever she had come from – looking for success in New York and, quite accidentally, finding it before she was twenty.

'The contract, Sarita?'

'My life is over. I've tried to learn to act. I have no talent, I have no voice—'

Arlette was growing nervous about Micah Benoni. She glanced around, trying to find him.

She had run away from him. Sarita had not been a reason for leaving him. She had been an excuse.

Now, ashamed of her fears that Anthony might read her thoughts, Arlette was ready to dispose of Sarita's problems and look for Micah.

There – Jeffrey Brooke. Jeffrey liked Sarita and he liked beautiful women, and when they were in trouble he liked to comfort them. But at the moment he was talking to Max Gilmore's wife, Susie Allen, whose new musical had lately made a star of her, playing Nell Gwynne in *The Protestant Whore*.

Arlette spoke quickly, but with a careful tenderness. 'Sarita, you must not—'

Arlette, I've been photographed too often and always with that same stupid smug stare—' Sarita gave an imitation of the beautiful, vague, arrogant young face which had stared into the eyes of millions of increasingly bored magazine readers. 'That's the way they told me to look. It was the Sarita Stanhope look. For a while I was a sensation, and then all of a sudden it was over.'

'No, no, Sarita.'

'Where is he?

He thinks I didn't want to see him – and he's left—

Arlette made a quick move to escape, and had become quite angry with Sarita.

'Arlette, that isn't all—'

'Forgive me, Sarita. I'm a little nervous tonight. We all are. Sarita! My brother is here. I must—'

'Please, Arlette, listen to me! Jerry told me to marry someone else!'

635

Arlette had reached out to touch Jeffrey's arm, hoping to give Sarita to him. 'When did he say that?'

'Last week. I suppose he's said it, one way or another several times. Why won't he marry me, Arlette? I'd let him have other girls.'

Arlette wanted to give Sarita a reason she could understand: 'Sarita – Jerry has *been* married—'

CHAPTER 80

What could be more logical? Even Sarita should be able to understand that.

There was Max Gilmore, not two feet away, talking to John Powell; Gilmore in his Roman armor, Powell in a dinner jacket. And John was nodding at what Gilmore was saying while thoughtfully, concernedly watching Arlette.

'Arlette—' he had asked her during the summer, when she had found several excuses not to visit his office, 'won't you see me ever again?'

They stood on the beach, a little distance from where the children and weekend guests had gathered for a late afternoon picnic.

The first few times, she had looked evasive, for Arlette had lost her appetite for revenge on Anthony once she had fallen in love with Micah. Falling in love with Micah Benoni, it seemed, had restored at least a part of her fidelity to Anthony. She had given John several answers: classes; dubbing sessions; study with Alicia – waiting for the great inspiration. One day, she would hear herself say it. One day, she did.

'I can't see you any more, John,' she murmured sorrowfully, Marguerite Gautier bidding the young Count farewell. 'It – isn't fair.'

That was the explanation, containing all the elements she had hoped for.

Unfair to whom? If unfair now, then why not three

years ago? But John was not a man to embarrass either of them with another question, and he never asked it. After all, he had not expected ever to be her lover.

John kissed Arlette. Max kissed Arlette. Both men kissed Sarita. And in the general confusion of embraces, Arlette escaped, made her way with that sinuous movement she had learned, passing through a crowd as if the crowd were not there:

Where is he? Where is he?

All at once there appeared before her an apparition from the past.

Like a balloon held on a string at the level of her own face: a face with a white skin and white teeth, green eyes and flaming-red hair, her bright pink mouth opened wide in a smile which was only too familiar nowadays: Deborah Crane.

Deborah's arms reached out as if to embrace her. 'Arlette, darling—'

Arlette smiled a little as she stepped quickly backward, as if mildly alarmed at the prospect of being embraced by this balloon which, after all, was not affixed to a string but to a body wrapped tight in gold cloth.

The bitterness and hatred she had felt against Deborah were gone. That impulsive telephone call to London had made possible her love for Micah. But for Deborah, she would have seen Micah Benoni only on the plane crossing the Atlantic, and never again; nor noticed the picture in the newspaper. Her love for Anthony had encapsulated her.

Arlette went on, and now caught sight of Dr Benoni, talking to four or five men and women, among whom she was horrified to see Anthony:

Now how in the hell did that happen?

At home, they had nothing to say while they undressed. Anthony went into his dressing room and Arlette heard the usual sounds of running water in the shower while she removed Cleopatra's wig and stepped into her shower.

It was four-thirty, and she found herself suddenly so

tired that, were it not for these rituals without which she had never once gone to sleep, she might have fallen asleep on the bathroom carpet.

It did not occur to her that this was normal routine, and at the same time absolutely abnormal, considering that it was the night of the greatest success they had shared so far.

Not a word.

Not an exchanged glance or smile. But no indication of hostility, either.

In the car, when they had driven Michael and Maura to their hotel – for although ordinarily they stayed at the house, on this night, Michael said, and tomorrow, guests could only be a nuisance – no words were spoken during the drive from the hotel. Arlette gave one long deep sigh, whether of relief or dread she did not know.

She came out of the bathroom to find Anthony in bed, eyes closed, his breathing regular, fast asleep – a trick he had learned and which he could do at will. She got into bed beside him, touching the light switch, and kissed him good night, as she did every night, whether he was awake or asleep, closed her eyes, and fell asleep.

She woke suddenly, sometime later, feeling herself being pitched over, thrown from her back onto her stomach, and her body was invaded with a sharp pain. She cried out, protesting, and his hand covered her mouth. The pain turned to pleasure, but pleasure was still a part of his rage. This lovemaking was punishment, a possession without mercy or pity, a revenge she thought might kill her.

Now and then she murmured his name, pleadingly – for as he controlled the pleasure, he controlled the pain – and when the pain came, sharp, sudden, profound, a sudden deep penetration while he held her in a vulnerable position, that pain was miraculously transformed into a pleasure which made her begin to imagine dying in his arms, obliterated by this rage of jealousy.

'There is some murder in love, Arlette,' he had said one day. A warning?

638

All at once it was over: She felt herself dissolving, disintegrating. He moved away swiftly, not lingering inside her as he usually did, and then the light shone in her eyes.

He stood beside the bed, looking down at her, while Arlette covered her face with her hands, vaguely aware that she was crying and had been crying for some time, whimpering sobs of protest, despair, helplessness.

That, he had told her, is what I can do to you . . . Didn't you know it?

His hand closed over her wrists and slowly, against her resistance, he forced her arms above her head. At last she opened her eyes, to see him kneeling above her, staring down at her grimly, without a trace of the tender smile of inquiry he had formerly given her after lovemaking.

'I hurt you?' The question was serious, concerned.

She nodded slowly, and closed her eyes again. 'Of course. You wanted to.'

'I wanted to kill you.'

'I couldn't have stopped you.'

After a long silence he answered her with Ming Huang's words to Jade Ring when she had lived with him in exile, letting him believe his soldiers had killed her: ' "You once gave me whatever value I felt myself to have." ' He let go her hands.

She covered her face and turned from the light. The room went dark again, and presently she felt him lie down, on the far side of the bed. He said nothing, but she did not fall asleep for several minutes.

When she woke it was one o'clock in the afternoon and she was alone. There was a note on the bedside table, telling her he had gone to discuss a scene with Jerry and would see her at the theater.

Suddenly wide awake, wondering what had happened to her, for she felt that he must have marked her permanently with those hard grasping hands, she ran into the bathroom.

There were blue marks, fingerprints on her breasts, on

the inner parts of her thighs, across her belly. But after careful inspection, she decided makeup would cover it.

Strangely, she felt refreshed. The pain had been intentionally produced, yet he had avoided doing her any real damage. It was what she would have done to him had she been capable of it when she had heard Deborah's voice.

But there was the difference between his admitted longing to kill out of pain and the committing of murder from some irrational flash of rage. He had known, at every moment, what he was doing – however vengeful. And he had not forgotten that although he wanted to kill her, he wanted far more to keep her.

He had left, perhaps, out of shame? Arlette smiled at the mirror. *Not Anthony.*

He was gone for the reason he had given: he wanted to talk to Jerry about a scene which had displeased him, or Jerry, or both of them.

Last night it had seemed, in those hallucinatory hours which followed any enthusiasically received play, that Jerry was satisfied for once, Anthony was satisfied, while she was too preoccupied with Micah Benoni and the sight of him talking to Anthony and Michael, Art Friedman and Malvina Brooke, to remember whether she had liked Cleopatra.

Arlette telephoned to Irma to order lunch served in the bedroom in an hour, and began very slowly the routine of exercises, bathing, making up her face, rolling up her hair – for her Cleopatra was a blonde Greek, except when she wore the Black Egyptian wigs of state.

While she worked through the phases, she tried to solve the puzzle: Anthony knew she was in love with Micah Benoni.

What had been said?

What had happened in those two or three minutes after she joined them, before Anthony, without a words, only a curt handshake, had left them and was not seen again until Michael sought her out to say he was waiting in the car.

There was no mystery about it.

Anthony had glanced at Micah Benoni, at her, and read their history in thirty seconds. The real puzzle was how she had been so foolish as to imagine that even in that crowd of two hundred people they would not meet:

Predestined enemies will always meet in some narrow alleyway.

She had wanted them to meet?

She did not like that idea. Her feeling for Micah had nothing to do with that ancient grievance against Anthony, which seemed, once and for all, to have vanished the moment she had confronted the balloon which had turned out to be Deborah Crane.

The culprit was Malvina Brooke, that painted ship upon a painted ocean.

Yet it struck Arlette, with some surprise, when the lunch arrived and she sat before the window glancing at the newspapers, that for Arlette Morgan she had made an extraordinary series of misjudgments last night. She had mixed the potion as clumsily as any amateur witch, and had created a situation out of which trouble would sooner or later and inevitably arise.

And so it had; and boiled over, in the form of Anthony's wild attack, part love, part hatred, part pleasure so intense as to become pain, part sharp, stabbing pain, caused by intent. He knew her body, and he knew what positions, what sudden changes, what unexpected jabs and thrusts would find her vulnerable.

Malvina Brooke. That bloody bitch.

'Oh, Anthony,' Malvina had been saying as Arlette joined them, standing opposite Micah and Anthony, who stood side by side. 'It really was the most interesting dinner party – and I think one of the most beautiful – Arlette has given. What a pity you were in Los Angeles.' Malvina gave her a small smile. 'Wasn't it beautiful, Arlette?'

'I suppose it was, Malvina, if you thought so,' Arlette replied softly, politely.

But she had seen, with a keen sense of pity, the look of pain and disbelief in Anthony's eyes, as if, finally, his enemy had arrived. He turned, shook hands briefly with Micah, saying, 'I hope we'll meet again, Dr Benoni,' and was gone. So was Malvina.

Arlette and Micah stood alone and looked at each other, curiously self-conscious.

'And did you find it?' Arlette asked him.

'Find—'

'The charm of the quark. Wasn't that what you were looking for?'

Micah laughed, the first free, spontaneous expression from either of them tonight.

'We're not sure. Some of us found it. Some of us didn't. The first three quarks are generally agreed to have no charm – some think the fourth has.'

Arlette continued to smile at him. 'The usual odds – even out there?'

Looking again at Micah, she had a disturbing memory of Anthony's face when she had met him at the hotel in London, two days after she and Micah had parted before the inn at Thyssen's Bougival.

Anthony, his face joyous as she opened the door, seizing her eagerly, and no doubt hopeful that this absence had obliterated her vengefulness.

She had thought, in astonishment: *The whole world has changed – and he doesn't know it . . .*

And so it had. For if it had not, then the Micah Benoni she was talking to at this moment would be a man who signified nothing more than Jeffrey Brooke, whom she saw over Micah's shoulder, holding Sarita by the hand and leading her about, trying to cheer her up, while Sarita smiled, laughed, and wiped away another tear.

'You'll be here—' With a slight nod Micah indicated the stage, the people in costume and evening dress, the theater, still brightly lighted, where some couples sat in the red velvet seats, drinking and talking. 'You'll be here until—'

'September twentieth. Then there'll be a few months for study. All acting and no study makes for bad acting,

Anthony thinks. Early in March we'll be in England for *Wuthering Heights*.'

Micah smiled. 'You've found a hard way to go through life.'

Arlette laughed softly. 'You, too. Half the people here live the same way.' She looked at him, talking tenderly, not concerned about the expression on her face. The damage had been done, if only by the quick renewed alertness on Micah's face as she came toward them. 'Anyway, most people don't go through life. Going through life is like going through a brick wall every bloody day.' As she said it, she was aware of an unexpected bitterness for the truth of what had been the course of her life. 'They prefer to pass through life. A mirage passing through a mirage.'

'Arlette – I've been trying to think of something to say to you about those women—'

'Women?' She was quickly alert.

'Your two Cleopatras.'

'You think the young Cleopatra and the older are two different women?'

'You played them as two very different women.'

'The young one had a chance to grow older, to find out who she would become, what she would do to life – and what life would do to her. Not everyone is that lucky. Or unlucky.' She made a little spiraling gesture with her forefinger, indicating smoke, or incense, sent upwards. 'One more incarnation—' She looked at him thoughtfully. 'The last responsibility the living owe the dead is – memory.'

CHAPTER 81

MALVINA CHANDLER AINSWORTH BROOKE.

Arlette sealed the envelope and looked at it thoughtfully.

It was a little after four, and she was dressed to go to the theater.

She opened the concealed drawer and thrust the envelope in amid two or three dozen others, not on the top, for should something happen to Arlette, when the drawer was opened – by whom? – they must not be able to decide that these enemies or friends had been entombed in chronological or any order. The scheme seemed clever to Arlette, or if not clever at least satisfying, despite the fact that she was sure of very few names consigned to perdition over the years.

These people might have prospered? Some might even have become her friends? Her lovers? One, of course, her husband.

She locked the drawer, swiveled the hinge which put it out of sight again – and left the room feeling that something had been accomplished. Something had: if Malvina did not die prematurely – she would, at least, grow old. That was one infallible curse it did not require Arlette to bring about.

Other people might waste their energies and sour their tempers, spoil their faces, freeze their smiles with ugly thoughts – but Arlette preferred to free herself by this simple formula, the great virtue of which was that it could not fail. Sooner or later, the curse must take effect. Upon her, too.

Anthony was not in the dressing room when she arrived at the theater, and she supposed he might be in Jerry Hoffman's office.

She undressed and looked at her body in the brilliant dressing-room lights, then took up a bottle of the lotion which was believed to be the actor's best friend, able to conceal dark circles under the eyes, signs of heavy drinking, bruises, abrasions – even old age – and began covering the prints left by his fingers.

Certainly, with those marks, there would be no immediate meeting with Dr Benoni. There would not have been anyway. For Micah had driven back to Princeton early this morning.

'When will you see me again?' Arlette had asked. 'Six months from now? A year?'

'When, Arlette? I can't call you. You must let me know. Your time, after all—'

He smiled, for she had described to him the way her time was consumed. When a play was in rehearsal or in production, she lost her identity and disappeared into the part; a young, vicious, ignorant, charming Cleopatra; an older, more sinister, more sensually alluring, more ruthless Cleopatra. These were the women who must occupy her thoughts and feelings every moment, lest she lose them and walk upon the stage displaying to the audience someone else. Arlette Morgan?

'I will, I will,' she told him, trying frantically to think of where she would find the hour, the two hours, the excuses, the lies. 'Next week?'

'I think so. I have—'

'I know. We both have too many responsibilities, and we both arranged it this way.'

'We had no reason to expect we'd ever meet.'

His smile made her uneasy. Was this a form of amusement for an astrophysicist – concentrating some brief attention upon a different type of star – one which had plunged to earth as the comet had plunged into the earth's atmosphere the night of Jade Ring's birth?

'You haven't forgotten me? Or have you?'

He looked at her with concentrated seriousness. Then he smiled, but the smile was also serious. 'I haven't forgotten – anything.'

As Arlette worked with her makeup, she found herself marveling that she could have stood there, staring at Micah Benoni with open helplessness; forgetting, or not caring, that Anthony might see her.

This man, Anthony De Forest, had a wildness in him, that same quality which let him become a savage Othello who had once or twice almost strangled Desdemona; who had played a raging Coriolanus whose hatred of the Roman mob terrified the audience, for it seemed a hatred of them, and it was; who had played Mike Chance as the

645

post-hedonistic modern man on his way to becoming the last truly wild animal left on earth – this man was not very likely to accept the idea that she had fallen in love.

Whatever he might have guessed before, Anthony's shrewdness would tell him at a glance when it was revenge and when it was love:

I wanted to kill you.

Arlette turned slowly before the mirror. Her costumes were as naked as she had been able to persuade Jerry Hoffman and the Hoffman-Repertory board to permit. They were made of transparent Egyptian cotton, transparent cloth of gold and silver tissues, jeweled, and where one breast seemed to have been left naked, actually it was covered with flesh-colored chiffon, the areola embroidered with bronze sequins. Camouflage was in order now.

'Tragic actresses,' Art Friedman had reminded her, 'may show their breasts, but not their tits.'

'Or their twats,' mumbled Jerry, still the bitter lover who had confessed that his pride was the bane of his life. 'One good fuck is worth all the phony pride I ever got drunk on.'

Cleopatra, in her young savagery, or later in her full power of sensuality, moved about the stage with the confidence of the woman who had left a magic trail through history.

We're too good, Arlette thought, dabbing with the lotion, *Anthony and I.*

When she was caught off guard, as she had been last night, when she had forgotten even her self-protective superstitions, then she was willing to admit that over the years of working, together and separately, living together and separately, she and Anthony had reached a harmony of understanding, the quick give and take of a man and woman who knew each other professionally as thoroughly as they knew each other privately:

We're too good to let anything interfere with us. No one else can do what we can now.

She was still naked, holding a hand mirror to make certain the actor's friend had done its job, concealed all traces of last night's holocaust, when she heard a key turn, and Anthony came in, locking the door behind him.

He stood motionless, and for several moments they studied each other in the mirror.

He walked toward her slowly, while she waited to see what his ingenuity might produce.

He stood in back of her, and Arlette's heart beat faster. She was a little afraid of him now. Gently he lifted the hair from the back of her neck and put his mouth to where the central triangle grew down the nape, and for several moments did not move or speak. She waited, rigid and unmoving.

He took a step backward and looked at her in the mirror. 'That will never happen again.' He spoke with the solemnity of a man taking a religious vow.

'*Do you need to be told that because something has happened once, it can happen again?*' she asked him.

'It won't. That's all there is to it. Now, let's not talk.'

They did not customarily talk during the hours before the curtain went up. Usually Arlette sat before the mirror and began the slow process of applying makeup, while Anthony read reports he took out of an attaché case, like any stockbroker.

They had nothing to say.

Then they were onstage, filing across in stately progression, accompanied by musicians and slaves, peacock feather fans, and a troupe of eunuchs and ladies, giggling and whispering, until their mistress began to speak: '*If it be love, indeed, tell me how much.*'

She looked at him curiously, as if not sure what his answer would be under the circumstances, and was aware that she had not entirely forsaken Arlette Morgan.

Jerry Hoffman had directed the play at a flashing tempo, cutting the brief scenes in and out, slowing the pace only where Cleopatra appeared with her women and eunuchs, or when she and Mark Antony were together. The brief scenes of battles and plans of battles came and went as if they were perhaps only imagined wars and rumors of wars.

Yet the pageant of the coronation was played at majestic

tempo, with a solemn dignity, the stage crowded with Roman soldiers, Egyptian ladies in brilliant robes, young boys waving fans, and Cleopatra covered from head to floor in a vast circular cape of crimson silk, sitting motionless while Antony placed the crown of Isis upon her head, the staffs of Upper and Lower Egypt folded across her breasts.

A quickly lowered curtain cleared the stage of throne and Cleopatra, and the armies were on the move again, marching and fighting. When Antony, having disgraced himself by deserting his men to follow the Queen's retreating flagship, at last entered her palace at Alexandria with his shamed cry of: '*No, no, no, no, no,*' as she approached him, it sounded like the protest of every man who had let love overcome his sense.

'*Pardon, pardon!*' she cried, piteous as the child queen she had long since abandoned.

He took her into his arms, still seated, bringing her to him between his knees, and kissed her with a slow steady pressure which continued until Arlette began to lose her sense of time, and her balance, so that when he finally released her, he had to help her to her feet.

Jerry Hoffman met them coming offstage, Arlette still looking uneasy and dazzled, Anthony with a grim smile.

'I was about to shout *fire*,' said Jerry.

Arlette looked at him questioningly. 'Did it last as long as it seemed to?' Anthony was watching the action on the stage, preparing for his next entrance.

'Sixty-seven seconds, as I clocked it. What the hell got into him?'

'What do you suppose, Jerry?'

The play proceeded, cutting from the battlefields to Cleopatra and her women, until Antony, defeated, launched into his diatribe against Cleopatra, which became so full of hatred that she ran from him, and when he fell silent, staring at her with what looked to Arlette like Anthony De Forest's hatred, she went to him slowly apologetically. '*Have you done yet?*'

Anthony's voice rang with a challengingly prophetic

648

sound she had never heard: *'Come, let's have one other gaudy night . . .'*

Arlette had the uncanny sense that all of this had happened to them some other time, some other place, and was returning now, as the universe turned itself inside out.

. *'Call to me all my sad captains . . .'*

Then, with Antony dead and Cleopatra dressed in her night-blue death robes, the crown of Isis on her black wig, she lay upon her bed, after kissing Iras and Charmian tenderly, reaching into the countryman's fig basket and placing the asp to her breast.

'As sweet as balm, as soft as air,' she murmured as the poison began its work, *'as gentle . . .'*

By that time, Minerva and Eva were crying, which they had not last night.

Arlette was borne off upon the litter as the soldiers onstage shouted in confusion at the betrayal of their anticipated triumph. She jumped from the litter and looked about in dazzled bewilderment, surprised to find she was where she should be, after all; in the theater – and still, it seemed, alive.

When the last curtain call had been taken, Arlette found herself embracing Minerva and Eva, while in the general confusion of soldiers dashing about, the audience still applauding, Anthony had disappeared.

'How strange, how strange,' Minerva was repeating. 'After all these years – the three of us together again in the same play.' She gave a broken sob.

Eva said, 'Five months more, and after that we'll never be on the stage at the same time.'

The reason, of course, was that this was the last time Minerva Grey and Eva French would play supporting roles, even to Arlette Morgan, and yet why the sorrow, premature, should have overtaken all three of them tonight, they did not know. Yet there it was: the end of something precious.

Arlette broke away and ran to the dressing room, crying. She went in swiftly and stood inside the closed door, head bowed. 'We'll never play together again,' she said, tragically as Cleopatra bidding her handmaidens farewell. He looked at her sharply, inquiringly. 'Minerva and Eva and I. Do you realize that?'

'I suppose you won't. It's what all of you have wanted, isn't it?'

'Everything we've wanted, and now that we have it – I can't tell you why – but somehow it seems like the end of the world.'

'Come here.'

She looked at him skeptically, but walked toward him. 'It's not the end of anything. This play has witchcraft in it. It's driven all of us a little crazy.' He placed his hands about her waist. 'Forgive me.'

CHAPTER 82

Arlette sat down opposite Anthony in the London hotel sitting room, idly listening to Anthony talking with a reporter. But she was concentrating not upon the words he was saying, but upon the words he had said to her late last summer at Montauk.

Outdoors, the light had gone from the sky and on the grass paper bags with sand in the bottoms, holding lighted candles, were appearing, magic earth-grown stars set out by the Webb children. The Powells and their guests had arrived, including Jerry Hoffman, without Sarita.

Jerry had finally convinced Sarita he was not going to marry her and she had married an airline captain, whom she had met on one of her fashion assignments.

As if perhaps Arlette could explain to him the way of a maid with a man, Jerry had told her what Sarita had said two days before the wedding: 'He'll be away a lot. I can come whenever you want me.'

'She's still in love with you.'

'Love – love. It goes better on the stage, or a sound

track. It belongs in songs and poems and plays and movies. It's credible there – it's not credible in real life.' He smiled, a somewhat curious smile.

'I hope you were gentle with her.'

'I guess I was. I said: "No, thanks, baby. It does nothing for me – poaching on another guy's preserves." '

What does he mean by that? What has he heard?

Nothing, of course. She and Micah had not met often. They had been extraordinarily cautious. So cautious that Arlette was almost convinced caution was a pesticide capable of killing the strongest love. Yet, it had not. It was Micah Benoni she loved – the inconveniences were only that. Inconvenient.

For love, she had discovered, had phantasms of its own: what did not please love, love turned to its own purposes, refusing the evidence of the shadows on the wall, the whispers from the sky.

While Jerry's pessimism – not only about love – had increased.

As his fame increased, as his abilities increased, so did that early pessimism increase. Arlette thought that perhaps he trusted and loved her more than anyone else he had known.

They were, in a sense, married by their past, by the year and a half they had been lovers. For although after his first announcement they had never made love again, it had been a perpetual affair, intimate, mutually trusting, mutually concerned. They wanted for each other the kind of happiness neither believed could endure for long once it was exposed to the remorseless addition and subtraction of everyday life.

She had left Jerry talking to Alicia and gone upstairs to dress.

She had not seen Anthony since they had come back from a ride on the beach with Malvina and Jeffrey. After lunch Anthony had excused himself, saying he had work to do.

During the ride, as she and Malvina had been cantering side by side, Arlette in blue denims and red sweater, her bare feet sometimes in the stirrups, sometimes not, Malvina had said: 'Arlette, I miss my picture.'

'What picture?'

'Jeffrey and I are in the Yellow Room.'

She did not ask Malvina what picture she missed, and set her horse into a gallop, catching up with Anthony and Jeffrey.

There was Malvina again. ' "The Prickly Revenge Wort." Did someone take it?'

Anthony had given Arlette a quick sharp glance, while Arlette's face remained expressionless, unconcerned about the disappearance of 'The Prickly Revenge Wort.'

Ordinarily their paths crossed during the day, coming and going, on the beach, hiking or driving the moors. 'The Prickly Revenge Wort,' she was thinking, had something to do with his unaccustomed absence:

I'll dress and then I'll look for him.

If he had something to say to her, she was not going to run away. But when she was dressed, he opened the door and came in, looking at her with an expression she knew: Othello entering Desdemona's bedroom: *'And are you honest, Desdemona?'*

'Who did you give it to?' He sat down, resting one ankle across his knee, waiting.

'Maybe someone took it.'

'We don't have guests who take things, even a little drawing – especially not one done by their hostess.'

Arlette looked at him steadily:

Now why the hell is he asking me this when he bloody well knows who I gave it to?

Her expression was slightly smiling, guiltless. She would not tell him who had the picture, inconsequential little watercolor she had painted after Deborah's voice had encouraged her superstitious belief that everything she loved would one day be taken from her.

More than five months had passed since the night he had met Dr Benoni at the opening-night party for the two Cleopatras. All that time he'd had nothing more to say, and she supposed he never would.

Now, when she was no longer waiting, he asked her this question.

He did not move, only sat looking at her as she stood before him, waiting.

'Where is it?' he demanded suddenly.

A small watercolor she had painted one afternoon, in this same room, looking through a book of fifteenth-century prints of plants and flowers, from which she had composed her imaginary plant: a wicked, erotic, cannibalistic little plant, strangely shaped, strangely colored, yellow and red and green and orange.

There was a humorous irony in it which, perhaps, made it attractive to Micah Benoni, who had remarked upon it the morning they left Montauk, asking where it came from. And when she told him and he laughed, as if to have found another unsuspected Arlette, she had slipped it into his attaché case, and he had since told her it hung in his office, where his students supposed the L.M. who had signed it must be an illustrator for science-fiction magazines.

'Where is it?' he repeated.

She started to walk past him and thought she would make a successful escape, but he seized her wrist.

Arlette did not try to free herself. 'Anthony, I'm not going to tell you. If it's gone, what difference does it make who has it?'

His hand on her wrist slowly relaxed, but when she started forward he seized her again and stood swiftly, looking at her with an expression of rage she had seen only once when he was playing a part – or when he had been angry with someone else.

Still holding her wrist, he leaned down, savage as Coriolanus denouncing the people of Rome. His voice was low, urgent, mocking.

'The guys before – Donahue and Brooke and Hoffman—' Arlette was surprised at Jerry Hoffman's name. 'Powell. Granville. They make no difference to me – any more than that first young jerk in high school—'

He hates me. He's hated me for a long time. I've hurt him badly.

He was speaking slowly. 'You thought I didn't know about them?' He was so near she could not see him clearly, only feel the force of his rage. 'What the hell difference did any of them make to me?' What difference did such men make to the Emperor of the Flowery Middle Kingdom?'

The tranquil smile either did not affect him or perhaps it made him angrier. 'If that was your idea of revenge – forget it! Powell, Granville, Hoffman – I saw it in their eyes when they looked at you.' He moved back and she could see his face again, smiling that same angry smile. 'Once a man has had a woman – fucked her flat – he's never able to look at her the same way again.'

He's right. They never do.

He had released her and she started forward, but once again he caught hold of her shoulder. 'I can't tell you not to see him. A woman will see a man when she wants to – there's no way to stop it. I'm not a guy to regard a woman as real estate. But remember this – he's god damn well not going to make any difference with us – with you and me or Hoffman-Repertory. Too bloody many years have gone into building it. Is that clear?'

'My years, too, Anthony.'

Anthony nodded brusquely, as if he had signed a contract with a business associate whose honesty he did not trust. 'Good.'

All at once he had become formidably mysterious. A man she had lived with for years had shown himself a stranger, shrewd, patient, able to contain a raging jealousy as she could not; and he became all the more mysterious as, during the next weeks, he seemed never to have spoken those words at all.

The episode began, after a time, to seem part of her imagination; her guilt had spoken – not Anthony.

Now, as she sat listening indifferently to Anthony and the London interviewer, she could not have guessed what he was thinking about or even if he was no longer concerned with her, except as she affected his professional life. There was no way of knowing, as once she had known so well, what he felt at any given moment; what he was thinking; what she meant to him.

'I'm late, I know,' she had said when she came in. 'The fittings—'

Anthony had looked at her with his face set, and might be suspecting she had been with Micah Benoni.

She had. Micah had driven from the Jodrell Bank Observatory, where he had spent the past several weeks doing research in new developments of radio astronomy.

Arlette listened again, forcing herself to come out of the dream-like state in which any meeting with Micah left her. The meetings occurred infrequently, and each time, began with the disappointed sense that soon it would end: they had met, made love, and parted, even before she knocked at the door of his hotel suite.

'Why is it,' the interviewer was asking Anthony, 'that all the Cathys, so Sir Charles' publicity states – except the twelve-year-old – will be played by Miss Morgan? Catherine at fifteen or sixteen, and later as a grown woman, are both played by your wife, as is Catherine's daughter. While you're to play Heathcliff only after he's run away and returned from London after several years, then later as a man of forty or forty-two.'

'It's much easier for a woman, my wife, at least, to look like a sixteen-year-old girl than it is for a grown man to look like a nineteen-year-old boy.'

Anthony gave a sudden flashing smile at Arlette, who, taken by surprise, smiled her thanks. It was quite true, as the tests had shown, that she could look like a sixteen-year-old Catherine Earnshaw, or like Catherine Earnshaw as a married woman. While, as Anthony had said, once a man had grown up, he could never again look like a boy.

'I see,' said the interviewer, and turned to Arlette. 'Miss Morgan, may I compliment you on your Marguerite Gautier?'

'Thank you.'

'I particularly liked this review.' He took from his briefcase a review clipped from a magazine. Arlette recognized it as Gordon Donahue's.

'A good review, that, wasn't it?' The interviewer glanced at Anthony. 'Mr Donahue was Miss Morgan's drama teacher in college?'

'He was also my drama teacher. He's had thousands of students. Have you heard of any of the others?'

Anthony stood up, preparing to dismiss the interviewer.

'I would like to know, Miss Morgan, something about your working habits.'

Arlette looked at him, all at once the imperious star. 'I don't have habits. I have discipline.' She smiled ingenuously. 'So much more reliable.'

'Do you regard acting as an art, or a profession?'

'I regard it as work.'

'You've never known failure, have you?'

'Not in the sense you mean.'

'Is success necessary to you?'

'Certainly.'

She gave Anthony a sideways glance. All at once Arlette leaned forward, and the pearls, with their central strand weighted by the goddess Kuan-Yin, swung forward as she placed her right forearm across her knee. 'I'm trying to tell you the truth,' she said gently. 'But the truth to me is ambiguous and paradoxical. And in my experience, all relationships are ambivalent.'

Anthony spoke up quickly. 'Miss Morgan means—'

'I meant what I said.'

'But surely there has been at least one person you have trusted without qualification?'

'Two. Dr Michael Malone, my brother.' The reporter looked surprised. 'And Professor Frederick Morgan, my uncle.'

'Michael Malone is your brother?'

Arlette smiled faintly. 'Yes.'

'How interesting. And, how unexpected.'

Arlette got up swiftly. 'Please, Miss Morgan – one more question. To what do you attribute your success?'

She turned, still smiling. 'To my acting.'

As they left the hotel room, the interviewer followed close behind.

In the street they encountered him again; as they approached their limousine, he stepped between them and the opened door.

'Please, Mr De Forest – do you have any advice to give young actors?'

Arlette stepped into the car and looked at Anthony looking at the interviewer. Ming Huang answered for him: '*I have no advice to give . . . I have learned nothing.*'

CHAPTER 83

Granville had bought a town house since Arlette had last been in London. Granville was sometimes convivial, surrounded himself with actors and celebrated painters, the party-going rich, and men and woman he met while traveling. But when he was working, he saw only the few people he trusted and needed for that project.

He showed Arlette and Anthony several dozen stills taken from scenes which had been filmed the summer before in the north, of the twelve-year-old Catherine Earnshaw and Heathcliff, thirteen. He showed them close-ups of the faces of the child actors. They had been sought to match pictures of Lily Malone and Pat Runkle at the same ages. The resemblances were so uncanny that although Anthony was enthusiastic and admiring of his young facsimile, Arlette studied the pictures without speaking, and placed them on the coffee table.

The children had finished their work. She would never meet this replica. But it disturbed her to know that somewhere in this world, in this same London, lived a twelve-year-old girl who might grow up to be another Arlette Morgan:

Where will I be then? How will I look? Will I still be acting? Will I, perhaps, no longer be alive?

There they were, blonde Catherine Earnshaw, with her long ringlets, and the dark-skinned, dark-haired gypsy brat, warily meeting. There were close-ups of them smiling at each other. Long shots of them running across the moors.

'Three minutes, in the final cutting,' said Granville, perhaps thinking that Arlette's eyes showed some concern about this young self, this Lily Malone.

By means of a photograph of Patrick Runkle taken when he was nineteen, Granville had discovered another young Heathcliff somewhat older – supposedly seventeen – but Granville said that a seventeen-year-old boy did not look seventeen when seen next to a sixteen-year-old girl.

This young Heathcliff would be Ian Flaherty, a dark-haired, dark-eyed twenty-year-old Irishman, and as she looked at his picture, Arlette's breath stopped. There was the past: Patrick Runkle, president of the senior class, football captain, scourge of the campus virgins. Ming Huang: Anthony De Forest to be.

Anthony had looked at the photographs of the young man who was to play a love scene while Arlette played the sixteen-year-old Catherine Earnshaw, and shook his head in amusement. 'Christ, you know, I think maybe I did look something like that.' He glanced at Arlette. 'Can you remember? Did I?'

'You did. I can remember. Ghosts, Charles. The picture will be a ghost story.'

'The past is powerful. The dead are powerful.' He glanced at Arlette sharply. 'You said that to me once. And the picture will say it more plainly – or more painfully. Lennox and I tried to find a way to keep Ellen Dean out of it, keep it all in Heathcliff's memories during the last few months of his life. But there were a few things Heathcliff could not have known. And Ellen Dean as housekeeper would obviously never know what was going on between those kids while they were running around the moors all day, or crawling across the rooftop to get into each other's rooms at night. We do. We know it's impossible for a man and woman to be crazily in love who've never fucked – and often. It doesn't guarantee love, but one thing's sure, without it no guy goes dashing around in a storm the night the woman he loves is dying, and he doesn't spend twenty years haunted by her ghost, either, unless there's something more than religious advice he wants from that ghost.'

'You believe in ghosts, Charles?'

'I don't know what I believe in. But this picture believes in ghosts. Ghosts that walk and talk and scream and bleed. I believe in those ghosts. And so do we all – for the next few months. Shall we go in to dinner?'

The scenes of Catherine Earnshaw as a young girl, with the young Heathcliff, were to be kept to a minimum, and when the Irishman, Ian Flaherty, was introduced to her, all at once the swagger his photographs had shown was gone.

Arlette smiled and shook his hand, and since he could find nothing to say, she began talking to the hairdresser.

'He's scared pissless,' Granville told her. ' "But, Sir Charles, I will never be able to handle Miss Morgan – that way." ' Sir Charles laughed. ' "Pretend she's the girl you had last night," I told him. We'll see.'

They saw that the young Heathcliff had forgotten how he had handled the girl he had last night when the time came for Catherine Earnshaw, in her long white nightgown, to climb in young Heathcliff's bedroom window.

'You're always getting me in bed with some guy I'd never go to bed with,' Arlette told Charles at the end of the day. 'This can take all summer.'

'All I ask, Arlette, is that we get one shot where it looks like he's screwing her.' And he loudly advised the disconsolate Heathcliff, fearful he was about to fail his first great opportunity: 'Just for once, Ian, tomorrow morning, kiss her as if nothing on heaven or earth could stop you. After all – this is your one true love and the rest of your life is going to be fucked up by it.'

'Yes, Sir Charles. I suspect it may.'

Arlette laughed, patted his shoulder, and ran off to her dressing room, where in five minutes she was out of Catherine's nightgown, into her black sweater and skirt, and the hairdresser was leaving when Charles Granville came in.

'May I drive you home?' he inquired, so solicitously she was sure he had come to try once more to make love to her.

Until she and Anthony came to London, she had not seen Granville since the New York premiere of *The Return of the Native*, and that was a long time ago, four years.

Before Micah.

That was how she counted time nowadays. Either something had happened before Micah or it had happened after Micah. They were two quite separate categories of time and significance and insignificance.

But Charles Granville had no idea that now she lived in a different time dimension which had obliterated Sir Charles Granville as a lover, past or present or potential.

He sat down, and while Arlette removed some of the makeup, began to talk as if this were any casual encounter between fellow workers. 'I tried to get Powell for this, you know.'

'I know.'

'But he's too bloody involved with that play which is going to show us we're headed for an apocalypse of murder, cannibalism, destruction of humanity and all its friends.'

'John is not optimistic.'

Arlette glanced at her watch. Seven-thirty.

Sir Charles quickly stood up. 'Anthony waiting for you?'

'We eat dinner about eight-thirty and talk a little, and—'

'And go to bed.'

'And go to bed.'

Arlette started to walk past him, but Granville caught her and kissed her, holding her in that determined embrace she all at once remembered very well.

Before Micah, she might not have stopped him; or she might.

Now she said: 'Charles – it wouldn't be fair—'

At that, Granville released her, looking at her as if one of them had lost his wits. 'What in Christ's name are you talking about?' He stared at her suspiciously. 'Arlette – what's happened?'

'We made a mistake, Charles, that's all.' There. A mistake. The magic word if ever there was one.

They looked at each other questioningly, a little sadly. 'I've loved you – did you forget that?' he asked, surprisingly gentle.

'I'm sorry.'

'Shut up, you little bitch.' All at once he kissed her, this time lightly. 'I've thought about you for a long time. Beat it, while you can.' As she went quickly ahead of him, he gave her a whack on the buttocks and got into the car beside her with a smile, not an entirely reassuring smile, but a smile; there were several months of work to be done.

He pushed the button to raise the window between them and the chauffeur and, quite as companionably as if the last few minutes had never happened, began to talk about his plans for the picture. 'Behind the credits I want your face, only your face, as Heathcliff talks, seeing your face everywhere – in the polished floor, in the flagstones, in the trees, the clouds, the air at night—'

At the hotel he kissed her, and all at once Arlette was contrite. 'I'm sorry, Charles.'

'It's over. Forget it. I'll pick you up at eight. Don't worry. The first thing I am is a director.'

Once young Heathcliff had contrived to kiss her as if his life depended upon it, he grew bolder, and by the time Granville decided to fly them north for the seduction scene, he seemed to have convinced himself – or been convinced by Arlette – that it was not Anthony De Forest who was the real Heathcliff.

'Twenty minutes, in the final cutting,' Granville told Arlette. 'But he may as well make the best of it. He may grow up to be an actor – or he may become so overbearing

661

as a result of having begun his career as Anthony De Forest that he'll never get beyond it.' He had come to the trailer which followed their jeep to the location site each morning, to watch the makeup man and hairdresser. 'The willingness to do whatever is necessary to get what the picture needs. That's the only actor worth his keep.'

Arlette smiled slightly. *Well, that's me. And Anthony.*

The Irishman was young and had not foreseen that the future eventually did arrive.

One convincing love scene from Ian Flaherty was all Granville needed – Arlette's face in close-up would do the rest of the work for him. But once, he must forget he was about to kiss, to touch, to lie on top of this woman he idolized – without the sheets and quilts which had simplified his job in the earlier sequence.

'The rest is up to you, Arlette. There'll be one cameraman only, and it will be a close-up. I'll talk to the kid. If he doesn't touch you he'll be too scared to look convincing. But once a man's hand begins to approach the great female mystery—' Granville was mocking and serious. 'He's young, he's perpetually randy – he fancies he's in love with you – nature is wonderful.' He laughed, but added seriously, 'There's no tragedy of the two Catherines without this scene. Remember that. Help him.'

'I know. I know. But why didn't you hire an actor?'

'He looks like Anthony. And he's a good enough actor when he's not terrified.'

By midmorning, the light was brilliant and slightly mauve, like the moors, and Catherine and Heathcliff ran over them, the camera truck following in the distance. They stopped when Granville's electronic voice called out, pausing to rest.

Granville ordered them on: Run up the hill. Run as fast as they could. Run all the way to the top. Throw themselves down, exhausted.

'Don't act exhausted. Be exhausted. Lie in the grass, or sit on it. Do whatever you feel like doing. If it doesn't work, we'll go back to the script. You're both looking better and better.'

By which he means we look more and more frantic.
If only he looked less like Pat Runkle.

The time seemed out of sequence, and it was at once disturbing and frightening. She was a grown woman – she knew what her life was to have been, many years of it at least. All at once, here was Pat Runkle, about to make love to her for the first time. The sequence of her life, her feelings, her growth into a woman, the painfully won confidence and capability, did not belong here, now. She longed to be Lily Malone again, unknowing of the future as Ian Flaherty was at that moment.

They began to run, Arlette running as fast as she could, sometimes holding Heathcliff's hand, sometimes pausing, gasping for breath. By the time they reached the hilltop she was excited by the running, the windy day, the fragrant air, the moors in all their shades of mauve and taupe and dull green.

In another moment there was the truck, the makeup man and hairdresser, jumping out to examine Arlette while Granville ordered them to leave her as she was, wet-faced, disheveled. 'Come here,' he said peremptorily to young Heathcliff.

Twenty feet away they stood talking, and when they returned Heathcliff was looking dazed and embarrassed, even younger than he should have. Granville climbed down the slight incline to where the bank had been prepared with its bed of ferns and moor flowers, stationed his cameraman, and summoned Arlette.

Arlette ran to the edge of the bluff and jumped down the six-foot embankment into a soft cover of moss and flowers. Heathcliff followed and, observing Granville's instructions, landed beside her with a determined bound, promptly seizing her by the hair and kissing her with more authority than he had shown before. They sank slowly to their knees, clinging together as if they were two drowning people who would end by drowning each other.

He bent over Catherine, quick and impetuous, as she looked up at him. Arlette's arms closed fast about his shoulders, the palm of one hand pressing against the back of his head as he forced her slowly backward and his hand pushed beneath her skirt.

Arlette had difficulty during any love scene in separating the actress from the sensualist, and as his hand paused on her thigh, she drew in a long deep breath and held him closer, their tongues mingling in swift excitement.

Granville's calm voice interrupted them. 'Cut. Got it?' he asked, and the young Heathcliff drew away as if accused. Granville was talking to the cameraman. 'Shall we try another?'

Arlette sat up. 'Another what?'

Heathcliff had walked several feet away, hands in his pockets, his back to them, head hanging. Arlette drew up her legs pulling the dress around her ankles, and gazed off into the distance.

Granville came to her and squatted on both heels, took a long stem of dry grass and stuck it between his teeth. 'Thanks. There's only one way to take the fear out of a young guy when he's terrified of a woman. We'd have shot that bloody scene a hundred times.'

Heathcliff was some distance away by now, and Granville called out: 'Come along, unless you want to walk back. It's fifteen miles.'

In the trailer young Heathcliff sat opposite Arlette, gazing at his muddy shoes, then casting Arlette a pained apologetic look, which she seemed not to see, as she chatted amiably with Granville, the *noblesse oblige* of the professional, compliant to whatever duty required.

She smiled at Ian consolingly when they arrived at the inn, took his hand as she jumped out, and whispered: 'Granville would chop of your head if the scene called for it—'

'Miss Morgan, please believe—'

'Good-bye. Good luck.' She kissed his cheek. 'Mr De Forest takes over from here.'

In the sitting room of their suite, Anthony was dictating letters to Eugene Cartwright, who had recently arrived from New York bearing mail and messages from Alicia

and Minerva and Eva and Jerry; business letters from
Friedman and Jim Brown; the contracts for the signatures
for *Medea*. New York. Was there such a place on such a
day?

She sat down, eyes still shining with excitement, and
looked at Anthony carefully:

*There he is: twenty-three years later. Except that the young
Irishman will never become Anthony De Forest.*

One Anthony in a hundred years.

CHAPTER 84·

After that, as Arlette told the young Irishman, Mr De
Forest took over.

Heathcliff had returned a grown man, to reclaim
everything Catherine Earnshaw's brother had taken from
him. Anthony had talked little about how he meant to
play Heathcliff, and now he made it obvious by his
makeup, the way he wore his early nineteenth-century
clothes, that here was a Heathcliff as savage, brutal,
vengeful, cruel, passionate, as the man described.

And the Catherine Earnshaw Linton who walked the
moors with Heathcliff after his return was no longer the
sensual young girl, but a woman who had learned by
marrying Edgar Linton that one man was not like another.

As they walked ahead of the camera, she glanced at
him, paused, and pointed.

'*There*,' said Catherine, indicating the mossy bank.
'*Nothing changes on these moors—*'

'*My God, my God, how I have thought of it—*'

Catherine Linton was not being played as a proper
young woman, brought up to become a lady, but as a
woman who could not have been brought up properly
anywhere, any time – a woman destined to destroy herself
and any man who loved her on her own terms; and there
were no others.

Heathcliff slid down the embankment first, and Catherine followed him. This scene was to be taken first from the angle of Catherine's back, and Heathcliff was to unbutton her dress as she knelt before him, pushing the dress to her waist, and only his face would be seen as he put his hands on her breasts.

Once again, there was Granville's favorite cameraman, guaranteed not to film anything he was not instructed to, for Anthony could keep an eye on an errant cameraman while acting a rape, a murder, a death scene.

The scene would be shot from different angles: the cameraman above, showing Heathcliff's back, Catherine's bewitched face, before it was blotted out by a movement of Anthony's head. There would be a very long shot, both the cameraman and Granville at a distance, with Anthony lying upon her and her legs apart.

This scene was to have an atmosphere of magical renewal of love – an evident belief on the part of Catherine and Heathcliff that her marriage, his six-year absence, had changed nothing. There was to be no tragedy on their faces, no fearful misgivings, only the tender, increasingly wild rediscovery of the love they remembered.

She remained motionless as he unbuttoned her dress, slid it off her shoulders and down to her waist, and his hands closed over her breasts, with that familiar gesture of his thumbs caressing the nipples, the faint smile increasing as their color deepened and they arose like buds. He forced her gently backward, lying over her, and Granville's voice spoke softly: 'Cut.'

The scene took the morning because Granville required many angles, many distances of the camera.

At one o'clock they climbed back up the embankment to summon the trailer with the hairdresser and fitter, and Arlette and Anthony and Granville sat on cushions eating a lunch of salad, Brie, flown up from London every other day, French bread, plums and peaches.

Slowly emerging from the spell, Arlette sat silent in Catherine's rumpled muslin dress, which must not be pressed, nor her makeup repaired, nor her hair combed and bits of moor grass removed from it. She sat eating slowly, facing the two men without clearly seeing them, or hearing what they had to say.

Two men, discussing gross receipts, brokers' tips, Swiss bank accounts, good investments and bad investments, and the best ways to avoid paying more than a minimum tax to either the English or United States government.

'Cut,' said the director – and *cut* went their minds.

They returned to their everyday selves in a few minutes.

But Arlette, captured by these women she played, by their unhappy lives, by the men who loved them, might – unless she was given a few days respite now and then once the shooting began – remain for weeks or even months, trapped inside Eustacia Vye or Emma Hamilton or Catherine Earnshaw Linton, or even Marguerite Gautier. In a play, although that happened for several hours before and after the performance, there were nevertheless a few hours she might claim to herself, talking to friends, laughing, studying with Alicia or one of the other teachers who rotated through her life.

Once, she had talked to Micah about it.

'I don't know how much longer I can keep it up. So much destruction must be doing something to me. Are we affected by what we pretend?'

He had driven from the Observatory when she called to tell him she would be free the next day: Granville was going to begin filming Heathcliff's death scene, and Anthony wanted privacy.

Whether these meetings were difficult for Micah to arrange, what he gave up, she did not know or ask, and he did not tell her. When a break came in her schedule, she called him and he arrived.

'The stars,' she said, smiling slightly, 'will be in their places when you get back.' She turned her head sideways as she sat before him naked, while he lay propped on one elbow, looking at her seriously: 'Won't they?'

'They may be a few more million light-years away. But it makes little difference to my work.' Micah's hand caressed her slowly, an artist exploring a sculpture, a

667

blind man finding the shape of beauty, and wherever he touched her, the touch trailed a magical current in its wake.

Neither his wife nor his children had come to England for the three months he planned to be there – and Arlette supposed he had arranged this, too.

'You, Micah,' she said softly, and was becoming drowsy as his fingers touched her temples, eyelids, lips, the bridge of her nose, as if he would explore her so completely that when they parted, the memories would have been sealed in her flesh, and his. 'You have freedom. I don't.'

'That's been your choice.'

'My choice? Yes. I chose my life, but everything followed from that. Actors need not only audiences – they need each other, they need their directors and coaches. Actors are the greediest people on earth. We need everything. We use everything. And sooner or later, everything uses us. If we convince them, the audience, about love or hate or dying, they give us awards. Money. Applause. Love.'

'Love?'

'Envy.'

Arlette continued to sit motionless, under the slow steady passing of his hands along her arms, across her breasts and thighs. There was a long silent moment.

'Love,' he said finally, 'when it's condemned to frustration, becomes envy. Most people don't call it that. They don't even like to believe they feel envy. They prefer to believe the icon is at fault.'

There had begun a faint ringing sound in her ears, some flute-like music of her imagination, distant, scarcely audible; and it seemed he would soon put her into a trance, a state where she would begin to comprehend that eternity of time and space he studied. Tears of pleasure formed in her eyes and ran slowly down her face.

Remorseful, Micah grasped her with both hands and settled her upon him.

Why do tears impress us more than laughter?

She bent over him, her hair covering his face, while her

muscles quivered and the sounds of a soft distant wailing made her wonder, in momentary stupefaction, where they were; if perhaps someone was hidden nearby.

At last, opening her eyes, as if she had been on a far interior journey, private as a dream, as an anaesthesia, returning to where they were when she looked at him as he lay on his back beneath her, she saw to her surprise a slight tender smile on his face.

The bewilderment increased. A smile? Now?

It appeared slowly out of the earlier expressions she vaguely glimpsed when, opening her eyes to look at him in those intervals when the interior journey brought her near enough to earth that she was reminded of her former life there, she found his face as contorted with painful pleasure as her own must be.

She found the smile reassuring. The quivering of her muscles subsided, the heavy beating of her heart slowed, no longer threatening to knock its way through her chest, burst forth: her last gift to him. They were safe, after all.

Never, it seemed, had she felt entirely safe during his lovemaking, for as the intensity increased, the sensations acquired a curious impersonality, too powerful to be endured without the reassuring knowledge that if terror intervened she could look out from that inner world and find him there, marauder and protector.

Now, having explored her body, a devout geographer discovering some new land of unexpected caverns, blooming fields, rising hills, he bit her nipples, not too gently, and after some time left her, but did not move from beside her:

Now, it might as well never have happened at all.

Memory is the worst pain. Now – weeks without him.

'You'll leave me again.' She knelt beside him, touching his hair, kissing his mouth lightly. 'Forgive me. I'm the one who's leaving – in a way.'

I'm going back to a different world: my real world.

As she sat with Anthony and Granville in that real world, not listening to them, those memories seemed to belong to some unimaginably distant past – eight days ago.

She did not know whether he would be there when she got back to London. Not if Granville kept them with his interminable quest for perfection:

Where is he going next? He told me. I've forgotten. Nova Scotia's new radio observatory? New Zealand? Moscow?

The search for a time to meet, a place to meet, would begin again.

When she was leaving, wearing the jonquil-yellow suit with the nephrite camellia pinned to its lapel that Anthony had given her, he had said: 'Someday, Arlette, you may find you've had enough.'

'Of what?'

'Your life, the way you live it now.'

And then what?

But she did not ask him that:

Enough? Enough of being Arlette Morgan? Who would I be then?

It's too late ever to be Lily Malone again.

She glanced now at Granville and found him watching her thoughtfully. Anthony had walked several yards away; he stood there a few moments, then turned and came toward them. Heathcliff ready for the next scene.

'We'll walk,' Granville told them. 'The more you walk in this sun and wind, the better for your faces in this scene – real sweat. Oh, much better, I assure you—'

'Poor Catherine.' Arlette looked at Granville, slightly surprised, for she had not expected to say it. 'Yes, she is a ghost. Even to me. And, oh Jesus – I've got to die again—'

However, she was not scheduled to die until they returned to London, since that was an indoor scene.

Something worse awaited her here: the opening of Catherine's coffin by the sexton, at Heathcliff's bribed demand. And Granville planned that for the first day when the light suited him.

'Once that's out of the way,' he told her as they walked

swiftly along. 'I think you'll be able to give more attention to the death scene.'

'No doubt. Once I'm dead, I can give my complete attention to dying.'

CHAPTER 85

'It's a mad idea. Not even Heathcliff would have done it.'

'Heathcliff did do it in the book. And by Christ, he's going to do it in the picture. Of course he's mad. This is a crazier love story than any you've played—'

'But he says she looks the same, and you know she would—' Arlette shuddered.

'I've done some research.' Granville sounded as if he were discussing research on furniture. 'It's possible she would have looked more or less the same. Scared?'

'I'm scared! Yes!'

'It's only a few seconds – and it must be shot here. We need the moors, the naturally increasing darkness – the wind. We can't fake this. There are air holes in the coffin. Jesus, Arlette, there's no risk. You did damn near drown in the weir, and were determined to do it.'

'I know, I know,' said Arlette, weaving her fingers nervously together. 'That was water. I can swim. This is different. The box.' She looked at him with her eyes wide and bright, vaguely aware that Anthony was standing near them. All at once she said angrily, 'The hell with it. What difference does it make? I'll never be buried.'

Anthony shook her shoulder. 'Arlette!'

She looked at him, eyes wild as Catherine Linton's the night she died, accusing her husband and Heathcliff of having killed her.

She glanced away. 'I'm ready.'

The small burial ground, with old headstones marked by the names of Earnshaws and Lintons of several generations, had been prepared more than a year before. There was one fresh plot where Edgar Linton had been buried that day, and the next night Granville planned to shoot the sequence of Heathcliff bribing the sexton to open Catherine's grave, waiting with a miser's greed for the sight of her.

The sun was gone, the light soft, pleasing to Granville, and Arlette declared herself prepared to enter the coffin, assuring herself it made no difference whether this be acting or reality; it came to the same thing, finally.

Giving one hand to Granville, one to Anthony, refusing to look at either of them, concentrating upon the earth, the box lined with frayed silk, she became unexpectedly tranquil, and lay on her back with her feet together, hands crossed over her breasts, closing her eyes.

She told them to give her a little time to become inanimate, fifteen seconds, no more, no less – and slowly she counted:

Mirror, mirror. Kashmiri. Cathay. Pagoda. Orange poppies. Bamboo. Deep water. Dark forest . . .

She heard the sound of the lid settling, and slowly reduced the level of her breathing, concentrating upon each vision as it appeared, distinct as a photograph, until her breathing had lowered to its least possible level, her eyelids were motionless, and the pupils of her eyes fixed steadily upon the orange poppies:

Suppose they can't get the lid open?

Suppose Anthony jumps on it and fights them off?

All at once it seemed this was something seized out of the future. She thought of Anthony:

What is he thinking as he looks at me? Does he wish it were true? All the fears, all the resentments, finally over?

Men had wished for worse things when jealousy gored them.

It had begun to seem peaceful, and perhaps more than fifteen seconds had elapsed. It even seemed quite likely this was her death, the end of her life, no scene she was playing.

She felt the light increase, although her lids remained shut, and heard Anthony's voice: '*Catherine – oh, my darling, darling—*'

672

'Cut.'

It was Sir Charles standing over her, not Anthony, watching her seriously and, to her astonishment, with a tenderness she had not seen on his face since they had been lovers.

'It's all over,' he said, a doctor speaking to a patient coming out of anesthesia. 'You're fine.'

Arlette sat up, and to her surprise, she laughed merrily and defiantly. 'Of course I'm fine! Did you think I was dead?'

The faces around her were solemn, their smiles tentative and slightly ashamed. And where was Anthony?

Anthony stood some distance away, his back to them. She approached him slowly, almost timidly, and he whirled around, took her in his arms, pressed her head against his shoulder, and held her for several moments, until Granville arrived.

'Let's talk about something cheerful,' suggested Arlette. 'Let's talk about how pregnant I have to look for my death scene.'

Seeing those faces struggling to lose their solemnity, respond to her effort to fling a little incense about and abolish the odor of death, Arlette decided she had acted the scene – if it might be called acting – with conviction.

Granville was still brooding. 'I should have used a double – or a wax dummy.'

'The hell you should! I'm Catherine Earnshaw. Nobody else.'

'I think you'd better get away from here, Arlette. I'll send you back when the plane comes tomorrow.' Granville's actors and technicians rode a shuttle service on his jet. 'There's just one more scene here – Anthony and the sexton. Take a day off. Do something—'

Something.

She sat across from Micah Benoni in the restaurant of the little inn where they had driven in a rented car, a few miles out of London. They were talking eagerly, laughing from happiness and relief. Arlette thought the reunion –

not yet consummated – combined with the scene she had played the day before and with Micah's anxiety that he might have been in Moscow before Granville set her free, had made them giddy.

The bubbling casserole of beefsteak and kidney pie stood on the table between them, and while they waited for it to cool they drank consommé and looked out the windows at this broad, still flowing tributary of the Thames, where wildfowl occasionally paused to preen their feathers and cruise about in search of edible morsels. The sky was gray and the water gray, and Micah's eyes were the same gray color, for it seemed they changed with the light reflected from the world outside. Or from the world inside?

'Shall we go to the same inn?' he had asked when she called. 'Did you like it?'

'I liked it.'

'Eleven-thirty? Same corner?'

'Good-bye, darling – thank you.'

Thank you. That was what she said to him each time. *Thank you.*

Thank you for being you? Thank you for loving me – for taking time off from your galaxies and superspace to talk my language, since I can't talk yours? Thank you.

It must mean something. She had never said it to another man.

In the taxi, on her way to the designated corner, dressed in black skirt and black sweater and flat-heeled black pumps, she took from her makeup bag a waist-length blonde wig – Catherine Linton's wig – straight as a silk scarf, and pulled it over her head. She wiped off the lipstick, but on dark glasses which covered half her face, and smiled with joyous anticipation.

Whether or not the taxi driver took notice of the transformation, she did not know:

He probably thinks I'm going to nothing more serious than a bank robbery.

Once in the car, she began by telling Micah about the coffin, the waiting, the counting, playing a game of telling him a story so he would tell her a story. And as she talked, glancing sideways from time to time to examine his face, she remembered what he had said: *Someday you may not need this.*

Did he suppose that she acted for the reward of being a star? Or having a famous name? That scarcely seemed possible, since he had said that the value of any art was in its giving to human life the dimensions which made it human.

She had thought about it, but now that she was with him, something prevented her from asking him. Did he suppose she acted for different reasons from those which had made him become an astronomer?

She looked at him carefully:

Yes, I love him.

Micah Benoni's remarkable face and elegantly shaped head seemed to contain puzzles within puzzles.

Even that great wordless confession of lovemaking, which said more than all the confidence of a lifetime, had not explained him to her; yet he seemingly concealed nothing.

In that first sudden glory she seemed to understand everything, not Micah Benoni only, but the world he studied, history of ancient explosions, mimicked everywhere in the universe; the sudden glory which came with a conviction that, finally, she had discovered him and that the discovery would not be lost this time.

Then it was gone, no more durable than the breaking of a wave.

What he wanted from her was not so clear.

Perhaps it was some comprehension of her capacity to portray other women so convincingly audiences temporarily forgot who was the actress, who was the character, and let her lead them toward unwelcome sorrows of self-knowledge.

Now, as they sat in the warm little restaurant, talking as if neither had other responsibilities, entirely concentrated upon those few hours, her descriptions of her work

675

omitted all mention of Anthony, as his references to his life did not include his wife or children.

She was glad to know so little of that life he lived when he went to his home. Unhappily, it was not possible for him to know so little about Anthony.

The world knew about Anthony; and despite his secrecy, Anthony, like herself, had been thoroughly revealed, turned inside out.

There could be nothing left of either of them.

Now, while they ate, she asked Micah one question and another; a child given an opportunity to catechize her favorite adult. She asked what he was studying at the Jodrell Bank Observatory, and as he talked she watched his face for clues:

How much he loved her. There was no way to be sure.

While he was paying the check, having answered her questions seriously, he said: 'All that we scientists — any of us — have learned or will ever learn can be only a whistle in the vast cacophony of nature. Don't expect too much of us. The puzzles multiply.'

Indeed they do.

Arlette started up the staircase, then all at once took them two at a time and arrived at the top to look down at him, her face joyous and brilliant, welcoming.

Great Solomon, let us try again!

Later, she felt it her responsibility to let him know that in her history love was not only one feeling; it changed as she changed; it changed as the people she loved changed.

'I've saved nothing to protect me. I love you, Micah.'

'You don't need protection.'

'If I ever should, I don't have it. You can kill me any time.'

'I'll never hurt you. You know that.' He glanced at her curiously, touching her chin to turn her face toward him. 'It's the first loss you're grieving for, Arlette. Not the second.'

'It's both,' said Arlette stubbornly, refusing to give up her claim to resentment against Anthony. After all, without it — what would she be doing here?

We live on separate planets. When we're together, it's an imaginary world. Even we may not be real, except to each other, and only for a few hours. These two people we are when we're together may not even exist for anyone else.

That was supposed to be the charm of a love affair.

With the others, that had been much of the charm.

Micah, however, aroused the need for possession which could be renewed, reaffirmed, displayed to the world, as a separate life; and a life they shared:

But which world would we live in? His – or mine? That's the impossibility.

What had Micah given up today, for example?

Whatever it might have been – stars tracking across a television screen in a quiet room, where he sat feeding a computer pulsars, quasars, galaxies; a page or two of his new book – he would not tell her. Confessed sacrifices had a way of becoming accusations.

CHAPTER 86

No one, it seemed, was prepared – even Arlette and Anthony, who sat in the back row of the projection room, Alicia beside Anthony and Jerry Hoffman beside Arlette – for the film Granville had contrived.

Anthony's death scene struck at them the moment the lights went down: a blast of music, wild and weird, perhaps something Granville had found among the country people and amplified into an arrangement which was primitive, crude, yet sophisticated.

In back of the titles, Arlette's face filled the screen, superimposed over clouds and polished flagstones, trees, and water: the girl the young Heathcliff had made love to, who had run about the moors with the *gypsy brat*; the sixteen-year-old girl who had climbed into his window, crossing the rooftop late at night to reach him. Her blonde hair surrounded her face, glimmering softly, and she showed a smile of joy, rapturous welcome.

677

Then Anthony's voice spoke, low, contemplative, tormented; *'God, it is a long fight! I wish it were over!'*

He lay on the bed, fully dressed, his dark hair unkempt as if he had not combed it for days. And as he lay there, following his visions of Catherine, a slight smile came to his mouth. He turned his head and she was beside him, a live woman, her eyes closed, sleeping, breathing deeply and slowly. He reached for her, put his arms about her.

She did not evaporate, as a proper ghost should. She was no longer there.

This ghost left the room like any ordinary visitor. She walked swiftly across the floor, opened the door, and went out, closing it quietly, while Heathcliff reached forth one hand pleadingly, calling her name, and fell back in despair.

As Catherine closed the door, Ellen Dean opened it, her face tranquil. She had seen no ghost pass by.

'Did you call, sir?'

Heathcliff raised his head, his face wild with the fury of frustration, and seeing the placid, quiet Ellen Dean, their childhood nurse, the nurse of Catherine's sixteen-year-old daughter, he gave a sigh. *'It's you, Ellen.'*

'Yes, sir.' Ellen approached the bed and looked at him as he gazed at her with an expression of horror and pleading.

'It is a long fight,' he repeated, more gently. *'I wish it were over.'*

They were silent, watching each other. Heathcliff, a dying man who willed his death; Ellen Dean still incapable of comprehending these savages she had spent her life caring for.

'Ellen – I wonder if you remember—' Heathcliff looked out the window, then back again to Ellen. *'When I was sixteen, before I ran away, and came back a rich man – by whatever means – there was one Sunday when she left me to be with the Lintons. She said I did not amuse her any more. I was dirty and sullen. It was true . . .'* A curious reflective smile lighted his eyes. *'Only you tried to comfort me. You told me I must not be despondent, that perhaps my father was Emperor*

678

of China, and my mother an Indian queen.' He smiled wryly. *'I've remembered that, Mrs Dean. It could be the truth. I don't know the truth.'*

Abruptly he dismissed Mrs Dean, telling her not to come back to trouble him. *'To die is not easy, Mrs Dean. I beg your indulgence—'* She left in silence, nor did she open the door again when his voice cried out in powerful summons: *'Catherine! Catherine!'*

Arlette leaned forward, her eyes wide and wet, horrified by the bitterness, the passion of savagery, the hatred of himself and Catherine:

No wonder he didn't want me there.

She was wondering how much of both her feeling and Anthony's about Micah Benoni had inadvertently been picked up by the camera, that treacherous contraption which victimized anyone who got in its path.

But if Anthony had any such misgivings about his own victimization, there was no sign of it.

He sat, muscles at ease, his expression that of a student listening to a professor with restful alertness, critical of each intonation, every sentence and idea. He was not participating in the Heathcliff who was no longer himself. He had become the critic, the aloof scrutinizer, concerned not only with his performance, but with hers, with the direction, most of all with the editing, which, in effect, made the film after their acting had provided the raw material for Granville's technical skills and imagination.

Anthony, true shaman, seemed to find it natural that a shaman should rip out his guts for the bastards. That was why he had become a shaman in the first place: to use all of himself; give all of himself, wring himself dry of emotion and energy, before at last he must leave the world and those bastards to their next devices. While Arlette's resentment never entirely left her. It scalded her before; muttered at her afterward.

This remote man was not the Anthony who had played the scenes in which she had participated:

The Heathcliff who had slapped Catherine's sixteen-year-old daughter hard enough to make her face swell.

The Heathcliff who had met Catherine Earnshaw Linton in the dark seclusion they had found while her husband was sleeping. The Heathcliff who had knelt beside Catherine's coffin in the Grange parlor, unfastened the locket about her neck, and spoken on the breaking edge of a sob: '*Catherine Earnshaw, may you not rest as long as I am living – haunt me – I cannot live without my soul!*'

This was not the Heathcliff who at last stood facing Catherine Earnshaw's daughter in the room where his son had just died, and the boy's father, despising him even when the boy could no longer suffer from his hatred, coolly inquired: '*Now – Catherine, how do you feel?*'

Catherine answered gently: '*He's safe, and I'm free—*'

Here was Juliet again. Arlette heard the young girl with surprise, for it was the tone she remembered from her first session with Alicia Fiedler, saying, at Alicia's request, Juliet's '*Amen,*' which told the Nurse in one word that Juliet was now a woman.

Catherine said: '*But you have left me alone so long to struggle against death alone, that I feel and see only death!*' She looked at him with the accusatory, resigned expression of a woman his own age. '*I feel like death!*'

Heathcliff had chosen, for his dying, the room Catherine had slept in as a young girl, the room to which he had come late at night, climbing through the window. Now, where the window had been black with a starless night, Catherine Earnshaw Linton's face appeared, her hair wet with rain, the gown in which she had been buried soaked through. The face was very clear, tragically alive, and her fist rapped upon the window, rousing him so suddenly that he sat up, plunging his fist through the pane – a real windowpane, real blood, and his own, Anthony had told her.

Heathcliff seized her wrist, to drag her through the window, into the bed with him.

'*Let me in,*' Catherine's voice pleaded. '*Let me in!*'

The two scenes had been shot separately and spliced later, because of Anthony's insistence that Arlette not be present. It had been someone else's hand he grasped. His blood, flowing steadily and profusely, soaked the counter-pane. He had told her of the scene when he returned to New York, for it required five stitches and the scar was still visible.

'A special effect,' he had explained, as if it were nothing out of the ordinary for an actor who took his work seriously to risk cutting an artery, 'would have been a special effect. This film can't stand special effects. It depends, in large part, on its crudity.'

The close-up of her face at the window came during Heathcliff's death scene, and while his hand continued to grasp hers, trying to draw her in to him, she disappeared. She did not fade into transparency; she was gone, and there was no reply, no vaguely floating face of his hallucinations as he threw the window wide and shouted, in the voice of a man begging for his life: *Come in, Cathy! Once more – hear me this time–'*

There was a close-up of the windowpane, as it stood opened to the stormy night, and the letters scratched upon it: CATHERINE EARNSHAW-HEATHCLIFF-LINTON: The record of the dead Catherine's hopes and indecisions.

The music stopped, there was a long silence, as he continued to lean out, straining, then threw himself back upon the bed and clenched his bleeding fist until, when he opened it, there were marks of nails cut into the palms. No special effects there, either, he had told her, somewhat grimly, but with the pride of a *torero* who had killed an unkillable bull.

They were Heathcliff and Catherine Earnshaw Linton; and they were Arlette Morgan and Anthony De Forest, bidding each other a final good-bye. A farewell without tenderness, accusatory, half mad, Heathcliff holding her in his arms, kissing her mouth and eyes, stroking her tangled hair; Anthony, playing Heathcliff with the pain he must have felt for several years as he tried again and again to bring her back to him – an effort as hopeless as trying to bring Catherine back from death; she wanted to die, as Arlette wanted never to trust herself to him again.

Catherine spoke in a low accusatory voice, staring down into his eyes as he knelt beside the bed. *'You have killed me – how many years do you mean to live after I'm gone?'* She seized his hair and clutched it until the pain showed in his eyes, while he stared at her steadily. *'I wish I could hold you until we were both dead!'* Her voice and face were bitter, condemning, and Arlette was astonished to find there on the screen, in that face which so uncannily resembled her own, the Arlette who had heard Deborah Crane's voice in London and then put down the telephone, whispering with incredulous conviction: *I will never be happy again.*

That Arlette had vanished little by little, first into the refuge of John Powell's love; into the anger she had never clearly spoken to Anthony out of her fear of giving him an ugly Arlette to remember: the Arlette lost to him once and for all in Micah Benoni's love.

There she was, disguised as Catherine Earnshaw, straining at Heathcliff's hair until it drew his eyebrows upward at the corners, her face cruel, vengeful, savagely beautiful.

'Don't torture me until I'm mad as yourself!' That was Heathcliff, and it was Anthony.

She listened in increasing wonderment to the words which had at last given Arlette Morgan and Anthony De Forest courage to speak to each other without the subterfuge of their lives as they lived them, all the concealed anger and pain from which they protected each other.

They embraced again, Catherine as violent as he, with a sudden renewal of vitality, this last surging strength and will to hold him to her. Catherine's sobs, as she kissed him, mingled with Arlette's seated beside him.

'Yes—' Heathcliff's voice and face showed angry bitterness again. *'Kiss me and cry – my kisses and tears will damn you . . .'*

It's all true.

Why was it that when they had played the scene, they had played Catherine Earnshaw Linton and Heathcliff, while now the picture she watched was Anthony De Forest and Arlette Morgan, meeting on the Montauk beach, as she watched him approach, moving toward him slowly, reluctantly, and when they came together, resolutely shutting him away from her?

Those two people had talked quietly, even occasionally smiling, as at some recognition of all the secrets held between them, Anthony somewhat angry with what he took for petulance, demanding that she get it over with, as a child gets over a colic.

'*You love me*—' Heathcliff said, shaking her by the shoulders, and her head fell back, eyes closed. '*Nothing could have parted us but you – you, of your own will*—'

Yes. He's telling the truth.

Or maybe we've all been everyone?

'*Let me alone*—' Catherine raged at him. '*You left me, too – I forgive you – forgive me!*'

Heathcliff kissed her, and Arlette again glanced sideways at Anthony. But if he saw Arlette Morgan and Anthony De Forest in those two lovers, his grim, critical, stolid expression gave no evidence of it. Perhaps the imagery of the screen was too vivid, and he could resist it only with anger.

Ellen Dean entered Heathcliff's room – their room, as he had called it – to find him lying fully dressed on the bed, the window banging in the wind, the rain pouring on his face and hair, his eyes wide and staring, a fierce unnatural grin upon his mouth. She approached him slowly, softly, touched him, and started back as she found him dead.

The picture was not quite over, as Anthony stepped across the back of his seat without a glance and disappeared through the exit door.

She started to get up, but Jerry grabbed her wrist. 'Sit still!'

The screen was suffused with that light over the moors which had come two or three afternoons in September, mauve, rose-colored along the horizon, as a sheep boy, driving his flock, stopped still, trembling, for the sheep refused the crossing.

A man and woman, Catherine and Heathcliff, walked

slowly along the path, not transparent ghosts but Catherine and Heathcliff; arms about each other's waists, a serene tranquillity in their smiles. They walked on, turning their backs to the audience, and when they had gone a distance, the sheep obediently made the crossing. The boy's piercing flute cut through the air.

There was a moment of silence before the lights went up, and Arlette tried once again to free herself of Jerry, to search for Anthony:

Granville got his picture. However he did it.

Unquestionably, this audience was the most emotional they would ever have, however successful it might prove – or even if the public decided it did not want to see two lovers crossed not by their stars, but by their own violent unforgiving natures.

'My God – what an actor he is—' That was Minerva.

'Where is he?' That was Eva.

'Don't look for him. Leave him alone,' Alicia said. 'That's why he left.'

For even when they went straggling out, as if they were leaving the scene of a disaster from which all bodies had finally been removed, they did not find Anthony in the lobby. The women, struck by the blinding light, quickly inspected their faces.

Art Friedman approached Arlette, who still held Jerry's arm, as if she might get lost, and told them that someone had seen Anthony go down a back staircase leading to the street.

Anthony's departure seemed that of a victorious gladiator who, having destroyed every enemy sent against him, had quit the arena in disgust, unable to endure the sight of his victims.

By the time she reached her voice teacher's studio, Arlette was convinced Anthony had been taken by surprise by Granville's picture, perhaps offended by it – for he was sometimes offended by what directors, producers, other actors, critics, considered his best work. That was often the work he disparaged as having been over-done, and then he compared himself unfavorably with Arlette.

Micah Benoni talked to her briefly about the film, the first time they met after its public opening, but Arlette was not eager to discuss it. 'Never a nice light drawing-room comedy, where the worst disaster is red wine on the Aubusson and the most terrible feelings are concealed behind a gay ironic laugh—' Arlette demonstrated the laugh she meant, unconcerned, nothing at all conspiratorial in it.

They had seen each other three times during the months since she had returned from England – a great luxury, she called it. This was Saturday, their fourth meeting, when she had found many excuses for not being in any of the places where people expected to find her on a Saturday.

They had spent little time talking, either about the picture or the trip he had made to New Zealand; and Arlette made no mention of the article about Zarah Benoni's debut as a solo pianist at a concert given at Princeton, where, the article said, *this girl of great beauty may also become one of our major musicians.* She had, the critic went on, the drive for it, the self-confidence, no diffidence about her when she walked onto the stage, or when she nodded, very slightly, at the end of the concert:
She's young. She has years to live – years I've spent . . .
And yet those years had provided her with everything she had wanted, and with much she had never thought of wanting during that time when Valerie was trying to make an all-purpose active independent young woman of her, suited for life among the aborigines.

And Frederick had instilled in her that learning was all, learning was everything – not so easy as it seemed, for learning was not words read and remembered, permanently put on file in the brain: learning engrossed the entire being, emotions, sensitivities, smells of the morning, intent delight in a flower or hummingbird. Learning, according to Frederick, proved the sum of living. It never stopped, even momentarily; a lapse of concentration, a few moments of unawareness, and worlds were undone.

Arlette and Micah met as if several thousand years had passed them by and there was all that time to be made up.

They met early in the morning in Micah's suite at the hotel – another of those conferences he attended, he had perhaps explained, provided he ever explained anything. She thought he did not. One thing a genius should surely be immune from was the necessity to wrack his over-crowded brain with domestic trivia. He left, and that was all there was to it. No questions. No excuses. No lies.

They made love, quickly at first, then after a while, for what seemed to Arlette some endless period of time during which, slowly, gradually, she lost awareness of where she was, who she was, and was filled with sensations which streaked through her veins and seemed to loosen every muscle in her body, until at last she fell into a state of near unconsciousness, lying beneath him, arms flung wide, motionless. There was at last the slowly gathering, slowly expanding release in her belly. She felt a sense of drifting, no fear, only a steady loss of self-awareness, as she gave herself over to the conviction that once he left her, she would be dead. Nothing would remain of her which would ever again move, talk, dance, laugh. And nothing left to conjure another incarnation.

They slept for some unknown time and awoke simultaneously, facing each other; and at last smiled – tentatively, as if inquiring of the other what disasters had been met and survived.

'I thought I was dead,' she whispered. 'I never expected to see you again.' She laughed softly. 'I didn't even blame you. It seemed quite natural. Maybe that's the logical ending.'

'I was going to stop, several times. But I wanted to get everything there was of you. And here we are. Two separate people – after all.' He sat up, running his hand through his black hair, the first time she remembered seeing him make the gesture, and was startled: Gordon Donahue.

Well, men had similar ways of identifying their maleness; no man had a lien on any one gesture, movement, smile. They all did the same things, it seemed, at different times.

686

With some absent part of her mind, Arlette had thought of Micah Benoni while she sat in the dark theater, watching Heathcliff and Catherine:

Micah is the classicist.

For all his gifts of passion, she and Micah were of two different species. His sense of form about life and the universe was strict. His conviction that each perfect form will be found, sooner or later, to contain other forms – the whole not so systemically perfect as some of his colleagues would like to believe. Still, he confessed that he, like most scientists, had a preference for symmetry:

Anthony and I are the romantics. We value more than anything our emotions and what we can use them for. We walk out on a stage, or stand in front of a camera.

No one can help us then.

'Next,' she told Micah, 'is *Medea*. It's going to take a long time to get ready for that one.' She was dressing slowly, reluctantly. The allotted sand had sifted through its narrow space. 'That Asiatic sorceress, that murdering woman whose murders must be justified – at least on her own terms. How will I ever find her? She's no one I know or ever knew. It's ridiculous, everything she does.'

She was at the door, wearing the black pleated skirt and sweater, the sable coat thrown over her arm. Her lips parted as she tipped her head and he bent, this tall, slender, elegant man, to kiss her.

'Don't forget me.' With another little smile, soft, wistful, she was out the door, running down the hallway, looking at her watch; guilty over the work she had not done that day.

CHAPTER 87

Arlette began her approach to *Medea* slowly, cautiously, convinced she would never be able to dredge up this murdering jealous woman:

*How can I reach back three thousand years and touch her –
understand what made her kill her children?*

A year had gone by since *Wuthering Heights* and Arlette's
Oscar had revived her other two films, and it had been
decided that an interim period was in order for her.
Anthony spent five months in England performing *Julius
Caesar*, another obligation he had been avoiding, while
Arlette's lessons continued. But the lessons with Alicia
had been exercises in Greek drama, plays she never
expected to appear in, a way of trying to sink herself into
that ancient world.

'Have you never been jealous, Arlette?' Alicia asked.

'Jealousy – jealousy—' murmured Arlette, glancing
about the dimly lighted room, the old photographs on
the black lacquer and mother-of-pearl tables, the Paisley
shawl thrown over the piano, the beaded flowers under
glass globes, the real flowers in mixed bouquets. This
room where she had slowly approached each new character and begun to peel that new character down to raw
flesh, revealing veins and muscles, bones and marrow,
leaving at last a medical drawing of a woman's body, then
to reconstruct a new self, fiber by fiber:

Jealousy.

Arlette continued to repeat the word to herself until it
had become a word in some unheard-of foreign language.

'Jealousy is a petty emotion.' She was ashamed of her
own defeat by this petty emotion. Yet she did not believe
it was petty; for, out of control, it was one of the sources
of the world's great tragedies – a kind of reverse hubris.

Alicia must be impatient by now, aware that for the
first time some barrier had come between them which
Arlette refused to try to break through. She seemed to be
building it higher, putting brick after brick in place like
a demented mason in a triple-speed motion picture. 'I'll
have to imagine it.'

'Everyone has been jealous sometime. Very often, the
most ferocious jealousy is experienced for the most
insignificant reason. Much of it is imaginary – Othello.'

Arlette smiled. 'Yes. Jade Ring and Mei Fei. Yes, I

know jealousy. I played it when I was nineteen. But this Medea is nothing but jealousy.'

At the end of the hour and a half nothing was resolved. Alicia walked with her to the door of the drawing room, and Arlette turned impulsively. 'I've disappointed you. I brought you nothing.'

'Did you expect a perfect performance this afternoon?' Alicia smiled. 'Friday, at three.'

Arlette paused as the butler opened the door, turned, and called: 'Pride! It's not jealousy, Alicia – it's pride! The pride of a barbarian princess. Not the same thing as middle-class pride. Jason is an ambitious bourgeois.' She laughed triumphantly and ran to the elevator, setting out for her next lesson.

By the time they had been in rehearsal for two weeks and still no sign of the real Medea had appeared, Jerry came late one afternoon to talk to her, and they sat alone in the second-floor library, Anthony's study.

The walls were painted the color of eggplant, dark and shining, and the rug was covered with white water lilies, with a tracery of green fronds. The furniture was big, upholstered with polished cotton in the same design, and all about the room were Chinese bibelots. Along the walls were some five thousand books. There were modern paintings, and vases filled with white peonies, for it was her favorite time of the year, the time of her birthday, which took her by surprise whenever the date arrived again:

I'm still here.

Arlette sat on the sofa. Jerry sat a few feet away, studying her as carefully as she had seen him studying a painting on one of their visits to the Metropolitan Museum. He still lived in the apartment Sarita had decorated with African and South Sea Island sculpture, and paintings twelve feet long. Yet what he loved and studied were the old masters – finding there, she supposed, material for his lighting effects.

'Rembrandt,' he said to her once, 'that's all.'

Jerry lived with Tracy Cochrane in the apartment Sarita had left.

Sarita had come to see Arlette once, had cried and threatened to commit suicide if Arlette could not make Jerry take her back, and Arlette had soothed her, marveling that this seemingly vapid young woman should have such a raging passion, for unquestionably it was real.

'I love him, Arlette. I really love the son of a bitch. I love him so much I'd like to kill him.'

Before beginning any discussion of Medea, Arlette asked if Jerry had heard from Sarita, and if Sarita was happy with her airline captain; or, at least, reconciled.

'She called the other day. She's decided to have a baby.' Arlette shook her head, as in wonderment at such a quixotic solution to lost love. 'She says she's pregnant. She sounded happy – I think.'

Jerry made a slight gesture. He was, at least, sorry for her. But it was a part of Jerry's gift that he pitied every man, woman, and child now alive, ever alive, ever to be alive. And that compassion permeated each play he directed.

Seated opposite him, vital, so intensely concentrated, Arlette knew what he was thinking about her: so much beauty, and the vividness which gave meaning to that beauty must one day be annihilated, as if she had never moved through the world at all. Very often, it seemed that she and Jerry looked at each other, thinking the same thoughts, and found it better not to speak them.

'Tracy will give you no such trouble.'

Jerry stared at her gloomily. 'I hope not.'

Tracy was as different from Sarita as one girl could be from another, and perhaps that was why Jerry had chosen her, hoping to avoid the problems which had plagued him for so many months: an unhappy girl, greeting his guests with wan smiles.

Tracy Cochrane was older than Sarita, thirty-four; and Tracy had inherited money. She had gone to schools and universities in France and Switzerland. She had been married twice: once to an Englishman; once to a Frenchman. She was black-haired and black-eyed, and used makeup which was slightly Oriental. Her hair was short and straight, curled over her cheekbones, swirling about her head like a thick silk fringe.

Several years before, she had begun to design jewelry, and in less than a year had become known for her inventive decorations, strung together of agates, gold balls, silk tassles, ancient Roman coins, partial garments in effect.

Tracy Cochrane looked as lazy as a cat but had the energy of a puma, and would, Arlette guessed, keep Jerry interested for as long as she chose.

Jerry grew increasingly attractive, more subtly charming, more casual and easy – except when he was directing, and then there was the Jerry Hoffman Arlette had first encountered: Jerry the whirling dervish, who slowly worked his cast to a pitch of hysteria.

'Well, Arlette?'

'She's not who you think she is.'

'Never mind who I think she is. I'm not playing the part.'

'The only Medea I can play is an incarnation of the mythological women of the ancient East – Lilith, giving a shriek and disappearing from Eden when Adam tries to dominate her. She's the Witch of Endor and Ishtar. She has changed the men she loved into birds with broken wings, into wolves, into horses to be beaten. She goes, out of love for Jason, to an unknown country. And she's abandoned there for reasons which are no reasons to her: ambition. Medea must be played as a symbol of a past far more ancient than Greece. As a woman, she's a monster. As a symbolic creation, she is a priestess whose cult is sexual love, whose pride is beyond the comprehension of Jason, whose ambitions seem to her so unworthy he must be destroyed. She destroys him.'

'What do you plan to do with what will cling to you of the twentieth century?'

'I'll tear it off.' She made a swift gesture, as if to tear the flesh from one arm, elbow to fingertips.

'Jason?'

'Jason and Medea have no common ground. They don't know each other and never have. Anthony will play that kind of Jason, although we haven't talked about it. I will play a woman whose pride has been destroyed, and who wants only to destroy everything Jason values – and then leave him to die.' Arlette jumped out of the chair. 'Maybe I can't do it.' She added, for good measure, 'I'm almost positive I can't do it: play a Medea who thinks she is blameless. We live by our own terms, after all.'

Anthony entered to find them standing face to face, serious as parting lovers. He smiled as he shook hands with Jerry. 'You've agreed?'

'We've agreed that Arlette will play the Medea she thinks is the only one she can play.'

'And I'll do the same for that prick, Jason. Stay for dinner.'

'Thanks – but—'

'I've been trying to convince him that Medea is not a woman.'

Anthony glanced at her alertly. 'No. She is not a woman. She is the dark side of every female.'

Now how in hell did he know that?

Jerry was faintly, secretively smiling, and Arlette, feeling herself at a sudden disadvantage, caught hold of their hands. 'Jerry, Anthony – did you know that when *Medea* opens it will be almost twenty years since we did *The Taming of the Shrew*?'

'No!' cried Jerry, as if this reminder had shattered him. He looked bewildered, disbelieving, despondent. He gazed at his shoes. 'Twenty years is' – he made a helpless gesture – 'gone.'

'Not gone, Jerry,' Arlette protested, 'it's all there. Everything we've done. All the incarnations, all the people we've been. Nothing is ever lost.' Her voice took on a ringing tone, which seemed to catch them by surprise. Medea's voice, though they did not know it yet.

Anthony walked downstairs with Jerry, and Arlette went to bathe and put on a robe before dinner, her new favorite robe, three kimonos, one over the other, each a'

692

shadowed mauve and purple chiffon, each colored a little differently, tied in back with a wide sash like a miniature obi.

When she returned to the bedroom Anthony was not there, and she sat at the desk and began to copy Medea's part where she had left it that morning: '*No one has ever injured me but suffered more than I had suffered.*'

She was concentrated upon this woman and her jealousy, which, she had decided, must be played with a continuous subtle rhythmic bodily movement, a prolonged orgiastic protest against what she had lost and longed for:

What the hell is jealousy about, if not fucking? I learned that a long time ago.

All at once she became aware that she was no longer alone, glanced over her shoulder, and saw Anthony in the doorway, staring intently at the portrait which hung at the far end of the room, the portrait of Arlette in the threadbare white silk robe Anthony had retrieved when she was ready to throw it away.

Arlette had become so accustomed to the portrait she was scarcely aware of it, and did not like to look at it: *the past never ends.*

Anthony continued his intent study of the portrait, and she was surprised to realize that he was, in fact, furious.

Had he heard something about her last meeting with Micah? But from whom? And that had been three weeks ago.

His face was grim, and she had a sudden surprised realization that in Anthony's belief it was she who was the destroyer of their relationship.

At the same moment, she knew he was right.

She stood up slowly: Nothing can be changed now. *It's become as much a part of our lives as everything else that's happened since Jade Ring met Ming Huang.*

He glanced at her, a flickering glance of hostility and rage.

'All those years,' Anthony had said, not long before they were married, talking of Jade Ring following Ming

Huang into exile, disguised as a serving girl. 'All those years – living with him, waiting for remorse to kill him.' She had been surprised at the change in Anthony's face and voice, as if that part of their college play had troubled him for a long time. 'The most terrible revenge one human being could take on another.' He had looked at her, his black eyes glistening. 'Only a woman would have the tenacity – or the bitterness – to do it.'

Remembering those words, she watched him warily, as if some dangerous animal had entered the room.

He walked slowly toward her and Arlette stood unmoving. They were silent, as if each were taking the measure of the other's susceptibility to anger.

'Tell me, Arlette,' he said now, and there was a slight curious smile, 'are you still getting revenge on Pat Runkle?'

Arlette stared straight into his eyes, determined not to quarrel: *Bonfire. Yellowbird. Red moon. Golden tassel. Dragonfly . . .*

He reached out quickly, seized one shoulder, and shook it hard. 'Answer me!'

Arlette was silent. They must stop here. The next boundary had no sure barrier to keep them under control. She said reasonably: 'You will never understand why I do what I do – or have done what I've done.' She paused. 'You've never lost anyone of crucial importance to you, Anthony.'

'I haven't?' He gave a soft incredulous laugh. 'I've lost you.'

'I'm still here.' She gestured, indicating not only the house, but their lives, their work, the notes on the desk.

Anthony gave a furious brush of one hand, which came near to hitting her. 'So was Jade Ring.' The look of fury disappeared so quickly she might only have imagined it. '*Tell me why I killed you!*'

With an uncanny accuracy he spoke in the exact tone with which Ming Huang had pleaded with Jade Ring's apparition, when at last she consented to appear before the exiled Emperor.

Arlette looked at him helplessly, and the reply came into her mind from that same play of Gordon Donahue's which had haunted their lives: *In the end, neither heaven nor earth can pity*. But she did not say it.

'*What enemy sent you to me?*' He stood looking at her, as if contemplating what harm he would do her: seize her by the throat, throttle the life out of her in a minute or less.

'Never mind. I love you still.' He turned and left the room.

CHAPTER 88

The set was somber. The façade of Medea's house stood at the center of the stage: the ivory-colored house, the blue sky of Hellas, across which passed an early morning mist and transparent clouds; white noon light, fierce enough to be almost palpable, under which Jason and Medea were to exchange their bitter dialogue. A slow softening into blood-red sunset; the starless night, lighted by torches at either side of the great door. There were the steps, the black door opening into the house, the black curiously shaped rocks upon which the women of the town squatted. There was little to distract from Medea.

'This,' Arlette said to Anthony in a tone of wonderment, 'is the first play I've had to myself.' Shocked by the tactlessness, so near to cruelty, she touched his hand. 'Forgive me, Anthony—'

'I wanted it for you, you know that. Anyway, Jason can be made less insignificant than he is.' He looked amused. 'You have your private notions about Medea. I have mine about Jason.'

Jason and Medea's two boys were to be played by John Powell's youngest sons. Jeffrey Brooke would play Creon, and Max Gilmore Aegeus.

There were still few clues to Arlette's Medea. During rehearsals she never howled, never writhed like a woman suffering from severe cramps, never fastened Jason with a basilisk's eye. She gave no indication she meant to copy other traditions.

She played with an air slightly dazed, slightly distraught, proud but not arrogant, bewildered and exalted, as by some divine inner conviction.

'Where's the hysteria? Where's the loathing? Where's the murder?' Jerry asked her a week before the opening.

The rest of the cast he had brought up to full pitch. The women of Corinth moaned, swayed in unison: the Nurse was distraught; Jason strode into his part, demanding brusquely of Medea what was ailing her, as any twentieth-century man might ask his wife why she was crying – just because he had forgotten their anniversary, or announced a plan to marry his secretary?

Jason was forceful, ruthless, uncomprehending of Medea's grief; unbelieving of her dangerousness. He was a man who esteemed position, not love.

As for the Golden Fleece, Medea's killing of her brother, the deception of her father, her following Jason to alien shores – all that had been her own doing. He had asked for nothing. She had thrown it all at him – Golden Fleece, murders, poisons – and if she now chose to claim to have done it for his sake, so much the worse for her.

At the end of Jason's recital of his virtues, Jerry laughed. 'Anthony, you could convince a man there's no sun or moon.'

'Jason's a Greek – the inventors of specious reasoning. He can explain anything to another Greek. Not to Medea.'

But Anthony was modest about this part. He knew its flaws. Jason was a petty man, and Anthony was accustomed to play men who dared greatly, achieved what they achieved without help from a magic-practicing woman or anyone else, and fell through the working of their own flawed natures.

Jason, though he would look magnificent, though Anthony's resonant voice would chill the flesh of women throughout the audience, though he would play Jason with Jason's own conviction in his righteousness – nevertheless, Jason was a part he had assumed as a gift to Arlette.

It was not until the day that Jerry wanted the lighting pattern set for Jason and Medea that Arlette appeared in each of her three costumes, with three different hairstyles.

Anthony had come earlier, and as she went to the dressing room she saw him standing in the fantasized Greek dress which displayed most of his body – one of the few advantages he had in this part – the short, wide-pleated bronze leather skirt, the sleeveless finely meshed shirt which opened wide, uncovering his torso to the waist, the ornate Greek sandals, and Anthony's black hair, unhelmeted.

Medea's makeup was similar to Arlette's usual stage makeup, but for a slight tilt at the outer lid corners, a slight golden sheen over her face and shoulders and arms.

She wore a body stocking the color of her skin, and she had coaxed the fitter to cut the neckline lower and lower, front and back, to make the straps thin as thread, to cut higher and yet higher over the thighs, until it was cut nearly to the waist.

'It doesn't leave anything to the imagination, Miss Morgan,' the fitter said when Arlette pronounced the garment satisfactory.

'It's really not needed at all,' Arlette confided charmingly, smiling at her with conspiratorial implication. 'With all those draperies—' She gestured at the three costumes, white, crimson, black – hanging like finely pleated handkerchiefs from hooks.

'All those draperies are transparent.'

'But they're in layers. Medea – please believe me – is not only a barbarian she is a priestess and a witch. She is part divine. Her sorrow is that, in the manner of ancient divinities, she took a fancy to a mortal man.' She shrugged. Arlette laughed merrily at the little joke between her and the fitter.

From her place in the wings, out of sight of Anthony, Jerry, or the electrician, she watched Anthony, walking, turning, and marveled that this man, so beautiful when

697

she had first met him, was even more beautiful today –
complete, adult, male power and confidence:

*Where are the lives we might have lived, Anthony? Where
did they go?*

She thought of what Micah had said on their first visit
to Montauk. They had gone out to watch the moonrise,
while he answered all the impossible questions she put to
him: 'In fact, we know very little. And some of us are
willing to admit that however much we may one day
know, we will never know final answers. This universe is
mysterious, strange and violent, beyond man's imagining. We cannot see the universe entirely. We get in our
own way.'

'We can't even see our lives, for getting in our own
way.'

Arlette looked at Jason, leaning one arm upon his leg
which rested on a rock, the exact stance of Ingres' Oedipus
speaking to the Sphinx, and there came a spasmodic fear
that, after all, it might be Anthony's show, not hers.

Panic set up a treacherous clamor, that dreaded feeling
which occurred as the opening night approached.

At that moment she could convince herself that if it was
not Jason who would steal the performance, then it would
be the two boys – those wretched children of John
Powell's, beautiful to look at, heartbreaking as they began
to fear their mother, to understand that she meant to kill
them. Or even Blanche Hart, the old Nurse.

Arlette waited as Jerry continued his lighting experiments. And the longer she waited the more hopeless it
seemed that she could play this enraptured princess at all.

'Where the hell is Arlette?' Jerry shouted. 'I told her to
be on deck at eleven-thirty!'

'I've been here since eleven-thirty,' Arlette called, her
voice clear, pure, impudently mocking.

'Where are you? We've got work to do.'

Arlette stepped barefoot onto the stage, head high,
arms at her sides, back straight, and faced Jerry, while
Anthony stood to one side.

'Holy Jesus,' said Jerry, 'we'll never make an honest witch of you.'

'The lights will take care of everything.'

She passed Anthony and he reached out one hand to touch hers.

Jerry began calling directions to his electrician, to Arlette, telling her to move there, stand there, turn around. 'All the lighting tricks in the world won't keep you from looking naked.'

'But will I look like Medea?'

There was silence from both Jerry and Anthony, while the electrician worked the controls, and at Jerry's instructions sunrise passed into bright morning sunlight, and Arlette moved slowly, with the implicit threat of a predatory animal, her face never changing expression, blameless, visionary, the white garments floating about her.

'Okay. Let's try it with the red one.'

As darkness settled she emerged from the house after the children had been killed, to confront Jason, showing him the blood on her garments, on her hands and arms.

In the black costume, she took the dead children with her, driving offstage in a chariot.

'That's it.'

While Jerry and the electrician made their final notes, Arlette slowly raised her head and began a long, eerie, minor-keyed wail, which caused the three men to glance up in alarm: a song out of the ancient past of Asia, prolonged, ululating, a sound which seemed scarcely human.

'*Ai!*'

They were the first sounds to be heard from Medea, inside the house, while the women of Corinth and her old Nurse had gathered outside, talking of the terrible curse which the voyage of the *Argo* had brought to her mistress.

'*Ai!*' came the banshee wail again. '*Ai!!!*'

As the first-night audience heard that mournful, inhuman protestation of love and vengeance rise into the air and hang there for what seemed an interminable time, no breath drawn to sustain it, then falling down the scale and rising again, there was a stir of uneasiness, as if they had indeed entered the presence of some practitioner of the black arts.

The barbarian woman, still unseen, struck them with a horror that her vengeance might reach them from across the footlights. Her golden net was flung over them at those first sounds – as it was later to be flung over Creon's daughter, turning her to a human torch.

'*Death. Death is my wish. For myself, my enemies, my children. Destruction.*'

The doors swung slowly open and Medea stood before them, gilt blonde hair swinging about her head as if the coiled ringlets, falling over her shoulders and down her back, twirling along the sides of her face, were alive with energy, hatred, sensuality.

'*As for me, I want simply to die.*'

The words sounded as a chant, a song, a curse, an imprecation.

She moved slowly down the steps, gazing straight before her as she spoke to the women, describing her gifts to Jason, his debt to her; and all the while her face had the trance-like expression of an enraptured witch, not responsible for her crimes, past or to come.

Her body moved subtly, the draperies swaying, and whatever ugly words she spoke, her face remained serenely enchanted, lighted as from an inner sense that revenge was her sacred duty. There was a look of uncanny joy, more terrifying than if her face were contorted.

These were the tones of a witch who had practiced good for Jason, but who could also practice evil – a witch who refused to comprehend Jason's Hellenistic morals, who listened with a slight smile of rapt incredulity as he explained, with all the solemn intensity of a man selling airplanes or tractors, that his marriage to Creon's daughter had not been made out of a young man's lust for a pretty girl – but a grown man's reasoned quest for power, authority, what he might give to his sons.

At last, Jason reached to touch her, sudden desire on his

face, and she smiled mockingly, moving away. His hand fell, his face turned despondent – the gesture had occurred spontaneously to both Arlette and Anthony during one of the last rehearsals.

As she appeared at the beginning of the second act, wearing the crimson gown, two bracelets winding from wrists to elbows, narrow golden serpents, she held the cloak of woven gold, and beside her stood two open cases, one containing a golden wreath, the other for the cloak – the fatal gifts for the daughter of Creon.

Jason had been sent for, and arrived, assuring her of the children's safety among Creon's friends, even though she must go into exile.

But, he seemed to ask, what was exile to a barbarian, born in exile?

Medea stood, reaching one hand toward him, palm upward, fingers loosely curled:

'Forgive me, Jason, as I do you . . .'

She kissed the two boys tenderly, warning them not to touch the cases; they walked away on either side of their father, who had coaxed them into loving him once again.

Watching them, she smiled faintly, saying slowly: 'Vengeance makes grief bearable . . .'

CHAPTER 89

Arlette and Jerry Hoffman were dancing slowly, holding each other close, in the small darkened room which had been cleared of tables and chairs, behind the main dining room. The orchestra was playing, although she was scarcely aware of it, the sweet morbid strains of that song from If I Should Die Before You Wake. It had been popular for so long now it was called a classic.

The girl singer held the microphone lovingly, as if it were a penis, and whispered to it her message of bitter humor and betrayal:

701

> *'There are lies that have a tender meaning*
> *That the eyes of love alone can see . . .'*

Arlette shook her head. 'That song. There must be a lot of suspicions and hurt people in this world.'

Jerry said nothing, perhaps because he could not. The Edmund Kean Award ceremony had ended less than an hour ago. The small seclusive society made its awards every two years. The award itself was only a small engraved card, embossed with the group's insignia, inscribed with the name of the recipient and a brief message of approval – scarcely enthusiastic enough to be a congratulation – for sustained work in the legitimate theater.

It could be framed; put in a drawer, or hung in a study or dressing room, like a doctor's diploma. But no one in the theater ever forgot who had it and who did not: it was as memorable as crossed eyes or Halley's comet.

Four citations were awarded every two years – two to women, two to men, but if one sex or the other had not produced a worthy recipient that award was lacking.

No compromise with quality was the motto of this century-old group; and even the members of its small committee must be speculated about but never known for certain. Nor was the identity of the recipients known until the master of ceremonies, chosen from among the season's most respected producers or directors, made the announcement at the ceremony, as unemotionally as if he were announcing an appointment to an inconsequential Congressional committee.

Anthony had received the award several years ago, for his energetically flamboyant playing of Henry V – the production in which Arlette had her small role as a Princess of France.

She had not been jealous, something of a surprise, since Anthony had an Oscar, and had been given it for his second picture, a freakish accident which had perhaps affected the fact that he had not received others for better performances.

Arlette took the card for his award to an antique dealer and had it set in an eighteenth-century gold frame, twice its size, studded with rough-cut semiprecious stones – something, the dealer said, which had been secretly conveyed out of Old Russia – and Anthony had returned home one night to find it hanging above his desk.

Whether she had expected such a tribute for herself one day, Arlette had not been sure. She still believed that too much good luck was dangerous. Then, a little more than an hour ago, she had, as from a great distance, heard her name spoken, and the master of ceremonies, Thomas Marvell, was reciting what sounded alarmingly like the roll call of her life's trespasses: 'Hedda Gabler . . . Desdemona . . . Millamant . . .' His voice continued, and Arlette's heart began to beat heavily.

'Who's he talking about?' she whispered to Anthony, who was watching Thomas Marvell with such intent concentration he neither glanced at her nor replied – only took her hand and held it.

'Lady Macbeth . . . Mary, Queen of Scots . . . Beatrice Cenci . . . the young Cleopatra . . . the mature Cleopatra . . .'

'Oh, Anthony,' whispered Arlette in despair.

Who else could it be? No one else had played those parts – and none of her motion-picture roles had been mentioned.

'Medea: Miss Morgan's finest work.'

As Arlette wondered how she could get past Anthony, who sat between her and the aisle, and escape. Thomas Marvell was walking to the edge of the stage, extending his hand, while from the other side she was dismayed to see Gordon Donahue walking onstage and smiling at her, a tender, encouraging smile, holding in one hand the dark red case in which the card was hidden.

'What shall I do?' she whispered.

Anthony was on his feet, offering his arm, escorting her to the stairs, where he left her. And then, all at once, with the keenest feeling she had ever had of that warning Valerie had given her long ago: *If this is the life you choose,*

Lily, you will always be alone, she slowly mounted the stairs:

Amida Buddha . . .

She crossed the stage with the smoothly flowing movement which was a part of the reason for this citation, accepted the kisses of Thomas Marvell and Gordon Donahue, murmuring to Gordon: 'What the hell are you doing here?' and then, as seemingly self-possessed as her first character, Antoinette, starring for the neighbors in Lily Malone's production of *Adventure*, she smiled, very slightly, and pretended to listen to what Gordon was saying.

She was not accustomed to looking at an audience, even during curtain calls, and now – as she did then – kept her eyes slightly above the level of their heads, slightly below the faces in boxes and balconies.

She stood straight, easily balanced, hands at her sides, and the beaded white chiffon evening gown, cut straight across her breasts and held up by invisible straps, swayed and glimmered, although she made no movement or gesture, only listened politely as Gordon Donahue described her history: all she had done for so many years, in all her incarnations.

Not a saint among them. Not even a victim of man's tyranny over womankind: goddesses, queens, whores. Those had been her gifts: murderesses; incestuous daughters; courtesans; strong, passionate, sensual women, most of them cruel and domineering; fierce violent women, whom she had portrayed with deceptive tenderness, using all the wiles they had needed to live such lives.

From time to time she heard, with vague interest, a phrase or a sentence of Gordon's. Much of it he had said to her, in other words, and much he had written:

. . . unquestionably Miss Morgan's finest performance, this princess, emblem of an ancient past intruding into the Greek attempt at ordering mankind's disorderly nature . . .'

She was thinking that it was true, in some way she did not understand, that as the play progressed toward the scene where she determined to kill the children as the one way to destroy Jason, root and branch, the rage for murder she had despaired of ever finding had flooded her, until she was unable to see clearly as she said to Jason: '*I have done it because I loathed you more than I loved them.*'

Now, remembering that this rage returned reliably to her at each performance, she was puzzled by the ferocity: *Where does this hate come from?*

Of course. But so long ago.

What we owe to our enemies . . .

'This splendid actress, capable of at once seeming to have herself in absolute control and to have lost all awareness of what she is doing . . . Arlette Morgan – with the esteem of . . .'

Something jogged at Arlette's consciousness. She turned to take the small red box, giving Gordon, for one quick movement, Jade Ring's dazzling smile.

In another moment she heard her voice, but not what she was saying.

She had prepared no speech. Nevertheless, she found herself speaking, swiftly, tenderly, almost placatingly, as if in apology for this honor she had done nothing to deserve.

The silence again began to seem to her unusual, and out of some fear that perhaps she had said something she ought not to have said, she raised her voice until it took on some resemblance to the final keening of Medea over her dead sons: 'All I have tried to do is to give back to them the lives they lost – those who walked before us.' She closed her eyes briefly and, finding nothing more to say, murmured, 'Thank you. God bless you.'

Somewhere, there was crying. That emotional nation of hers would laugh or cry for anything or nothing: Minerva. And Eva. Blanche Hart. Not Alicia Fiedler. Alicia had never been known to cry offstage.

Slowly as a willow bending before a steady wind, she gave them the bow which brought her forehead to her knees, then rose slowly and stood, palms together in the Buddhist salutation.

She turned to Gordon, giving him the Buddhist salute, which he returned readily, having taught it to her; then to Thomas Marvell, whose reply was a little awkward. And then, slightly smiling, she walked down the stairs as the audience began to applaud, and was immediately following Anthony, who held her hand, through the corridors beneath the stage.

Out of doors, Anthony took the sleeveless floor-length ermine coat from Conrad and tossed it over her shoulders, gave her a convivial slap on the buttocks, whereupon she was in the car and they were on their way. Anthony was laughing, delighted as if he had outwitted some mortal enemy, as he had – the television cameras, still photographers, reporters, waiting in front.

Arlette leaned back, Anthony still clutching her hand, to reassure her or himself, and as they drove through the heavy traffic toward the East Side – Arlette supposing they were going home to the little dinner they had arranged, since everyone was dressed up anyway – she had the stunned sense of having, for the first time in her life, committed some unknown gaucherie onstage:

Of course. It's because the words were my own. I've never spoken my own words in public before.

'Anthony – what did I say?'

'What difference does it make?' He was smiling with a triumphant pleasure she had not seen on his face – except when a part called for it – for a very long time. The smile was joyous, proud; but the words seemed ominous.

'Did I make a fool of myself? What did I say? Tell me!'

She was convinced that as her voice had gone out over that preternaturally silent audience, it had carried some sinister message:

You bastards – you took long enough to get around to it. What did you think I've been doing all this time?

Sensing that she did not know what she had said and might burst into one of those tear storms which could overtake her after any intense excitement, even love-making. Anthony quickly stroked her hand. 'I can't remember, darling. You heard the applause. Jesus, I was as knocked out as you were. Alicia will remember. Ask her.'

'Yes. Alicia will remember.'

They were on the East Side, and in the Seventies, not the Sixties, and nearer to Second Avenue than to their own house. She was thinking of something Alicia Fiedler had said to that young girl who was still hovering between Lily Malone and Arlette Morgan, who came to her each day eager for wisdom, catching every word as if it contained a precious stone, stringing the sentences together on unbreakable thread.

'There is a sixth sense which every real actor has,' Alicia had said. 'The ability to detect the forming emotions of the audience, and to guide them.'

The second piece of information Alicia had given her some weeks later. 'No one but an experienced player can tell how he can be at the same time lost in his part and yet conscious of everything around him.'

Remembering those words, put away for safekeeping long ago, until their message should be recognized as applying to Arlette Morgan, she smiled.

Sometime, sometime during the first night of *Medea*, there had appeared – like a fully blooming flower before her – this rapport between Arlette Morgan the actress, Medea the barbarian princess, and the audience. It had come unbidden, after years of searching, and would never leave her.

Tentatively, as if to make certain they were still there, she folded her arms and slipped her fingers above her elbows, to touch the two bracelets Anthony had given her on opening night, three and a half months before.

They were delicately woven bands of platinum, half an inch wide, from which hung threadlike chains, each ending with a ball of ivory, each ball carved with the name of one of the characters she had played.

'There are enough left for all the parts to come,' he had said.

'No, no, Anthony. Never speak of the future – this is so much—'

She touched them wonderingly. This night seemed full of portents, strange, wonderful, possibly ominous. Awards, gifts – and now some mysterious trip, not to their home. Another present – a very special party, no doubt, although she must not let him know she had begun to suspect it.

The car stopped, and as Arlette got out another car stopped beside them.

'Alicia!' She sounded as if seeing Alicia in New York, on Second Avenue – and, yes, outside Le Muguet, ostentatiously unobtrusive with its white plastered walls and black iron grille over the door – was the world's least likely coincidence. 'And Jerry!'

Arlette embraced everyone who came her way, laughing, and all at once, as she went into the restaurant, closed to the public that Sunday night, she seemed swept forward on a joyous wave of all the friends she had ever had, everyone she had ever loved. She turned, kissing Anthony quickly, and embraced first Valerie and then Frederick – this was indeed the one certain surprise.

'You came so far – for only this.' It sounded vaguely familiar, some quotation from her high school reading, from the years they had guarded her with care. 'How I love you!'

The humble, frightened, superstitious, haunted woman was gone.

She was playing the role she sometimes thought had always been her best: Arlette Morgan, star. The only one which had been easy to learn.

CHAPTER 90

'You?'

Arlette turned as a hand touched Jerry's shoulder and he released her to Micah Benoni.

Her head rested lightly against his shoulder, and for two or three minutes they moved in silence.

Anthony had invited him? Michael had invited him? But Michael would not invite a friend to a party given by Anthony.

They had last seen each other in his hotel suite a little more than three weeks ago. It was the day he had come to hear Zarah perform at Carnegie Hall – and she suspected the rest of the family was also in the city, at some other hotel.

He said nothing about why he was there, and Arlette would not ask. This troubled her, making her wonder if she was doomed to go through life in a dark jealousy of a twenty-one-year-old girl she had never seen.

No doubt, she reasoned, if once she saw the girl, the fears would be gone. Twenty-one. She would be half finished, her manners young and gauche, and her fears of Micah's love for this daughter he did not talk about would vanish.

Not likely.

For in Zarah's latest photograph, accompanying an article about her performance, the girl's face had a solemn beauty, like her father's.

Micah had outlined his program for the next two years: New South Wales. Los Angeles. British Columbia. Sweden. Puerto Rico. Three months in his study at Princeton, to complete his book.

'Micah – when will we see each other?'

'We will. We have.'

Arlette moved back a little, looking up at Micah with a wondering smile. 'You were in the audience?'

'Yes.'

'Anthony invited you?' Incredible as it seemed, there was no other explanation.

'Everything was very efficiently arranged. I sat with Michael and Maura.'

'Men. Men – are remarkable.'

Micah was smiling, trying to keep his expression unreadable.

Once, as they walked the beach, he had bent suddenly, picked up a stone, and thrown it a long distance into the water, saying: 'Let's go away.' She had smiled, as if he had remarked on the weather, and said nothing; after that she began to be afraid he might say it again. So far, he had not:

We met too late.

Susie Allen was singing, in her lyric soprano, which had made a star of her when she played Nell Gwynne in *The Protestant Whore*, the hit song: 'Spend a Little Time with Me.' Nell, pleading with the Merry Monarch to give her a little more of his time. The song was witty and plaintive; every love song seemed to have been caught up in it, mocked a little, then given back its underlying plaintiveness.

You need a great deal, Arlette.

Yes, you do.

For all your Chinese conviction of not needing or desiring wealth or fame or power or expensive objects.

'Only to live in harmony with my own nature,' was the answer she had once given Micah when he had asked what further ambitions she had.

The ambition was so modest, so inappropriate, no sooner had she stated it than she was embarrassed. It had been true once, at least in her idealistic reminiscences of what had seemed, while she was living with Valerie and Frederick, the only respectable guide for her life, and it clung now, a persistent fragrance, a memory of some imagined early existence.

'What did you think of my speech tonight? I don't know what I said,' she added, to explain the question, so childish, so immodest she was ashamed of it.

'I thought you were beautiful.'

'But my speech? What did I say?'

'You don't know?'

'I don't know.'

'At the end you said: "Farewell, gentle friends." '

'Farewell – but why? Why would I say *Farewell*?' She smiled a little, surprised, and curiously pleased. 'Well – now it's been said.'

'Sorry.' That was Anthony, touching Micah's shoulder.

Arlette's heart gave a quick anxious beat, as if some old atavism had warned her that two men in love with the same woman in the same room meant trouble. Micah smiled, releasing her, and Anthony nodded:

That's all?

No rapiers, no fisticuffs? Not even: What the hell are you doing here?

Ah, but then pride has its uses among men which no woman was likely to fathom. A slight curtness, a slight restraint in the smile, a slight exaggeration of the punctilio of all such ancient customs as had survived long enough to have been transmuted from abduction to shoulder-tapping for a change of dancing partners.

Remarkable, mused Arlette, moving easily with Anthony, who held her hard against him: that had been his style since college, one which had brought him in those days a certain notoriety, for he put his arm around a girl on a dance floor as if he knew exactly where they would be and what they would be doing in two or three hours.

She looked at him: *Is this the same man? Is he possibly that same Pat Runkle? No, of course not. I'm not the same. He's not, either. We call each other Arlette and Anthony. We sleep in the same bed and make love and get up and eat together and work together.*

And we will for as long as we live . . .

Perhaps that was what this party was meant to signify; the clans had been summoned – the nation was there in force: There was one outsider only: Dr Micah Benoni.

For Michael and Maura, Valerie and Frederick, Anthony's father and mother, belonged to that nation by blood or marriage – although it was the first time in two or three years that she had seen Anthony's parents, who stopped in New York now and then on their way to France or England. The rest of the world had ceased to interest them long ago.

The party, Arlette guessed, had been outlined by Anthony, the restaurant selected by Anthony, and the most important guests listed by Anthony. The details had been planned by Edna Frazier and Eugene Cartwright, assisted by the interior decorator who had redecorated Le Muguet for this night, and the musicians, chefs, two or three florists.

When the sketches of the bouquets, the interior, the menu, the wine list were ready, Anthony had studied them, corrected them – since there was nothing anyone had so far discovered which Anthony did not correct but Shakespeare's lines – and the work was overseen by Edna and Cartwright.

The walls of the smaller dining room, which had been cleared for dancing, were lined with mirrors, as were the walls and ceiling in the large dining room, which seated at tables of ten about one hundred and fifty people. In the center of each table was a bowl of yellow lilies. The tablecloths were thin yellow linen. If anything had been left to chance, it seemed unlikely. Arlette's favorite colors; Arlette's favorite flowers; Arlette's favorite food; Arlette's favorite people:

Even to Dr Micah Benoni.

Anthony had been convinced she would win the Edmund Kean Award, and if she did not, then this would celebrate *Medea*, Thanksgiving, Christmas, and the New Year, not to mention birthdays past and to come.

Arlette leaned back against Anthony's hand and looked at him. 'Who invited Dr Benoni?'

Anthony smiled, as if at a private amusement he did not plan to share. 'Who the hell would invite him? I did.' Arlette was silent, and Susie Allen's voice continued trying to wheedle more time from His Majesty; life's perennial problem, especially where monarchs of one kind or another were involved. 'If you don't understand that – you're pretending to know less about men than you do.'

Anthony took her hand. 'Come on, let's eat before dinner's over.'

The rock band took over, and while some couples were leaving the floor, Sarita, visibly pregnant, with her handsome white-haired airplane captain, paused to kiss

Arlette and Anthony. Jerry Hoffman was dancing as if it gave him some opportunity he had known would come along if he waited for it with Tracy. Eva French danced with John Powell, who had been obliged to learn the dances for Clarissa, while Walter Hodges sat talking to Minerva and Thyssen.

As they went through the doorway, Arlette turned, whispering, 'Thank you, Anthony, thank you—' There was that bewitching smile of Jade Ring's – *flowers added to embroidery* – this night's true beginning, however many years had elapsed between the smile and the reward.

Anthony kissed her briefly and Arlette glanced across the room, to see Micah Benoni, seated with Malvina and Jeffrey Brooke, look quickly away. His head had been slightly lowered, and as she looked at him his face flushed dark. Arlette had a moment's despairing conviction he would never see her again.

Or a moment's hope: no more disappointments. A cure no doubt worse than the ailment.

After Arlette had stopped several times, kissing and being kissed, pretending to talk about the music, Anthony left her, and it was twenty minutes – after embracing Jerry and Eva and Minerva, her favorite fitter, her favorite hairdresser, her favorite cameraman, Edna and Irma, Brian and Rhoda O'Neil – that she arrived at the family table, where she and Anthony sat with his parents, Michael and Maura, Valerie and Frederick, and Gordon and Marian Donahue.

Arlette stood in back of Gordon and bent to put his arms around him. 'Everyone I love most is here.'

That was before she saw Deborah Crane, closely followed by her escort, Thomas Marvell, advancing in a billow of bounding gold-red curls, bounding breasts, teetering hips, with all her teeth showing in that wide deceptive smile which almost closed her eyes.

'Congratulations, darling!' Deborah threw her arms about Arlette, who hesitated, and then cautiously placed her cheek at a distance from Deborah's. 'You should have had it years ago.'

Arlette backed away, and Frederick stood to hold her chair. 'Thank you, Deborah.' She smiled slightly, not unkindly:

After all, I do owe you more than you can ever guess.

But what she owed her – Micah Benoni – she saw only in brief glimpses during the next two or three hours.

Once she became immersed in playing this favorite part, Arlette forgot everything else, while the world – whichever one she was in at the time – went whirling by as if she had fallen into a spinning kaleidoscope. She lost all self-awareness, and seemed possessed of an energy which might last her until eternity.

Then, sometime around three o'clock, she looked about, remembering Micah, as one remembers at some unexpected moment an old friend or lover not thought about for years, and could not find him. When she and Anthony, the Donahues, and Michael and Maura went drifting out near five o'clock, she had not seen him again.

The next night, it was *Medea*, as usual. And the next, and the next.

Except that the reports of the award, and the few photographs caught as she dashed in and out of the restaurant, brought a larger than usual standing-room crowd.

Less than three weeks later, after she and Anthony had returned from the theater and had been asleep for two or three hours, the private telephone rang. It rang several times before Anthony picked it up.

'Hello . . . Yes . . . Yes . . . Yes! . . . *What?* . . . What, Jerry? . . . Speak up, for Christ sake, I can't hear you! You're at the theater? . . . Yes! . . . And what the hell did you say? . . . Good Jesus Christ! We'll be there . . .' He slammed the telephone into the receiver, shook Arlette's shoulder hard, and was out of bed at a bound. 'The theater's on fire!' He shook her again. 'Arlette!'

'What?' Arlette was sitting up, looking for him, but Anthony was in his dressing room.

'It's going up like a torch! The bloody place has half burned down!'

Arlette woke up as if she had fallen through a hole in the ice, leaped out of bed and ran to her closet, pulling out a heavy sweater and skirt and tights, for the night was windy and bitterly cold, and there was hard snow still on the ground from a recent heavy fall.

CHAPTER 91

A large area had been cordoned off by the police, for the cold windy night sent sparks flying like red snowflakes from the burnt-over roof of the Alicia Allerton.

Arlette and Anthony had run out of their house less than five minutes after Jerry's call, telling Conrad to meet them with the car when he could get there – they would find a taxi. After running seven or eight blocks, slipping over the sidewalks, stumbling into snow-piled gutters, dancing along in what seemed a drunken desperate ballet, Anthony whistling at every passing cab, they finally stopped one, only to be obliged to get out five blocks from the theater and begin making their way through the crowd.

Standing at the crowd's edge, Arlette stared up at the flames pouring from the roof of the theater and began to cry despairingly.

Anthony seized her hand and forced their way through the crowd.

It was snowing again, soft white flakes, which settled and melted, and through the flakes the flames mounted steadily higher, writhing and twisting, gold and yellow and pale red, blue and green tines streaking through them against the black sky.

They stood, Anthony holding one arm fast around her, now and then absently kissing her face, a reassurance of some kind, watching the theater, now a black charred shell, burning out its guts.

The sparks flew, and now and then came soft explosive sounds, as of breaking glass inside the theater – lights, mirrors, perhaps. The smoke billowed around the flames. At times only the bottom half of the theater could be seen, flames eating steadily through the smoke, seemingly impervious to the great jets of water from the fire hoses. Policemen pushed the crowds backward, starting small stampedes of panic and hysteria.

The firemen could be seen with their ladders thrust against the sides of the building, and from time to time charred and burning pieces tore loose and were carried off by the high wind, sailing above them; but now and then one came plummeting to earth, starting other stampedes.

Arlette cried steadily, silently, giving little moaning gasps of which she was unaware. The Alicia Allerton had evidently become fully human to her, not a building, not an inanimate object, but someone she loved.

The crowd was noisy, shouting, sometimes laughing, sometimes giving awed sighs, as another shower of sparks broke into the wind, like Fourth of July fireworks spraying upward, falling back to earth.

That they should be enjoying it infuriated her. She clenched hard with both hands to Anthony's forearm; she wanted to strike out at them, scratch their faces, hit them with her fists, scream at them to go away, this had nothing to do with them.

'What a great show!' a man shouted in back of her.

Arlette raised her booted foot and brought it down hard on his instep and he gave a shriek of pain. In that crowd there was no way to be sure who had committed the assault. Nevertheless, he was soon gone. But others were jubilant, and she could not obliterate them all.

Anthony glanced at her as she pressed her face against his shoulder, shutting her eyes. 'Don't cry – what's the good? It's happened.' She cried more loudly. And Anthony, for all his philosophy, said through clenched teeth: 'That ass-hole watchman and his fucking pipe.'

She stood straight, no longer crying, and watched the flames begin to die slowly, leaving the charred outer shell; nothing could have survived the heat of the fire inside the theater.

There were protests that the fire was going out, the fun would soon end, and Arlette said: 'Who would have thought it could burn so long?' She recognized, with surprise, the sound of Lady Macbeth's sorrowing plaint: '*Who would have thought the old man to have had so much blood in him?*'

Jerry was the first to find them, appearing out of the crowd by some magical feat. He seized both of them at once, throwing his arms around them. He looked distraught, his eyes wild, a Jerry Hoffman they had never seen before. 'You missed it!' he yelled.

'Missed what?' shouted Anthony.

'The lights! The marquee lights! They kept on burning and burning: ARLETTE MORGAN ANTHONY DE FOREST MEDEA. And then – just like that! Out!'

He made an explosive gesture of doubling his fist and letting his fingers burst wide apart. 'Out! Oh, Jesus! It was—' His voice sounded as if he were strangling himself against the need to cry. 'Terrible,' he said softly.

The crowd was slowly, reluctantly, drifting away, although hundreds were still there, milling about. Few sparks flew now from the blackened walls, and Arlette cried aloud and covered her ears as a part of one wall fell inward; she stood rigid, waiting for the building to collapse. But no other part fell.

Jeffrey Brooke found them next, with Alicia. He explained, somewhat embarrassed, that Malvina was sleeping. Arlette was glad she was not there. Malvina was no part of their nation. This was no tragedy in her life – another building on fire, nothing to shed tears over.

Alicia, as Arlette embraced her, tenderly, as if the loss of this building called the Alicia Allerton might be experienced by Alicia as some wound to her own person, looked at Arlette with her eyes bright, but she was not crying. She smiled a little, and Arlette understood the smile: *You see how easy it is to lose a thing you love?*

The crowds continued milling about, moving and drifting; the fire trucks were beginning to pack their equipment, leaving only four hoses trained upon smoldering areas, and the theater stood in black silhouette, half its former size, its outlines jagged, broken, a weird piece of ruined architecture designed by some mad fantasist of the high Romantic era.

Other members of the company began to appear, emerging from the thinning crowd. It was nearly five o'clock, but the night was still black.

Tracy had arrived, running up breathlessly and embracing Arlette. And all at once Arlette understood that this young woman breathed the same air they did; her needs and beliefs were theirs.

Edna Frazier and Eugene Cartwright found them, and for the first time Edna spontaneously embraced both Arlette and Anthony, and to Arlette's disbelieving astonishment, Edna Frazier could cry.

Minerva appeared with Eva French and Walter Hodges, and the three women embraced, crying as they had the night after the second performance of *Antony and Cleopatra*. It had been, at the time, an ending which had seemed nearly fatal in its implications, and yet nothing had changed.

By now, they were being recognized, Arlette and Anthony first, then Eva and Minerva and the others. It was not often a street corner gathered so many famous stage faces at one time, and Anthony said it was time to get back to the house, drink coffee, eat something, and talk.

The car was located and Anthony sent the women off in that, while the men found taxis.

At home Irma was ready for them. The dining table had been set with piles of plates, cups and saucers, cold roast chicken, platters of thin sandwiches; cheeses and breads, bowls of fruit; an urn of coffee, and a large pot of tea.

The fire was burning in the fireplace and the women converged upon it, throwing off their coats, shivering and holding out their hands, discovering for the first time that their feet were numb. Arlette and Tracy sat on the floor and pulled off their boots, and the men began to arrive, tossing their overcoats down in the foyer, leaving their boots at the doorway.

They were all there: the Hoffman-Repertory.

John and Margo Powell came in; Art Friedman had brought Blanche Hart, and after the handshakes and kisses were repeated, they fell into an almost instantaneous and, it seemed, unbreakable silence which began to threaten to last forever.

They filed about the dining-room table and, after several minutes, during which only occasional murmured comments were exchanged, seated themselves in a powwow circle in the drawing room, cross-legged or kneeling, and began to eat.

Anthony sent Conrad to bring legal note pads and pens and pencils, which Conrad passed as ceremoniously as cocktail napkins and after-dinner cigars.

Before there was anything to write – except for some desultory doodling by those who doodled automatically – it seemed they must first try to solve the one question which absorbed them to the temporary exclusion of everything else: How, exactly, could the fire have started?

'The whole place was fireproofed: scenery, chair cushions, curtain—'

'That ass-hole watchman—'

'He was sitting there half asleep when I left.'

'Half drunk—'

'He was sober enough to put in the alarm.'

'It was a short circuit—'

'It was arson. I saw a suspicious-looking character.'

'You saw a suspicious-looking character in New York?' asked Jerry. 'Don't be paranoid.'

Arlette had nothing to say.

She ate eagerly, the food seeming to spread through her body like a fluid of magical properties, warming her, restoring her, bringing her to life again, after shock had seemed to deplete her of all energy and even the capacity or wish to think about what had happened.

'It was sabotage.'

'Once and for all, that ass-hole of a watchman was drunk—'

Jerry got up and started for the dining room, then paused and turned. 'The theater's burned out. It's happened, and that's all we'll ever know. That's all!' He turned away. 'It was an accident.'

'An accident—' repeated Arlette, with deep bitterness.

Swift as a cat, she sprang up and rushed at him, striking him on the chest with her fist as Jerry staggered backward a step, staring at her as if she had gone insane.

'Oh, yes!' The others turned, dumbfounded, and gazed at her. Arlette? The fire had driven her quite wild, hysterical. 'Yes, god damn you! An accident!'

She stopped pounding at him. Anthony had not moved, only watched her carefully, thoughtfully. This was no time to explain that accidents were one thing to most people, but the entire course of a lifetime to Arlette.

Any explanation was preferable to an accident for her: sabotage, careless watchman, faulty wiring. Any concrete explanation would be preferable.

She went back to where she had been sitting between John Powell and Max and sank slowly to the floor, the sole of her right foot against her left inner thigh, her torso falling forward until her forehead touched her left knee.

She spoke softly, in the voice of Medea, forgetting she was Arlette Morgan. 'Everything's over – all those years – all that time – all the hope—'

Alicia looked shocked. The others gazed at one another in bewilderment. And Anthony spoke loudly. 'It's not over, Arlette. The Alicia Allerton has burned down. But that doesn't mean the end of Hoffman-Repertory.'

Jerry, apparently understanding why she had flown at him, came and knelt on one knee beside her, gently stroking her back. 'We'll finish the run in another theater – I'll have one for us tonight—'

She sat up abruptly, wiping her face with the palms of her hands. 'Tonight?'

'Or tomorrow or the next day – you're god damn right. What time is it?'

He went dashing up the stairs to Anthony's study, followed by Eugene Cartwright, to put in calls to costume makers, wigmakers, the set designer, theater rental agents, and all at once there was a surge of optimism.

Jerry came back downstairs. 'I haven't got hold of Lowenstein, but I left word. He'll get something for us. Let's see – what's dark right now—'

Jerry had begun a sketch. Anthony was talking to Jim Brown and the two Hoffman-Repertory lawyers about insurance. Andrew Thyssen had put in a call from Los Angeles, and Minerva ran upstairs to talk to him.

In three minutes, there it was, on Jerry's legal pad – a small Greek temple; four Doric pillars on either side of the main doorway, with a pediment and some squiggles to indicate he meant to find a decoration for it. He passed the paper around.

'I'll get hold of Bernie today. Arlette – when will you be ready for fittings?'

'Whenever you say.' She stood up. 'It's eight-thirty. Scrambled eggs? Bacon?'

While Edna Frazier was talking to Irma and Conrad was gathering the trays, the talk went on, all of them becoming increasingly excited, charged with new energy, as if life were about to begin again.

The disaster was turning into a triumph, and Arlette stood a moment looking at them: Anthony talking seriously and rapidly; Jerry at work on another version of his design; Max and Susie and Alicia facing each other – Alicia in the lotus posture, fresh as if she had just gotten out of bed after a sound night's sleep.

The room was filled with their voices, those beautiful trained voices she loved as she had never loved the sound of any musical instrument. She sometimes thought that of the men she had loved, it had been their voices she remembered most vividly: Frederick, Michael, Anthony, Jerry, Gordon Donahue, Charles Granville, Micah Benoni . . .

And all at once, Micah seemed more than ever distant, uninvolved in her life. She had a strong premonition that, by some series of coincidences, they would never meet again:

What a ridiculous idea. He wouldn't let it happen even if that were what I wanted.

She went to stand behind Jerry, to watch him sketching, then knelt beside him, kissed his face, whispering, 'I'm sorry, Jerry—'

With a quick embarrassed grin, Jerry held up his sketch. 'It'll be ready before Anthony's finished *Lear* or Arlette's finished shooting her film.'

And at this, which they took as no hope, no bravade, but a contractor's sober estimate, there was applause. They settled down to the scrambled eggs and bacon and toast and coffee, convinced this was no disaster but a glorious opportunity.

Then all at once they began to grow tired, to eat without having much to say. The Alicia Allerton had meant as much to any one of them as it had to Arlette, and now, after the hysteria of excitement, there had come over them a formal feeling, an acceptance with dignity, a sorrow without words to express it.

Arlette was thinking that there, in that dressing room, were the charred bits of all the mementos she had put in every dressing room she had occupied, from the first part she had played. Photographs of Valerie and Frederick, taken twenty-five years ago. Photographs of Michael and Maura taken on their wedding day. A photograph of Gordon Donahue, which had been on the dressing table in her first New York apartment. The green-fringed Spanish shawl that had belonged to her mother, in which Lily Malone had danced a Spanish dance in a high school recital. The red-framed page of Jerry's illegible notes for *Hedda Gabler*, with an elaborate drawing of a Victorian house in one corner. The photograph of her parents, taken when she was three, seated between them, smiling straight at the camera.

They left the house, all of them at once, suddenly tired.

Jerry had found a theater. The fitters and wigmakers for Arlette and Anthony would be there at one-thirty –

and it was nine o'clock. They went dashing into taxis, disturbing the peace and quiet of Sixty-second Street, calling out their good-byes, waving, laughing . . .

CHAPTER 92

'Think about it, Arlette.'

She had thought about it. And sometimes it seemed she thought about it continuously:

Flying to Los Angeles; reading her lines for the next day's schedule; talking to Thyssen and Max Gilmore and Grant Evans. She thought about it when she was having fittings for her elaborate wardrobe – Faustine was a rich French woman, or so she said, who had left her husband and children before the end of the Second World War and, by means unspecified in James Lennox's script, taking with her and her lover clothing and jewelry enough to establish her in any world capital, only to find herself in Guatemala, living on a *finca* near Lake Atitlán.

That lover, or husband, General Charles Delorme, either was a member of the French underground resistance movement, who had escaped in time to save his life, or was he someone else: the commandant of a Nazi extermination camp?

Lennox and Thyssen were no more explicit about these facts than others in this most mysterious of all Thyssen's films. And Arlette suspected it was some part of Thyssen's own history.

His family, German Jews, had left Germany in the early thirties. But Minerva had told her that Thyssen's first wife, a French woman, had refused to leave with him; had later been reported dead, and that was when he had married Thea Barlow. Thyssen had transferred a successful motion-picture career in Berlin to an even more successful motion-picture career in Hollywood, and Arlette suspected that this mysterious woman, Faustine,.

723

was perhaps some bitter recollection of his first wife. No one would ever quite know that, either.

Thyssen intended doing neither the audience nor his actors any favors by solving the script's multiple puzzles.

'These three people don't have to know what they're doing, any more than any of us knows what he's doing. They live on hope and lies,' Thyssen told them at the first conference. 'That they believe Mexico will give them political asylum is enough. Whether it would have or not makes no god damn difference – to me, to you, or to the picture.'

Ghosts, again.

But this was the ghost of a woman she could understand better than she had ever understood Medea.

When the run ended, she stood naked in the dressing room and detached Medea's quivering coils of hair. She unwound the golden serpent bracelets from each arm and threw them among the curls.

'Medea, you haven't been my favorite incarnation.'

Anthony was smiling. He had said, more than once, that she became too intimate with the characters she played.

'Think about it, Arlette.'

So Micah had said the last time they had met, when she returned alone to New York after three weeks in London with Anthony, talking to Granville about *Anna Karenina*. While she was filming *Faustine*, Anthony was to play *King Lear*, in London with the National Theatre. After that, Anna and Vronsky for them and Granville.

When she had got off the plane at Kennedy a voice was paging Miss Lily Malone.

Suddenly uneasy, trembling inside as if she were about to encounter some desperate danger, she picked up the telephone:

Why do we fear what we want most?

Yet the conspiracy, the mystery, the excitement of planning and having the plan work was as delightful as if she had set out in a moon capsule and landed exactly according to calculation at the edge of the Valley of Musical Dreams.

She gave the operator her name and, after a minute or two, heard his voice. 'Arlette – was it a good flight? I'm in the passengers' lounge. Wait there, I'll be down.'

Each new meeting seemed the first. Weeks had elapsed, or months. Everything was new, to be discovered again. They must retrace the past, in their feelings; her history until this moment, and his; her character, and his:

Is he the man I thought he was last time? Has he changed?

She looked at him steadily as he walked nearer and then stood directly before her; that face, a stranger's, yet it occupied some part of her mind at every moment: the high cheekbones, tanned clean-shaven skin; the elegantly formed head, the look of authority, and the tenderness as he bent to kiss her:

Yes. You and I, Micah – we're among the life-wounded.

She did not say it, but perhaps he sensed what she was feeling, and he kissed her carefully, then waited for her to suggest what they would do, where they would go.

'Think about it, Arlette.'

Whether she was sitting for publicity pictures, standing for fittings, dictating to Edna Frazier. Whether she was trying to balance her professional relationship with Grant Evans – a very different man now that he was current idol of all girls between twelve and twenty-nine, and yet a serious actor. Whether she was taking a singing lesson, French or German lessons, practicing Yoga or ballet exercises – and by now she had gurus and teachers of several disciplines on each coast – she thought about it.

She was interested in Faustine, and she was interested in *Faustine*, as James Lennox and Thyssen had worked it out. It was as ambiguous, as puzzling, as filled with the commonplace fears and the grave terrors, the dubious loves and unequivocal lusts, as she believed life itself to be:

Faustine could be me. Give or take a few of those accidents of fate, I could be Faustine.

725

That troubled her only because she was afraid she might play herself inadvertently, and not the character. And while Grant Evans had assured interviewers that the secret of screen acting was simple: the actor must play himself, and the character would fall into line with him – that was the opposite of all Arlette's training.

'I'm sorry to advise you,' Thyssen said the first day, when they met to have lunch at his house, 'that I'm going to do something I don't believe in. We will have to shoot some of the difficult scenes fairly early in our schedule because of the rainy season. We must work around the weather.'

'Good,' said Arlette.

Thyssen smiled curiously. 'Good? Why?'

'The difficult scenes are the most interesting.'

'But first,' said Thyssen, 'we'll do a few easy ones, here on the sets. Film actors, like theater actors, need to get the feel of their parts. Too many directors expect them to start from a standing jump into the middle of the most difficult scene in the picture. We'll begin with two indoor scenes.'

'Which ones?'

'Charles and Faustine are living at the *finca* when he has the attack of appendicitis. We'll begin there.'

Gilmore grimaced. 'We'll begin with me clutching my gut and groaning – while we're getting acquainted with Charles and Faustine and the Doctor.'

'The other scene will be Faustine's first visit to the Doctor's house, after they've met on the road. She says she has a sore throat. This is the scene where she tells the Doctor she came with Charles because her husband was killed by the Germans and her children sent away to the country and could not be found. He doesn't believe it, and says so.'

'But he believes the way she looks,' said Grant.

This young man has grown up since I taught him to cry.

During the filming of *The Lady of the Camellias*, she could feel him trembling each time he touched her. Now, Grant Evans was not only older, he was better-looking;

726

he was not only better-looking, he had become accustomed to adulation himself.

Thyssen gave them their scripts for the next day, told them what time to be on the set, and Max Gilmore set off to join Susie Allen at the house they had rented. Edna had gone ahead to Thyssen's guest-house, which Arlette was occupying again, to make telephone calls.

Arlette started toward the guesthouse and Grant Evans followed her. 'Will you – have dinner with me tonight?'

She smiled at him, thinking of Armand and Marguerite, meeting in this new incarnation.

'I'm having dinner with Edna. She reads my cues for tomorrow.' He looked slightly embarrassed, as if he had not expected the refusal. 'But thank you.'

How, she supposed he was thinking, could she have refused to sleep with a man whom millions of American women fantasized about? How many disappointing husbands and lovers had he replaced in how many otherwise boring encounters? How many beds did he occupy in one day or night, coast to coast?

She ran into the house. 'Here I am!' she announced to Edna, the two fitters, the hairdresser, the German teacher, the French teacher:

Think about it, Arlette.

And who was this Faustine Delorme she was expected to become at ten o'clock tomorrow morning?

The script gave her few clues.

Faustine was a refraction, a kaleidoscope of colors and responses from the two men she spent those few weeks with. Somewhere she must be found, and she had not found her yet.

'She'll be there when the time comes.'

It was Micah who had reassured her while they walked the beach.

He had seen her now in several plays and the three movies.

She had been a part of his world long before she had seen him on the plane, glanced at the notes he was reading, and begun to puzzle over those hieroglyphics upon which

727

he concentrated so intensely that it seemed a bright light was burning beside her.

And she, who never talked to strangers or acknowledged their presence, passing through and among them as Micah said neutrinos could pass through solid objects without affecting them, nevertheless she had surprised herself by telling him her story of having once lived in China:

'Recently?'

'Not more than twelve hundred years ago.'

If he had smiled skeptically, she would have said nothing more, and probably never thought of him again.

Instead, he had looked at her with the suggestion of a smile, and at that moment the plane banked sharply, sending the brilliant late sun into his eyes, and she had seen them emerald green and glittering.

That, I suppose, should have warned me.

After all, no one's eyes should turn from gray to green for any reason whatever.

Surely there was something miraculous in having such eyes. She had convinced herself it had something to do with a mind which required such eyes to see so far into space and time. But he assured her there was a simple explanation: too much blood to the head under stress or excitement, for example; a certain light – a lamp, a shaft of sun. Nothing strange at all. Genes and chromosomes might be added to the recipe if desired.

'Think about it, Arlette,' had been the last thing Micah had said to her when they had driven back from Montauk, after two days, during which he had called to tell his secretary he would miss his Monday class: no reason.

Midway down the island they stopped for dinner at about nine o'clock. And for a time, it seemed to her the dinner would carry them through to a slightly melancholy but gallant prospect of another farewell.

She became aware that Micah was watching her, steadily, intently, and she smiled at him almost timidly, sensing that he was about to say something she would not want to hear.

'I want to live with you.'

Arlette studied the steak, the broiled tomatoes, concentrating as upon a Dutch still life. 'I wish we could, Micah.'

There was a silence of several seconds, while her heart had begun to beat with an anxious force.

Why should this love of a man she loved in equal degree terrify her more than facing the most demanding audience; more than the day she left the hotel and set out for the town where Lily Malone was to marry Patrick Runkle; more than the opening night of *The Taming of the Shrew*, when she had experienced the first recognition that now she had sold herself to this profession, into the voluntary enslavement of discipline? But there it was. The fear was the fear of herself.

What he wanted was what she wanted: there it stopped.

Micah Benoni carried the entire apparatus of his life, his gratifications and disappointments, his hope for future glories, if he entertained such hopes, in his head.

'I can work anywhere in the world. All I need is the equipment. It's everywhere – New Zealand, England, Canada, France. And it's at my disposal. The work I've done these past thirty years has given me that much freedom.'

'And the work I've done has taken my freedom. With every play or picture, I'm wrapped closer into it, wound around and around, an Egyptian mummy, swaddled – immobilized.' She laughed at the image, but he did not. He was watching her with the first anger he had shown.

'Then what?' he demanded.

'I don't know.'

If we talk, we'll quarrel—

'Micah – please—'

His eyes gleamed, and it seemed there could be no love behind that still intent face. She looked away, afraid of seeing that this love was after all something they had both imagined, the actress and the genius, enchanted by each other's accomplishments.

'We met too late, Micah.'

'Not necessarily. Think about it.'

CHAPTER 93

On the set representing a patio in Guatemala, Arlette sat across the table from Max, dressed in a long white sheer linen dress, off the shoulders and low on her breasts. The long full skirt had two feet of embroidery around the hem; a white rose was between her breasts, and she was barefoot: Faustine to perfection, they had agreed.

Magenta bougainvillaea blossoms covered the table, and votive candles burned amid the crystal and china. The set was a replica of a house on the *finca* near Lake Atitlán, where shots of adobe Indian houses and mountain trails would, as he said, open the picture up.

How it was that Max Gilmore, accustomed to Jerry Hoffman's sparse settings, did not immediately translate himself into General Charles Delorme, or his alias, clearly puzzled and annoyed Thyssen.

Thyssen relied upon facial expressions, large disturbing enigmatic close-ups which contradicted the dialogue, questioned the action, emphasized the aloneness of each character in a Thyssen film.

When Arlette had appeared from her trailer dressing room, Thyssen had examined her carefully, and nodded. 'You've got it. Faustine is beautiful, and wants to be admired. She has reason to please this guy – all the time.'

'Even,' said Max, 'if we don't know what the hell the reason is.'

'I know,' said Arlette. 'Well enough, anyway.'

After an hour or more, Max astonished Arlette and Thyssen by clutching his side, grinding his teeth, and saying in perfect German: '*Mein Gott, ich kann nicht. Faustine, ich glaube das ich sterbe!*'

Arlette moved near, touching his shoulder as he bent double. The Spanish-Indian maid appeared with the next course and Arlette dismissed her, speaking to the General in English. '*Don't move, Charles. I'll bring the Doctor. If it's appendicitis, it could rupture.*'

There was a sound of a motor starting, Arlette backed the car swiftly into view and off the set. She stopped the motor.

'We've got it.' Thyssen never embarrassed his actors by asking them why, if they could get it after fifty failed attempts, they had not done it the first time. 'We'll go on. It's only twelve-thirty.'

In another scene Arlette would park the car in the Doctor's courtyard, run into his bedroom, seize him by the arm, and tell him that her husband was dying.

But here there would be no more of what Thyssen called traveling.

No getting the General out of his dinner jacket and into bed. The next scene began with the Doctor and Faustine in the dimly lighted bedroom where the General lay with his face turned to the wall and made no reply to the Doctor's greeting.

By the time Thyssen was satisfied with that, the sky had begun to change color. 'Tomorrow night. Same time.'

Faustine kissed Delorme tenderly. '*Mon cher, il faut le faire. Vous avez cent-quatre degrés de fièvre. Le médicin est excellent et expérimenté – l'opération tout ce qu'il'y a de plus simple.*'

Max's voice rose. '*Il me faut un anesthésique local! Faustine! Que je ne commence pas à babiller—*'

Grant spoke soothingly, and placed his hand, holding the syringe, upon the General's arm. '*If you talk – speak German. I won't understand a word—*'

Another spasm of pain, and Max seized the bedposts, his body rising. All at once he fell back inert, the Doctor thrust the needle into his arm, out of camera range, since Thyssen believed that too many effects of pain lost the audience to their own fears or memories.

'*Begin to count slowly, General Delorme—*'

'*Ein, zwei, drei—Schweinhund, Scheisse! – vier—*'

Thyssen's schedule was timed to take all shots which

required the interior of the General's patio and house, and so there began what he called the 'night watch': Faustine and the Doctor waiting in the patio, lighted by a few candles and the dim electric light from the interior.

From time to time they were to go to the General's room, then return to the garden to talk – in a few sparse sentences by which they were to learn as much about each other as Thyssen wanted them – or the audience – to know.

She would play and sing a French song, composed for the picture from a poem of Lamartine, and there would be the beginning of lovemaking between them.

'In other words,' said Grant Evans, somewhat defensive over his Dr Lawler, 'this bastard has never heard of the Hippocratic oath? He'll let his patient go into coma or delirium while he's screwing his wife.'

Thyssen replied softly. It was growing light. They were tired.

'He's not going to screw her that same night. He may not touch her. But I don't want a movie set in cement before the first reel is filmed. We'll see. That's all. Lust and responsibility are not necessarily incompatible. The woman is tempting – isn't she?'

For four nights they sat in the patio, Dr John Lawler and Faustine Delorme, Dr Lawler asking questions, Faustine answering evasively, the Doctor making repeated visits to the General – Faustine continuously present.

They shot the scenes in brief fragments. Thyssen dismissed as many technicians as possible, sending for a hairdresser or makeup man only when he needed them.

The quiet of the patio, the sense that they were alone, or nearly alone, gradually lulled Arlette and Grant Evans into a hypnotic sense of having become Faustine Delorme and Dr John Lawler, waiting for her husband to come out of the anesthetic.

Faustine and the Doctor were in the General's room, where he lay moaning, occasionally mumbling in German. She quickly covered his mouth with her hand and bent over him, whispering.

Then they were in the patio again.

Faustine took up the guitar and sat with one leg crossed over her knee, picking out the lyric, and began to sing. The man in the bedroom might be dying. It was, she explained, his favorite song:

> *'Aimons donc, aimons donc! de l'heure fugitive,*
> *Hâtons-nous, jouissons!*
> *L'homme n'a point de port,*
> *Le temps n'a point de rive:*
> *Il coule, et nous passons. . . .'*

Another long silence. Faustine murmured: *'You understand what it says?'*

'I speak French. And German.'

'You son of a bitch.'

'I came here to perform an operation. Not to take the witness stand.'

'You're not an American. Are you a doctor?'

There was a moan from inside the house, and the General's voice rose to a pitch of rage: *'Ich hab meine Pflicht getan – alles, alles, was ich könnte—'*

They went on to other scenes:

Faustine talking to the Doctor the first day she saw him on the road near Lake Atitlán; Faustine on horseback; the Doctor driving a jeep; Faustine seated at the fragment of an outdoor café which was a replica of one they would use in Guatemala, suspicious of two men seated at a table nearby.

As the technicians were making their preparations for the café scene, Edna Frazier arrived in the chauffeured car which Thyssen had left at her disposal. Anthony had called from London – it was the opening night of *King Lear*. He was waiting for her call at Granville's house.

Arlette ran into Thyssen's trailer office, and while Edna put in the call, she waited, her heart beating as if this were the first time she had talked to Anthony since that day when Gordon Donahue introduced Jade Ring to Ming Huang.

They had said good-bye in London two months and a

half before, and the last few minutes at the airport had left her uneasy, as if she had something to apologize for. *Is that what he expects?*

She had decided before they left for the airport that when the time came, she would say that she loved him. As they waited in the lounge he watched her. His face was anxious and pain showed in his eyes, and that was not Anthony as she thought of him, or as she wanted to think of him:

Yes, he loves me. But then – he has nothing ugly to remember.

His fingers touched her chin, lifting her face, and she closed her eyes as his mouth touched hers:

Now, I'll say it: I love you—

But the words, after all, remained unspoken, and instead she left him with Jade Ring's bewitching smile, a slight wave, then a kiss blown from her fingertips as he stood motionless, nodding slightly by way of good-bye:

And so I couldn't do it, after all.

It was not so very different, she had thought, from her inability to speak to Micah about Zarah's complimentary reviews; or about her prettiness.

But, unluckily, the girl was not merely pretty, she was beautiful, and Arlette felt a jealousy of a kind quite different from what she had felt about Deborah Crane. Deborah had not been worth taking seriously. This Zarah would go through the world like Arlette herself, being taken seriously by everyone who met her. Men would fall in love with her, and perhaps never quite extricate themselves. The compliment about Zarah was impossible to give.

And so it had proved with the simple statement: *Anthony, I love you.*

Anthony would not be fooled. He would not be grateful. And, in a sense, she blamed Anthony for not having learned, even yet, what she had known since she was five: happiness was not to be depended upon. And the people you loved and needed most would one day be lost to you.

To her. To anyone else. But not, he clearly believed, to Anthony De Forest.

'Arlette?' Anthony's voice was strong, clear, full of triumph. 'Arlette – darling, how are you? Where are you?'

'I'm in Thyssen's trailer. I'm about to see two men I think are members of the Irgun, maybe looking for us. Tell me – you're pleased? It went well?' They had always been careful not to admit to success, not to admit real satisfaction – that was a superstition which even Anthony De Forest, shaman though he might be, scrupulously observed.

'Jesus, I wish you'd been here! I did it – I played a guy thirty years older than I am. I played him, so help me, God, I think I played him like Lear!' The joyousness, the pride in his increasing skills, delighted her, even while she felt a sudden dread of the future:

What will I play when I am old?

She was ashamed of the thought, arriving unexpectedly, and yet she had asked herself that many times.

Anthony's plans seemingly extended until he reached the age of ninety-three, when he would play *Oedipus at Colonus*. And he had no misgivings, no premonitions, no fears, no suspicion that his talent might weaken one day – any more than it occurred to him that his health or his looks might eventually betray him:

The shaman who had gone into the cold wilderness of the Chosin Reservoir and emerged two months later with his collection of magic talismans, carried not in a bundle of buffalo hide, but in the cells of his brain.

Anthony read two or three paragraphs from a review of his *Lear*, and then, reluctantly, it seemed, he concluded there was nothing more to say.

'I'm keeping you, Arlette. They're waiting.'

'Yes. I won't be able to talk to you until we get back from location.'

Something went out of his voice. Confidence. 'I know. You're enjoying Faustine?'

'I'm not sure who she is – and I don't think I will be when the picture ends. Sometimes I think she may be a German Jew—'

735

Anthony had read the script. 'The script contradicts it – Arlette – Arlette—'

'I – love you—'

She hung up and dropped into the chair:

My God! I said it! And I wasn't even thinking about it. Where did it come from? What will he expect of me! Something – different . . .

Perhaps it had been a way of sealing herself into a cocoon, beyond possibility of Micah's luring her out into his world of stars and bent space.

Arlette went out slowly, thoughtfully, then became aware that they were waiting and ran toward them gaily. 'The reviews are marvelous! If I could ever learn as much about acting as Anthony knows . . .'

'Over there,' said Thyssen. 'Sit at the café table, cross your legs. Gesture at the waiter. Faustine believes the common people are common. Don't notice the tourists at first.' He bent over her. 'You know everything Anthony knows. Now, just a slight smile, thinking about something, not too pleasant—'

CHAPTER 94

'This is your picture, Andrew,' Arlette told Thyssen on the plane en route to the high Sierras. 'More than any you've made; what the world becomes when people dare not trust each other.'

'I've been there.'

By that time they had filmed several love scenes: Arlette and the Doctor; Arlette and General Delorme, photographed in a variety of situations and places, hours of the day or night.

'Those scenes are crucial. Unless he was raving-mad with lust for the woman, the Doctor would never hit on the crazy notion of getting the General across into Mexico. He uses the guy's guilty conscience to get at his wife. Delorme uses the Doctor's desire for his wife to get himself into Mexico. Obviously, he's no safer there than anywhere else if they're after him. And they are.'

'Sex and suspicion. Suspicion and sex.'

'The two have a remarkable affinity.'

There had been discussions of the General's fears of being followed; his brooding guilt about his participation in the German death camps.

The location in the Sierras looked like a safari campsite. There were trailers: one for Arlette – Edna had returned to New York; one for Thyssen; one to be shared by Gilmore and Evans. There were tents: small ones for the crew, a large one to eat in, and a special tent for Thyssen and the cast and the head cameraman. Six Indian ponies grazed on the mountain grasses and drank from the stream, neither wide nor deep: Thyssen's choice for the frontier.

The mountains delighted Arlette, who roamed like a child taken into the forest for the first time, sniffing the leaves, caressing the soft furry needles, applying her open palm with care to test the prickly ones.

When Grant Evans slipped his arm about her waist, she looked at him with a gay and happy smile. 'Arlette, I do love you. I'll love you all my life. You've taught me more about acting than all the directors, all the— That's not why I love you, though.'

She kissed him lightly, and felt a particular happiness that this bouquet, so quickly arranged, and with most of her reliable ingredients missing, would nevertheless prove imperishable: Grant Evans would like to think that once upon a time he had had a special relationship with Arlette Morgan, unknown to the rest of the world.

The picture was built of lies; its only reality was the feeling between the three principals, their fears of one another and the world; their guilts; their cross-fertilization of suspicion and terror.

In Chichicastenango, Faustine, concealed by a rebozo, had knelt among the praying Indians in the church, its interior dim with incense and heavy with the smell of flowers strewn over the floor, an offering to the pagan gods, and there she had taken Doctor Lawler's passport from his pocket, returning it while he was engrossed with watching the men they thought might be members of the Irgun. But whose name the passport carried, she had never told Lawler or Delorme. And Thyssen had not favored the audience with an informative close-up.

The rest of the film had yet to be completed, but the weather had been right in the Sierras, and so they had come to film the final scene.

They sat around the campfire, speculating.

Arlette stared into the fire, thinking of her telephone conversation with Micah the day before: he would meet her in Los Angeles when they left location, and they would have the two days together which Thyssen had promised his tired actors.

Arlette stood up. 'Faustine is a woman who long ago stopped trusting or loving anyone. The world has become an enemy.' With a gesture of good night, she went into her trailer.

The next morning she appeared in the dusty mud-spattered black leather riding habit, weathered to Thyssen's taste, but still one of the handsomest costumes she had worn: black leather, soft and supple, flaring and divided for riding, mid-calf length, the edges cut into a four-inch fringe. She, as well as the Doctor and the General, wore a holster across her hips, each holding a pistol.

They were to ride in single file, Faustine first, the Doctor second, the General last – an order of march dictated by the General – and the cameras were set at varying angles and distances.

They plodded along until they heard running water.

'*There it is!*' Evans shouted. '*The frontier!*'

The three dismounted and, pulling on the bridles of the stubborn ponies, proceeded on foot to the stream's edge.

Max, as Delorme, spoke to Faustine: '*I'll go ahead to be sure the water's not too deep. You follow.*' He looked with a strange blank savagery at the Doctor. '*You're coming?*'

The General kissed Faustine, who gave him a brief gesture as he started across. *'Vaya con Dios.'*

The stream was narrow and shallow, the crossing soon made, and as the General proceeded the Doctor followed him, then stopped, three or four feet into the stream. The General turned from the far side, beckoning, and the Doctor raised his pistol and fired point blank. The General pitched forward into the water.

The Doctor stood motionless, holding the pistol. There had been no sound of alarm or protest from Faustine, standing on the bank behind him.

She called out: *'Achtung, Herr Doktor – Herr Major Joseph Meyer!'*

The Doctor turned swiftly. Faustine's pistol was leveled at arm's length. She fired directly at the Doctor, who did not raise his pistol. There was a brief look of astonishment and he fell, while Faustine stared at him, her face serious, enigmatic, as she lowered the pistol.

The camera continued what would later become a long close-up of Faustine's face, her serious expression, without triumph or sorrow, while the music would begin, softly with the song 'Et Nous Passons,' with Faustine's voice singing as she had sung for the Doctor in the patio.

Thyssen said: 'Good. We'll try it once more – when you've put on dry costumes. And this time, Grant—'

Arlette gave a burst of laughter. 'Oh, Micah! If you could have seen Grant's face. Six more takes. *Six . . .*'

Micah was smiling; amused, she hoped, for this meeting had not begun as happily as she had anticipated.

They were late in coming back from the mountains. The schedule had been extended because of Thyssen's passion for being sure he had every possible angle, every nuance of expression – Faustine's cool executioner's stare across the pistol held at arm's length.

'You tell me, darling,' she continued, hoping to coerce Micah into playing the game with her. 'Why did she kill Lawler? Was he Meyer, or was his passport forged? Was

739

she German? Did she think he would kill her? I wonder if Lennox and Thyssen have ever decided.'

Whenever they came together after a long absence, there was once again the helpless distrust.

When he arrived at Thyssen's guesthouse and was met by Arlette in blue denims and a white wool sweater, his face was grim:

What good is it to either of us – this way?

'Let's pretend, Micah,' she said eagerly when he had kissed her. 'Let's pretend these two days are – all our lives.'

She had wanted him to go to the bedroom, assuring him no one would come, but he picked up her bag and walked out. 'I want to be alone with you in a place neither of us has been in before.'

She had told Thyssen she was going to visit her brother and his wife at La Jolla. And she had taken the precaution of putting in a call to Anthony as soon as they had returned from the mountains.

He was at Granville's house, discussing the script of *Anna Karenina*.

'Anna is your part, Arlette,' Granville said. 'You'll make her believable – I never did think she made much sense – now she will.'

'You're all right, darling?' Anthony asked. 'You're happy?'

'Happy, happy,' murmured Arlette. 'Is there such a thing?'

She should not have said it, for that would set Anthony to thinking disturbing thoughts. No one knew better than Anthony that happiness, wherever she could find it, however she could conjure it, had been her only antidote to the old unmitigable conviction that some unexpected disaster would take her by surprise:

Happy? Of course I'm happy. Why shouldn't I be? I'm loved by quite a few people a little, and by three or four or five a great deal. And I'm me: Arlette Morgan.

She had not been so confident while she waited for Micah to register at the motel with small white bungalows, where children were screaming and laughing in the swimming pool and women with hair dyed blue and orange were lying, apparently unconscious from the spell of the sun:

Browning was right. You can never get it all together.

Dr and Mrs Benoni were shown a room with a double bed, where a radio was playing. The bellhop switched on the air-conditioner and the television set as Arlette turned off the radio, and Micah ushered him quickly out, pressing a bill into his hand.

'Arlette – Arlette—' His hands were on her shoulders, and his voice spoke her name quietly, between yearning and reproach. 'Here we are – again—'

He smiled, and she closed her eyes, for his smile was ironic, saying:

Here I am – a man who it seems has nothing better to do than wait for you to call.

'Micah – you're angry?'

'I'm angry, I suppose. I love you – and it's a more bitter pain than I was ready for. I had always supposed that pain was about – other things—'

'I know: the suspicions beginning again, leaving one country for another country your father hoped would be safer – that was pain enough. Forgive me – I've brought you more.'

He smiled; the smile was tender now. 'Let me look at you. I've almost driven myself crazy, wanting you with me – five months—'

Arlette followed him as if it were a choreographed ballet, moving with his movements; motionless when he was, holding his head between her hands, giving a low outcry at that joyous disaster, the end as it seemed of all lovemaking and the end, perhaps, of all life. She became aware that she had begun to cry, sobs that were full of pity for them both.

After some time, while it seemed she must have been near unconsciousness, he brought her to life again with sensations that began softly, little more than insinuations. The feeling intensified, and Arlette drew a mournful-sounding sigh, staring up at him with a look of fear, pleading for keener pleasure, until after some interminable time, he fell asleep.

Her body seemed to have spilled its contents against the walls of bone and flesh, all that prevented her from melting into the world outside.

She lay beside him, silent, staring straight at the ceiling, and all at once was struck with what seemed the answer to her life's search.

Her mind seemed to be numb and only her body lived, heart pounding, the pulse showing its beat beneath her navel. The secret evolved, clear at last. She gave a soundless, mirthless little laugh:

The secret is that there is no secret. I'm the secret as much as anything is. I must tell him before I forget . . .

She turned, but he was asleep; she would tell him later.

The light had gone from behind the flowered draperies he had pulled across the Venetian blinds, and she could not read the watch on the bedside table.

She bent over him and studied his face, longingly, disturbed by some premonitory sorrow – that same sorrow which came each time they were together:

Why can't I feel it only once – when it happens? Good-bye?

She fell asleep, peaceful, relieved that she need never wonder again about the secret, having solved it finally: all the mysteries unraveled at once, to betray that small seedling at their core: no mystery; no secret.

When she awoke the great discovery had vanished.

Micah was dressed, in slacks and a blue shirt, tying a dark blue tie with that brief intense concentration it seemed even a genius must give to his necktie. She smiled, watching him.

The knowledge she supposed she had put on with his power was gone, irrecoverable, but there remained the relieved wonder that she no longer need look for it.

It was late by the time they set off, after dinner, down the highway, the cars passing so swiftly it was possible to imagine they were unoccupied. Then, the long slow climb up the mountain.

Finally Micah turned off the highway. 'There it is.'

The observatory was quiet, serene. They ascended to the cage set high beside the great telescope, Micah saying only that she must sit down, look into it, out into space, backward into time.

She obeyed, catching her breath at the billions of stars which floated before her.

There was the future, in the limitless bleak distance: there was the future and the past; there was the land of lost content.

Arlette felt that she was trespassing upon a sacred domain, a magician's lair, set with gigantic eyes pointed outward, while cameras worked in silence:

Where is our life before we have lived it? Out there?

After we have lived it?

There, too?

She thought of Lily Malone, in Jade Ring's black lacquered coiffure, with depending strands of wisteria blossoms, dressed in a crimson silk gown, stepping forward to meet the Shining Emperor, Ming Huang, Patrick Runkle – asking herself that question in all the ignorance of youthful optimism.

Now the question had been answered. Or at least a large part of it, and the loss was a permanent one for her and Micah Benoni: the loss of the years which had been sloughed off in the living of them, leaving them unable to give to each other unused selves.

'Where are the astronomers?' she whispered.

'Astronomers are invisible people. Only other astronomers are able to detect them. They are, you might say, a kind of quark – more hypothetical than real. And their charm is often more hypothetical than real.' That was his apology for the earlier grimness. 'Put to the test of patience in real life, we don't always hold up so well as we might wish.'

Arlette laughed with relieved delight, warm again with gratitude and trust.

He explained to her how the telescope functioned, what it recorded, how the photographs were studied, and

Arlette made a passionate effort to understand. Yet the mystery began to terrify her with increasing intensity.

She asked questions, but the answers made her dizzy:

'Ten thousand million years ago the universe began to evolve from the initial explosion. We think—'

'But what do we know? For sure?'

'Nothing, for sure.' Micah smiled, somewhat wryly, a man who had pondered the imponderables and concluded that they were, in fact, imponderable. 'Some astronomers think the sequence of universes will never end. Some think the universe will reach its state of maximum entropy and die a heat death. Some think the universe will annihilate itself. This troubles them – it makes the whole effort somewhat pointless, doesn't it? And some think that eternal darkness and indefinite expansions are its destiny. Many of them find this notion repellent. Those are the scientists who forget that their first and essentially only responsibility is to eliminate themselves from their judgments.'

'I see only one thing out there, one question: Where did yesterday go?'

'You're looking at it. Come, you've had enough. I'm not your teacher – you're not my student. I only wanted to give you a clue to how I spend my time.'

'Tell me one thing more, Micah: where is the day after tomorrow today? Where is it going to happen? Out there – too?'

He laughed softly, kissed her, and slipped his arm around her. They started out. 'I know a way to answer all those questions—'

They walked through the silent building. All at once Arlette turned: '*I hear there's a hell of a good universe next door!*'

'*Let's go!*'

He caught her hand and they began to run toward the car, Micah's flashlight guiding them in the dark.

CHAPTER 95

Back in New York, through with Faustine, Arlette embraced Irma and asked about her vacation with Conrad.

Irma began to describe it, and as she talked Arlette wandered about the drawing room, enjoying it as if she had never seen it, promising herself to return for a complete inspection tour a little later. All the while she was moving with a soft restless glide, glancing appreciatively now and then at Irma, murmuring: 'Marvelous. Wonderful. Fantastic!'

Irma, knowing the exact time – eight minutes they had tacitly settled upon for these reunions – since Miss Morgan was always in a hurry to run upstairs, study her schedule, and be on her way again, gave Arlette the sealed envelope left by Edna Frazier when she had set out for London four days ago with Arlette's suitcases; they expected to be there no less than nine months.

'Please tell Conrad to wait. I have to go somewhere.'

Where? That was the answer she would find in the envelope.

She dashed up the stairs and in the bedroom, stopping in the doorway as if she expected Anthony to put aside the book or script he had been reading and ask what all the excitement was about.

For excitement shone in her smile, in her eyes, in the eagerness of her gestures.

The room was empty. No one there but the furniture. The bed, with its yellow silk hangings and spread; the late nineteenth-century French paintings; the cabinet which contained the names of those she had supposed to be her enemies. On a table, a silver-framed photograph of Anthony, taken when he was playing Othello, ferocity glittering in his black eyes; that same dark and somber Anthony she encountered every now and then:

So beautiful, so beautiful, this house is. I could never have guessed I could come to love beautiful objects. Valerie wouldn't approve . . .

She tore open Edna's envelope and sat at the desk to study it: if anything untoward should ever happen to Miss Morgan, it would certainly not be the fault of careless planning by Edna Frazier. She could not be late. She could not be surprised — at least, professionally. She could not be left to search for what she had not guessed she might need. Edna Frazier had guessed.

The schedule was a work of art: from this moment until she took the plane to London, arriving in time to see Anthony's last performance of *King Lear*, every appointment was listed. The envelope contained her passport, the airplane ticket, the seat reservations; Edna had even selected the dinner menu. There was the hour when Conrad would leave for the airport; the hour when Anthony would meet her in London. There were the tickets for her and Alicia to see tonight's performance of Minerva as Violaine. There was the hour for tomorrow morning's directors' meeting, where she would sign contracts for the future.

Romeo and Juliet was scheduled to begin rehearsal in two years; it would alternate with Anthony's *Oedipus Rex*.

'It's the time for you,' Jerry had said, 'to play Juliet.'

'I played Juliet.' The memory was still hurtful.

'You were too young then to play a fourteen-year-old girl.'

There were other contracts: John Powell's play, *The Witness Rose*: the single rose pinned to the leading lady's dress — the only witness to her murder by her husband, or their joint suicide; another of Powell's mordant views of matrimony. She would play that with Max Gilmore, in alternate weeks while Anthony played *Richard II*.

There it was: the next three years of both their lives, signed and sealed, delivered over to Hoffman-Repertory.

There was other information in Edna's schedule, but Arlette put it aside, took Edna's telephone book for hotels and restaurants, and dialed the Hotel Pierre.

Three months earlier, they had driven down from the observatory, Arlette in a stupefied wonderment at the billions of stars, the years flowing away from them, as if they were being abandoned to some especially sinister and solitary fate. They had stopped at another motel, where they stayed until it was time to start back to Los Angeles.

As the time for parting approached, Arlette had begun to grow restless. Micah, seemingly amused – although she thought it unlikely the amusement was real, only for the purpose of maintaining these last few hours on even keel – suggested they leave an hour early:

'A tire might go flat. The gas tank might run dry. The carburetor may be rusty. The motor might conk out – motors sometimes do.'

'It may not seem like work to you, Micah. But it's work to me and to the people I work with.'

'I take your work more seriously than mine, if that's possible. You speak to the imagination. And when we stop talking to the imagination, we stop living.' He kissed her gently; tears had appeared, and this curious weakness, helplessness, so it seemed to her, was evidence of some mythological power he exerted. He was silent, studying her with that wonderful gravity. 'I'm not what you think, Arlette. You've invented your idea of me. I'm a guy with work to do who likes to do it.'

'The Pierre,' he reminded her when she left him at Thyssen's guesthouse. 'If the plane's delayed I'll send a cable for my secretary, Miss Lewis. New Zealand is a long way.'

Now, in New York, Arlette asked for Dr Benoni.

Dr Benoni was not due until tomorrow. A cable had arrived today. Addressed to a Miss Lewis? In fact, yes.

'I'm Miss Lewis,' Arlette told the girl and, when she hesitated, added: 'Hurry up – read it! You're wasting my time!' She was surprised at Miss Lewis. But then, the girl would never guess she was talking to Arlette Morgan, possibly a heroine of hers:

'PLANE DELAYED. ARRIVE KENNEDY ON 30TH 9:12 PM. WILL

747

TELEPHONE YOUR HOUSE PRIVATE NUMBER.' Nothing left out there, either.

Arlette drew a deep breath and looked at her watch. *All is destiny.*

Edna's schedule was intact.

Tonight: *The Tidings Brought to Mary*, with Alicia. Tomorrow at ten the board meeting. In the afternoon Jerry was to give her a private tour of the new Alicia Allerton Theater. And then, Edna had written, Mr Hoffman wanted her to reserve an hour and a half for a 'surprise':

He's decided to marry Tracy?

No. Whatever the surprise, it was not that.

It was Minerva's performance of Violaine that she would have been most disappointed to miss, and her throat swelled with pride as she watched Minerva's conquest of this difficult part – ripe fruit of the years spent with Alicia.

Arlette and Minerva threw their arms about each other, laughing and crying a little, as they did at each triumph the other had. Jeffrey Brooke came in and embraced her.

'Thyssen called this afternoon,' Minerva told Arlette when they could get into a corner and whisper. Thyssen had no doubt spent the hours since she had left Los Angeles studying the first several hundred feet of film. 'He said: "We've got some sensational stuff here." '

'What does he mean?' She was not entirely emancipated from Faustine.

'I'm leaving for the Coast after the show closes in January – but I won't be able to tell you anything for several weeks. As soon as I can, I'll call.'

Arlette smiled. 'Call me – but only because I want to talk to you. By then, I'll be Anna. I'll have forgotten who Faustine was.'

There was Eva, followed by her husband, and she was wearing a dress which appeared to be melted silver, which nearly matched her hair; around her neck were emeralds as precious as anything Anthony had given Arlette.

Arlette felt a wave of warmth and love, and as she went

from one to the other, discussing the experiences of the months she had been away, their future plans, laments that there would be no spring or summer at Montauk this year – Micah Benoni suddenly appeared before her, a Micah Benoni so real she closed her eyes.

Jerry glanced swiftly around for what had caused that unexpected defensiveness, something like fear. 'Clap your hands, Arlette.'

She smiled. 'It wasn't an evil spirit, Jerry. I – remembered something.' That man of glittering intensity, who could disrupt her in the midst of anything but her work – and perhaps that came next.

She remembered Micah in the observatory, showing her the empty spaces in the sky which might or might not be black holes, that potential fatal ending of the universe, capable of sucking everything into itself, where time might hang for eternity – and yet seem only an instant.

The observatory had terrified her, and he had sensed this, saying that perhaps it had been a mistake to bring her there. 'It's the kind of thing you have to take for granted, I suppose.'

'Like taking birth and death for granted. Like taking love for granted. Like taking life for granted.'

'I know. We never do – not even those of us who are farthest gone in scientific objectivity. As I once supposed I was.'

They had run out of the observatory, then walked to the car and started down the mountainside to search out a place to spend what was left of the night. Arlette sat in stunned silence, horrified by this glimpse into infinity – only three quarters of the way to the end of the universe. Or so we think, he had said. If the universe has an end.

She had persisted in her questions, finding each answer more painful, wishing she had not asked it, yet going on to ask another.

Finally Micah had said, slowly, as if he were not entirely convinced he should say it: 'It's cost me quite a long struggle, because the end of it has proved to be an unscientific conviction – a species of renunciation, I suppose, of my life's work. I'm like a priest who leaves the priesthood but remains in the monastery, muttering his prayers and confessions, participating in the mass, illuminating the manuscripts, and not believing a bloody word of it.'

Arlette sat, stiffened with fear. 'Micah, don't talk like that. It's – dangerous.'

He laughed softly. 'You've turned me into a magus, Arlette. Don't do it, for both our sakes. I've got a certain brand of information – that's all. But my unscientific conviction, if you will, is that I can no longer believe in anything but subjective experience. And of those subjective experiences, the most powerful is what can be experienced sensually.'

She was suddenly exhausted, shocked in some curious way she did not understand; for all he had said was what she had believed ever since – if not before – that first afternoon when Jack Davidson had forced his way, with little effort, through the filament, emblem of ignorance, and opened her to the world; made her vulnerable, and brought her fully alive.

Once experienced, she still believed, the sexual bond might be broken, as it had been with Jack; with Donahue and Jerry Hoffman and Powell and Granville, even the bond of trust she had formed with Anthony might dissolve, but the essential bond of having once loved sexually was eternal.

Now, in the midst of this gathering of her nation, these people Micah Benoni would not understand, nor understand what they meant to her, he had appeared, Egyptian pharaoh, medieval monk – a description which had occurred even to him.

'Live with me,' he had said to her on the drive back to Thyssen's. 'You can work anywhere in the world. So can I.'

She had smiled sadly, shaking her head in the darkness of the early morning. 'No, Micah. You'd be in New Zealand. I'd be in New York or Los Angeles or London: *I am what is around me . . . One is not duchess a hundred yards from a carriage.'* She was afraid to look at him, thinking that his patience extended to eternity, but not to days and months and the fragile years which might still be left to them. One day, she would lose him.

'Anthony?'

'Anthony, of course. And I'd lose my people – the Hoffman-Repertory. Oh, no, I'm not so free as you imagine, Micah. And suppose it should turn out that the best directors and producers didn't want me: alone – Arlette Morgan—'

He laughed briefly. 'They would.' But then, stopping in front of Thyssen's guesthouse, he turned, his arm across the back of the seat. 'Forgive me, Arlette – I promised I wouldn't talk about it again.'

'I'm never happy when I'm away from you, but I'd be even less happy – away from them—' She got out, not finishing the sentence. 'I love you, Micah.'

I love you, Micah.

I love you, Anthony.

You love a lot of people, Arlette.

It was true, she thought, looking around the room.

Jerry was beside her. 'Ten o'clock tomorrow morning. And when we've got the contracts lined up, I want to show you the theater. I can't wait to see you on that stage—'

CHAPTER 96

It was Saturday, and when Jerry and Arlette reached the theater it was empty and quiet.

They stood for several minutes across the street, peering through the crowds.

The theater would seat fourteen hundred, a number Jerry and the architect had decided was the optimum to hear by natural means the subtleties of English diction.

'They can see you clearly. They can absorb the character's personality.'

751

'It's truly beautiful, Jerry. A Greek temple – perfectly proportioned.'

She was dressed to go to the airport: mauve silk sweater over a mauve wool skirt, and a coat of green cashmere lined with dyed mauve moleskin, into the center back of which had been worked a large white lily of ermine, a baroque flower with a twisting green stem and two green leaves.

Looking at the building, she thought of that girl, Lily Malone, eager to challenge the world and afraid to try; the girl who had spent a year convinced she was haunted. She had cured herself by deciding to become Arlette Morgan, and it had taken all the years between for her to come near accomplishing the transformation.

As they stood, peering through the traffic, studying and admiring the Greek temple Jerry Hoffman had built, she found herself thinking again that she was a little afraid of seeing Micah.

That brain, continuously at work in the finely shaped head, had solved every problem he had invented, sooner or later, even if he might eventually find reason to discard the solution and construct a new one in its place. Only this one problem could not be solved.

Their two different lives, too different, could not be patched to make one life – as once she and Anthony had done; and had gone on mending the rips and tears as they appeared. There was no such possibility for her and Micah.

They crossed in the middle of the block, Jerry holding her hand, darting among the cars, and led her around to the back of the building. Inside it was chilly, dim, damp with the smell of wet cement, none of the usual smells of an empty theater: the audience, the odors of its breath and skin, sweat, cigars and cigarettes, liquor, perfumes; that smell of humanity which came, after years, to permeate the chairs they sat in, the curtains which separated them from the stage.

Jerry showed her with excitement and pride how the intricate machinery would operate, explaining that the stage would partly revolve, to accommodate the swift scene changes so many classical plays required. The curtain would be blood-red velvet with a gold monogram of two joined *A*'s, large enough to cover half its center. He showed her where the dressing rooms would be, and indicated hers and Anthony's; the empty space where a stairway would lead to more dressing rooms, enough to accommodate large casts.

He described the lighting, the miracles it could perform: an entire play could be described by the lighting; even actors were scarcely necessary with this miracle of light. He looked at her with that whimsical smile which said he was teasing her.

Listening to him, it began to seem the theater was complete. The walls and seats in place; the sets ready for the first night's performance: Minerva Grey playing Joan to Jeffrey Brooke's Warwick. Arlette and Anthony would still be at work on *Anna Karenina*.

'After that, it's all yours – if you can learn to resist that siren song—'

'Thyssen's. Granville's. No. We'll spend most of our time here. I don't think Anthony will play very much in London. Maybe not at all. He's learned all they had to teach him.'

'Come out here. Walk carefully, the floor's uneven. The acoustics aren't right yet. But I want you to be the first actor to stand on this stage.'

Arlette looked down into the orchestra pit, afraid to look outward into the vast empty space, which would be filled with red velvet chairs next time she saw it, then up at the semicircular balcony, designed to give almost everyone the same view of the stage.

Jerry let her hand go, and she started to retreat, as if this were opening night and she had never before set foot on any stage.

'Arlette!' His voice spoke sharply, and she paused at midstage.

His arms were folded, and he was looking at her in the way he sometimes had when he wanted a particular performance from an actor but was determined they discover it themselves. She looked up and out, feet together, hands lightly clasped, like a young girl about to begin her high school graduation speech. She stood silently, her face sorrowful; then all at once turned to Jerry, who was watching her with the curious brooding expression she saw occasionally, when he thought she was not looking at him.

'How wonderful if we could always play to this audience!' There it was: her perpetual ambivalence about the people who came to watch her, take everything she could give. After a moment she asked: 'May I say something?' She smiled, a little apologetic to be usurping this stage before the building was complete.

'That's why I brought you here.'

'What do you want me to say?'

'Whatever you want. It's yours.'

She closed her eyes, then opened them and heard a voice coming from long ago, more than seven years: Mary of Scots, warning the lords who had tried and found her guilty: *'Look to your consciences and remember that the theater of the world is wider than the realm of England!'*

She was silent another moment, and a different voice came from a more distant past: *'The Thane of Fife had a wife; where is she now?'* She paused. *'All the perfumes of Arabia will not sweeten this little hand. Oh! Oh! Oh!'* She paused again, and her voice faded, as if she moved into the distance. *'To bed, to bed, to bed.'* She stood motionless.

She was as frightened as she had ever been before a full house. She turned to leave the stage, then glanced at Jerry. 'One more?'

The next moment she was gay, impudent, vivacious; Mrs Millamant teasing her adored Mirabell: *'Why, one makes lovers as fast as one pleases, and they live as long as one pleases, and they die as soon as one pleases; and then if one pleases one makes more.'* Mrs Millamant's conspiratorial laugh rang out, taunting, light, glittering like sunlit water.

She clasped her hands, raised her head, and closed her

eyes. Medea's keening voice implored Hecate: '*Help me now: to remember . . . the use of the venomous fire, the magic song and the sharp gems.*'

Medea's voice faded slowly, the incantation ending in a low shuddering sigh.

After a long still moment, Arlette bent forward until her head touched her knees, she remained motionless, then straightened with the quick familiar flourish.

She ran toward him, plunging into his arms as he opened them, and they stood, holding each other fast, until, she sensed, he began to be afraid of being alone with her – the same proud man who had declared he would make love to her no more because she was in love with another man.

'Come along.'

He had another plan – the 'secret' of Edna Frazier's schedule. They were going somewhere.

He hailed a taxi, and while they headed downtown and east, they talked easily – not of the secret, but of the meeting that morning. The signing of Minerva's contract for the opening night. The signing of Ian Flaherty to play Romeo opposite Arlette – and they laughed at Flaherty's awestruck bewilderment, for he must have been supposing that in the past years since he had been the young Heathcliff he had become a seasoned man of the world, twenty-four and master of all females he surveyed.

As the discussion went on, rehearsal dates, costume designers; lawyers objecting for lawyers' reasons; actors objecting for actors' reasons, only Arlette sat quiet, slightly smiling, thinking of her meeting with Micah Benoni.

She had begun when she awoke to count the hours, telling herself she must not believe in the meeting at Kennedy Airport at nine-twelve that night, for any plane coming from New Zealand was going to stop for one or the other of those reasons which stopped planes. She would not see him at nine-twelve, and so she need not fear the meeting. She might not see him at all. There could be further delays. Perhaps she would be on her way to London before he arrived in New York:

A fear – or a wish?

As the conference continued, Arlette emerged from her reverie and answered promptly: Yes, she would be ready for rehearsal for *The Witness Rose* on March 1, two and a half years from then. Yes, the opening date was satisfactory. Yes, the closing date of alternating Anthony's *Richard II* with *The Witness Rose* was satisfactory.

Eva French was going to make a film while Minerva was playing Joan. After the closing of *Richard II* and *The Witness Rose*, Eva would appear in *She Stoops to Conquer*.

The taxi had reached an area of lofts and warehouses, but Jerry still talked of contracts, the theater, her impromptu performance, and held her hand in the companionable way he had, not caressing it, only holding it for mutual comfort and reassurance.

'Do you think Flaherty can learn enough in two years to play a Romeo to your Juliet? He's got the moxie – he's got the balls. Has he got the fire in his gut?' The taxi stopped before an apparently deserted building.

'I think he'll be a good actor one day.'

She got out, asking no questions, for Jerry's face now had a tense, secretive excited expression, and a sly smile. He ushered her into an elevator, and a man set the creaking machinery in motion.

'Afternoon, Mr Hoffman.'

'Afternoon, Joe. They've gone out?'

'Hour ago. Said you'd be here at two.'

'I know. We're late. I have the key.'

Jerry unlocked the door and they entered a vast room, crowded with stone torsos and figures, each in a state of partial completion – a crowd of maimed naked warriors, turned to stone.

'Why, it's beautiful work. Is he a friend of yours? Who's the sculptor?'

'You don't recognize him?'

'Let me look a little.' She went on to another, a man, somewhat larger than life size, naked, standing simple as

756

Michelangelo's David, and yet for some indefinable reason completely modern, with a face which could belong only to a contemporary man: a model, or friend of the artist. 'Sol Edelstein?'

'Yes. You've met him.'

'I know. You have some of his work.'

They walked on, slowly, studious as if they were in a museum, and stopped at last before the figure of a woman, the stone polished until it was smooth as marble, and Arlette stood gazing at it with interest and bewilderment. There was something strange about it.

The statue was exactly her height, and when she looked into its face, the face was on a level with hers. The figure stood erect, gracefully easy, and the body was both revealed and covered by the stone draperies, which seemed to cling as if they had been wrung out and put on wet; her breasts were clearly defined, the hips, the navel, and the draperies over her legs showed the right knee, slightly bent.

The arms were extended a few inches at either side, and the fingers of each hand rested lightly on a mask: the Greek masks of tragedy and comedy.

She studied the face, that colorless stone face. It emerged before her slowly, until she found herself looking into a mirror.

The face was her own; yet – without color – not her own. Or perhaps this sudden meeting with a permanent self had frightened her, made her reluctant to recognize it. She felt an eerie conviction that if she should commit an act of vandalism – pick up a mallet and strike the stone figure a hard blow – the layer of stone would crack, fall away, and a live woman would be released:

Who is she?

Me, of course.

She turned to Jerry, who was looking intently at the statue. Sensing her movement, he answered without looking at her. 'That's it. That's the statue that goes in the pediment. Are you disappointed?'

'It's beautiful. How did he do it?'.

'Anthony gave him a hundred photographs. And he's met you several times. No one else will know who it is – unless they use a telescope. Or we tell them.'

'But we won't tell anyone, will we? Anthony, Alicia – no one else?'

'No one else.'

The statue had a curiously disturbing quality. There she was: Arlette Morgan. And there she would be, above the theater, standing at the center of the triangle, that sketch Jerry had refused to describe, saying only that when the time came, a statue would be there.

At last, smiling, although she felt a strong unexplainable sense of despair, she turned away. 'Thank you, Jerry.' She glanced at him with an apologetic smile. 'I'm sorry I can't say anything else.'

'I don't want you to say anything else, darling. I did it as much for myself as for you. For myself, to be truthful.'

They started toward the door, and when they reached it turned once more. They looked at the stone figure for a moment. Arlette bowed her head, and walked out as Jerry opened the door. 'It will last such a – long time. Won't it?'

'It will last a long time.'

At home, she found herself unexpectedly tired, and thinking of the twenty-six hours before she would be likely to sleep again – on the plane – she called the airport, was told the plane from New Zealand was expected on schedule, then undressed and went to bed.

She awoke in a dark room and sat up. She rang the kitchen. 'My God, Irma, what's happened? Did I miss it?'

'Did you miss what, madame?'

'The plane! The plane!' A thousand years had passed while she had lain there. The world had changed. Empires had risen and fallen. The pyramids were dust. Seasons had come and gone, springs and summers and winters innumerable. 'What happened?'

'Nothing, madame,' Irma replied soothingly. 'Nothing has happened out of the ordinary, madame. It's exactly six-thirty.'

Arlette sighed. 'Oh, Irma, thank God, thank God. Irma, I'm starving! Literally starving!'

'Yes, madame. Dinner will be ready at seven.'

CHAPTER 97

Her anxiety over the meeting, her precognition that no sooner would Micah walk into the club lounge to meet Miss Lewis than he would be back there again with Arlette Morgan, waiting for her plane to depart for London, those concerns had turned everything into possible sinister omens:

It's over before it begins.

She had called the hotel. No messages. She called the airport again: the plane from New Zealand was still scheduled to arrive on time.

When Conrad brought dinner, she told him she would take the Mercedes because she was going to meet her brother and sister-in-law.

Now what the hell kind of lie is that?

She returned to the dressing room while the table was being set, leaned close to the mirror, and began to correct her makeup, aware that she was singing very softly. Presently she heard the song:

> *'L'homme n'a point de port,*
> *Le temps n'a point de rive:*
> *Il coule, et nous passons. . . .'*

She smiled, undisturbed by the song, for the first time since she had heard it. She shrugged and turned away from the mirror.

Et nous passons. And so we do.

With a volume of nineteenth-century Russian history before her, she ate Irma's delicate dinner: cold cucumber soup; cold jellied chicken; endive salad; out-of-season raspberries sprinkled with framboise brandy.

At eight o'clock she made one final survey in the mirror, slipped on the coat, and ran downstairs. She opened the front door, then paused.

She closed it and ran back to the kitchen, where Irma and Conrad were having dinner in their dining room. They got up as Arlette came in swiftly, smiling brilliantly, reassuringly. 'I'm leaving now. Dr and Mrs Malone are spending the next two days with friends on Long Island and I'm driving them out. My brother will drive me to the airport tomorrow. You can pick up the Mercedes there tomorrow night at nine, Conrad.'

Irma and Arlette embraced, and Arlette shook hands with Conrad, the ancient ritual of arrival and departure.

'Good-bye, Irma! Good-bye, Conrad! We'll call when we can—'

And with that same brilliant reassuring smile, she left them.

There. It was still a lie, but it was a lie that felt better.

'Here we are,' Arlette said. She smiled at Micah, in a chair facing her.

She sat on a sofa in the lounge at the airport, legs crossed, the green cashmere coat thrown back so that its inset white ermine lily with the twisting green stem and curling leaves surrounded her. Anthony's pearl necklace was wound around her neck three times, the Goddess of Mercy, Kuan-Yin, between her breasts. They were waiting for her plane to London to be called.

There was no disguise of wigs or dark glasses. She wanted Micah to remember her looking like Arlette – one more small flower for the bouquet which was prospering in its growth and beauty; for never had it seemed fresher, more fragrant, more permanent a creation than during these past twenty-three hours.

This was where they had met, the night before, to his surprise and a pleasure so intense that she felt guilt that this man, who had such a great capacity for happiness, had never had the opportunity fully to develop or express it.

He had been smiling as he came toward her then, had taken hold of her quickly and kissed her, in that darkened corner of this room where men and women waited to board planes or meet arriving lovers or friends, husbands or wives, drinking, reading, gazing vacantly, talking quietly, all with fatalistic acceptance of whatever might be their lot.

He held her away from him and looked at her, as if to make sure there was no mistake: this was Arlette. Then he had kissed her again, a kiss so profound that she whispered: 'Micah – there are people—'

'What of it?'

He kissed her once more, but then took her hand, as if there were more important things to do than to stand here kissing in public.

Micah, too, traveled without luggage, only an attaché case, which held his papers, toothpaste, electric razor, one or two shirts – he left clothing in hotels all over the world. They walked quickly out of the terminal, turning every few moments to look at each other, as if wondering at so successfully accomplished a conspiracy. And so it was.

No small feat for them to have discovered a space in their lives which might have lasted two days, except for his plane's delay, but which still left them with twenty-three hours, if her plane was on time.

'And it will be,' said Arlette. 'They always are – just when you wish they were hung up over Chicago or Boston.'

Again she felt that slight fear, fear which accompanied the eagerness, putting a dangerous cutting edge on it, fear that one day, one time, one of them would say some small word or phrase, and it would be the final one.

They required that each take care of the other's fragility.

And when he was angry, however carefully controlled the anger might be, she felt threatened: one word, one gesture, would be there between them forever, the sword placed by Tristan between himself and Isolde. And so their love had ended – even if Wagner did not see it that way.

Now, once again in the passenger lounge, she looked at Micah. 'It was the happiest time ever, for me.'

'For me, too.'

She took up the little statue of Kuan-Yin, studied her a moment, and replaced her between her breasts.

'We meet to part, Micah.'

'But we did meet. We were born in the same country – not too many years between us. Have you ever considered that unlikely miracle?'

'Yes, I have. And others.' She was silent a moment. 'I do love you.'

It was true, as he had said. All the odds of their lives had been against such a meeting. It was impossible to make an inevitable chain of events or destiny.

She was going back to Anthony, and could never explain to Micah that there was no way to break the De Forests apart without destroying not only their two careers, but damaging those of all the actors and directors and technicians who depended upon them. The discipline and work which had gone into their creation had become a cement, strong enough to weld together a great building.

This time, to her intense relief and gratitude, there had been no need to explain.

They had disposed of Faustine before they were halfway to Montauk; they had finished with the conference in New Zealand, the resistance of half the astronomers to an open universe which, Micah said, made them nervous.

'Why, I don't know. There's no more comfort to be found in a closed universe than an open one. Still, many of them evidently think it's cozier in the long run. The long run they won't be allowed to wait up for.'

After that, there was no more discussion of work.

And except for a walk on the beach they made love until they fell asleep, and made love when they awoke. They were surprisingly lighthearted, as if this were no brief chance in their lives, but a reward they might have whenever they chose.

Micah had arranged to spend several weeks working at the Jodrell Bank Observatory, and he would be in London in March. That posed problems, and for a moment she was almost sorry to hear it, for once work began on a Granville production, it proceeded remorselessly: When he arrived she must find a way to manipulate the schedule.

She sat on the bed in the yellow guest room, wrapped in a towel tied about her waist, cross-legged, and looked at him lying with arms behind his head. She leaned her elbows on her knees, bending forward, studying intently the black eyebrows, the high-bridged nose, the slight smile which showed the tips of his teeth, alluring teeth, she thought, if teeth could be said to be alluring. 'Can they?'

Micah laughed, one of those rare, hearty laughs, which she loved to hear, remembered when they were apart, and was sometimes afraid she might not hear again.

'Can teeth be alluring?' she asked again, with the deep seriousness of Lily Malone asking her uncle Frederick if butterflies could be induced to return to their cocoons once they had seen the outside world.

'If only I could show you to some of my doubting colleagues, they could stop their quibbling over whether or not there is such a thing as charm.'

This also delighted them; but not for long, for the clock had a warning. They must leave in an hour and a half, and Arlette needed time to dress. 'Come here.' He untied the towel with one forefinger and brought her downward so that she was kneeling over him, her mouth on his; and when they separated, she got out of bed, made a mock stagger, and ran into the bathroom to begin the ritual. She wanted him to remember her as he supposed she was with or without the subtle camouflage of professional makeup.

Now, sitting in the club lounge, they looked at each other, silent, serious:

All this time, and not one word about Anthony. Not one word about 'this kind of life.'

He had surprised her more than at any time since the first night he had made love to her and she had decided that a magician had invaded her, producing pleasures and agonies of pleasure of which no mortal man was capable:

He's strong. He's reckless. He's of yang. Like me. Jade Ring had recognized him.

'I warn you,' Michael had said, 'he's a formidably serious man.'

And part of his seriousness had been demonstrated by his capacity to spend these last twenty-three hours with her and never ask the questions he longed to ask; never try to persuade her of what he wanted to persuade her.

She glanced at him now and then. His face was not easy to read. Indeed, it was impossible to read; and she was that accomplished reader of faces whose infallible skill awed and intimidated her fellow actors, even directors.

He was sad at the prospect of parting soon?

He was thinking of what he must do tomorrow and six months from then?

He took it for granted that people came and went in one another's lives, giving themselves with unconscious abandonment, which seemed at its highest moments nothing less than the unity of mythological rumor, where two became one, then drew apart: the magical performance had once again run its course.

There were times when she retained the feeling that the act of love would remain with them for the rest of their lives; all at once, it was gone.

He was perhaps a man of formidable stoicism, prepared to accept what life allowed him with grace and dignity, without complaint, once his theorem had been clearly expounded. Or he was a man of formidable persistence, prepared – like any disciplined scientist – to try first one means of gaining his objective and, when that failed if he had not lost belief in the theorem, to try another, then another.

She was watching him steadily, luxuriating in the sound of his voice as it seemed to flow through her – yes, this Dr Micah Benoni was the one real mystery she had encountered: priest, sensualist, cynical idealist, who took for his

764

province nothing so small as the world, but the universe and all possible universes.

And who was yet capable of the deepest, strongest love for a woman's body, her emotional responses, her beauty: 'Micah Benoni,' she said softly. '*Who is like God.*'

He was standing, his hand extended, for she had missed the announcement that it was time for passengers to board Flight 877 for London, Munich, Istanbul.

'Oh!'

So it had come, after all. This moment she had convinced herself would never arrive. She stood, throwing the coat over her arm, picking up the handbag, and she and Micah went out together, walking slowly. She glanced up at him, tears in her eyes, and gave a quick apologetic smile.

'I'll be there in three months, more or less,' he reminded her.

They stopped at the entrance of the security gate, looking at each other silently, and he kissed her, letting her go only when the final announcement was made.

'Be happy, Micah.'

She smiled, the best imitation she could give of Jade Ring's smile, and had one last glimpse of him, his face somber, thoughtful.

Then she was through the perfunctory security process and on the plane, taking her seat in the bulkhead section; no one in front of her. She gave the stewardess her coat, covered her eyes with dark glasses, took a newspaper from her bag and held it before her face.

When the stewardess asked Miss Malone if she wanted a drink she replied only by a great effort, stunned by the sense of emptiness: 'Nothing, thanks. I'd like to sleep.'

She turned her face toward the window. The lights inside the plane were on, and she raised the dark glasses to see if she looked like the Arlette Morgan she remembered, or if perhaps these last hours had changed her beyond recognition. She was the same. At least she looked the same.

Before the plane took off she was asleep.

She awoke at what seemed a sound of distant thunder, a low rumble. The plane shook as if it had come alive, a great animal shaking itself, trying to shake itself apart. She sat straight and looked around. There were screams, glasses and trays of food had fallen to the floor, and she realized that the plane was descending very swiftly.

'Ladies and gentlemen – there is a technical problem.' Please keep your seats – fasten your seat belts securely—'

The plane's wings pitched from side to side. The plane plummeted, like a rock falling from a great height.

The stars, through the window, looked tilted out of their normal positions, and were passing swiftly, seeming to fall through the sky at the speed of a comet plunging to earth.

She tossed away the dark glasses and sat rigid, clasping the arms of her chair, pressing backward because of the swift descent.

She had less a feeling of fear than of surprise at the screaming pandemonium behind her, people yelling, cursing, praying. There had come over her a stunned disbelieving wonderment:

So soon? And it's over?

She never doubted the plane would crash, drown them all. There were no survivors from plane wrecks at sea; not when the plane was disintegrating in midair. She never doubted her life would end in two minutes, six minutes.

She sat in wondering silence:

Suddenly a sharp protest arose: *But who will play Anna for me?*

The noise increased. Screams and sobs and yelling curses grew louder. It seemed to Arlette in some moment of irrational concern that it was her responsibility to find another Anna—

The captain's voice could scarcely be heard.

She began her patience count: *Flame. Feathers .   .*

She stopped:

Patience for what? There's nothing to wait for—

The stars rushed by, the plane was descending at a steeper angle. The captain's voice spoke, repeating: 'Flight crew prepare for a water landing . . . Flight crew prepare for a water landing . . .'

She had a quick vision of Anthony receiving the news, reflecting, saying, as Anthony had said at word of Cleopatra's death: *Dead, then?* Or Heathcliff, of Cathy: *She's dead?*

We've played it so often – it may not seem true – at first—

A stewardess fell to the floor, sobbing. Arlette looked away, out the window, at the rushing stars, the night passing by them, as if they had left the earth and were sailing outward into limitless space – not downward, more and more precipitately:

Now it's over? There will never be anything more?

Where did my life go?

The plane smashed into the water with a force which cracked the fuselage.

In a moment, water had filled the cabin, rising to the top. The stars were gone. There was blackness outside and inside. The screams had stopped.

The front section of the plane split away; it continued its plunge. The ship fell silent as it rode downward, steadily traveling.